Until T

BY THE SAME AUTHOR

Bath Intrigue
Lady Aurelia's Bequest
Insubstantial Pageant
Incomparable Miss Brady
A Highly Respectable Marriage

UNTIL TOMORROW

Sheila Walsh

CENTURY
LONDON SYDNEY AUCKLAND JOHANNESBURG

First published in Great Britain in 1992 by
Random House UK Limited
20 Vauxhall Bridge Road, London, SW1V 2SA

Random House South Africa (Pty) Ltd
PO Box 337, Bergvlei 2012, South Africa

Random House Australia Pty Ltd
20 Alfred Street, Milsons Point, Sydney, NSW 2061
Australia

Random House New Zealand Ltd
18 Poland Road, Glenfield, Auckland 10,
New Zealand

A CIP Catalogue Record for this book is available from the British Library

Typeset by Deltatype Ltd, Ellesmere Port
Printed in Great Britain by
Mackays of Chatham PLC, Chatham, Kent

For Des – with love

Acknowledgements

I would like to thank my daughter and son-in-law, Fran and Andrew Gregson, of Ball and Gregson Ltd., Southport, for their encouragement and help. Also, Mr Frank Willett, who so generously shared with me his memories of baking in the thirties and forties.

PART ONE

KATHLEEN
1936

Chapter One

The warmth from the bakehouse still lingered along the passage, taking the chill off the small washhouse. Liz Ryan heaved the last of the towels from the copper into the first dolly tub and from there to the second one, each time paddling them round vigorously before feeding them through the mangle. 'Amo, amas, amat,' she chanted, forcing the handle as it baulked at the thicker parts, before dropping the towels into the waiting basket. Then it was through the scullery and into the living room, to spread them out on the rack with the rest of the washing. With an ease that belied her slight frame, Liz hauled on the rope and the rack lifted, creaking, to the ceiling. 'Amamus, amatis, amant.' A couple of deft twists of the rope round the hook on the wall, and she knotted it and stepped back.

'Well done,' she said, with a satisfied nod, there being no-one else present to applaud her efforts.

Dad had been grunting in his sleep when she crept past the front bedroom on her way to swop her school uniform for the green wool frock her sister, Rita, had recently outgrown. Everyone else was out except her mother, who was serving a customer. Liz glanced uneasily at the clock. Mam was cutting it fine, if she wanted to avoid a long wait in the doctor's surgery. Oh, please God, she prayed urgently, please make her go this time – and without an argument.

'Perhaps I won't bother, after all,' Kathleen Ryan said, coming through from the shop, brushing aside her daughter's over-eager reminder. 'The surgery's always packed of a Monday evening, and in this weather it would be just plain daft to sit there picking up germs, when there's any number of jobs need doing here. The washing for one. I never did get it finished – oh, you've done it.' She stopped, relief vying with vexation. 'You're a good girl,' she said grudgingly. 'Truth to tell, it's been one of those days when I couldn't seem to get on for customers, and we're bound to get busy again near closing time. I'd better leave going till later in the week.'

'Oh, no, you won't, Mam.' Liz was firm. 'I can look after the shop and everything just as well as you. Well, almost,' she amended hastily, not wishing to provoke her mother in her present mood. 'Ah, listen, you've put off going to Dr Graham twice already, and anyone with half an eye can see that you're not yourself. Besides, I had to ask off school early on your account, and if you don't go, Sister Imelda is sure to find out. I think she must have a direct line to God, that one – she always knows everything! I don't want to be accused of telling lies.'

Her mother bridled. 'That's no way to talk about a good and holy nun, Liz. And I do wish you'd stop exaggerating. I'm tired, that's all, and the last thing I want is to have that old woman, Graham, fussing over me. I know already what he'll say: "You're a bit run down, Kathleen" ' – she mimicked the gruff Scottish voice – ' "You need to put your feet up more often." I could tell him that for nothing, and save myself taking his precious coloured water!'

It wasn't true, of course, and Kathleen knew it. A nagging ache was draining the energy from her even as she spoke. She was by nature a plain-speaking woman, and she knew full well that a bottle of coloured water wasn't the answer to her problem, so why was she fooling herself? Just as she knew, after the fright she'd had that morning, that it would be stupid, if not downright dangerous, to play the ostrich any longer. Anyway, from the set of Liz's mouth, she wasn't going to be given the chance.

There was no getting anything past this middle daughter of hers, the very spit of herself at sixteen – sharp as a needle, and so eager for life, her supple body growing shapelier by the minute, the way her own had been before the years of childbearing had thickened her waistline. Liz was impulsive, outspoken and chock-full of impossible dreams. And stubborn. Looking at her now, with her shining brown hair imperfectly confined in two thick plaits, her brow a troubled furrow above a short straight nose, and determination written all over her, was like looking into a distant mirror. Except for Liz's eyes. No-one else in the family had eyes that colour: dreaming tea-coloured eyes that took on the sheen of liquid gold the instant her emotions and enthusiasms surfaced – which they frequently did these days, for Liz was at an age when life was a challenge and there was no such word as impossible. Oh, God, Kathleen thought. What I'd give to be sixteen again!

The thought brought a rasp to her voice. 'I'd be just fine, if you lot wouldn't keep on at me. I'm sick and tired of being nagged at, morning, noon and night!'

But Liz was not put off by her mother's brusqueness. A great one for giving you the edge of her tongue, was Mam, even more so of late. What did trouble Liz, because she was dead straight-talking as a rule, was Mam's evasiveness – the way she wouldn't quite meet your eyes. And for weeks now there had been a weariness in her voice that even sharp words couldn't disguise, and black circles under her eyes. Alice Regan's mother had looked exactly like that last year, and six months later she was dead. A small hollowing of fear lent increasing urgency to Liz's argument.

'It's no use, Mam, you're going if I have to shut the shop and take you myself! You promised Dad, and I'll not be the one to help you break that promise.'

'Oh, for pity's sake!' snapped her mother. 'I never heard such a fuss about nothing. It's plain there'll be no peace for me in this house until I get it over with.'

'Great. I'll fetch your coat.' Liz took the stairs from the living room two at a time, before Mam could change her mind.

Ryan's, Bakers and Confectioners, on the corner of Fortune Street and Great Homer Street, enjoyed a regular passing trade, so that people were in and out of the shop fairly frequently after her mother had gone. But she was glad to be kept occupied – it meant there was less time to brood on the fate of Alice Regan's mother.

Liz usually enjoyed having the place to herself. She loved the comfortable familiarity of the living room – the big oak dresser almost filling the wall that backed on to the shop, its polished cupboard doors reflecting the firelight. The top was cluttered with family photographs, trophies and mementoes, and in the centre, a small red lamp burned beneath a picture of the Sacred Heart. Mam's piano, which had accompanied many a sing-song, occupied the wall facing the big kitchen range, leaving just enough space under the window for the treadle sewing machine that had been Grandmother Power's. The window gave instant warning of anyone coming through the back gate and across the yard to the door or bakehouse, whilst the heavy lace curtain drawn across it prevented nosier folk from peering in, and helped to soften the starkness of the long bakehouse wall.

Light brown lino, still damp in places from its daily mopping, covered the floor, and in the centre was a large table with a much washed red chenille cloth thrown over it. Even the shabby sofa under the stairs had an endearing squashiness.

The smell of the potato and onion pie that Mam had put in the oven ready for supper was already beginning to mingle with the traces of hot crusty loaves, yeast, and all the other indefinable smells that filtered through from the bakehouse. Soon the washing would begin to steam gently, adding its soapy aroma to the rest. And beyond the passage, the bakehouse waited, scrubbed and clean and resting, its fire banked down until the night's work began.

On a quiet day, Liz would maybe snatch a few moments to curl up in Dad's old armchair by the fire, set within arm's reach of his pipe-rack above the bookshelves where Dickens rubbed shoulders with Trollope, Yeats, G. K. Chesterton and Gerard Manley Hopkins, who was a priest as well as a poet. A great reader, was Dad. She would watch the flames playing over the gleaming blackleaded range, and dream of a time when the name Elizabeth Ryan would be famous. She never quite got as far as deciding how this goal was to be achieved. Such mundane considerations had no place in dreams.

Learning had never been any problem to her, though art was her favourite lesson, and Sister Barbara, her art teacher, had on several occasions hinted that she could go far. But art wasn't for people like her – unless, of course, she turned her skills to confectionery. Dad always said she had a fine light touch with pastry and fancies, as well as the passion for perfection and eye for presentation that her brother, Chris, lacked. *Elizabeth Ryan, Confectioner – by Appointment to His Majesty the King*. She declaimed the words aloud. They sounded good – except that there hadn't been much call for fancies, artistic or otherwise, in this part of Liverpool over the last few years, with so many folk out of work. And although times were improving, Chris was still having to work for Lunt's in Latimer Street so as to bring in a wage.

Besides, Mam wouldn't hear of her wasting a good scholarship and five years at Everton Valley Convent of Notre Dame on any airy-fairy artistic nonsense. She had always been in the school's upper band, and was expected to matriculate next summer with the same ease that Rita had. Rita had gone on to sixth form college to get her highers, and was now in her first year at Mount Pleasant College, training to be a teacher.

But then, Rita always wanted to teach, just as Clare, Liz's best friend at school, had her heart set on becoming a doctor. Whereas Liz, for all her dreaming, and a great need inside her that often burned for expression, hadn't the first idea what she really wanted to do. So there'd be no highers for her, which was a pity; she quite enjoyed school. But Mam reckoned the time would be better spent at a secretarial college, where she could get a whole string of qualifications to fit her for a good office job – an idea Liz found vaguely depressing.

Mam set great store by qualifications. Liz could still remember how she had carried on seven years back, when Big Murray, the head teacher at St Anthony's, had advised against Chris trying for a scholarship – as if it was a personal insult to her! After all, Rita had passed easily enough. Surely Chris deserved an equal chance. But for once Dad had properly taken the wind out of Mam's sails.

Liz hadn't meant to eavesdrop, but it was almost impossible to have a private argument with only the scullery, the living room, two bedrooms and an attic to accommodate the seven of them. On that particular day Liz had been in the bedroom she then shared with Rita and Shirley Anne, and only a wall as thin as paper between it and her parents' room.

'We all know you're a great one for education, Kathleen,' Dad was saying, quiet enough, but with the Irish coming out in him, the way it always did when he was moved or meaning business. 'But don't be trying to make an academic out of young Chris. He sets great store by your opinion, but he's just not bookish – expect too much of him and he'll end up with the notion he's failed you.'

'He won't fail, not if he works hard . . .'

'You're deluding yourself, *acushla*. Our Rita's the brainy one. And Liz, too. She'll surprise us all one day, I'm thinking – ' Listening, Liz had blushed. 'And we'll have to wait and see how the little ones turn out. But Christopher is different – he's a doer not a thinker, and he knows what he wants.'

'I don't understand you, Michael Ryan,' Mam had thrown back at him. 'He's your son. Don't you have any ambition for him at all?'

'Ambition?' he repeated. 'No, not a scrap. I don't hold with being ambitious for others. But I have hope. I hope all my children will succeed – that they will be whatever it is in them to be to the best of their ability. For Christopher that means making good bread. He's halfway there already, but then, he's had the knack of it from the day he first climbed on to a stool to get his hands in the dough trough.'

'Only because you've encouraged him. Getting him up at five in the morning to help you before he goes to school – small wonder his work's suffered!' Her mother's accusation sounded bitter. 'God only knows why you're so keen for him to follow you! It hasn't got us very far.'

'Is that how you see it? I hadn't realized – ' Liz heard the hurt in his voice, and longed to rush in and comfort him. But her mother must have heard it too, for she exclaimed: 'That isn't what I meant at all, and you know it! It's not your fault times have been bad. But they will get better, and – oh, Michael, don't you see? With a really good education, there are going to be so many more opportunities for our children than we ever had! I just want them all to have the chance of a good job that will lead somewhere!'

'Of course you do, Kathy, my love. Do you think I don't? But you must understand that baking isn't simply a job. It's a gift, something born in you, like painting or music. And when you have such a calling, you have to follow it, no matter what. Because at the end of the day, knowing what you want out of life is more important than passing a few ould exams for the sake of proving how clever you are.'

There had been a passion in Dad's voice when he spoke of his work that Liz had never heard before – a poetic eloquence that made her heart almost burst with pride. It must have had a similar effect on her mother, for she allowed him to continue unchallenged.

'And I think Chris should work somewhere else for a while

when he does leave school,' he said. 'The experience will be good for him, and he'll be bringing in a wage which we can't afford to give him at present. But who knows – in a year or two, when the better times do come, we can maybe run to a bigger shop altogether; maybe even be like Fred Munnings, and have *Ryan and Son* above the door in fine gold letters. You'd like that, wouldn't you, *acushla*?'

Only then did Mam speak. Liz wasn't sure she believed they could ever compete with Mr Munnings, who had three shops, including one in Church Street where all the posh people shopped, and lots of wholesale customers besides, but she said with an odd sort of laugh, 'Well, that's being ambitious with a vengeance! But we'll see. You're a smooth-tongued rogue, Michael Ryan, when you've a mind to be.'

And Liz heard the smile creep into her father's soft Irish voice. 'Amn't I just, though? And all without passing a single exam in me life! But, sure, a little thing like that didn't stop you making shameless eyes at me the moment we met . . .' And that had been the end of the argument, except for a lot of muffled laughter and scuffling.

Over the next few years her mother had certainly redoubled her own efforts, driving everyone else as hard as herself. Then, last winter, Mrs Heap died. She had kept a run-down grocer's next to them on Great Homer Street, and Mam had been forever complaining that Heap's shabby window was a disgrace that did their own trade no good at all.

They were in the middle of Sunday dinner when Dad mentioned that he had been talking to the old woman's son, who was wanting a quick sale of the premises. Without a word Mam got up from the table and went upstairs. They heard the creak of the top drawer of the bedroom chest, and a minute later she was down again, laying a small Post Office savings book on the table beside Dad's plate. Liz, as curious as the rest of the family, craned forward to look. They watched him open it, and saw his face go blank.

Finally he looked up at Mam, disbelief changing to awe. 'But this is – There's almost enough here to – ' She nodded, and a slow smile lit his eyes. 'Begob, but you're a crafty one, Kathleen Ryan! You must have been squirrelling money away for years!' He got up and put his arms round her in a way that brought a lump to Liz's throat, and said softly, 'I don't know how you did it, but I'm glad it's my side you're on, woman!'

Mam had actually blushed. 'I know it isn't exactly the grand expansion you had in mind, Michael, but with a bit of help from the bank we could perhaps lay the first brick in the foundations of the Ryan Empire.' And everyone had cheered, though the younger children weren't quite sure why.

For a while after that things became quite exciting, as walls were knocked down and others built up. Everyone helped, even the little ones, and there was whitewash everywhere. At the end of it, there was lots more room in the house, and the shop looked twice the size, all light and airy, with the counters extended and new shelves put up to display the groceries.

Best of all, Mam now had the two things she had secretly yearned for – a bathroom, converted from the second scullery, with a gas geyser to heat the water, and a tiny parlour of her very own, out of what had been Mrs Heap's living room.

Mam had had to be coaxed over the parlour, which she said was a needless extravagance. But – 'Sure, it'll be worth every penny, *acushla*,' Dad had said softly, watching her expression, 'if it brings that lovely sparkle back into your eyes.'

'Wasn't that the most romantic thing you ever saw?' Liz whispered to her sisters in bed that same night. 'Mam's face was a sight – all pretty and rosy-cheeked.' Rita, ever practical, pointed out that everyone flushed up when they got excited, and if Liz spent less time at the pictures, or with her nose in a book, she might be better able to distinguish between real life and sloppy romance. An argument ensued, with Shirley Anne for once taking Liz's part – though she thought it a bit much, calling Mam pretty.

Liz smiled, remembering, and took the kettle into the scullery to fill it from the tap at the wide stone sink so that she could set it on the fire ready to mash the tea when her father came downstairs.

That had been the start of better times. It was as if Mam had been given a new lease of life. Like a bee in clover, she set about making the expanded shop pay its way. She got up very early to help Dad in the bakehouse, and most days Liz did her share of baking, too. Jobs were allotted with rigorous impartiality, and any pocket money had to be earned by taking extra Saturday jobs.

'This isn't a hotel,' Mam would say briskly. 'The good things in life have to be earned. And our Rita's board and lodging at Mount Pleasant still has to be found.'

Dad bought a big covered handcart, and spent every spare moment carrying samples of bread and confectionery to all parts of Liverpool – not just the ordinary loaves, but some of the traditional recipes he had brought from Ireland; the soda and wheaten breads, the farls and barm bracks, and a special kind of potato cake called boxty, which he made to order. Liz would often grate the raw potato for the boxty, singing the rhyme he had taught her. 'Boxty in the griddle, boxty in the pan. If you can't make boxty, you'll never get your man.'

Lots of general stores agreed to give his samples a try. In fact, the venture proved so successful that Dad had to start at two o'clock in the morning to get all the baking done in time, and Joey, and sometimes Liz herself, helped with the early deliveries. He'd even begun to talk about looking for a second-hand van.

The shop trade increased too, as folk, liking what they'd bought from the new outlets, came to see what else Ryan's had to offer – such as the real home-cured ham, the eggs and cheese that Mam bought from Cousin Tom, who had a farm at Melling.

When Dad applied to join the National Association of Master Bakers, Mam's cup was full. 'You should have done it long since,' she'd said with satisfaction. 'You've as much right to call yourself a Master Baker as Fred Munnings.'

The jangle of the bell cut into Liz's thoughts. She flicked back a straying pigtail, smoothed her pinafore and hurried through to the shop. Already the steamy windows were bejewelled with medallions of frost against the street lamp beyond. A shawled figure hovered near the side counter, one hand furtively outstretched towards a barm brack, only to be swiftly withdrawn.

'On yer own, are yer, Liz gairl?' Nora Figg's voice oozed weary resignation, but the eyes of Fortune Street's busybody, darting this way and that, were needle-sharp. 'I just come ter see if y'd gorr'any of them penny bags yer mam has of a Monday.'

Liz knew there were some under the counter, mostly buns left over from Saturday. But she didn't see why the likes of Mrs Figg should benefit. 'I'm sorry,' she said. 'Anyway, Mam says you've not to have any more till you've paid off your tally.'

Fury flared, but the retort was bitten back. A sigh swelled the thin bosom confined beneath the shawls. 'She's an 'ard woman, your mam – God-fearing, but 'ard. It's ter be 'oped she never lairns whar'it is ter be left a poor lonely widder woman, wid only the paltry Relief between 'er an' deggeradation.' Mrs Figg paused to gauge the effect of her oratory on the young girl.

But Liz had heard it all before. She might have shown more sympathy, had she not so often seen that same 'poor widder woman' leave their shop, stopping only to light a furtive fag before scurrying into the public of The Grapes on the corner opposite.

'Perhaps,' she suggested innocently, 'if you were to pay something off what you owe? There's more than eight shillings on the tally . . .'

'*Eight shillin'*! And where would the likes o' me get eight shillin'?'

Liz eyed the nicotine-stained fingers clamped over the jaws of a shabby purse which bulged noticeably in the middle. The woman followed her gaze. 'It's only pennies, an' them mostly spoken for.' Defensiveness turned to cunning. 'If yer was ter slip me a couple of them ha'penny farls, mind, I could likely manage.'

'Oh, for heaven's sake!' Liz seized the scones from the counter, dropped them unceremoniously into a bag, twirled the corners deftly and held it out of reach until the penny was safely in her hand. Grumbling, Mrs Figg opened the purse a crack and fished out the single coin. Liz took it and handed over the bag. 'And don't you dare tell Mam I let you have them!'

The paper bag disappeared rapidly beneath the folds of the shawl, but still Mrs Figg made no move to go. 'Nor' ill, is she – yer mam?' Her shifting eyes were suddenly intent upon Liz's expressive face. 'Only I could of sworn I seen 'er goin' inter the doctor's sairgery earlier – an' she's been lookin' as sick as a sow's ear fer a while now . . .'

Liz realized too late why the wretched woman, known to all as 'Nosey Nora', had come into the shop. 'Mother's just fine, Mrs Figg. Now, if you don't mind, I've work to do.'

The woman bristled and drew her shawl tight around her. 'Well, I 'ope she's wearin' summat warm,' she said spitefully. 'It's brass monkey's out there, an' there'll be a freezin' fog comin' in off the Mairsey any minute, mark my words!'

As she turned to leave the door burst open, letting in a rush of cold air and the pipe of treble voices irreverently rendering the unauthorised, but highly topical, version of a well-loved carol – '*Hark the herald angels si-ing, Mrs Simpson's pinched our king* . . .' – currently popular among the young.

'You wanna watch wur you're goin', Joey Ryan!' she snapped, as two well muffled schoolboys, their bright faces pinched with cold, tumbled into the shop, almost knocking her down. 'No consideration f' yer elders! What's more, the scuffers'll 'ave you up fer treason if they catch yez singin' that blasphemous rubbish! An' serve yer right!' She left, banging the door behind her.

Liz was round the counter in a flash. She grabbed a fistful of collar in each hand, and frogmarched her brother and his inseparable best mate through into the living room, her tongue-lashing punctuated by the occasional sharp shake.

'Leave off, our Lizzie! You're chokin' us!'

'Serve you right if I did, my lad!' she retorted, giving him a final shake before releasing them both. 'And don't call me Lizzie! How dare you shame us in front of that woman with that mockery of a carol!'

'Don't talk daft, it's just a bit of fun. Everyone's singin' it.'

'You're not everyone. Anyway, it's not just the carol,' Liz said – though she hated them making fun of the handsome young king, whose voice had sounded so sad on the wireless last Friday night when she'd sat with Mam and Dad listening to his abdication speech. She thought it terribly romantic that he was giving up his throne for the woman he loved – a bit like Rudolph Rassendall in *The Prisoner of Zenda*, who'd had to give up the throne *and* Princess Flavia, except that fiction wasn't quite the same thing. Mam, of course, being Mam, said that King Edward should have put duty before love, and Dad agreed with her. But all Joey had worried about was whether they would still be able to have the street party for the Coronation, like they'd had for the late King's jubilee.

The recollection sharpened Liz's voice anew. 'I mean, just look at you! And you're no better, Eddie Killigan – a pair of scruffbags sent to frighten the customers. And another thing,' she prodded the air with an accusing finger. 'You know full well you're forbidden to use the shop entrance, let alone drag every Tom, Dick and Harry in with you, trailing your muddy feet all over the place and knocking customers over.'

With an air of angelic innocence, Joey opened wide his luminous blue eyes, with the dark curling lashes that were the envy of every girl in his class at school. 'Nor I haven't, neither, cos Eddie isn't a Tom, or a D . . .' He ducked the cuff she aimed at him, darted out of reach behind the table with the eel-like agility of an active ten-year-old, and saw her mouth twitch. 'Anyhow, I don't know what yer makin' such a fuss for – it was only Nosey Nora!'

'Don't call her that! And don't take your coat off, either. Mam's left some messages for you to do.'

'Aw, no! Why does it always have to be me? Our Shirley Anne's four years older than me an' she's *never* made to do messages!'

'Shirley Anne's gone to her dancing class . . .'

'Ooh er!' Joey pulled his mouth into a prissy pout and teetered round on the toes of his boots. Eddie, his sandy hair standing up in spikes, fell about laughing, and even Liz found his antics hard to resist.

'It's a good job she can't see you, my lad, or she'd thump you black and blue.'

'Gerroff!' scoffed Eddie. 'Your Shirley Anne couldn't batter fish!'

'That just shows how little you know her, my lad.' The shop bell rang again. 'Come on, off with you now. I'll have to go,' she said, and twitched a piece of paper from behind the clock. 'Back door this time. Here's the list, and the basket's on the table – '

'But we're starving!' Joey clutched his stomach in mock agony. 'An' it's *freezin'* out there!'

'You'll soon get warm if you run,' Liz called hard-heartedly, already on her way, her plaits bouncing against her shoulders. And then, relenting a little, 'Oh, go on with you. If I've time, there'll be hot Bovril for you both when you get back – I might even let you make dripping toast.'

'Great!' The door banged. Liz winced and went through to the shop.

*

It had been a long uncomfortable wait, made worse by a room full of wheezers and scratchers, as well as the usual crop of work-shy men with hangovers and hacking coughs, and fractious children. Kathleen Ryan had deliberately taken a seat near the door, avoiding the area round the small gas fire where most people congregated. Even so, it wasn't long before the stench of unwashed bodies filled her nostrils, penetrating the double layer of scarf held tight across her face. She had tried breathing through her mouth, but it made little difference. To make matters worse, her corsets were digging in something cruel, even with the laces let out as far as they would go and the two bottom buttons of her bust bodice undone. Above the fireplace an ancient wooden clock ticked sonorously, and as each minute passed, the finger jerked forward: One more an' then I'll leave, she kept telling herself, her stomach close to heaving.

Now, at last, she sat in the starkly lit surgery, surrounded by the familiar clutter of books and patients' files, all kinds of paraphernalia spilling over every surface and on to the floor. It had looked exactly the same for as long as she could remember. In fact, the whole house, as far as she could see, was crying out for a duster and a bit of elbow grease. That housekeeper had a cushy job, all right.

Kathleen's gaze returned to Dr Graham, who was writing in a swift spidery hand, and her knuckles whitened as she clutched the handbag lying in her lap. The desk lamp made a halo around his bent head, and illogically she found herself remembering a time when that unruly white hair had been black and wavy, and she had tugged at it with baby fingers. Where had the years gone?

She still felt uncomfortable after his examination – and, to be honest, was deeply ashamed at the need for it. What must he be thinking, after putting the fear of God into us all those years ago?

As if reading her thoughts, the doctor laid down his pen, a reassuring smile replacing the look of preoccupation. 'Well now, Kathleen – ' He spoke with fatherly familiarity – and why not, for hadn't he brought her into the world, and her children too, and seen them through all their childish ailments? 'It's not the end of the world, though I'll not insult your intelligence by pretending I'm happy about it.'

'You and me, both,' she said flatly. 'It's been so long. I ought to be ashamed – a woman of my age.'

'My dear Kathleen, women of your age are having babies all the time.'

'That's not what I mean, and you know it. But you'd think after more than ten years – well, nine, I suppose, if you count the miscarriage . . .'

Dr Graham did not miss the suppressed hint of pleading, almost of panic, in her voice, and his heart went out to her. He remembered her last three increasingly difficult pregnancies, with intermittent bleeding, the one still-birth between Shirley Anne and Joey, and the final traumatic miscarriage to which she referred, resulting in a haemorrhage that had almost killed her. He had told her and Michael quite bluntly then that there must be no more babies. Sterilization had been firmly rejected, as he'd known it would be, as had the use of any so-called unnatural devices. He sighed. The situation was all too common among his Catholic patients, and the outcome inevitable, for even if the husband took to seeking his pleasures elsewhere, sooner or later the marital bed beckoned, with disastrous results.

But the Ryans were different. No one could doubt their great love for each other. Michael in particular had aroused Dr Graham's admiration. His faithfulness was never in question, yet he had somehow managed to sublimate the physical expression of his love for the best part of ten yeras. Graham knew of very few men capable of sustaining that kind of voluntary abstinence for one year, let alone ten. Ah well, good man though Michael was, he was only human. One careless moment was all it took, and Fate had a way of playing some pretty rotten tricks.

'No need to tell you, I suppose, that you're almost four months gone?' He fixed Kathleen with a baleful eye before concluding ambiguously, 'It's a pity you didn't come to see me sooner. Not that it's too late, even now – '

She smiled faintly, in spite of her distress. 'You're a great trier, doctor, I'll say that for you. But you know the answer.'

Dr Graham had long ago rebelled against his own Calvinistic upbringing, and what faith he retained was somewhat insubstantial, leading him into frequent conflict with the Almighty. He'd known he was on a hiding to nothing even hinting at abortion, but even so, he had to stifle the impatience which unquestioning obedience to the edicts of Holy Mother Church always evoked in him. If those who made the rules were required to suffer one quarter of the agonies that women endured – mostly through the selfishness of men – they would maybe amend some of their more sanctimonious utterances. Of course each new life was sacred. His whole profession was founded on the precept of caring, on the preservation of life, so that he suffered agonies of conscience whenever, like Solomon, he was forced to make a choice. But he had watched too many women like Kathleen die needlessly – and weren't their lives sacred, too?

Kathleen, of course, had a way of defying the odds. Almost any other woman he could think of with her medical history, working the hours she worked, would probably have aborted naturally weeks ago. Even as a child, she had shown herself to be spirited and courageous. But this time a heart as big as a bucket and a capacity to endure might not be enough. He found himself hoping, with unusual fervour, that he would be proved wrong.

'I was tired, and my breasts were a bit tender, but there was no morning sickness like I always used to have,' Kathleen was explaining, 'so when I had almost non-existent periods for a couple of months, it was easy to kid myself that it was the change starting early.' And oh, God, didn't I pray that it might be so! she thought. 'But by the third month, I knew – the way I felt, it was no use fooling myself any longer. I suppose I should have come to see you then . . .'

'It would have been more sensible,' he agreed.

'Well, I'm here now.'

It was ungraciously said, but Dr Graham ignored the uncharacteristic lapse of good manners, which doubtless arose from apprehension and guilt. How much longer, he found himself wondering, would she have gone on putting off this visit, had not some intermittent bleeding over the past few days culminated in a bleed that finally put the fear of God into her?

'True enough,' he said. 'And I'm sure I don't have to spell things out for you. We'll just have to see what can be done to diminish the risk of aborting. Thankfully, no harm has been done – as yet.' He let the last two words lie, and saw a shadow cross her face.

'Tell me, how has Michael taken the news?'

It was immediately obvious from her face that she hadn't told her husband, and this time a small 'tch' of impatience did escape him. 'Oh, Kathleen, girl, what am I to do with you? Well, he'll have to be told, because if this poor child is to have any chance at all, you're going to have to make some pretty drastic alterations to your life from now on.'

Chapter Two

'Hush now, Freddie,' the young woman waiting to be served told the grizzling toddler balanced on her jutting hip, as he lurched forward to grab a jam doughnut placed tantalizingly beyond the reach of his wriggling fingers. 'Mammy hasn't got any pennies to spare today.' She smiled wanly at Liz. 'They don't understand at his age, do they? I wouldn't have brought him, only his grizzling gets on Arnie's nerves . . .'

Liz often wondered how Ellen Cassidy, who had gentility stamped all over her, had come to marry her big roistering docker husband. They lived at number twenty-seven, four doors up from Nora Figg. Ellen couldn't be much above her late twenties now. She had once been pretty in a fair, delicate way, and still could be, but five children in quick succession had left their mark, and since Arnie's accident her blonde hair had dulled to mouse, and she had aged years.

'Every tragedy 'as its blessin',' Liz had overheard one customer confide to another after it happened. 'At least there'll be no more babbies for that poor lass.' Looking at Mrs Cassidy now, thin and pinched with cold in her threadbare coat, it seemed to Liz that it was a queer kind of blessing.

'How is Mr Cassidy?' she asked.

'Much as usual. But it's kind of you to ask.'

'You've come for your bread.' Liz reached for the large loaf Ellen had brought in earlier to be baked, something Dad only did for a few special customers.

'Thanks, love. And a tin of conny.' Ellen seemed to hesitate, as Liz reached down the condensed milk, her glance strayed towards the living-room door. 'Your mother wouldn't be about, would she?'

Liz, wrapping the loaf, guessed why she wanted to know. She reached beneath the counter and brought out a couple of the bags she had denied to Mrs Figg. 'Mam's out, I'm afraid, but she said to be sure to give you these if you came in. One of broken biscuits and one of buns. And you might as well have this, too,' she added impulsively, reaching for a solitary currant loaf on the back shelf. 'It's an order someone didn't collect, and it'll only go to waste. Call it fourpence – that's a shilling altogether, with the bread.'

A faint flush of embarassment ran up under Ellen Cassidy's skin, and she made no immediate move to open her purse. 'Are you sure about the currant loaf? You'll be open for a good while yet.'

'Course I'm sure. Honestly.' Liz crossed her fingers. It was only a white lie, she told herself, although there was no such thing according to Father Clarkson; in his book all lies were wicked. She'd get a terrible telling-off and at least five Hail Marys as a penance at her next confession, but it was worth it. Anyway, she didn't see how God could possibly damn her for performing a Christian act. Still, as a kind of extra insurance, she kept the fingers of one hand crossed as she took the shilling. Then, in an excess of generosity, she recklessly reached for a doughnut, ducked under the counter flap and held it out to Freddie. 'My treat,' she said. He snatched it from her with fingers like icicles, and immediately his face was covered in jam.

'Oh, bless you, Liz, but you shouldn't have.' Ellen's voice was taut with emotion.

'Whyever not?'

'Because I don't want him to grow up thinking that he only has to crave something . . .'

'I'm sure he won't. Anyway,' Liz eyed the child's smeared face, and grinned infectiously, 'it's a bit late to try to take it off him now. You'll just have to tell him I've decided to give my Christmas presents a bit early this year.'

A tug hooted mournfully on the river as she held the door and watched them disappear down Fortune Street, followed by the first creeping swirl of fog. She shivered and hurriedly shut it out.

In the living room, Liz found her father thrusting a taper into the fire to light his pipe, his sandy hair curling damply on the nape of his neck where he'd given himself a quick swill under the tap.

'Dad. I didn't hear you come down.'

Michael Ryan straightened up, ducking to avoid the rack of washing with a deftness unusual in so big a man. He drew unhurriedly on his pipe, tamping it down until, satisfied at last, he pinched out the flame and returned the taper to its place on the mantelshelf. Only then did he turn, pipe in hand, eyes narrowed against the wreathing smoke.

'Well, you wouldn't, would you? You were busy in the shop.'

It was a perfectly reasonable reply, but something in the soft Irish voice made Liz look at him suspiciously. 'How long have you been here?'

'Long enough to discover that, left to yourself, you've a fine free way with the profits,' he said in the mildest of tones. 'If you mean to treat all our customers so magnanimously, I'm thinking we'll be a long time making that fortune your mother's always on about.'

'It was only a currant loaf an' a doughnut,' she said defensively, 'and I'll pay for them out of my own money.' One shaggy eyebrow twitched and she ran forward impulsively to throw her arms round him, relishing the rough texture of his cardigan against her cheek, with its familiar smell of Wills Gold Bar tobacco, and loving him quite fiercely. 'Oh, Daddie, I suddenly thought how awful life must be for Ellen Cassidy. There's only her struggling to keep that whole family together, and nothing to look forward to. I thought how lucky we were, and I just wanted to *do* something! Giving Freddie that treat was such a little thing.' When he didn't answer, she said in an anxious, wheedling voice, 'You won't tell Mam, will you?'

'That is not a thing you should be asking of me,' he admonished, but his hand was gentling her hair, for this was his Lizzie – generous to a fault, and he wouldn't have her any different. Liz sighed and relaxed. 'Did you have much trouble getting your mother off to the doctor's?' he asked presently.

She drew away at once, hearing the special softness that always crept into his voice when he spoke of Mam. But a sudden need to reassure him overcame the gnawing worm of jealousy. Putting on her best James Cagney impression, she said, 'Well, I had to threaten her a bit, but she went quietly in the end.'

He managed a smile, but Liz noticed that it didn't quite reach his eyes. And he began to fiddle with his pipe again, sucking at it and tamping it down as he so often did when he was bothered. Apprehension returned, churning her insides.

'Mam will be all right, won't she?'

Sighing, he laid his pipe on the mantelshelf and pulled her close again, this child who was his favourite, though he loved them all. His chin sank to rest against her hair. 'Don't ever be doubting it, Lizzie, my love. She's just a bit run down, I reckon. But, sure, isn't your mother Dandy Power's daughter, and the very spit of him? The Powers are bonny fighters, every one.' The raw emotion in his voice was almost more than Liz could bear, for it told her that in spite of his apparent confidence, he was as unsure as she was herself.

It had always been the same between Mam and himself. Grandma Power had told Liz often enough, before she went to God, about the big quiet young man from Connemara with eyes as soft and blue as cornflowers, who had taken a room next door to them, and lost his heart utterly and completely to their daughter Kathleen the moment he first laid eyes on her. Their wedding photograph had pride of place on the kitchen dresser, and Liz would often stand and look at it, the raw-boned young man with the shy smile, the sleeves of his coat not quite long enough for his arms, and the girl with pretty dark hair cut fashionably short and curling round her face. You could see the love shining out of them. To see them now, her father's shoulders beginning to hunch a little after long hours in the bakehouse, and Mam, hiding a heart of gold and her weariness behind a brisk driving manner and sharp tongue, it was sometimes hard to believe they were the same two people. Yet only recently, at Uncle Nick's wedding breakfast in the church hall, she had watched them dancing, folded very close, with Dad crooning 'I'll take you home again, Kathleen,' softly into Mam's ear, and a lump had come into her throat. Rita said it was embarrassing, them carrying on like that at their age, but Liz blinked away a tear and wondered if anyone would ever love her like that.

By the time Joey and Eddie came back, Michael had mixed his starter dough and gone on his rounds, to collect the money and any unsold goods. Liz made the promised Bovril for the boys, and left the two of them listening to Children's Hour on the wireless while fighting over the toasting fork. 'Don't make a mess,' she said. 'I've put the dripping bowl out on the side, but I'll thank you not to go digging down for all the juicy bits from underneath.'

'Can we go and play ollies in the bakehouse after?'

She eyed the shiny marbles chinking in Joey's hand with misgiving. 'Only if you promise not to leave them lying around. We don't want any broken legs this close to Christmas. And watch out for Missy's kittens. They might just be daft enough to swallow one.'

When Shirley Anne came in, banging the back door behind her and muffled to the eyebrows in a thick woollen scarf for fear of germs, Eddie had gone home for his tea and Joey had vanished upstairs. Complaining bitterly, the younger girl unwound the scarf and left it in a heap on the floor with her dancing shoes, then rushed to the chair by the fire, pulled off her boots, and sat wriggling her feet in their thick black stockings as close to the flames as she dared, half crying as they began to thaw and hot aches set in.

'You'd do much better to give them a brisk rub,' Liz admonished, coming through from the shop. 'You'll get terrible chilblains doing that.'

'I don't care. Rubbing them hurts just as much.' Shirley Anne pulled at the ribbon that tied back her shoulder-length flaxen curls, and they sprang free to cluster about her face. At just fourteen, she was already bidding to be a beauty – and knew it. 'Besides, I've see you toasting your feet often enough.'

'Please yourself. Only don't be too long about it; there's the table to lay and bread and butter to be cut. And I'll thank you not to leave those things on the floor. Chris is bringing Jimmy Marsden home for supper.'

This news effected an immediate transformation. Her sister rose in a graceful swoop, all discomfort forgotten. 'Isn't he the one whose father has that big butcher's shop near Lunts? The good looking one?'

'If you happen to like boys who plaster Brylcreem on their hair and talk all smarmy . . .' Liz said dismissively.

'Well, Lily Killigan and me both think he's smashing!'

' "I," ' she corrected absently. 'Anyhow, Lily Killigan thinks anything in long trousers is smashing.'

Shirley Anne chose to ignore this slur on her best friend. She drifted across to the staircase, pausing two steps up, with one hand on the banister rail to say in her best stage voice: 'I think I'll just go and change my frock. This old serge isn't fit to be seen. It needs washing.'

'Well, you'll have to wash it yourself,' Liz snapped. 'And don't be long changing,' she added, peeved that Shirley Anne could somehow manage to look ethereal even in her old serge and woolly stockings. 'Mam's out, and I don't see why I should do everything!'

'No need to snap. Anyway, I'll be finishing school in a few days, so it's hardly worth bothering.'

It had long been a source of grievance to Liz that her sister was accorded her full Christian name while her own much nicer Elizabeth had been shortened. At least she no longer got called Lizzie, except occasionally by Dad, and she didn't mind that, because it was said with love. But in her less charitable moments, she resented the fact that, because Shirley Anne had been a delicate baby, she had been indulged from the first. Admittedly Liz, little more than a baby herself, had been enchanted by the tiny angelic bundle, who had learned early to exploit her fragile appearance and enormous blue eyes to good effect – and had continued to do so throughout fourteen years, both at home and at school, whenever anything in the least taxing was demanded of her. But somehow she was never too tired to dance.

It was when she was four that dancing lessons had been advocated to strengthen her under-developed limbs. Shirley Anne's talent showed itself at once, evoking eulogies from Miss Eglantine, her teacher, and she quickly became the star of the dance school's small concerts. When the remedial need for lessons passed, Miss Eglantine had argued that it would be criminal to stifle such a gift: Mam had refused to spend hard-earned money on what could no longer be justified as a necessity, but Shirley Anne made herself ill with crying, and finally promised that she would earn the money for her lessons.

Even then she had found a really cushy Saturday job, doing light shopping for one of Miss Eglantine's wealthy patrons. And not only did she get a shilling a time, but Mrs Frith also gave her little presents – a white frilly blouse that she no longer wore, a glittering evening purse with only an odd bead or two missing, and lots of other things – that Shirley Anne accepted prettily, then pawned at Mr O'Hare's on Benledi Street corner, making herself a nice bit extra. Liz sometimes thought that if Shirley Anne fell into a midden, she'd come up smelling of the Californian Poppy scent she was so daft about. And immediately she despised herself for succumbing to the sin of jealousy.

No-one came into the shop for ages. Liz looked at her pile of homework, resolved to do it later, and finally, out of sheer restlessness, wandered through and opened the shop door to peer out. You couldn't see more than two houses down Fortune Street. The fog lay like dirty cotton wool, carrying the soot from a thousand belching chimneys, and the taste of it caught in her throat. Liz hated fog. She always felt as though there were something evil just beyond her reach – something that distorted sound, making the hollow rattle of the trams down on Scottie Road seem much closer, while traffic in Greaty itself swished up on you without warning; disembodied voices drifted back and forth, and the foghorns, increasing in urgency, spawned distant plaintive echoes. She didn't envy anyone out on the river tonight – or anywhere else for that matter. Oh, Mam, hurry up, she cried silently.

'Hey, our kid – do us a favour and shut that door before we all freeze to death back here!'

'Chris!' Liz turned joyfully as her brother put his head into the shop. 'I didn't hear you come.'

Chris was tall and sandy-fair like his father, with the same slow beguiling smile, the same easy manner – in his overalls and baker's hat the likeness was almost uncanny. Liz often wondered if that was why he was Mam's favourite. 'I was just wondering if there was any point keeping the shop open this evening, but Mam's not back yet, so I suppose we'd better carry on as usual.'

'She'll come,' he said confidently. 'A bit of fog won't trouble Mam. I'd go and meet her if I knew which way she was coming, though she'd not thank me for it. She's likely called in to see Dandy.'

'Yes, of course.' Why hadn't she thought of that? Liz walked briskly to join him, and he flung a casual arm round her shoulders.

'We aren't going to wait supper, are we?' he said with a grin. 'It'd be a pity to let that pie spoil.'

'Greedy pig!'

'Just trying to be practical, with Jimmy being here an' all. We were thinking of going down to the Stadium later.'

Liz rather wished Jimmy Marsden *weren't* here this evening. Not that she disliked him exactly; she just wasn't in the mood for visitors. 'Come on, then. As it happens, Mam said not to wait on her, and I've no idea when Dad'll be back. I don't suppose for one moment that Shirley Anne has laid the table?'

Chris chuckled. ' 'Fraid not. She's wearing her best Sunday pink, and the last I saw, she was giving Jimmy the full Hollywood treatment.'

Laughing, they went through to the back, where they found their young sister perched on the table, swinging her legs and talking animatedly to a stocky young man with bold dark eyes and glistening black hair swept back to give him a passing resemblance to Clark Gable. Next thing, he'd be growing a moustache. He was lounging back in the armchair, clearly amused by Shirley Anne's antics, and contributing the odd teasing comment. Suddenly, illogically, Liz wished she had taken that bit of extra time to brush out her plaits.

'Hi, Liz,' he said, lifting a casual hand.

Jimmy Marsden was the same age as Chris, but a lot more sure of himself. And flashy, Liz decided, eyeing the sharp crease in his grey flannels, the Fair Isle pullover and boldly checked sports jacket. Yes, he was too flashy by half.

'I thought you were supposed to be setting the table, Shirley Anne,' she said more sharply than she intended, as Chris went to change out of his work clothes.

'Sorry.' Shirley Anne stopped swinging, and grimaced as she dropped lightly to the floor. 'Poor Liz! Have you got one of your headaches? You look ever so pale, doesn't she, Jimmy?'

'Put your claws away, little cat,' he said with a grin. 'Your Liz looks fine to me.'

Far from taking offence, she tossed her head provocatively, gurgled with laughter, and pulled the tablecloth out of the dresser drawer. 'If you want some tea, you'll have to work for it. Come and help me with this,' she said, shaking it out.

Kathleen had no clear recollection of leaving the surgery on Rose Hill, nor did she notice which way her feet were taking her. She had pulled her scarf over the lower part of her face to keep out the fog, and walked aimlessly, head down, only half aware of shadowy figures jostling her as they scurried home out of the choking pea-souper with its numbing cold. The raucous shouts of '*Y'echaw . . . Y'eckspress*' came and went. Every so often a pool of lamplight revealed a shabby news vendor hugging the *Evening Echoes* and *Expresses* close to his body for warmth, hopping from one foot to another in a vain attempt to stamp some vestige of life back into them. Once she was dragged back from under the front of a tram. She stared vacantly at her deliverer, who was mouthing something about strawberry jam, and then asked, sharply: 'You all right, gairl?' Without answering she withdrew her arm from his clasp and moved on. 'Ey! Don' strain yerself ter say thanks!' he shouted after her. 'Tell yer what – next time I'll let the tram 'ave yer!'

But she scarcely heard him. Her mind was incapable of coherent thought, battling with a confusion of anguish, fear, ice-cold anger and raging indignation – and over it all, she heard the voice of Dr Graham quietly but firmly spelling out exactly what she must, or to be more precise must *not*, do for the next five months.

What he prescribed was impossible, of course. A whole month in bed – and that only the start of it! It couldn't be done, for how would Michael manage without her? Yet if she defied his warning, she would almost certainly end up killing the unborn child within her. And that would be murder, which was equally unthinkable.

It wasn't fair, just as they were beginning to taste the fruits of success. But perhaps that was it. Perhaps she wanted success too much, and God was punishing her for it . . .

Kathleen came to a halt, and saw with vague surprise that she had come home – not to the shop, but to her father's house in Virgil Street where she had been born and raised. Had she been drawn here by primeval instinct? For surely every woman needed the comfort of her mother at a time like this. Except that her own mother was long gone.

There was a lump as big as an egg in her throat as she rattled the knocker. Light from the lobby slanted suddenly across the uncurtained front parlour as the door to the back room opened, throwing up shadows on the walls.

'God save you, whoever you are, on a night like this,' said Dandy Power, turning the lock, his neat figure framed in the narrow opening, familiar and reassuringly pugnacious, his bald head gleaming beneath the lamp. 'Kathleen, girl? Is that you? Come away in, for the love of God!'

And with a strangled sob, she stumbled forward into his arms.

*

Michael Ryan pushed his handcart home by way of Rose Hill, though he guessed that Kathleen would be long gone. Still, he couldn't shake off his worry. It was so unlike her to be lack-lustre. Maybe it was her age. Sometimes, it was hard to remember that twenty years and more separated the girl he had married from the woman she was now; in his eyes she was always his own lovely Kathleen. An only child, he had little experience of women's problems: his mother had died giving him life, and the aunt who reared him had abhorred weakness of any kind. He had heard other men complain of their wives' irrational behaviour when they reached 'a certain age' – but, sure, his Kathleen wasn't like other women.

When he reached Dr Graham's, he saw that the lights were out in the front of the house, where the waiting room and surgery were situated. He toyed with the idea of calling in anyway, for reassurance. But the doctor would most likely be at his supper, and he'd be none too pleased to be summoned from it by an over-anxious husband.

With his coat collar turned up and his hat pulled well down, Michael shook the life back into his numbed hands and resumed his journey. It was no easy matter, pushing the cart in this weather: if he kept to the road, even close into the kerb, he was in mortal danger of being knocked down by any eedjut crazy enough to be driving a car, and if he took to the pavement, he could well take the skin off some poor devil's shins.

Even so, nothing could quite dispel his glow of satisfaction that there were so few unsold goods to be carried home. Kathleen would be pleased, he thought, feeling the comfortable weight of silver coin dragging at his pocket – and on a Monday at that. Trade was getting better all the time. A few more weeks and he could maybe start looking for that van. Meanwhile there was Christmas to be thought about, and he was resolved that this year everyone would have something special. He already knew what he would get for Kathleen – and Joey, too, was easy. The lad had been haunting them for a bicycle for long enough, and hadn't he seen the very one yesterday in a second-hand shop over Toxteth way? He'd go in first thing tomorrow and put a deposit down for it. Dandy would be happy to keep it for him until Christmas Eve.

Michael had a great regard for his father-in-law. When they first met, Dandy had been a riveter by trade and a pugilist by inclination, though it was many a year since his last appearance at the Stadium. Michael had never seen him in action, but knew that in his day Dandy had been a bonny featherweight, much sought after by agents who begged him to turn professional. This he had done for about ten years, often fighting twice a night to bring in the money, but nowadays he contented himself with coaching youngsters in the noble art. It kept him young in his retirement, he said, and certainly his sixty-seven years sat lightly on him. He was Dandy to all, even to his grandchildren, and to see him striding out, you'd know at once how he came by his nickname: trim figure neatly suited, curly-brimmed blocker at a jaunty angle on his head, and always the colourful waistcoat proudly ornamented by a gold-plated half-hunter and chain, presented to him after his last fight by his enthusiastic supporters, as a mark of their esteem.

It occurred to Michael that, as he would be passing close to Virgil Street, he could drop by this evening to ask Dandy about keeping Joey's bicycle safe till Christmas. With luck he might even be offered a welcome nip of whisky to warm him.

The living room was quiet. The older boys had gone out at last, Chris reluctant to leave, with Mam not yet home.

'Come on.' Jimmy had finally become impatient. 'You're not doin' any good sittin' here, an' we'll miss the main bout if we leave it too late. If you like, we can go round by way of your Grandad and the doc's.'

Joey had been packed off to bed, and Shirley Anne, having cleared the table and washed up, departed with an air of silent martyrdom to rub some Pond's cold cream into her hands. Liz finished drying and stacking the dishes, and got out her homework. But Homer's *Iliad* failed to hold her attention, and the French translation fared little better. Her glance strayed more and more often to the clock on the wall.

When the shop bell went, she jumped. It was an age since anyone had been in. She put down her book and hurried through, to find her mother pushing home the bolts.

'Mam, at last! I was beginning to think . . .' It seemed foolish now to admit to her worry, with her mother there safe and sound. She finished lamely, 'Is the fog still as bad?'

'It's worse, if anything. There's no point in staying open any longer.' Kathleen straightened up, not quite meeting her daughter's eyes. 'Your Dad's putting the cart away.'

'Oh, you came home together!' Liz made no attempt to disguise her relief. 'What did Dr Graham say? Did he give you a tonic?'

Kathleen didn't answer. Instead, she pushed past her daughter, making for the stairs, and Liz saw that her eyes were all red and blotchy. 'Mam? What is it . . . what's wrong?'

'For the love of God, don't fuss me, child. I just want to go upstairs for a while.'

'But you haven't had anything to eat.'

'I'm not hungry.'

Dismayed, Liz watched her go. Shirley Anne, who was curled up in the armchair, looked up from her new copy of *Picturegoer*. 'Whatever's up with Mam? Isn't she well?'

Liz whirled round, eyes blazing. 'Of course she's not well! She hasn't been well for ages, as you'd have noticed if you weren't so wrapped up in yourself!'

'No need to snap. You've been wrong side out all evening.'

It was true. Liz bit her lip and was on the point of apologizing, but her sister already had her nose stuck back in her magazine. Indignation surfaced again, and might have exploded if she hadn't seen that the light was on in the bakehouse.

She found her father standing motionless, his big frame bent over the table, head down, his hands splayed out, as though supporting an unbearable weight. The sight of him brought a lump to her throat. Something awful must have happened to make him look like that. The fear made her want to turn and run, but he sensed her presence and turned.

'Ah, Lizzie, my love, it's you. I've been cutting back the dough.' He looked around blankly, as if he weren't sure what to do next, though the open flour sack stood ready by the trough, waiting to be used. 'Everything all right, is it?'

And suddenly, Liz knew nothing could be worse than not knowing. 'No, Dad, everything isn't all right – not all right at all. What with you looking like someone's just kicked five bells out of you – and Mam in a right state and gone rushing off upstairs!' He just went on standing there, staring through her with that awful, defeated look. 'Please, you must tell me, even if . . .' Liz couldn't finish.

But Michael couldn't seem to take in what she was saying. He couldn't rid his mind of the memory of his Kathleen sitting in Dandy's back parlour, her eyes swollen from weeping – Kathleen who had always been his strength, who hardly ever cried. Never would he forget the way she had thrown herself into his arms the minute he walked in, fresh sobs wracking her body at the sight of him.

And then it had all come pouring out of her, about the baby – as if it was herself to blame, until at last he grew quite angry with her. He'd held her very tight. 'Hush, now,' he'd said in a strangled voice. 'No-one is to blame, *acushla*, least of all you!' And he recalled those nights without number when he had sweated out his agony of longing, denying his own body because of the love he bore his wife; and on the very few occasions when temptation had proved too much he had been *so* careful. There was just that one night, after her brother Nick's wedding four months back, when they'd all got a bit merry and he had maybe grown a bit careless. One night!

The whisky Dandy thrust at him, too quickly swallowed, loosened his tongue and he, who never swore, had glared hard-eyed at his father-in-law over Kathleen's head. 'Ten long years of celibacy I've endured, as near as dammit – and for what?'

'Michael!'

But for once, his wife's shocked voice made no impression.

'I'll tell you for what – sodding all, that's what,' he concluded bitterly. 'You know what I think? God must have a bloody sadistic sense of humour, else why would He make us for coupling an' then kick us in the teeth for doing it?'

'Stop it, Michael!' Kathleen had been appalled and embarrassed by his frankness in the presence of her father – to say nothing of his language. She wasn't even aware that he knew such words! But in a curious way, his outburst helped her to pull herself together. 'I won't listen to such wicked blasphemous talk!' she cried, looking at him for a moment with something of her old fire. And then her face had softened. 'Ah, listen now, Michael – it's not for us to question God's design,' she said resolutely, putting him to shame. 'It'll be all right – He'll not let us down, you'll see.'

'Dad!' Liz was shaking his arm.

'Oh, I'm sorry, child. I was miles away. It's just that I – we've had a wee bit of a shock.'

'What kind of shock?'

'Well, the long and short of it is,' he said awkwardly, 'your mother's to have a baby, after all this time – ' He shrugged, his voice flat. 'Seemingly, she's known of it for some weeks, and kept the knowledge to herself so as not to be troubling me.'

And Liz, who had been prepared for the very worst, felt a great weight lifting off her. 'But that's wonderful!' And then, noticing that he wasn't sharing her mood; 'Isn't it?' she demanded, drawing on her limited knowledge. 'I mean, like you said, it's been a long time since Joey, but Mrs Killigan had Maisie last year, and I'm sure she's older than Mam . . .'

'It isn't simply a question of age, girl dear.' He turned with a sigh and drew her close. 'Listen now, while I explain to you the best I can.'

A short time later, Liz stood at the top of the stairs, Mam's stone hot-water bottle in its blue flannel jacket tucked under one arm, and a mug of hot Ovaltine clasped in her hands. She nibbled nervously at her lip as she hesitated outside the closed door of her parents' room, then she knocked softly and went in.

It was a smallish room, with the bed taking up most of the space. On one side of the bed a narrow wardrobe stood against the wall, cheek by jowl with a tall thin chest of drawers. On the opposite wall was a little bow-fronted dressing table with an oval mirror.

Her mother sat motionless on the bed, beneath the picture of Our Lady of Perpetual Succour, recipient of many a novena on behalf of one or other of her family. She was staring into the mirror, and in the poor light her face seemed full of hollows, almost skull-like. Liz shivered at the unfortunate comparison. Kathleen's eyes lifted briefly to acknowledge her daughter, but she made no attempt to move.

'Mam – ' Liz summoned all her reserves of courage and walked across to put the mug down. 'I've brought you a hot drink,' she said.

It was as though her mother had not heard. She went on gazing at her reflection, just looking and looking, and her daughter, feeling helpless in a situation she still didn't fully understand, bit her lip and turned away to slide the bottle under the bedclothes.

At last Mam spoke. 'How old would you say I am, Liz? Seeing me as I am now, this minute?'

Her voice was devoid of expression. Liz didn't quite know how to answer. Mam had never been one for making a fuss over her appearance. The pretty dark hair that had curled round her face on her wedding day now had silver threads in it, and was pulled back into a kind of bun. It was obvious, too, that Mam was feeling bad just now, and it showed. In an effort to make her feel better, she said awkwardly, 'I never really think of you as being any particular age – you're always the same to me, to all of us. You're our mother.'

Kathleen swallowed. 'You're a good girl, Liz. But the truth is, I'm too old by a long way.'

'No, you're not!' Liz cried passionately. 'That's a stupid thing to say!' She dropped to a crouch at her mother's knee, looking up. 'Oh, Mam, listen to me. I know – about the baby and everything. Dad explained it all to me . . . and I want you to know that you're not to worry. Everything's going to be all right. Get to bed, now – I've put the bottle in near the top, so you'll have a nice warm patch to get into – and you've to stay there and rest for as long as Dr Graham says you must. I'll get the others organized, and between us we'll manage fine.'

'Oh, my dear girl!' Kathleen bent and gathered Liz convulsively to her, pressing her daughter's head against her breast. 'What would I do without you? I have so much to be thankful for!'

Liz kept quite still, half smothered in the folds of her mother's best white silk blouse, which was warm and soft to her skin and exuded faint traces of the 4711 Eau de Cologne she always used. It was a long time since Mam had given her more than a quick hug. She felt strange, even a little embarrassed, by this sudden intimacy. Yet the part of her that was still a child savoured the comforting swell of her mother's breast, the heartbeat fluttering fast and faint beneath her cheek. And then, gradually, she became aware that warm tears were soaking into her hair.

'Mam?' she whispered, her own throat closing up fast with fear. 'Mam, you are *pleased* about the baby, aren't you?'

Chapter Three

Liz tossed restlessly far into the night, for once not noticing that her side of the bed was stone cold, until Shirley Anne, already in sole possession of the hot-water bottle, grabbed back her share of the bedclothes for the umpteenth time and mumbled crossly, 'Give over, our Lizzie – you'll give us pneumonia!'

It had been an odd kind of evening, and as she drifted in and out of sleep, dream and reality became muddled in her mind. But always, she came back with a jolt to face the certainty that from now on life was going to be different. Dad had said as much, though she still didn't fully understand why having a baby was so dangerous for Mam.

Liz had told Shirley Anne about the baby, leaving out the more worrying aspects, whilst explaining that Mam would have to stay in bed for a while. 'Which means there'll be no burying your head under the blankets of a morning. Joey can't manage all the early morning jobs on his own, and you'll have to help a lot more in the shop, too.'

Shirley Anne didn't mind about the shop, but she protested loudly about the rest, and went flouncing off to bed in a huff, leaving Liz to reflect ruefully on her own lack of tact. Oh, well, least said, soonest mended. It had been a long day, and tomorrow would be even longer, so she'd better shift herself. She stifled a yawn and went into the bakehouse.

It had always been her favourite place, especially at night, but tonight it seemed more welcoming than usual with the oven roaring away, a strong aroma of yeast in the air, and Missy in her basket under the big scrubbed table, ruthlessly grooming her latest kittens. Her number one son, now fully grown and sleekly black, stalked the corners in search of mice.

'You've made an early start,' Liz exclaimed, seeing that her father had already tipped the dough out of the trough on to the table and covered it with sacks, and was scaling off and handing up his second batch of four-pound loaves. The first batch had been set to prove, and covered with a cloth to exclude any draughts.

Michael looked up briefly. 'I thought it best. There's more than usual to be got through. The orders are up again.'

'I'm not surprised. Folk aren't so daft they don't appreciate quality when they see it,' Liz said with a swiftness that drew from him a reluctant smile. She ran a quick eye down the outside orders, not counting the bread and barms, and totting up the rest in her head – 'four dozen of Eccles, the same of Nelsons for the "wet nellies", three dozen each of vanilla slices and scones, jam tarts, meat and potato pies . . .' the list went on and on, and that wasn't counting what they'd need for their own shop. For a moment the sheer quantity almost daunted Liz. It wasn't the first time she had helped with the confectionery, but always Mam had been there, and she hadn't realized how much the business had grown in the past few months. 'I see what you mean,' she said, hoping she sounded confident. 'Here, I'll help with that – two pairs of hands are quicker than one.'

Without waiting for his consent, she took a piece of dough and began handing it up into a tight ball with all the ends tucked underneath. She popped it under the waiting cloth to prove and took another piece. 'As a matter of fact, I came to tell you that I'd be down by five to make a start on Mam's baking.' She hesitated. He hadn't mentioned Mam, and for some reason she felt awkward doing so. When he still said nothing, she hurried on. 'But looking at that list, I think I'd better take a leaf out of your book and get a biggish batch of puff paste ready prepared when I've finished this. It'll save time in the morning.'

Michael looked up again, brows drawn together, though his hands never faltered in their rhythm as they continued to mould the scaled dough. 'Lizzie, my love, this really won't do,' he said, the soft brogue very pronounced. 'I'll not deny that extra help would be welcome, but what you're suggesting – Well, it's a grand idea born out of a fine generous heart, but it would be quite wrong of me to let you do it. I'll not have you wearing yourself out, not now or in the morning. Your teachers won't be best pleased if you start falling asleep over your books.'

Liz heard him out impatiently. 'Well, that's the other thing I came to tell you, Dad. There's no way I can possibly go to school in the morning.' The words came out in a rush, driving home her point before he had time to object. 'Well, I can't, can I? I mean, just think. There's the shop itself for a start – someone has to take charge of that. And as for "extra help", it seems to me, looking at that list, you're going to need all the help you can get. You'll have to take a break some time during the night if you're to cope with the deliveries as well, and not get near killed with it all!'

'I'll rest for a while on the sofa when I've the best part of it done,' he promised absently.

But Liz wasn't convinced. 'So you say. But you won't. I know you. Ah, listen, now – let me help. I know I'm not Mam, but you've kidded me often enough that I've got magic fingers.' She couldn't tell if her words were having the desired effect, except that her father's hands stilled momentarily, and his face took on a funny, faraway look. She resorted to coaxing. 'It'll be all right about school, honest. Sister Imelda already knows Mam isn't well, so she won't be surprised.'

I know I'm not Mam. The words reverberated through Michael's head. There was so much that he had wanted to say to Kathleen when they got home, but in spite of his great love for her, or perhaps because of it, the right words eluded him. And so he had come in to start the bread: there was something infinitely calming about working the dough. Liz wasn't Kathleen, right enough, but just for a moment there, listening to his daughter, his thoughts had gone winging back across a space of more than twenty years – hearing the eager voice of his new young bride, so confident, and with the same uncanny knack of going right to the nub of things, as she prodded him into more ambitious ways. She hadn't been that much older than Liz was now . . . So maybe it would be wrong of him not to give his daughter a chance to prove what she could do – for tomorrow, at least. He simply couldn't bring his mind to look beyond tomorrow, not yet. Kathleen's role in the steady growth of the business had always been crucial, but it was a role that must inevitably change from now on, and he had no way of knowing how that would affect the future – a future which, only last evening, he had viewed with such rosy optimism.

Slowly, he straightened and resumed his task. 'God only knows why you should be so keen – it's terrible hard work. But you've a mighty devious way of getting round a man,' he said with a wry smile. 'And things being the way they are, the sheer logic of your argument doesn't leave me with much of a leg to stand on.' Liz reached up to plant a smacking kiss just below his ear. 'Give over, now – we've had enough soft soap for one evening. And think on – I want a clear understanding that you'll stop work the minute you've had enough. I'm sure if I ask him, Chris will put in an hour or so before he leaves for work – '

'Of course he will. And if we all pull together, everything'll be fine. There, that's done.' Liz pushed the last piece of dough beneath the cover and moved down to the marble slab beyond the big wooden table. 'I've already told Shirley Anne she'll have to be up early, ready to shape herself and do her share.' As she talked, she began to assemble and weigh out her ingredients.

Michael turned his attention to the oven. There was a great blast of heat as he opened the door. The soot on the back wall had turned to grey ash. Swiftly he raked away all the coals that smoked or flamed, and threw a small bowl of water over the hot ashes that had fallen through into the pit. As the steam rose he shut the door and closed down the damper to let the heat build up again. He paused in turning back to watch Liz lift the four pounds of flour from the scales, and tip it on to the slab. Not wasting a moment, she rubbed in the cake margarine, made a well for the cream of tartar and the water, and brought it all together into a nice clear paste. Finally she dusted it with flour, brought it swiftly and lightly into a ball, and covered it with a damp cloth.

The weight of his misery was momentarily lightened by a glow of pride. She had the gift, right enough – a true Ryan to her fingertips, with an expertise beyond her years. Even so, it felt strange, not having Kathleen at his side. If anything were to happen to her . . . He pushed the thought away and drew the first proving towards him, swiftly remoulding the dough to fill the waiting tins, then threw the cloth over them again to give them time to recover before putting them in the oven.

'Seems you've got everything all worked out,' he grunted. 'But heaven knows what your mother will say. She won't be pleased to know you're missing school.'

'Don't worry about Mam. I'll talk her round.' Liz sounded more confident than she felt. She reached for the big slab of butter, squeezing it to make sure there was no water in it, then moulding it into a nice neat block. There was a precision about making puff paste that she particularly enjoyed – pinning out the dough to an exact rectangle on the slab, thicker in the middle, thinner on the outsides; shaping the butter to the size of the inner rectangle and placing it in the centre, folding the sides over it like a parcel; then rolling it out once more into a larger rectangle, using as little flour as possible and brushing off any that remained.

But now, as Liz worked, folding one end to exactly two thirds of its length and bringing the other end neatly to cover it, her mind was elsewhere. Dad was really down – and he hadn't been near Mam since they came home, not even to say goodnight. He couldn't be angry about the baby, not Dad. She wondered if she should tell him how miserable Mam was, but that might just make him feel worse. Liz sighed and gave her mind to other, equally pressing, problems.

Dad hadn't been altogether wrong when he jokingly accused her of having things all worked out – up as far as Christmas, anyway. It was obvious, when you thought about it. Mechanically, she turned the paste round, letting her thoughts run on as she pinned it out again, keeping the edges straight, and repeating the folding operation.

Mam would raise Cain, of course, if she had the least inkling of what her daughter was contemplating. Tomorrow morning would be all right; she could talk her way round that one. But there was next week to be thought of, too. Dad would have to write to Sister Imelda – it might take a small miracle to persuade him it wasn't a mortal sin, going behind Mam's back, but it was the only way to solve the immediate problem. And after tomorrow, after she had proved she could cope, they would both see it was the only sensible thing to do . . . With the sublime optimism of youth, the possibility of failure never entered her head.

The last fold completed, Liz set the paste aside, covered it with a dry cloth and then a damp one. 'There,' she said. 'I can finish it off in the morning.'

'That you can, girleen,' Michael said, his voice tight. He seized the scuffle pole with rather more vigour than usual, dunked the sacking on the end of it in a bucket of water, and sloshed it over the base of the oven to clean away any lingering ash ready for the bread. 'But don't be doing another thing now. Tomorrow will be a long day, so you're going to need all the sleep you can get.'

It was growing light when Kathleen woke, and for a moment she panicked, thinking she had overslept. And then she came fully awake and remembered, and a different kind of panic took hold of her. Oh, God! she prayed, show me what to do for the best . . . Not just for me, but for the family and for Michael, especially for Michael. He's such a good man, a simple honest man, and this has hit him hard. He's hurting inside, having taken the blame to himself. But we'll get that idea right out of the way, once I have him to myself for five minutes. I know well enough he didn't mean all those things he said, not really. If I could just . . .

Tears thickened Kathleen's throat, but she refused to give in to them. Feeling sorry for herself was stupid and unproductive, and she could not abide waste. Even stuck up here away from it all, there'd be things she could do – decisions to be made, the accounts to be kept in order, the kind of things Michael never gave a thought to.

It was going to be unbearably frustrating, having to lie back and watch others doing her work – and likely making a pig's ear of it, most of the time. But, please God, when the month was up, Dr Graham would allow her to resume at least a part of her daily routine. In the meantime . . .

Her thoughts were disturbed by a curious scrabbling at the door, which opened with a jerk to reveal a blurred figure clutching a tray. 'Are you awake, Mam?' Liz whispered.

'Well, if I wasn't before, I am now,' Kathleen said drily.

Liz hugged the tray to her with one hand while she switched on the light. 'Sorry. I'm not awfully good at this. I didn't mean to wake you.'

'You didn't.'

'Oh, good. I've brought you a fresh hot-water bottle and some breakfast. Tea and some toast and marmalade. Is that all right?'

'Splendid,' said her mother, swallowing the faint nausea that rose in her at the mention of food. She levered herself upright, removed the rosary beads which had slid beneath her, the crucifix digging into her side, and pushed them under the pillow. 'I can't remember when I last had breakfast in bed – certainly not since Joey was born. Here, give me the bottle – that's right, and the tray.

And while you're at it, you'd better fetch over that fancy bed jacket you knitted for my last birthday.'

Liz ran to open the bottom drawer of the chest and drew out the dainty blue jacket wrapped in tissue paper. The wool felt soft against her fingers as she helped Mam slip it on over her flannel nightie. 'It looks beautiful,' she said shyly. 'The colour really suits you.'

'I don't know about that, but if you mean to keep up this kind of treatment I'll be getting properly spoiled.' Kathleen's shrewd eyes had not missed the slight unease beneath her daughter's brightness. 'What time is it?'

Liz hesitated. It seemed a terrible long time since she had climbed out of bed, teeth chattering, fumbling in the dark for the vest and knickers and the hated liberty bodice that she had pushed under the eiderdown to keep warm, while Shirley Anne slept on, curled up like a dormouse.

Her mother still waited patiently for an answer.

'Time?' she said vaguely, peering through the curtains. 'We've been so busy, I've hardly noticed the time. Getting on for nine, I should think. The fog's gone, thank goodness, but it's very frosty. Chris was up before four to give Dad a bit of a hand, and I've managed to get all the wholesale orders done, and the rest are baking now.' Liz knew she was gabbling, but couldn't stop. 'What do you think? Grandpa Dandy turned up to help Dad with the deliveries. Isn't he a brick? They went off together about an hour ago. And he said he'd help in the shop later. I couldn't manage to prise Shirley Anne out of bed in time to get the milk, but Joey managed the lot – he's worked like a little Trojan. They've both had their breakfast and gone off to school, and she's promised to help when she comes home this evening.'

The mention of school brought her to a halt, and at last she met her mother's eyes. It was impossible to guess what she was thinking. Even when she spoke, her voice was expressionless.

'You seem to have everything under control.'

'I hope so,' Liz said. And then, head high, 'I may as well own up, Mam – I'm not going to school today.'

'No. I think I'd already guessed as much.'

'Well, I couldn't go really, could I? Not with all the extra there is to be done.'

'No,' Kathleen agreed quietly, sipping her tea.

The mild acceptance startled Liz. It wasn't at all what she had been expecting. Perhaps, after all, she might risk broaching her other idea.

'Mam . . .' she began.

Kathleen patted the bed beside her. 'Sit down here a minute, Liz. There's something I want to say to you.'

Liz sat, warily, ready to do battle if necessary, and determined to stick to her guns, no matter what Mam said.

Kathleen set her cup back on the saucer and put the tray to one side. It was a great act this daughter of hers was putting on, but she could have no idea how much those eloquent tawny eyes gave away.

'You've hardly touched your toast!'

'I'm sorry, dear. I'll do better another time.' Kathleen's smile was strained as she took her daughter's hand. 'Listen now, last night I was a bit upset, and what I said then – well, it's best forgotten. I'm thinking a lot straighter this morning, and there's a suggestion I want to put to you. I wouldn't even consider it if I didn't know you'd finished your exams, but as it is, it seems I've little choice. Liz, how would you feel if I were to write to Sister Imelda, asking her to excuse you from school for the rest of term?'

To Kathleen's astonishment, her daughter began to laugh.

'Well, I don't see what's funny about it! If you get behind with your lessons, you'll have to work much harder later on to make up. We'd have to put it to your father as well, of course, for it's not a decision to be taken lightly. But if he did agree . . .'

'Oh, Mam! I know it's not really funny. It's just that I was trying to pluck up courage to suggest the very same thing.'

'Two minds.' Kathleen's mouth quirked. 'To think of it, St Anthony's probably wouldn't miss Shirley Anne if she did the same. With Christmas so close, you'll need help with the shop.'

Joey, in blithe ignorance of the drama taking place around him, knew only that Mam was poorly, which meant he'd had to do extra early jobs.

'Our Liz was busy queening it in the bakehouse an' ordering everyone around,' he told Eddie when they met later at school. 'Shirley Anne was supposed to help, but getting her out of bed of a morning's more trouble than chopping wood. Anyway, she's useless.'

'If yer Mam's still bad termorrer, I don't mind givin' you a hand,' Eddie said off-handedly.

'Hey, that'd be great! Dad might even pay you. Not much, mind – I only get a tanner a week meself.'

'That's all right. I've got plenty of good ideas for making an extra bob or two. For a start, I thought we might buy some candles with what we made last week sellin' all them chips. I know a place I can get candles really cheap, and we can go round people's houses, selling them. Everyone's sure to be wanting extra candles for *Chrizzy*.'

The 'chips' in question were bundles of firewood. It had been awful hard going chopping all that wood, but Eddie, always quick to spot a good little earner, assured Joey that, like candles, everyone needed firewood at this time of year, and had urged him on until his arms ached. And as usual, Eddie had been right. If they did half as well out of the candles, he'd be able to give Mam an extra prezzy, and have a bit to put by besides, which might cheer her up.

By the time Shirley Anne and Joey came in for dinner that first day Liz was almost light-headed with exhaustion, and she began to wonder how her mother had managed for all these years, with the cooking, the cleaning, the washing and the bakehouse work as well as the shop. She was certainly in no mood to suffer her sister's complaints about the blind scouse she served up to them.

'I didn't have time to go for meat, so you'll just have to put up with vegetables and dumplings for once,' she snapped. 'I can't pretend to make it like Mam does.' Things might not have been so bad, she thought, if it wasn't for all the do's and don't's constantly being shouted down the stairs. She had to keep telling herself that Mam was only trying to be helpful, but it was really getting on her nerves.

'I can't see why Mam has to stay in bed,' Shirley Anne grumbled. 'Mrs Killigan is forever having babies, and Lily says she's never had to stay in bed for weeks on end.'

Liz turned on her furiously. 'Shirley Anne – you've never told Lily Killigan about the baby? Oh, how could you? You promised not to breathe a word to anyone!'

'Nor I haven't!' cried her sister, guilt making her defensive.

'There wasn't a soul anywhere near when I told her. An' Lily isn't *anyone* – she's my best friend!'

'Yes, and she'll go straight home and tell her mother, and Mrs Killigan's got a mouth like a trapdoor. I bet the whole of Fortune Street knows by now!'

'Well, I don't see why you wanted to keep it such a dead secret in the first place. I bet *Mam* never said not to tell.'

Mam hadn't, which did nothing to improve Liz's temper. But before she could say more, their raised voices attracted their mother's attention. 'Is everything all right down there?'

'Yes, Mam.' She glared at Shirley Anne. 'There, now see what you've done,' she hissed.

Shirley Anne pushed her plate away in disgust, picked up her hat and coat and rushed out, banging the back door behind her. Joey carried on eating, finishing his own and Shirley Anne's fast-congealing helping, and wiping both plates clean with a piece of bread. 'It wasn't that bad, our Liz,' he said magnanimously, and wondered why she hugged him. 'Gerrof,' he said, sliding out from under to follow in his sister's wake.

'Everything all right, chuck?' Dandy asked, coming in to find Liz regarding the greasy remains of the scouse with loathing.

'Fine,' she said with bitter sarcasm. 'I'd offer you some of this, but you wouldn't thank me for it. It's disgusting. I think I'll put the snib down on the door while I run and get Mam a nice bit of fish from Mrs Mac's.'

'Go easy on yourself, Liz, love. You've already done wonders. Don't try to be a miracle worker.'

'Oh, it isn't the actual work, Grandpa Dandy,' she exclaimed with sudden passion. 'In fact, I'm enjoying that, really I am, though it's harder than I expected, only don't tell Dad I said so – or Mam. Especially Mam. It's bad enough with her constantly . . .' she stopped short, biting her lip. 'Anyway, like I said, it's not the work, it's all the extra things. I daresay I'll speed up quite a bit with practice.'

'I daresay you will,' he agreed quietly, and added, after a moment: 'It's even harder for her, you know, Lizzie.'

'Oh, I *do* know! It just . . .' she shook her head. 'If you're going up, you won't say anything? I wouldn't want to hurt her feelings.' The shop bell jangled. 'I'll have to go.'

'Never fear. Mum's the word.' He tapped his nose and grinned. 'Anything you want me to take up?'

'I don't think so. Just tell her everything's fine, and her dinner'll be up soon.'

Kathleen was sitting up in bed, viciously stabbing a needle in and out of a patch on Joey's second-best trousers. When Dandy knocked and put his head round the door she gave a guilty start, then raised her head as though prepared to do battle.

'Oh, it's you, Dad,' she said, relaxing as he did no more than lift a quizzical eyebrow at the pile of mending awaiting her attention. She resumed her patching with less venom. 'If I sat here twiddling my fingers, I'd go mad. I need something to take my mind off things. Heaven knows what that boy does, to get his clothes in this state.'

Dandy chuckled. 'Much the same as boys have always done, I daresay.' He threw her a sly look and perched on the end of the bed. 'There's a certain girl, I remember, who wasn't so very different at his age.'

'Well, at least I always mended my own clothes.'

'Aye, that you did, thanks to your Mam's training, God rest her.'

He fell silent, thinking of the pretty red-haired girl he'd met all those years ago on a jaunt to Tralee. Within a month of meeting he had married her and brought her back to Liverpool. Seven children she had borne him, and all but two had grown strong and healthy, and in time scattered like the good seed, to multiply – all except Flora, their eldest, who had married late and well, and lived very grandly down the line in Southport. Liam, Dandy's eldest, was in Chicago with half a dozen children he might never live to see, and his middle daughter, May, had moved to Toronto. But he still had Nick, his youngest, who had been a late starter in the marriage stakes. He and his Laura lived in Bootle. But of all his children, Kathy was his favourite, the most like her mother, God rest her.

'There was hardly fourpenn'orth of your Mam in those days,' he mused aloud. 'Or later. The two of you together wouldn't have made a decent shillin's worth, but she did a bonny job of raising you all, just like you are with this lot.'

Kathleen frowned. 'I'm not so sure. The two girls were going at it hammer and tongs down there a while back.'

'Well, everything's peaceful now,' he said airily. 'Got her head screwed on right, has young Liz. She's doing a grand job.'

'Perhaps, but I'm afraid it's asking too much of her – trying to put an old head on young shoulders.'

'Not a bit of it. Liz knows what she's doing, right enough, if she's left to get on with it.'

The needle stilled in Kathleen's hand. She could feel the stupid tears thick in her throat. 'You mean I shouldn't keep interfering?'

'I didn't say that.'

'But it's what you meant! It's what she thinks. I'm only trying to help – there's so much to remember . . .'

'True. And she's made herself a list of all the important things, very businesslike. By the by, you're getting something special for your dinner, so try to look pleased.'

She threw her sewing down in frustration, squeezing back the tears. 'Oh, Dad, what am I to do? This is only the first day, and I'm nearly climbing the wall. I'll never stick it for a month!'

That you won't, girl, Dandy thought. After Christmas, we'll maybe have to see what we can do about giving you a little help along the way.

'Of course you'll stick it,' he said firmly. 'Many's the time I got walloped in the first round of a fight and thought me number was up. But after a while you learn to ride the punches, to pace yourself – '

She choked on a despairing laugh. 'You and your old boxing! This isn't quite the same thing . . .'

'Don't you believe it. Life's pretty much like a prize fight when you think about it. The harder it gets, the more your need to survive outstrips everything else.' His voice softened. 'Michael's a good man. You'd go a long way to find better.'

'D'you think I don't *know* that?' Kathleen's voice rose and cracked. 'But how can I tell him so, when the big fool won't come near? I haven't seen him at all since last night, and it isn't just that he's busy. He's still blaming himself, I know he is . . .'

Dandy heard the suppressed anguish behind the words. 'Well, blame is maybe too strong a word, but I can remember how I felt when Mary lost our second baby – I felt so helpless, I went out and drunk meself paralytic. It certainly did the trick, though I'd the mother and father of a hangover to show for it. Fortunately – or maybe unfortunately in this case – that's not Michael's way.'

'Dad, *please* find him and ask him to come up.'

A few minutes later, her husband was in the room, filling it with his presence. He had removed his baker's overalls, but his sandy hair was still standing on end where he'd pulled his hat off, and his face was creased with weariness, so that he looked a curious mixture of man and boy.

He came and stood by the bed, his eyes, the only alive thing about him, raking her intently. 'I looked in on you sometime in the early hours, *acushla*,' he said. 'You were fast asleep. Already you look more rested.' There was relief in his soft voice, and a kind of diffidence, too. 'I like that blue thing you have on. You look as pretty as a picture, sure enough. I remember you were wearing blue the day I first saw you.'

'Oh, Michael' Trust him to pay her compliments at such a time! Laughter that was very close to tears caught in her throat. 'Will you sit down, for pity's sake, before you fall down? You look exhausted.'

'It was a long night. But young Liz has done us proud.' He hesitated before lowering himself onto the bed beside her. 'I suppose we'll need to talk – '

'Tomorrow,' she said.

'Yes, tomorrow,' he agreed. 'I'll think more clearly after a few hours' sleep. I can use Chris's bed.'

'In a minute,' she said and held out her arms to him. Wordlessly he reached for her, and then they were locked together, heedless of anyone who might come in, his head cradled against her breast.

The blue bedjacket was soft and warm against his unshaven cheek. '*Acushla*,' he murmured – and was asleep before the word left his lips.

That was how Liz found them, going up a little time later with the steamed fish and some bread and butter, cut very thin. She had taken great pains with the tray, laying it with a pretty lace traycloth. But as she pushed open the door, Mam put a finger to her lips and Liz instantly withdrew, feeling she was intruding on something very private. Downstairs she sighed, and put a plate over the fish to keep it warm, knowing that for all her care, it would go dry and curl up at the edges.

Chapter Four

Sister Imelda wasn't pleased, but then Liz had never expected that she would be, even though she had popped into St Anthony's on her way to the tram to light a candle to Our Blessed Lady.

She had made an effort with her appearance. Her coat was neatly buttoned and the hated uniform hat sat squarely over her plaits like a black pudding basin with a brim. Even so, her courage was already wilting by the time she got off the tram halfway up Everton Valley, Mam's letter crackling in her pocket, and crossed the road to the Convent of Notre Dame, whose forbidding walls dominated the corner ahead of her.

Liz made her way along hushed corridors, past closed classroom doors, beyond which she heard the scratching of nibs, the odd nervous cough. A new young nun enquired her business, and went ahead to prepare the way. 'You may go in now,' she whispered on her return, in reverential tones.

Sister Imelda's austere face, rigidly cocooned in white linen beneath her neat coif, gave nothing away as she listened to Liz's halting explanation, and she read Mam's letter in silence. For several moments afterwards the headmistress stood staring out of the window, struggling to subdue her anger. She ought to be used to it by now. The excuses, always the same – just a few days off to mind the young ones, feed the family, run errands. And in too many cases, it was the last she saw of her promising young students, their talents blighted before they had ever been tried. Surely, that wasn't going to happen with this child. . . ?

Liz shifted her weight from one foot to the other and allowed her gaze to stray round the room with its aura of polish and piety – the big, imposing desk covered with papers, a statue of Our Lady of Lourdes in one corner, the holy water font beside the door and the picture of Blessed Julie Billiard above the fireplace, bearing the words, *Ah, quil est bon, le bon Dieu* – How good is the Good God. Now might be the ideal time to prove it, Liz thought – and almost immediately caught her breath as the flames curling round the coals in the hearth sent up a shimmer of heat, which just for an instant gave the illusion of movement to the plump benevolent features of the Order's founder, as though she were nodding and smiling encouragement.

'You know the gist of your mother's letter, Elizabeth?'

Liz jumped. 'Yes, sister.' Only the nuns ever used her full name.

'And there is really no alternative to keeping you off school?'

'No, sister. Someone has to take Mam's place, you see, and it wouldn't be fair to ask our Rita to give up college – and Shirley Anne's too young for anything but minding the shop . . .'

'I see.' Sister Imelda paused. 'And after Christmas?'

Liz admitted that they hadn't got around to thinking that far ahead.

'I hope you will bear in mind that this is an important year for you,' the stern voice continued. 'Every day lost will be a setback.'

'I'll be able to study at home, sister,' Liz promised, eager to placate.

The headmistress appeared not to have heard. In fact, she spent so long staring down at her desk that Liz wondered if the interview was over; she was about to sidle quietly out when Sister Imelda suddenly came back to life. She flicked back her veil with an imperious finger, adjusted the starched white collar that swept down from her shoulders like a breastplate, and bent a particularly piercing look upon Liz.

'You are a bright child, Elizabeth – brighter in some ways than your sister. Does that surprise you?'

It flabbergasted her. Not that she didn't enjoy school work on the whole, but Rita was the brainy one in the family. In the distance, the bell for dismissal rang, but Liz was hardly aware of it.

'I have been going through the examination papers. As the results were given out this morning, I may tell you now that you have come top of your class in all but two subjects. If you continue to work well, you should have no trouble matriculating with excellent grades and going on to highers. You might even, if it could be managed, try for university.' After a significant pause, she concluded, 'I would ask you to bear that in mind.'

University! The revelation left Liz totally bereft of words. Sister

Imelda looked at her for a long moment then, more abruptly than usual, said: 'That is all, child. You may go.'

'Thanks – I mean, thank you, sister.' At the door, Liz paused; turned. 'Excuse me sister – Which were the two subjects – the ones I didn't come top in?'

There was an infinitessimal pause. 'Chemistry' – Liz could have sworn the austere mouth twitched – 'and Scripture.'

She left in a daze, mingling with the steady exodus of chattering, darkly uniformed figures hunched against the cold like a flock of crows as they straggled out of the building.

'Hey! Are you deaf, Liz Ryan?'

There was a tug on her arm and she turned to see her best friend. 'Sorry, Clare. I was miles away.'

'That's nothing new.' Clare Whitney tucked a flyaway strand of straight fair hair firmly behind her elastic. They were opposites in almost every way – the private pupil and the scholarship girl – yet they had been firm friends from their very first day, when they had been put in the upper band and given adjoining desks.

'When you didn't come in, I though you must be ill. There's a lot of flu about. I was going to call . . .'

'I'm fine.' Liz made sure they weren't being overheard, and quickly explained what had happened.

'How rotten for you all – so close to Christmas, too. I bet the Holy Dragon wasn't too pleased. I say, you did awfully well in the exams – did she tell you?'

'I still can't quite believe it,' Liz said, wondering what her friend would think if she told her what else Sister Imelda had said. 'Listen, keep my exam results to yourself for now, will you, Clare? It'll only set Mam worrying, if she gets to know. She's bad enough as it is.'

'If you say so.' Clare looked troubled. 'And, if I can help at all, you've only to say.'

'Thanks.' But Clare wouldn't be a ha'pporth of use in the present chaos of shop, home and bakehouse. Her father was a solicitor, and they lived in an ordered world, in a large comfortable house. Mrs Whitney had always made her welcome, just as the living room behind the shop had been a second home to Clare. But Clare was neat and precise by nature and – as Liz was fast discovering – with so many things to be done at the same time, you had to think fast and be ready for anything.

As the news about Mam got round, customers were very sympathetic. Mrs Killigan, chief spreader of the word, whose own large and ever-increasing brood had left her enormously fat, commiserated good-naturedly, and there was a wealth of kindness from folk with worries of their own.

'If there's anything at all that I can do, Liz,' Ellen Cassidy had said diffidently the moment she heard, 'you know you've only to ask. If nothing else, I could maybe take some of your washing home with me. You must have a lot of big stuff, with all that gets used in the bakehouse on top of your normal family wash.'

'But you've got more than enough already,' said Liz, thinking of all her children and Arnie, whose washing must be a day's work on its own. Yet the offer tempted her. It was one of the daily chores she least enjoyed, and it was no good relying on Shirley Anne. But it still didn't seem right to impose on Mrs Cassidy, who looked permanently tired. Even as she wavered, however, the young woman pressed home her offer.

'I wouldn't say it if I didn't mean it. It's something I *can* do, you see, and' – embarrassed colour flooded her face – 'I wouldn't want paying, just the soap. In fact, I couldn't take any payment. Arnie never got any compensation, you see, 'cos they said the accident was his own fault – he'd been at the drink and was larkin' about. So I only have the Relief, and I'd lose that if I was to take money. But your mother's done me many a kindness, and now I'd like to do something for her. I could pick up what you have of an evening in the pram, and bring it back the following day, if that's all right.' And so the matter was settled, though Liz knew she'd have to pick her moment to tell Mam.

Clare's mother did a lot of entertaining, and scarcely a week went by without at least one special order on top of her usual. She, too, was full of sympathy. 'And you will let me know if there is anything I can do to help?'

The thought of Mrs Whitney's elegant, rather statuesque figure behind the counter almost sent Liz into peals of laughter, but the offer was quite genuine.

'Such a difficult time, too – for all of you. I suppose your mother's indisposition will affect the amount of Christmas orders you can undertake?'

'Oh, no,' Liz was quick to reassure her. 'If there's anything you specially want, we can do it.'

'You're sure? I am entertaining quite a large number of friends on Christmas Eve. Cook is getting a little past it, you know, and I had thought, perhaps – some of your excellent vol-au-vents, amongst other things?'

'If you can let us know what you want in good time, and perhaps pick the order up, I'm sure we can manage most things.'

Liz made the promise with perfect confidence. After all, once Rita was home, she could foresee no real problems. At least, none before Christmas.

'We make a good team, don't we, Dad?' she said, as they worked together in quiet harmony the next morning. 'You and me together, with our Chris helping out.'

Michael looked up, his eyes soft as they rested on her. 'We do that, girl,' he agreed. 'And it's certain you'll be hard to replace. Our Chris is a fine baker, and we'd not be managing so well without him, but he doesn't have your particular skills. I'm thinking it will be hard to find a craftsman willing to work part time who can do as well as you. They mostly want full time work.' There was an agony of uncertainty in his voice.

'What exactly did Dr Graham say to you the other night?' she persisted, and when he didn't answer: 'I'm not a child, Dad – and I'm not blind, either. You've had something on your mind ever since his visit. Mam isn't going to be able to do much even when she's allowed up, is she?'

It was as if something inside her father suddenly let go, and she was shocked to see him grow haggard before her eyes. 'No, Lizzie love, she isn't. It's a difficult few months she has ahead of her.' He sighed deeply. 'We'll not be seeing the old days back for a fair while, I'm afraid. In fact, I doubt they will ever be quite as they were. But don't be lettin' on to her that I've said so. She worries enough as it is.'

'As if I would,' Liz said lightly, but her heart was being squeezed with her love for him. She wanted so much to lighten his burden, for she sensed that he didn't know which way to turn for fear of upsetting her mother. In that moment all her agonizing was at an end; the seeds, already sown in her mind, sprang to life.

She heard herself say calmly: 'You can stop worrying, Dad, because I've made a decision. I'm not going back to school after Christmas – in fact, I'm not going back at all.' She heard his swift intake of breath and hurried on. 'And before you start raising objections, it's not a case of me making sacrifices for the family.' Liz grinned self-mockingly. 'I'm not the sacrificial type. The thing is, I've never quite known what I wanted to do, except that I had this . . . this feeling worrying away inside me. And now I know why.' As she spoke, she felt a surge of excitement rising in her, the words spilling out of their own volition. '*This* is what I want to do. In time, I mean to learn everything there is to know about the making of beautiful confectionery.' She was surprising herself almost as much as her father, but suddenly it all made sense. 'And one day, Dad,' she concluded triumphantly, 'not next week or even next year, but one day, I'll make the name of Elizabeth Ryan famous far beyond Liverpool, you'll see!'

Michael stared at her, his heart beating fast, scarcely able to believe that this was his Liz. Her eager face was flushed, her eyes alight with enthusiasm – so sure of herself, she almost had him believing every word, for he knew as sure as anything that hers was no young girl's immature dream. She had set her sights impossibly high, sure enough, but her feet were firmly on the ground. If nothing else, she was learning the hard way that she faced long unsociable hours of often back-breaking work. There was, however, one big snag.

'Kathleen will have a fit!'

'We won't tell her. Not before Christmas, anyway. Let her think that you're looking for someone.'

Michael's brows came together. 'Liz Ryan, am I hearing right? You wouldn't be inciting me to lie to your mother?'

'Not at all. Just don't go out of your way to tell her the truth,' Liz said, quick as a flash. 'It's for her own good, after all.'

He spluttered, tried hard to be angry, and finally succumbed to unwilling laughter. 'Heaven help me, if I haven't spawned a true Daughter of Eve! Well, well, we'll just wait and see.'

And Liz, exhausted by her outburst, held her peace, knowing that the battle was more than half won.

*

By mid-morning on Saturday, she seemed never to have stopped running. Then at last, the shop was free of customers. 'Be an angel, Shirley Anne, and make us a cup of tea.'

Her sister went willingly for once to put the kettle on, and Liz followed her, flopping down on to the settee. Her head was spinning, and there was a throbbing over her left eye – the kind she got after too much studying. 'Please God,' she groaned, 'don't let anyone else come in for at least ten minutes.'

'You'll feel better when you've had a drink,' Shirley Anne said, eyeing her worriedly. 'At least I hope you will, cos I'll have to go when I've had mine.'

Liz sat up abruptly, and wished she hadn't. 'Go? Go where?'

'I told you early on, only you never listen. I've got to go and do Mrs Frith's shopping – she relies on me, Saturdays.'

'Well, so are we relying on you,' Liz retorted. 'Surely Mrs Frith could manage, for once? She's not helpless. You can write her a message, and get your friend Lily to take it. If Mrs Frith's that desperate, Lily can do her shopping – or she can send her chauffeur.'

But this didn't suit at all; Shirley Anne wasn't having her friend poaching on her preserves. 'Mrs Frith's promised me a permanent job after Christmas, so I don't want to go offending her now. Anyway, it's my tap dancing class at twelve o'clock, and I can't miss that. There's only one more practice before our concert.'

Liz found all her old resentment boiling up and spilling over. 'Well, you'll just have to miss it – like you'll just have to stop being such a selfish little pig and wanting everything your own way! There's less than a week to Christmas, which means we'll be busier than ever, and I've got more than enough on my plate already!'

'And whose fault is that, Miss Bossy-boots? You couldn't wait to show everyone you could take Mam's place, so it jolly well serves you right! And if you think I'm going to let you lord it over me, you've got another think coming!'

Shirley Anne tossed her head, so the silvery waves fanned out into a provocative shimmering halo. It was the last straw. 'You're stupid and unfeeling and I hate you!' Liz cried, and slapped her face.

Kathleen heard the shouting, culminating in the noisy sobs of her youngest daughter, and her own frustration reached breaking point. She climbed out of bed and ran to the head of the stairs. 'Stop that dreadful row at once, Shirley Anne! And I want the both of you up here – this minute!'

In the commotion, neither girl noticed the arrival of their grandfather. He stood in the scullery doorway, his bare head rising to a shining peak above jug-handle ears, giving him the look of an amiable pixie – an illusion that had caused many an unsuspecting opponent in the ring to underrate him, to their cost.

'Go back to bed, Kathleen,' he called up. 'I'll sort these two out and be with you in a brace of shakes.'

But he seemed to be in no hurry to begin, surveying his warring granddaughters – Liz, flushed, her eyes over-bright with anger, and Shirley Anne's face distorted and ravaged by tears. The latter, seeking to engage his sympathy, prepared to shatter the silence once more.

'That's a grand pair of lungs you've got there, girl,' he observed pleasantly, 'but one more peep out of you and I'll give you something you can really cry about.'

Shirley Anne, her mouth wide open and on the point of drawing breath, choked, and Liz, already half-ashamed of her outburst, whispered in awe, 'Grandpa Dandy, you wouldn't – would you?'

His keen eyes looked back at her, unblinking. 'Well now, since I trust the two of you are going to use what little sense God gave you, I reckon we'll never know, will we?' He gave the words time to sink in before proceeding. 'Now, you just listen to me, the two of yez – your Mam's got enough on her mind without you addin' to it, and so has your Dad, so we'll have an end to all this right now. In future, if I get even a sniff of trouble, it's me you'll answer to.' Dandy looked from one to the other, and neither was foolish enough to doubt that he meant every word. Satisfied, he nodded. 'Now, win or lose, I never allow my lads to end a bout of sparring bad friends, and no more will you, so I'll thank you to shake hands or whatever it is that girls do.'

There was a tense moment, then Liz flung her arms impulsively round her sister. 'I am sorry, truly. I know I go on a bit, but I didn't mean to be so bossy . . .'

Shirley Anne sniffed and then, with a sudden burst of affection, returned the hug. 'And I didn't really mean all them things I said.'

'Of course you didn't.' Liz looked at her wan, contrite face and sighed. 'Oh, go on. If you shift yourself, you should be able to get to Mrs Frith's before your tap class.'

'Oh, Liz – are you sure?' As always when she got her own way, Shirley Anne was all sunshine again. She kissed her sister and danced away. 'Lovely Lizzie! I'll be back by three at the very latest, an' I'll do extra next week – honest!'

Dandy eyed her balefully. 'Be off with you, baggage,' he grunted, catching her with the flat of his hand as she rushed past. 'And think yourself lucky. Aye, and you'd best splash that pretty face with cold water before you go. You don't want folk seeing it all blotched.'

Her laughter floated back from the scullery. The tap splashed, and a moment later they heard the door slam.

'You're a fool, young Liz, d'yer know that? Lettin' her get away with it. She's spoiled to death, that one.'

'Just listen who's talking!' Liz exclaimed. 'You're as bad as the rest of us.' She shrugged, deflated once more. 'I don't know how Shirley Anne does it, but sooner or later we all end up giving in to her.'

Dandy looked closely at her. 'That was a bonny thing you did. It's never easy being the first to say sorry.'

'Oh well, I shouldn't have gone on at her like I did. She's only a kid.'

His eyes twinkled. 'Oh, aye? And what are you, then, girl?'

She half smiled. 'You know what I mean. I'd never have let fly in the first place if she hadn't caught me at a bad moment.'

'Well, you're tired, and small wonder. You've worked yourself into the ground this morning. I hope you're not doing too much.'

The kettle began to whistle, and Liz laughed suddenly, the tension released. 'She never even made the tea.'

When Chris came in that evening, he told Liz to put on her glad rags. 'Jimmy and me are taking you to the pictures. We reckon you deserve a treat,' he said, lifting her up and enveloping her in a great bear hug. Liz, more flattered than she would admit by Jimmy Marsden's apparent interest, went to a lot of trouble to make herself look really nice. But to her everlasting mortification she slept right through the second half of Fred Astaire, with her head on his shoulder.

'And after I'd been waiting ages to see it,' she wailed.

But Jimmy didn't seem put out. He just grinned, and said maybe they'd take her again when she'd caught up on her beauty sleep.

Chapter Five

Sunday came as a blessed relief to all.

In spite of her exhaustion of the previous evening, Liz was up in time to go to early mass at St Anthony's with her father. And by the time the others got back from the later one, Rita was home, and it seemed to Liz that the whole house breathed a sigh of thankfulness.

Rita, being the eldest, was upset not to have been told the news at once.

'Your mother didn't want you worried,' Michael said. 'Knowing how important your work was, what with all that teaching practice you've been doing, and your exams on top. And there was nothing you could have done.'

'Even so, I had a right to know.' It wasn't easy to tell what she thought about the baby, but as usual she was forthright in expressing her views about the situation in general. 'At least this will put an end to Mam wearing herself out in the shop like she's been doing all these years.'

'I hope you don't mean to tell her that,' Michael said with deceptive quietness, 'for I know fine what her reaction will be.'

Rita flushed. In some ways she was very like her mother, being small and dark and equally outspoken, but where Kathleen was impulsive, she tended to be dogmatic, her opinions tending very much towards black and white, with little consideration for the greyer areas between. 'I only meant . . . It wasn't a criticism . . .'

'I know fine what you meant, love. But it's the way your Mam's always wanted things – the way God made her – so just mind what you say. She's not ill, not in the strict sense of the word, and it's hard enough for her being stuck away up there, without feeling that *her* business is being taken out of her hands. For make no mistake, it's her drive, not mine, that's made the business what it is, and enabled us to put you through college.'

'You shouldn't run yourself down like that!' cried Liz, leaping to his defence so that they all turned to stare at her, her father's eyes gently quizzical. She blushed, but insisted: 'Mam couldn't have done any of it without you.'

'For goodness sake, don't let's start an argument,' said Rita. 'I'm sorry if I spoke out of turn.'

'You didn't,' Michael assured her. 'Sure, it's grand to have you home, and no-one will be more glad to see you than your mother, so don't be keeping her waiting now.'

But still she lingered. 'I suppose all this is going to make things very difficult for you, once Liz goes back to school. Perhaps I should ask if I could have a leave of absence – perhaps even take a year off and go back . . .'

'No. That really *would* break your mother's heart.' Michael's voice was stern. 'You know how she feels about you and your teaching.'

Liz flew on to the defensive, without stopping to question the wisdom of it. 'What's more, it'd be plain daft. You're nothing like as good as me in the bakehouse, and anyway, Mam and Dad will be glad of your wage when the baby arrives,' she said practically. 'You're as bad as Chris – he was all for throwing up his job, too, the minute he heard. But it isn't necessary. The way we've got things running now, I can manage perfectly well. Dad'll tell you.' She encountered a curious expression in her father's eyes.

'Liz has been a treasure, right enough, and if I were to tell you the number of compliments I've had about the quality of our goods this past week, you'd never believe me.' He smiled as she turned pink with pleasure.

Rita was very aware of the look that passed between them, and just for a moment it made her feel like an outsider.

And then Liz saw the way her shoulders were sagging. Poor Rita. It wasn't exactly a happy homecoming. 'I'm sorry!' The words came out in a rush, 'I've been looking forward to having you back, really I have. You'll be a lot more help than our Shirley Anne, and it'll be great to have someone sensible to talk to for a change.' This made them all laugh, and the atmosphere lightened.

The three sisters were washing up after dinner when there was a clatter of boots on the stairs, and Joey irrupted amongst them.

'Hey, you'll never guess what! Aunt Flora's car's just stopped outside. Honest! I seen it from Chris's window!'

'Saw,' corrected Liz and Rita in unison – and exchanged a smile.

Liz threw down the cloth and ran towards the shop door, beyond which an elegant figure could be seen getting out of the gleaming black limousine, helped by Peters, her chauffeur, in his smart grey uniform. Liz tugged at the bolts in order to be the first to greet her favourite aunt: to be enveloped in soft fur and hugged to a musky-scented bosom.

'Liz, child, let me look at you!' Bright dark eyes very like Dandy's appraised the slim figure in a Sunday best dress, the shining face whose childishly rounded contours of cheek and jaw were beginning to fine down into purer lines. 'Hm – shaping up nicely. Almost a young lady, in fact.'

'Shirley Anne's prettier,' Liz said honestly, though she glowed with pleasure at the compliment.

'Pretty isn't everything. I was never pretty.'

And then everyone was crowding in, eager hands dragging Flora through to the back room, where the appetizing smells of dinner still lingered, and the fire burned bright. There was much talk and laughter, for Aunt Flora was always a welcome visitor. She saw that the sofa was piled high and spilling over with brightly coloured paper streamers and tinsel. 'Someone's been busy,' she chuckled.

'Mam helped to make them, and we're putting them up this afternoon,' Joey explained. He liked Aunt Flora. She was so full of fun, and never went away without giving him at least a shilling to spend, as well as sweets.

Aunt Flora came into their lives like a whirlwind at irregular intervals, showering them with presents and bringing with her the aura of a whole different world. She was the eldest child of the Power family, who had gone into service straight from school. A bright girl, not beautiful – which might have been a disadvantage, for rich women didn't like their maids too pretty – but clever, and determined to better herself. After several moves, always upwards, she had become housekeeper to a Mr and Mrs Hetherington, who lived up the coast at the Birkdale end of Southport.

It had proved to be a happy association all round, and for ten years she had enjoyed privileges not accorded to many in her position. Mrs Hetherington, a sweet, delicate lady who had been unable to have children herself, had always welcomed Flora's nieces and nephews to the large Victorian house, and loved to watch their uninhibited pleasure as they explored house and gardens, or came back from sorties into the nearby sandhills dishevelled but happy. When she died, Flora stayed on to keep house for Mr Hetherington, and after a decent interval he surprised her and shocked his large circle of acquaintances by asking her to marry him, and they had lived amicably together until his death two years ago. Now well turned forty, Flora had acquired a degree of chic that sat as easily upon her as the black saucer hat with its brief veil, wickedly tilted over one eye, perched on hair unashamedly bleached and crimped into stylish waves. Yet there was nothing stuck up about Aunt Flora.

'Can I go out to see Peters an' have a sit in the car?' Joey clamoured to be heard.

'Yes, of course. And the rest of you can make yourselves scarce, too,' she said, shrugging off her fur coat, which Liz seized and draped reverently over the back of a chair. Flora sat at the table, resting her arms easily on the dark red chenille cloth. Without appearing to look, she noticed that everywhere was spick and span; the big dresser gleamed with polish, and, Sunday or no, the cheerful range had been blackleaded. That would be young Liz's hand, no doubt. 'Tell your mother I'll be up in a minute. I want a word with your father.'

'Now then, Michael,' she said when they were alone, 'I won't beat about the bush. Dad telephoned me last night and told me about our Kathleen. It's a right pickle, and no mistake.'

Michael liked his sister-in-law, but he occasionally found her a bit overwhelming. And now, because of his own raw feelings, he imagined a note of censure and became defensive.

'Oh, good grief, I'm not here to chuck me weight around! I wouldn't presume. It's Himself up there' – the little black hat bobbed – 'He has an infuriating habit of throwing a spanner in the works, just when you think you've got everything sorted. He's done it on me a time or two.' His look of disbelief unsettled her. She took an enamelled cigarette case and lighter from her handbag. 'Can I tempt you?' she asked, flicking the case open with painted fingernails.

'Turkish – very exotic!' He smiled and fumbled in his pocket. 'Thanks, but I'll stick to my pipe, if you don't mind.'

As he reached for the tobacco and matches from the shelf over the fireplace, Flora said: 'You're thinking I've done well for myself, and you're right, but many's the time I'd have changed places with our Kathleen, or Liam or May. Sure, I've got money – more than I know what to do with, in fact. And no-one but meself to spend it on, since certain stuck-up people in this family won't have any truck with it. And I'll not deny I've been lucky. But even luck has its price – ' She blew a gentle cloud of smoke and her voice grew husky. 'John always thought his friends accepted me, and his few real friends did, but the rest – when he wasn't around it was a different story. Now I'm a rich widow, of course, they'd like to curry favour, but it's too late. I don't need them any more. I've got all I want' – here for the first time her narrative faltered – 'except children. And all the money in the world won't buy them.'

In the silence that followed, the coals settled in the hearth and voices came faintly from upstairs. Michael didn't know what to say. He had known Flora for more than twenty years, on and off, but here was a glimpse of a woman he didn't know at all. At last he said softly, 'There's the pity of it, for you'd have made a bonny mother. But if it's any consolation at all, there's a pack of children here who love you dearly, and I am deeply grateful to you for all your many kindnesses to them.'

'Oh, drat you, Michael Ryan.' She stubbed out her cigarette and sat up straight. 'I'll never forgive you if you make my mascara run! I can't think how we ever got on to all that maudlin rubbish. Listen now, and I'll tell you why I've come.'

Kathleen quelled a small rush of envy at the sight of her sister's slim black dress, the diamond pin at her neck, her high-heeled patent shoes. She reckoned it must be all of two months since she had seen Flora, just before she'd gone gallivanting off with friends to foreign parts. But it didn't take any great feat of imagination to guess what had brought her today.

'Dad told you, I suppose,' she said, when Flora had settled her trim, well-corseted figure in the one and only chair, and the rest of the family had been dispatched elsewhere. 'I can just hear him shouting his orders down the telephone – "Get along there and cheer our Kathleen up. She's had a bit of a setback." '

Flora grinned. 'Something like that. But I was intending to come, anyway, before Christmas.'

'Well, you'd no need to rush on my account. I'm not exactly going anywhere.'

Flora heard the underlying tension in the flippant remark. It merely confirmed that she was doing the right thing. 'Don't be too sure, our kid. I haven't been idle since Dad called. I've had a long talk with Doc Graham, and if you behave yourself, I have his permission to carry you off to Rose Lodge for a few days in the New Year.'

Her sister's reaction was predictable, for even if Michael hadn't already warned her to expect resistance, Flora knew well enough that Kathleen wouldn't take kindly to having matters decided behind her back. She waited patiently for the tirade to end; only when every last objection had been voiced, did she attempt to speak.

'I bet you've been bursting for an excuse to get all that off your chest. But it won't do you any good. Michael thinks it's a great idea.'

'It's a conspiracy,' Kathleen accused.

'If you like,' Flora agreed. 'But only because you're so pig-headed! Ah, come on, our Kathy, admit it. It'd be a lot easier for everyone here if you came to me for a while.' She let the words sink in, then said casually: 'Besides, when did you and I last let our hair down and have a good old sisterly heart to heart? At least think about it. I'll be over again before Christmas.'

When Peters had driven Aunt Flora away, the younger members of the family set about the decorating, organized by Rita in her best schoolmarm manner. Michael left them to it, saying he was going to sit with their mother in peace and quiet. But everyone else had a splendid time – including Jimmy Marsden, who arrived, uninvited, just in time to see the Daimler disappearing from view.

'What a car!' he exclaimed. 'That aunt of yours must be worth a packet.'

'I wouldn't know, and anyway, it's none of your business,' Liz returned, quick as light. 'So if you've only come to be nosey, you can go away again.'

'Liz!' Rita frowned at her rudeness.

But Jimmy wasn't in the least put out. 'When Chris said last night what you'd be doing, I thought another pair of hands might get the job finished quicker,' he told Liz with a grin. And, lowering his voice so that only she could hear: 'Then you and me could maybe go for a bit of a walk.'

Liz wasn't often lost for words, but this time his audacity took her by surprise. The lofty disdain with which she usually dismissed his brash manners deserted her. 'Just you and me, d'you mean?' she stammered.

'Well, I wasn't plannin' on taking the whole family. I thought we might go as far as the Pier Head, wander along the Landing Stage to see what ships are in.'

The amusement in his eyes made her notice them for the first time: grey blue, they were, with darker rings round them and thick dark lashes. Their expression deepened into something tantalizingly different as he appeared to read her thoughts, and immediately she was thrown into confusion.

'Here, then,' she commanded, to cover her embarrassment, and thrust one end of a paper chain into his hand. 'If you've come to make yourself useful, you'd better get on with it.'

'And afterwards?' he persisted from two steps up the ladder.

'We'll see. I'll have to ask Mam.' And, as his smile deepened: 'There won't *be* an afterwards, if you don't help us get these chains pinned up.'

She flounced off, crimson-cheeked, but very much aware of his presence. An hour or so later, when the last piece of tinsel was in place, she dragged Rita into the scullery on the pretext of making a pot of tea.

'Listen, can I have a lend of your coat? I've only got my uniform one that's fit to be seen, an' I can't wear that.' Then she had to tell Rita why she wanted it, and her sister's eyebrows shot up. 'Well, I don't see why I shouldn't go. I'll ask, of course, but Mam's always saying I don't get enough fresh air, and Jimmy's not exactly a stranger. Anyway, there's not much chance of him trying anything silly at three o'clock in the afternoon down the Pier Head, is there?'

An hour later, resplendent in Rita's brown tweed coat and with a gold-coloured beret she had knitted herself pinned to her unruly hair, she was strolling with Jimmy down Water Street, into the teeth of an icy wind off the Mersey, and feeling very strange.

'Help!' Liz turned back on a sudden violent gust and clutched at her beret, while he laughed at her predicament.

'Come here. We'd better have that off,' he said, a wicked glint in his eyes that made her blush without knowing why it should. Before she could stop him, he had removed the pins and the beret, and was pushing them into her pocket in a familiar kind of way. The wind tumbled her hair forward in a tangled mass around her face. He gathered it with practised fingers and tucked it behind her ears, letting his hands rest either side of her face for a long moment. Looking up at him, Liz felt a frisson of sensation so odd, so unexpected, that it half-scared, half-exhilarated her. For a moment she was sure he was about to kiss her, and her heart began to thump.

Then: 'Give over,' she said imperiously, and pulled away. 'I thought we'd come here to see the ships. It'll be dark before we've done, and there'll be ructions if I'm not back by then.'

'Right. Come on.' Jimmy took her hand and tucked it under his arm, seeming amused by her sharpness. As they passed the bright red Nestlés chocolate machine, he stopped and put two penny coins in the slot. 'One for you and one for me,' he said.

Liz, munching thoughtfully on the chocolate bar, was quite pleased with the way she had handled things. Her voice had sounded surprisingly normal. Jimmy wasn't so bad, she decided. Like Chris and Joey, he just needed taking firmly in hand. Except that, for a few moments, there had been nothing sisterly in the way she felt about him.

Sunday or no, the river was busy as ever, its pewter waters choppy and capped with a murky froth. With dusk already threatening, the sky was just as grey, streaked with yellow – the only lingering evidence of a feeble winter sun. But out in the river, a big liner stood out against the gloom, blazing with lights from stem to stern, her many coloured flags standing out stiffly in the wind. It was a sight Liz had seen many times, but it never failed to thrill her.

'That's the *Athenia*,' Jimmy said. 'She's one of the Donaldson Line, down from Glasgow. One of the tenders, most likely *Skirmisher*, 'll be taking the Liverpool passengers out to her in the morning.'

Liz was impressed by his knowledge. 'Wouldn't you just give anything to be aboard her?' she said dreamily. 'Sailing off to exotic places, your every whim indulged . . .'

But Jimmy wasn't watching the liner; he was watching Liz's face. Such a giveaway face, so at odds with her often sharp tongue. And it had given her away earlier this afternoon, right enough, for all her bluster. Her eyes, reflecting the twinkling lights, glowed like molten gold. He wondered how it would feel to have her in his arms, looking up at him like that, kissing her sweetly curving lips. If it wasn't for Chris, he might be tempted to find out. But you didn't mess about with your best mate's sister, so he'd have to be patient.

'It's a great idea, cruisin',' he said. 'Except the only way the likes of us will ever get aboard is by doing the indulgin'. Matter of fact,' he said casually, 'I have thought about giving it a go. It's not that difficult to get taken on as a butcher or a baker. Friends who've done it say it's a great life.' He grinned at her. 'Maybe me an' your Chris'll take off one day. We'd only need a candlestick maker. Fancy the job?'

'You do talk a lot of nonsense sometimes. Besides,' she said with confidence, 'our Chris'd never leave home.'

Only three days to go. Michael was sitting having a quiet smoke before going out on his rounds, his gaze following Liz as she laid the table for tea and carried on a conversation with Rita, who was busy in the scullery. Once as she passed, her eyes met his, a hint of pleading in their depths, and his thoughts returned yet again to the envelope, still crackling in his pocket. It had come early in the day along with a few Christmas cards, while he was snatching a bite of breakfast. Rita had taken Kathleen's breakfast upstairs, and for those few moments he and Liz had been alone.

'Take those up to your mother,' he had said, while his daughter leafed eagerly through the pile to see if any were for her. 'It'll give her something to do for a bit.'

But Liz didn't answer, and when he looked up, she had a long official envelope in her hand. For a moment he thought she was about to throw it on the fire. 'Liz?' he said sharply.

She jumped: then thrust it at him, her whole body tense. 'I think you'd better have this one.'

He opened it and read the contents through in silence – twice. Without looking up, he asked quietly, 'I take it you already know what this is?'

'Yes. I recognized Sister Imelda's writing. It's my report.'

'And a letter as well.' Michael ran a hand distractedly through his hair, a whole range of conflicting emotions flooding his mind. 'Oh, Liz, Liz! Don't you see – this changes everything! I can't possibly keep this from your mother. It's not just the report – it's what she's written. Kathleen'll be so proud to know what hopes your headmistress has for you!'

'I know.' Liz groaned. 'But that only makes it worse, don't you see? Like giving a baby sweets with one hand and taking them away with the other! An' it's no good telling her I don't mind, because, right or wrong, she'll still blame herself. Dad, she mustn't see it. Nor our Rita, either.' Her father looked so distressed that she ran to put her arms round him, her face against his stubbly cheek. 'I'm sorry. You've got so much to worry about already. I shouldn't ask you to deceive Mam, but – oh, it isn't fair!'

His hand came up to cover her clasped ones. 'Ah, girleen, when was life ever fair?' She moved her head away and he turned to look up at her. 'Listen now – don't be upsetting yourself. And don't be worrying about me – or your mother. One lesson I've learned over the years – most things have a way of working out, given time, so nothing will be done in a hurry.'

Liz gave him one last fierce hug, and let him go.

That same evening, as Michael was on his way out, Shirley Anne burst in from her concert rehearsal in a state of almost incoherent excitement.

'Will you draw breath, child, and begin at the beginning,' said her father.

'It's about the pantomime at the Empire . . .'

Joey looked up from sorting through a box of Christmas tree decorations. 'Oh, yeah! Are we going to see it, Dad? It'll be smashin' – Sandy Powell. *Can you 'ear me, Muther*?'

He had the voice perfectly, and they all laughed except Shirley Anne.

'Oh, do shut up, Joey! Dad, this is really important. The producer came to Miss Eglantine's this afternoon – one of his juvenile dance troupe has gone down with chicken pox, an' he's desperate to find a replacement . . .' She paused for dramatic effect. 'He picked me, straight off. At least, he wants me to go to the theatre in the morning for a proper audition!'

The two older girls, drawn by their sister's explosive outburst, came to the scullery door as Michael removed the pipe from his mouth, and regarded his flushed daughter in silence through the curl of smoke. She rushed over and clutched his arm.

'Oh, Dad, *please* say I can go! It's the most fantastic thing that's ever happened to me, an' if you say no, I'll die!'

But she had gone too far. 'Be quiet, girl,' he said sternly. 'I'll not have you talking of dying in that wicked hysterical way.'

'I didn't mean it, really! It's just . . . Well, it's what I've always dreamed of . . . An' I'd get paid and everything, just like a real dancer.'

Liz could have told her that being paid was not likely to endear her father to the idea. But she could see how desperately her sister longed to be given this chance. She said quickly: 'It *is* a wonderful opportunity, Dad. And if it's only for a short time, I can't see any real harm.'

Shirley Anne sent her a swift, grateful glance.

'Well, I can,' Rita said. 'She's got enough daft notions as it is.'

'How would you know? You don't know anything about how I feel. Listen Dad, it'd only be until the other girl's better. Mr Grace – that's the producer's name – is coming round later this evening with Miss Eglantine to see you. If you'd just listen to him . . .'

Her father was quiet for so long that she was in despair. Then he stood up. 'Time I was away. I can't say I like the idea of my daughter prancing about on the professional stage, but you'd better go and talk to your mother about it. And don't, for the love of heaven, upset her. Go with her, Rita, there's a love.'

Shirley Anne would rather have had Liz, who was clearly sympathetic, but it wasn't worth arguing for fear of upsetting Dad.

Kathleen's instinctive reaction was the same as Michael's. There was a whole world of difference between performing at small local concerts and 'going on the stage', mixing with professional actors and dancers.

Rita wasn't in any doubt about it. 'Dad's right. Shirley Anne's bad enough now, and she's barely turned fourteen – too young to be mixing with stage folk. Give her a sniff of greasepaint and who knows where it will all end.'

'That's not fair!' Shirley Anne exclaimed. 'Why shouldn't I be allowed to do the thing I do best? You don't know anything about actors, our Rita. They're only people, same as everyone else.'

Rita and her mother exchanged glances. But then Kathleen looked into her youngest daughter's impassioned face, and a curious feeling stole into her heart. A week ago she would have agreed with Rita. Now, finding her own dreams thwarted, she was torn. Dancing and singing were Shirley Anne's only real talents, yet Michael would never countenance the stage as a career, any more than she would herself. Shirley Anne knew that. Which meant that her young daughter was destined to work in a shop or factory when she left school. Would it not be unnecessarily cruel to crush her dreams without ever knowing whether they had any substance?

'I think we had better see this Mr Grace,' she said – and, as the light leapt into Shirley Anne's eyes – 'But it doesn't change the way your dad and I feel, so don't be getting any silly ideas about the future.'

Later, when the visitors had been and gone, Liz took her crochet hook and a ball of red wool and went upstairs to sit with her mother. 'That Mr Grace seemed a nice enough sort,' she said. 'I'm glad you talked Dad into letting Shirley Anne go for the audition.'

'I only hope I won't regret it.' Kathleen watched her daughter's busy fingers, and the long red worm that grew and curled across the bed. 'Liz, whatever are you making there?'

'It's a kind of experiment – a special Christmas line for the shop. I'll show you tomorrow, if it works out.'

Kathleen watched her daughter closely. Responsibility was already changing her – she was growing up fast. But they mustn't lose sight of the fact that she would be back to school in a couple of weeks. Michael was going to miss her. He hadn't said much, but she guessed he would be having trouble finding someone to replace her – craftsmen were snapped up fast, and few would look twice at poorly paid part-time work. The shop too was a problem. Dr Graham had been evasive about the future, but lying in bed with plenty of time to think, she was becoming convinced that a month's rest would not be the end of it. She guessed, with a feeling of helplessness, that Liz was already contemplating sacrificing her chances of matriculating, and that would be a wicked waste.

'You really enjoy it, don't you?' she said abruptly. 'The business, I mean. Your father doesn't go in much for compliments, but I know he's proud of you.' What Michael had actually said was: 'Our Liz is a great little worker, right enough. And she's her mother's daughter. It's a formidable combination. Sure, she has me organized to a T.' But Kathleen knew there was more to it than that – Liz possessed skills that she herself lacked.

'I enjoy making confectionery look attractive,' Liz was saying eagerly, pleased by the compliment.

'Well, don't get too fancy in your ideas,' Kathleen said with unaccountable sharpness. 'Most of our customers still like good plain fare.'

But when Liz brought the results of her labour for inspection the following morning, Kathleen had to admit they were attractive. Liz had used every spare minute experimenting, and had finally come up with a meringue snowman. He had a round body with a smaller round for his head, the two stuck together with chocolate which spilled down to make his coat. He wore a chocolate cap, and round his neck she had tied a muffler of red wool.

'I've made these gingerbread Christmas trees as well, with white icing for snow. None of them cost much to make, so I reckon we can sell them at two for a ha'penny.'

'Children will love them,' Kathleen said with genuine admiration. 'What does your father think?'

'He agrees with you. I'm only sorry I didn't think of them sooner.'

Over the rest of the week they sold so well that Liz was hard-pressed to meet the demand – and with Shirley Anne rehearsing most of the day, it was just as well that Rita was there to mind the shop and prepare meals. At this rate, Liz thought, we'll all be exhausted by Christmas.

Chapter Six

By eight o'clock on Christmas Eve, they *were* exhausted. There had been a non-stop stream of customers throughout the day, eager to spend what remained of their money from the Christmas Club that Kathleen always ran, and Liz was touched by the number of gifts that were shyly pressed into her hand across the counter.

Several times, the shop had come close to running out of luxury items such as tinned salmon, tinned fruit and decorative boxes of sugared fruits and chocolates, and Joey had been hastily dispatched to the wholesalers to fetch more. The boiled ham, too, was in demand, as well as Christmas cakes and mince pies, and the special large pork pies that Michael only made for high days and holidays.

In the middle of all this chaos, Mam was to receive Holy Communion early on Christmas Eve, before the shop opened, and nothing short of a virtual spring-clean of the whole house would satisfy Rita if the priest was to be suitably received. In the circumstances it was hardly surprising that tempers became frayed.

'Do give over, our Rita,' Liz protested, as her sister flicked a duster round yet again before going to wait near the shop door, candle at the ready. 'The place already reeks of polish. This isn't the first time Father Clarkson's brought Communion to Mam, you know. Anyway, if a stable was good enough for the Holy Family, Our Blessed Lord won't turn his nose up at a bit of honest dust!'

'Liz! Don't be disrespectful.'

'I'm not. But anyone with half an eye can see there's enough to be done without making work.' Liz tossed her head and marched back to the bakehouse.

She was still fizzing when Mrs Whitney sent Clare down, later that morning, to collect her order. Her brother was driving the car. Liz had forgotten that Francis would be home from college. He was nineteen, a rather aloof young man, with hair as fine and fair as Clare's, which flopped across his forehead, making him look a bit like Gary Cooper. Liz had long ago realized that he wasn't stuck up, simply shy, and perhaps because she was Clare's friend he had always been at ease with her.

As Clare now dragged him through to the back to carry the trays of pastries, she said, 'Mother wondered whether you might manage to come this evening, Liz?'

'I can't – honest! It's been bedlam here all morning, and Shirley Anne's neither use nor ornament with the pantomime so close to opening, so it's almost certain we won't be finished till late.'

'Poor Liz,' Francis said. 'It doesn't seem right, you having to work while everyone else is having fun.'

He actually sounded as though he minded. Liz felt a tingle of pleasure. 'Oh, well, it can't be helped.'

But just for a moment she wished it could; just for a moment she longed to be free to please herself.

'Well, how about New Year's Eve?' he persisted. 'Surely you can be spared to see that in with us? You could even stay the night.'

'That's a great idea, brother dear!' Clare grinned at Liz. 'He does have them occasionally. Oh, do come, Liz. It's going to be a proper party, with lots of people, not family and neighbours like tonight.'

Liz's heart leapt. It would be fun to let in the New Year in real style, and Francis sounded as if he really wanted her to be there. Dad and the others would be able to manage, just for once. And then she realized that everyone else would be in party clothes, and she had nothing remotely suitable.

'It's no use. I can't,' she said flatly.

'Oh, surely,' Francis sounded impatient, but received a piercing glare from his sister, and closed his teeth on what he had been about to say.

'You take those trays out to the car. Liz hasn't got all day to stand here talking.' He muttered something about bossy sisters, but when he had gone, Clare said quickly, 'I know what's eating you, so just listen a minute. You remember that lovely dress Gran bought me for my birthday – the pale green taffeta? Well, I've never worn it; it looks horribly insipid on me, but with your colouring, you'd look fantastic in it. No-one but Mother need know, and she wouldn't tell.' She saw resistance fighting longing in

Liz's eyes, and took her by the shoulders. 'Oh, come on, Liz – we're friends. There's no room for pride between friends. You don't get that many treats, so why not let yourself go for once, and have a little fun?'

'All right, I'll ask Mam.' The words spilled out of Liz before she could change her mind.

Michael came in late, tired but happy: trade had been way above anything he could have expected. He took his cup of tea upstairs to share the good news with Kathleen, and found her busily separating ten shilling notes from pound ones, clipping them together, and putting them on a tray at her side already stacked with mounds of coins. The past few days had given her more to do, and put the sparkle back into her eyes.

'Michael,' she said, looking up as he came in. 'Will you just look! We've never done so much business! And this is only what we've taken up to five o'clock.'

'It's a grand sight, right enough. and that's not the end of it, *acushla*,' he said, stretching himself out in the chair beside her. 'There's plenty more for you to count downstairs. I'd hardly a crumb to bring home. And nothing but praise all round – to say nothing of a bottle or two of whisky, and other marks of appreciation from grateful customers. And it's all thanks to your foresight. I'd never have dreamed of expanding the business without the confidence you had in me.'

'Rubbish,' Kathleen said, but there was a catch in her voice. 'It's young Liz you should be thanking – the others, too, but Liz most of all.'

Michael's eyes warmed. 'Oh, I know fine the treasure *she* is. Haven't I watched her – the way she puts that little bit extra of herself into all she does, and every day growing more sure . . .'

'Michael?'

There was an urgency in Kathleen's voice. But before she could say more, there were feet on the stairs and Liz was in the room, filling it with a different kind of urgency as she tugged at her father's arm. 'Dad! You'll never believe . . .' When he failed to move, she tugged again. 'You must come down, this minute!'

'Give over, child. Lord knows where you get your energy after the day it's been. Can't a man get a few minutes peace in his own home to rest his weary bones?'

But Kathleen was already pushing back the bedclothes. 'Liz? What is it? What's wrong?'

'Nothing's wrong, Mam. In fact, it's the most wonderful thing in the world! Aunt Flora's just arrived with her presents, and . . . Oh, Dad, do come on!' As her father got reluctantly to his feet, she grabbed his hand, calling over her shoulder: 'If you look out of Chris's window, Mam, you might be able to see it.'

In the crowded shop a buzz of excitement filled the air, and outside another small crowd had gathered on the pavement, heedless of the cold, all talking at once. Liz hurried her father to the door, where he stopped in his tracks, his face robbed of colour and expression.

Parked by the kerb, under the gas lamp on the corner of Fortune Street, was a spanking new van with an enormous bow of red ribbon tied to its bonnet.

'Come an' have a close look, Dad.' Joey seized his hand.

With Liz holding on to one arm and Joey tugging him forward, Michael was drawn, unresisting, down the steps to the accompaniment of much cheering. Flora had already climbed out and stood at the kerb, wrapped in furs, the smile in her eyes betraying a mixture of mischief and bravado. 'Happy Christmas, brother dear.' She touched her scented cheek to his as she pressed the keys into his hand.

Michael was in a daze. 'Flora? This is madness – you shouldn't have done it! We can't possibly accept . . .'

She laughed. 'Oh, stuff and nonsense! I knew that's what you'd say, so I've had it registered in your name, and – well, I'm afraid there's no taking it back to the garage now. There – d'you see?'

And he did see, sure enough. Emblazoned on the van's side, gold lettering proclaimed: MICHAEL RYAN, MASTER BAKER OF QUALITY AND DISTINCTION – and underneath in smaller print, the address of the shop. Flora hooked her arm through his.

'Come along,' she said, urging him back inside. 'You can't quarrel with me comfortably with all the street looking on, and anyway, our Kathleen should be allowed to have her say – it's her present, too.'

But Michael was in no state to quarrel at that moment; a very private man, the emotions he found himself experiencing were impossible to analyse, though disappointment played a large part. He had wanted the van so much, but not this way, and certainly not in the humiliating glare of publicity. Now, those long months of saving, and their climax – the thrill of actually choosing it and buying it – had been denied him. He was very quiet as he led the way up to the bedroom where Kathleen waited.

Kathleen, too, was lost for words, though there were tears in her eyes, and she hugged her sister so tightly that Flora was almost moved to tears herself.

'Well,' she said huskily, 'I never thought I'd succeed in silencing the two of you.'

'I never thought you'd do anything so crazy,' Kathleen exclaimed, regaining some of her spirit. 'Honestly, Flo – what sort of reaction did you expect?'

Flora grinned. 'To be honest, I expected to get me head blown off. But if I'd offered you money, you'd have said "Thanks, but no thanks," right? So I had to think of something you couldn't refuse.' She glanced at her brother-in-law, whose face was still dauntingly inscrutable. 'I know you do drive, Michael, and Dad happened to mention you were saving for a second-hand van, so, being a practical woman, it seemed to me that a new one would be much more sensible – save you buying someone else's troubles.' His lack of response was like a slap in the face, and disappointment thickened her voice. 'I've done the wrong thing, haven't I?'

'No, Flora, indeed you haven't!' Kathleen looked beseechingly at her husband. 'It's – well, it's such a surprise, that's all.'

'Don't flannel me, our Kathy. You always were a rotten liar. What's more, you're too damned proud, the both of you – and in case you've forgotten your seven deadly sins, pride's not a virtue. So, you just listen to me for a minute. For years now I've watched you build this place up from nothing, and for all that I grumbled when you refused to take a pennyworth of help from me, I've admired you for it, too. But it's no fun having money if you can't spend it on the folk you love, and this year, just for once, I wanted to do something really special for Christmas, to make up for the rotten trick Fate's played on you.' She met Michael's eyes with a self-deprecating shrug. 'Okay, maybe I did have a sudden rush of blood to the head. Dad warned me I'd gone right over the top with all the razzamatazz – he said you'd hate it. But it *is* Christmas – and anyway, subtlety never was my strong point.' A wry smile curved her mouth. 'He was dead right about that stupid ribbon, though – it was a daft idea. I'll get Peters to take it off before we leave.'

Her disappointment made Michael ashamed of his own ingratitude. He stooped to kiss her cheek. 'You'll do nothing of the kind. Sure, you're a devious woman, Flora Hetherington.' Over her head, his eyes met Kathleen's. 'It's a trait that runs in the family, I'm thinkin'. But your heart's in the right place, which is all that matters. So I do thank you most warmly. And you will kindly leave the ribbon where it is. A present is not a present without a bit of fancy wrapping.'

Kathleen, her ear attuned to every nuance of Michael's voice, knew just how much it cost him to make that speech, and as she added her own thanks, she loved him all the more fiercely for the generosity of his gesture. And it didn't seem to matter any longer that their own gift to Flora – a pair of soft black kid gloves and some pretty lace handkerchiefs – was insignificant by comparison, for like hers to them, it was given with love.

Flora, reassured, was herself again. 'I'd better be off,' she said. 'I've got a big dinner party tomorrow.' But first there were the remaining presents to be exchanged. She gave Michael the large carrier bag she was holding. 'They're all there – the things you asked me to get, together with my own presents for the children. At least *they* enjoyed the spectacle.' Suddenly she began to chuckle. 'But honestly, I never expected the whole of Greaty and Fortune Street to join in.' The chuckle became a laugh, and then they were all laughing. 'Oh, my!' she gasped, tears threatening to ruin her carefully applied make-up. 'The only thing missing was a brass band!'

Downstairs, the shop had filled up again. Some were genuine customers; others, a small group near the door, had simply come in out of the cold to carry on their gossip and conjecture. Rita and Liz were kept busy, but every now and then, snatches of conversation filtered through to them, one voice lifting above the rest.

'. . . alwiz the same, it is, when Lady Muck from Bairkdale comes slummin' in that great 'earse of a car with 'er Fancy Dan at the wheel, bestowin' favours. I'm not the only one oo's seen 'er sweepin' in 'ere, decked out like a bleedin' May'orse . . . all fair coat an' no drawers!'

This brought loud protests from those who knew of Flora's many acts of kindness to old friends in need, and a fierce argument ensued, but Nora wouldn't be silenced. 'Ah, shurrup! Crawlers, the lot of yer! Well, I 'aven't fergot, if you 'ave, as she wus once plain Florrie Power, in sairvice ter scratch a livin' like the rest of us – tharris until she gorrin cosy-like with 'er boss an' ended up livin' the life of Riley!'

'You rotten old cow!' Liz exclaimed furiously, forgetting all about being grown up and responsible. 'Nosey Nora fits you a treat – you're never happy unless you're poking your nose in other people's business!'

This raised a chuckle or two, and cries of 'Good on yer, Lizzie, love – you let 'er 'ave it!' Rita, scarlet with embarrassment, nudged her hard in the ribs.

'I don't care,' Liz muttered, unrepentant. 'I'd like to *choke* her with her own miserable lies.'

Dandy sat beside Peters in the Daimler, cushioned from the rattle of the cobbles by soft leather and superb springing, and looking every bit as much at home amid such luxury as when pushing Michael's handcart or riding the delivery bike. The King himself wouldn't scorn such a vehicle, he thought with satisfaction. Flora had done well for herself, right enough. Too well, some might say, but he'd no truck with such mealy-mouthed philosophy, for hadn't he brought the lot of them up to work hard in order to better themselves? There was nothing wrong with ambition, as long as you remained true to your roots and never forgot the bottom line – that wealth brought obligations. And they'd done him proud, the lot of them.

The car drew soundlessly to a halt behind the new van, and he could see, beyond the steamed up windows of the shop, the vague shapes of a great many people.

'Business is booming, by the look of it,' he said, as Peters came round to open the car door for him.

Peters grinned. 'It is that, sir. And if the din's anything to go by, they're all fighting over last minute bargains.'

Pushing his way up the steps, Dandy caught the tail end of Nora in full flight, followed by Liz giving her what for. At first everyone was too engrossed to notice him. Then a hush fell as the group by the door parted to let him through, and pressed in behind him, eager not to miss the fun.

'Mindin' other folk's business as usual, eh, Nora? One thing's for sure, there's small chance of anyone forgettin' you.' Dandy's voice was pleasant enough, yet a nervous titter nearby was quickly stifled as everyone hung on his words, waiting for the fireworks to begin. 'Tell me, now – was it my daughter's name you were taking in vain? If so, p'raps you'd care to repeat the gist of your argument, so there's no mistake. Because if I *did* hear you aright, Christmas or no, I'd consider it me bounden duty to break me lifetime vow never to strike a woman, and ram that scurrilous lying tongue of yours down your throat.'

Liz held her breath – and so did everyone else. And then the click of high heels on the lino broke the silence. Flora was among them, and a great sigh spread through the shop, followed by a renewed buzz of expectation. 'It's berra than a pantomime, this! Best seats, and all fer nowt!' someone was heard to mutter.

'No need to be putting yourself to the trouble on my account, Dad. After all, this *is* the season of goodwill. Isn't that so, Nora? When we try to be nice to everybody? So I think we ought to have some consideration for Harry Carney over at The Grapes. If you were to cut Nora off from her swallow, the profits in his Public would drop by half overnight, and most likely wreck his Christmas for him!'

The whole shop erupted with laughter, and in a moment Flora was surrounded by old friends, all talking at once, eager to back her up and openly fingering her fur coat with an envy untinged by malice. Nora Figg's vituperative retort was lost in the noise, and by the time everything had settled back to normal, she had gone.

'Listen, can you manage on your own for a bit?' Liz asked Rita, when Aunt Flora had left and things were back to normal. 'I've those few special orders to take up Fortune Street. I'll not be long.'

She had packed the boxes earlier, ready to put in the handcart. One was for Mrs Carey at number 15, whose daughter, Mollie, was the same age as Liz. Rheumatic fever when she was five had damaged Mollie's heart, and that, together with repeated attacks of bronchitis, had taken its toll, making her seem much older. Yet she was unfailingly cheerful and always looked forward to Liz's visits, and the gossip she brought.

Now, as Liz carried the box through to the tiny back room, and put it down on the table, she heard the frightening rasp of Mollie's breathing from her chair drawn up close to the fire. Her dark hair hung lankly round her face and her eyes seemed too big in the cavern of her face, but they glowed with pleasure at the sight of her friend. Her mother shuffled over to sit in the only other chair.

'I can't stay this evening, I'm afraid,' Liz explained. 'We've been mad busy.' It grieved her, the way Mollie seemed to grow thinner every time she saw her. Several spells in hospital didn't appear to have done much good, and Liz sometimes wondered if Mrs Carey fed Mollie properly. But it couldn't be easy for her, either, crippled as she was by arthritis.

'It's good of you to come at all,' Mollie said. 'And to bring Mam's shoppin' an' all.' She paused and said quietly: 'I wondered if your Chris might have brought it.'

Liz's heart went out to the fragile girl who worshipped her brother. 'He's working late tonight, but he'll maybe slip in over the holiday. Anyway, it's probably the only chance I'll have to wish you Happy Christmas. There's a small present for each of you in the box – ' She grinned suddenly. 'Not to be opened till morning.'

'Thanks.' As Liz turned to go, Mollie begged her to wait, and reached into a work bag beside her chair. Even so slight an exertion brought on the racking cough that was never far away these days. Hiding her distress, Liz waited for the girl to catch her breath.

'It isn't much, but I made it myself.' Mollie pushed the small, carefully wrapped parcel into Liz's hands, and smiled. 'Not to be opened till morning.'

Liz got through her other calls quickly, leaving Ellen Cassidy's to the last. Mam had taken the news about Ellen helping out with the washing surprisingly well, and had agreed with Liz that to take the Cassidys a really nice hamper of food for Christmas would be a practical way of saying thank you. It included a capon which Cousin Tom had brought in from the farm with their turkey. Liz had surrounded it with lots of trimmings, as well as tinned fruit and condensed milk, and cakes and sweets for the children. And for Ellen, a pair of warm gloves, and fifty Player's Weights and a bottle of Guinness for Arnie.

In contrast to the dinginess of the other houses Liz had visited, every inch of Ellen's was scrubbed clean, and as sparkling as she could make it. In the back room, a fire burned brightly behind a guard, and a full rack of washing hung above it. Arnie's bed, set against one wall, took up nearly half the room. There was a low cabinet beside it to take his wireless, a half empty pack of cigarettes and a saucer, presently overflowing with fag ends and ash. Under the window stood a table with assorted chairs and boxes scattered around it, and on the table a tray of crudely modelled lumps of plasticine left unfinished by the children.

But no amount of elbow grease could disguise the worn furnishings, just as no amount of disinfectant could quite remove the smells of a sickroom. Liz often wondered about all the intimate and unpleasant things Ellen must have to do for her husband. It was bad enough, with Mam in bed, having to empty her chamber pot several times a day, but Liz's mind shied away from the awfulness of Ellen's lot. One would have to be a very special kind of person to perform such tasks without flinching.

Arnie had the wireless on very loud, and made no attempt to turn it down for Liz's benefit. He was a big man. His outline beneath the blankets stretched right to the end of the bed, his movement restricted to his head and shoulders and right arm. Ellen kept him shaved, and his hair neatly trimmed. But it was his eyes that Liz always noticed: they were like the eyes of a trapped animal, blazing with impotent rage. Ellen must love him very much to put up with his ill temper, and all the nursing, with such unfailing patience. Liz felt a great surge of pity, remembering the fine swaggering fellow Arnie had been before his accident.

She put the box down on the table. 'This is just a small thank you for all you've done.'

'Liz, we can't possibly accept all this!' Ellen's voice shook as she saw the chicken and accompanying luxuries.

'I don't see why not. You more than deserve it, and it was the only way I could think of to say thanks. We've been so mad busy that if you hadn't taken on the washing, I don't see how I could have managed. And Mam said if you want to bring the chicken up and roast it in our oven, you're welcome.'

'That's good of her, but it'd be best done in the pot on the fire – that way we'll have some good nourishing soup as well. This is a bit like a dream. I had got us a bit of belly pork, but now – ' Ellen looked up, her eyes shining with tears. 'Oh, Arnie, we'll be able to have a proper Christmas for once!'

'What d'yer expect me to do – bloody cheer?' He ground the words out, and immediately began a fit of coughing. Through it he gasped, 'Gorra new arse fer me in there, 'ave yer, gairl? A new paira legs, too, so I can stroll up t' The Grapes fer a bevvy with me mates? Cos that's about worrit'd take to make a proper Christmas fer me!'

'Arnie!' Ellen was scarlet with shame.

'It's all right, Ellen.' Liz was close to tears, though who for, she couldn't be sure. Pity and indignation were equally strong in her as she moved impetuously towards the bed, shouting above the music on the wireless. 'I'm truly sorry, Mr Cassidy. I know how terrible it must be for you . . .' Her eyes met his for an instant. If looks could kill, she thought, with a shudder, and rushed on before the sky fell on her. 'All right, then, I don't know, not really, but it's pretty terrible for Ellen, too, you know. And it would mean so much to her if you could just try to make Christmas a bit brighter for her and the children.'

Oh, Lord, me and my tongue, she thought, as Ellen drew a whimpering breath and sank on to the nearest chair: I've gone and done it now. From the crackling wireless came the intermittent sound of a choir joyously singing *Glo-or-or-or-oria, in excelsis De-eo* . . . It was one of her favourite carols, the one she loved to let rip with. Now, suddenly, Liz felt sick, hearing those paeans to the glory of God ringing out in a room where there was little, if anything, to praise God for – and she knew that never again would she sing the carol with the same fervour.

She hardly dared to look at Arnie, yet she couldn't not look. His eyes burned into her, and it was like the end of the Saturday afternoon serial at the pictures, when the monstrous creature from space turns his demonic gaze on Flash Gordon and you just *know* that he's about to paralyse your hero with a mesmeric beam of light.

And then, quite suddenly, the fire went out of him. 'Aw, gerrout,' he muttered, and turned his face to the wall. But not before Liz had seen a tear roll down his face.

She stared, horrified at what her words had done. 'Oh, Ellen, I'm sorry!' she whispered, tears now streaming down her own face. 'I don't know what got into me. I didn't mean . . . I didn't . . .' She turned blindly towards the door.

'It's all right, love. You meant well.' In the cramped lobby, Ellen put her arms awkwardly round her. 'Arnie can't help the way he is. And maybe what you said needed saying.' Her voice wobbled slightly. 'Only I could never bring meself to do it . . . So, who knows – it might even do a bit of good.' She drew a breath. 'And I do bless you for the parcel – and the thought.'

Liz trundled the cart home in abject misery. But when she had almost reached the dark back-crack behind the bakehouse, someone tugged at her arm. 'Hey! Have I suddenly become invisible or something?'

She turned at the sound of a familiar voice. 'Oh, Jimmy,' she said, her voice catching on a sob.

'What's all this, then? Lost a shillin' and found sixpence?' He took the cart from her, set it down and, putting an arm round her, turned her face up to the moonlight. 'Hey, this isn't like you. Someone been havin' a go at you, have they?'

This brought a wail of despair, from which he assumed the worst.

'Tell us who it is and I'll kill 'im! I'd kill anyone who messed with you.'

'No, no,' Liz cried, even as a secret part of her warmed to his outburst. 'It's me that's been having a go. I've been so unkind!' She poured out the whole story.

'Well, that's not so bad. Cassidy'll get over it,' he said, enjoying the feel of his arms around her and her pressed tight against him. 'Cheer up. Christmas is coming.'

Liz looked up with a hiccuping laugh. 'You are daft,' she said, 'but nice daft.' Held there in the circle of Jimmy's arms, her cheek against the damp tweed of his overcoat, she felt her heart beat a little faster. Her earlier opinion of him forgotten, she was warmed by his vehemence on her behalf – a knight defending her honour. Looking up, she saw his face, etched like smooth marble in the moonlight, his eyes shadowed by the peak of his cap which, just for an instant, resembled the upraised visor of a knight's helmet. It was a face at once familiar, yet with the fleeting unreality of a romantic stranger. And when he kissed her gently, a proper kiss on the mouth, she didn't think it at all fast of him. It was a night when nothing seemed quite real; even the higgledy-piggledy slate roofs of Fortune Street shone bright as silver, transforming the shabby, tight-packed houses beneath into palaces.

'Come on,' Jimmy said, shattering her fanciful illusion. 'I'll wheel this cart home for you. I guess your dad won't be needing it any more, now he's got that smashing new van.'

In the end, it was a lovely Christmas. Out into the cold clear night for Midnight Mass, and then back to Mam. It was the first time she had missed going in years, but she wasn't asleep and they all piled into her room and sat on her bed, feasting on sausage rolls and mince pies, and drinking hot milk laced with the whisky Dad had received from grateful clients, while they told her all about the singing, and how lifelike the crib was, and how everyone, including all the priests, had sent her their best wishes.

In the morning there were new dresses for the girls and pullovers for Chris and Joey, as well as a collection of parcels under the small Christmas tree. There was a watch each for Chris and the two elder girls, and a pair of new tap shoes for Shirley Anne. Joey thought he had been left out, until he was taken through to the bakehouse where the longed-for bicycle leaned against the wall, greased and polished by Dandy until it looked almost new – and with proper brakes, unlike the 'Penny rips' he and Eddie occasionally hired from Kew Street for a penny an hour. His face was a picture, and everyone agreed there'd be no doing anything with him until he was allowed out for one quick round of the block before breakfast.

'But no stoppin' anywhere, mind – especially not at the Killigans'!

The living room was awash with hand-knitted socks and scarves and discarded wrapping paper. Michael had a new pipe from Chris, and tobacco from Joey. He caressed the smooth bowl of his pipe lovingly, placed it between his lips for a couple of experimental sucks, and then put it in his pipe rack along with the others.

'Aw, no, Dad!' Joey cried. 'You always do that, an' then go on usin' yer old one!'

'Not this one. I'll break it in this very day, after dinner,' Michael promised, ruffling his hair.

'Dad, when are we going to try out the van?' Chris said.

'We, is it?' Michael gave him a quizzical look. 'Ah, well, maybe there'll be time, after we've been up with your mother's presents. It wouldn't do to be making her feel left out.'

So everyone crowded into Mam's room again, and soon her bed, too, was piled high with talcum powder and knitting wool for the baby, and a new nightdress, patterned with tiny flowers and with a pretty lace-edged collar. But the most exciting gift of all was from Michael – a gramophone, something she had been wanting for a long time.

'The handle winds quite easily,' he said, 'and then you move this arm across and let it down very gently.'

There was a faint hissing sound, followed by the unmistakable voice of Cavan O'Connor singing *I'll take you home again, Kathleen*. Her eyes filled as she held out her arms to him.

'Come on.' Rita beckoned the others from the room. 'There's breakfast to get and the turkey to prepare.' Their departure went almost unnoticed.

'It's really meant for your parlour.' Michael's face was half-buried in Kathleen's hair. 'But we can fix a place here where you can reach it for the present, and it'll maybe help to pass the time. I've several more records to start you off – a couple of John McCormicks, a Nelson Eddy and Jeanette MacDonald, and a Gracie Fields for laughs.'

'Michael Ryan, have I ever told you, you're a lovely man?' she whispered.

Dr Graham had agreed that Kathleen could come down for dinner, so long as she promised not to lift a finger. It was to be a real family dinner, augmented by Dandy and Kathleen's brother Nick, with his wife Laura, whom they hardly knew. The numbers stretched the living room to its limits and overflowed into Mam's parlour when they all assembled to cheer as Michael and Chris, deaf to Kathleen's protests that a few stairs wouldn't kill her, vied for the privilege of helping her down.

Liz had always liked her Uncle Nick, and wished she saw him

more often, but since he and Aunt Laura had married, they had gone to live in Bootle. Her father was something important in the building trade and had given them a two-up and two-down house as a wedding present. Nick was a louder, jollier version of Aunt Flora, a big man with twinkly eyes – 'a bit of a devil', she'd heard Dandy call him more than once. She couldn't understand what he saw in Laura, who was pale and quiet and wore her straight fair hair pulled back into a tight roll. She hardly opened her mouth, and Liz wondered whether it was because she too was having a baby, and felt embarrassed about Mam's trouble, though Mam went out of her way to make her feel at ease.

'I'm a lucky man,' said Dandy, leaning back later, replete with turkey and plum pudding, and growing loquacious with a few jars under his belt, 'to be celebratin' this day with so many of me family gathered around me. And' – lifting his glass to absent loved ones – 'the rest with us in spirit.'

Joey, knowing from past experience that they were in for a long, and to him tedious, bout of reminiscence, wriggled restively on his chair. 'Please, Dad, can I leave the table?'

'Now, why would you want to do that, I wonder?' asked Michael.

'Aw, Dad, yer know why. I want to go and show Eddie me bike. You wouldn't let me go callin' this morning.'

Rita frowned. 'It won't hurt you for once to stay until the rest of us have finished and grace has been said.'

'Oh, let the boy say his own grace and be away.' Dandy waved a dismissive hand. 'He'll go off pop if he has to sit there much longer.'

'Mam?'

Kathleen heard the note of pleading and, beguiled by those wide dark-fringed eyes, smiled with more than usual benevolence at her young rip of a son. 'If your father says you may.'

'Thanks, Mam.' Eagerly Joey sought confirmation from his father, and receiving it, ducked his head, eyes screwed shut, then blessed himself with exaggerated piety and scrambled down.

'And don't you let that Eddie ride your bike, or it'll come back in pieces!' Liz called after him.

When Dad had taken Mam back upstairs, he and Chris and Uncle Nick had a bit of a discussion about enlarging the back gate, so the van could be run into the yard. Then they took the van out for a spin while Dandy and the girls tackled the mountain of washing up. At first Laura hovered, offering to help.

'That's all right, lass. You go and talk to our Kathleen. We'll soon get to the back of this lot between us, won't we, Shirley Anne?'

Shirley Anne, who would cheerfully have handed over her tea towel to Aunt Laura, muttered agreement and carried on with reasonably good grace. She could count the time in hours now to the opening of *Puss in Boots*, and already her head was filled with dreams of becoming famous overnight. Of course, everyone kept impressing upon her that she was only in the pantomime until the other girl was over her chickenpox, but once he had actually seen her perform in public, Mr Grace would recognize her superior talent. She might be younger than the rest, but she was the only one in the troupe who could kick her leg right up over her head like Jessie Matthews, and she had made sure he'd seen her do it at rehearsal.

So buoyed up was she that she had even overcome the disappointment of getting a silver locket from Aunt Flora, instead of the pure silk stockings and lacy suspender belts and cami-knickers her sisters had received. It was a pretty locket, and if she really wanted silk stockings, she could break into her five pound note. Aunt Flora always gave them each a brand new one, white and tissue crisp, for Christmas and birthdays, to spend as they pleased, though Mam usually made them put most of it in their Post Office savings. Anyway, when she was famous, she would be able to have a new pair of silk stockings for every day of the week.

'Your father said to come up, but if you'd rather rest . . .' Laura still couldn't bring herself to call him Dandy. She hovered diffidently in the bedroom doorway, as yet showing little evidence of her condition.

Kathleen, propped up against her pillows, still wearing her best blue frock that was getting too tight, was tempted to seize on the excuse. She was tired. And anyway, they had so little in common that conversation would be hard going. But poor Laura looked so dejected that she hadn't the heart to reject her company.

'Come and sit down. I do nothing but rest, and I'm heartily sick of it, I can tell you. That's the only chair, I'm afraid, but it's quite comfortable.'

Laura sat, but continued to look ill at ease.

'I expect you find the family a bit much, all together like this,' Kathleen said, feeling sorry for her. 'But you'll get accustomed – we're not so bad when you get to know us.'

'Oh, I never thought . . . it's just . . . I'm an only child, you see.'

Kathleen did see. She thought back to the wedding – Laura's stuck-up parents, making little attempt to mingle with their daughter's rather boisterous new relations, other than Flora, who was obviously worth cultivating. 'Well, if you ever feel the need of a chat, you're welcome to pop in any time. It's not far on the bus, and I'd be glad of the company. After all,' she patted her stomach ruefully, 'we do have something in common just now . . .'

For the first time Laura smiled, and Kathleen began to see why Nick had fallen for her. There was a certain innocence behind her reserve that would appeal to his big generous nature. But innocence soon palled – it was to be hoped there was more to Laura than that.

'A first baby can be a bit daunting,' she went on, 'so if you want advice or reassurance – well, I reckon I'm something of an expert by now.'

'Thanks, I . . . There isn't really anyone I can ask. Mother doesn't seem to like talking about it . . .'

That figures, thought Kathleen. Laura's mother was the kind of woman who would shy away from any mention of bodily functions.

Encouraged by her sister-in-law's friendly overtures, Laura hurried on in a sudden rush of confidence. 'I'm sorry things aren't going very well for you just now. I think you're being terribly brave about it.'

No, I'm not! Kathleen wanted to scream. I'm scared silly. But I can't tell anyone that, not even Michael – especially not Michael. Not anyone, so I'll just have to get on with it.

Chapter Seven

The New Year's Eve party the Whitneys held to usher in 1937 was to remain forever in Liz's memory. It was her first experience of the kind of party she had imagined existed only in films, in a house where flickering log fires were reflected in polished mahogany and gleaming glass; where an enormous Christmas tree filled one corner of the drawing room – and where, to her delight, she was accepted, not as the middle Ryan girl, but as a young lady in her own right.

The frock helped, of course. Gazing at her reflection in the full length mirror in Clare's bedroom had been like coming face to face with a stranger. Clare had been right – the pale green taffeta gave a delicacy to her complexion and brought out the bronze lights in her hair, held back by an Alice band of matching material. The sweetheart neckline exposed an awful lot of her chest and, with the sash pulled close at the waist, emphasised the growing shapeliness of her figure. And suddenly it didn't matter that she wasn't pretty, or that the other young women present far surpassed her for elegance. Nor did she mind that the equally elegant men, Fred Astaire look-alikes in white tie and tails, gave her no more than an indulgent passing glance. She would probably have died of fright if one of them had asked her to dance.

She was more than content to sit on the stairs with Francis, who, self-effacing as ever, showed little inclination to mix. They talked about a lot of things – her decision to leave school for one.

'But don't you mind at all?' Francis asked. 'You must be clever – Clare says you beat her hollow in the end of term exams.'

'Oh, anyone can pass exams if they swot up hard enough,' Liz said airily. 'And I see no reason why my brain should stagnate just because I've left school. To be honest, I shall miss my friends, and there is a part of me that occasionally wonders how far I might have gone if circumstances had been different, but' – her voice took on a note of defiance – 'it just means I'll have to get to the top by another route.'

'I wish I had your kind of certainty.' Liz heard the disillusion in his voice. 'My father's always taken it for granted that I'll read law and join his firm, and he can't understand why I'm dragging my feet.'

Liz caught sight of Mr Whitney across the hall; bluff, genial, gregarious – a successful man in every way. But she could quite see how impossible Francis would find it to emulate him.

'Perhaps if there was something else you really wanted to do?' she suggested.

'Oh, but there is. I want to fly aeroplanes.' He watched her tawny eyes grow wide, and groaned. 'You see, even you think it's a crazy idea.'

'I don't – not really. It just came as a bit of a surprise.'

'Well, you can just imagine how Dad would react. But ever since I had my first joyride a couple of years back in the Southport beach plane, I haven't been able to think of anything but becoming a flyer.' Liz had never heard so much enthusiasm in his voice. 'There's a chap here tonight, an American called Leigh Farrell – I don't know if you've met him yet? He and his father are staying next door with the Hazletts. They design and build aeroplanes, and Leigh test-flies them. Can you imagine how I feel, just listening to him talking about it! They've been down in London having discussions with someone about long-distance chartering. Leigh's promised that if he can hire a plane from the flying club at Speke before they sail home next week, he'll take me up and show me the basic procedures.'

Clare put her head round the banister rail. 'Hey! You shouldn't be hiding away there. Come and join the fun. We'll be eating shortly.'

Liz jumped up. 'Is there anything I can do?'

'No, there isn't. You've done your bit. Enjoy yourself. Don't let that brother of mine bore you.'

'I'm not bored.'

Francis, too, had risen. He put a hand on Liz's arm. 'You won't tell, will you?'

'Of course not. What d'you take me for?'

A little while later, she was waiting her turn to get close to the dining table, groaning under the weight of more food than she'd ever seen outside of Cooper's, and contemplating the back view of the young man in front of her, who had hair even redder than Eddie Killigan's. I bet he was called 'Carrots' at school, she thought, stifling a giggle. He had obviously attempted to slick it down, but it still showed a distinct tendency to curl up at the nape of his neck. So preoccupied was she that, when he turned without warning, she wasn't quick enough to get out of the way. A well-filled patty shot off his plate, up-ended itself, and landed with a squelch in the hollow of her neck before sliding down to lodge in the dipping sweetheart neckline. He muttered something soft, short and, Liz suspected, extremely rude under his breath, then said ruefully, 'I'm terribly sorry.'

'Oh, no! It isn't your fault!' she exclaimed, intrigued by his deep easy drawl, whilst the practical part of her mind wondered how best to remove the patty without damaging Clare's beautiful frock. 'Accidents are bound to happen in such a dreadful crush.'

'I guess so. But if you'll just hold still a minute,' he said, 'I think I can – ' He took a clean plate and held it close – so close, in fact, that his hand rested feather-light against the curve of her breast. 'There!' he exclaimed triumphantly, as with a neat flick of the finger he tipped the pastry on to the plate. With great aplomb, he then drew a spotless white handkerchief from his trouser pocket and presented it to her with a flourish. 'I guess I'd better leave the mopping up operations to you.' His long mouth curved away into deep humorous creases. 'It would be a pleasure to oblige, but folk might get quite the wrong idea.'

Scarlet with embarrassment, Liz seized the handkerchief and quickly wiped off the small amount of filling, then stood, not quite knowing what to do with it. He took it from her and pushed it carelessly back into his pocket. His eyes, a clear penetrating green, continued to regard her in a lazy, amused way that sent a tingle right down her spine – as if he was waiting for her to speak.

But Liz was quite untypically tongue-tied. Finally she blurted out, 'You must be the American flyer.'

'Must I?' The laugh lines fanning out at the corners of his eyes quivered. 'And you are Clare's young friend – the one who prepared much of this splendid supper.'

Liz stared. 'However did you know that?'

'I asked. Mrs Whitney told me all about you.'

'Oh.' For the life of her, she couldn't say more. He was just being kind, of course, but . . . He had actually asked! Her pulse raced and she could feel herself blushing again.

And then there was some good natured grumbling about people hogging the food, and they became separated. He didn't seek her out again, nor did she really expect him to, but even so, Liz floated through the rest of the evening on air.

Mrs Whitney, coming upon her much later all alone, staring out of the dining room window, was concerned. 'Liz, my dear? Is everything all right?'

'What?' Liz swung round, her eyes still full of dreams as she reluctantly dragged her thoughts away from the slim, clear-eyed American, whose long-jawed face was thick with freckles, whose rather dominant nose looked as though it had been on the receiving end of one of Dandy's famous left hooks, and who, for all his apparent air of indolence, was one of the most vitally alive people she had ever met. 'Oh, yes. Everything's fine, thanks. I was just looking at the stars – they're so bright tonight, don't you think?' She saw Mrs Whitney regarding her in a very strange way, and added hastily, 'I'm having a wonderful time, honestly!'

'Well, I'm glad to hear it, but you mustn't hide away here on your own. It's almost midnight, and you'll miss the first-footing.' Clare's mother shoo-ed Liz before her into the hall where everyone had gathered. Clare pushed her way through to join her, and Liz tentatively mentioned the American.

'Oh, you mean Monica Hazlett's beau – at least that's what she'd like to think. Honestly, it's pathetic, the way she clings to him, making sheep's eyes!'

Monica Hazlett was almost nineteen, slim, blonde and, to Liz's eyes, terribly sophisticated in an oyster silk frock cut on the bias so that it clung and swirled. And Liz was philosophical enough to accept her own encounter with Leigh Farrell for what it was – the stuff of dreams.

As the grandfather clock began to chime the hour, the excitement mounted, and on the first stroke of twelve, a cheer rose, almost drowning out the knocking on the front door. A dark-haired man Liz knew only as Charlie was admitted, bearing the obligatory gifts of coal, bread and salt, and was dragged into the crowd. Then, somehow, everyone managed to link hands for the singing of 'Auld Lang Syne', and there was a great deal of kissing and laughing and shouts of 'Happy New Year!'. The crowd ebbed and flowed, and for the second time that evening Liz found herself crushed against Leigh Farrell. His body was surprisingly taut and muscular, and once again, in spite of all her fine reasoning, she was filled with the oddest tingling sensation.

'Hello, again. Liz, isn't it?'

And because she had never felt quite this way before, she said, 'Elizabeth, actually – Elizabeth Ryan.'

He smiled. 'A beautiful name for a beautiful young lady.'

It was, of course, the intoxication of the moment that made her accept the compliment without argument – that made her stand quite still, her eyes shining like liquid topaz as they lifted to his. And the same intoxication must have infected him, she later told herself, for one of his hands came firmly about her waist. 'A very happy New Year to you, Elizabeth Ryan,' he said softly, and, bending down, touched his lips to hers.

Michael soon adapted to the van, with only one minor disaster when he braked too suddenly and shunted a whole tray of custards into a congealed heap. Dandy and Chris had helped to fit out the interior with shelving, which meant they were able to get an amazing amount into a small space. Deliveries became much quicker, and in no time at all he was wondering how he had ever managed with the handcart – which he had put away in the cellar, just in case. He also invested in a delivery bike for short runs.

Liz had expected ructions from Mam over her decision to leave school. But for all her hopes and expectations, Kathleen was nothing if not a realist, and a further visit from Dr Graham had confirmed what in her heart she already knew.

'I'm sorry, lass,' the doctor had said, 'but you can put all thought of working out of your head. I did warn you that it wouldn't be easy. So far, so good, but for the next few months, a little light exercise and a great deal of rest is going to be the order of the day, if we're to bring you and the baby safely to full term.'

She had opened her mouth to protest, but he forestalled her. 'The best thing you can do for now is to take up your sister's suggestion – go and stay with her for a week or two. Life won't seem half so bad away from here, where you'll not be seeing what needs doing.' When she still looked set to argue, he sat down on the bed. 'Now, listen to me, Kathleen – I know how you feel, but no-one is indispensable, and to be brutally honest, do you not think it's time you gave some thought to your family? They're feeling the strain, too, you know – especially Michael. So go to Southport, and give them a bit of a break.'

She was very quiet for a moment. Then: 'You don't pull your punches, do you?' she said.

'Not with Dandy Power's daughter, I don't. We've known one another too long to start treading on eggshells now. Besides, you know I'm right. Your sister's a sensible woman, and her doctor happens to be a friend of mine, though he shouldn't be needed if you behave yourself.' He patted her hand and stood up. 'The time will pass surprisingly quickly.'

So, when Liz finally got round to breaking the news, Kathleen's reactions were less dramatic than she had expected, though her disappointment was obvious. 'It's such a waste!' she wailed.

'I don't mind, Mam, honest. If you really want to know, I'm quite excited by the whole idea. I've already got some thoughts about extending the confectionery side of the business.' Liz, thankful that only she and her father knew the contents of her school report, tried to instil as much enthusiasm as she could into explaining her ambitions, but got little response. 'Anyway,' she said in a final effort to please, 'it's never too late, so they say. Maybe Sister Imelda'll let me go back next year to sit my exams. And if she won't, there are other places I can do it.'

Rita, saying her own piece before she went back to college, poured scorn on this suggestion. 'People who talk that way seldom do anything about it, as well you know. You're being incredibly short sighted, Liz; making an unnecessary sacrifice for a matter of a few months. Dad would get by . . .'

'Maybe he would, but you can lose a lot of trade just getting by,' Liz argued with surprising percipience. 'And that would be a pity, just when the business is becoming known for quality, the way Mam always dreamed it would. You know as well as I do Dad doesn't have that kind of imagination. He makes the best bread in town by far, but he'd never blow his own trumpet. He's like a ship without a rudder unless someone organizes him.'

'Oh, you – you're as bad as Mam where he's concerned. She

could still do any organizing that's necessary. Now Dad has the van, he can get round a lot quicker, and with the money that's saved, and Dandy and the rest of you helping out when you can, he could afford to take Chris into the bakehouse full time – maybe pay for a bit of part-time help in the shop as well.'

'And the house will run itself, I suppose?' Liz retorted. 'The meals and the cleaning, looking after Mam, as well as the shop and all the unexpected things that crop up – not to mention the baby when it arrives? And I thought you were the practical one!'

'So I am.' Rita flushed, driven to defend herself. 'It could be managed, if everyone pulled their weight. Shirley Anne doesn't do half enough. She should be here full time instead of smarming up to that Mrs Frith.'

'She works mornings in the shop,' Liz said. 'Mrs Frith does pay her a small wage, and there's the little concerts for her good causes – Shirley Anne will get extra for those.'

'That's not proper work. She should be here, where she belongs. A right little madam, she'll be, if you don't watch out.' Rita's tone was scathing. 'Five minutes in the limelight, mixing with the likes of Sandy Powell, and she already thinks she's God's gift to the stage. But that Mr Grace was quick enough to chuck her out when the other girl came back.'

'That's not fair, Rita. We always knew that would happen. And even you have to admit Shirley Anne *was* good – no, she was more than good, she was brilliant!'

'Well, I hope you haven't told her so. It's high time she gave up mooning around, chasing dreams . . .'

But Liz was remembering again the thrill of seeing her sister on stage, being applauded by a full theatre, with all the family, except Mam, in the best seats, courtesy of Mr Grace. For the first time, perhaps because of the growing changes in herself, Liz was beginning to understand the burning ambition that drove Shirley Anne, and it made her more sympathetic than she might otherwise have been.

'You know as well as I do that Shirley Anne'd be hopeless at running things here. And besides, far from making a sacrifice, I have ambitions of my own for this business. I'm going to be a great confectioner one day. That's *my* dream, if you like. We all need our dreams. And in keeping Mam's alive, I'll fulfil mine.'

'Oh, I give up! You're acting like a fool, Liz, throwing away a fine opportunity to make something of yourself for some woolly-minded fantasy. People like us don't get second chances, as you'll learn to your cost. And it's a wicked shame, because you're really quite bright – you could have made something of yourself.'

'I still can,' Liz was stung into retorting. 'And what's more, our Rita, I will. You just watch me.' She was tempted to reveal what Sister Imelda had said about her being brighter than Rita, but bit back the wounding comparison just in time. 'I know you can't see it, but there's more roads to success than by passing exams. And one day I'm going to prove it to you!'

Sister Imelda's reaction was fairly predictable. It was an interview that Liz, for all her bravado, had been dreading. The loss of this child in whom she had placed so much hope came as no surprise to the headmistress; it had happened before and would happen again. But the waste of a good brain, for whatever reason, was to her unforgivable, and bitter disappointment found expression in cutting brevity. She made no comment on the tentatively voiced suggestion about coming back next year and, faced with the nun's cold disapproval, Liz found her arguments trailing away. Swift dismissal came as a merciful release.

Meanwhile, Chris had been making a few decisions of his own. Dad had made it quite clear that they couldn't yet afford to have him give up his job, but he reckoned he'd be of more use working nights and being around during the day, catching some sleep when he could. He began making enquiries as soon as Christmas was over, but it was a quiet time and there were no night vacancies at Lunt's. But through a fellow worker he eventually heard of a bakery down Walton way that was always wanting nightworkers.

'You must've heard of it. It's norra union place – not your sort of place at all, I'd have thought. They've gorra huge cellar lay-out – more like a fact'ry, really – an' send vanloads of stuff out all over the area. The pay's not bad, but talk about sweated labour! Badger don' 'alf gerr 'is money outa yer the hard way, so no-one sticks it fer long.'

'I hope I won't need to stick it for long,' Chris said with a grin. 'So it's worth a try. I'll get along there after work.'

The woman behind the shop counter looked him over with a knowing eye. 'Yer'd best come through,' she said, lifting the flap and nodding towards a trapdoor in the floor. 'The old feller'll be down there somewhere, crackin' the whip.'

Chris hesitated. 'Is this the only way in?'

'What d'yer expect, lad?' The woman sniffed. 'A posh staircase?'

He knew about places like this, where the bakery was built right out under the street, so the snow never got to lie in winter, but – a trap in the floor! His mouth had gone very dry, and his ears went funny, but he smothered the beginnings of panic and climbed down the inadequate wall ladder. At the bottom he found himself in a world of heat and noise made up of several huge cellar rooms. He hesitated, unsure which to choose.

'Hi. Lost yer way, sunshine?'

Chris turned to see a bright-faced girl eyeing him with lively interest from the doorway of a room that echoed with women's chatter. Her red springing hair was imperfectly restrained by a white cap, and she didn't look much above Liz's age.

He grinned. 'I'm looking for Mr Badger.'

'You poor sod!' She eyed him pityingly. 'He's well named, that one. Always on at us. Yer'll likely find him in there.' She nodded towards the opening opposite, and another curl dislodged itself, coming to rest on a flushed cheek.

'You there, gairl!' A fleshy, strutting man had come up behind them, and was waving an angry fist at her. 'Get back ter work if y'don't want ter be out on yer backside. Y've been told more'n once, I don't pay yer t' flirt with my men. An' you – ' he jerked his head. 'Come with me.'

Without waiting, he strode away. Behind his back, the girl pulled a face and mouthed 'What did I tell yer?' and Chris just had time to ask, 'What time d'you get out?'

'Six, if I'm lucky.' She ducked back into the room.

'Come on, lad. I 'aven't got all day.' The irate man was beckoning him into a cavern of a room, where the biggest ovens Chris had ever seen ran the whole length of one wall, giving off a stifling heat. Around a large table, about twenty men were working like automatons. Several were scaling off with rhythmic precision, throwing the dough to the centre, where the nearest pair of free hands moulded it and put it into tins. Others were moving tins on to the setters, and then on to big trolleys, until all the shelves were full. There seemed to be a constant procession of trolleys laden with proved dough being wheeled to the nearest free oven, where the huge drawplate was pulled out and two men standing either side of it took the setters, shelf by shelf, and tipped the tins on to it until it was full. Further along at another oven, two more men were reversing the process, laying a long piece of wood across the drawplate between the baked loaves, pulling on to it as many as the wood would hold, and tipping them on to a movable table to be wheeled away to the cooling and packing department. Again claustrophobia threatened; as Chris wondered what would happen if there should be a fire, and they were all caught down here with only that narrow trapdoor to the shop for escape. The sweat ran down his back.

'Well, lad – d'yer want the job or not?'

Chris hesitated.

'Yer'll find nights hard goin', but I can start yer Friday. Three pound ten the first week, an' if yer shape, I'll maybe raise it to four. But I want no larkin' about with the judies, mind – not that they're around of a night time.'

It was good money, more than he was getting at present, but he didn't know if he could stick the conditions. He muttered something about not being sure.

'Suit yerself, lad. Only don't expect me ter keep the job on spec.'

Chris hung around outside, taking great gulps of fresh air, and stamping his feet against the cold, until at last the girl appeared amid a small chattering group. She was wearing a brilliant pink muffler and beret that should have clashed terribly with her hair, but didn't. Chris saw her point him out, and there was much whispering and giggling. Suddenly his legs seemed too long and spindly, and he was glaringly aware that the cuffs of his working jacket didn't reach his wrists. Unlike Jimmy, he'd never bothered much with girls; three sisters were more than enough for him. But this one was different. She reminded him of a small irrepressible bird, and he found himself prey to the strangest sensations as she left her friends and came sauntering across.

'Hello – yer waited, then,' she said pertly. 'You blushin'?'

'Of course not,' Chris lied, feeling the tide of colour surge afresh. 'It's just that I'm still sweating from being in that hell-hole.'

'It's not so bad when you get used. You been taken on, then?'

He shrugged. 'I haven't made up my mind.'

'Well, I'd better be knowin' yer name, just in case.'

'It's Chris – Chris Ryan.' He swallowed. 'And yours?'

'Sally Forest. Come on, you can walk us to the tram, if yer like – we'll freeze, standin' here.' She tucked her arm through his and, looking up, gave him a bright slant-eyed look. 'Any relation to Ryan's in Great Homer, are you?'

He hesitated. 'Why?'

'No reason. It's just you bein' a baker. Me Mam often gets Ryan's bread. Reckons it's a cut above most others. Still, it stands to reason, if you were one of them, you wouldn't be working fer an old slave-driver like Badger.'

She was laughing up at him, but in an admiring sort of way that made him straighten his shoulders and gave him the courage to say, 'Listen, I have to get home just now, but I'd like to see you again.'

'Well, yer will, won't you? On Friday, if yer take the job. I work late, Fridays.'

Again the colour ran up under his fair skin. 'You know what I mean.' He cleared his throat. 'Are you doing anything Sunday afternoon?'

'I might be,' she said teasingly. 'And then again, I might not.'

'Well, then – we could maybe go out somewhere . . .'

Sally grinned. 'I'll think about it.'

'But . . .' Out of the corner of his eye, Chris saw the tram coming. 'Look, I don't know where you live or anything.'

She swung herself up on the step, and called over her shoulder, 'I'll meet yer two o'clock by the Rotunda. Don't be late.'

Chapter Eight

On the day before Kathleen left for Birkdale, she ran everyone ragged with a list of instructions as long as her arm. But it was Liz who bore the brunt of them.

'Mam! You're only going for a couple of weeks,' she was at last driven to protest. 'The place isn't going to fall apart in that time.'

'No, of course not.' Kathleen sank back against the pillows. 'I'm doing it again, aren't I? Fussing, I mean. It's just . . .'

'I know. But it'll be all right, I promise.'

Kathleen looked into her earnest face, and capitulated.

On Monday morning Flora's sleek black Daimler arrived, and Michael was back from his rounds in time to help his wife downstairs and see her safely settled, wrapped in rugs, with a hot water bottle to keep her feet warm during the drive. His heart was heavy, for they had never been apart for more than a day or so in all the years of their marriage, and he would be bereft without her. But he put on a brave show, waving her off with Liz and Dandy, enthusiastically supported by half of Fortune Street.

'Honestly, this is ridiculous!' Kathleen protested. 'If this is what royalty have to go through, I pity them.'

'Stop grumbling and make the most of it,' Flora said, not a whit dismayed by her ingratitude. 'Whether you like it or not, my girl, for the next week or so you're going to be cosseted. Peters and Caulderbank have brought a bed down into the small back parlour, so you'll have a nice view of the garden. And the downstairs cloakroom is right next door . . .'

Kathleen closed her teeth on the retort that sprang to her lips. She didn't want nice views, or to be fussed over by Flora's servants, good as they were. And as for *downstairs cloakrooms* . . . she sometimes wondered if Flo remembered what life was like in the real world. She shut her eyes and feigned sleep until she felt the car slow and turn in between the wide gateposts to draw up in front of the big, creeper-covered house.

In no time, it seemed, she was sinking into a luxurious feather mattress, with downy pillows plumped up behind her so that she could appreciate to the full the large expanse of lawn and shrubbery, while the motherly housekeeper, Mrs Meadows, tucked in the blankets, put away the meagre contents of her suitcase, and poked the fire into a cheerful blaze before departing to make her 'a nice pot of tea'.

Flora, observing her sister's drawn face, said she would tell Mrs Meadows to leave the tea until later, and abandoned her to a solitary contemplation of the view, and of the *small* parlour – with its blue carpet, so soft to the feet, its pretty chintz sofas and curtains and mahogany what-nots – into which the whole Ryan family, house and all, could have fitted with ease.

She had never felt so alone, or so utterly miserable.

The house seemed very empty without Mam. They all felt as though the heart had gone out of the place, and in a curious way it drew them closer together. Business was quiet but even that had its blessings – Nora Figg hadn't been near since Christmas Eve.

'Decided ter give Lunt's the benefit of 'er custom,' announced Mrs Killigan, always first with the news, when she came in for her bread. 'Tekken umbrage proper, she 'as, after the way she wus treated – bin slaggin' you off all over the place. Not that anyone takes notice.' The folds of fat beneath her tightly stretched coat heaved with merriment, and Liz found herself wondering if Lily, already growing plump, would end up like her mother. 'Eh!' she wheezed, 'but I'll not forget that set-to in a hurry – a show an' a half, that wus!'

But Liz gave her no encouragement to continue. 'Well, as far as I'm concerned, it's good riddance to Mrs Figg. Except that she'll be back, as sure as eggs is eggs, if only to poke and pry. Besides, no-one else'll put up with her pinch-penny ways for long.'

With Rita back at college, life settled into its former pattern, and Liz was once more obliged to cook the meals. 'The job's yours any time you want it, my lad,' she told Chris tartly when he enquired of no-one in particular how anyone who made such mouth-watering pastry could produce a tapioca pudding solid enough to be made into bricks. 'In fact, I'm thinking seriously of making out a rota, so you can all take a turn.' From that moment, all criticism ceased.

What little spare time she had went on giving Mam's bedroom a good going over, so that it would be all fresh and clean for her return. Ellen came in to help her, and took the curtains and bedding, including the bedspread, away to wash. She also offered to come and spring clean the rest of the house before Mam returned, an offer gratefully accepted by Liz.

'I find I've got a bit more time since Hester Whelan moved in next door. She's been a godsend. What with her being a widow, and her only son away in the Navy, she's got lots of time on her hands. She loves having the two little ones, and she's ever so good with Arnie – better than I am, sometimes.'

Although Arnie's name came into the conversation several times, Liz didn't like to ask whether there had been any repercussions as a result of her thoughtless remarks.

'We had a lovely time,' was all that Ellen said. 'I've never seen the children so excited. All that food, the Christmas cake and mince pies and the bars of chocolate – I was afraid they'd be sick, but they weren't! And as if they hadn't enough, some of Arnie's old mates came round with toys for them and a jar or two for him.'

Joey remained his usual cheerful self, and as for Shirley Anne – well, Liz didn't know quite what to make of Shirley Anne. She had expected her to be inconsolable when her spell at the Empire came to an end, and so she had been for a day or two. But after one great outburst of tears, there was nothing worse than a tendency to go round in a dream half the time, and Liz could only suppose that her sister had come to terms with her disappointment.

This was true up to a point, but no-one, not even Miss Eglantine, knew of Mr Grace's final words of encouragement to Shirley Anne; of the card he had given her, with his name and address on it; or ofhis promise that, when she was a little older, he would be only too ready to help her launch herself on a stage career.

She had hidden the card away in a secret place, and no-one, not even Lily, had been permitted to know of its existence. In the meantime, she was enjoying working for Mrs Frith. You couldn't really call it work, though she didn't tell Liz that. But she had proved to be quite a dab hand at sending out invitations and helping to entertain guests.

'I can't imagine how I ever managed without you, dear child,' Mrs Frith exclaimed. A pretty, rather plump woman, she had been widowed at fifty, and lived alone with a maid and a cook in a big house in Faulkner Square. 'It was always a sadness that we were never blessed with children. But now – well, you are almost like a daughter to me.'

Shirley Anne, for whom drama and reality almost always became intermingled, played her part with great enthusiasm, pandering to Mrs Frith's every whim, and was overjoyed whenever a concert was arranged and she got a chance to perform. And, although she always demurred when Mrs Frith insisted upon paying her extra for her delightful singing and dancing, she always ended up taking the money offered.

'I don't see why I shouldn't. She must be ever so well off,' Shirley Anne told Liz. 'You should see her wardrobes – whole walls of them. She's got more clothes than Aunt Flora.'

Liz was becoming resigned to the fact that Shirley Anne always managed to fall on her feet. 'As long as you don't take advantage of her. And don't forget, we want a proper morning's work from you, here. *We're* not made of money.'

As might have been expected, Michael was the worst affected by Kathleen's absence: a quiet man at the best of times, it now took all Liz's coaxing to get two words out of him.

'Honest, Grandpa Dandy, but for visiting Mam, the only time he's content is when he's in the bakehouse. And even there, he's only half there, if you see what I mean.'

'What your father needs is motivation,' Dandy said. 'Give him something to occupy his mind – preferably something that'll be a nice surprise for Kathleen when she comes home. How about hintin' that he and Chris might like to carry on where you've left off with that bedroom you've been so busy making spick and span? A lick of paint would finish the job a treat.'

Liz thought that was a great idea. And it might help to clear the air between the two of them – there had been ructions when Chris had announced he was thinking of changing jobs.

'Badger! I didn't teach you all I know to have you wasting your time on trash like Badger.' Dad seldom raised his voice, but you were never in any doubt when he was angry.

'I know, Dad, but if I work nights, I can be around more during the day, and the money's good . . .'

'Money! Lord save us, boy, if you've learned nothing else from your mother and meself, I thought you'd have learned that money isn't everything. We're managing fine the way we are. It'd do our name no good at all if word got around that you were working for Badger. That place of his should have been condemned years ago – would have been, except he has friends in high places. He's no business taking you on nights, at your age.'

'I'll be eighteen in a few weeks.' Chris had sounded unusually truculent, and Liz prudently intervened.

'Ah, come on, Chris,' she'd said lightly, thinking how alike they looked, glowering eye to eye across the table. 'Dad's right. You're too good to waste your talent on the likes of Badger. Anyway, I've got plans – and if they work out, we'll soon need you here full time.'

Chris hesitated. He could be stubborn, for all that he was easy-going. But the more he thought about Badger's, the more he hated the idea of working there.

'Besides, Mam would be so ashamed.'

That did it, as Liz had known it would. 'All right, Miss Bossy-boots, you win,' he said with a sheepish grin.

Liz was also the first to notice that Chris was taking more pains with his appearance. On one occasion she caught a distinct whiff of *eau de cologne*. When she teased him about it, he coloured up.

'If it was anyone else, I'd say you've got yourself a girl friend.' To her amazement he turned bright red. 'You have! Hey, that's great. What's she like? When are you going to bring her home?'

'Never, if you keep on like that,' he muttered, and rushed out, slamming the door.

When Jimmy popped into the shop on the pretext of buying a seedy cake for his mam, Liz said wretchedly, 'I never meant . . . I didn't stop to think. He must be badly smitten. Have you met her?'

Jimmy grinned. 'A bewitching little redhead, name of Sally. Got all her cards at home, that one. I reckon she'll lead him a bit of a dance.'

'She'd better not!' Liz rushed to her brother's defence, immediately hating the unknown girl. 'If she breaks his heart, I'll kill her!'

'No danger of that. There's no harm in Sally, and I think Chris quite enjoys her teasing.' He leaned across the counter, his bold eyes smiling. 'Tell you what – how about a foursome next Sunday, you and me and the two of them? Then you could look her over for yourself.'

'Well, I don't know.' Liz was flustered. He was always hanging around, but this was the first time he'd asked her out properly. 'Sunday, Dad'll be going to see Mam, and I might be going with him.'

'Ah, come on. Your Mam wouldn't mind.' His voice became softly persuasive. 'I'd really like you to come.'

Her heart skipped a beat. 'Well, I'll think about it,' she said off-handedly.

There and then, she made up her mind to do some shopping. Dad had given her four pounds at Christmas. 'You've more than earned it, girleen,' he'd said. 'And your mother agrees with me that from now on, you should have a regular weekly wage. We thought thirty shillings to begin with, which isn't a lot for all you do, but the way business is improving, we can maybe increase it soon.'

Thirty shillings every week! And nine pounds already hers, counting Aunt Flora's fiver. Some would have to go into the Post Office, of course, but she desperately needed some new clothes. Apart from her Christmas frock, almost her entire wardrobe was made up of school uniform and hand-me-downs.

She confided her intentions to Dandy when Dad had gone up to rest. 'Will you mind the shop until Shirley Anne comes home? I won't be any longer than I can help.'

'Take all the time you want, chuck.' His pugnacious face broke into a grin. 'I reckon it's time you thought about yourself for once.' His hand moved to his trouser pocket. 'An' if you're short, just say the word.'

'Thanks, but I've got enough, really!' Liz gave him a swift kiss.

It wasn't the best day to choose, with snow on the ground and more on the way from the look of the sky, and her feet had outgrown her wellingtons which meant she'd have to borrow Mam's galoshes. But nothing could quite subdue the bubbles of anticipation as she took the tram from Scotland Road to Whitechapel. From there, with her purse stuffed deep in the pocket of her school coat, safe from pickpockets, she squelched her way through the slush round Bunny's Corner into Church Street, and decided to have a good wander before getting down to any serious business. But first, she allowed herself to be lured into Cooper's by the wonderful smell of freshly ground coffee, past the page boys delegated to stand near the doors, ready to relieve wealthy customers of their parcels and carry them to the waiting line of cars.

This store had fascinated her from early childhood, especially the section which housed the singing canaries. Inevitably, she found herself drawn to the confectionery department, an Aladdin's cave of mouthwatering displays designed to tempt the palate; mounds of crystallised fruits and ginger, exquisite sugared plums, and Turkish Delight dredged with dust-fine sugar, nestling in exotic wooden boxes decorated with strange squiggly writing that looked as if a snail had crawled across the surface; chocolate so satin-dark and rich it made you want to stroke it; displays fashioned with incomparable artistry, from the small and simple to the most intricate works of art. She had once heard that you could buy every kind of food at Cooper's, delicacies from all parts of the world – no matter how rare or exclusive – and if they hadn't got it, they would get it for you. Looking around her, Liz could well believe it, and like Saul on the road to Damascus, she saw with blinding clarity that this, on a smaller scale, was the goal she must strive to reach. The revelation so beguiled her that she stood quite still in the middle of the centre aisle to contemplate it further.

'Would you kindly move out of my way?' The cut-glass voice rudely penetrated her reverie, and Liz turned to find her nose within snapping distance of a fox's muzzle, its jaws firmly clamped round its own bushy tail across a well-corseted bosom, whose heaving indignation gave an uncanny ripple of life to the gleaming fur. The face above it was pinched with annoyance.

'I'm ever so sorry,' she gasped, caught between embarrassment and mirth, and ran out into the cold to resume her window shopping.

Of all the grand department stores, Hendersons was Liz's favourite, with Bon Marché running a close second, both equally beyond her means. Even so, it was the window of the former that drew her attention, and with her spirits still buoyed up from her visit to Cooper's, she succumbed yet again to temptation.

With an air of bravado, she outstared the disapproving doormen and sauntered past to drift through each department, her nostrils assailed by subtle perfumes, the expensive kind used by Aunt Flora. A distinctive smell of leather drew her to a counter where, among a selection of rejects, she spotted an elegant black handbag, reduced to ten shillings because the leather had been badly scarred by something sharp. It was a lot of money to spend on such a frivolous purchase, but she had never owned a proper handbag, and it would be worth every penny to own one from Hendersons. As for the scratch, she reckoned a bit of black boot polish would disguise the worst of the damage. The longer she stared at it, the more of a talisman it became. Recklessly, she proffered her brand-new fiver.

Then, bearing her prize, she set her sights lower. Across the road in C & A Modes she discovered, after much trying on and discarding, a serviceable brown skirt and russet jumper which together cost less than ten shillings; a dress patterned in reds and golds for seven and elevenpence, and a warm woollen coat, close fitting, with flaring panels and a double row of buttons up to the neck, in a pretty soft green, which had been reduced to half price and was a real bargain at just over a pound. There was a matching beret for one and sixpence, and in the haberdashery department she found some speckled wool that would be just right for gloves. All she needed now was a pair of shoes, and Timpsons provided a really cheap black pair with a neat bar fastening.

Her purchases complete, Liz began to make her way back towards Whitechapel against a snow-laden wind coming straight off the river. The light was going fast, and already the slush under her feet was beginning to freeze into crunchy peaks of ice, transformed from grey to glittering silver by the opalescent light filtering from shop windows. For the second time that day, the tantalizing smell of coffee wafted beneath her nostrils, and a sudden craving for something hot and sweet made her mouth water. The windows of Reagan's Café were steamed-up like all the rest, but with her nose pressed to the door she could see there were several empty tables.

Inside, well-dressed ladies sat wreathed in cigarette smoke, sipping coffee, and deep in conversation, surrounded by a collection of exclusive shopping bags. As the bell tinkled, all eyes turned towards her, making Liz instantly aware of her unprepossessing appearance. A thin-faced man in a formal black-striped suit eyed her with distaste from behind the pay desk before lifting a finger to beckon a waitress, also clad in black beneath her spotless white apron and cap. 'A table for one, if you please, Annie,' he said in a falsely posh voice. Liz blushed, but instinctively straightened her back. Head high, she followed the waitress to a corner table, almost obscured from view by a pillar. Without allowing her time to settle, the waitress whipped out pad and pencil.

'What would Miss be requiring?' she enquired in frigid tones.

Momentarily unnerved, Liz dropped her packages and seized the deckle-edged menu. 'Coffee, please,' she said, adding with sudden bravado – 'and a toasted teacake and some cream cakes.'

While she waited, she looked about her. It was a nice little café, small and tastefully decorated. A sign on the rear counter caught her eye. *High quality cakes and pastries supplied by Munnings of Church Street*. She picked up the menu again.

Tuppence for a cream cake! That was daylight robbery. Someone was making a hefty profit. Two cream cakes later, as she sipped her second cup of coffee, she was torn between the satisfaction of knowing that Mr Munnings' pastry wasn't a patch on hers, and a niggling feeling that there ought to be some way she could prove it.

It was still snowing when Liz began to make her way home. She turned the corner into Whitechapel and was about to cross the road when she saw the hunched figure of a man being pelted with dirty wet snowballs. Several people passed by, averting their eyes, which made her mad. Without stopping to think, she ran forward, waving her shopping bags and shouting, 'Give over, you little thugs, or I'll box your ears, the lot of you!'

'Gerrof, yer big Wet Nelly!' sneered the biggest boy. 'You an' 'ose army?'

Before he could draw breath, Liz swiped at him with the largest of her parcels, and caught him flush in the face, drawing blood. He staggered back, scattering his accomplices. 'And that's only for starters,' she threatened. 'I've learned plenty of dirty tricks from me brothers, so I'd shift now, if you don't want a demonstration.'

They scuttled away, muttering.

'Are you all right?' Liz turned her attention to the man. His hat had been knocked off, and she saw that his hair was quite white and worn rather longer than was usual. He straightened slowly and turned. There was a trickle of blood coming from one high jutting cheekbone. 'Oh, they *have* hurt you, the devils. I wish I'd thumped them harder!'

He probed the area with fingers that shook, then reached into the pocket of his overcoat and drew out a neatly folded white handkerchief. 'It is but a scratch, my dear young lady,' he said, dabbing his cheek. 'A stone gathered up with the snow, no doubt. Nevertheless, I am most grateful for your intervention.'

His voice was gentle, with a pronounced accent which intrigued Liz. She looked at him more closely. He might have been as tall as her father, had not a slight stoop foreshortened him, and in spite of his shabbiness, there was an air of dignity about him, and a quiet strength in his face. She put her parcels against the wall and picked up his grey felt hat, wiping the slush off with her sleeve.

'I'd have thumped them twice as hard if I'd known,' she declared, handing it back to him.

He shrugged. 'A childish prank, nothing more. I have known worse things.'

The bleakness in his voice made Liz curious, but a rattle in the overhead wires galvanized her into action. 'There's my tram . . . I must go,' she said, gathering her precious parcels to her as she began to run. 'Goodbye. I'm glad you weren't badly hurt.'

'Ah, but, my dear young lady . . . one moment, I beg of you . . .' His voice followed her as she clambered on to the step, and turned to wave.

Chapter Nine

The dance hall above the corner shop was crowded when Chris and Jimmy shepherded the girls to the place where they could leave their coats. It was a very ordinary room, but it didn't seem so to Liz, whose only previous experience had been of church hall hops – and you couldn't call them real dances, with a three piece band and everything. The dimly lit room was wreathed in cigarette smoke and there was an excited buzz of conversation.

It was Sally's seventeenth birthday, and Chris had persuaded Dad to let his sister make up a foursome with himself and Jimmy. It wasn't the first time they had been out together, but Dad wasn't keen on dance halls.

Liz had taken to Sally at once. She was bright and outspoken, but although she teased Chris, you could tell she liked him a lot, and now, seeing them dancing together, it was obvious that Chris more than liked her. Liz felt a twinge of possessive jealousy.

'Come on, daydream.' Jimmy was tugging at her hand, leading her towards the floor.

Liz held back, feeling suddenly shy and talking fast to cover it. 'I'm not very good at dancing – our Shirley Anne says I've got two left feet, and she should know.'

'Your Shirley Anne knows nothing. Just you let me be the judge.' His arm was round her waist, pulling her gently towards him. 'Come on, relax. That's it – let yourself go, follow me, and you'll be fine.'

And because the tune was one of her favourites, she did as he said, and found it wasn't a bit like learning the steps with her young sister. Jimmy was an excellent dancer, and as he steered her skilfully past less accomplished couples, Liz found her body becoming attuned to his. Her head drooped against his shoulder as the words of the song came softly to her lips – *Red sails in the sunset, far out on the sea, oh, carry my loved one home safely to me . . .*

'That's nice,' Jimmy murmured, and imperceptibly drew her

closer. 'There, what did I tell you? You're doing great.' His breath was warm against her ear. 'M-m, you smell nice.'

'It's *Evening in Paris*,' she said dreamily. 'Chris bought it me for Christmas.'

And then her state of bliss was rudely shattered, as she realized that his hand was straying away from her waist to wander where it shouldn't.

'Jimmy Marsden, you stop that at once!' she said, pulling back, with colour flooding her cheeks.

'O.K. Sorry.' He grinned down at her, not looking at all sorry. 'But you can't blame a fella for tryin'.'

It was hard to stay cross, especially as such compliments were still enough of a novelty for Liz to cherish them. She knew the dress from C & A suited her, as did her hair. Shirley Anne had done it for her, with a deep wave on top, and caught up at the sides with gold-coloured slides.

It was Sally who first noticed that someone else was taking an interest in Liz. 'Hey, I don't know what you've got that I 'aven't,' she said, nudging her in the ribs, 'but that fella by the door hasn't taken his eyes off you all evenin'.'

Intrigued and not a little flattered, Liz glanced casually across the room to where a slim, good-looking young man, who seemed vaguely familiar, lounged against the wall, his blond hair slicked back, and a cigarette dangling from the corner of his mouth. Their eyes met, and he smiled and bowed mockingly.

'Wow!' Sally breathed. 'D'you know him?'

'Not really, and Liz doesn't want to, either.' Chris's voice was unusually curt.

'Whyever not?' Liz looked at her usually easy-going brother in some surprise, and glanced across the room again. 'I know. It's Alec Munnings, Mr Munnings' son. I haven't seen him for years, what with him going away to that fancy private school.' She thought of Mr Munnings, dark and thick-set, a bit smarmy with the customers, and looked again at the son who was a couple of years or so older than Chris. 'He's not a bit like his dad.'

'He's ever so handsome.' Sally was in provocative mood.

'He's a toad,' Chris said. 'You keep away from him, both of you.'

Sally bridled. 'You're very free with your orders, Chris Ryan! I don't know who you think you are, but just stick ter bossin' your Liz. I can look after myself.'

'Chris's right, though,' Jimmy said placatingly, seeing that his friend was set to argue. 'Alec Munnings has a bad reputation. They say he's got more girls into trouble than I've had hot dinners.'

Far from putting Sally off, this information merely made her look at him with fresh interest.

'Matter o' fact,' Jimmy continued, 'I'm surprised to see him here. Blair Hall's a bit beneath his touch – an' if I'm not mistaken, he's already paid one visit too many to Arthur's across the road, so you girls just take care.'

Certainly, as the young man straightened up and began to make his way between the dancing couples towards them, he seemed to weave a little.

'Well, well.' He stopped in front of them. 'What have we here? If it isn't young Christopher Ryan and party.' His light blue eyes seemed almost transparent – like ice, Liz thought, as they looked her over in a way that brought the colour to her face. Sally returned his stare pertly when she received the same treatment, but it was to Liz that his gaze finally returned. 'Can this be your little sister, Christopher? My, how she's grown.' He invested the words with a double meaning. 'I think the occasion calls for a dance.'

'Go away, Munnings,' Chris said. 'She doesn't want to dance with you.'

'Doesn't she?' His voice was casual, but his eyes were hard. 'Is that true, little Lizzie Ryan – or do you let your brother make your decisions for you?'

If he hadn't called her Lizzie, the outcome might have been different. As it was, her resentment against Chris for depriving her of any say in the matter was swamped by a fury of indignation. How dare Alec Munnings, a virtual stranger, address her with such odious familiarity! *And* she could smell the drink on his breath.

'I don't need anyone to speak for me,' she said. 'I'm quite capable of recognizing a drunk when I see one. They're two a penny down Greaty most nights. If I were you, I'd go outside and get some fresh air.'

She heard the sharp intake of breath as all around them ears came out on stalks, and dancers close enough to hear seemed to be marking time in anticipation of a bit of excitement. Sally's eyes had widened in a kind of half-awed admiration at Liz's outspokenness. And Liz knew she had gone too far. But apologize she would not.

'I'll dance with you, if yer like.' Sally, in an attempt to avert disaster, gave Alec Munnings a swift bright smile of invitation.

'You will not,' muttered Chris. 'Just keep out of this.'

Sally tossed her head angrily. 'I've told you more than once, Chris Ryan, to mind your own business.'

'Shut up, Sal,' Jimmy warned her. 'You'll only make things worse.'

But it was doubtful if Alec Munnings had even heard. His pale eyes, narrowed, were fixed on Liz. 'Seems to me you need a lesson in manners, little girl,' he said softly.

'Stop right there, you weed, if you don't want a fist down yer gob.' This time Jimmy got in first. 'No-one talks to my girl like that. An' as for lessons in manners, p'raps you'd care to come outside an' discuss who needs to learn what?'

There was a tense moment, made incongruous by the band's enthusiastic rendition of *Somebody stole my gal*. It was Alec Munnings who finally backed off. 'I wouldn't waste my time on the Ryans or their friends,' he drawled, turning on his heel. 'Who are they, anyway? Papist trash with a rich relation daft enough to buy them a brand new van to pander to their inflated idea of their own importance!'

'Better that than a jumped-up proddy with a mouth full of ollies!' Liz flung after him.

He turned back with such venom in his eyes that she thought he would hit her. But he thought better of it, and moved away.

Chris, red in the face, had to be held back by Jimmy. 'Let him go. He's not worth getting chucked out for.'

'Jimmy's right,' Liz said. 'His kind usually end up wriggling out of trouble.' Over near the door she could see Munnings surrounded by a group of friends. 'I'm glad I said what I did, though. Come on, big brother.' She tugged at Chris's arm. 'Time you had a dance with me. Don't give him the satisfaction of spoiling our evening.'

Several times, Liz was aware of glances being cast their way, but nothing happened, and a short time later Alec and his friends left. She and Jimmy tried to inject some enthusiasm back into the occasion, but Chris remained quiet, and she could tell that Sally was disappointed, so it was almost a relief when the time came for them to leave, too. Dad had only agreed to Liz going to the dance on condition that they were home by ten-thirty.

Jimmy had borrowed his father's Austin Seven, and no-one spoke much as they made their way to where it was parked, in a quiet side road well away from the attentions of the rough element milling around in the vicinity of the nearby Pacific pub, known affectionately to the locals as 'Arthur's'. They had almost reached the car when four figures moved out of the shadows to confront them.

'Oh, no!' groaned Jimmy. 'Stand well back, girls. This could get nasty.'

For Sally, it was the last straw. 'Some ruddy birthday, this is! I'd have had more fun stayin' at home!'

'I'm sorry, Sally.' Chris sounded harassed, as well as apprehensive. 'I'll make it up to you, I promise. But Jimmy's right. You'd better do as he says.'

Liz was angry. As if Chris had spoiled Sally's wretched birthday on purpose! Couldn't she see how awful it was for him? Chris wasn't a fighter. Sure, Dandy had taught him to defend himself, but he was too much like Dad – he hadn't an aggressive bone in his body. Even Jimmy wouldn't stand a chance against four of them. She ran back in the direction of the pub, shouting for help, but there were enough fights going on there to keep everyone busy. 'Oh, Sal, you'd think there'd be a policeman around, with that lot creating mayhem,' she cried in despair.

'Scuffers are like trams – never one around when yer need 'em. God, that lot'll murder Chris and Jimmy.'

Liz thought of burly Sergeant McNaughten, who came into the bakehouse most nights for a cup of tea and a warm. She would give anything for a sight of his great powerful shoulders now. But wishing was pointless. The boys seemed to be holding their own, but with two against four, it could only be a matter of time. She winced with every thud and grunt, and knew she couldn't stand about doing nothing while her brother and Jimmy got beaten senseless. What she needed was a weapon of some kind.

'Sally, see if you can find something to hit them with.'

But Sally wasn't listening. The fight had excited her, and she was dancing around, yelling encouragement. 'Go on, bash 'im, Chris . . . hey, that's great! Look out, Jimmy – ouch! Gerrup . . . yer not hurt . . . land 'im one back!'

'Oh, do be quiet!' Liz shouted. 'You'll only make matters worse.' And then she heard Sally kick something metallic. She was down on her knees in a moment, scrabbling round until her fingers closed on what felt like a piece of rotten iron railing. She got to her feet, wielding it triumphantly. Now, if she could just make out who was who . . .

It was then that she glimpsed the fifth man – a slim figure near the far wall, just beyond the pool of lamplight, watching intently but making no effort to intervene. And she recognized him at once.

He was so engrossed that he didn't hear her until she was upon him, eyes ablaze – an avenging angel brandishing something long and hard within prodding distance of the most vulnerable part of his anatomy. He swore, and made a half-hearted attempt to reach out.

'Don't,' Liz said softly. 'My hand might slip, and you wouldn't like that, would you? Now, call off your bully boys, Alec Munnings, before I make your eyes water.'

'You little slut!' He mouthed the word through shut teeth, but she could smell his fear, and laughed.

'Sticks and stones!' she scoffed. 'I've got two brothers, remember? And in the rough and tumble of growing up, I learned quite a few handy tricks. So you'd better do as I say – ' She prodded him very lightly and he flinched, moaned what sounded like 'Jeesus', and tried to press himself back into the wall. 'Now,' she said.

'Right, lads . . . that'll do . . .' His voice came out as a mere squeak, and they appeared not to have heard. She prodded him again, and in sheer panic, he screamed, 'Stop, for God's sake, stop! Scuffers!'

The last word acted like a charm. As the sound of running feet died away, Liz heard Chris and Jimmy groaning and picking themselves up, and she eased back a bit with the rail. 'You'd better get after your mates, if you don't want my brother to find you here.'

Alec was breathing fast as he edged away from danger. 'You'll be sorry for this . . .'

'Oh, aye?' She laughed contemptuously. 'Well, it's easier picking on girls than fellas, isn't it? Most times. But if I were you, I wouldn't press my luck. As it happens, this is your lucky night, because I'm not going to tell anyone you were here. Not that I give a damn for you – but, if Dad got to know, gentle as he is, he'd kill you, and I'd not wish him to have blood on his hands – even yours. But I might not be so fussy another time, so don't get any funny ideas.'

They had hoped to sneak in unnoticed, but Dandy was in the living room with Michael, enjoying a tot of whisky to celebrate the completion of the newly painted bedroom.

'Saints preserve us! What have we here?' Dandy was on his feet in an instant, reaching up to turn Chris's face to the light. 'Well, there's no skin broken, thank the Lord, but you'll have a lump like a duck egg under that eye termorrow.' He clicked his teeth. 'Did you not have the sense to keep your guard up, like I taught you? Wait now, while I fetch the first aid box.'

Michael, too, had risen, but more slowly, his face expressionless.

'He couldn't help it, Dad,' Liz rushed in, knowing how he felt about brawling. 'There were four of them set on him and Jimmy, when we were walking to the car. It's a mercy they weren't killed!'

Michael's lips twitched slightly. She was a great one for the odd exaggeration in a good cause. Even so, it was fair to assume the lad'd had no choice. 'You aren't hurt anywhere else, Christopher?'

Liz sighed. Chris only got called by his full name when Dad was moved – by anger or some other emotion. But now, he didn't sound angry.

'No, Dad. I'm fine.'

'Well, if that's the truth of it, at least some of what I taught you must have stuck, for all that you were never that keen,' said Dandy, coming back into the room with a pad of lint soaked in arnica. 'Here – hold that against your cheekbone while I cut the plaster.'

'I suppose you didn't recognize the men?' Michael asked.

Chris shook his head – and winced. 'It was too dark. But I'm pretty sure there was a fifth man as lookout – I definitely heard someone call them off.'

And Liz, who hadn't dared to ask that same question, carefully let go the breath she had been holding.

Chapter Ten

With its huge box carrier between the two back wheels and another carrier to take a basket in front, the delivery bike wasn't the most elegant of vehicles – in fact, it bore more than a passing resemblance to Boadicea's chariot. But it did have a lady's mounting bar, and elegance was the last thing on Liz's mind as she pedalled the half mile or so to the centre of town along Greaty.

A grand plan had been forming at the back of her mind for some time. She hadn't told anyone, even when Chris teased her about the time she spent perfecting and extending their range of fancy cakes.

'Don't be working yourself into the ground, now,' Dad had said, catching her in the bakehouse one evening, shedding tears of frustration over a batch of fondants that hadn't come up to expectations. 'You're doing a grand job, but you know what they say about all work and no play – at your age, a girl should be out enjoying herself now and again.'

'I am enjoying myself,' she had sniffed defiantly. 'I'm just furious because this fondant won't come right. I followed the directions ever so carefully and the Genoese shapes were fine, with absolutely no loose crumbs. I even managed to spread the apricot jam on top beautifully, but as soon as I dipped them – Well, look at them now; you can see the edges of the sponge showing through. They're hopeless.'

'Nonsense,' Michael said. 'They're entirely acceptable.'

'Acceptable isn't good enough, Dad. They have to be as near perfect as I can make them.'

'Ah, well, Lizzie, my love, perfection is something else – achieving that can take a lifetime of striving.' He peered into the *bain marie*, giving the icing an experimental stir. 'At a guess, I'd say you've added a bit too much syrup. But you know fine what the real trouble is.' His expression was stern. 'You're too tired to concentrate.'

She opened her mouth to deny this, but he wouldn't let her speak.

'No, I'm putting my foot down this time, girleen. It's grand to see you so eager to learn, and coming on by leaps and bounds. But with your mother away, I've grown a bit lax, letting you work all the hours there are. You've been on the go, one way or another, since five this morning, and it's now gone eight o'clock. I wonder you can see straight at all. Which brings me to another thing – I've no wish to stifle all this enterprise, but I'll have to be setting a limit to your more extravagant experiments. We can't afford to waste ingredients.'

Liz recognized the finality in his voice, just as she acknowledged the truth behind his words. She was too impetuous, too ready to allow her imagination free rein. At school, this tendency had been curbed. She could hear Sister Imelda now – 'Slow down, Elizabeth – read, absorb and practise.' Perhaps the time had come to apply that kind of discipline to her present efforts. It had been good to learn, as she had done, from watching others, but already her mind was teeming with ideas for more ambitious projects, and in her eagerness to proceed she was in danger of dissipating the talent she knew she possessed.

Dad's old recipe book was her only source of information. It wasn't exciting, but it did contain a lot of good common-sense advice, which she read and re-read until it was thoroughly absorbed. Then she worked on one or two items with a view to perfecting them. Her care paid off. Now, her cakes not only tasted good, but looked professional enough to compete with the best that Munnings could provide, and the time had come to put their quality to the test. Dad and Chris had both been too busy to notice that she was making more cakes than usual that morning, and although it wasn't normally in her nature to be secretive, this time was different. Shirley Anne, lounging in Dad's chair between customers, showed no curiosity when Liz announced casually that she had a special errand to do.

'You'll have to cope on your own for a bit. Dad's gone, and Grandpa Dandy isn't coming until later, but I'll be as quick as I can.'

Shirley Anne uttered a long-suffering sigh. 'It's my poorly time, but I suppose I'll manage.'

'You'll have to, like we all do. Just thank your lucky stars you don't get stomach cramps like our Rita.'

Her sister just sighed again. She deeply resented her periods, the messiness and discomfort – and most of all, the awful home-made towels she had to wear, that had to be washed and re-used. With Mam and Liz and herself, and Rita too when she was at home, there always seemed to be a bucketful of them soaking in salt water in the wash house. 'I don't see why we can't have the kind you throw away,' she'd complained to Liz more than once.

'Because they'd cost the earth for all of us, that's why.'

'Miss Eglantine says you can get special ones that fit inside you and don't show at all. I don't quite understand how they work, but she said that, as a dancer, I'd find them much more comfortable. I might try when I can afford them.'

Of course Liz already knew about them. There had been a lot of silly giggling among some of the sixth formers at school who swore they'd tried them. But the whole procedure sounded distasteful. Miss Eglantine's advice was gospel to Shirley Anne, but Liz was sure Mam would be livid with her for putting such ideas into Shirley Anne's head.

She said: 'I haven't got time to argue. But you want to watch what you do. Anyway, your *poorly time* never seems to trouble you when it comes to doing the things you really want to – like going to posh houses to give concerts.'

'That's different. The concerts are important to my whole future and not just for Mrs Frith. Word's been getting round since the pantomime. Miss Eglantine says she's being asked all the time if I'm available for evening engagements. I could get anything from a pound to three pounds a time, so I'd soon be well off.'

'Sounds wonderful.' Liz meant it, in spite of the irritation that her sister's complacency still aroused. 'As long as Dad didn't object. He doesn't mind you giving concerts for a good cause, but he may not be so keen on you going just anywhere.'

'Miss Eglantine wouldn't let me go just anywhere, and she'd come with me.' Shirley Anne preened. 'So you see,' she said piously, 'with what I earned, I could give Mam quite a bit most weeks, and still put some away in the Post Office for when I can go on the stage properly.'

Whatever else Shirley Anne might be, she was certainly an optimist, Liz thought, stopping outside Reagan's Café and kicking down the bike's parking legs. But good fortune seemed destined to shine on her sister, no matter what. Perhaps a little of it might rub off on me, she thought, smoothing down the three-quarter length navy coat she'd sneaked out of Mam's wardrobe, in the hope that it would make her look older. She straightened her bright red beret, lifted the basket from the front carrier, and approached the door with a carefully assumed air of confidence. It was early and there was only one customer, an elderly gentleman at a crumb-scattered table in a corner, reading his morning paper over a pot of tea. She quelled a flutter of nerves and stepped inside.

At the sound of the bell, a woman who looked like the cleaner popped her head round the door to the kitchens at the back. 'Yer'd best take a seat, while I tell 'imself. He'll be with yer in a jiff.'

She had hardly finished speaking when the thin-faced man appeared, minus his formal coat, and with shirt sleeves flapping. He eyed Liz with a distinct lack of enthusiasm.

'Good morning,' she began brightly. 'I wonder if . . .'

'I can only do tea and toast,' he said, not bothering with his posh voice. 'We don't get many folk this early.'

'Thanks, but that's not why I'm here. Are you Mr Reagan?'

'I am – and before you say any more, I've no staff vacancies.'

'I don't want a job, thanks. I've already got one.' Liz stifled the temptation to add 'and I wouldn't work here if you had.' She wondered how the place had become so popular, when its owner was so churlish. 'The fact is, Mr Reagan . . .' It had seemed so easy when she'd rehearsed the speech in her mind, but already she could see suspicion clouding his eyes.

'Haven't I seen you before?'

It had never occurred to Liz that he would remember her. But she was spared the need to reply by the old gentleman, who appeared beside her, *harrumped* to gain attention, and slapped his money down on the counter. Liz waited impatiently for him to leave, and hurried once more into speech.

'My name is Elizabeth Ryan, of Ryan's Bakery in Great Homer Street. We are expanding our business, and wondered whether you might care to sample a selection of our wide range of cakes and pastries with a view to adding them to your menu.'

'Nothing doing, my girl. Mr Munnings supplies me with all I need.'

It sounded very final, but Liz wasn't about to give up that easily. 'Yes, I know,' she continued persuasively. 'But our reputation is growing fast, and you would find us very competitive, both for quality and price.'

Mr Reagan opened his mouth, and shut it again as the significance of her words sank in. Anxious not to give him time to think, Liz lifted two cake boxes from her basket and set them on the counter.

'Anyway, I've taken the liberty of bringing a small selection for you to try out – with our compliments. And Dad's bread is very good, so I've brought a couple of loaves, too. I won't detain you any longer. I'm sure you're busy, and so am I. But I'll call again and perhaps then we could talk about costs. In fact, if you were to give me a rough idea now of what you're paying Mr Munnings, I could be putting together some figures.'

Out in the street, her knees turning to jelly, Liz couldn't believe she'd really done it. Dad wouldn't like her poaching on Mr Munnings' preserves, but business was business, and after the way Alec Munnings had behaved she had no qualms – well, only a few. And her cheek might yet pay off, for Mr Reagan – driven, she suspected, by the possibility of making more profit – had grudgingly given her the information she wanted. Ninepence for a dozen cream cakes! Ryan's could certainly better that. Buoyed up by this thought, she mounted Boadicea again and pedalled up Church Street and across into Bold Street to make her next call.

It always gave her particular pleasure to take this route, for here she was among the truly exclusive dress establishments such as Bacon's, Gladys Drinkwater, Cripps, Sons and Co. – and De Jong et Cie, who, she had heard, sold the most exquisite silk lingerie. Fancy being rich enough to pay the earth for wisps of silk and lace that most people would never see! But because everything was way beyond her reach, she was able to view each display with a fascination devoid of envy. She rode along, pausing entranced to watch the lady assistant at Bartram Orchard's dressing the window with a single gown, complemented by a frivolously elegant hat and a furled parasol. Liz recognized this to be style at its very best – something each shop in its own individual way possessed.

Which made the shabby Candide Café and Patisserie look all the more incongruous, rubbing shoulders with these doyens of fashion – like a parlour maid taking tea in the drawing room with her mistress. Liz braked suddenly and studied the café in more detail. It had never occurred to her to look as high as Bold Street, which had several smart cafés. And yet, why not? The pretty mullioned windows of the Candide were sorely in need of paint, but it must once have been as prestigious as its neighbours, for even now, it managed to convey a faded air of gentility – as did its owner, when Liz finally plucked up courage to enter.

Mr Morgan was probably no older than Mr Reagan, but everything about him drooped a little: from the yellow hair turning to grey which flopped across his forehead, to his straggly moustache, to the hunched shoulders, he resembled nothing so much as a benevolent, slightly bewildered buddha. But his eyes were nice, a surprisingly bright blue, and there was nothing in the least patronizing in his manner, or in the gentle, melancholy smile with which he greeted her breathless proposal and invited her to be seated.

'It is very kind of you, my dear young lady, to wish to include me in your enterprising project, but I fear you would find me a disappointingly unfruitful participant.'

'Oh, surely not, Mr Morgan. Why, with so many wealthy ladies passing your door, I'd have thought you were ideally situated.'

A faint smile touched his lips. 'You sound exactly like my dear late wife when we started out – a little gold mine, she said. And she was right. For many years we had a thriving business – until, in fact, almost eighteen months ago, when she passed away.'

'Oh, I'm sorry. I didn't know . . .'

'Why should you, my dear child?'

Her fingers encountered a neat darn in the spotless white tablecloth. She smoothed it thoughtfully. 'Was her name Candide?'

'It was. We first met in 1914 when my regiment passed through Paris. I fell quite immoderately in love the moment I saw her.' His blue eyes grew dark with memories. 'Her father kept a small patisserie on the outskirts of the city. After the war I returned, to find that her father had succumbed to influenza and Candide was alone. But, in spite of her grief, she was young and bursting with optimism and ambition, as you are now, my dear young lady. Also, she had an unerring feel for business – a true Parisienne, in fact. And so beautiful!' He chuckled. 'I still don't know how I found the courage to propose, for I was convinced she would laugh at my presumption. But she did not.'

Mr Morgan seemed to have forgotten Liz was there, and she, though impatient to get on, hadn't the heart to prompt him. In any case, his story intrigued her, and she was curious to know more. She looked around. It was a lovely room, quite large, with a desk near the door at the end of a long glass counter, lots of little intimate corners, pillars, and a small white grand piano on a dais in one of the corners.

At last he looked up, his eyes overbright. 'This café was her idea, you know. I was to manage it and she would practise the skills learned from her father. We would advertise it as a little corner of Paris in the most exclusive part of Liverpool. It couldn't fail, she said. "All those rich and fashionable ladies, they will not be able to resist such a lure!" And she was right. They came from miles around to sample her *brioches*, her feather-light *palmiers* and the *mille feuilles* that were her speciality. And I would play the piano – all their favourite tunes. Ah, me! Those were good days.'

His voice tailed away, and Liz felt a curious frisson of affinity, as if she had been meant to come here. When Mr Morgan spoke of Candide's relationship with her father, he might almost have been describing the closeness between herself and Dad. This is it, she thought. This is where my dream will begin. She cleared her throat.

'Do you have any children?'

Mr Morgan shook his head. 'We had each other, and the business. Nothing else seemed to matter. Perhaps it was for the best, as things have turned out. I can no longer compete with so many smarter establishments, though I have managed to retain a few faithful clients – splendid ladies who shop at Sloans, and seem to enjoy popping in here afterwards for a chat over their Darjeeling tea. But nowadays they are content with buttered toast, or maybe a toasted teacake.'

'Oh, we do teacakes, as well. I'll bring some tomorrow, if you like, so you can try them out as well as the cakes.' Liz looked into his sad eyes and thought that, rather like Dad when Mam wasn't around, the poor man was fast sinking into a slough of despond.

'Well . . .'

'It won't cost you anything to try,' she said persuasively.

Mr Morgan seemed not to have heard her. He was looking around, as though seeing the shabbiness for the first time. 'I ought to have sold this place long ago, of course. There have been offers, some of them excellent – one would-be purchaser is so persistent that I am very tempted to accept.' He sighed. 'If only I could rid myself of the foolish notion that the spirit of my Candide is still lingering here, reproaching me.'

'Perhaps it isn't so foolish. I know that in her place I would hate you to give up,' Liz said firmly, trying to quell the excitement welling up inside her as ideas, new and far more ambitious than she had ever anticipated, began to stir. She leaned forward. 'Listen, you're no older than my dad, and if you ask me, it would be criminal to give up when, with a bit of imagination, a lick or two of paint, and the right supplier, this place could be every bit as successful as it ever was.'

The Ryan children were no strangers to Mrs Meadows, but over the past week or two she'd had a constant succession of them trooping in and out of the house. And although she occasionally grumbled to Peters and the maid, Gracie, about the state of her floors, there was no doubt that the youngsters brought the old place alive, in a way Mrs Hetherington's fine friends never could.

'I've always said this was meant to be a family house.' She paused in her vigorous polishing of the silver to jerk her head in the direction of the upper hall. 'Just as she was made to have children, never mind swanning off on fancy cruises and the like to fill her time. It's funny, the way things turn out – there's her sister with more than she can rightly cope with, while she . . .' Mrs Meadows sighed. 'If only Mr H. had met her first, instead of that poor frail soul . . .'

'It's the way of the world, Mrs Meadows.' Peters was philosophical. 'Always was, and always will be, I shouldn't wonder.'

They might have been surprised to know how closely their mistress's view accorded with their own. The mutual affection that had always existed between Flora and the Ryan family seemed to have developed into something rather special during Kathleen's brief stay. She and Kathleen had been able to talk more freely than they had done for years. Her nieces and nephews, too, visiting in higgledy-piggledy fashion, had brought a gust of fresh air blowing through the house, and over the weeks had come to regard her as a kind of confidante, their eager – 'You won't tell Mam and Dad, will you Aunt Flora, but . . . ' prefacing many a disclosure of their most intimate hopes and fears. In such a way had she learned how much Chris adored his Sally – who, if Flora was any judge, was flighty enough to break his untried heart – and how that pert little minx Shirley Anne had her sights fixed on fame and fortune, so different from Rita, who took life altogether too seriously and was apprehensive about her finals. Only Joey was still young enough to take life as it came. How different they all were. But the prize of the bunch for her money was still Liz; Liz of the deceptive dreaming eyes. Liz, who was unquestionably her favourite, and would yet confound them all.

Flora had even been honoured by a couple of visits from her young brother and his wife, supposedly to see Kathleen. Nick had acquired a soft-topped Morris second-hand, egged on no doubt by Laura at the instigation of her mother. She still remembered the wedding, and how Mrs Burchall had smarmed all over her – the kind of woman, Flora thought, who would take great delight in boasting to her friends about 'my daughter's sister-in-law, you know, who lives in Birkdale.'

Still, Laura was inoffensive enough, even if she was making a bit of a meal of her pregnancy – going on quite tiresomely about Nick painting the nursery primrose yellow when he wasn't waiting on her hand and foot. Nursery, indeed – they only had the two tiny bedrooms. Flora could have hit her brother when he'd grinned sheepishly at Kathleen and said, 'Got to keep the little lady happy, our Kath. She isn't an old hand like you.'

But today Kathleen was going home. Michael was coming by train so that he could travel back in the Daimler with them, and Flora suddenly realized how much she was going to miss her sister – all of them, in fact.

And tomorrow? Tomorrow she would take up the threads of her life once more; go shopping, pack her bags, and set out as she always did at this time of year in search of the sun. I'm a lucky woman, she told herself. I'm forty-two, free as air, enjoy excellent health, and have as many friends as a woman of my age needs. She caught sight of herself in the hall mirror, and paused. Perhaps it was a mere trick of the light that, just for an instant, the face staring back at her looked uncertain, vulnerable – and was developing wrinkles. You're a daft beggar, Flora Hetherington, she admonished herself, and went to change her frock and put on her warpaint.

When Michael arrived, she was wearing a cream woollen suit and tan court shoes in soft calfskin, and her golden hair clung as neatly as ever about her head.

'You look nice,' he said, as if her suit had been bought at Lewis's, instead of from Elsa Schiaparelli during her last visit to Paris.

Flora regarded him with affection and, not for the first time, felt a twinge of something less definable. They had grown somewhat closer over the past week or two. Michael, in his quiet way, possessed qualities that were strong and enduring – and there had been times recently when she had fallen into the dangerous trap of wondering what it might be like to be loved as Kathleen was loved.

She touched her cheek to his, then gently pushed him towards the parlour. 'Go on in while I tell Peters to bring the car round. Kathleen's case has been packed for hours, and she's been like a cat on hot bricks, waiting. I don't know how much longer I'd have been able to keep her pinned down.'

But Michael didn't go at once. Instead, he took her by the shoulders. She could not quite match him for height, but they were near enough eye to eye, and his were as vividly blue as she had ever seen them. 'And never think I don't know fine how much of her improvement is down to you, Flora, girl,' he said, deep-voiced with emotion.

'Rubbish. A few trips out in the car – the odd visit to town to have tea in Thoms, and a lot of chat which we both enjoyed.' Her tone was self-mocking. 'A bit of a rest and a change was all she needed. I can hardly take much credit for that.'

'Ah, Flora, Flora.' Michael's fingers tightened their grip. 'Why do you always have to cloak your good deeds in flippancy? You are a fine generous woman, and this is one debt I can never repay.' He drew her close for a moment, then kissed her gently and let her go.

Flora stood quite still, with tears choking her throat, flooded with unfamiliar emotions. Any minute now she'd be making a fool of herself. She pulled herself together.

'Get along with you,' she said briskly. 'Our Kathleen'll be climbing the wall.'

Chapter Eleven

Michael still had to pinch himself occasionally to convince himself that Kathleen was back where she belonged. Not that the children hadn't rallied round splendidly, especially Lizzie. They would need to talk about Lizzie, he thought, secure in the knowledge that, with Kathleen's return, their home was whole again.

It would have distressed him immensely to know that his wife's feelings were much less clear-cut. Her arrival had been greeted with so much spontaneous joy that it had been easy for her to profess delight over the freshly decorated bedroom, and she had been genuinely touched by Chris's gift of a pram and a cot, bought cheaply from the sister of a friend and lovingly restored in his spare time. Even the business was going from strength the strength. How could she possibly tell anyone, especially Michael, of the strange depression that hung over her?

As ever, it was Dandy who spotted that all was not well. 'D'you want to talk about it?' he asked as they sat in her little parlour one afternoon.

She looked up quickly. 'Is it so obvious, Dad?'

'Only to me, girl. Your Michael is that over the moon at having you back that nothing else matters very much to him at present.'

'Oh, Dad!' Her throat was choked with tears. 'I don't know what's wrong with me. I've had a good long rest, the baby's kicking like Stanley Matthews, and I'm back where I longed to be every minute of the time I was away, with Michael and all the family around me, and so many things done for my comfort and pleasure. They've even done up this old sofa so I can rest. I should be the happiest of women!'

'But instead, you feel like a stranger in your own home,' Dandy said, as usual putting his finger on the nub of the problem. 'All decisions made for you.'

'That's it, exactly! Oh, everyone means well, but our Liz in particular is a young whirlwind – she's got everything so well organized, I'm beginning to feel like a spare part, fit only to knit baby clothes.' And a clumsy, blown-up spare part, her thoughts ran on, as she fought down the panic that threatened more and more often as the days passed. Never before had she been so big or so uncomfortable at seven months, but not to anyone could she voice her hidden fear that she might be carrying twins. That really would be the last straw. She had almost blurted it out when Flora, in jovial mood, had suggested she must be incubating a football team, and had brought a dressmaker in to run up a couple of loose dresses in soft, becoming colours. But one word to Flora, and she'd have had her tame doctor round like a shot. So instead she had reached for her rosary beads, never far from her fingers these days, and begun yet another novena to Our Lady of Perpetual Succour, praying as she had never prayed before that she was wrong, and everything would be fine once she was home.

But it hadn't been that simple. 'I sometimes wonder if it wouldn't have been easier all round if I'd stayed away.'

'I never thought I'd hear that kind of talk from you, our Kathy,' Dandy said sternly. 'The Powers have never been quitters, and you'll not be the one to break the mould.' He stood up, his voice softening. 'Ah, just give it time, girl.'

But afterwards he sought out young Liz. 'Have you a minute, chuck? Because I think you and me are going to have to put our heads together.'

About an hour later, Liz took her mother a cup of tea, and hovered indecisively until Kathleen said with a trace of exasperation, 'For pity's sake, Liz – whatever it is you want to say, say it and have done.'

Liz blushed, and came with alacrity to sit on the end of the sofa, nervous fingers smoothing the lovely mohair rug that had been a gift from Aunt Flora. 'I've been wondering, Mam – d'you feel well enough to help do the stocktaking? I haven't a clue how to go about it. I mean, I know you're not supposed to do anything energetic, but you could take little rests in between.'

Kathleen regarded her daughter in silence for a long moment. 'Have you been talking to your grandad?'

Liz nibbled her lip furiously. 'Grandpa Dandy did say you were feeling a bit low, but I really mean it about the stocktaking. I know it has to be done at our year end, which is now, but . . .'

This brought a smile to Kathleen's lips at last – a real smile. 'Oh, come here, you daft thing, and give us a kiss.'

Dr Graham came to see how Kathleen was. 'Splendid. You look better than I've seen you for ages. But that doesn't mean you can do as you please.'

He quickly dispelled her fear about twins. 'No, no, lassie. It's just that you're carrying a lot of water, and the baby's lying a bit awkwardly, which is why you feel so uncomfortable. But you aren't due until May, so it's got plenty of time to right itself. Just go easy. Plenty of rest – these last weeks are going to be crucial. I'll be in to see you regularly from now on, and at the least sign of bleeding, or if your ankles swell unduly, anything at all – I'll want to know at once.'

'Old fusspot,' she grumbled, and received short shrift from Michael.

'He's a good man, Kathleen, and well you know it.'

Kathleen didn't tell him about the stocktaking, but she felt a lot better, being where she belonged, at the centre of things.

'Hey, Mam, it's good to have you back,' Joey exclaimed, coming in from school to find her on the parlour sofa, propped up by cushions in fresh bright covers – made up by herself and Liz some time back from a bag of Lewis's remnants, and stuffed with goose feathers from Cousin Tom's farm – and surrounded by account books. 'Doesn't she look smashin', Eddie?'

Eddie, embarrassed by the need to comment, shuffled his feet and muttered, 'Aye, yer look great, missus. Can we got out and play, now?'

'Half an hour,' Kathleen said, asserting her authority right away. 'Joey has homework to do, remember. He's not got a lot of time left before he sits his scholarship. And don't get dirty,' she called after their fast-retreating backs.

'Ah, Joey, yer don't really want ter go to a posh school, do yer?' Eddie pleaded when they were out of earshot. 'Yool 'ave ter wear a cap an' a nancy boy uniform!'

'So what?'

'Our mates'll catcall after you, that's what.'

'An' I'll tell 'em what they can do with their stupid catcalls, cos gettin' me scholarship's the only way I'm ever goin' to learn all the things I really want to know about – things they don't learn you at St Anthony's.'

'What sorta things?'

Joey wriggled uncomfortably. 'Oh, I dunno – algebra and physics and geometry, stuff like that. Our Liz has a smashin' goemetry set she's goin' to give me if I pass me exams.'

'Huh! That's bribery, tharris.' Eddie scuffed his feet along the pavement. 'Yer won't catch me stayin' at school a minute longer'n I have to. I've got big plans, an' I bet I end up richer'n you.' His boast met with silence. After a moment he said disconsolately: 'You'll still play with us, though, won't you?

''Course I will.'

'That's all right, then.' He tugged at Joey's arm. 'Well, cum on, or we won't have time to do nuttin'.'

Kathleen discovered Sister Imelda's letter quite by chance. She had been looking for a missing account from the flour mill, and knowing Michael's habit of stuffing things in his pockets and forgetting them, had gone to the wardrobe in search of it.

She stood with the report and the letter in her hands, tears clogging the back of her throat. Her first instinct had been to confront her daughter, to rail at her for the chance she was deliberately giving up. Kathleen had not the least doubt that the decision had been Liz's, and that she had talked Michael round, for left to himself, Michael would never have kept the letter from her.

But as the tears forced themselves through tight-shut eyelids, Kathleen knew that she must not reject this unspoken act of love, could not throw back at Liz the generosity that had prompted it. Someday, please God, she would make it up to her, but for now, the child seemed happy and fulfilled – and anyway, she was in no position to offer any alternative.

So Kathleen took her place once more at the hub of things, doing what little she could to help, offering advice when it was asked for, and biting her tongue when it was not – and if her back sometimes ached abominably, she kept the fact to herself, resolved that no-one should have cause to say she was doing too much. Whether the stay at Flora's had conditioned her to inactivity, or whether it was simply a manifestation of her advancing pregnancy, she soon discovered that patience came easier than she had expected.

Michael, reluctant to let her out of his sight for long, found many an excuse to come in for a brief sit down and a warm by the fire, although with the new outlets discovered by Liz, he was never quiet for long.

'It's been a revelation to me,' he said, in one of the few moments they had to themselves, 'the way young Lizzie's set about things. She seems to have grown up overnight. There's no resting on her laurels for that one – she's got another firm commitment from a small place up Everton way this very day. That makes four in all. Reagan's was never on, of course, and I can't help wishing she'd left well alone there, for all that it was his café first gave her the idea. Fred Munnings is none too pleased. Seemingly he's been obliged to trim his profit in order to keep Reagan's custom.' Michael shook his head. 'Liz meant it all for the best, I know, but it wouldn't do to get a reputation for trying to undercut our fellow bakers.'

Kathleen swallowed her impatience. A sense of fair play was all very well, but she had a sneaking admiration for the initiative her daughter had shown, and if some of it were to rub off on Michael, so much the better.

'Rubbish,' she said. 'Folk in the trade aren't blind. Everyone knows that Reagan's café is worth a mint to Fred Munnings in advertising alone, and since he was obviously charging well over wholesale rates, they'll think as I do – that it serves him right. There's nothing wrong with healthy competition. Liz was a bit over-impetuous, that's all. Now I'm back, I'll be able to keep a steadying hand on the rein.'

Michael looked up from scraping out his pipe, his eyes warm in the firelight. 'And it's glad I am to have you back, *acushla*.'

'No more glad than I am to be here,' she said quietly.

He cleared his throat, leaning forward to tap the bowl of his pipe against the fire basket until he had command of his emotions. 'I was hoping you could maybe caution Liz over her plans for the Candide. That place seems to have taken a powerful hold of her, what with talking Morgan into restoring it to its former glory, an' all.'

'But you've had a word with the man. He's straight – he wouldn't try to con our Liz?'

'Oh, he's straight, right enough. As for conning, it seems to me the boot's on the other foot. The fellow is so taken with our girleen and her notions, she could tell him black's white, an' he'd believe her. And that's what worries me, because for all that she's made great strides in a short time, that's all Liz is – a bit girl, not yet seventeen.'

It crossed Kathleen's mind that he might be jealous of the way Mr Morgan and Liz had taken to each other. 'I agree she's young, but is age so important? I wasn't that much older when we started here, and I was just as bursting with ideas.'

'True again. But you know fine what Liz can be like when she gets an idea into her head. I suppose I don't want her to be disappointed. Every spare minute she's experimenting, asking questions, and now she's mastered most of the ordinary run of confectionery, she's wanting to know, if you please, how to make fancy foreign confections like *palmiers* and *mille feuilles*.'

'Goodness!' Kathleen chuckled. 'And were you able to tell her?'

'Not to her entire satisfaction. Luxuries of that kind don't figure much on our customers' shopping lists. But Mr Morgan was able to oblige.' Again, Kathleen noted that faintly disapproving note in Michael's voice. It was not like him to harbour jealousy. 'Seemingly Candide Morgan was a dab hand at such delicacies, and had them all written down in French in a little book.' At this point, pride replaced disapproval. 'The language was no trouble at all to our Lizzie, of course.'

'Of course not,' Kathleen echoed gravely. 'You know, I remember the café in its heyday. I used to walk down Bold Street with the pram, just so I could peer in to watch the nobs sipping their tea. I often thought it a pity Morgan let the place go after his wife died.'

'Understandable, though. I know if it were me . . .' Michael stopped, a sudden blankness in his eyes as the impossible for an instant reared its head.

Kathleen recognized his fear, and beneath the rug, her hand closed convulsively on the crucifix of her rosary, its hard edges biting deep into her flesh. Ah, Jesus, Mary and Joseph, she prayed inwardly. It's not for myself, but don't let that happen, *please*! Anything but that!

Aloud she said calmly, 'Well, it's not you – and it isn't going to be. Look, I know you think our Liz's biting off more than she can chew, and maybe she is, but there's no harm in aiming high. Next thing, she'll be wanting us to instal a telephone . . .'

'It has already been mentioned,' he said drily, and she laughed.

'Poor Michael, no peace for the wicked! It's clearer by the minute that whatever ambitions you or I may have entertained for her, Liz has her own plans well and truly in hand. She's becoming almost as single-minded as Shirley Anne, for all they're not the least bit alike in other ways . . .'

'And who is it they get it from, do you suppose?' Michael's tone was dry, though she was relieved to see that the warmth was back in his eyes.

'You can be pretty stubborn yourself, given cause,' she retorted. 'If you ask me, it's a powerful combination, the mix of Ryan and Power blood that our children have inherited – powerful enough to withstand any knocks life may dish out.'

'You sound just like your father.'

'Do I? Well, I'll take that as a compliment. Anyhow, if the last few months' accounts are anything to go by, young Liz might well have the right idea. And think on – if she succeeds, so does Ryan's. In which case, I was wondering if the time hasn't come to take our Chris into the business?'

He chuckled. 'You'd always a knack of knowing me own thoughts. It's hard going for the lad, trying to do a job and a half most of the time, and on top of everything else, we're getting more and more catering work coming in. Dandy does all he can to help, but this week alone we've a couple of big orders in for St Patrick's night ceilidhs, and there are several wedding breakfasts booked during the weeks after Easter.'

'Goodness!'

'Liz came to an arrangement with Harry Carney over at The Grapes. He has this big room upstairs doing nothing, and he decided to turn it into a function room, with a separate entrance. Liz heard of it and told him we'd do the catering. It's proving to be a great success.'

'Then we're definitely going to need a telephone, for if I know Liz, it'll not stop at Harry Carney's. You'd better make enquiries. Seems I've come home to a regular hive of industry,' Kathleen said, resolved not to feel jealous that they'd done it all without her.

*

Jimmy had plans for going to Southport on Easter Monday. 'That new ride opens at the Pleasureland on Good Friday, but you and Chris'll be up to your eyes in hot-cross buns, then – and we'll be mad busy at our place, too, with everyone wanting extra meat for the weekend.'

'We couldn't go on Good Friday,' Liz said reprovingly. 'There's church in the afternoon. Anyway, I'd rather go Monday. It's a more celebrating sort of day.'

Jimmy's eyes crinkled up. 'You're a funny girl, d'you know that?' And he put his arms round her waist and kissed her.

She no longer pushed him away and told him not to be daft – at least not often, only when he started getting too fresh. Among their friends they were regarded as a pair, though Dad insisted she was much too young to be courting. He didn't mind them going for walks together like now, in daylight, but of an evening he still insisted that they should be part of a group, preferably with Chris there to keep an eye on them.

In some ways she was relieved. Not that she didn't enjoy Jimmy's company. In fact, she was quite fond of him, really – he was handsome and good fun to be with, even if he did know it – but there were times when his behaviour was unsettling.

'Sometimes, when he's had a bit to drink, he tries to push his tongue into my mouth,' she whispered to Clare in the anonymous darkness of the Great Homer cinema. 'It's ever such a queer feeling. Has anyone ever tried it on you?'

'Certainly not!' Clare, whose current project in Biology was hygiene, found the mere thought distasteful. 'I hope you don't let him.'

'Course not. I always shut my teeth tight. Last time, I got fed up and bit him. You should've heard him!'

They collapsed into giggles, and a voice from behind told them to shurrup or get out.

'D'you remember Maggie Harris in Form Four?' Clare whispered. 'She thought that was how you got babies . . .'

'Or poor old Sister Benedict who was always telling us we must never permit a man to touch us in certain places . . .' Again the giggles threatened. 'She never could bring herself to tell us where.'

'I won't tell yous two again!' the irate voice threatened.

Up on the screen they were showing the trailer for next week, and Don Ameche had Alice Faye in a passionate embrace. Liz unwrapped a toffee, and watched them speculatively. 'D'you think *they* do that sort of thing?'

'Wouldn't be surprised, if half the things you read about film stars are true.'

Liz found her thoughts wandering, just for a moment, to Leigh Farrell. His New Year kiss had hardly been a kiss at all, yet she had never forgotten the clean fresh smell of him, and the way his mouth felt on hers.

And then the big picture came up on the screen, and she slid down in her seat and gave herself up to Nelson Eddy and Jeanette MacDonald.

Chapter Twelve

The train was packed on Easter Monday, even though they'd set off early, loaded down with sandwiches and thermos flasks. When they arrived in Southport, trains from other towns were already disgorging hordes of passengers, who surged out of the station into the sunshine, across Chapel Street, causing havoc amongst the traffic as they made for the beach. Buckets and spades were much in evidence, their stalwart young owners undeterred by the fact that it was only March.

'Come on,' Liz said, tugging at Jimmy's arm. 'We'll cut through the arcade and up Scarisbrick Avenue – that way we won't get our legs prodded black and blue by the bucket and spade brigade.'

Chris put an arm round Sally, hung on to his new trilby, and together they too dodged between the hooting cars. 'Whew! that's better,' he said, when they reached the comparative shelter of Cambridge Arcade. 'That wind's like a knife. I suppose you realize we'll probably freeze to death up there on the fairground?'

'Listen to him,' Sally scoffed. 'Proper misery-guts, he's gonna be. It's as well we didn't come Good Friday – you'd have had snow an' all, then.'

The sun filtering through the glass roof made a halo of her thick curls as she laughed up at Chris. He was wearing his one and only suit and looked very dashing, a bit like Douglas Fairbanks. Though he always took Sally's teasing in good part, Liz sometimes wished he'd stand up to her a bit more. But he was like Dad, easy-going, and as long as Sally was happy, so was he.

When they reached Lord Street, it, too, was blocked with cars. There were policemen on all the crossings, ushering people across, and in Scarisbrick Avenue, the little shops were doing a roaring trade in buckets and spades, windmills and little coloured flags. Children were nibbling away at sticks of rock to see if Southport was written all the way through, as they giggled at the postcards with fat ladies on, running away amid shrieks of laughter when the shopkeepers shouted at them to keep their sticky fingers to themselves. The traffic was even worse on the promenade, and horns were blaring.

'I've never seen so many cars in one place!' Jimmy exclaimed. 'They seem to be coming all ways.'

The Pleasureland was very busy, though not as packed as they had feared, perhaps because people with young children had made straight for the beach. All the old stalls were operating, and some new ones as well, the paint barely dry on gleaming woodwork. They went first to admire the new giant Big Dipper, its great rails shimmering against the blue sky. As they watched, a carriage packed with excited people came hurtling along the high straight section and swooped down a giant silver curve, the screech of metal almost drowned out by shrieks of terrified delight.

Liz shuddered. 'Ugh! You're not going to get me on that!'

'Cowardy custard!' Jimmy chanted the old childish insult at her, but his eyes were laughing: 'We'll go on the Helter-Skelter instead, and come back later when the queue's gone down.'

The Helter-Skelter was almost as bad, but Chris and Jimmy were quite ruthless, pushing the girls up the steps with taunts of 'Coward', and dispatching them, squealing and clutching their coats about their legs with mock-modesty, to follow round and down until they all landed in an undignified heap at the bottom. As they picked themselves up, a sign for Winchester Repeating Rifles caught Jimmy's eye.

'That's for me,' he said, and the two boys were soon engrossed in a shoot-out to the death, with Sally egging them on to win her a giant teddy bear. Jimmy was only too eager to display his skill with a rifle, and in his made-to-measure shrimp tweed sports jacket, matching cap set at a jaunty angle, Liz thought he looked every inch the sporting gent.

But eventually she got bored, and drifted away to the other stalls. She made sixpence on the roll-a-penny, promptly lost it at the coconut shy, and then just wandered, enjoying the crowds and the sunshine, and wondering how Mam and Dad were enjoying their bit of peace and quiet. Rita had gone out with a friend, Shirley Anne was helping Mrs Frith with an Easter Fayre, and Joey had gone to New Brighton with the Killigan family.

Liz was wearing her best green coat, but had tucked her beret in her pocket to let her hair blow loose. Above, the beach plane circled the Pleasureland and then headed off towards the far end of the Marine Lake, the sound of its engine growing fainter. It reminded her of Leigh Farrell, and she wondered if he had kept his promise to Francis. The Whitneys were spending Easter in the Cotswolds with Mrs Whitney's mother. Clare had been studying hard all term, and on the few occasions they had met, there'd been so much to talk about that the subject had never come up.

Lost in thought, Liz realized she had wandered some way from the others. By now they'd probably be going mad, looking for her. She turned to retrace her steps – and found her way barred by a tall, well-dressed figure.

Alec Munnings. He had a couple of friends with him, and Liz felt a small frisson of fear. But Alec wouldn't be daft enough to make a scene in such a public place, would he?

'D'you mind?' she said pointedly, when he made no attempt to stand aside. For answer he took her arm, while his two companions closed in on her other side. Her heart began to thud uncomfortably, but she wasn't going to let him see she was scared. 'If you don't let me go at once, I'll scream blue murder,' she threatened.

'Go ahead,' Alec said in his cultured voice, so different from his father's. 'Everyone will think we're just larking about.'

'Or that little girls who go wanderin' off on their own are askin' for trouble,' said one of the others.

'Shut up, Mal. And you – ' Alec squeezed her arm until it hurt, and smiled. 'There's a lot of things I'd like to do to you, my girl. I owe you, remember? But I'll pick a better place than this to pay my debts, so do as you're told and you won't get hurt – this time.'

Liz believed him. She ought to have been reassured, but something in the way he said it made the skin down her spine shiver. They were moving away from the main area when suddenly he pulled her towards a gap between two shuttered stalls and swung her round, standing very close with his hands pressing her shoulders against the rough panels to stop her from struggling. If they had been alone, she would have attempted to knee him – something Chris had taught her to do in just such a situation – but with Alec's two companions blocking her only means of escape, it would be pointless.

'Now, listen to me, Lizzie Ryan . . .'

'Don't call me that!'

'I'll call you what I damn well like. In case you haven't already guessed what this is all about, I'll spell it out for you. It's about queering other people's pitches.' As realization flared in her eyes, he nodded. 'Good, I see the penny's dropped. My Dad's not best pleased with you, and when he's ratty, the whole family suffers, including me.'

Liz looked up into the pale, handsome face, into eyes rendered almost colourless by the bright sun. 'I didn't do anything underhand. I simply gave Mr Reagan the chance to choose – and as it happens, he chose to stay with your father, so I don't see what you're on about.'

'This isn't about Reagan, although having to re-negotiate terms with the man has meant a loss of face as well as profits. It's about your other busybody activities. There'll soon be bloody Ryan's cakes everywhere you look.' The pressure of his hands increased. 'But it's your deal with Morgan that's really got up Dad's nose. He's been wanting a place in Bold Street for years, and ever since Candide Morgan died he's been pressuring Morgan to sell him that café. And then, just as he was beginning to weaken, what happens? You walk in there, an interfering little school brat with damn-all experience, and fill the old man with dreams of reviving the place.'

'Mr Morgan didn't want to sell his café – not deep down,' she said through teeth clenched to control the shake in her voice. 'I just gave him a bit of encouragement, that's all. He's free to do as he pleases.'

'And what does please him, eh? What kind of encouragement did it take? Offer him more than a few cakes, did you? Got a special liking for little girls, has he, lonely old sod?'

The sneer in his voice and the crude laughter of his friends brought the blood rushing to Liz's face, and with it an anger that spilled over into words, making her forget her fear.

'That's a terrible thing to say! Mr Morgan is a nice, gentle man. He would never dream of. . . ! Oh, never mind. Just go away, you . . . and take your dirty mind and your sniggering hangers-on with you!' Tears of fury blocked her throat.

'I'll go when I've finished.' Alec's hand was under her chin, now, pushing her head hard against the woodwork, his voice an angry rasp. 'Our name stands unrivalled for quality in Liverpool, and beyond. And that's the way it's going to stay. Because the business will be mine one day, so what happens now matters very much to me, which is why I'm telling you – your deal with Morgan is off. You'll have to tell him you can't supply him, after all.'

The heel of his hand, pressing hard against her throat, was beginning to restrict her breathing. Liz could feel the sweat running down her back. Common sense told her to give way, but the old stubborn streak decreed otherwise, and she heard herself croaking defiantly, 'Oh, give over. You've been watching too many gangster pictures.'

She regretted the words the moment they were out. She watched, mesmerized, as his face began to waver in a red mist. And then another voice came to her, a voice she was sure must be a cruel illusion born of desperation, for in spite of being distorted by anger it was blessedly familiar. 'What the hell's going on here? Let her go, damn you!'

And the pressure instantly eased.

Liz blinked to clear the mist, her body sagging, with the release of fear as much as anything else. She was dimly aware of raised voices, but was convinced that they were all part of her distorted imagination, for it couldn't be Leigh Farrell – he was thousands of miles away. And then, very close and very real, she heard him demand: 'Elizabeth, are you all right?' Firm hands were supporting her, shaking her.

'Yes, thank you.' Her eyes cleared suddenly. 'I . . . is it really you?' What a stupid thing to say. But he seemed not to notice. Of Alec and his friends, there was no sign.

'That guy didn't hurt you?' he persisted.

Liz took a deep breath and pulled herself together. 'No, honestly, I'm fine.'

Only then did he let her go – almost thrusting her away. 'Well, you've no business to be fine! I thought – hell, I don't know what I thought! What in the name of all that's holy were you doing in a place like this on your own?'

Liz was taken aback by his anger – by the bright shards of green in his eyes, the dark mass of freckles standing out aggressively across his forehead; even his hair, ruffled into disorder by the wind, glowed red as fire. But because she was beginning to tremble with delayed reaction, his unprovoked and quite unjustified rebuke infuriated her, and she found herself responding in kind.

'You don't have to shout at me, Mr Farrell. I'm very grateful you came along when you did, but I'm not a child, nor, as it happens, am I alone. My brother and our friends are around here somewhere – we j-just got separated, that's all.' The chattering of her teeth rather lessened the impact of her retaliation, and she saw that he wasn't wholly convinced.

'Really? And the guy who was choking hell out of you?'

'An acquaintance. We had a slight difference of opinion, but I was never in any real danger.'

'A slight . . .' Leigh broke off and ran a hand through his already dishevelled hair. 'You English and your understatements!' But the edge had gone out of his voice and he laughed suddenly. 'Well, you're cool, I'll say that for you.'

Liz was aware that her reaction must make her appear ungrateful, if not downright rude. She bit her lip, flushing with sudden embarrassment. 'I'm sorry, Mr Farrell. I didn't mean – I really was very glad you arrived when you did.' It wasn't much of an apology, but she didn't know what else to say.

He looked different from the other men around, in his soft brown leather jacket and pale corded trousers, a colourful scarf casually knotted and tucked into the open neck of his shirt in place of a tie. With reluctance, she said, 'I suppose I'd better look for Chris and the others.'

'Sure. And I'd better go find my party. I'll walk with you, if I may. And the name's Leigh.'

His easy familiarity disarmed Liz, and a curious melting feeling coursed through her. 'You know mine,' she said.

'Sure do. Elizabeth. Though I noticed everyone at the Whitneys' called you Liz. Would you rather I did the same?'

'Oh, no. I've always wanted to be called by my full name, but no-one ever did, except the nuns.' She giggled at his wry grimace. 'Anyway, I like the way you say it,' she added shyly.

'Right. You've got it – a pact between the two of us. You're in good company as it happens. Elizabeth was my grandmother's name.'

Maybe he was just being kind, but she didn't care. It was like being granted a special privilege. Yet she felt bound to say, 'You don't have to – to escort me, you know. I'll be quite safe now.'

His lazy grin was immensely reassuring. 'Sure you will, but two's more fun.'

Leigh was surprised to find that he meant it. Frank Hazlett must by now be convinced he'd taken leave of his senses, he thought wryly, for he had dashed off with no more than an incoherent apology. But if he were to be totally honest with himself, he was already regretting his offer to accompany the Hazlett family on this day out. Not that he didn't like kids. But Monica – well, nineteen was a dangerous age, old enough to mistake infatuation for something more, and too old to be teased out of it.

Somehow, this child beside him seemed a whole lot more mature. Mrs Whitney had filled him in on her background at New Year, and he remembered thinking then what a gutsy kid she was, taking on all that family responsibility – which maybe accounted for his fury when he found that young thug threatening her.

'You seem to spend an awful lot of time in England,' Liz said.

'I suppose it must look that way.' He put a hand under her arm as they pushed a path through the crowds. 'Actually, this time I flew over. We landed at Speke on Saturday – me, my navigator and two crewmen.'

'All the way from America?'

He chuckled, hearing the note of awe in her voice. 'Every bone-aching, exhilarating mile.'

'But isn't it dangerous? You must be terribly brave.'

The chuckle became a full-throated laugh. 'If you'd said crazy, I might agree with you.'

'That, too,' she agreed sternly, as if reproving him for misplaced levity. 'I've read about aviators getting lost, drowned, even, crossing the Atlantic.'

'You don't want to believe all you read, honey. Most things worth doing have an element of risk, but I've no hankering to be a dead hero, believe me. Aviation is making great strides, and with better planes and the improved blind-flying equipment, the good old water jump is getting safer by the minute. Even the once dreaded northern route is becoming less hazardous, except in winter. There's a lot of haggling going on between the big boys over who gets to do what, and where and when, but they'll have to reach agreement soon on the carrying of goods and passengers. We've been operating a Pacific service for several years now, just as your Imperial Airways has its Empire run. And I intend to see that, when the commercial race across the big pond really does get under way, Farrell-Drew Aviation will be able to offer the best planes flying the safest and fastest route.'

Leigh stopped and looked down with a rueful smile. 'I'm sorry. You must be bored out of your mind. Once I get going, there's no stopping me.'

'Oh, no! It's fascinating. Honestly.' Thrilled by his vitality and enthusiasm, Liz longed to be able to respond, to sound knowledgeable, but although she had heard Chris and her father arguing the pros and cons of long-distance flying often enough, the whole idea still seemed to her far-fetched. 'Is Farrell-Drew your own company?'

'Sort of. It began as the brainchild of my Dad and Charlie Drew – Dad's the ideas man, and Charlie's the designer. I do a bit of both these days, and get to experiment with the results.'

'A bit like Mam and Dad and me,' she said.

He chuckled. 'Right.'

To mask her ignorance of aeronautics, she side-tracked slightly to ask about Francis and his longing to fly.

'Oh, he's a natural. You see, it's not just a matter of mastering the instruments, you need to have a feel for it, too – you know what I mean, a kind of instinct that can't be taught. And Francis has it. Getting his father to see things his way is a different matter, though. I was hoping to have another go at Mr Whitney, persuade him at least to let Francis take lessons; but it seems they're away. Maybe, with this civil war in Spain, he's afraid his son may end up doing something stupid. But he isn't going be able to stop Francis forever. Far better to encourage him, let him join the RAF when he's through with college.'

Liz was immensely flattered that he should be talking to her seriously, as though she were an adult. She found herself telling him about Mr Morgan and the Café Candide, and of her hopes for the future, with the same enthusiasm. 'The café reopened this weekend, which meant I had to be up early this morning to make sure they had enough cakes to see them through today.'

'Six throws for a penny – every guardsman knocked down wins a prize!'

The raucous voice from a nearby booth almost drowned her words. Leigh glanced across at the stall, with its swaying row of red-coated soldiers lined up along the rear wall. The stallholder, quick to spot his interest, yelled, 'Come along, sir – win a priceless gift for yer young lady. Score with six and she'll become the proud owner of a genuine antique musical box.'

Leigh followed the man's glance to where the little box sat, complete with pirouetting ballerina on top, a crude toy that had probably been mass produced in some grubby foreign sweatshop. 'In a pig's ear, she will,' he murmured, and lifted a laconic eyebrow at Liz. 'What d'you think?'

'Oh, yes, do.'

'O.K., you're the boss. Let's give it a whirl.' He collected the six soft balls, and a small crowd collected behind them, roaring encouragement which turned to cheers as all six soldiers were felled with deadly accuracy. The stallholder's smile faded as he grudgingly handed over the prize.

'That was wonderful!' Liz exclaimed.

'Not bad for a pitcher out of practice,' he said smugly. And as she glanced up enquiringly, 'Baseball. I used to pitch for my school team.'

'Baseball. That's a bit like rounders, isn't it?'

'Young lady,' he growled. 'Smile when you say that.'

Her giggle was infectious. She turned the key on the side of the box and the little figure on top revolved jerkily to the tinny strains of the Blue Danube waltz.

'That's terrible,' he said. 'Throw it in the first trash bin we come to and I'll buy you something better.'

'Certainly not.' She could probably have bought better in Woolworths for threepence, but Liz cradled her prize as if it held the crown jewels.

A roving photographer took their picture and handed Leigh a card. 'Ready in a couple of hours, sir. Booth near the entrance.'

Leigh grinned and pocketed the card. 'What now?' he asked.

Liz knew she ought to find the others, but she hadn't had so much fun in ages. Alec Munnings was forgotten. 'We could go on Noah's Ark,' she said.

So they went on Noah's Ark, collapsing into gales of laughter as they were rocked every which way, clinging to the rail and each other to keep their footing. From the Ark, they went on to other sideshows, until they had amassed such a haul of prizes that they had to buy a bag to put them in.

'This one has to be for you.' She pulled Leigh towards the sign which proclaimed, 'American Bowling Alley'. And he laughed, and taught her how to hold the bowl so as to knock down the most pins at the other end.

It was as they turned away that she caught sight of Chris, anxiously scanning the crowd. It was tempting to pretend she hadn't seen him. But that would be mean, and anyway, even the best things couldn't last forever. So she waved, and eventually Chris waved back.

'I'd like to meet your brother,' Leigh said.

She turned quickly. 'You won't tell him, will you? About Alec, I mean – what happened.'

'Not if you don't want me to.'

'You sound disapproving, but it isn't the way you think.' Liz searched for the right words. 'If Chris knew, he'd get mad and go chasing off after Alec, and there'd be a fight – and that would upset Mam and Dad . . .'

Leigh lifted a placating hand. 'O.K. I get the picture.'

The plane came flying over yet again, and at once his head lifted and he stopped, alert, shielding his eyes with one hand. 'The good old Fox Moth's keeping busy, I see. It sure brings back memories – many's the time I've taken folks joyriding to earn the odd extra dollar.'

'It flies from the beach,' Liz explained. 'Monsieur Giroux, the pilot, takes passengers up for five shillings, and gives them a signed postcard certifying that they're actually flown with him. He's got another plane, too, that he sometimes uses to give flying instructions and displays.'

'Giroux? I wonder. Dad knows a Norman Giroux – I met him once. French Canadian, quite a character.' There was a curious note in Leigh's voice. 'Have you ever been up?'

'Heavens, no. I'd never dare – not that I ever had five shillings to spare.'

'D'you want to go now?' His eyes were suddenly very bright and challenging.

Her heart missed a beat, and then began to thud. Was it the thought of flying, or the unexpectedness of his asking her as if he really meant it? 'I'm not sure. The idea's a bit scary.'

'Even if I promised to hold your hand?'

'Oh! Would you, really?' She hadn't meant to sound so eager. Whatever must he think? She couldn't stand people who gushed. Embarrassment brought the colour flaming vividly into her face. But there was only amusement in the faint smile that lit his eyes, and that confused her more than ever.

In the end, she was spared having to answer by Chris, who pushed his way through to her with Jimmy close on his heels, and Sally a little way behind. 'Liz – are you all right? Where on earth have you been?'

'We've searched the place for you.' Jimmy glared suspiciously at Leigh.

Guilt made Liz defensive as she introduced her companion, very aware of her flushed cheeks. 'Well, there's no need to make a drama out of it. I just walked farther than I meant and then I met Leigh and he won all these for me – ' She held up the bag of prizes, including the musical box, and as Jimmy's scowl deepened, she said quickly, 'Leigh's a flyer, he knows all there is to know about aeroplanes. He was just offering to take me up in the beach plane.' She met his amused gaze and her chin lifted. 'Weren't you?'

'Sure was.'

Sally had been eyeing Leigh with blatant interest. 'Can we all come?' she asked pertly. Liz looked daggers at her, and Chris muttered 'Sally!' She became all wide-eyed inocence. 'Well, why not?'

Leigh betrayed a momentary flicker of something resembling exasperation. Then, with a coolly-drawled, 'Sure. Why not, indeed?' he looked to Liz.

'Thanks,' she heard herself saying, 'but I don't think I want to go, after all, if you don't mind.'

One eyebrow quirked. 'Just as you please. Some other time, maybe.' He saw Monica Hazlett homing in on him, her blonde hair lifting in the wind, her fur jacket clutched tightly about her. 'Just now, it looks like I'm wanted anyway.' He smiled at Liz.

'Bye, kid. We had a great time, didn't we?' Then he lifted a hand in salute to the others, and strolled away. A few moments later, Liz watched Monica Hazlett slide her arm possessively through his.

She was quite unprepared for the jealousy that shot through her. And because she couldn't take it out on the person concerned, Sally found herself on the receiving end. 'How could you be so brazen? I didn't know where to look!'

'Hey, now, hang on a minute, Liz,' Chris protested. 'Sal didn't mean to . . .'

'Oh, of course she meant to. Trust you to stand up for her.'

Sally's eyes opened wide again. 'I don't know what you're on about. It just seemed like a fun idea for us all to go.'

'Rubbish! It's quite obvious why you made the suggestion, so there's no need to play the innocent!'

Jimmy could contain himself no longer. 'Never mind Sally – it seems to me you're the one who needs to do some explaining, Liz. Picking up a bloke like that – old enough to be your father, and a Yank to boot! We all know what they're like!'

'Yeh, who'd have thought it.' Sally giggled. 'You're a sly one, Liz Ryan, gettin' off with a Yank – and what a Yank!'

'You mind your own business – and as for you, Jimmy Marsden, you're talking out of the back of your head! Leigh's a perfect gentleman, and he's only about twenty-five.'

'Twenty-five or thirty-five, *perfect gentlemen* don't go round picking up sixteen-year-old girls,' Jimmy sneered. 'Not without some encouragement, anyway.'

It was Chris's turn to take exception. 'Now, just you hang on a minute, Jimmy. You're talking about my sister.'

'Oh, shut up, all of you!' Tears of anger and disappointment choked Liz as she and Jimmy stood glowering at one another, oblivious of the blue sky, and the sunshine, of the plane droning steadily above, and the laughter all around them. It would have been so simple for her to put the matter right, to explain that Leigh wasn't a stranger, but she was too incensed by Jimmy's accusations and too confused by a variety of emotions even to try.

'Well, if that's what you think, you know what you can do.' She turned on her heel and marched away, still clutching her prizes.

Jimmy was already in pursuit when Chris caught at his arm. 'No, wait. You've got our Liz really mad, now. She doesn't often lose her temper, but when she does,' he grimaced, 'skin and hair fly. Best if you take Sally on the Dipper and I'll go and sort her out.'

'She'd get a clip round the ear if I had anything to do with it,' Jimmy said savagely.

'Precisely – and much good that would do.'

Chris caught up with Liz near the Water Chute, where the squeals were almost as loud as for the Dipper. He grasped her arm. 'Hold up, our kid.' He swung her round and saw her tears. 'Oh, come, it's not that bad.'

'We were having such a lovely day,' she wailed, 'and now it's all ruined.'

'No, it isn't. Not if you don't want it to be.'

'Why should it be up to me? Jimmy Marsden's got no right to preach at me!'

Chris looked uncomfortable. 'No, but it's understandable – seeing you so friendly with a perfect stranger. He's jealous, Liz. I wasn't too happy about it myself.'

'Well, he's no business being jealous. And anyway . . .' She stopped, biting her lip.

'And anyway what?'

Liz heaved a great sigh and explained to Chris about meeting Leigh at Clare's party, and why he was here. 'He's really nice.'

'Well, why on earth didn't you tell us, instead of letting Jimmy get hold of the wrong end of the stick?'

And she couldn't explain why, not just because of Alec, but because even she didn't understand this possessive urge that made her want to keep Leigh to herself. So she tossed her head. 'Because you all immediately thought the worst, that why. Anyway, I'm not Jimmy Marsden's property.'

'So you're going to ruin the day for all of us, just to spite him?'

Put like that, it did make her sound like a spoiled child. 'No, of course not. I'm sorry, Chris. Come on, I'll make things right with the others.'

They walked back, arm in arm, towards the Big Dipper, and watched as the carriage swooped past with Sal and Jimmy hanging on to the bar and screaming with the rest. Liz felt even more guilty, for it should have been Chris up there with Sally. Mr Hazlett was there, too, with the whole family, plus Leigh, to whom Monica was clinging for dear life, alternately screaming and hiding her head against his chest in the most sickening way.

Jimmy accepted Liz's explanation, but it was an uneasy truce. He was accustomed to calling the tune where girls were concerned, and with a blend of charm and cheek, often managed to keep several girls happy at the same time. But Liz wasn't like other girls. She never appeared particularly flattered by his attentions, nor did she make flirtatious overtures of her own. Yet, young as she was, he had got into the habit of thinking of her as his steady girl – always there when the others palled. And it surprised him to discover how much he minded her making sheep's eyes at the American.

Liz, having apologised, considered the matter at an end. That was how family arguments were always settled, she told him, and as far as she was concerned, this was no different. And wasn't it time they were thinking about having their picnic? To carp further would have put him in the wrong, but he couldn't help noticing how carefully Liz guarded her prizes.

They decided to have their picnic on the beach, in a quiet corner sheltered from the wind, where Liz laid out a white cloth and began dispensing sandwiches and lemonade with her customary good humour. Soon they were all squabbling like children over who had eaten all the salmon paste and left the egg, as though nothing had happened, and afterwards the boys lay back replete, with their collars turned up and their hats over their eyes – like gangsters, Sally said – and Liz and Sally entertained themselves by criticizing the various fashions, shuddering as several heroic souls trotted towards the distant waves in swimsuits and caps, with no more than a towel for protection.

'They want to be careful,' Liz said. 'You can run into patches of quicksand out there.'

'Serve them right for being so daft.' The shrieks from the fairground continued unabated, and all around them children's voices filled the air. Sally glanced at the two prone figures and lowered her voice. 'Go on, then – tell us about him – the Yank. What was he really like?'

'There's nothing to tell – and don't call him that,' Liz said sharply. She stood up, brushing the sand from her coat.

'All right, no need to be so touchy. I still think you were dead selfish – keeping him to yourself. I reckon you've got a crush on him.'

'You do talk a lot of rot,' Liz muttered, bending down to collect up the cups, and hide the betraying flood of colour. 'If you want to make yourself useful, you can help me clear up this mess, then we can go down the pier while the sun's shining.'

'O.K.' Sally gave the boys a nudge with her toe. 'Did you hear that, lazybones? Liz wants to go down the pier.'

'Does she, now?' Jimmy raised himself on one arm, his cap pushed back at a rakish angle. There was wariness behind the challenge in his eyes, narrowed against the sun to look at Liz. She wondered if he had heard Sally's comment about Leigh. But he only said, 'Right. The pier it is. But only if we can have a cup of tea in the café at the end and ride back on the little train. I'm not walking the best part of a mile twice.'

It was freezing cold on the pier, in spite of the sun, but Liz didn't mind. She was quite happy to lean on the end rail with the whole expanse of the bay spread out before her, and nothing in sight but the odd ship trailing smoke on the horizon and Blackpool Tower pointing skywards in the distance, away to the right. She felt uplifted, as though she had only to stretch out her arms to go soaring off into infinity.

With the wind in her ears, she didn't hear the plane until it soared over them, heading out to sea. It wasn't the ordinary beach plane that gave rides, but the special one, and as she watched it began to perform the most intricate dives and turns, looping the loop, and swooping down to skim the waves. On the sands below, people were clapping and cheering for more. Jimmy shouted something to her, but his words were carried away on the wind, and she was too absorbed to care. For the first time, she began to see what it was that made people like Leigh and Francis so passionate about flying. There was something wonderfully carefree about the gyrations being performed by the little plane; just watching it thrilled her to the core. And she knew, without a doubt, that it was Leigh at the controls, joyously flinging that fragile-looking collection of spars and rigging about the sky like a paper dart.

Jimmy's arm came round her waist. 'Liz – I'm sorry I was rotten to you earlier.' The brashness was for once absent – in fact, he sounded almost diffident. 'Are we friends again?'

Liz watched the little plane grow smaller as it flew off in the direction of Blackpool. Leigh was as far beyond her reach as that plane – an insubstantial dream. Jimmy was the reality. She smiled at him and laid her head on his shoulder. 'Friends,' she said.

Chapter Thirteen

There hadn't been a king crowned since 1911, and the whole country was in the grip of Coronation fever. The Duke and Duchess of York were already much loved, and new-born girl babies stood a better than even chance of being christened Elizabeth or Margaret Rose.

Liverpool, renowned for 'putting on a show', was about to irrupt in a riot of pageantry, colour and gaiety that would surpass all previous celebrations. And the people of Fortune Street were determined to put on the best street party in the whole city. Liz had started a fund for that purpose straight after Christmas.

Michael had been totally against Kathleen having anything to do with the arrangements in her present condition.

'Small chance I'd have. With you and the family and Doc Graham all watching me like hawks, it's as much as I can do to blow my nose without permission. But folk need to have a meeting, to decide how best to use their Coronation club money. And this is the logical place to hold it, like they did for the Jubilee . . .'

'Don't remind me – bedlam, it was, with everyone arguing like the divil. I'll not have you upset with the baby due in a week or two.'

'Five,' she corrected him. 'And I won't be upset. If they hold it before our Rita goes back to college, she'll keep things under control, and Liz will help. I'll even promise to go to bed before they begin, if that'll please you.'

So Michael had given in. It was frustrating for Kathleen, listening to the voices below and not being able to participate, though she was treated to a running commentary from Joe and Eddie, who sat enthralled at the head of the stairs. 'Hey, Mam – Eddie's Mam's just gone for Nosey Nora, 'cos she said we'd got too many jellies on the list an' not enough ale,' Joey snouted.

'An' Dad's sidin' with Nora,' Eddie put in. 'Our Mam'll half murder 'im when she gets 'im 'ome!' But Kathleen's conviction that her daughter would be more than equal to the occasion was later confirmed by Eddie's mutter, 'I tell yer what, Joey – it's God 'elp any kids your Rita gets charge of. Go through 'em like Syrup of Figs, she will!'

The meeting was soon over. Kathleen heard the sound of many feet trooping back through the shop, then all was quiet, except for Liz's voice telling the boys to scoot. She put her head round the bedroom door.

'Can Mrs Cassidy have a word, Mam? She seems really upset.'

'Yes, of course. Ask her to come up, and pull that chair forward a bit. Perhaps you could make us a cup of tea.'

Ellen sat twisting her fingers in her lap, not knowing quite how to begin. Her face was blotched and puffy, as though she had recently been crying. 'It's the washing,' she began at last. 'I feel awful, knowing how you're placed, and after I offered to do it in the first place . . .'

'But now you find you can't manage it any more.' Kathleen's voice was reassuring, though her heart sank. The news couldn't have come at a worse time. She felt suddenly very weary.

'Oh, it isn't that I can't manage, but Arnie's got himself in such a state that I had to come and see you. It's the Relief, you see. We had a man round late this afternoon, and he says they'll have to dock our money if I don't give up, and I can barely get by as it is. I tried to explain, but he refused to believe you weren't paying me . . .'

Liz, coming in with the tray, was in time to hear Ellen's tale of woe. 'I bet Nora Figg put him on to you – she was dropping hints like mad the other week.'

'Don't jump to conclusions, Liz,' her mother said sharply. 'Nora has her faults right enough, but any number of people must have realized what Ellen was doing.'

'It really doesn't matter how it happened,' Ellen said. 'What's done is done. Only it grieves me to have to let you down.'

'Now you're being absurd.' Kathleen's voice sharpened. 'I don't know how we'd have managed without you these last few months. As Liz well knows, I've never been happy about letting you do all that washing for nothing. So, from now on, if you really want to carry on, and Arnie is agreeable, we'll put the arrangement on a proper footing, so that you can straighten matters out. Otherwise we shall have to look for someone else.'

'Oh, I wouldn't want that.'

Ellen's face was full of conflicting emotions, and Kathleen, quietly sipping her tea, pressed home her point. 'Any more than we want to lose you. In fact, once the baby comes, we are going to need more help rather than less. The business is growing, and taking more of Liz's time, and although Shirley Anne's worked mornings in the shop since she left school, I doubt we can rely on her indefinitely.' Kathleen's voice grew dry. 'Her concert work is so well paid that it would be foolish to try to hold her back. She's already talking about keeping us in our old age.' She shrugged. 'So, you see, even when I'm back on my feet, there'll be plenty to be done. We should be able to offer you at least a couple of hours work a day on a regular basis.'

'That would be splendid,' Liz exclaimed. 'And you could bring the little ones with you, if it would help. They wouldn't be any trouble, would they, Mam?'

Kathleen gave her daughter a look of exasperation. But Ellen was too overcome to notice.

'I'm sure I could manage that. Our Dot's ever so good with the younger ones, so getting them to school and back'd be no problem. I wouldn't be far away, and I'm sure Hester would look in on Arnie now and again. They get on ever so well – they play poker and gin rummy for hours on end, sometimes, *and* she won't let him cheat. I'd need to discuss it with Arnie, of course, but you know how he feels about being beholden to the Parish.'

She suddenly noticed how tired Kathleen was looking, put down her teacup and stood up. 'Speaking of Arnie, I've left him on his own. I must go.'

'Yes, of course. Well, you talk to him, and I'll have a word with Michael. And then we'll see. Now, about the washing – suppose I pay you ten shillings, starting this week? And if your horrid little man wants confirmation, he can have it.'

Liz was relieved at the prospect of having some help. Rita ran the house so efficiently while she was home that it freed her to spend more time in the bakehouse, where she was at her happiest and most creative. She had been secretly dreading the thought of having to cope with everything again, once her sister was back at college.

Dr Graham had been keeping a very close eye on Mam, and

eventually confined her to bed for a few days. Mam knew better than to argue; in fact, Liz had the feeling that she was relieved to have the decision taken for her. She didn't seem to be able to get comfortable anywhere, and she wasn't sleeping at all well. It made her snappy with everyone. And her mood wasn't improved by Uncle Nick calling in to say that Laura was expecting twins, which was why she hadn't come with him.

'Poor love, it's made her a bit scared, like. The doctor says she's fine, but her Mam's is about as far as she feels like going at present.'

'And much good that'll do her. You want to watch it, Nick. That woman'll make an invalid of Laura, which won't be good for either of you – unless you want to spend the next three months waiting on her hand and foot.'

Nick grinned sheepishly. 'Oh, well, you know how it is.'

As the days went by, Michael could think of little except Kathleen, and Dr Graham's concern that the baby was still lying badly. Not that he said as much in Kathleen's presence.

'I'd as soon she wasn't worried at this stage. There's time enough yet for the head to engage . . .'

'And if it doesn't?'

Dr Graham gave him a straight look. 'We'll give it another week. If nothing's changed by then, I'd like her to see a friend of mine. Latimer is a specialist. Excellent man. It could be he'll want to have her admitted to hospital, just to be on the safe side.'

'Look now, if there's something wrong, I want to know.'

'And if I knew for certain, I'd tell you, Michael. Let's just say that I'd be happier to have her in the care of experts for the last couple of weeks or so.'

The doctor's words had an ominous ring, but Michael could get no more out of him, and so he kept the worry to himself. Rita was studying hard for her final exams, and Liz already had more than enough on her mind. As for Chris – Chris, like himself, would feel helpless. They were all helpless.

But Liz had eyes in her head. And she'd felt the cutting edge of her mother's tongue more often than usual. 'Mam *is* all right, isn't she?' she asked Dr Graham on his next visit.

He smiled encouragingly. 'She's doing fine, lass – if we can just keep her quiet for the next week or two.'

'Honestly,' she exploded to Clare, who came round at the weekend, 'I may not know very much about having babies, but I wish he wouldn't treat me as if I were a complete ninny, incapable of understanding.'

Clare was sympathetic. 'I'm sure you've no need to worry.'

'Oh, not you, too!' Liz cried in disgust. 'You're already beginning to sound like a doctor yourself. Just remember, when you *do* qualify – that kind of patronizing attitude makes people worry all the more.'

Clare laughed, and in an effort to divert her friend's mind, said 'Leigh Farrell flew back to America last week. They had some trouble with the plane's engine, and he thought he might have to stay even longer. Monica Hazlett wouldn't have minded in the least.'

Liz hadn't seen Leigh since the day at the fairground – indeed, there was no reason why she should. It had been fun, but she was under no illusion; she had been no more to him than a likeable kid, to be indulged. Still, it would have been nice if he'd said goodbye. Sometimes, when Shirley Anne wasn't around, she would take the little musical box from under her side of the bed, and turn its key to make the ballerina dance. Her head told her that it was just a cheap toy, but the memories evoked by the tinny music filled her with confusing emotions that made her hide the musical box from prying eyes; that caused her heart to skip a beat every time she caught sight of a head of red hair lifting above its neighbours in the street ahead of her, and sent her running in pursuit, just in case.

'Francis was pleased as Punch,' Clare was saying, 'because Leigh finally talked Daddy into letting him take flying lessons. There's a small airfield near his college.'

'Oh, I'm glad. That will mean so much to him.'

'You seem to know more about my brother than I do!'

Liz pulled herself together and grinned. 'I'm just naturally nosey. It's not easy to keep secrets in our house.'

A couple of weeks later, she had an airmail letter with a Connecticut postmark. It was from Leigh, enclosing a copy of the photograph the man on the fairground had taken. She looked terribly childish, clutching the musical box, but it was very good of him. Her heart leapt with pleasure, and because the letter had his address on, she answered it, filling a whole page with all sorts of trivial news.

The spring weather was tempting people to shake off their winter blues, and as a result, the café trade increased almost daily. Liz, spending more and more time perfecting her range of cakes, sometimes wondered if she hadn't bitten off more than she could chew, but pride would never allow her to admit it. Now that Arnie had agreed, it would be a help having Ellen around. Shirley Anne seemed to be spending more and more of her time at Mrs Frith's these days so that Liz wondered how long it would be before she tried to wriggle out of her responsibilities altogether. Chris and Dad now shared the bulk of the everyday baking and the deliveries between them. The installation of the telephone had brought a further increase in trade, and the van seemed to be forever coming and going.

But Liz was still loath to surrender responsibility for the Candide, which she regarded as her own special project. For the time being she preferred to deliver their daily order personally, carefully wrapped and stored in Boadicea's capacious containers.

The sight of the café, restored to its former elegance, never failed to fill her with pride. She loved the way the pretty shell wall lights cast a blush of colour across the white walls and fluted pillars. The tables were covered in white linen and the fragrance of fresh flowers mingled with other tempting aromas. A huge bowl of daffodils stood near the paydesk, and each table had a centrepiece of violets, bought daily from a flower-seller in Clayton Square.

Mr Morgan had spent almost every penny he possessed on the restoration. It frightened Liz, just thinking about the risk she had persuaded him to take. But, once she'd convinced him, he had thrown himself into the venture with an enthusiasm that more than matched her own, and seemed to thrive on the challenge.

'My dear Elizabeth, I haven't enjoyed myself so much in years. I've even taken to playing the piano again. If the venture fell through tomorrow, I would still consider the attempt worthwhile.'

But it wouldn't fall through. The early takings were excellent and, to Liz's relief, there had been no repercussions from Alec Munnings, in spite of his threats. Mr Morgan had found the perfect lady to help him run the Candide as it should be run – Alice Tremain, a widow in her late thirties, with a willowly elegance and a pleasant way with customers. Already the Candide was being talked about in the more affluent areas of town; which had to be good news for Ryan's, too, Liz told herself as she wheeled Boadicea down the jigger into Fortune Street.

With only a day or two to go, Coronation fever was reaching its peak, and lines of bunting flapped above her head as she pedalled along Great Homer Street. Like most people, she and Chris had spent half of Sunday afternoon pinning a string of tiny Union Jacks all round the window and along the front of the counters, and she had made a special red, white and blue display, featuring pictures of the King and Queen and the two princesses, to stand in the centre of the window.

Most of the shops on Greaty were gaudily arrayed, and she viewed them with a critical eye as she rode past. None, so far as she could see, was as fine as their own . . . So engrossed was Liz that she didn't hear the car coming fast behind her until it was too late. Within seconds she was sprawling on the pavement, her legs still entangled in the bike which lay half on top of her, whilst the car sped on its way, the driver apparently oblivious of what had happened.

The heavy fall had knocked the wind out of her, and as willing hands came to help, she became aware of a warm trickle of blood on her cheek.

'Eh, yer in a right ol' pickle 'ere, Liz, gairl!' Nellie from the newsagent exclaimed, her voice warm with sympathy. 'Crazy young bugger! Didn't ought ter be purr'in chairge of anythin' faster'n a pram. Think 'is da'd know better. Tell yer wot, 'e's made a right mess of yer cakes an' all.'

'Oh, no!' Liz struggled to get to her feet, and a man's voice, gentle, with a pronounced accent, warned her to take care. Tears stung her eyes as she saw the cakes she had made with such care, assorted creams, flung willy-nilly in all directions. 'Oh, no!' she wailed again, hardly aware of her various aches and pains in her distress at losing her precious cargo. She was down on her knees again, reaching for them, one after another – seeing, through a blur, the grit embedded in the cream.

'Come,' said the gentle voice, and a hand beneath her arm urged her to rise. 'First we will assure ourselves that no bones are broken, and then we shall see what can be done to minimize your loss.'

'I'm all right. Just a few grazes.' But Liz allowed herself to be helped up, wiping the blood from her cheek with the back of her hand. Someone had already righted Boadicea, but the bike looked almost as much of a wreck as she felt, and although the back carrier was still closed, she shuddered to think what she would find when she opened it.

'Will yer cum inside an' sit down fer a minute, Liz?'

'Thanks, Nellie, but I haven't time.' Liz gazed about her in despair, as curious people paused, commiserated, and then stepped carefully around the mess.

'Forgive me, but I believe you should make time. That was a bad fall.'

There was genuine concern in the man's voice. It was a voice that was vaguely familiar. Curiosity overcoming all else, she looked up to see a tall figure in a long dark coat . . . white hair beneath a grey homburg. 'Of course! I know who you are,' she exclaimed, momentarily diverted. 'The snowball man . . .'

'You remember.' He smiled. 'I am flattered. I recognized you at once, my young saviour. My name is Fritz Lendl, and I have wished many times that I could thank you more fully.'

'But you did thank me, at the time.'

'Well, now perhaps I can make proper recompense. Ah, yes – ' he turned, as Nellie came out of the shop with a chair in one hand and a cup and saucer in the other. Mr Lendl took the chair and set it down. 'How sensible – and so kind. My dear young lady, you will sit now and drink this tea that your kind friend has made, and we will then decide what is to be done.'

'That's right, gairl. You do as 'is nibs says, an' get that down you. White as a ghost, yer look.'

Liz was suddenly too dispirited to argue. What did a few minutes matter, anyway? The cakes were ruined, and her knee throbbed like anything. She pulled up her skirt. 'Oh, damn! A good pair of stockings ruined, too!'

Her new friend chuckled. 'That is better. A little healthy anger is good, even at the price of a sore knee. Now, tell me about these cakes – you were delivering them somewhere, yes?'

Liz told him, explained who she was and where she had been going, and in the telling, the colour came back into her cheeks. 'Poor Mr Morgan! Whatever am I going to do?'

'It is a matter of some urgency? Then, if you will permit, let us first discover the extent of the damage.'

The chair and cup were returned, and together they took stock. Almost everything in the front basket had tipped out on to the pavement, and was beyond saving, and when Liz lifted the lid of the rear box, the top tray was at first sight a jumble of cream and pastry.

Fritz Lendl removed it carefully and peered underneath. 'Ah. Not good, but I have seen worse.' He glanced up. 'These are your own work, yes? Most interesting. Come, we must return to your bakehouse without delay. It is not too far for you to walk?'

'No, I'm fine . . .' Liz was by now bemused. 'But. . . ?'

He smiled. 'I am being mysterious, but I will explain as we go.' Ignoring her protests, he began to push the bike while she limped along beside him. 'You must know that until last year, I too had a flourishing patisserie. It is no exaggeration to say that in Vienna, Fritz Lendl's confections were a legend. So you see, already we have something in common.'

'You said "had"?' Liz prompted as he fell silent.

He was so long replying that she wondered if she had said the wrong thing. 'There was – trouble.' Again, as on their first meeting, there was a bleakness in his voice. 'First it was bricks through the window, and later a fire, which destroyed everything.'

'You mean someone deliberately set fire to your shop? That's terrible! But why?'

'Why?' He turned his dark eyes on her and she saw the sadness in them. 'I am a Jew, my child. For some, that will always be reason enough.'

Liz was appalled – and, remembering the circumstances of their first meeting, embarrassed. There were many Jewish people in Liverpool, and she had occasionally heard people disparaging them, even calling them dirty. But to go to such lengths?

Hoping to make him feel better, she said impulsively, 'Jesus was a Jew.'

'So he was.' Fritz Lendl smiled a little sadly. 'He wasn't treated so good, either, and by his own people.' He shook his head, and Liz had the feeling that he was miles away. 'There are many bad people in my country, Nazis, who speak with admiration of the way Adolf Hitler's Germany has flouted all the treaties and rearmed the Rhineland. They would like to see Austria as a part of Hitler's great Aryan dream. There would then be no hiding place for Austrian Jews.'

'Is that why you left?'

'Not entirely.' Her question jerked him back to the present. 'Forgive me, Miss Elizabeth. My problems can be of no interest to you.'

'Oh, but they are,' Liz insisted. His distress made what she had read in the newspapers seem suddenly real. 'So many awful things seem to be happening in the world, with civil war in Spain, and Italy bombing Addis Ababa. I remember seeing the Emperor, Haile Selassie, on the Movietone news at the pictures – such a sad, dignified little man. Grandpa Dandy reckons the rearmament of the Rhineland is a direct threat to France, and could lead to war, and if it did, we would be drawn in, like last time.' She stopped, looking up into her companion's expressive face, suddenly desperate for reassurance that her safe, comfortable little world would remain secure. 'It won't come to that, will it?'

'Who am I to know such things?' He shrugged. 'I know only that I had no heart to begin again. My dear wife died some years ago. So when my daughter and her English husband, who have a nice little cleaning business here in London Road, begged me to come and make my home with them, I agreed. They are very good and do all for my comfort, and my grandchildren are a joy, but often my heart is like a stone. I miss Vienna and my old way of life . . .'

There was so much yearning in his voice that Liz found a lump in her throat, and was quite relieved to see that they had reached home. The van was parked in Fortune Street, and she led the way through to the bakehouse.

'Dad?'

Michael looked up from the batch of barms he was making and saw that she was not alone. 'Come in,' he said, 'and don't be making a draught.' His interest was centred on her companion; only as she came nearer did he notice the blood congealing on her cheek. 'Lord save us, girleen, what's happened to you? Are you hurt anywhere else?'

'Only a grazed knee – and my pride.' She forced a grin, and introduced Mr Lendl. 'He's been ever so kind, Dad,' she said, explaining briefly what had happened.

'Then you are doubly welcome, sir. Lizzie, love, take Mr Lendl through to the house. Chris is there, having a break; he'll make Mr Lendl some tea while you clean up those grazes.'

But the old man put up a hand. 'Thank you, but I can perhaps be of more use here. The matter, I believe, is urgent – and I have some considerable experience . . .'

The next hour passed so quickly that Liz had no time to feel sorry for herself. She cleaned up her grazes, changed her stockings, and reassured her mother that she wasn't hurt. Then she telephoned Mr Morgan to explain what had happened, and promised that she would be along very soon. Meanwhile Mr Lendl, clad in one of Michael's overalls, had unloaded the cakes, separated the badly damaged ones from the rest, and was working with deft fingers to cannibalize them, making one good cake or pastry from two or three damaged ones in a way that was little short of miraculous: with the application of a little fresh icing and cream, they were soon almost indistinguishable from the originals. After this, it only took a moment to examine, and where necessary touch up, the undamaged ones, before re-packing the order. It was by no means complete, but Mr Morgan would have enough to be going on with until more could be made.

'I wouldn't have believed so much could be salvaged,' Liz exclaimed.

Chris was equally impressed. He had been having a cup of tea with Mam when she arrived, and had accompanied her back to the bakehouse to meet her intriguing new friend.

Michael too had been watching keenly; it had not taken many minutes for him to recognize the hand of a master.

'You have my thanks, Mr Lendl. This particular venture means a lot to my Lizzie.'

'Indeed. It gives me much happiness to be of use.' Although he smiled, there was sadness in his eyes as he glanced at Liz. 'I have been much impressed by your daughter – it is not often that one discovers such a talent in the making. It must not be neglected. You are fortunate in your children, Mr Ryan. I have only the one child, a good and loving daughter, but alas, she did not inherit my gift.'

Mr Lendl's praise filled Liz with pride. But, as Grannie Power used to say, 'Fine words butter no parsnips', and if she didn't get a move on, his praise would be of little avail. 'I must get these cakes to Mr Morgan,' she said.

'Give them here,' Chris said. 'I'll take them in the van. I've told you often enough, you should send the order on the van with the rest instead of making that long trek with Boadicea. Think of the time you'd save.'

'I like going myself.'

'Then the sooner you learn to drive, the better.'

'Stop squabbling, the both of you,' said Michael sternly.

'Sorry, Dad,' Liz said with a grin. And to Chris, 'Come on, then. I'd better come with you, so I can explain properly. I'm sorry to rush off, Mr Lendl.' She glanced at her father. 'But I'm sure you'd be welcome to stay. I'll be back in a jiffy – I'll need to be, if I'm to complete the order.'

Fritz Lendl held up his hands, 'My dear young lady, you must not consider me. I wonder . . .' He hesitated as they all turned to look at him. 'It is only a thought, but I would be happy to be of service.'

'Would you, really?' Liz cried.

'Hush, Liz,' said her father. 'It's a kind thought, sir, but we mustn't impose any further on your time.'

'It would not be an imposition,' the old man insisted. 'Can you not see, it is you who would be doing *me* the kindness! Just to be here – to involve myself . . .'

There was a yearning in his voice, an intensity in his eyes, and Michael recognized the man's need, as if it were his own. 'Very well, so,' he said quietly.

In the van Chris was full of questions, about Mr Lendl, and about the accident. 'You didn't get a look at the driver, I suppose?'

'Well, hardly . . . it all happened so fast.' Which wasn't entirely true, for his question prompted a fleeting memory of those brief seconds as she was falling; a glimpse of fair hair, a pale profile turning towards her as the car shot past. An illusion, or something more? Nellie, too, had spoken as if she recognized the driver.

'What kind of car? What colour?'

'I don't know. I'm not daft about them like you and Jimmy. It was dark – black, perhaps. A kind of sports car,' she added when pressed. 'I'm sure it had a cloth top.'

Chris was quiet for a moment. Then he said slowly, 'There aren't many cars like that hereabouts, but I know who's got one. And so do you, Liz.'

'No,' she said flatly, wishing she'd been less explicit. 'What's more, I don't *want* to know. So if you're thinking what I think you're thinking, forget it. Just leave it. I'll be more careful in future.'

From very early on Coronation Day, you could feel the whole of Liverpool pulsating with excitement. Liz was up earlier than ever. All the cafés were expecting to be busy, and Dad and Chris had their hands full supplying extra bread for the many sandwiches that would be made for their own street party and countless other celebrations, together with meat pies and iced buns decorated with little red crowns. And all to be finished by midday, when they hoped to be able to close. Again Mr Lendl had offered to help, and Liz could hardly believe her luck. Just to watch him work was a delight.

'Are you sure?' she asked. 'Won't your family want you to join in the celebrations?'

'For you it is a celebration,' he said. 'And for my Mitzi and Joe and the children, too. But for me, it is just another day.'

At 9 a.m. bells began to peal all over the city, great paeans of triumphant acclamation. Later, Joey put his head round the door.

'Hey, our Liz, come and look! There's planes, lots of them – bombers! Dad, Mr Lendl, come and look.'

Michael glanced at his companion's austere profile. In many ways, he and Fritz Lendl were two of a kind – both quiet men, with a great love of their work. And, having by now learned something of his background, Michael guessed that a display of warlike machinery would hold little appeal for this man, who longed only to live out his life in peace. So he shooed his young son away, saying they had better things to do.

Chris was already outside, shading his eyes with one hand. 'It's the 610th Lancashire Bomber Squadron of the Auxiliary Air Force,' he shouted above the noise. 'I read about them in the *Echo*. What a sight, eh? Your friend Farrell ought to be here to see them.'

'He's not my friend,' Liz protested, but her words were drowned by the throb of the engines.

The excitement over, Joey and Eddie set off to watch the parades, and Rita said she'd like to go along to St John's Gardens with her friend Margaret, to listen to a relay of the Coronation service from Westminster Abbey.

'You don't mind, do you, Liz? I'll leave dinner in the oven, and we'll be back in time to help with the party.'

'Of course I don't mind. You didn't have much of a holiday over Easter. I'm going to wait and see it in the cinema with Jimmy. There's a whole lot of us going. I wonder if we'll be able to pick out Aunt Flora in the crowds.'

Their aunt had breezed in a few days ago, a vision in cream wool, glowing with good health from her recent cruise, and as always her arms were full of presents. 'I can't stay,' she said. 'Some people I met on the cruise have invited me down to London to see the Coronation. They have a flat overlooking the processional route.'

'Well, don't let us detain you,' Kathleen had said with a sharpness born of disappointment. She had been looking forward more than she had realized to having her sister home again, with her unfussy brand of common sense.

'That's me, tactless as ever.' Flora sat down beside her. 'Feeling rotten, are you, Kath? Listen, I tell you what – I'll ring the Madisons, tell them something's come up. To be honest, it'd be a treat to put me feet up.'

But Kathleen knew she didn't mean it. Flora radiated energy. 'Don't talk daft,' she said. 'Of course you must go. I'm not fit company for anyone at present. The last few weeks always did make me snappy.'

So Flora had gone to London, not entirely reassured, and making a mental note to give Dandy the Madisons' telephone number – just in case.

Michael had fixed the wireless up in the bedroom so that Kathleen could listen to the Coronation service, although Liz had the impression that her mother didn't care much, one way or the other.

'Are you all right, Mam?'

'Fine, love,' she said. 'I've just got a bit of a headache.'

Chapter Fourteen

By mid-afternoon, the party was in full swing. Dandy was in his element, organizing games for the children, leaving the parents free to set out the mountains of sandwiches and cakes, the jellies and the bottles of pop, and position the crates of beer at regular intervals along the street. Above their heads fluttered the red, white and blue bunting, the streamers and the Union Jacks which stretched back and forth across the street, from house to house. The lamp posts at each end of Fortune Street had been wound from top to bottom with crepe paper and tied to each, out of reach of greedy fingers, were great bunches of balloons, to be distributed later in the day. Every house shone – the windows sparkling, the ledges and doorsteps donkey-stoned to a brilliant white, and the flagstones swilled down with water.

Each front door stood open, so that people like Arnie and Mollie shouldn't feel left out. It hadn't been a good winter for Mollie. She had recently spent several weeks in hospital, and looked little better for her stay when Liz and Chris popped in the night before the party.

'I thought I could maybe have me chair pulled up ter the front winder,' she said, every breath an effort. 'That way I'd feel part of the fun.'

Liz looked at her brother. 'Great idea,' Chris said. 'I'll come and move it for you after dinner tomorrow.'

Mollie's expression betrayed her feelings as she gazed at Chris. 'Would yer? Honest?'

'Scout's honour.' Chris crossed his chest solemnly. 'What about your Mam?'

'She says she's not bothered.' The thready voice was determined. 'But you 'ave to make the effort, don't yer?'

Shirley Anne had been feeling sick with nerves ever since she got up, knowing that she was to perform that evening at a very special Coronation concert, at the home of Mrs Frith's main benefactress.

Mrs Frith was sending the car for her at four o'clock, and because the house was right out in the country, near Ormskirk, they were to stay the night. As if that were not excitement enough, Mrs Frith's dressmaker had made Shirley Anne a dream of a gown – pure white and very full, so that when she danced it would float. If she ever got to dance. The way she felt at present, it might never happen.

Still wearing her nightdress, she drifted, white-faced, into the scullery, where Rita was peeling potatoes ready to go in a pie later.

'I can't possibly serve in the shop this morning. I keep coming over hot and cold.'

'Don't be stupid.' Rita had no patience with histrionics.

'It's not stupid. You don't understand how much this means to me! Lady Prunella is an earl's daughter, so there's bound to be lots of important people invited. It could be my big chance – and if I'm ill . . .'

'You're getting to be a right little snob. The sooner you get dressed and behind that counter, the better you'll feel. There's nothing like work for taking your mind off things.'

Liz put her head round the door. 'Rita's right – at this rate, you'll be a gibbering idiot by this evening, and there's the party this afternoon to get through first.'

'You've got no soul – either of you.' Shirley Anne flounced towards the stairs. 'If I collapse on stage tonight, I'll never forgive you.'

But Liz only laughed. 'Come off it. You know as well as I do, you'll knock 'em cold.'

It was after two o'clock when they finally shut the shop, by which time the sounds of revelry were already mounting. Hester Whelan's son was home on leave from the Royal Navy. He had wheeled their piano out on to the street, and Hester was playing a medley of lively music hall tunes like *Waiting at the Church* and *Knees up Mother Brown*, to get everyone in the mood. Harry Whelan, a fresh-faced young man with a wicked glint in his eye, and the irresistible rolling gait of a sailor, was creating quite a stir among the girls. 'It's the bell-bottoms,' his proud mother said with a chuckle watching the children run up to touch his collar for luck. 'It always gets them.'

Shirley Anne took one look and went back to change into her prettiest frock – a floral print with a flaring skirt and a belt that made her waist seem impossibly tiny. She had recovered from her bout of nerves, and had washed her hair, using rainwater from the barrel in the yard, which always made it extra soft and silky. Now, she brushed it until it shone. She sauntered casually past Harry Whelan, and paused to smile up at him from under her lashes.

'You're Mrs Whelan's son, aren't you? You're ever so like her.'

He blushed. 'Should I know you?'

'I'm Shirley Anne Ryan, from the corner.'

'Can I get you a drink – some lemonade, perhaps?'

She touched his arm. 'I think I can just about spare the time. I'm giving a very important concert tonight, but the car isn't coming for me just yet.'

'It's really quite an education, watching her go to work on a fella,' Jimmy murmured, as the young sailor, wearing a dazed look, pushed his way through the crush, and returned to present Shirley Anne with a glass of lemonade. 'Poor besotted fool probably thinks *he's* making the running.'

Liz pretended indignation. 'I've seen you respond to Shirley Anne's flirting often enough.'

'Sure I have. It amuses me.'

'That's a terribly cynical thing to say.'

'Rubbish. Your little sister knows the score. Whereas you, my lovely Liz, are so innocent it isn't true.'

Liz never knew how to take Jimmy when he talked like this, cocksure and calculating – part of his Clark Gable image, in pursuit of which he had recently grown a pencil moustache. She wasn't sure she liked being called innocent. It made her sound childish and unattractive, 'lovely Liz' or no, just when she'd been thinking how grown-up she looked in her new pleated frock. Then Jimmy grinned. The music changed to *Sally* and, as the voices rose in chorus, he grabbed her round the waist and danced her down the street.

'You know your Shirley Anne can't hold a candle to you,' he said in her ear, executing a nifty side-step to avoid a clutch of small figures who erupted almost under their feet. Nora Figg was already well away on the ale, and almost merry, her cracked voice droning half an octave below the rest as she made a bee-line for the nearest crate to exchange her empty bottle for a full one.

As they passed the Cassidys' house, Liz tugged at Jimmy's coat, shouting above the lusty thumping of the piano and even lustier singing. 'Wait – let's take Arnie a beer.'

He grinned. 'You're very brave, all of a sudden.'

'Oh, Arnie and me settled our differences ages ago. Hello – can we come in?' She ran ahead of him down the lobby into the back room, and found Arnie already well away with a couple of his mates. Her bottle was added to the ones already spilling over the table by the bed, the top of the wireless and the corner of the sideboard.

'Cheers, gairl.' Arnie slopped ale over the sheet as he raised a tankard with his good hand. 'A' nangel of mairsy, tha's what you are. An' good luck ter 'Is Majesty, Go' bless 'im.'

'An' so say all of us,' echoed the others, the nearest planting a beery kiss in the vicinity of her ear.

'Oh dear,' Liz said. 'It's great to see Arnie enjoying himself for once, but poor Ellen's going to have a terrible time with him tonight.'

'It's not your worry, pet. Come on, this is still my dance. And your brother should be around here somewhere.'

They found Chris at last in Mollie's front room, slowly waltzing her round and round. Sally was standing to one side, her trim figure a vivid slash of light in the shabby room, her painted lips pressed very tightly together. But Liz hardly spared her a glance. She was watching Mollie, whose stumbling ill-shod feet trod an ungainly measure. Her gaunt cheekbones were flushed, and her eyes held an expression that almost moved Liz to tears.

'Eh,' Mollie gasped as Chris set her carefully back in her chair, 'I won't never forget that!'

'No more will I,' Chris said. And meant it.

Outside, Sally turned on him accusingly. 'That was grotesque – I didn't know where to look. The poor creature's in love with you!'

'I know,' Chris said quietly.

'You know?'

'Mollie's always had a thing about Chris,' Liz said. 'And she's not a creature.'

Sally flushed. 'I think you're all barmy.'

'That's enough, Sal.' Chris sounded just like his father as he met her contempt squarely. 'Mollie's dying by inches. So don't begrudge her a few moments of happiness.'

She stared back, her colour heightened, her eyes over-bright. Then she bit her lip and flounced away. Chris shrugged unhappily at his sister's 'Well really!', and followed in Sally's wake. And Liz, watching him, swallowed a lump in her throat.

'Quite a brother you've got,' Jimmy said.

Michael was not one for a lot of noise and fuss, so he was only too happy to stay with Kathleen. They talked quietly together about the changes they had seen, and wondered about the new King, who had never looked to inherit. 'Though with God's help, he'll do us proud, I'm thinking.'

'How could he fail, with such a good wife to support him?' Kathleen said with a hint of her old teasing spirit.

Michael enfolded her hand in his. 'As I have, *acushla*. No man, not even the King himself, has better.'

Kathleen turned her hand and their fingers entwined. 'Do you think Dad's right – about there being another war?'

'A week ago I'd have said not, but talking to Lendl has certainly made me think.'

Her grasp on his hand tightened. 'It would mean that Chris . . .'

'Don't go worrying yourself.' Michael quietly berated himself for fuelling her fears. 'Fritz Lendl is an unhappy man, and who can blame him. Did I tell you, now, that he has offered to take our Lizzie under his wing – teach her all he knows?'

'You wouldn't mind?' Kathleen watched his face. He hadn't been too keen when Mr Morgan had taken such a shine to his favourite child. But this, it seemed, was different.

'How could I mind, when he so clearly recognizes the artist in Liz? Haven't we talked often enough of late about the need for more expert tuition? Now she has the chance to learn from a top Viennese confectioner.'

'You might almost call it Fate.'

Shirley Anne came running up the stairs, her face pale, her blue eyes enormous with excitement. 'Mrs Frith's car's here. Oh, Mam, I feel awful! I've got cramps in my stomach. Suppose I'm sick in the car – ' she gasped. 'Or worse still, when it's time to go on and perform.'

'Not you, my girl. You'll be just fine. And mind you behave yourself.'

'I will. Oh, Mam – Dad!' She hugged them both, her blonde hair brushing against them as soft as silk. 'I'll tell you all about it t'morrow.'

'Get along, and don't keep that driver waiting,' Michael said gruffly. 'At this rate you'll have yourself worn out entirely.'

'If she doesn't wear us out first.' Kathleen winced as she heard the door slam. 'Thank heaven there's only one of her. Listen now, Michael, you really ought to go out and show your face – just for a short while.'

'I'd rather stay here with you.'

She smiled. 'Maybe. But you should go, just the same, in the interests of good business. I can hardly go myself.'

Left to herself, Kathleen shifted her position to ease the niggling pain that had been plaguing her, glad not to have to put on an act. Much as she loved Michael, it was a relief to be alone, just for a little while. She leaned back and closed her eyes, letting the silence of the house settle round her. Beyond the window, a rousing chord on the piano was followed by the opening of *Land of Hope and Glory*, which soon had everyone joining in. That's our Rita, she thought.

The pain eased and Kathleen drifted on the edge of sleep with no thought of time, until gradually she became aware of a warm wetness spreading beneath her on the bed. Her heart lurched and steadied again, and then a great calmness came upon her as she realized that the long wait was over – her waters had broken. She was the best part of three weeks early, but the baby couldn't come soon enough for her. For a few moments she lay, uncomfortable, but only slightly apprehensive at the thought of being alone. There was no hurry. Michael or one of the girls would come soon – they never left her for long.

But soon the soaking bed grew cold and clammy and she decided to get a clean nightdress from the drawer. She swung her legs round cautiously and sat up – and a violent pain almost tore her in two.

Liz had seen her father across the road, talking to Ellen Cassidy. He waved and she waved back. 'Our Rita's getting ready to play the piano, so Mam must be on her own. I think I'll go and make her a cup of tea.'

'Now?' Jimmy said, reaching for another bottle of beer. 'Couldn't it wait a bit? You're always busy, always on the go. Even out here, I've hardly had you to myself for a minute.'

Her eyes, golden with sunlight and laughter, were unintentionally provocative. 'Well, you could always come and help me. In fact, it's probably the best hope you've got of getting me to yourself.'

In the scullery, he wasted no time availing himself of her invitation, but when he tried to kiss her, she fended him off and handed him the kettle. 'Fill that while I lay the tray.'

'There's a name for girls like you,' he muttered. 'Girls who promise more than they deliver.'

'Kettle,' she said firmly. 'I'll just pop up and see Mam.'

She was still smiling as she pushed open the bedroom door. Kathleen was sitting on the edge of the bed, slumped forward with her hands folded across her stomach. 'Mam?' She ran forward. 'Mam, whatever's the matter?'

Kathleen didn't move at first. Then slowly she straightened up, and managed a weak smile. 'It's all right, love. The baby's decided to come a bit early, that's all. If you could get me a clean nightie – this one's wet through – the bed, too, I'm afraid.'

'Oh, never mind that.' Liz flew to the drawer, grabbed the first nightdress that came to hand, and began to help her mother out of the wet one. 'Easy does it,' she said, pulling it from under her. And then her mouth went dry as she saw the large, crimson stain. Surely that shouldn't be there? With heart beating fast, she slipped the dry nightdress over her mother's shoulders, eased her arms in, and wrapped a blanket round her. 'Listen, I'm going to telephone Dr Graham,' she said. 'I'll be back in a minute. Don't move.'

Kathleen's laugh was forced. 'I don't think I'd be able to move just at present.' She swallowed. 'Your father . . .'

'I'll get Jimmy to fetch him. Everything's going to be fine.'

Jimmy heard her flying feet on the stairs, and knew something was up even before he saw her face.

Dr Graham was having his tea when Liz rang. He made a couple of quick phone calls, and the ambulance was already on its way as he drove his car between the throngs of merrymakers. Michael met him at the door, his face ashen.

'Steady man. You'll not want Kathleen to see you worried. I've already been in touch with Latimer – he'll meet us at the hospital. He's an excellent surgeon.'

The word surgeon struck fresh terror into Michael. 'Does it have to be an operation? Oh, dear God! You knew this might happen, didn't you? You've known all along.'

'Not for certain. And until I've seen Kathleen, I'll not commit myself.' But his brief examination was a mere formality. 'There's a small complication, Kathleen, so I'm moving you to the hospital,' he said gently. 'Just lie quietly and take deep slow breaths until the ambulance gets here.'

Kathleen's heart lurched, but one look at Michael's face steadied her. 'This small complication?' She met Dr Graham's eyes with a calmness she was not feeling. 'Is it to do with the discomfort I've been having?'

He hesitated, choosing his words with care. 'It could be . . .' With relief he heard the clang of the ambulance bell. 'Ah, at last. Don't worry about it. We'll have you round to the hospital in no time, and in good hands.'

'But you'll be there, too?' For the first time, there was panic in her voice.

Dr Graham laid a hand on Kathleen's shoulder. 'I'll be right behind the ambulance, with Michael.'

But Michael held him back a moment. 'Well?' He saw Graham hesitate. 'For pity's sake, man, don't you see, I have to know!'

The doctor sighed. 'If I'm right, and I won't know for sure until Latimer's seen her, Kathleen's condition is what we call placenta praevia, which means that the afterbirth is lying below the baby instead of above . . .'

'And?'

'An emergency Caesarian section is our best hope of saving the child.'

It was like being in a nightmare. He was hearing the words, but they seemed to be coming through a blanket of cotton wool.

'Michael?' Dr Graham's voice penetrated the blanket, urgent – there was a hand on his arm, gripping it painfully tight. 'Do you have any brandy? Listen now, we must go. Do you have any brandy – or whisky?'

Like a wounded animal, Michael slowly shook his head and looked up. 'It's not brandy I need.' His eyes met Graham's, his agony apparent in their desperate appeal. 'Just tell me – what chance does Kathleen have? *I have to know*.'

In Fortune Street, the word ran round quick as fire. The clanging of the ambulance bell brought people running, and as the men carried Kathleen out, the revellers gathered in silence near the end of the street to watch her go.

Chapter Fifteen

Michael scarcely left Kathleen's side throughout that long night. Her face wore a mask-like stillness. They had put her in a small side room, where it was quiet. Every so often a nurse or a doctor would banish him while they did whatever they had to do, and occasionally someone would bring him a cup of tea, but no-one suggested that he should leave. The specialist had been kind, but he hadn't minced words. The operation had gone well, and the baby – a boy – though frail, was holding his own. But now there had been another complication. A post-something haemorrhage, he'd explained. An immediate blood transfusion had been given, and another might be needed. One of the nurses with the same blood group was standing by, but Michael had insisted that, if at all possible, his own should be used. And in the small hours he had lain close to Kathleen, watching his blood flow into her. After that they wanted him to rest, but he had continued his vigil.

They didn't understand, of course. He didn't really understand himself, but every instinct told him that Kathleen knew he was there, his blood mingling with hers, joining battle with her, enabling her to draw strength from him. He could feel the pull of it deep inside him. Many times it seemed that she had stopped breathing, and he would fall on his knees, holding her, willing her with every fibre of his being not to leave him. Nothing else mattered at that moment; not his family, not his business, not even his newborn son, fighting his own battle for life. If he prayed at all, it was not a conscious act. Kathleen alone filled his mind, and nothing must be allowed to break the link. That's what he told Graham when he called in. That's what he told the priest, a stranger, who, after baptizing their baby, came to anoint Kathleen.

Michael knew it ought to mean something to him, but it didn't, and to all the murmured platitudes counselling faith and the acceptance of God's will, he answered with dead-eyed calm, 'My wife will not die.'

At some point earlier the children had come in, but the sight of their mother distressed them deeply, and he had sent them home. And later, Dandy had arrived; he stood at the bottom of the bed, not speaking, and then he, too, left.

And as Michael continued to watch and wait, he knew that as long as he lived, he would never forget the smell that clung to his clothes and penetrated the very pores of his skin – a fetid, stomach-turning mixture of ether and antiseptic, of lingering cooking odours, and other nameless things.

The rowdier inhabitants of Fortune Street were still whooping it up outside when, with aching throat, Liz held a council of war in the living room. Rita should have taken charge, but for once her practical sister had been knocked sideways. Neither she nor Chris seemed capable of thinking straight, let alone taking decisions, since that awful visit to the hospital.

'Look,' Liz said. 'We can't just go on sitting here. It's getting late, and it's up to us to carry on as if – well, you know.'

Rita stared at her out of red-rimmed eyes. 'I don't know how you can think about the shop or anything, with poor Mam . . . Oh, Liz, seeing her, lying there like a c . . . corpse . . .'

'Stop it, Rita.' Liz was sharp, sounding so like her mother that they all turned to stare at her. She blocked the unthinkable from her mind. 'Someone round here's got to be practical. There's lots of people depending on us.'

'They'd all understand.'

'That isn't the point. If we let them down, they'll go elsewhere, and we might not get them back. Then where would be?'

'Is that all you're worried about – losing trade? You're getting hard, Liz, d'you know that?'

The accusation stung, yet Liz held her ground. 'Maybe I am, but Mam and Dad sweated blood building up this business, and Mam'd be the first to give us gyp if we didn't do all we could to keep it going until – ' She swallowed hard. 'But I can't do it on my own. And anyway, we'll all be better off keeping busy. Grandpa Dandy's already away to tell Mr Lendl what's happened. Poor Grandpa – I've never seen him so upset – ' Her voice faltered, and steadied. 'So let's get on with it, shall we? Chris, will you fire up the oven, and make a start on the dough?' He was staring into the fire, his face haggard. 'Chris?'

'What?' Her brother dragged his thoughts back from contemplation of the impossible. 'Oh – the oven? Yes. Right.' He left the room, dragging his feet like an old man.

Ever since the visit to the hospital, Joey had been so quiet as to be almost invisible. Throughout the present painful deliberations he had sat hunched over the table, chin in hand and knees drawn up, his feet hooked over the chair rail. Now he turned towards them, his blue eyes wide, his silky lashes spiked with unshed tears. The words burst from him, his Adam's apple working convulsively. 'Is Mam going to die?'

Rita and Liz exchanged a despairing glance, then Rita ran to gather him up, her voice husky. 'Of course not, chucky. Didn't we all go into church and light candles to Our Blessed Lady? If we pray very hard, God will know how much we need Mam and He won't let her die.'

Joey struggled out of her embrace, rubbing his nose fiercely with one arm and leaving a snail-like trail of silver the length of his sleeve. Unhooking his feet, he upturned the chair and rushed to the stairs, flinging over his shoulder, 'I'm norra baby, so you needn't soft-soap me! An' what's more, if Mam does die, I'll never believe in stupid old God, ever again! Not ever!'

His outburst had a devastating effect on Liz. She gasped, 'Oh, Rita!' and as Joey's feet thudded up the stairs, she flung her arms round her sister, and they clung together in a paroxysm of noisy, heart-wrenching sobs.

Liz was the first to pull away. 'No, I mustn't cry.' She blew her nose fiercely. 'If I cry, I'll never get through. Will you go up to Joey?'

But Liz did get through. She even found a moment to go up to Joey herself, later. He had already cried himself to sleep, but she covered him up and kissed the damply curling hair. Fritz Lendl's help that first night was invaluable, and Chris did the work of two, so that all their orders for the morning were met, and she was able to work out a proper schedule for the bakehouse until Mam was out of danger and Dad could think straight again.

Dandy had been jolted to the core by the very real possibility that his darling Kathy might be taken from him. His visit to the hospital and the spectacle of Michael, so totally oblivious of all that came and went around him, left him feeling old and defeated. But not for long. By the time he got home he was already beginning to think more positively. He'd been down for the count before, hadn't he? And always he had picked himself up and come out fighting. It was his proud boast that he'd never been knocked out, and he didn't aim to surrender that record now. So maybe he was no spring chicken any more, but the gut feeling was still there, and there were things he could do. With Michael so preoccupied, the youngsters would be looking to him for a lead. There was one positive thing he could do right away.

Liz was feeling less than tolerant when, long before opening time the following morning, she heard a repeated knocking on the shop door. No-one else was down, so she'd have to go, but if it was Nora Figg, she'd get short shrift.

The figure outlined against the glass wasn't Nora, however. The bolts flew back.

'Oh, Aunt Flora!' she sobbed against the scented bosom. 'Oh, Aunt Flora!'

'There, child, there.' Flora held her niece close, and cleared her throat. 'Dad called me last night, so I hired an aeroplane to fly me to Speke first thing this morning. Peters met me, and here I am.' Dismayed by the drawn look on Liz's face, she feared the worst, but could not ask. 'Come on, now. Get that door locked again and we'll go through to the back. I could murder a cup of tea.'

'Yes, of course.' Liz pulled herself together and led the way through. She boiled the kettle, set out the cups and saucers, and warmed the pot.

Flora made no attempt to help. Instead, she drew out a chair, loosed the button of her grey flannel coat and sat down, hitching her skirt, and crossing one silk-clad leg over the other, as she gave her niece an animated account of her flight from London, and the wonder of watching the sunrise from thousands of feet up. Liz wouldn't hear a word of it, of course, but it served to keep her own fear at bay, and filled the awkward silence until Liz carried the teapot to the table and sat beside her.

And then the words came out in a rush. 'I telephoned the hospital about half an hour ago, Aunt Flora . . . I had to know . . .'

Flora let go the breath she had been holding; against all the odds, it seemed, Kathleen had survived the night. And as she pieced together the more coherent parts of Liz's rambling account, what came through most vividly was the remarkable strength of character shown by this, her favourite niece. It had always been there, of course, but now it was as though Liz had grown up overnight. With this thought came the realization how very like Kathleen she was.

'Dr Graham called in last evening to tell us that Mam and the baby were still very poorly.' The milk jug rattled the rim of the cup as Liz poured. 'He said something about blood transfusions, and that Dad was staying on . . . He said there was no way they could have made him leave, short of carrying him out.' Her voice trembled. 'It sounds very bad.'

Oh Michael! Flora's heart contracted. 'It does, child. But your mother's a bonny fighter, for all that she's given us a few frights in her time. I remember, when she was about nine, she caught scarlet fever. Her temperature raged for days, and Dr Graham could do nothing for her. The priest was on the point of giving her the last rites that time, too. But she confounded everyone by pulling through. She did it then, and she'll do it again, you'll see.'

Liz wanted to believe her. Oh, how she wanted to believe! She watched her aunt take out her pretty cigarette case, and light up a cigarette with fingers that shook. As the grey whorls of smoke curled upwards, Flora blinked several times and said 'Oh, damn – I'm always getting the smoke in my eyes!' And then she smiled at Liz in wry recognition of the lie, and in a curious way it bound them together.

'Oh, Aunt Flora, I am *glad* you came.'

'Well, that makes two of us. How has Dad taken it?'

'He was ever so upset last night, but by the time he went out on the rounds this morning, he was busy trying to cheer us all up.'

'Good for him. Now, when I've had another cup of this excellent tea, I'm going straight round to the hospital to find out what's happening.'

They let Flora in at once.

The sight of Kathy lying so still, so frighteningly white, as if she hadn't an ounce of blood left in her, set her trembling. Hospitals – how she hated them. She remembered the night John had died, and, for one awful moment, feared that she would faint. *Daft besom, you're not the fainting kind! You'd be no use to Michael or anyone, then*. Not that Michael was even aware that she was there.

She went quietly to his side, and laid a hand on his shoulder. A quiver ran through him, but he didn't take his eyes off Kathleen, or in any way acknowledge her presence. And so she left the hand where it was, making no further attempt to break his unnerving concentration. Only when a nurse brought cups of tea for them both did he come to, with a kind of shudder. The nurse drew forward a chair and whispered to her, 'See if you can't get the poor man to have a bit of a rest.'

Flora studied her brother-in-law's haggard face as she sipped her tea, and would have given anything to be able to take him in her arms. With little hope of being heeded, she cleared her throat. 'Michael, listen to me. This can't go on. You need a break – a sleep. I know well enough that you've not left Kathy's side for the best part of fourteen hours.'

There was no sign that he had heard.

'It's not as if she even knows you're here.'

'She knows.' Michael's voice was expressionless, but his eyes, red-ringed and bloodshot, burned with a certainty that gave Flora goose pimples.

'All right – if you say so. But if Kathy does know, she won't want you wearing yourself into a state of collapse. Look, I'll stay with her for a bit . . .'

'No. The blame is mine, and there's only me can hold her safe.'

'Oh, give over, Michael. That's daft talk, if I ever heard it. Blame, indeed!'

'You don't understand. Go home, Flora. You're very good, but . . .'

'No, dammit, I'm not good!' she declared angrily, beginning to wonder if he was unhinged by grief. 'But I *am* bloody-minded. And for all that you might tell me to save my breath, Kathy is my sister and I want to help. I've a right to help!' Her words made little impression. 'Oh, why will you *never* take anything from me?' She stopped, appalled, the tears running down her cheeks.

Into the uncomfortable silence that followed, came a thin thread of a voice, 'Stubborn – the both of you.'

Once Kathleen was out of danger, everyone grew more cheerful.

Michael resumed work, and his frightening air of remoteness gradually left him. Even Shirley Anne did all that was asked of her without complaint. She had come home, brimming over with excitement, eager to tell of all the grand people she'd met and the praise that had been heaped upon her, only to find that overnight her whole world had shifted.

Mam was very quiet when Liz visited her, but that was only to be expected, and one of the nurses had let her see Baby George, named for the King. George, like Mam, had retained a tenacious hold on life. He was asleep when she peeped into the cot, and seemed incredibly tiny, but he had a silky cap of gingery hair, just like Dad's.

They all longed for the day when Mam would be allowed home. But when she did bring George home, she was listless and prone to tears, showing little interest in what had been happening in her absence, and none at all in the business. Liz had desperately wanted to talk to her about Ellen, who had quietly taken to coming in for a couple of hours here and there, to relieve her of some of the household chores, and do whatever else was needed.

Liz knew that Ellen must be paid, and she'd hoped that Mam would tell her how much. Her own instinct was to make it sufficient for the Cassidys to be able to do away with the Relief altogether, as it seemed likely that Ellen was going to become an indispensable part of their lives for the foreseeable future. Liz had tried broaching the subject with Dad, but he just said he'd leave it to her. So in the end, she and Ellen settled the matter between them.

It worried Liz, too, that Mam's rosary beads had lain unused on the small table beside the bed since she came home. A great one for saying the rosary, was Mam, and she almost always had a novena on the go – to Our Lady, or the Little Flower of Lisieux, or St Jude. But now even that seemed to be too much trouble for her. If matters don't improve soon, Liz thought, I'll be sending up novenas to St Jude, patron of hopeless cases, myself.

'What's wrong, Dad?' she asked in despair, after Mam had given Father Clarkson short shrift when he'd called to see her. 'It's not like Mam to be rude to a priest.'

Michael was evasive. 'Father was very understanding about it. They must be used to such things. It's just a phase your mother's going through, Lizzie, love. It'll pass.'

Kathleen seemed to be using her weakness quite deliberately as an excuse to get out of nursing the baby, no matter how much the doctor tried to coax her. Time after time Liz prepared Georgy's bottle, only to have Mam say fretfully, 'Oh, you feed him, love. He gets too heavy for me.' And because Liz couldn't bear to see the tiny scrap rejected, she did so, giving him extra cuddles for comfort.

'She is very anaemic still,' Dr Graham told them, 'and that makes her very tired. The iron tablets will help, and you must get her to eat lots of good nourishing food to build her up – as much raw, or very lightly cooked liver as she'll take, and things like spinach, watercress – I'll make you a list. A tonic might help, but it's a slow business, I'm afraid – you'll all need a lot of patience.' He hesitated, his glance resting on Michael and Liz in turn. 'What concerns me more is Kathleen's reluctance to nurse baby George. You must try to encourage her, or we could have a tricky situation on our hands later.'

Michael heard the words, but felt powerless to act. He had used up all his reserves, and no longer seemed to be able to get through to Kathleen. An undemonstrative man at best, he found himself tongue-tied and afraid when faced with her lack of response. He had been sleeping on the sofa downstairs since she came home, so as not to disturb her, and as the weeks passed, a chasm grew between them. Increasingly, he took refuge in work, or in his books.

Sometimes, when they were alone, Liz would come and sit on the arm of his chair, coaxing him to talk, even taking issue with him over something quite trivial in order to get a response. This didn't always work, but he would hug her and say, 'You're a good lass, Lizzie,' before retreating into silence again. Once she found him standing beside the pram, watched him pick Georgy up – arms that could lift a two-hundred-and-eighty pound sack of flour handling the baby with exquisite gentleness. And the sadness in his face almost broke Liz's heart.

'Honestly, Aunt Flora,' she was driven to confide on one of her aunt's frequent visits, 'I don't understand. Mam must see she's hurting Dad. She knows how much he loves her.'

'Maybe she does, but the mind's a complex instrument, so the Freuds and Jungs of this world would have us believe, and there's no knowing what mixed-up notions your Mam's got swimming round in her head.'

But Flora didn't understand it either. She had already made tentative enquiries of her own doctor as to who was the top man in the psychiatric field, and if matters didn't improve soon, she would insist on a consultation, whether Michael liked it or not.

'It's the same with Georgy. Even though Mam's up and about, now, she doesn't seem to want him near her.' Liz leaned over the pram, jiggling the blue woollen ball she had made and hung on a ribbon for him. 'And he's such a placid little soul.'

A sight too placid, Flora thought, not for the first time, as Georgy's eyes watched the movement without curiosity. But then, what did she know about babies? At six weeks, maybe she wouldn't have shown much enthusiasm, either.

A couple of weeks later Flora jiggled the ball herself, and this time she knew what it was that bothered her; there was an apathy about Georgy's response, or lack of it. Had no-one else noticed? She said nothing, but the moment she got home she rang Dr Graham, and asked him straight out. There was silence at the other end.

'Come on, Doc. You know me – there's no way I'm going to be fobbed off.'

Again there was a pause. A sigh. 'I think you had better come and see me.'

'Tomorrow,' she said. 'Better still, come over and dine with me in the evening.'

Alec Graham's Scottish dourness grappled with the temptations of the flesh. It was a long time since he'd had a really good dinner. His housekeeper's fare tended towards the practical – hotpots that would survive erratic hours and the inevitable call-out. 'Mrs Hetherington – Flora – I can't just drop my evening surgery.'

There was exasperation in his voice, but she could tell he was tempted.

'Rubbish. I'm sure you could find someone to take it for you for once. The change would do you good.' Flora played her trump card. 'I happen to know that Mrs Meadows has an excellent piece of sirloin in the larder.'

They dined in the morning room. 'Much cosier. The dining room's like a barn with less than eight people.' Flora wore a gently flowing gown of soft green, he a dinner suit from which the odd stain had been ineffectually sponged. The sirloin was medium rare, accompanied by an excellent claret, and followed by one of Mrs Meadows' special apple pies with cream. Flora, adept at entertaining, made sure that the conversation remained stimulating, but light. Only when they had moved to the drawing room, and Dr Graham was settled in a comfortable chair with coffee, a Havana cigar, and the whisky decanter at his elbow, did she turn to more serious matters, by which time some, if not all, of his scruples had been overcome.

'It's much too early to be certain. We can only watch and monitor the child's progress. Like you, I have observed a certain sluggishness – but it could just be that he's a lazy baby.'

'Or there could be something wrong?'

Graham ran a hand over his thick white hair, drew on his cigar and chose his words with care. 'There is no physical disability, nor any obvious indication of mental deficiency, as with mongolism. So any damage, if damage there is, should be slight. On rare occasions a baby is unavoidably deprived of oxygen for vital seconds, but Latimer is of the opinion that this was unlikely in your nephew's case. A deficiency occasionally presents when the mother conceives rather late in life – in such cases, there is often no known cause.'

'I see,' Flora sighed. 'And Kathleen and Michael know nothing of this?'

'As yet, my dear Flora, there is nothing to know.'

Flora sat forward suddenly. 'This may sound crazy to you, but I think Kathleen may sense something, deep down – a kind of mother's intuition?'

'I have had that thought myself,' he said slowly. 'It might account for her reluctance to accept the child. But it changes nothing, and I would still prefer to bide my time.'

'Fair enough. You're the doctor.' Flora stubbed out her cigarette. 'But if and when you should come to any conclusions, I want the best advice there is – money no object.'

'Michael is a proud man.'

'Damn his pride,' she said.

Chapter Sixteen

The atmosphere at home soon began to affect them all. Joey found numerous excuses to be out with Eddie, and Shirley Anne spent more and more time at Mrs Frith's. 'I don't know how you stick it,' she retorted, when Liz took her to task for not doing more to help. 'This place doesn't feel like home any more.'

'That's a terrible thing to say!'

But there was a grain of truth in Shirley Anne's words. They all felt it.

For Chris, it spelled the end for him and Sally. Things hadn't been the same between them since the disagreement about Mollie on Coronation Day. And the extra hours he'd been putting in since then, plus all the worry, had finally led to a tremendous row in the yard outside the bakehouse. Liz, coming through from the shop, heard Sally at the height of her tirade – in fact, the whole street must have heard.

'I'm sick of it!' Sally was pummelling Chris's chest with her fists, her face almost as red as her hair. 'Sick of hangin' around till you condescend to find time to take me out! I'm sorry about yer Mam, but it's family first with you Ryans, you an' yer flamin' business! Always was and always will be! I've had it up to 'ere!' Her hand flashed under her chin.

Chris, as pale as she was flushed, with a white line round his mouth, was just standing there, making no attempt to fend her off. 'If that's the way you feel, you know what you can do!'

'Yeh, yer right, I do know! Fer a start, I can find someone who'll give me a good time – somethin' I'm sure as hell never goin' to have with you!'

Before Liz could fly to her brother's defence, Sally tossed her red curls and was away down the street, her high heels clattering. 'Well, it's good riddance to bad rubbish, if you ask me!' she said.

And Chris, her mild brother, who hadn't a violent bone in him, turned on her with something close to a snarl.

'It was awful,' she blurted out to Jimmy later. 'He said no-one had asked me, and it was time I stopped trying to mind other people's business!'

Jimmy pulled her close. 'Yeh, well, tact never was your strong point, was it, kid?'

A wry affection in his voice, combined with the feel of his arms around her, brought all her careful defences crashing down. Jimmy was familiar and safe, and even if he did occasionally go out with older, more sophisticated girls, at least he never made any secret of it. Her tears soaked into his jacket as she sobbed out all her pent-up misery. 'Oh, Jimmy, everything's so awful, with Mam hardly speaking, and Dad grieving inside . . .' Her voice rose to a wail. 'No-one remembered my birthday – and Shirley Anne says I'm beginning to smell of baby-sick and nappies . . .' She lifted a tear-streaked face to him. 'I'm not, am I?'

Jimmy made an incoherent sound and drew her closer. They were alone in the living room, and after a moment's hesitation he picked her up and carried her across to Michael's chair. As he held her and shushed her gently, Liz's arms wrapped themselves convulsively round his neck.

'I wonder you haven't g-got fed up, too.'

'Would it matter to you if I had?'

In the comforting warmth of this new intimacy, Liz suddenly realized that it would matter quite a lot. She drew a hiccuping breath and tried to sit up to tell him so, but Jimmy's hand was behind her head, guiding it towards him. He began kissing her, gently at first, and then, as she didn't resist, with more insistence, until she found her mouth opening quite naturally to him. Although it still made her feel very peculiar, the sensation wasn't half as disagreeable as she had once thought. Furthermore, her body was behaving in the oddest and most pleasurable way . . . and so, she realized, turning hot with embarrassment, was his. Sister Benedict's grim warnings flashed through her mind, yet she seemed incapable of movement. Jimmy's breath, close against her ear, sounded as if he'd been running very fast, and his free hand moved to cup her breast, his thumb insistently stroking her nipple. And it was then, shocked by what was happening, that she struggled to pull away. At once he stopped.

'It's all right, Liz – it's all right.' His voice was oddly husky. 'I'm sorry, I didn't mean for that to happen, honestly I didn't. It was just having you so near – I got a bit carried away.'

But when he tried to settle her back in his arms she resisted, and he finally let her go. She scrambled to her feet, hardly able to look him in the eye. When she did, he was grinning at her, and indignation immediately replaced embarrassment.

'How dare you laugh at me? You ought to be ashamed, taking advantage!'

Jimmy, unabashed, stood up and straightened his jacket. 'Oh, come down off your high horse, Liz, it's no big deal. I reckon you enjoyed it, really. Go on, admit it.'

'I did not!' she exclaimed. But his grin was infectious. 'Oh, you!'

'Maybe it's time we stopped messing about and considered getting engaged.' The words came out spontaneously, taking him by surprise.

Liz was equally taken aback, new colour flooding into her face as her heart began to thump. 'You mean. . . ? Oh, no, we couldn't. Not now – I'm not . . . not . . .'

'Not in love with me?'

She heard the slight grate in his voice, and became even more confused. Was what she felt for Jimmy love? But even if it was, at the back of her mind an insistent voice was whispering that marriage would probably spell the end of all her ambitions and dreams.

'I don't know,' she said with incurable honesty. 'I'm very fond of you, but I'm only just seventeen, and there's so much I want to do. Besides . . .' She looked around helplessly.

'Yeh. I know. Bad timing.'

Jimmy was piqued. He could think of half a dozen girls who'd leap at the chance of marrying him. Still, on reflection, the blow to his pride was outweighed by relief. Sure, a part of him did want Liz; they'd kind of grown together. They both had drive and ambition, and with their combined skills, there was no knowing what they might not achieve. But although life with Liz would never be dull, the world was a big place, and he still had some living to do before he settled for marriage – and babies.

'It's all right,' he said brusquely. 'Forget I spoke.'

'I don't want to forget! I'm . . .' She searched for the right word. '. . . honoured.'

Their eyes met, and they both laughed suddenly at its pomposity.

'My pleasure. Maybe I'll try again next year. I don't give up easily.'

Liz didn't tell anyone what had happened, not even Clare. But just knowing how Jimmy felt about her did wonders for her morale, and for a while everything seemed a little brighter.

But the problem remained, and on an oppressive Sunday late in July, with thunder in the air, matters finally came to a head.

Once Mam was up and about, Sunday dinner resumed its usual ritual – though for all their efforts to tempt her, she mostly picked at her food. On this day, apart from her and Dad, only Liz, Rita, Chris and Dandy were home. Joey had been invited to spend the day with the Killigans, who were going on a charabanc trip to Blackpool, Shirley Anne was away helping Mrs Frith with a luncheon party, and Jimmy, who came round most Sundays, wasn't arriving until later.

Rita had insisted on cooking a roast, though no-one really wanted a hot meal. Liz could feel her new square-necked gingham dress sticking to her back. Towards the end of dinner, as the first rumbles of thunder echoed in the distance, she pushed her meal away, half-eaten, and took a deep breath.

'I know we don't usually talk shop on a Sunday, but these days it's the only time we seem to be together.' She looked round the table, half defiantly, her eyes coming at last to Michael. 'It's about the bakehouse, Dad. I have mentioned it before . . .'

Her words dropped like stones into a pond, and she could feel the reaction rippling outwards. Chris, who was still upset at losing Sally, as well as being worried about Mam, gave her an exasperated look.

Rita said, 'Do we have to talk about it now?'

'Yes, we do. With four of us working in there now, we're bursting at the seams, and if we don't do something about it soon, there's going to be an accident. Ask Chris – ask Dad. It's a wonder Missy and her kittens haven't been squashed under foot, we fall over them that often. And there's the van . . .'

Michael laid down his knife and fork and folded his serviette before looking up to meet the challenging eyes of his daughter. 'What you say's true enough, Lizzie, love, but I'm not sure now is the time.'

'You keep on saying that, Dad. But there never will be a right time unless we make one. You've as good as admitted we need another van. Jimmy thinks he might have found one, *and* he's been teaching me to drive. We will need it. Mr Morgan is very keen to start selling more high class confectionery this autumn, and there'll be lots more interest, nearer Christmas.'

'Oh, really!' Rita pushed back her chair and began to collect plates, clattering the cutlery in her agitation. 'I sometimes wonder what's got into you, our Liz, you and your obsession with that Café Candide. As for all your talk of *tortes* and *milles feuilles* and *petit fours* – that's not what Ryan's is about. Ever since that man Lendl came . . .'

'Don't you dare say anything about Fritz!'

'Easy, girls,' murmured Dandy, though without any real expectation of being heeded. The quarrel had the makings of a good honest-to-God ding-dong, and there was nothing like a full-blooded row for clearing the air. What effect it might have on his Kathy was debatable, but he was fast coming to the conclusion that it was going to take more than time and a lot of fancy doctors to cure her malaise, whatever Flora might think. So he was not entirely displeased when no-one took a blind bit of notice of him.

'. . . we owe a lot to Fritz, and what's more, he's a brilliant confectioner.' There was a vivid flash of lightening. Liz flinched and automatically paused to count the seconds before the clap of thunder came. 'If even a fraction of Fritz Lendl's skill rubs off on me, I shall be undyingly grateful! No business can stand still, it has to grow – and he's made me recognize something inside me, a – a *need*. I can't describe it . . .' Liz swung round to her mother, desperate for her support. '*You* know what I'm talking about, Mam. Tell her!'

But the woman who stared back at her from lacklustre eyes, whose blue shantung dress, once a perfect fit, now hung from her shoulders, bore no resemblance to the woman whose sharpness and drive had always kept them on their toes. And suddenly Liz couldn't bear it – she couldn't believe her mother had changed that much. 'Mam, you *know* I'm right. This is what I want, what you always wanted, dreamed about – that Ryan's would one day become known for quality.'

It was Rita who answered for her. 'Yes, but honest-to-goodness English quality, not fancy foreign rubbish!'

'Mam?' Liz was insistent. Lightening flashed again, the crackle of thunder following almost at once, but this time she didn't even notice. 'Mam?'

All Kathleen's nerve ends were silently screaming. She didn't want Liz reminding her. All those years when she had allowed ambition to drive her, and where had it got her? Nowhere. Dreams – what use were dreams to anyone? Peace and quiet, that was all she asked for now; to be left alone . . .

And then she looked into her daughter's eyes, and found herself unable to look away. Such eloquent, pleading eyes, passionately willing her to respond. Something stirred deep inside her – something that she thought had died giving her baby life – and, like a birth pain, wouldn't be pushed away. Liz's face became a blur.

'Enough, girls, the both of you.' Michael could not endure the sight of Kathleen's pale face a moment longer, the tears filling her eyes; the anguish of it was in his voice. 'I will not have your mother upset. God in heaven, has she not enough to bear?'

'Dad's right,' said Chris, unnerved by the pressure building up. 'You're just making everything worse, Liz.'

His accusation brought Liz to her feet, tears thick in her own throat. 'That's not fair! I wouldn't upset Mam for the world! But what about *me*? I have such plans, but they'll never see daylight at this rate. It's fine for Rita, scoffing at my ideas – her future's all sorted, and she doesn't have to bear the brunt of running the shop, the house, as well as looking after the baby, an' – an' everything.'

The storm building outside seemed to be having an effect on what was happening in the stifling living room, where tempers were well and truly boiling over. Like the tears that were spilling over, running unnoticed down Liz's cheeks.

'It's the way you wanted things.' Rita was full of righteous indignation. 'You aren't the only one who's been working all the hours there are – and I more than pull my weight when I'm here!'

'I *know* you do! I wasn't getting at you, honest. You've been smashing! It's this place – the atmosphere. Our Shirley Anne was right for once, when she said it wasn't like home any more – and I don't know how much longer I can stand it!'

'Lizzie, for the love of God, will you be still!' Michael's voice was almost unrecognizable.

'No, Dad, I won't! I can't. We've tried being patient like Dr Graham said, but it's not getting us anywhere.' Liz was frightened by the hysteria she could feel building up inside her, but she was powerless to stop it. Her voice shook with the force of holding it at bay, and she gripped the table edge. 'Mam, we need you back with us – really back, like you used to be, shoutin' and telling us off. Surely this can't be the way you want things – you like a stranger, and Dad keeping out of your way so you won't be disturbed? Mam, he's so unhappy, I can't bear it.' Her teeth were beginning to chatter. She heard her father's chair scrape back, and knew her time was up. And still Mam's face remained a blank. Had anything sunk in? In a last throw of despair, she rushed on. 'If you don't care about the rest of us, what about poor little Georgy? He's the sweetest baby, I love him, and I'll do anything for him for as long as I have to – but he's not *my* baby, he's yours, and it's you he needs.'

The silence that followed was palpable. Liz sat down abruptly, shaking from head to foot as she realized the enormity of what she had done. She wrapped her hands round her head, tears locking her throat, stifling her – unable to look up for fear she might have sent Mam right over the edge.

Into the silence rose a thin wail, gathering momentum as Georgy awoke and demanded his dinner. *Oh, damn*. She wiped a shaking hand across her face and muttered thickly, 'It's all right. I'll go.'

But Dandy, who had been watching Kathleen closely, put out a staying hand. 'Wait, now, young Lizzie.'

They all watched as Mam got up and moved like a sleepwalker into the scullery, where the pram was beginning to rock vigorously.

'What have you done?' Rita whispered. 'May God forgive you, Liz, if you've driven Mam too far! There's no knowing what mischief she might do him.'

But Michael was right behind his wife, the tears running in rivulets down his cheeks as he watched Kathleen lift the baby out and hush him gently. And as the first heart-wrenching sob broke from her, he held her and the baby close.

'Oh, Michael – the poor helpless wee mite!'

'It's all right, *acushla*. George will be fine. Everything will be fine now.'

In the living room, Dandy said quietly, 'God is good.'

And then the rain came – blessed healing rain, bouncing off the rooftops so that the ground was awash within moments. And the tears Liz had been struggling to contain flooded out too.

She pushed back her chair and ran upstairs to fling herself on her bed, sobbing uncontrollably. She hadn't known there were so many tears in her. Rita came, awkwardly apologetic, for clearly this was no ordinary outburst, and after her came Dandy, then Dad. She was aware of the emotion in his voice as he stroked her hair and assured her that everything was going to be all right. She heard the words, but they didn't stop the flow. And then Mam came, and sat on the bed beside her.

'My poor Liz,' she said, sounding tired, but already more like her old self. 'So eager to give, and I've taken so much. I don't know how I'm ever going to make it up to you.'

Liz turned to bury her head against her mother's knee, her voice muffled. 'No, no, no! That isn't what . . . I didn't expect . . . I just want you to be yourself again! That's all any of us want.'

'Yes.' Kathleen uttered a great sigh, and raised her daughter up. Her eyes were tired, but clear. 'You may have to bear with me for a little while, yet – just till I'm stronger.'

'Oh, I will – we all will!' Liz flung her arms round her mother, clinging to the brittle frame, sobbing afresh as guilt and pity and love welled up in her.

'Hush, child – you'll make yourself ill.'

But Liz couldn't stop crying, and in the end Michael sent for Dr Graham. He gave her a thorough going-over, after which he pushed his spectacles down his nose and looked at her over the top of them.

'Exhaustion,' he said. 'You've been doing too much for too long, young lady.'

So she was packed off to stay with Aunt Flora for a whole blissful week, to be fussed over by Mrs Meadows and have breakfast brought up to her bed, all beautifully laid out on a tray by Gracie. But, best of all, she had Aunt Flora to herself.

At her aunt's insistence, Caulderbank had put a couple of deckchairs under the hawthorn tree at the far end of the big oval lawn, grumbling all the while about the marks they would make in his lawn. He had been gardener at Rose Lodge for as long as anyone could remember, and was as gnarled and crabby as the great trees he tended with such loving care.

'Take no notice,' said Flora. 'He enjoys a good grumble.'

The weather was fresher after the storm, and they spent several days picnicking and talking about everything except the recent past, which was a forbidden subject.

And when her niece's skin had taken on a faint dusting of tan, and the light was back in her eyes, Flora took her shopping in town, where they spent a whole afternoon going into one exclusive dress shop after another. Liz managed a token protest, but her heart wasn't in it. By the end of the afternoon, Peters had enough boxes to fill the trunk of the car – hat boxes and dress boxes with names like Cannell and Broadbents and Bobby's scrawled elegantly across them. Liz drew a laughing breath, and wondered how she would justify so many lovely things to her sisters.

'I think we've earned a cup of tea,' said Flora, who hadn't enjoyed herself so much for years. 'Where is it to be, Thom's or Woodheads? Or we could go into the Leyland Arcade and maybe have music with it.'

It was a difficult decision. 'Oh, Woodheads, I think. Their cakes are so good, and I'd like to cast a critical eye over them.'

Flora laughed. 'Weighing up the opposition? You're going to make a fine businesswoman one day, Liz Ryan.'

Her words encouraged Liz to confide some of her ideas to Aunt Flora over dinner that evening – including her long-term aim to have a series of small shops in selected areas, selling her own exclusive confectionery.

'I'm not belittling what Dad and Chris do – it's fine, the best of its kind. But I don't believe it's where my talents lie – and I'm learning so much from Fritz, Aunt Flora. Later on, he is going to teach me to make chocolates and bon-bons – the way he made them in Vienna. And one day I shall sell them in elegant boxes, with *Elizabeth Ryan* in plain gold letters across the lid.'

'Goodness!'

Liz lifted her chin. 'I haven't told a single soul about this.'

'My dear, no-one will hear it from me.'

Liz had the grace to blush. 'I'm sorry, Aunt Flora. I didn't mean – It's just – well, I know it all sounds terribly far-fetched. Our Rita's already accused me of dreaming impossible dreams, and she doesn't know the half of it. But I'm not, truly. Oh, I know it won't happen tomorrow, or even next year, but I'm convinced that nothing is impossible, if you really believe you can do it.'

Flora applauded her tenacity, and made a mental note to contact her man of business, to set him looking for likely properties in which she might invest.

PART TWO

LIZ
1938

Chapter One

May 1938

'See, Georgy – see the pretty candle?' Liz held the cake just out of reach, a prettily-iced white confection with one blue candle in the middle.

Georgy, firmly strapped into the padded high-chair, watched the flame flicker, but made no attempt to reach for it like a normal, curious one-year-old.

'Shall we blow it out together?'

'Yeh, come on, Georgy,' Joey encouraged him. 'All together, now – ready, steady, blow.'

'Easy, lad.' Michael's quiet voice intervened. 'Don't get him over-excited.'

Kathleen smiled faintly at the protective concern in his voice. Dear Michael – always patient, always caring. So different from her. The anaemia that had plagued her since Georgy's birth had taken its toll. She was still impatient, still driven mad with frustration at times, but in her heart she knew that the old whirlwind Kathleen had gone forever. And although she wasn't yet ready to sit back and smell the roses, life at a slower pace had brought compensations. She was blessed in so many ways – there was Michael, of course, and Dandy, who was a tower of strength these days. And how many women could claim to be so fortunate in their children?

It had taken her a long time to come to terms with the guilt that still lay uneasily on her conscience, despite the consolation and expiation gained under the seal of the confessional – guilt that she had resented Georgy from the moment of his conception, that throughout her pregnancy, she had put the reality of his existence second to her love for Michael. And yet, thanks in great measure to Liz, it was Georgy with his limited intellect and great capacity for affection, who had forged new bonds of love between herself and Michael, and had, in a curious way, brought the whole family closer.

Liz was never sure how much Georgy understood, but apart from the odd tantrum, he was a placid, lovable child, and there were times when she was sure she glimpsed a flicker of awareness – like today, when he seemed to know that he was the centre of attention. The specialist Aunt Flora had insisted they should see wasn't committing himself as yet, but he did seem optimistic that with lots of stimulation, Georgy might eventually show considerable improvement.

She was glad everyone had made an effort to get home in time for the birthday tea – Shirley Anne had actually stayed home for the day, and Rita managed to get back early from the school in Toxteth where she now taught. Even Aunt Laura had driven over from Bootle, though without the twins, Martin and May.

'Mother's looking after them,' she explained diffidently. 'They were both coming down with colds, and we wouldn't want to give the birthday boy their germs, would we?'

'Small chance of that,' said Aunt Flora, blunt as ever. 'It's a constant source of wonder to me, how those two of yours manage to get colds or tummy upsets to order.'

'Flo,' Kathleen pleaded, because Laura looked flushed and close to tears.

'That's very considerate of you, Laura,' Michael said quietly, knowing fine how embarrassed she must feel about Georgy's disability, when she had two lively children. 'It was good of you to come.'

Even Joey, now in his third term at St Francis Xavier's, had foregone his beloved Scouts for once.

Joining the Sea Scouts had become a serious bone of contention between him and Eddie.

'Wat'yer want ter do a daft thing like that for?' Liz had heard Eddie mutter in disgust. 'All that *dib-dibbing* an' doin' good deeds!'

'It's not like that,' Joey explained. 'You join a patrol and learn all kinds of useful things, like tying different knots and learning to sail a boat. *And* you get to go camping.'

'We done that plenty o' times without joinin' any flamin' scouts.'

'I mean proper camping, for several days at a time – not messin' about down the *Cassie* with a couple of Tate and Lyle sacks held up by sticks.'

There had been an ominous silence, followed by a full-blooded raspberry that obviously came from the heart. '*That* fer yer precious scouts! Yer know somethin'? Yer gettin' dead borin', you are!'

It seemed to Liz that the friendship was doomed, which might be a blessing in disguise. She set great store by loyalty to friends, but Eddie Killigan kept dubious company these days, and seemed likely to end up like his older brothers, who were frequently in trouble with the police, in which case, Joey would be well out of it. But she didn't want him turning into a snob, either, like Shirley Anne, who had already dropped Lily in favour of more affluent friends. Liz occasionally saw the over-plump Lily, who was finding it hard to get a job, hovering outside the shop looking lost, and couldn't help feeling sorry for her.

The past year had seen great changes, not least in the bakehouse. Liz had returned from her visit to Birkdale to find plans for expansion already well under way, and just for a moment she had felt aggrieved – after all, it was her persistence that had prompted Dad to act. But how could she say so, when he so obviously hoped to please her? So she flung her arms round him instead, and he held her very tight.

'Eh, Lizzie love, we've missed your bright spirit about the place. But you're looking great now, girleen, that you are.' He stepped back in order to see her better, and Liz was shocked by how much white now peppered his hair. Surely it hadn't been that way a week ago – or had she just been too preoccupied to notice? 'And not too disappointed, I hope, that we've gone ahead without you?' She shook her head, but her eyes gave her away, and he drew her close again. 'To be honest, I'd no notion of moving so fast, only for Fritz pointing out that the solution was staring us in the face – and at a fraction of the cost of building new premises.'

He had been right, of course. The cellars that ran beneath the house and shop were dry and had easy access from the yard, as well as from the passage behind the shop. The largest one even had a window. Part of the area had been used as a coal store, but that was easily blocked off, and Missy's latest progeny made short work of any vermin.

So now Liz had her very own workplace – she and Fritz, for it had seemed sensible to fit the new premises out specifically for the making of confectionery, with the best equipment the firm could afford. The outlay had been worth every penny spent. Within the first six months, Ryan's new exclusive range had proved an unqualified success, Christmas being the high point.

That same autumn, one of Dad's oldest and best customers – a grocer in Everton, who had built up a steady market for Ryan's bread and cakes – had decided to retire, and after a lot of thought, Michael had acquired the lease. And with two shops, and a second van, a little of the old fire came back into Mam's eyes. She still lacked energy, but as the financial situation steadily improved, there was enough bookwork to keep her busy without entailing too much physical effort.

Mr Morgan had been delighted with the new ranges, for which the Candide was still the main showcase. 'I am already considering ways to enlarge my display counters in order to accommodate your delightful confections. The petit fours did particularly well at Christmas, and the demand continues.' He put an affectionate arm round her shoulders. 'Dear girl, I can never thank you enough for coaxing me into bringing this place back to life. Sometimes I can feel Candide's encouraging presence so strongly.'

The luxury range was beginning to sell well in other outlets, too, and in early spring, Ryan's opened a small shop near Sefton Park – part of a small block of property owned by Aunt Flora. Michael had eyed his sister-in-law with deep suspicion when she mentioned that it was coming up for letting.

She met his blue stare unflinchingly. 'You needn't look so po-faced, Michael Ryan. For your information, my business adviser suggested some time ago that I should put more money into property' – And may God forgive me for the white lie – 'This block was one of a group he bought up then. I have another in Waterloo, if you ever want to try your luck further afield. Anyway, it occurred to me that this particular shop is ideally placed for Lizzie's new project – subject to agreement on a fair rent, of course.'

Liz could have hugged her aunt. It was a darling shop, all freshly painted, and Dad had insisted that it should bear her own name, with 'Ryan's of Great Homer Street' in smaller lettering below.

ELIZABETH'S was open in time for Easter, and was destined to succeed from the very first day. Fritz made lots of chocolate

Easter eggs, from tiny to large, from very simple shapes to ornately decorated works of art. These, together with all their established lines, sold as fast as they could be made, not just there, but in all the shops.

The chocolate work fascinated Liz almost more than anything else. She spent every free moment watching Fritz stir the glossy mixture of cocoa butters and solids in a bowl over a pan of hot water, gently so that no bubbles should mar its smoothness. She listened as he explained about couvertures and the importance of temperature – how the butter was made up of a complexity of fats, each with a different melting and setting point.

'Now,' he said, 'we help this process by pouring it on to the marble slab and spreading it swiftly with the palette knife, making very sure that no water or steam comes near it. Then, as it begins to set, we gather it just as swiftly and put it back into the bowl to heat it up again, but to a lesser temperature this time.'

When it was ready, he polished the insides of the Easter egg moulds until they shone, and carefully brushed a thin layer into every crevice, letting it set and then repeating the process several times.

'One may, of course, pour the couverture in and run it round before tipping out the excess. It is quicker certainly, but there is not so good a finish. And I am used to the old ways.'

Fritz explained, too, how a wonderfully smooth filling could be made by mixing cream into the couverture and allowing it to set. 'This we call *ganache*. It can be varied with the addition of ground almonds or hazelnuts, or perhaps a little liqueur. It is then cut into shapes and dipped into the couverture to make chocolates.'

Liz longed to experiment, to learn more about fillings like praline and truffle, but although everyone in the family except for Joey was now gainfully employed, costs still had to be considered, and she knew that she must be patient.

By the time Georgy's first birthday came round, everything was going so well that Liz sometimes had to pinch herself. She and Fritz were having to work longer hours to meet the demand, and the shop still took some of her time. Ellen worked tirelessly, dividing herself between shop and house, popping home now and then to see that Arnie was all right. She looked brighter and more alive than she had for years, and she and Mam got on really well, while Dandy made himself responsible for Freddie and Georgy, who had established a definite rapport.

In one way the extra work was a blessing, for it helped to take Fritz's mind off less pleasant things. In March, Hitler had occupied Austria, and a brief shudder of apprehension had run through the country.

'Always it is March when that madman strikes,' Fritz had declared, weeping unashamedly for his homeland. 'And this will not be the end of his ambition. The Czechs will be next, you will see – he will take back the Sudetenland.'

A number of people seemed to share his view, and Liz felt the shadow of war come a chilling shade nearer. Dandy, of course, had always been pessimistic about Adolf Hitler and his 'goin's on', as he called them.

'But it won't really come to war, will it, Grandpa Dandy?' she'd asked him, almost pleadingly. 'I mean, isn't the League of Nations supposed to stop such things happening?'

'The League is dead, chuck. Has been for a long time, only no-one's got round to givin' it a decent burial. Most folk are a bit like old Canute, y'see – they think a few bits of paper will work miracles. An' they might, if you was dealin' with anyone but a jumped up little meglomaniac like Adolf – eats bits of paper for breakfast, he does, an' you can't reason with that kind of a man.'

A bit like Alec Munnings, in fact; he hadn't exactly been open to reason, either. Liz hadn't thought about Alec for some time. Shortly after the incident with Boadicea and the cakes, he had inherited quite a lot of money from a godparent, and gone swanning off to London and the good life. Chris knew someone who worked in Munnings' bakehouse, who reckoned Mr Munnings had got to hear about his son's reckless driving, and there'd been a blazing row. Whatever the whole truth, it was good riddance, as far as she was concerned.

'Come, come – we do not fall into daydreams.' Fritz recalled her to what she was doing. He was a hard taskmaster. She watched, and attempted to copy, as he piped meringue into the exquisite shapes outlined on a large floured baking sheet, so different from her pathetic attempts of two Christmases ago. She marvelled at his sure touch, his ability to concentrate, even though his mind must be far away, and she despaired of ever achieving his degree of excellence.

'We do not speak of failure,' he reproved her. 'It needs only time – and practice, practice, practice. Now, we will make up the tortes that are ordered for tomorrow, and then I will show you how to make Fritz Lendl's special strudel pastry.'

Liz watched his nimble fingers lightly drawing together the butter, the flour, the water and the eggs, until they became a smooth dough which he formed into two round balls.

'So, we leave it to rest while we prepare the filling. There are many versions, but for now, it shall be my simple *apfel-streusel.*' Together they sliced the apples thinly, toasted breadcrumbs in butter, and measured sugar and cinnamon. 'And, for special occasions, we add a little rum.' His eyes twinkled. 'Now the paste should be ready. We spread a cloth – so – and dust it well with flour.' Fritz took one of the balls of dough and pinned it out thinly on the cloth. Then he slid both hands underneath and began to work it out with his fists, thinner and thinner, tossing it round until Liz was sure it would break. By the time he laid it back on the cloth, it was almost transparent.

'Now you will try,' he said, indicating the remaining dough.

The pinning out was easy, but when Liz came to lift and stretch the paste, it wrapped itself round her arms – went everywhere, in fact, except where it was meant to be. 'Oh, no!' she cried. 'I'll never be able to do it.'

'Never,' said Fritz inexorably, 'is a word we do not permit. It requires only practice. Now, we finish the first strudel.'

Chapter Two

It was early July, and the ballroom was a sea of brilliant summer voiles and ninon as the Saturday night crowd, ignoring the lure of the warm evening outside, danced to some of the finest dance music in the country.

'The Grafton?' Liz had squeaked when Jimmy first suggested it. 'We can't go there.'

'Why not?'

Liz couldn't think of a convincing reason, except that they'd never been anywhere quite that posh. They had long since graduated from places like Blair Hall, with its unpleasant associations, and she was by now a reasonably accomplished dancer.

'What's wrong with Burton Chambers?'

'Nothing. But an eighteenth birthday is special, so just give in gracefully.'

Liz hadn't really taken much persuading. The Grafton Rooms had style, and you could dance to wonderful bands like Mrs Wilf Hamer's, or visiting ones like Joe Loss and Billy Cotton, who broadcast regularly on the wireless. It was the kind of place where 'real' ballroom dancers went. They had floor shows, too.

'We could ask our Rita and Chris – make a family party of it.'

This wasn't exactly what Jimmy had envisaged, but as Liz began to wax enthusiastic, he knew better than to argue. Rita had always been a bit too sharp-tongued for his liking, though she'd mellowed a bit in the last few months, especially since she'd started going out with Frank Duncan, the brother of a fellow teacher. As for Chris – he'd been avoiding dance halls like the plague since Sally'd jilted him. Jimmy doubted whether even Liz would be able to talk him round.

But Liz was determined that Chris would join her birthday celebrations. 'It's high time you gave over feeling sorry for yourself,' she told him with sisterly candour. 'There's plenty more fish in the sea.' This hadn't gone down too well, so she resorted to guile.

'If you must know, Chris, I'm counting on you to help me out. I want to ask Clare – she *is* my best friend, and we don't see half enough of one another these days. But she hasn't got a boy friend, and she won't want to be odd girl out.'

Chris still looked wary. 'What about Francis – isn't he at home?'

'No, he isn't, and besides, it wouldn't be much fun for Clare, coming with her brother. Anyway, it's my own big brother I want, not someone else's.' She saw he was wavering. 'Oh, come on, don't be a spoilsport. It's my birthday, and it's not as if you don't know Clare – she's practically family, for heaven's sake.' Which seemed to settle the matter.

The evening began awkwardly, with everyone feeling a bit self-conscious among the Grafton's regular Saturday night crowd, but as she and Jimmy, followed closely by the others, took to the floor for a lilting waltz, Liz knew everything would be fine. She had grown a good couple of inches in the last few months, and now her head was almost level with Jimmy's, cheek against cheek. She even had the perfect frock for the occasion – a floaty voile in soft gold, with narrow shoulder straps and a matching bolero jacket, a present from Aunt Flora. And she was wearing the little pearl earrings Jimmy had given her earlier.

'I'm ever so glad you thought of coming here.'

Jimmy's arm tightened. 'So am I. What's more, I've got myself the most luscious armful in the whole room.'

She giggled 'Flatterer. Are you going to propose again?' It had become a kind of joke between them.

'Would you say yes, if I did?'

'I might,' she whispered teasingly again his ear. 'It's just the night for it. Soft lights, sweet music, a new moon outside – what could be more romantic?' When he didn't answer, the laughter bubbled up again. 'You'd have kittens if I said yes.'

'You're a hard woman, Liz Ryan.'

'And you're a smooth-tongued rogue, Jimmy Marsden.'

They completed a full circle of the floor before he spoke again. 'What would you say if I told you I was thinking of applying for a job as a butcher on one of the Cunarders?'

Liz almost missed her step. 'I'd say – I suppose I'd say how much I'd miss you.' She realized that she meant it. 'But if it's really what you want, then I'd wish you luck.'

'I feel I'm in a rut. And all this talk about war has made me want to see something of the world while there's still a world to see.'

'Jimmy, don't! Not tonight.'

'Sorry, pet. Anyway, If I did decide to go, it'd probably only be for the one trip.' He drew her close. 'And it's nice to know you care.' With his face against her hair, he spun her round so that her dress lifted and swirled around her legs.

Leigh Farrell was waltzing in a more leisurely manner, enjoying the feel of black satin, warm and smooth as a second skin beneath his hand, as it rested in the curve of Monica Hazlett's back. He'd lay odds she wasn't wearing a stitch underneath. What a difference twelve months could make! Monica moved seductively against his hand, and he smiled, wondering how many more tricks she'd picked up along with this new veneer of sophistication.

As if aware that she was the object of his thoughts, Monica's mascara-laden lashes quivered and lifted, revealing reproachful blue eyes. 'Did you have to stay away so long?'

'That's life,' he murmured. 'A lot of things have changed back home. But we don't want to go into that just now.' His hand slid a fraction lower and he felt her breath catch. 'Quite a few changes round here, too, it seems. Your mother tells me you've got yourself a fine young beau – an Honourable, no less.'

'Oh, Edward's a sweetie.' She didn't exactly sound wildly in love. 'He's not here tonight.'

'I guessed as much.' Leigh thought of the gaggle of young men who hung about her, all eager to supplant the absent Edward. 'So when's the happy day?'

Monica shrugged and the satin rippled. 'We haven't decided. Probably in the autumn.'

At that moment Leigh's attention was caught by a swirl of gold; on the far side of the room, a couple were clearly enjoying themselves. They made a handsome picture. The young man, dark and sleek, was very sure of himself. But it was his partner who drew the eye – a graceful creature enveloped in spun gold, her hair fanning out and rippling in the soft light as she moved. At first he didn't recognize his young fairground companion of the previous year in this will-o'-the-wisp creature. Only when the music came to an end, and she stepped back from her partner, did he get a really good look at her. 'Well, I'll be . . .'

'What did you say, Leigh?'

He dragged his attention back to his companion. 'Sorry. . . ?'

'I thought you spoke,' she said.

'Not really. I just thought I saw . . .' Saw what? Some kind of transformation? For the child was a child no longer; in her place stood a young woman, not pretty exactly, but with a face that would make a man look – and look again.

He watched her thread her arm through the young man's, leaning towards him as they made their way across to the other side of the room, where her brother and Clare Whitney and another couple presently joined them.

Chris hadn't expected to enjoy the evening. The place might be different, and Clare was certainly no Sally, but he was bound to be reminded of times he was trying to forget. Only when Liz made up her mind about something, it would take a better man than him to deny her.

To be honest, the thought of spending an evening with Clare had terrified him. Clever people always made him feel thick, and it stood to reason that a girl who was set on being a doctor, no matter how often he'd said 'Hi' to her around the house, had to be above average clever. She was posh with it, too, which made him even more wary. So it came as a relief to discover that, in her own quiet way, Clare Whitney was surprisingly good company. She wasn't a bad little dancer, either, though some of the time they just sat and talked. He liked the way she had of lowering her head after making some dead serious comment, so that her straight fair hair slipped forward to conceal her expression. Then, just as suddenly, she would look up with a smile.

'You don't have to be polite. Chris. If I'm boring you, just tell me to shut up, and we'll go and dance.'

He blushed. 'I wouldn't dream of it. I mean, we can dance, by all means – but I like listening to you talk.'

Clare grinned. 'Our Francis calls me a pompous little know-all.'

'Yeh, well he's your brother. I'm forever calling our Liz "Miss Bossy Boots".'

They both laughed. Soon Chris was telling her things he could never have told Sally. He told her about dancing with Mollie at the Coronation party. 'It wasn't a bit like this.' He waved a hand in the direction of the dance floor crowded with well-dressed couples. 'Most folk'd have thought it a bit weird, really – Sally certainly did . . .' For the first time he uttered her name without a qualm. 'But for Mollie, just for a few minutes, that grotty little front parlour was the Grafton Rooms and heaven all rolled into one. She'd always taken a shine to me, you see – I don't know why . . .'

'I do,' Clare said softly.

'Well, anyway, Liz says we all need our dreams, and Mollie needed them more than most. She knew she hadn't got long . . . in fact she died a few months later.' It wasn't the sort of thing to be talking about in a dance hall with the lights and the music and everyone enjoying themselves. But Clare didn't seem to mind – she listened and sympathized in a way that made him feel good.

On the other side of town, in one of the grand houses that skirted Sefton Park, Shirley Anne was coming to the end of her twenty-minute act. She could tell from the volume of applause, and the rapt faces among the audience, that it had gone well. With a voice that was clear and true, her blonde hair threaded, Deanna Durbin style, with a simple ribbon, she was all things to all people; elderly ladies, dewy-eyed, remembered the innocence of youth, whilst their male counterparts found all their most chivalrous instincts surging to the surface – with just the occasional provocative frisson to give the whole thing a dash of spice.

As Shirley Anne went into her high-kicking finale, she was very much aware of the gorgeous young man with hair almost as fair as her own, who lounged against the wall nearby. He hadn't taken his eyes off her once throughout the whole twenty minutes. There was something vaguely familiar about him, but she couldn't place him.

'You're good,' he said, extricating her at last from the crowd, and guiding her to a seat in the corner.

'I know,' she said, studying him from under her lashes.

One eyebrow lifted. 'Modest, too. So why these twopenny-ha'penny concerts, when you could be going places?'

She leaned forward eagerly. 'Oh, I shan't be doing this for ever.

I know exactly where I'm going – right to the top. It's only a matter of time – and convincing my parents.'

His mouth quirked. 'Yes. I don't see the Ryans being too keen to put their little girl on the stage.'

'You know Mam and Dad?' And then the penny dropped. 'Of course! You're Alec Munnings. You're not a bit like our L . . .' She stopped, biting her lip.

'Don't leave me in suspense. What am I not a bit like?'

Shirley Anne tossed her head. 'Like our Liz said you were. She goes all po-faced whenever your name is mentioned.'

Alec smiled; a lazy, almost dangerous, kind of smile that made her catch her breath. 'And you?' he said. 'How do you feel about me?'

Shirley Anne felt herself colouring up, but she returned his look with a pert lift of her chin. 'I don't know you well enough to say, do I?'

'Well – ' He laughed softly. 'That's soon remedied.'

Rita's eyes were very bright when she and Frank returned to the others just as the floor show was finishing. Liz thought she had never seen her sister look prettier.

'We thought you'd got lost,' Liz said, and watched with interest as a blush ran up under Frank's fair skin. 'Hey, our Chris, did you ever see a more guilty-looking pair?'

'Give over, Liz,' Rita whispered frantically. 'Everyone's staring.' But her mouth was curving irrepressibly upwards. 'If you'll promise to behave, I'll tell you. Frank's asked me to marry him.'

'Oh, Rita!' Liz flung her arms round her sister. 'I'm so thrilled for you. And on my birthday, too!' She turned to kiss Frank's cheek. 'It couldn't happen to a nicer bloke.'

'Well, keep it to yourself. Frank hasn't spoken to Dad yet.'

But as Rita was kissed by each of them in turn, and Frank's back was slapped, and they all admired the sapphire ring with its circle of tiny diamonds, the people round about them could hardly fail to notice. Word eventually travelled as far as the band. Public congratulations followed and, to general applause, the spotlight was directed on them while the band played *If you were the only girl in the world*, followed by a rousing chorus of *Happy birthday to you* for the bride-to-be's sister.

'I'll kill you when I get you home, Liz,' muttered Rita, scarlet faced.

Liz laughed. She was still laughing when a familiar voice said, 'If I'm not butting in, may I be allowed to add my congratulations?'

And she stood quite still, her heart flipping over.

Chapter Three

It was Clare who exclaimed, 'Leigh! What a surprise! It's ages since we saw you – ' and made the introductions, whilst Liz stood apart from it all, feeling curiously light-headed.

So much had happened in the past year that reality had inevitably become more absorbing than make-believe. She had long since given up searching for a red head among the crowds and although the little music box was still hidden beneath her bed, it hadn't seen the light of day in months. Now, the time between vanished as if it had never been.

'And, of course, you remember our birthday girl – my friend, Liz?'

His eyes were deceptively lazy, assessing every detail. 'I surely do. At least I thought I did. But the Elizabeth Ryan I remember was kind of younger and smaller, somehow.'

He had remembered her. He had even called her Elizabeth. Suddenly, she was able to meet his scrutiny without embarrassment. 'I've grown up.'

'You surely have.' The creases at the corners of his eyes deepened.

How could she have forgotten that sensitive mouth, the slow smile that had the oddest melting effect on her bones? And his freckles . . . Oh, this was ridiculous. Suppose those all-seeing green eyes of his were able to read her inner confusion, the panicky feeling that welled right up into her throat?

But, illogically, Leigh's immediate sensation was one of relief. She hadn't changed – not really. Sure, her face had lost its childish plumpness, leaving that lovely pure line of jaw, which gave her a new maturity. But the moment she spoke, with direct simplicity, he knew that she was still the Elizabeth he remembered. It oughtn't to have mattered one way or the other, he told himself. Yet now, seeing her again –

'I don't want to break the party up,' he said, as the band arranged their music for the next number, 'but would anyone mind if I danced with the birthday girl?'

There was no reason why anyone should mind, but Monica, who had followed him, murmured, 'Must you, darling?' It was a mistake. Leigh lifted a speculative eyebrow, then turned his back on her to say, 'Will you dance with me, Elizabeth?'

'Thank you. I should like to, very much.'

The music was already beginning – an Astaire-Rogers number – and her left hand was firmly clasped in his as they joined the couples surging towards the dance floor. Leigh gathered it close against his chest, turning her towards him, with his free hand resting lightly in the middle of her back – a hold at once casual and intimate, unlike any Liz had experienced before. She had shed her bolero and was very conscious of her bare shoulders, his fingers warm against her skin through the thin voile. The top of her head brushed his chin, and his breath moved softly in her hair as he murmured, 'Comfortable?'

'Mm.' He was no Astaire, but he was every bit as good as Jimmy, and the slow foxtrot was her favourite dance. She ought to pinch herself – but if it was a dream, she didn't want to wake up.

'I almost didn't come tonight, you know. It seemed crazy to waste such a lovely evening indoors.'

'Well, I'm glad you changed your mind. It's like being given an extra birthday present.'

Leigh leaned back slightly to see her face. Her eyes were liquid gold under the soft lights. 'You really mean that, don't you?'

Liz blushed. Why had she never learned to think before speaking? 'Yes, I do, but . . .'

'It's O.K.,' he said, smiling. 'I won't get any wrong ideas.'

She settled back, reassured, and the smile was still in his voice as he began to sing the words of the song softly against her hair, *Oh, but you're lovely, never, never change* . . . just as if he really meant it.

Jimmy fumed inwardly as he watched them. His glance strayed in Monica Hazlett's direction – a right snobbish little bitch, but oh, what a body! Her kind often went for a brash approach from the lower orders – got a kick out of trying to put them down. But he'd willingly swop a snub or two for the pleasure it'd give him, just running his hands over that slinky body for five minutes.

*

In bed that night, Liz lay with sleep far away, the musical box clasped in her hands. She daren't play it for fear of disturbing Shirley Anne – who, as if echoing these restless thoughts, sighed and turned over, dreaming dreams of her own. That's all they were, of course, Liz admitted – dreams. She knew in her heart that seeing him again wasn't a good idea – playing with fire, Mam would call it.

But reason and commonsense had flown out of the window when his hand had tightened on her arm as they left the dance floor. 'Listen, honey, I'm off to London for a few days, but I'd like to see you again before I take off home – catch up on all you've been doing. Next Sunday, perhaps? I could phone you when I get back – make arrangements. We could take a run over to Southport.'

Liz could hear his voice now, filling her head with its soft resonance. She had hardly known how to answer him, and he had mistaken her hesitation for reluctance.

'Maybe it isn't such a good idea. I guess your Jimmy wouldn't be too thrilled . . .'

'Oh, no.' She had rushed in headlong before he changed his mind. 'Jimmy and I aren't – That is, we're just – Yes, Sunday would be fine. I'd like to see you again, really.'

A few miles away in Everton Valley, Leigh couldn't sleep, either. The night air was heavy with the perfume of roses as he stood by the open french windows, smoking yet another cigarette, and calling himself all kinds of an idiot. The smoke drifted upwards, untroubled by even the faintest of breezes, towards a sky brilliant with stars – a perfect night for flying. That's what you do best, fella, he told himself. So why don't you stick to it, instead of getting yourself involved with a girl, barely eighteen? True enough, Elizabeth Ryan wasn't your average eighteen-year-old, but sweet and wholesome for all that, with the innocence shining out of her. And he had a ten year start – ten hard-working, hard-playing years. If he had a grain of sense, he'd back off before she got any wrong ideas – better a little hurt now than a whole lot of heartbreak later. But even as he tried to convince himself, he knew that he wanted to see her again.

*

It was the longest week of Liz's life. Mam and Dad would have to know, of course – Jimmy, too. But long before Sunday, she had convinced herself that Leigh would have forgotten, or changed his mind, and anyway, everyone was so taken up with Rita's news that it didn't seem fair to spoil her sister's big moment.

It never ceased to amaze Liz how fast news got around. First thing Monday morning, the shop was buzzing with it. And because Shirley Anne was late down, Liz got the brunt of it.

'Your Rita's gor 'erself a fella, then. Named the day yet, 'as she?'

'Not that I know of, Mrs Figg,' she said, wrapping Nora's loaf and weighing out a quarter of broken biscuits. 'Some time next year, I expect, when they've saved up.'

'Insurance clerk, so I 'eard. Done 'erself all right there. Coin it in, them kind do.'

But Liz wouldn't be drawn. Mrs Killigan, standing alongside Nora, chuckled, setting her rolls of fat wobbling beneath a faded cotton blouse. 'Not from the likes of us, they don't. My Arthur don't 'old with insurance . . .'

Liz hid a smile. Feckless Mr Killigan would be an insurance company's nightmare – though at least he didn't resort to crime, like his two eldest sons. Dandy said it was only a matter of time before the scuffers caught Frank and Jacko bang to rights, and then it'd be a spell in Walton Gaol for them. The eldest girl, Grace, wasn't much better; seventeen, and as pretty as Lily was plain, she was known to the local lads as 'Grace and Favour'. It wasn't much of an example for the younger ones.

'Has Lily got a job, yet?' she asked as the door closed behind Nora.

'Norra proper job. Jus' three days a week down Tate and Lyle's, baggin' sugar. Still, anythin's better'n nuthin', an' it keeps 'er off the streets. I'll take a four-pounder an' one of them currant loaves. Your Shirley Anne's doin' all right fer 'erself, so I 'ear, an' good luck to 'er. Be a proper star like *Our Gracie* one day, I shouldn't wonder.'

To her credit, Mrs Killigan didn't seem to bear any resentment against Shirley Anne for dropping Lily, any more than she did over the growing estrangement between Eddie and Joey. 'Kids 'ave minds of their own these days,' was all she said.

When the phone rang late on Friday evening, it was Chris who answered. He put his head round the door. 'Is there a Miss Elizabeth Ryan here?' he asked in an exaggerated drawl.

Liz put down the skirt she had been hemming and flew to the passage between shop and living room, heedless of her astonished family.

'Leigh?'

'That's me. Nice to know you haven't forgotten me.' There was a laugh in his voice, which sounded deeper, even more attractive over the phone . . . 'How about Sunday – do we have a date?'

A date! 'Oh, yes. That is, yes, of course, if you still want to go.'

'I'm counting on it, honey. I'll pick you up about ten-thirty, O.K.?'

'Fine.' She'd have to go to early Mass and miss the choir. 'If you come to the shop, I'll be there to let you in.' She couldn't ask him to come round the back. For once she found herself in sympathy with Shirley Anne, who was forever bemoaning the lack of a proper front door. 'I'm sure Mam and Dad would like to meet you.'

There was a small silence. 'Want to look me over, do they?'

'Sort of. Do you mind?'

'Not at all. Don't worry about it. I'd want to do the same in their place. Ten-thirty, Sunday, then. Take care.'

Dad's reaction had been predictable. Liz watched him unhurriedly going through the ritual of filling and lighting his pipe – something that usually gave her pleasure. But now, she wanted to scream and dash it from his hands.

'I *am* eighteen, Dad. I'm not a child any more.'

'You're still in my care, girleen – and I'll not have you taken in by any smooth-talking Yankee stranger.'

'Leigh isn't a stranger. I told you, he's a friend. And he's nice. Ask Chris. He's a friend of the Whitneys, too. You can ring them up and ask them if you don't believe me.'

'Don't speak to your father like that, Liz.' Kathleen's voice cracked like a whip, but inside she was thinking, 'Oh, girl, girl, I know exactly how it is with you. I can hear it in your voice, even if you aren't aware of it yourself. And if you get hurt Michael will be hurt even more.' She turned to her son. 'What do you think of him, Chris – this American?'

Chris flipped a swift glance at Liz, whose eyes held an agonized plea. 'He seems a good bloke, Mam. Honestly. I'm sure Liz won't come to any harm with him.'

The glance had not gone unnoticed. 'I see. And Jimmy? Have you thought about him at all?'

Liz tossed her head. 'Jimmy will just have to understand, Mam – the way I'm supposed to understand when he sets his cap at other girls. It's only one day, after all – Leigh goes back to America next week, and it could be months, years, even, before he comes again.'

'Well,' Kathleen glanced across at Michael, 'your father and I will reserve judgement until Mr Farrell comes on Sunday.'

It wasn't the most satisfactory outcome, but Liz had no doubt that once they met Leigh, everything would be all right. Chris had been fairly quiet about the whole thing. But when they were alone, he spoke his mind.

'I don't care what you say, Liz, it's not fair to Jimmy. I know what it's like, being let down . . .'

'Oh, come on, Chris. Sally was never good enough for you. If she was, she'd have stood by you – helped, even. But Jimmy's not like you. He might make a fuss, but his heart won't be broken.'

'I'm not sure. He really cares for you, you know.'

'Maybe, but he doesn't want to settle down, any more than I do – so I don't see that either of us has any right to play dog in the manger.'

But Liz had underestimated Jimmy's reaction. They had the father and mother of a row, which ended with him slamming out of the house. Mam didn't say 'I told you so', but her expression said plenty.

'Comfortable?' Leigh asked.

'Um,' Liz murmured, snuggling down into the squashy seat that smelled of real leather.

'Not cold with the top down?'

'No. Just right.' It was going to be a glorious day, as she had known from the start it would be. When she went to early Mass there had been a kind of magical haze over the morning, the kind that promises heat later. She had changed her frock at least three times after breakfast, before deciding on a newish green-and-white cotton sundress with a square neck. She could take her white cardigan, just in case, and her Hendersons' handbag would hold all her bits and pieces and a clean handkerchief. A touch of pink lipstick, and she was ready.

'Anyone'd think you were being honoured by royalty, the way you're carryin' on,' Shirley Anne scoffed. But she sang a different tune when she saw Leigh climb out of his car, wearing immaculate cream flannel trousers and a tan shirt, with a brightly patterned scarf at the neck. 'You jammy beggar, where did you find *him*?' She craned her head out of Mam's parlour window. 'And will you look at that car!'

Liz was nervous, as she introduced Leigh to Mam and Dad, but she needn't have worried. He really did have the most beautiful manners. He handled Shirley Anne's blatant flirting with tact and humour, and was good with Georgy. 'I have a nephew just like you, back home, young fella,' he said, lifting him high in strong gentle hands. Liz could have hugged him. By the time they left even Dad seemed reassured.

'You'll need a scarf, if you don't want your hair getting tangled into knots,' Leigh said with a grin. But though Liz had brought one, she scorned the use of it, loving the feel of her hair blowing freely in the wind.

'Shirley Anne is pea green with envy,' she said with satisfaction.

Leigh laughed aloud. 'She is precocious, that one. I bet she has the fellas toeing the line.'

'And that's where they'll stay, unless they have some influence in theatrical quarters. Very single-minded, is our Shirley Anne.'

He remarked on how unalike she and her sisters were, and Liz said wasn't that true of most families, and that three of Shirley Anne would be a bit much for anyone. As she talked, a strong sense of family came through. She touched only briefly on Georgy's backwardness, saying how much it had pleased Mam and Dad, the way Leigh had singled the child out.

He found himself glancing at her from time to time, liking the way the wind whipped her hair away from her animated face, leaving her profile clear and uncluttered.

'I guess you've had a pretty rough time of it, this past year,' he said, and again she answered for the family.

'I guess we did. But it wasn't all bad. The business is expanding in all directions, and now we have Fritz, who is teaching me so many new and exciting things.'

'And that young thug?' he asked casually. 'Had any more trouble with him?'

'No. I doubt we'll hear any more from him.'

'And good riddance, huh? So, what do you want to do today?'

'You mean I can decide?'

'Absolutely. I am yours to command.'

This was a novelty in itself. Jimmy usually had everything planned. 'Could we stop at Formby, and have a walk through the pine woods? I haven't been for ages. We used to go by train in the holidays, armed with mounds of sandwiches and bottles of pop, and we'd spend the whole day looking for squirrels and collecting pine cones and paddling in the sea.'

'To the woods it is,' he said with a demonic leer. 'And if I have my wicked way with you, you have only yourself to blame.'

'Idiot,' she giggled.

It was still early enough for them to wander undisturbed along paths thick with pine needles. 'It's like walking on carpet, isn't it? And the smell!' Liz knelt to scoop up cones, making a well for them in her scarf. 'You're supposed to know when it's going to rain by whether they're open or shut' – she giggled again – 'only I can't remember which is which. They make good Christmas decorations, too.'

'It's a long time to Christmas.' Leigh leaned against a tree trunk, watching her with detached indulgence. 'I like it here – peaceful.'

'It won't be when the hordes descend.' Liz stood up, brushing needles from her skirt. The sunlight bounced off the distant sea, sending brilliant shards of light between the ranks of tall trees, fading into mote-filled ribbons as they reached the ground. Above, the thick green branches intertwined, obscuring the sky. 'When I was very young, I used to think this place was like the medieval cathedrals we had pictures of in our history books – great gloomy caverns with light streaming through slits in the walls.'

'And now you're a staid old lady,' he mocked.

She pelted him with pines cones and ran away, laughing. He retaliated, and the chase was on, ducking and weaving between the trees, their laughter filling the air, until she could run no more and collapsed against a tree trunk, gasping 'Pax!'

'And suppose I demand a forfeit?' Leigh murmured, standing very close, his hands braced against the rough bark behind her head, disturbingly aware of the rise and fall of her breast, the glow in her cheeks, and the way her breath caught and her eyes widened at his audacity. Everything about her pulsated with the joy of life – and he very much wanted to kiss her. But that would change everything. He opened his arms and stepped back. 'Pax it is,' he said.

Liz felt cheated, without quite knowing why. In the car later, she said, 'I'd like you to meet Aunt Flora. She's Mam's sister, my favourite aunt. You'd get on great, the two of you.'

'It's your day,' he said, resisting the urge to keep her to himself.

'She may be out, of course, but I could telephone her when we get to Southport.'

Flora was home, and said she would be delighted to see them later in the day. Meantime, they walked the whole length of the pier and back, and Liz pointed out the various landmarks and told Leigh how she had watched the gyrations of the plane, that last Bank Holiday. 'It was you, wasn't it?'

'A great guy, Giroux. Talked me into it. Speaking of which – ' His bright eyes challenged her. 'We never did take that joyride. What say we do it now?'

Chapter Four

The drawing room was cool and restful.

'I would have suggested the garden,' Flora said, as Gracie brought in the tray and set it down on the long sofa table, 'but you both look as though you've had enough sun and fresh air for the present. Liz, you'd better go upstairs, when you've had your tea, and put some cream on those shoulders; you don't want them to burn.'

'Yes, Aunt Flora.' Liz was watching Leigh. He hadn't seemed the least bit surprised by Rose Lodge, or the elegant woman who made them both so welcome, and she had been right in thinking that they would get on.

'Tea or iced lemonade, Mr Farrell?'

'Oh, tea, if you please, ma'am.'

'Sensible man. Much more refreshing on a hot day. And do help yourselves to sandwiches. Mrs Meadows will take it as a personal affront if you don't eat them.'

Leigh flicked an amused glance at Liz, did as he was bid, and settled back on the comfortable sofa, stretching out his long legs. 'You have a lovely house, Mrs Hetherington.'

'It is nice, isn't it?' She was bland. 'Not quite what you were expecting, I daresay, when Liz said she'd bring you to see her old Aunt Flora.'

Leigh grinned. 'Life would be very dull without a few surprises.'

'So it would.' His answer clearly delighted her. 'I seem to remember Liz telling me that you're a flyer. And no ordinary one, by all accounts.'

'I doubt there's any such animal. I guess what she really meant was that she thinks I'm crazy.'

'I'm sure of it after this morning. I nearly died!'

His eyes danced with laughter. 'We went joyriding with Giroux, but it wasn't quite your average trip round the bay, and your intrepid niece hasn't quite got over it, yet. I've been trying to convince her ever since that what I do isn't at all like that – '

'Probably much more dangerous,' Liz insisted.

'Not if you know what you're doing, honey. And it stands to reason, if you've helped to design and build a plane, you have sufficient faith in the workmanship, and your own judgement, to put it through its paces.'

Listening to their spontaneous banter, the way he called her Elizabeth, Flora began to wonder. They seemed to know one another remarkably well. Or was she reading more into it than was there?

'Incidentally, the old firm is now Farrell, Drew and Farrell.'

'So it should be. It's no more than you deserve. I hope that means someone else will be doing the test flying from now on?'

'Not while I've got breath in my body, they won't. Those are my babies, and no-one, but no-one, other than me gets to put them through their paces.'

'You see, Aunt Flora?' Liz helped herself to another sandwich. 'He's hopeless.'

'It seemed a good time to expand. The market place is wide open, and if the current situation doesn't improve, we could have our work cut out to meet the demand for planes.'

Flora's interest quickened. 'Would I be right in supposing that your recent visit to London was connected with such a possibility? Or am I being nosey? If so, just tell me to go boil my head.'

Leigh smiled. 'Ma'am, I wouldn't dream of telling you any such thing.'

'Of course you wouldn't,' Flora said amiably. 'You're much too well-mannered. Have another sandwich. No? A slice of Mrs Meadows' seed cake, then?' 'What about you, Liz? She cut it unhurriedly. But a war in Europe would affect your business considerably, Mr Farrell?'

He paused, the cake halfway to his mouth. 'You don't give up, do you?'

'Not often. Oh, I won't press you about your London visit, if it's terribly hush-hush. But you must surely hold views of your own about the possibility of war?'

The conversation had suddenly taken a turn Liz hadn't envisaged and didn't want, today of all days. 'Aunt Flora, do we have to spoil a nice afternoon with gloomy forebodings?'

'Of course not, child. But I'm interested in the American

viewpoint, and it isn't often I have the chance to pursue it. Mr Farrell?'

He laughed, shook his head, and grew suddenly serious. 'Well then, my opinion, for what it's worth, is much the same as most people's. I can see no other course of action if Hitler forces the issue – and he will, sooner or later. It's the question of when that's the real cruncher. I know a lot of people here think Chamberlain is weak – that the whole damn government is weak, in fact – and that, sooner or later, he'll sell Czechoslovakia down the river, but, to be blunt, he doesn't have much choice. This country isn't ready for the kind of war it's going to have to face. The more time your government can buy, the better chance it has of being somewhere near prepared to withstand Germany's Luftwaffe.'

'Is it really that serious?'

'It's that serious. And it isn't just the Luftwaffe. Shipping is going to be at the mercy of U boats, so regular commercial haulage flights between here and America will become vitally important – as important, in the long term, as the fighters and bombers Britain so desperately needs.' Leigh leaned forward, now totally engrossed, passion in his voice. 'I've been to Germany, ma'am, and seen some of what Hitler has lined up – and it scared hell out of me, I can tell you! This country is going to need all the planes and armament it can lay its hands on, because the destruction in Spain will be nothing to what German bombers could do here . . .'

They had become so engrossed that Liz's plea had been forgotten. In fact, as she listened, the seed cake turning to dust in her mouth, it seemed that she, too, had been forgotten. Aunt Flora and Leigh were talking to each other as equals, and she began to feel like a child with nothing to contribute – a child, to be seen and not heard. Finally she could bear no more.

'Stop it! Stop it! Stop it!'

They turned, staring at her.

'This is . . . w-was my lovely day,' she shouted, 'and you're ruining it w-with all your stupid talk about war.' Wild-eyed, tears threatening, she choked to a halt, appalled by her outburst – and then ran from the room.

'Oh, damn! Why can't I hold my tongue – ' Flora was out of her chair in an instant, but Leigh was even quicker, his distress obvious.

'No, it was my fault, ma'am. I got carried away, but I had no idea Elizabeth would take it so – oh, the poor kid.'

'I don't care who's to blame – and do stop calling me *ma'am*, for God's sake, it makes me feel about a hundred. My name's Flora.' She stopped, drew a breath and shook her head. 'I'm sorry. There's no call to vent my exasperation on you. It's just that I love that child as if she were my own.'

'I'm pretty fond of her myself. Look, if there's anything I can do?'

Flora sighed and shook her head. 'Later, perhaps. Stay here and have another cup of tea – or maybe something stronger.' She went across to a small cocktail cabinet. 'There's whisky, brandy, whatever you fancy. I'll go and find Liz. She doesn't often let fly . . . and it never lasts.'

Liz sat hunched up on the window seat in the blue bedroom which had been hers when she'd stayed at Rose Lodge the previous year, the handkerchief in her hands twisted into a damp mangled ball.

Her day was ruined – and she'd no-one but herself to blame, throwing a tantrum like that. It wasn't the talk of war, or even Leigh sounding as though he might relish the chance to get involved. The jealousy and confusion in her mind had no rhyme or reason to it. Tears threatened again.

'I thought I'd find you here,' said Aunt Flora, coming in and closing the door.

After a brief glance, Liz turned back to stare stubbornly out of the window. There was a thrush on the lawn, feeding a demanding young chick almost twice as big as itself.

'It's no good turning your back on me, young lady.'

'I can't go downstairs. You'll have to tell Leigh I'm not well or something.'

'Will I, now?' Flora heard the desperation in her niece's voice, and her heart ached for her. 'Well, you've come to the wrong shop, miss. I've never told a lie to save my own face, and I'm certainly not going to tell one to save yours. You must fight your own battles.'

Liz whirled round. 'But I can't meet him! Not after I've behaved so . . . so childishly.'

Flora's mouth twitched. 'Well, that's a pity, because he's

down there blaming himself, and probably drinking all my whisky.'

'It wasn't his fault!'

'The *adult* thing would be to go down there and convince him of that. He won't take my word.'

'I'd feel such a fool. We were having such a lovely day.'

'It isn't over yet – or at least, it needn't be.' Flora eyed her niece's blotched face. 'Oh, for heaven's sake, Liz! Give your face a good splash with cold water and brush your hair – you can help yourself to anything you need from my dressing table. A touch of powder and lipstick, a dab of perfume, and you'll feel as good as new.'

Liz came to fling her arms round her aunt, and Flora wondered if she was being altogether wise. The child's eyes earlier had given away more than she knew, as had this present emotional outburst. Leigh Farrell was a pleasant young man, but he was light years away from Liz in age and experience. Perhaps, a word in his ear? She disliked meddling, but just a hint about how easily young girls could be dazzled? Maybe she should just mind her own business – except that Liz was her business. Drat Leigh Farrell – drat everything. She pushed the girl away and walked to the door.

'Chop, chop, now – and put a bit of cold cream on those shoulders while you're at it.'

Leigh was alone in the drawing room when Liz went down. He turned from the window, glass in hand, and for a moment his closed expression daunted her. But apologize she must, so the quicker it was over, the better.

'I don't blame you for being angry,' she blurted out. 'Our Shirley Anne'd get a piece of my mind if she behaved like that!'

It wasn't at all what she'd meant to say. Her stomach churned as she waited.

The smile began slowly in his eyes, and spilled over into the creases of his face, curving his mouth into a broad grin. 'That's a neat apology, but you can throw away the hair shirt. You had every right to get mad – I was way out of line with all that war stuff.' He came close and put one finger under her chin, tilting it upwards. 'What say we forget the whole thing, and end the day with a slap-up meal?'

'Yes, please!' Liz looked into his laughing green eyes, and told herself it was relief that made her dizzy.

Some time later, Liz was enjoying dinner at the nearby Palace Hotel. Her spirits had taken a slight dive when Leigh asked Aunt Flora to join them, but, after a moment's hesitation, her aunt declined. It was a heady experience, sitting across the table from Leigh, who had produced a discreet tie and jacket from the boot of the car – as if, she thought, he had intended to end the day this way. She was even more impressed when he ordered a bottle of champagne, though it was disappointing to find that it tasted like fizzy lemonade.

'Savage. I'll have you know this is vintage Bollinger, and you get just one glass. Your Dad'd have me for breakfast if I took you home legless.'

But Liz didn't need champagne. She sparkled in Leigh's company, and scarcely noticed what she ate. But the meal couldn't last forever, and nor, Liz realized, could her lovely day, though she might try to stretch it a little longer.

'Come.' She seized him by the hand as they left the hotel. 'We're just in time to see the sunset. It's only a few yards to the shore.'

The tide was well out, leaving a wide expanse of golden sand that stretched in all directions. Behind them the sandhills, deep-shadowed, looked like a desert landscape. Apart from a diminutive figure walking a dog near the sea's edge, they appeared to be quite alone. The sun hovered just above the horizon, a huge orange ball gilding the tips of distant waves, and streaking the sky with every shade from palest amethyst to vivid scarlet.

'This is quite something,' Leigh said, his arm reaching out quite naturally for her shoulder, drawing her close.

Liz stood very still, not wanting to lose the moment, wondering if it was the champagne that bubbled so wildly in her blood. 'It's as though we had the whole world to ourselves,' she whispered at last. 'Can't you almost feel the peace of it soaking into your bones?'

'The perfect end to a perfect day.'

She didn't want it to end. Not now – not ever. The sun dipped lower and lower until it was a mere sliver of light on the horizon, and then it was gone.

Leigh sighed, and removed his arm. 'Time we went, too.'

'Oh, no – not yet.' Without pausing to think, she turned and ran up into the sandhills, pursued by his voice, now near, now distant.

'Elizabeth! Come back, you crazy girl.'

'Find me,' she called, exhilarated by the chase. As a child she had played this game a hundred times, scrambling up one side of the hill, hanging on to a tuft of grass to sight one's quarry before sliding down the other side, showering the occasional pair of lovers with sand.

Leigh had stopped calling, now. She knew that trick, too – the silent stalking, listening for the sound of breathing. The sand was clogging her sandals, and she stopped to drag them off, hooking them over her wrist. And that was her undoing.

'Got you,' he said from behind, his fingers closing inexorably round her arms, tumbling her into the sand, and losing his own balance in the struggle. He half sat, half lay, his features in shadow as he loomed over her. 'And what the hell was all that about?'

Her face was uplifted to him in the half light, her breath ragged, her wide eyes reflecting the lingering gold of the sunset and the full extent of her emotions. 'I didn't want to go home,' she said on a half sob.

'Oh, my dearest girl!' Leigh groaned and gathered her close, until they lay together with the sand still warm beneath them. But her mouth was cool and fresh and oh, so eager as he explored it with a questing thoroughness. Her hands pushed under his jacket, fingers digging into his back, and all his good intentions melted away.

It wasn't like anything Liz had ever known. She had no sense of right or wrong, time or place – only this great need in her that had to be satisfied. Her body arched to the touch of his hand, pressing closer, closer to him . . .

It was a shower of sand, followed by a small dog slithering down the sandhill, that shocked Leigh back into his senses.

'Oh, God,' he muttered, and rolled away, to sit with his head in his hands, leaving Liz in a limbo which swiftly turned to painful embarrassment as the yapping dog was followed by its master. The man muttered apologies and scuttled away, but from the way he averted his eyes, she knew how she must look, sprawled in the sand with her dress awry. Ecstasy turned to shame. Yet, seconds before, she had been on the verge of something wonderful.

Leigh neither moved nor spoke until the man was out of earshot. Then he got slowly to his feet and held out his hands to pull her up, releasing her the moment she was steady, as though the merest contact with her burned his fingers. 'I'm sorry, Elizabeth. That should never have happened.'

He sounded so formal, like a stranger. Didn't he understand that she had wanted it to happen? But he was already telling her to put on her sandals, anxious to get away. And that made her angry. 'Oh, do stop apologizing. I was the one who started it. It's my fault, if it's anyone's.'

'I'm not getting into an argument,' he said. 'Let's forget the whole thing and go home.'

It was like a dash of cold water. Shame engulfed her as she realized that what she had done, or been about to do, was not only a sin in the eyes of God, but had put her beyond the pale in Leigh's eyes, too. She had read enough novels to know that what some men classed as an amusing diversion, instantly branded a girl as cheap. Was that how Leigh saw her? In silence she fastened her sandals, brushed the sand from her frock, and retrieved her handbag.

They drove home in silence, broken only by the occasional enquiry as to whether she was warm enough; Liz, a permanent lump in her throat, replied with grunts. When the car arrived back in Great Homer Street, she sat, knowing she should say: 'Thank you for a lovely day,' but unable to get the words out.

'Elizabeth . . . do we have to part bad friends?'

Leigh's voice was surprisingly gentle, but it was the gentleness of an adult towards a child, and she found herself answering with a child's politeness. 'Of course not. It was a lovely day. Thank you very much.'

In the half light, she saw him bite his lip. 'It *was* a lovely day, honey – one I'll never forget.'

The words had a terrible finality about them. 'Shall I see you again?'

'Not for a long time. We have a full order book – you know how it is.'

'Yes, of course.' Desperate, she threw pride to the winds. 'I could write to you.'

He said nothing for a moment. Then: 'You'd be wasting your time, honey – when I get busy, I'm a terrible correspondent.'

So that was it. He didn't want to know. All she wanted now was to get out, before she made a complete fool of herself.

As she fumbled with the door, he came to open it for her. 'I'd better see you safely in.'

'You needn't bother,' she said, turning away. 'I'll be quite safe. I know where I am with the folk round here.'

Chapter Five

As the summer continued, the news from across the Channel made many people uneasy. And the weather didn't help. In June there had been gales, and in August came hailstones as big as golf balls that shattered many a roof down Fortune Street, followed by torrential rain.

Ellen's house was flooded, as were many others, and she sent one of the older children along to the shop to say she'd be late. A couple of Arnie's mates turned up to help, and said they'd fix the roof, too – and Mrs Killigan chivvied her idle brood into doing the same for neighbours who had no man.

'The children thought it was great fun,' Ellen said, when she finally arrived. 'But that flood water had all the muck of the streets in it – you wouldn't believe the mess it made. And the smell!'

'I know,' Kathleen agreed. 'We had the same problem with the cellars. The main bakehouse isn't affected, thank God. Liz and Fritz are having to manage there until we've time to deal with the water.' Georgy began to make small grunting noises, which she tried to ignore. 'We can't sweep the water out, so it'll have to be mopped up – and every surface scrubbed before they can use it again.' She saw that her small son was turning red in the face. 'Oh, Georgy, not again!'

Ellen heard the angry frustration in her voice. 'Shall I lift him?'

'Thanks, but he needs changing.'

'I'll do it. Then we'll have a nice cup of tea.' Kathleen didn't argue. She had done more than usual that morning, and was feeling the effects. She filled the kettle and set it to boil before sitting down. Ellen laid the piece of blanket on the table, and lifted Georgy on to it, her hands deft from constant practice. As mine were once, Kathleen thought with a sigh.

'Michael said some of the roads are badly flooded. That's the third dirty nappy today.'

'Poor little chap. Teething, I expect. We'll soon have you more comfy, won't we, chuck? No, Freddie, leave the pins alone.'

'Georgy *poos*!' said Freddie, wrinkling his nose as his mother dropped the offending nappy in the waiting bucket.

'Yes, well, you'd know all about that, wouldn't you? Now, just be a good boy, and you can have a biscuit and a drink of orange.'

'Anyway, Dandy's got it all organized,' Kathleen said. 'So, once they've finished in the bakehouse, they can get cracking. Rita's Frank has promised to come as soon as he's able, and Shirley Anne can give Mrs Frith a miss for today and get stuck in with the rest. Many hands make light work, as they say.'

'There, that's better.' Ellen put Georgy back in the pram and gave him a rusk. 'Is Liz all right? She looks proper peaky – not her usual cheery self at all.'

Kathleen sighed. 'I'm afraid she fell pretty hard for that American. He was certainly attractive enough to charm any young girl – really nice, too, but much too old for her. It's as well he went home when he did. And, then, of course, to add insult to injury, Jimmy took umbrage and got himself that job on the cruise ship, so now her pride's well and truly dented.'

'Poor kid. Young love can be awful painful.'

'Liz'll get over it. Our Chris is great with her. He's been through it all, himself, of course. And there's nothing like hard work for curing a broken heart. She's already planning for Christmas.'

'If they let us have Christmas in peace,' Ellen said with a sigh.

Francis was home, and at Clare's instigation he called round to see Liz. He was a fully fledged RAF pilot now, with his wings proudly displayed on his uniform coat.

'You do look smart,' she said, surveying him critically, surprised by her pleasure at seeing him. She was missing Jimmy more than she would have thought possible. Only after he had gone did she realize how much she had taken him for granted. No more emotional entanglements for me, she told herself bitterly. There had never been any danger of that with Francis; he was totally single-minded about flying, which suited her just fine. The memory of Leigh threatened to intrude, and was firmly rejected. 'How long are you home for?'

'Ten days.' He made it sound about ten days too long away from his precious aeroplanes. 'I wondered if you'd like to come out with me one evening? We could go to the pictures, or have a meal – anything you fancy.'

She could almost hear Clare saying, *Poor Liz needs taking out of herself. Be a dear and make a fuss of her*. Still, they had always been at ease with one another, and it would be fun to hear about his new life. 'A meal would make a nice change, on one condition – that the word *war* is never mentioned.'

Two nights later, Francis took her to a small restaurant on West Derby Road, where the atmosphere was pleasantly intimate and the food excellent. The fact that he was now doing what he wanted to do, and was good at it, had given him an assurance he had previously lacked. He would always be a loner, of course, but Liz enjoyed the evening, and his laconic descriptions of some of the crazier tricks his fellow pilots got up to. Francis must have enjoyed it, too, because he suddenly said, 'Liz, will you write to me?' And she said she would.

'We must do this again,' he said when he took her home. 'At the weekend, maybe?'

And, so that there should be no danger of a misunderstanding, she said, 'Lovely. Why don't we make a foursome with Clare and Chris?'

In early September, there were fresh scares about war, with talk of Civil Defence, of air raid precautions, and trenches being dug in London parks for protection in the event of bombing. Later that same month, the Government issued thirty-eight million gas masks. An appeal went out for volunteers to assemble them, and be trained to fit and distribute them. Dandy was one of the first to offer his services.

'I may be too old to fight for my country,' he said jauntily, 'but this is one way I can help to put a spoke in Adolf-flamin'-Hitler's wheel.'

Already a well-loved member of the community, Dandy was a tremendous asset to officials at the Civil Defence centre; trusted by the elderly, who remembered the successful young boxer who had done Liverpool proud, and by their children and grandchildren whom he had coached. He could coax even the most apprehensive into letting him fit the grotesque-looking masks, with their ugly snouts and nasty rubbery smell. 'Come on, Nellie, get yer chin well in first – now, wait while I spread the straps an' run me finger round the edge of the rubber to see if the size is right. Great. Now, just take a deep breath while I put this piece of paper over the mouthpiece – no, gairl, *breathe in.* Don't hold yer breath, for pity's sake, we don't want you turning blue, you'll clash with the curtains! That's the ticket.' Then he'd show them how to do it for themselves.

He made a game of it for the children, encouraging them to pretend they were monsters, but some of the mothers with young babies came near to breaking his heart. 'But worr'about 'im, mister? Yer can' put one on 'im.' He had to tell them what he'd told Kathleen. 'They're working on one with bellows that you can put the babby inside. But if the worst should happen, God forbid, just cover Georgy's face loosely with a good thick blanket and get him down the cellar quick as you can.'

In spite of the growing signs all round her, like the big new aircraft factory near Speke Airport, and lots of firms going over to arms production, Liz stubbornly refused to believe that war was imminent. Even Fritz's growing pessimism failed to daunt her as, obstinately, she continued her Christmas preparations. She had set her heart on producing their first boxed collection of luxury chocolates as well as some of the petit fours, and had gone to a lot of trouble to find someone to produce a box to her own design.

'Are you sure the time is right, Lizzie, my love?' Michael studied her determined face, his heart aching for her. That American had a lot to answer for, half-breaking his dear girl's heart. 'I know how you feel, but it's a lot of money to lay out.'

'We can just afford it. And there should be more money about, with factories taking on extra workers to make munitions and things. In fact, there'll never be a better time, because everyone'll need cheering up with something really extravagant. Mr Morgan thinks I'm right, and so does Aunt Flora.'

'Oh, well, if they're both encouraging her, you might as well save your breath,' Kathleen told Michael drily. 'Not that she needs any encouragement. She has a very strong will, has Liz – and, to be fair, her judgement is almost always sound.'

'I know that fine. Just like her mother, as I've said often enough.'

September seemed a long month, but at the end of it, after a lot of bargaining and sabre-rattling, Mr Chamberlain went to see Hitler and, at the price of a dismembered Czechoslovakia, came back with a document in which Hitler agreed to negotiate on any further disputes. The nation cheered him, the gas masks were packed away, and the fear of war receded. But the euphoria didn't last, as people began to read between the lines.

'Chamberlain must think we're daft,' Dandy said. 'That document isn't worth the paper it's written on. I tell you, Adolf Hitler couldn't keep a promise if his life depended on it. A few months to gobble up the rest of that poor country, and then he'll go after Poland.'

This made Liz all the more determined to pursue her plans, and Fritz became obsessed with teaching her all he could. In their spare time, they worked on the couverture and perfected the fillings – the praline and ganache and truffle, and the many kinds of paste work. 'And in the New Year, if time and fate permits, we shall deal with spun-sugar work and icings. My Mitzi is helping me to write it all down for you in English, so that you will at least have the knowledge, should anything happen to me.'

'Why should anything happen to you?'

There was sad resignation in his smile. 'You think they will permit me to remain here, if war comes?'

'Why not? You aren't German.'

'I am Austrian. I suspect it comes to much the same in the minds of the authorities. And in other minds, also. Already I have heard whisperings – you must have heard them, too.'

Liz was vehement in her denial, though there had been one or two snide comments about his presence in the bakehouse. But a few weeks later there was an incident in the shop that brought his words to mind again.

'That Jew-boy you got working for you?' It was Nosey Nora, as she was leaving – who else? But the shop was full and ears were pricked. ' 'ow d'you know 'e en't a spy, working for the Germans?'

There were one or two murmurs of agreement. Liz was so angry she could hardly speak – which was probably as well, since it gave her time to collect her thoughts. 'Apart from the fact that he hates the Nazis more than we do, and with good cause,' she said coolly, 'what could he possibly tell them that would be of use? D'you think, maybe, the Nazis would like to know how many loaves of bread you get through in a week? How much you spend at The Grapes of an evening? I haven't time to stand here talking nonsense. Next please.'

There were titters of laughter, and the matter was dropped. But not before she had heard other mutterings.

'Honestly, Dad, it's so unfair!' Her indignation surfaced again later. 'I just wish they could have seen him weeping over that photo in the *Picture Post*, those poor old men down on their knees, scrubbing the pavements in Vienna while the Nazis stood over them, laughing. Fritz said he felt he'd betrayed them by leaving. I didn't know how to comfort him. He's so gentle, it makes me angry that anyone could think ill of him.'

Michael took her face in his hands, his voice mirroring the compassion in his eyes. 'Ah, Lizzie, you have a generous heart. It is difficult for you to understand that when people are frightened and confused, they have to find someone to blame.'

Shirley Anne had been behaving strangely for several days. So, when she came home early one afternoon and shot straight upstairs, Kathleen said, 'That girl's up to something. I can always tell.'

'She's growing up fast,' Ellen said, shrugging on her coat.

'Too fast for my liking. I mean, you've only to look at her – she looks nearer eighteen than sixteen.'

'But so very pretty.'

'Oh, aye, she's that, all right. That's what worries me. With all these concerts, it's hard to know exactly how much money she's earning. I do try to keep a check on her savings, but she can be very close. Not that she doesn't pay her share, and more, but there's as much going on her back as she gives me.' Kathleen sighed. 'I just don't want her to be taken advantage of, and there's plenty ready to do that.'

'But Mrs Frith will see that doesn't happen, surely – and her dance teacher?'

'Perhaps.' Georgy was in one of his clinging moods, and Kathleen moved him from one side to the other.

'He's getting too heavy for you to hump round.' Ellen was torn between the need to get home and a desire to help. 'I could stay a bit longer. Our Dot can cope with most things.'

'I won't hear of it. You do more than enough as it is.' Kathleen walked to the foot of the stairs. 'Don't stay up there, titivating, young lady. We're needing another pair of hands down here.'

'I won't be a minute, Mam.'

Shirley Anne curled up on the bed to read again the letter that had come that morning – the second in a matter of weeks.

'I'm not sure that I should permit you to have your mail sent here, my dear,' Mrs Frith had ventured in gentle reproof. 'I do hope you are not concealing anything from your parents?'

Shirley Anne thought quickly, crossed her fingers and opened her blue eyes very wide. 'Well, as a matter of fact, I am. That is, I'm trying to arrange a little surprise for them, and you can't keep anything secret in our house.'

'Dear child. Well, in that case . . .'

Silly old fool, Shirley Anne thought. Anyway, it wasn't really a fib. She *was* planning a surprise – only not quite the sort she had allowed Mrs Frith to think. For a moment a pang of guilt assailed her, but excitement soon smothered it.

After that first talk with Alec, she had met him several times more, and at his suggestion had written to Mr Grace to ask if there was any chance of stage work if she came to London, allowing him to think she had her parents' approval. At the time he had advised her to stay put until the political situation resolved itself one way or the other, but now he had written again to say there might be a small part for her in one of his pantomimes – subject to audition, of course – if she could be in London by the 20th October. She could assure her parents that secure accommodation would be provided for her. And Alec had promised to see she wasn't lonely. She had only to let him know when she was coming and he would meet her. If you didn't take chances, he had told her, you didn't deserve to succeed.

It wasn't easy to keep secrets when you shared a room with someone, but Shirley Anne had discovered a loose floorboard under her bed, with a hole underneath large enough to keep things she didn't want anyone else to find – like these letters, and a purse full of money, and an extra Post Office Account book that no-one knew about, into which she had put all the tips given to her by Mrs Frith's friends. Many an elderly gentleman, enchanted by her performance and her pretty manners, had pressed money upon her for no reason at all that she could tell, except that she had occasionally sat upon the arms of their chairs and flirted harmlessly with them. As a result, she had amassed the handsome sum of ninety-eight pounds, four shillings and sixpence – more than enough, surely, to see her through until she was established.

The shop bell rang twice in quick succession, and she hastily stuffed everything back into the hiding place and carefully replaced the board.

The scullery door slammed shut behind Chris as he came in, half hidden behind an enormous cardboard box. Seeing his mother struggling under the weight of sixteen-month-old Georgy, he slid the box on to the table and hurried across to take the child from her.

'Give him here. Dad'd go mad if he saw you carrying him round like that.' Kathleen smiled and relinquished Georgy without protest, and Chris lifted him high. 'Hey, young fellow-me-lad, time you were chasing us all round the room.'

Kathleen sat down in Michael's chair and leaned back, waiting for her heart to settle into its normal rhythm. 'Dad was making really good progress with him, before he got so involved with his Civil Defence. Still, now the panic's over, maybe he'll have a bit more spare time.'

'Where is everyone?'

'Ellen's gone home, Michael's resting, Liz is downstairs working – she never seems to tire, that one' – a note of envy was quickly stifled – 'And Shirley Anne is upstairs, doing heaven knows what. I've called her once already. Rita won't be home for another half-hour, and Joey is at Scouts.'

The shop bell rang again, and she made her way through to answer it just as Shirley Anne came running down the stairs, wearing a pale blue frock that Chris hadn't seen before. It had a square neck, and gathers at the waist, and looked highly impractical for working in the shop.

'Hi, Georgy-Porgy,' she sang, giving the baby a smacking kiss. 'Who's a lovely boy, then?'

Chris lifted an eyebrow. 'You're in a good mood. Someone left you a fortune?'

She wrinkled her nose at him. 'Ha, ha. Sarcasm doesn't become you, brother, dear.'

'Aye. And work doesn't become you, it seems. You're up to something.'

'Rubbish. Can't a girl be happy without everyone getting suspicious?'

But Chris had seen the betraying trace of colour run up under her skin. 'Not when the girl is you. Anyhow, you'd better get in there and relieve Mam. She's looking whacked.'

Shirley Anne tied an apron over her frock, made a face at him, and whisked through to the shop. A moment later, Chris heard her voice, bright and cheerful as she chatted to the customers. He shook his head. She was another Sally, he thought – and was surprised, and relieved, to find that he could at last think of Sally without bitterness.

Georgy was making sounds which seemed to denote frustration. 'Well, our kid, I don't know what magic Grandpa Dandy employs, but let's see what you can do.' Chris lowered his baby brother gently until his feet touched the floor in an attempt to get him to walk, but he continued to slither until he was lying on the floor, where he rolled on to his tummy and wriggled along like a worm. Chris sighed and got down beside him on his hands and knees, no easy task in the limited space. 'See,' he said. 'This is how you crawl.'

And that was how Liz found them. She giggled. 'Your turn to play bears, is it?' Her eyes lit up as she saw the parcel. 'Are these my boxes? Oh, Chris, I must see them!'

She ripped off the brown sticky tape and pulled back the lid. 'Oh.'

Chris stood up. 'Something wrong?'

Liz drew out a flat sheet. 'They need folding.'

'Well, of course they do. What did you expect?'

'But it'll take hours!'

He grinned. 'What an impatient girl you are. I daresay we'll all give you a hand.'

Her eyes shone as she flung her arms round him. 'Oh, Chris, what a nice brother you are.'

'Well, if you're going to make all our fortunes for us, it's the least we can do.'

'Pig. I must have a try – see what they look like.' It was a bit like doing a jigsaw puzzle, but once she got the knack, the box was soon finished. It wasn't quite as elegant as she would have liked, but it did have the right classic look, with its glossy white finish and plain gold lettering. Across the top left corner, THE LENDL COLLECTION – she had insisted on that – and across the bottom right, ELIZABETH RYAN. 'Oh, Chris!'

'Looks great,' he dutifully obliged, thinking it a bit too plain. 'What you wanted, is it?'

Shirley Anne was less tactful. 'It wouldn't tempt me to buy. You should've had lots of gold roses on the lid. '

'I'm not aiming to sell to the likes of you,' Liz retorted.

But when Aunt Flora saw the boxes, she pronounced them to be exactly right for the kind of market Liz was aiming at. 'If you like, I could investigate the possibility of finding one or two outlets in Southport,' she offered, delighted to see her niece animated once more.

Liz wanted the boxed chocolates on sale as soon as possible – there would be more than enough to do in the bakehouse, come December. So, for the next few days, everyone lent a hand in spare moments, making up the boxes, lining them with gold edged tissue, and arranging neat rows of chocolates in their little frilled paper cases. The chocolates would also be displayed loose in ELIZABETH'S and the Candide, along with the petit fours, for customers to make their own selections.

In the excitement, no-one noticed that Shirley Anne was behaving rather more oddly than usual. They were by now accustomed to her comings and goings, and although Michael had grave misgivings about her being allowed so much licence, he was forced to admit that there was no way they were ever going to make her conform.

'Heaven knows where she gets it from,' Kathleen said, 'but the theatre's in her blood, and sooner or later, she'll be off, whether we like it or not. Perhaps we should ask Miss Eglantine's advice.'

The fact that Shirley Anne's bed hadn't been slept in rang no warning bells in Liz's mind; she quite often stayed the night with Mrs Frith after a late concert. But the chauffeur almost always brought her back in time to help in the shop. However, it wasn't until half the morning had passed without any word that

Kathleen's annoyance became a nagging unease, and she telephoned Mrs Frith.

'But I'm sure she left here at her usual time.' Mrs Frith sent for her chauffeur. 'Yes, Max is quite certain of it. He did say she asked him to set her down some way short of home, to get a little fresh air before being cooped up for the morning – those were her own words,' Mrs Frith said hastily. 'I do hope – oh, dear me. Surely nothing can have happened to the dear child?'

Kathleen reassured her, and promised to keep her informed. But she already knew what must have happened. She and Liz hurried upstairs, where it took only a moment to discover that most of Shirley Anne's clothes had gone from the cupboard, and her Post Office book was missing from Kathleen's drawer.

'Oh, Mam, she wouldn't?' Liz sat down abruptly, ashen-faced. 'Not without a word.'

'Oh, yes she would. That's exactly what she'd do. However am I going to tell Michael? He'll never understand.'

'No more will I. Honest, Mam – at this moment I could kill her! The heartlessness – walking out like that!'

'Single-minded. It seems to run in the family,' Kathleen said, her mind working fast. 'It's quite obvious she's gone to London. To tell the truth, but for the shock of it, I'm not altogether surprised. If I know Shirley Anne, she'll have had the whole thing planned. The theatre's been drawing her like a magnet ever since that pantomime. It was merely a question of time.'

Her mother seemed to be taking it very calmly. 'But she's sixteen, Mam. And alone in London.'

'Oh, I doubt she's alone. Whatever else, our Shirley Anne's not one for roughing it. I think we'll find that Mr Grace at the back of it, and, whatever I think of the man for encouraging her, I'm certain he'll see she's properly looked after.'

Sure enough, they got downstairs to find Lily Killigan at the back door with a letter. 'Shirley Anne give me a shillin' ter keep her case in our back shed overnight, an' bring this for yer, late mornin'.' Lily thrust the letter at Kathleen. 'Y'won't tell our Mam, will yer? She'd give us a thick ear.'

Kathleen waved her away, and she turned and ran.

Dear Mam and Dad, the letter read, *I have to go. Please*

forgive me and don't think badly of me. You know how much I want to be a star, and one day you will be proud of me. Don't worry, as Mr Grace has found me a place to live and has promised me a job. Lots of love to you and everyone, and a big kiss for Georgy.

Michael took the news in silence – never a good sign.

'Oh, Mam!' said Liz in distress.

'Leave him be, child,' Kathleen said, her heart heavy as she watched Michael walk back to the bakehouse. 'He'd never turn against any of you, no matter what. He just needs time.'

At around the time that Lily was delivering the letter, Shirley Anne was well on her way to London. The journey, indeed the whole escapade, had been very exciting, but now she was tired and hungry and a little frightened. She had told Mr Grace she would be met by a friend. But when she arrived, Euston station seemed like a vast cavern of steam and noise, and she remembered lurid stories about young girls being accosted in such places and taken away for the White Slave Trade, never to be heard of again. Until that moment she had loftily scorned such tales. Now, suddenly, everyone looked suspicious.

Then she saw Alec pushing his way through the crowd, tall, debonair and reassuringly familiar, his long tweed overcoat swinging loose. She dropped her case and flung herself into his arms.

'Hey, what's all this?' he said, dismissing her incoherent fears. 'You'll feel much better when you've had something to eat. Everything's going to be fine.' And above her head, he smiled.

Chapter Six

In November Jimmy came home, lean and bronzed, full of all that he had seen and done. There had been a couple of cards for Chris, and the occasional one to her – 'having fun, wish you were here' cards, giving no indication of his feelings, so that Liz had not known quite what to expect when he returned. But he breezed in as though nothing had happened, sharply suited, and laden with presents, and she was suddenly shy of this new, more adult Jimmy.

And when he smiled at her, she forgot the bitterness of their parting and greeted him, literally, with open arms.

'Hey! If this is the kind of welcome you give the traveller home from the seas, I think I'll go away more often.'

'Oh, no you won't,' Liz said, without looking up from opening her present. 'We're counting on having you around for Christmas. Oh . . .' The last piece of tissue fell away, and she held up a heavily fringed shawl in vivid shades of orange and gold and flame that shimmered in the firelight. The material was incredibly soft and light, and felt warm against her cheek. 'Oh, Jimmy, it's beautiful!'

All the time he was away, he had carried a memory of an impetuous girl growing into womanhood, so it came as something of a shock to him, also, to discover how smoothly the transition had been accomplished in his absence. Liz was now a young woman glowing with warmth and confidence. His pulse quickened. 'I thought they were your kind of colours. It's Turkish – pure silk.'

He had something for everyone. Kathleen was touched by her mother-of-pearl brooch, and the soft toy for Georgy. And while Liz draped the shawl across her shoulders and sashayed round the room as she brought him up to date with all the news, Kathleen thought that she hadn't seen her daughter look so happy in months – and the way Jimmy was eyeing her, she began to wonder. Liz never mentioned Leigh Farrell: it would have worried her less if she had. But now Jimmy was back, perhaps old ghosts could finally be laid to rest. She had not always approved of this rather brash young man, but he seemed to be improving with age . . .

Jimmy didn't seem a bit surprised when Liz told him about Shirley Anne sneaking off to London in search of fame.

'Little madam. Still, it was bound to happen, sooner or later. Very single-minded, your Shirley Anne.'

'It was a nine-day wonder in the shop, of course.'

He grinned. 'I bet. So what happened? Did your Dad go after her?'

'He would have done. In fact he was all for calling in the police, but Mam calmed him down – suggested she should go and have a word with Miss Eglantine first. But before anyone could do anything, Shirley Anne was on the telephone to say that Mr Grace had created a part specially for her in one of his pantomimes – only a small solo song and dance spot, but in one of the theatres on the outskirts of London, where she might be noticed – and if she couldn't stay and do it, her heart would be broken forever!

Jimmy grinned. 'Sounds like she's landed on her feet as usual.'

'It was touch and go. But Mam reckoned that if we dragged her home by force, she'd only run away again. And it all seems above board. She's to get six pounds a week, and has a room in a very respectable boarding house, with a dragon of a landlady, so we needn't worry about her. She said Mr Grace doesn't put himself out for just anybody, and if she works hard, she'll be a star one day.'

He laughed. 'How like Shirley Anne to turn the whole place upside-down, run everyone ragged, and then tell them not to worry! Still, I wouldn't put it past her to succeed. The family could have a star in the making.'

'I don't know about *could*,' Kathleen said drily. 'If you believed the few brief notes the young madam has honoured us with, you'd think she was already famous. At least Mr Grace had the goodness to write and reassure us that she was quite safe. But I do worry about her – she's too young to know if folks are exploiting her.'

Jimmy had his own views about Shirley Anne's ability to look after herself, but he wasn't about to air them here.

And then Chris came in, and after a riotous few minutes, the two young men went off together to celebrate Jimmy's return with a jar at The Grapes.

'I'm glad Jimmy's back,' Kathleen said casually, watching the pink deepen in her daughter's cheeks. 'Our Chris has really missed him.'

Liz had judged right in supposing that people would be in a spending mood that Christmas. There was a definite 'let's enjoy ourselves while we can' air abroad, and luxuries in particular were snapped up.

'It's as well we boxed so many chocolates ahead of time,' she said, coming back from a visit to ELIZABETH'S early in December. 'They've only got two dozen of the half-pound size left, and even the larger size is selling fast. Mr Morgan has had people ordering two and three lots at a time. I do hope we'll have enough boxes. It's a bit late to get more made now.'

'I think we'd better order them, just the same,' Kathleen said 'The demand won't necessarily stop the moment Christmas is over.'

When Kathleen settled down to do the books in February, she already knew that both sides of the business were in a healthy state, but even she was surprised by how much the luxury side had grown in so short a time.

'Oh, Mam, isn't it great?' Liz's eyes were golden in the lamplight as Kathleen went through the figures with her. 'Now I know how you felt when your plans for Ryan's began to succeed.' She didn't notice her mother's stillness as she rushed on, 'I've a long way to go, of course, and none of it would have been possible without you and Dad letting me try new ideas. And I admit that Fritz has done a lot of the creative work, but I'm learning fast.'

'I didn't know what to say to her, Michael,' Kathleen confided later, when they were alone in her parlour, with John McCormack singing *The Rose of Tralee* softly in the background. 'It's true that I was ambitious for you, but Liz has taken things a good few steps further than I would ever have dreamed of. I mean, you've only got to think back a couple of years. We thought things were going well then, but suddenly everything seemed to conspire against us. That's when Liz took charge. Now we have two vans, three shops and even more outlets – it may sound far-fetched, but it's as though Liz's dream has somehow lifted and inspired the lot of us.'

Michael had been watching Kathleen's face, which had become quite pink and animated, so that, just for a moment, he glimpsed the girl he had first fallen in love with – the girl who had been, and would always be, his inspiration. The gramophone record came to an end and the needle scratched. He got up to lift it and set it back on its rest, then turned back to her, his eyes warm.

'Maybe so. But even Liz needed someone to show her the way. Haven't I said often enough that she's her mother's daughter? And she's proved it, though to tell the truth, I'm not sure I'm comfortable with all this change at my age.'

'You're not old!'

'I'm no spring chicken, either. But even with youth on her side, I'd give the devil an' all to know how she's managed it.'

'By using every ounce of the wit and intelligence God gave her. Oh, Michael,' she burst out, 'I still can't help wishing, sometimes, that things had been different. There's no knowing what she might not have achieved if she'd gone on with her schooling.'

'It's no use looking back, Kathleen.' He searched in his pocket for his pipe, as he always did when discomfited or embarrassed. 'Liz is happy and fulfilled doing what she wants to do.'

'Yes, but if there is a war, everything she's achieved is likely to go down the drain. Remember how it was last time? There'll be no fancy cakes, no chocolates, everything rationed. What will Liz do then? She'll have nothing to show for all her hard work.'

'She'll do what we'll all have to do – bide her time.'

'But it needn't have come to that, don't you see? A good education, a string of certificates to your name – they're never wasted. And that's what she should have had – it was her right.' Kathleen hesitated, and then leaned forward, the words dragged from her. 'I know, you see – what Liz gave up. I've known for the past two years.'

'Beddam!' he said softly. 'And us thinking we'd been so careful.'

She choked on a laugh that was half a sob. 'I was missing an invoice one day, and I looked through your pockets – you never were one for tidying them out. And I found Liz's last school report, and Sister Imelda's letter.'

'Ah.' The tobacco glowed in the bowl of his pipe as he drew on it. 'You never said.'

'There didn't seem much point. By then, it was too late for her to go back and sit her exams, and I was in no state to offer any alternative. I convinced myself that it could all be put right later. But life has a way of thwarting the best laid plans, and by the time there was even half a chance, Liz had practically doubled the business and seemed to be thriving on it . . .'

'And still is.' Michael reached for her fingers, twisting in her lap, and stilled them with one large, competent hand. 'Listen, now, Kathy, my love, it was her choice. Otherwise, do you not think I'd have moved heaven and earth to find a way round the problem, knowing how you would feel? But it was Liz who decided what she wanted to do – just as she will go on deciding. And if, God forbid, Hitler should scupper her plans, she will simply bide her time, then begin all over again – because that's the way she is.' His eyes met hers. 'Just like her mother.'

Nobody now doubted that war would come. It was simply a question of when, and Rita, ever practical, decided to move her wedding from August to Easter Monday.

'I'm not going to risk having my day ruined. It means giving up teaching a term earlier, which hasn't pleased the head, but the school authorities are adamant about employing married women, though they may have to think again if war comes. It also means I won't have time to make the dresses, but I've found a good dressmaker in Toxteth, who says she can easily manage them. And Frank is on the lookout for a house or flat to rent. We haven't enough saved to consider buying, and anyway, Frank thinks we'd do better to wait – see how the situation develops.'

'You seem to have everything organized,' Michael said. 'And I've no doubt Frank will know what he's doing.'

They were all together for once in the living room, waiting to listen to the news, which was seldom cheerful these days but which, on Thursdays, was followed by the much-needed tonic of Tommy Handley in *ITMA*. Chris had washed and changed, ready to go out as soon as it was over. Kathleen was by the fire, undressing Georgy, who lay on her knee, pink from his bath, his nightgown warming over the fireguard, and Joey was doing his homework on the only bit of the table not occupied by the girls, who were poring over patterns suggested by the dressmaker.

'I've already decided on ivory satin, and I thought, being Easter, daffodil yellow might be nice for the bridesmaids. Hilda and I went round the shops last Saturday, and there was some very pretty material in T. J. Hughes. Could you come with us this weekend, Liz, to see if you like it?' Rita's voice took on a censorious note. 'I suppose it's no use even asking Shirley Anne?'

'Oh, but she won't want to miss being a bridesmaid at your wedding!' Liz exclaimed.

'She may have to. This new show she's in is set to run until July. We'll be lucky if madam makes it for the day.'

Shirley Anne had been spotted by an impresario when the pantomime was in the last couple of weeks of its run, and won a part in his new musical revue, so she had gone more or less straight from the pantomime into rehearsals for *Stepping on Air*. Again the part was small, but this time the theatre was in the West End itself, and had attracted more attention.

Kathleen took the safety pin out of her mouth. 'All the same, Rita, you'll have to ask her.'

'I suppose so. But I'll want a straight yes or no.'

Joey looked up. 'I won't have to wear a posh suit, will I?'

'Do you good to look respectable for once,' snapped Rita in her best schoolmarm manner.

'Yes, miss.' Joey grinned.

He was growing up fast, Liz thought; those thickly-lashed blue eyes were already breaking hearts. At thirteen, his easy-going nature had remained unchanged, but he was now in long trousers and had become one of the senior altar boys at St Anthony's, where most of the Guild of St Agnes and not a few of the Children of Mary were daft about him. She was never sure whether he was aware of their adulation, but it wouldn't have made much difference; apart from the Sea Scouts, Joey's interest was concentrated almost entirely on things mechanical. Machinery of all kinds, and engines in particular – the greasier the better – were a constant source of joy and discovery to him, and he was forever in trouble for getting oil on his clothes.

Eddie Killigan, seeing him one day up to his elbows in engine oil beneath the raised bonnet of one of the vans, had wandered across, his fertile mind busy with schemes to revive their flagging friendship. 'Aw, Joey – it'd be easy as fallin' off a log. There's always old cars to be had if you know where to look, an' if you was to tart up the engines an' I gave 'em a lick of paint, we could sell 'em again, easy, an' be quids in.'

'I hope you told him what to do with his idea, our kid,' Chris said when Joey jokingly passed on the gist of the great plan. 'It doesn't take a genius to work out who'll be "getting" the cars for Eddie. Those brothers of his'll have him as bad as themselves, soon. You want to keep well out of it.'

Joey was scathing. 'Honest, Chris, I know Eddie better than you do, so there's no need to try teachin' your grandmother to suck eggs. I'm not so daft that I can't see through his little schemes.'

Rita wrote to Shirley Anne, who sent back a note, obviously scrawled in haste, saying that there was no way she'd be able to be a bridesmaid, but she would try to get to the wedding. It would depend on the trains, because she would have to travel up on the Sunday and leave straight after the wedding next day to get back in time for the evening show.

'*Try*! I hope she's going to do more than try,' Liz protested to Aunt Flora during her weekly visit. 'You'd think she'd move heaven and earth to get here.'

'I dare say, love, but you have to see it from Shirley Anne's point of view. It isn't just selfishness, you know. Like it or not, your sister's first commitment has to be to the show.'

'I suppose so. You really think she's good, don't you?'

Flora had been to London for a few days, and had gone to see *Stepping on Air* with friends. She had been more than a little impressed by the ethereal creature with the piquant face and huge eyes, who had graced the stage with her effortless dancing, and had been described by one critic as 'light as thistledown'. Shirley Anne's stage presence was so assured, it was hard to recollect that she was only sixteen – though Flora suspected that few people apart from Mr Grace actually knew her true age. She had been less happy, however, when she went backstage to see Shirley Anne after the show. Her niece was sharing a dressing room with several other girls, and although she greeted her aunt enthusiastically enough, there was a distinct edginess about her, and the delicate features looked drawn beneath the make-up.

'You've lost weight, child,' Flora had said in her forthright way. 'I hope you're eating properly.'

Shirley Anne pouted, exchanging glances with a young man lounging against the wall, who raised an eyebrow in return, but made no effort to come across. At the time she had found the experience faintly disturbing. Now, she kept her fears to herself.

'Oh, Shirley Anne's good, all right,' she told Liz. 'With luck, she'll go places.'

And how about you, young Liz? Flora wanted to ask. Many a time she had turned that episode with Leigh Farrell over and over in her mind, wondering if she had done the right thing, especially when he had gone back to America, leaving Liz looking like a ghost. But Liz had come through, apparently none the worse, and maybe a little wiser – wise enough, she hoped, not to let Jimmy Marsden sweet-talk her into marriage. Liz had her sights set every bit as high as her young sister, even if she didn't recognize the fact – and she was much too young to be thinking of marriage and babies.

Nothing, in fact, could have been further from Liz's mind. With the Easter trade on top of the wedding preparations, her only concern was to see that everything got done in time. Everyone was working flat out, one way or another. The Easter eggs had gone better than ever this year, as had the chocolates, and Dad and Chris were up to their eyes with shop orders, plus several buffet suppers for Easter week.

Fortunately Dad had made Rita's wedding cake ages ago, to give it time to mature, though it still had to be iced – a task reserved for Mam. But Liz had been watching her mother. It didn't take a lot to tire her out these days; Dr Graham said it was the anaemia, which had never really cleared up. And with the wedding brought forward there was a lot to be done in a short time. Mam had managed to go shopping with Rita to choose her own wedding outfit but, although Dandy took his young grandson off her hands for much of the day, she was still kept fairly busy with all the paperwork and the ordering for the shop, as well as helping when needed. Liz feared that, when it came to the point, the prolonged standing and the concentration involved in icing the cake might prove too much for her.

'If she didn't feel able, would you do it, Fritz?'

The old man paused in his work to look at her. 'Me? You are asking me to perform this most important of tasks?'

Liz thought how drawn his face had become since what he called the *Anschluss*, when the Nazis had walked into Vienna. Now Hitler had further confirmed his predictions, by taking over what was left of Czechoslovakia.

Impulsively, she continued, 'It's asking a lot, I know. You do so much . . .'

'It is not that, *Liebling*. I would consider it an honour. But your parents may not wish that an outsider . . .'

'Outsider? But you're almost one of the family!' Liz exclaimed. 'You must know that's how we all think of you.'

'Such goodness.' His eyes filled with tears, and he brushed them away with the back of his hand, leaving a streak of flour. 'And I am a foolish old man. If it is what your mother wishes.'

Liz hadn't actually consulted her mother, but when she put the suggestion to her, there was no mistaking the fleeting look of relief in Kathleen's eyes. 'I get so cross with myself. A couple of years back, I'd have managed everything with one hand tied behind me. I can hardly blame Georgy – he spends more time with Dad than he does with me, and Ellen takes care of most of the heavy work . . .'

'You expect too much of yourself, Mam,' Liz coaxed her. 'You always did. But you want to be fit for the wedding.'

'Yes, of course.' Kathleen forced a smile. They didn't understand, any of them, what it cost her to practise patience. 'I'd be delighted if Fritz would ice the cake. I'll come and tell him so.'

The river was busy with traffic as Dandy wheeled the pram along the landing stage to where the Birkenhead ferry was preparing to cast off.

'Here we are, then, lad. Over an' back for tuppence, so long as we don't get off. How does that sound, eh?'

Georgy stared solemnly back at him.

'Morning, Dandy. Takin' the little'un for a blow?'

'Just there an' back, Alf – get a bit of air in his lungs.' He handed over his money and the pram wheels rattled over the slatted gangplank, bouncing Georgy up and down. 'All right if I stow the pram here and take him up top?'

'Right as rain, la.' Alf had seen Dandy box many times at the Stadium in his heyday, a hero to his generation. Watching the old timer now, climbing the steep stairway with the plump, rather ungainly child clasped to his chest, Alf thought there was something equally heroic about the way he coped with that grandson of his, who must be getting on for two years old and who anyone could see was tuppence short of a shilling.

'Here we are then, Georgy.' Dandy sat down on the wooden bench with the child, wrapped in a blanket, firmly held on his knee. 'An' we've got it all to ourselves. Listen, now. You see them two birds perched up there on the twin towers of that big building, with their wings spread out, an' lookin' up river and down like they was on guard duty? The liver birds, they are. Unique to this great city. Homecoming sailors scour the skyline from Formby Point on for a first sight of them, cos it's said the day they disappear'll be a bad day for Liverpool,' Georgy yawned. 'That's the ticket, lad, get some of that good Mersey air in your lungs. We'll have you boxing for England one day, you'll see. There goes the gangplank. We're off.'

As the ferry boat shuddered into life, Dandy slid the child gently down until his feet touched the deck. 'Can you feel the throbbing, Georgy?' And when his grandson looked up, vaguely questioning: 'That's the engines.'

He encouraged Georgy to put one foot in front of the other until he tired. The ferry ploughed its way towards the open river, weaving a path expertly between the tugs and dredgers and other tiny craft which seemed to be going in all directions, churning up foaming waves that sparkled in the sunlight. Dandy sat Georgy on the rail, as he always did, pointing out the different sights – the smoke issuing from the funnel, grey-black against the blue of the sky; the cargo ships; the Isle of Man ferry, *Mona's Isle*, getting under way; and the big white liner coming in to dock. 'How's that for a lovely ship. An Empress, that's what she is. A real lady. It's a grand sight, don't you think – all them ships, coming and going? Ah, and see, up ahead there – that's Birkenhead.'

And Georgy smiled one of his rare smiles.

It was a lovely wedding; everybody said so. Even the telegram arriving late on Saturday – SORRY CAN'T MAKE IT HAVE A

LOVELY TIME LOVE SHIRLEY ANNE STOP – couldn't spoil things, though Rita was a bit short with her when she rang on Sunday afternoon to wish her happy. Liz, in a sudden burst of sympathy for her young sister, managed to speak to her briefly before she rang off. Shirley Anne was full of bravado, but Liz could have sworn that she was crying. It wouldn't do to spoil the happy atmosphere by saying so, but the thought continued to trouble her for some time.

The sun shone from early on, and all the local people, as well as most of Rita's pupils from the school in Toxteth, came to pack the corner of Greaty and Fortune street. 'Just like the 12th of July,' some wag observed, and was promptly rounded on for trying to stir up trouble. The crowd cheered impartially as each member of the family left for the church, moving slowly down Fortune Street in the big black car decorated with white ribbons – Kathleen in a powder-blue swagger coat with a matching dress and a hat with an eye-length veil, accompanied by her two dark-suited sons, and the bridesmaids, the epitome of spring in their sunshine yellow.

But the greatest cheer was reserved for Rita, who finally emerged with Michael in her simple ivory gown, her face, as pale as her dress, framed by a cloud of veiling, and a bouquet of spring flowers clutched in her hand. 'Be 'appy, gairl,' they shouted. Schoolchildren, frantically waving, yelled, 'Hey, Miss, over 'ere! Ooh, yer luk like the Queen!' as the car moved away.

Michael saw his daughter's flowers were trembling, and sought her hand. 'All right, Rita love?'

'Oh, Dad, I swore I was going to be perfectly calm, and here I am, shaking like a jelly.'

His hand tightened on hers. 'You'll be fine, girleen, once you see your Frank. And if you're half as happy as your mother and meself have been, you'll not go far wrong.'

Liz had vowed she wouldn't go all soppy, but St Anthony's was full and the Nuptial Mass was so beautiful, the exchange of vows so moving, that she had to swallow hard a couple of times. Outside the church afterwards, the rejoicing was unconfined as photographs were taken and well-wishers pressed forward to congratulate the happy couple. A devout agnostic, Nora Figg had felt unable to bring herself to enter a Catholic church, but she was well to the fore with her confetti, her raucous comments, tactless as usual, rising above the rest. 'Y've bairned yer boats, now, gairl! Yu'll just 'ave ter make the best of it.'

They used Harry Carney's big upstairs room at The Grapes for the reception. It was a comfortable room, panelled in dark oak with red plush furnishings and, in pride of place on the mantel-shelf, a glass case containing a model of one of the early Cunarders, in which Harry Carney's father had sailed as a chef.

Frank didn't have many relations, apart from his sister Hilda and their widowed mother, but all who came were made welcome as family and friends collected to toast the happy couple, and admire the wedding presents laid out the previous night, including the beautiful linen that had arrived from Toronto and Chicago, from Aunt May and Uncle Liam. They admired, too, the cake, in the centre of the buffet table. Fritz had decorated both tiers with exquisite basket-work and hand-worked flowers, and topped it with an intricate archway under which stood figures of the bride and groom.

He had also helped Ellen with the food, which she somehow managed to organize whilst taking charge of Georgy and the twins. Nobody knew what Michael had said to Nick and Laura, but for once they not only brought the children, but consented to leave them in Ellen's care.

'That's your Michael all over,' murmured Aunt Flora to Kathleen. 'Gentle as a lamb, but heaven help any of us when he digs his heels in.'

'I've never noticed you being daunted.'

'Oh, well, you know me – fools rush in, and all that.'

Kathleen smiled at her sister, who was nobody's fool – as elegant as ever today, in a wide-brimmed black straw hat swept up at one side to reveal a single beige rose which exactly matched her tailored coat and skirt. 'Laura can't help the way she is. It's her mother's influence. Perhaps it would be no bad thing if she did accept our May's offer to take her and the twins, if war should come.'

'Put the Atlantic between them, you mean? That should do the trick, as long as mother didn't decide to go too. How has Nick reacted to the idea?'

They both turned to watch their younger brother, who was encouraging the antics of his children. 'He says he's all for it, though he'd miss them like mad. Laura's such a bag of nerves, I'm not sure which scares her most – the thought of the sea journey, or the risk of being bombed.'

'Silly woman.' Flora transferred her attention to Kathleen. 'And what about you? Would you be tempted to take Georgy to Canada?'

'Certainly not!' Kathleen was shocked. 'We're a family – and if push comes to shove, we'll see it through together as a family.'

'If things did get nasty, you could always come to me, you know.'

'Oh, really, Flora! However did we get on to such a morbid subject? I refuse even to think of war on my daughter's wedding day.'

Dandy, dapper in his best suit, his watch and chain proudly displayed, had taken change of Georgy so that Ellen could pop home and check all was well, but soon Michael came to claim his son, hoisting him high on his shoulder.

'You go and get yourself a drink, Dad. We'll just stay here and watch everyone, eh, Georgy?'

But his young son was more interested in something over his father's shoulder. 'Sip.'

Michael and Dandy stared at one another in disbelief. Georgy stretched out grasping fingers. 'Sip,' he lisped again, quite distinctly.

'Well, God be praised!' murmured Dandy. 'D'you not see there, behind you? It's the old Cunarder. When I take the lad down to the river, I point out the ships and tell him all about them. Kathleen, come here, girl. How's this for a wedding present?'

When the excitement had died down, and all the toasts had been drunk, it was time for Rita and Frank to leave for a short honeymoon in Llandudno. Liz went across the road with Rita to help her change into the smart but practical navy blue suit she had bought to go away in. It was Liz who took the navy and white hat which her sister had set primly and squarely on her head, and tilted it saucily over one eye. 'Go on,' she said. 'Be a devil for once.' And then, realizing that their relationship would never be quite the same after today, she hugged her fiercely. 'Be happy, our Rita!' And Rita hugged her back, and said if she wasn't careful, they'd both start blubbing and ruin their make-up.

Flora had insisted that the couple should be driven to Lime Street Station by Peters in the Daimler, so after tearful farewells, Rita threw her bouquet, which Liz caught, and they were away, the two bridesmaids crammed in with them, and Chris and Jimmy bringing up the rear in the van.

By the time the seeing-off party returned, the pianist and accordion player were in full flow, and the atmosphere had mellowed, with most of the men at one end of the room, amiably arguing Everton's chances of winning the League Championship, and the women at the other dissecting every detail of the wedding, while the children ran wild and got under the feet of the few couples who were dancing.

'Come on,' Jimmy said, putting an arm round Liz, and propelling her, unresisting, towards the dancers. 'I've hardly had you to myself all day.' And because the wedding had left her thoughts in turmoil, she welcomed the comfort of his arms. 'Hey, this is nice,' he said softly. 'You know, I've been thinking . . .'

'Not now, Jimmy,' she murmured. 'I might be tempted to say yes, and regret it tomorrow. Just hold me and dance.'

In the corner, she glimpsed her mother, Georgy lolling sleepily on her knee. Mam was drooping too, taking little part in the conversation. In that instant, she seemed isolated from the rest. Suddenly Liz couldn't bear to see her looking so worn. A great surge of anger and love and pity – even fear – threatened to swamp her as she realized that everything dear and familiar was changing much too fast.

On an impulse, she broke away from Jimmy and ran towards the pianist, bending to whisper in his ear. He nodded, and as Jimmy caught up with her, the music came to an end. 'What was all that about?'

'You'll see,' she said.

The two musicians went into a huddle, and then the pianist said, 'Can I have your attention, ladies and gentlemen? I have had a request from a beautiful young woman – and I never refuse requests from beautiful young women. I'm told the people concerned will know it's for them. Are you ready, Mike?'

They began to play, and Liz saw her father's head come up first; saw him turn to look at Mam. 'Go on, Mam,' she said, taking Georgy from her. 'It's a special request.'

'Oh, really, I don't think . . .' Kathleen began, turning pink. But Dad was already there, waiting to take Kathleen in his arms, holding her with that special closeness turning back the years. And it didn't matter that Mam's lovely dress was all creased, or that Dad's movements were slightly less than fluent, because Liz knew that, for them, the old magic was timeless. She doubted if they even heard the clapping and cheering as they circled the floor alone, to the familiar strains of *I'll take you home again, Kathleen*.

Chapter Seven

There was a curious air of unreality about that spring and summer, as though people were determined to enjoy themselves, come what may. With many factories well into the production of munitions and aircraft parts, and with fighters and bombers being turned out as fast as possible, there was less unemployment than of late, which meant that there was a bit more to spend.

'It's an ill wind,' said Kathleen.

Even the imminence of conscription was regarded by many young men as a passport to adventure. Jimmy and Chris had already joined the Territorials.

Kathleen turned pale when Chris first mentioned it. He'd not been the same since that Sally girl had messed up his life. But she only said abruptly, 'Well, if they mean to call up twenty- and twenty-one-year-olds, I suppose you'd have to go, sooner or later. But for heaven's sake, why meet trouble halfway? Your Dad's likely to have enough problems as it is.'

Chris just grinned. 'Don't worry. We'll both end up in catering, and that'll be a doddle.'

'War is never a doddle, lad,' Dandy warned him.

Jimmy had been restless ever since his spell at sea, and it was he who had suggested the Territorials.

'At least we'll know what we're doing when it does happen,' he said, determined to use the intervening time to wear down Liz's resistance.

'It's always been you for me, lovely Liz – even if I have had the occasional fling.'

They had taken a picnic to Eastham woods on a Sunday, early in May, crossing on the ferry in perfect weather, and wandering through thick carpets of bluebells and primroses, pursued by the voices of children playing 'tag' among the trees.

Liz felt she was being pressured. She was very fond of Jimmy – no, she was more than fond of him. A small voice whispered that there was none of the magic she had felt in an earlier time, in a different wood. But this was real life. She and Jimmy knew one another so well that there would be few surprises in store for either of them, which, she supposed, ought to make for a happy marriage. So why did she find the prospect vaguely depressing?

'Jimmy, I'm sure it's not a good idea to rush things – marriage is so permanent.'

He drew her down among the bluebells, and his caresses were very persuasive. 'I'd hardly – say – we've been – rushing,' he murmured, punctuating the words with ever more urgent kisses. 'We've been skirting round one another for years, on and off. It wouldn't have lasted this long, if we weren't meant for each other. And you can't let a fellow go off to war without someone to fight for.'

'That's blackmail!' Liz tried to pull away, but he was too strong for her. 'Jimmy, please. I can't think with you so close.'

'Then don't think. Just say yes. Please.'

His face, close to hers, was very serious and unexpectedly vulnerable. It was the vulnerability that did it. 'I suppose we could get engaged – but that's all,' she added hastily as his ardour increased.

'I hope you know what you're doing,' Mam said, when they got home and broke the news. 'You're not yet nineteen.'

'You were only nineteen when you married Dad.'

'That was different. The war was still on, but your father wasn't involved. He'd come over from Ireland in search of work, and the moment we met, we just knew, right off. But we were courting for two years. There was none of this rush-rush, now-or-never attitude.'

Kathleen knew she was being illogical, but the speed at which her children were growing up and leaving home was suddenly escalating. First Shirley Anne, then Rita – and every morning, she dreaded the sound of the postman in case he'd brought Chris's call-up papers. Now here was Liz contemplating marriage. Soon there would only be Joey and little Georgy left. It wouldn't be so bad if she could be sure that Liz was really in love with Jimmy, the way she and Michael were. But a love like theirs didn't happen very often, and she'd seen no sign of it with these two.

'Don't worry, Mam. We won't be doing anything daft,' Liz said, guessing her thoughts. She looked Jimmy straight in the eyes. 'We're getting engaged, that's all.'

Reassuring her mother was one thing, but she sensed that Dad's feelings went much deeper. He did not object to her engagement, but the closeness between them had always been special, and she knew that the thought of losing her would be hard to accept. While the rest of the family were merrily celebrating, her father quietly left the room.

Liz caught her mother's eye, then went after him, knowing where he would be.

'Dad?' He was standing aimlessly in the bakehouse, as though he wasn't quite sure what he was doing there. She went up and put her arms round him, and was instantly caught and held. 'It's all right, Daddy, you aren't ever going to lose me,' she said, her voice muffled against his shoulder. 'I'll always be here – always your Lizzie, no matter what.'

Michael stood unmoving for a moment. It was wrong to have favourites, he had told himself so often enough. But this child, his lovely Lizzie, was special, and he couldn't gainsay it. His hold loosened. 'I know it fine, girleen, but I know, too, that you have your own life to live, as I have mine. And if you truly love Jimmy, it would be very wrong of me to begrudge you your happiness.'

'As if you would! Anyway, we won't be getting married for ages yet.'

'Ah, Lizzie,' he laughed softly and kissed her cheek. 'You're a grand girl.'

'Have you heard?' Chris let the back door bang to behind him; Liz hadn't seen him so flustered in a long time. 'There's a submarine in trouble out in the bay, with over a hundred men on board.'

Kathleen came through from the shop as he was speaking. 'Ellen's just told me. It's the *Thetis*. Poor Hester Whelan – her only son's on board. Ellen's trying to make sure she isn't alone, but they say it could be ages before anything's known . . .'

'Oh, Mam! Not that nice Harry – the one our Shirley Anne took such a shine to?'

'That's him, God keep him. Only twenty and all his life before him. No wonder Hester's distraught.' Kathleen looked at her eldest son, every day growing more like his father, the very first time she had seen him, with the same long limbs and shy charm and smiling blue eyes. Her heart turned over. Suppose it had been Chris in that submarine?

'I did hear it wasn't in very deep water,' he said, 'so with any luck they'll get it up all right.'

'Never mind luck, just pray as hard as you can, the both of you,' Kathleen said. 'I know how I'd be feelin' if it was one of you.'

She picked up Georgy, and felt a great rush of love as he rewarded her with a sticky kiss. He was getting heavy for her to carry, but his sweet nature was a blessing that outweighed most of his shortcomings. They were all delighted with his progress since Rita's wedding; by his second birthday, last month, he could say all their names after a fashion, and was walking better with every week that passed. The specialist was equally pleased with him. 'Love can move mountains, Mrs Ryan,' he said – though they both knew that Georgy's particular mountain could only be moved so far.

The news about the submarine ran through the community like fire. When Liz went out later, it seemed the whole city was holding its breath, and for the next couple of days all kinds of rumours circulated. Marker buoys had been sighted – divers had been down and the men were alive – they were going to burn a hole in the submarine's side and get the men out that way . . . Throughout that time Hester clung to hope, keeping her vigil along with other families and the patient crowds who bore them company. But in the end the vigil became a wake: only four men escaped, and Harry was not one of them.

'She's so calm, it's not natural,' Ellen said, when at last Hester was back home. 'I told the doctor when I fetched him to her – she hasn't slept a wink in days. But he's given her something, and she's gone out like a light.'

'It's a terrible tragedy. Makes you wonder if the authorities couldn't have done more.'

Ellen shrugged. 'There's a lot of folk saying the same. But we'll probably never know the answer to that one.'

As the summer progressed, the news got worse. Chris and Jimmy had been placed on stand-by orders. They tempted Clare away from her studies and all went out for a final fling, Liz wearing her engagement ring, a pretty opal surrounded by tiny diamonds.

Nora Figg, seeing her wearing it in the shop one day, had peered at it and muttered, 'An opal, is it? Bad luck, is opals.'

'Mrs Figg!' Ellen had been incensed. 'How can you say such a thing?'

'Oh, let her say what she likes, Ellen. I'm not superstitious.'

Nora had sniffed. 'Suit yerself. I'm only repeatin' worri 'aird from them as knows.'

But Liz refused to let the old misery-guts spoil her pleasure in her lovely ring.

'It'd look even better with a nice gold band next to it,' Jimmy murmured persuasively on that last evening out.

'Maybe, but I like it the way it is for now.'

Jimmy grinned. 'Ah, well. It was worth a try.'

'Will you write to me, Clare?' Chris asked diffidently as the last waltz began.

And Clare, who had little contact with young men, apart from Chris – and Francis, of course, although brothers didn't count – felt a small glow of pleasure. 'Yes, of course I will.'

Shirley Anne lay in her shabby bed in the shabby room that constituted home, and fought back the panic that had been building in her for the past month. Each night she danced and sang her heart out, and each morning she woke hoping – praying, even – that the exertion would have done the trick: only to face fresh despair. This couldn't be happening to her, screamed the little voice inside her head. It was a mistake – a terrible mistake. Everything had been going wonderfully. London was crammed with people out to enjoy themselves, *Stepping on Air* was still playing to packed houses, and she had made lots and lots of friends.

She had tried telling herself that there could be any number of reasons. But she was never late. Her mouth went dry and she felt sick again. He had sworn to her that she needn't worry, that he always took precautions – and Alec wouldn't lie to her. He adored her, he had told her so hundreds of times. And she had been madly in love with him almost from their very first meeting – his amused indolence, the way he flicked his straight blond hair away from his forehead with one finger; even the hint of danger about him fascinated her.

He seemed to have money to burn, yet hardly ever seemed to work. He introduced her to his sophisticated friends at tea dances in smart hotels. And then one day, saying he was tired of sharing her with others, he swept her away, slightly tiddly with champagne drunk in celebration of someone's birthday, to his luxurious apartment in St John's Wood.

He had been so persuasive that afternoon, so tender, that she had offered no more than a half-hearted resistance when he begged for more than mere kisses. 'I only want to look at you, my beautiful one . . .' She could hear the seductive voice now, feel his long sensuous fingers bringing her to wild peaks of excitement as they explored her body before slipping the straps from her shoulders, sending her new satin and lace cami-knickers to join her dress on the carpet; kneeling to undo her suspenders, and rolling down her stockings, one by one, his lips, feather-light, tracing their progress. 'Oh, yes . . . you are very lovely. Please let me love you, darling.'

And moments later, he had carried her, shivering violently with something more than cold, into the bedroom, and laid her on the bed. A part of her mind kept telling her that this was wrong, that she ought not to let him, but her body was on fire and Alec was whispering, 'You'll be quite safe – I won't give you a baby, I promise!' and she had no power to resist.

They had spent many afternoons in his apartment since then. He had not always been so gentle, but she was so besotted that even his small cruelties had a kind of sensuality.

If I don't go down to breakfast soon, she thought, that old cow of a landlady will be up to see why not. The mere thought of greasy egg and sausage in a dining room that smelled perpetually of stale cabbage was nauseating. A sudden longing for home, and Mam, and all that was familiar, overwhelmed her. But that was impossible, too. If she ran away now, left the show before it finished, she'd never get another chance. I'll get through somehow, she told herself. I'll stick to toast for breakfast, and later today, I'll go to the flat. Perhaps there's something wrong with Alec's phone.

Six times Shirley Anne pressed the bell, heard it ring. She was about to turn away when the door opened. Alec stood there, wearing the black silk robe with the gold dragon snaking down the back that made him look like Noel Coward, one hand raised, smoke drifting from a Turkish cigarette glowing in its gold-tipped ebony holder. His eyes narrowed slightly, but he made no move to let her in. And beyond him, she glimpsed dark hair spread across a cushion, a matching drift of smoke.

'Alec . . . I must talk to you!' She began, incoherently, to babble her fears.

'For God's sake, keep your voice down!' he snapped, pulling the door to behind him, and glancing up and down the corridor, which was for the moment deserted. 'Pull yourself together.' Shirley Anne swallowed back a sob. 'That's better. Now – have you seen a doctor?'

'No, but . . .'

'Then you'd better – as soon as possible, if you're to get rid of it.'

She stared, not understanding what he meant. 'Get rid of it?'

His lip curled. 'Such innocence! A trifling operation – there are practitioners who will oblige for a price. I may even help you pay for it, if you're sensible.'

Shirley Anne was horrified, not wanting to believe what she was hearing. 'B-but that's murder!' she whispered.

'Very melodramatic, but a bit late in the day for scruples. Still, it's up to you. I'm sorry, but . . .' The tip of his cigarette glowed red as he slowly inhaled.

'Sorry? How can you just stand there and say you're sorry? You promised me it wouldn't happen,' she sobbed. 'I can't – can't do what you said! You'll have to m-marry me.'

'*Marry you*?' Smoke curled upwards from his flaring nostrils as he looked her over coldly. 'Whatever gave you such a bizarre idea?'

'Well, because it's your – our baby.'

'So you tell me. But even if you could prove it, which you can't, a man can't be expected to marry every bit of skirt who throws herself at him. You were begging for it, sweetie – even you can't deny that. How am I to know how many other men you might not have – er, pleasured?' He ignored her gasp. 'Take my advice – have the abortion, and put it down to experience. You have a glittering career ahead of you if you play your cards right, and no- one need ever know that you're nothing but a cheap little Papist tart.'

'Oo-ow!' The sound, a mixture of bitterness and fury, echoed down the corridor, as she lunged towards him, her long fingernails upraised. But he caught her hands and imprisoned them in one of his, forcing them down, his cigarette held menacingly close to her face.

'Better that than a foul-mouthed proddy pig!' she screamed, the last vestige of poise deserting her. 'I know now why our Liz hates you! She'd kill you if she was here!'

There was a flicker of malevolence in his eyes, and for a moment he looked anything but coolly sophisticated. 'Well, why don't you go home and tell the bitch?'

'Alec, darling, whatever's keeping you? Do hurry up . . .' The husky summons sounded querulous.

'I'm coming, my pet.' Alec's voice was silky once more. 'As for marriage, you silly gullible child, not a chance. I am already engaged, have been for some time – to a young lady of impeccable background. We are to be married quite soon.' His grip tightened momentarily. 'And don't try to make trouble for me, or you will be very sorry.'

Shirley Anne never knew how she got back to her digs, or how she got through the show that night. It was as though someone else inside her took over, someone who kept reiterating 'I'm damned if I'll let that creep get the better of me!' And although several people remarked that she looked tired, no-one could fault her performance.

'A real trouper, that Shirley Anne,' she heard one of the backstage crew say admiringly. 'Never short-changes her audience – not like some prima donnas I could mention.'

In July Mr Morgan died, quite suddenly, in his sleep. He had been looking frail for some time, but made light of it whenever Liz or Alice suggested that he should employ another assistant so that he could take life more easily.

'This *is* my life,' he would insist with a quiet twinkle. 'What would I do with myself? And what would my ladies do if I were not here to chat with them, and admire their hats?'

Alice rang to say she had found him sitting peacefully in his chair when she arrived, and wasn't sure what to do. He had never mentioned any family, and no-one had ever visited him. They agreed that she should contact Mr Morgan's solicitors, and that the café should remain closed for that day, at least, as a mark of respect. Then, if there was no objection, Alice would carry on as usual until Mr Morgan's affairs were resolved.

Liz could scarcely take it in at first. Her affection for Mr Morgan had been such a warm, living thing. Knowing him had changed her life, for if she had not gone into the Candide that day two years ago, she might never have been inspired to strive for something more than a modest improvement in the business. But after the first shock had abated, Liz was able to take comfort in knowing that he would at last be reunited with his own beloved Candide.

In the following day's post, there was a letter for Mam and Dad from Chris, and two for Liz – one from Jimmy, and an official-looking buff envelope. She opened Jimmy's letter and compared notes with Mam. The two lads were somewhere near Norwich, and having a great time, by all accounts.

'Not that our Chris is any great shakes as a letter-writer, beyond telling us that the weather's hot, his feet are sore from marching, and there's a great pub in the nearby village,' Kathleen said drily. 'I hope yours is a bit more interesting.'

'A bit.' Liz blushed, grinned, and folded Jimmy's letter away in her pocket to read on her own later. The buff envelope was from a firm of solicitors in Castle Street, dealing with the estate of the late Charles Morgan. 'What do you make of this, Mam?'

Kathleen scanned the few sentences couched in legal phrases which told one nothing. 'Alice may have put them on to you, if Mr Morgan had no relations. Perhaps he's left you a memento. He was very fond of you.'

Liz had never been to a solicitor's office. She dressed with care that afternoon in a navy-blue tailored dress with a short swing-back tartan jacket and a shallow-brimmed navy hat. It was by Dorville, one of the most expensive outfits she possessed, and always made her feel confident.

An hour later she returned, to find Dad in the living room with Mam, having a quick cup of tea – a rare treat since Chris had left. They were making enquiries about getting someone part time, an older man who might be glad of a few hours' work. If rationing came in, they'd maybe not need anyone full time.

'That was quick,' Kathleen said, looking up briefly. 'There's tea in the pot, if you want a cup.' When no reply was forthcoming, she looked again at her daughter. 'Are you all right, love?'

Liz sat down at the table, and burst into tears. They both stared.

'Lizzie?' Michael's voice was gentle.

She lifted her flushed face, her eyes brilliant with tears, her hat askew.

'He's left it to me,' she said in a dazed voice. 'Mr Morgan's left me the Candide. It's mine.'

It took two cups of tea and a lot of talk, much of it incoherent, before the reality sank in. Liz said she would have to go and see Alice at once. 'Mr Morgan apparently left her some shares in the business – I don't quite understand yet how it will work – ' She looked across at her mother. 'Oh, Mam, you don't suppose she might feel slighted? Alice has done far more than me to build the place up.'

'There's only one way to find out,' Kathleen said.

'Yes, I suppose so.' Liz jumped up and tossed her hat on the table, shaking her hair loose. 'Can I take one of the vans, Dad?'

'I suppose you'd better,' Michael agreed. 'But go easy, will you? The state you're in, you'll be running someone down.' When she had gone, slamming the door behind her, he knocked out his pipe, put it in his pocket and looked across at Kathleen. 'Well now, who would have thought it? Not the best time, perhaps, to inherit a business, but that will be the last thing on her mind.'

By the time Liz reached the Candide she was already beginning to feel calmer. Alice was pale, but elegant and composed as always.

'My dear girl, of course I don't begrudge you your good fortune. I would hate that kind of responsibility. As a matter of fact, Charles told me what he intended to do, but it wasn't my place to mention it – for all I knew, he might not have got round to making a new will.'

'I still can't quite believe it. You *will* stay on and run the café?'

Alice smiled. 'Of course I will. I have a stake in its future, after all.'

Liz glanced round the unlit café, which looked somehow forlorn. 'Oh, dear – it's going to seem very strange without him.'

When she got home, the telephone was ringing. Ellen was in the scullery and her mother was in the shop.

'It's the fourth time that wretched thing's rung in the last half hour,' Ellen said, exasperated. 'And every time we answer, it goes dead. The operator's as fed up as we are.'

'Could be a fault on the line. It's all right, I'll take it,' Liz said.

She hurried into the passage and picked up the receiver. 'You're through,' said the operator.

'Ryan's Bakery,' Liz said. 'Can I help you?'

There was no immediate answer, though she could hear breathing at the other end. 'Look, whoever you are, stop playing silly beggars. Either say what you want to say, or put the phone down.'

'Liz? Oh, Liz, at last!'

'Shirley Anne? Is that you? Are you the one that's been driving everyone daft?'

'I couldn't . . . I'm sorry. Don't tell Mam, but it was you I wanted . . . I must . . .' She sounded odd, uncertain, almost pleading – not at all Shirley Anne-ish. ' . . . must see you, now!'

'Now? Where are you, for heaven's sake?'

'I'm at Lime Street Station. I've been here for simply ages.'

It was on the tip of Liz's tongue to tell her to find her own way home, but there was a despairing edge to her sister's voice, and she found herself saying instead, 'I'll be there as soon as I can.'

The station was full of bustle and steam, and clouds of acrid smoke that caught in Liz's throat. A train had just arrived, spilling its contingent of travellers out on to the platform to swell the crowd, making it difficult to find anyone.

'Liz, oh, Liz!'

Shirley Anne came from nowhere, flinging herself at her sister in a storm of weeping which, even by Shirley Anne's standards, threatened to reach histrionic proportions. Liz, thoroughly alarmed, could only hold her tight, hushing her like a baby, while passers-by looked on curiously. 'Hey! Nothing's that bad. You'll make yourself ill.' Finally, she said sharply, 'That's enough, Shirley Anne. If you don't stop, I shall slap you.'

She sounded so like Mam that the younger girl stopped in mid sob, hiccuped, and drew a shuddering breath. They located Shirley Anne's luggage, left abandoned on a bench, and made for the refreshment room and a restorative cup of tea.

Liz didn't try to hurry the explanations, beyond establishing the fact that the show had closed. But she was appalled to see how sickly her sister looked, surely due to more than the effect of all that crying. If this was what going on the stage did to you, she couldn't see what was so wonderful about it. 'The sooner I get you home and start feeding you up, the better,' she said at last.

'No!' Shirley Anne exclaimed. 'I can't face Mam and Dad, not yet!'

And then it all came pouring out, and Liz listened in growing dismay, not attempting to interrupt until at last her sister's voice tailed away. One corner of her mind was screaming, 'This can't be happening, it's all a mistake – she's an innocent, she doesn't know what she's talking about' and another was saying over and over, 'Oh, poor Mam and Dad! Dear God, haven't they had enough?' And then she looked into Shirley Anne's red-rimmed eyes and saw a frightened little girl who didn't know what to do.

'Oh, love!' she said, stretching out a hand. 'They'll understand. They'll be disappointed, but they'll understand.'

But Shirley Anne knew they wouldn't – not in a million years. Oh, they'd forgive her, they'd support her, but they wouldn't understand. She had come back prepared to blacken Alec's name, to make him pay. Yet, now it had come to the point, she couldn't even bring herself to *speak* his name. What good would it do? He would deny everything, and no-one would believe her.

Chapter Eight

It seemed a bitter irony that almost before Liz had time to savour her inheritance, events were conspiring to diminish her pleasure. Shirley Anne's homecoming was only the first.

She had begged Liz to go in ahead of her, to break the news, but Liz was adamant. 'We'll go together,' she said, taking her sister's hand. 'It won't be easy, but you'd best just come straight out with it. Mam's got a sharp tongue, but she loves you – they both love you, and that's all that matters in the end.'

In fact, it wasn't necessary to speak the dreaded words. Kathleen, coming through from the shop, hardly even had time to register surprise. One look was enough. It was all there in Shirley Anne's face – guilt, shame, even a hint of truculence. It was every mother's nightmare, and for one instant she was tempted to implore *Why me, Lord? Haven't I had more than my share*? But her daughter looked so very young and scared, that in the end she simply held out her arms.

'Oh, Mam!' sobbed Shirley Anne, rushing to cling to her. Liz, watching her graceful sister stoop to be encompassed in Mam's fierce no-nonsense embrace, felt her own eyes sting.

'Come along, now, child,' Kathleen said at last, her tone deliberately matter-of-fact to discourage the onset of histrionics. 'Tears never mended anything. What's done is done. You aren't the first, and you certainly won't be the last. How far gone are you?'

Shirley Anne sniffed. 'I'm not sure. About seven or eight weeks, I think. I – I haven't been to a doctor.'

Kathleen uttered a faint 'tch' and said, 'Well, that's the first thing. We'll go along and see Dr Graham tomorrow. Meanwhile, you'd best let me break it to your father. We'll need to have a talk later, but for now you cut along and wash your face, then get some rest. You look exhausted. And heaven knows what they've been feeding you on – you're nothing but skin and bone.'

When Shirley Anne had left the room, she turned wearily to Liz. 'I suppose she hasn't told you who the man is?'

Liz shook her head. 'She said there wasn't any point – he was about to get married, and anyway, he'd been horrible to her, and she hated him. Oh, Mam, how could she do it?' And then, remembering herself and Leigh in the sandhills, and how close she had come to letting go all reason, she turned away to hide her blushes.

She didn't quite succeed, but Kathleen, seeing the flood of colour, mistook guilt for embarrassment. 'All too easily, I'm afraid. Still, we'll get over it,' she said bracingly. 'I never did hold with shotgun weddings – two wrongs seldom make a right. There'll be talk, of course. Shirley Anne's fall from grace will be a nine day wonder, and once word gets out, Nosey Nora'll have a field day. Still, at least it'll make a change from her ranting on about the folly of employing Germans, and how we might all be found dead in our beds one morning.'

'The evil her kind plant in other people's minds infuriates me,' Liz exclaimed.

'Some folk are just plain scared, love – they don't stop to think.'

But there were good people, too, people who turned out on a lovely sunny day to mourn Mr Morgan's passing. His funeral was attended by many of 'his ladies', fluttering handkerchiefs much in evidence, and a great many other people, too. Liz was moved to discover how many friends Mr Morgan had made in his own quiet way. The size of the congregation seemed to her a fitting tribute to a thoroughly good man.

Michael was finishing off a batch of Victoria sandwiches when Fritz put his head round the door.

'Is this a convenient time to speak with you, my friend?'

'Surely.' Michael dragged his mind away from Shirley Anne. 'There may well be a cup of tea going, if you'd care for one but, of course, I forgot, you're more of a coffee man. What can I do for you?'

'There is nothing you or anyone can do, I fear.'

Something in his voice made Michael look at him more closely. There had been several incidents recently, young louts catcalling after Fritz, the odd obscene message scrawled on the shop front. The latest attack had been more physical, and unpleasant. 'If you're worrying about that business this morning, Fritz, I've had a word with Sergeant McNaughton . . .'

'I worry only for you and your family, Michael. The situation can and will get worse. And so, much as it grieves me to add to your present problems, I believe it is better that I do not work here with you any longer.'

'There is no need . . .' Michael said, a shade too quickly, and saw the understanding of his friend's sad smile.

'There is every need. It is enough that you lose customers because of me, but tomorrow it could be a brick through your window. Once this kind of sickness takes hold, all reason is lost – believe me, I have seen it before. And, much as I value your loyalty, we both know how little time is left to me.'

'Liz will be heartbroken.' It wasn't what Michael had meant to say, and he saw the old man's face crumple a little, heard the pain in his voice.

'Ah, yes, Liz. Such a joy she has been to me. She will take it hard, I think. I wonder' – here the voice almost failed – 'would you be so kind as to explain to her? I lack the courage . . .'

'The devil take Adolf Hitler!' Michael burst out in unaccustomed rage.

'He will, my friend, without a doubt he will – in God's good time.'

Liz didn't take it well.

'I never heard such a pack of nonsense, Dad. Whyever didn't you stop him?'

'Don't talk to your father like that, Liz,' Kathleen said, even as Michael put up a calming hand.

'I'm sorry, but . . .' Liz's eyes glittered with fury, not against her father, but against the narrow-minded spite that had driven Fritz away. 'I'll go round to his daughter's this evening – make him see sense.'

'No, girleen. You will do nothing of the kind.'

She stared. 'You mean you're going to allow a few louts to frighten you into letting Fritz leave?'

'Liz!' Kathleen's voice sharpened, but again Michael calmed her. He took his daughter gently by the shoulders, feeling the resistance in her.

'It isn't that simple, Lizzie, my love. Oh, maybe I could have talked him round, but Fritz Lendl is making the one and only gesture he can make to protect us. It is important for his pride – and for the love he bears you in particular – that we allow him to make it.'

Tears glistened in the golden eyes. Liz's voice was thick with them, and her mouth went all awry. 'But it's so unfair!'

Michael kissed the top of her head. 'I know, girleen. I know.'

Dandy was now busy helping to organize the ARP, and enjoying the challenge. He followed the news avidly, always ready with his own views on each new development. 'Didn't I say Chamberlain'd never get Russia to join us and the French in supporting Poland?' he declared, when it was announced that Ribbentrop had gone back to Germany and signed a peace pact with Russia. 'There's parts of Poland the Russkies'd love to get their greedy paws on, so if it's true about the pact, we've been out-manoeuvred again, and Hitler can march into Poland any time he chooses.'

'There's still us and the French,' Nick argued, more to convince himself than anyone else. 'Chamberlain's guarantees to Poland still stand.'

Dandy uttered a derisive grunt. 'Adolf Hitler doesn't give a toss for Chamberlain's guarantees. Oh, there'll be a lot of diplomatic clap-trap, but it won't make a ha'porth of difference. I give it to the end of the month.'

'As soon as that?' Nick and Laura exchanged anxious glances. They had come over to Fortune Street for the evening, leaving Laura's mother to babysit. George was in bed, and Joey and the girls had gone to the pictures. The family knew Shirley Anne was back home, but only Dandy and Flora knew why, and Kathleen had no wish to make her daughter's misfortune known to her prudish sister-in-law, who would carry it home in turn to her mother. Though Laura was for the present far too preoccupied with her own problems to waste time or thought on anyone else.

'I wish I knew what to do,' she said. 'Nick thinks he can get us a place on a ship, and your May has written again, urging us to go over there.'

'Well, no-one else can make up your mind for you,' Flora said, blunt as ever. 'We none of us know what to expect, though plans for the evacuation of schoolchildren seem to be going ahead. I've had several lots of officials round, assessing how much of my home they might consider leaving to me – so if any of you want a bed, you'd better say so now.'

Laura's face was an agony of indecision. Kathleen remembered her apprehension during her pregnancy, her almost paranoid avoidance of Georgy in those early days, as if he might somehow contaminate her precious twins. She guessed that Southport would not be far enough from danger for someone like Laura – egged on by her mother, who was the root cause of most of her problems.

As if proving her point, Laura stammered, 'Mam says if they bomb Liverpool, we might not be that much safer in Southport.'

'How reassuring,' murmured Flora, and received a gentle shake of the head from Michael.

'It's just that I don't know your May. And then there's the journey – I've never been on a ship, and it's such a long way. Suppose they sink it, like they did the *Lusitania*, last time? If Mam could go, too, perhaps I wouldn't feel so bad, but she won't go without Dad, and so far he won't budge, even though he's retired and they could let the house . . .'

Kathleen looked across at Nick, whose face was blank. But his knuckles were white. And she suddenly tired of trying to pander to her spoiled sister-in-law. 'And what about your husband?' she said tartly.

'Oh, he can't come. They wouldn't let him, in any case. He says he'll be needed on the docks . . .'

'I wasn't suggesting he should. It's just that in all you've said, I haven't heard one word about Nick's feelings, or how you feel about leaving him. Working on the docks could be a lot more dangerous that joining the Forces. Doesn't the thought of him having to face that alone bother you?'

'Leave it, our Kathy!' he muttered, red-faced, not looking at his wife.

'I'm sorry, Nick, but I'll burst if I don't say something. When I married Michael, I married him for better or worse, because I loved him – and like most, we've had our share of both over the years. I could no more think of leaving him than I could stop breathing, so if the bombs do come, we'll face them together as we have everything else, because for me that's what loving someone is all about.' She heard Michael trying to silence her, but ignored him. 'But I can understand your concern about the children – I've got the same worry, and if you and Nick both truly feel that taking them to Canada is the safest course, then fine. Do it. There's no call to feel guilty about it, and no-one'll think the worse of you for it. But, for God's sake, stop all this selfish humming and hawing, and try giving a little thought to what it will cost Nick to let you go.'

In the silence that followed Kathleen was aware of all kinds of tensions. Flora, resisting the urge to clap, lit a cigarette and observed the various reactions through the curling smoke; in other circumstances, it would be the stuff of pure farce, she mused, surprised to find that she was even a little sorry for Laura, who seemed on the point of hysteria; Nick's handsome features showed a mixture of fury and embarrassment; Dandy, lips pursed, gazed heavenwards in apparent resignation. Michael's face was, as ever, hard to read, but he would be assembling his thoughts. And she suspected that Kathleen herself, having finally rid herself of a great many festering grievances, was already regretting her outburst.

Laura broke the silence by clambering to her feet, her normally pale face almost puce, her mouth quivering. 'Nicholas – take me home this minute!'

'Aye, girl, I will,' he said, sounding dispirited rather than angry. 'We came here for advice and support, not to be insulted.'

'Sit down, Nick – you, too, Laura.' Michael's voice was deceptively quiet. 'No-one will leave this room until peace is restored. We're all under a strain just now, and maybe it's beginning to tell, but if families start falling out, what hope is there for the country or the world?'

'That's all very well . . .' Laura interrupted peevishly.

'Quiet, now. I'm callin' this meeting to order.' Dandy stood up, all five feet seven inches of him, aware that the time had come for him to assert his authority. He hooked his thumbs in his waistcoat pockets and looked at each of them in turn. 'As all but a couple of you are flesh of my flesh, and the rest as near as dammit, I make no apology for pulling rank. I may even bang a couple of heads together, if it's the only way to make you see reason.' Small as he was, he cut as indomitable a figure now as he had in his days in the ring – and, as then, he sensed that he had them all where he wanted them, even Laura, who sat down abruptly. 'We've had a lot of plain speaking here this evening – and maybe some of it needed saying – but that isn't the issue right now. Time is short for all of us, getting shorter by the minute, and our tempers with it, perhaps. So, one way or another, pride will have to go out the window.' He looked at his daughter and daughter-in-law in turn. 'So, who's going to be first to say sorry?'

Kathleen stood up slowly and went round the table to where Laura sat, still rigid with injustice. 'I'm sorry, Laura. I had no business to preach at you like that. Only you and Nick can decide what's best for you. I can't think what came over me, except, like Dad and Michael said, we're all a bit on edge, all have difficult decisions to face . . .' She was about to add 'like what to do with Shirley Anne,' but family reconcilation could only be taken so far, and the longer she could keep that news from Laura, the better. She kissed her sister-in-law's averted cheek, and turned to hug Nick. 'Sorry, love.'

He put up a hand to cover hers, giving it a quick squeeze, and she smiled at him before going to Michael's side, feeling the warmth of his arm close round her.

Laura was not entirely mollified, but she could tell that Nick was wanting to settle – always the one for the easy way, was Nick. 'Very well,' she said grudgingly, 'we'll say no more about it. I'm sure I've no wish to drive a wedge between my husband and his family. But we'd better be going, just the same. Mother doesn't like to be out too late.'

'If you must,' Dandy said. 'But not until we've drunk to your great magnanimity.'

The sarcasm was totally lost on Laura.

Chapter Nine

'I am speaking to you from the Cabinet Room of Number 10 Downing Street . . .'

They had been to Mass early that Sunday as a family, and they now clustered round the wireless to listen as a family, Kathleen sitting in Michael's chair holding Georgy on her knee, and Michael standing behind, his hands resting on her shoulders. Mr Chamberlain's schoolmasterish voice, though calm, betrayed an occasional tremor of weariness . . . '*that unless we heard from them by eleven o'clock*' . . . all eyes instinctively turned to the clock, which showed eleven-fifteen . . . '*that they were prepared at once to withdraw their troops from Poland, a state of war would exist between us. I now have to tell you that no such undertaking has been received . . .*'

'Well, that's it, then.' Dandy sounded almost cheerful as he switched off the BBC announcer, who was starting to list the air raid precautions they already knew by heart. 'At least now we know where we stand.'

Shirley Anne instinctively moved closer to her father, who put a comforting hand on her shoulder. 'There now, girleen, we'll be just fine, you'll see.' And Joey nudged her in the ribs and said bracingly, 'Yeh. We'll soon have old Adolf licked.'

Kathleen's first thoughts were of Chris. *Dear God, keep him safe*. She got up and handed Georgy over to Michael. 'I'm going to put the kettle on. We could all do with a cup of tea. It'll be rationed soon enough, so we might as well enjoy it while we can. And another thing,' she said, quietly, but firmly, 'from now on we'll be saying a decade of the rosary together each evening after tea, for ourselves and for those we love who are not here with us.' She looked at each of them in turn. 'Prayer is as powerful a weapon as anything Hitler can devise, and Our Blessed Lady's never let this family down yet.' No-one disagreed.

Liz had listened to the news without emotion. I ought to feel something, she thought. This is probably the most momentous hour in my life so far, and I don't feel any different. The truth was, of course, that for almost everyone, the Prime Minister's announcement was a mere formality. The threat of war had been around for so long, that air raid shelters and sandbags were now a familiar part of the local landscape. They had even grown used to newer innovations, such as the barrage balloons lazily drifting above the city, like silver-skinned airborne whales.

For weeks the Ryans, like everyone else, had been involved in hectic preparations, criss-crossing the windows of their shops and the house with brown sticky tape, and making and hanging blackout curtains. Once that was done, Kathleen and Liz turned their attention to trying to assess how rationing might affect business.

'The petrol is going to be a problem. But there'll soon be less to deliver, so we can lay up one of the vans, and keep the other for the longer distances.'

'Maybe you could find a way of fixing a box cart on the back of the van, and we can bring Boadicea out of retirement. She'll need a bit of a spring clean, of course . . .' Liz looked meaningfully at her young brother.

'Yeh, O.K.,' Joey agreed amiably. 'I don't mind.'

'And I must remember to ask Cousin Tom about the chickens for that splendid poultry run you and your Dad have built out the back,' Kathleen said. 'It should take at least two dozen good layers, and there'll be no shortage of scraps to feed them on.'

The beginning of September brought the heartbreak of evacuation. Children, with the cardboard cases containing their gas masks slung across their shoulders and labels tied to their coats, each clutching a small case, pillowcase, or pathetic paper bundle, some in tears, converged on Lime Street Station, accompanied by teachers, and waved off by mothers trying to put on a brave front. Rita's Frank had decided to volunteer for the navy, and Rita was off to Shropshire with her old school, who found themselves several teachers short.

'I might as well go, Mam,' she said. 'We never really settled in those rented rooms, and I'd not want to stay without Frank. Besides, I'd have to do some kind of war work, so why not do what I do best? I reckon those kids need me as much as anyone does.'

Ellen, usually so strong, came close to breaking over what was, for her, an agonizing choice. 'I'm sorry. I can't seem to think straight,' she had confessed tearfully to Kathleen some weeks before, after giving the wrong change for the umpteenth time. 'I know I'll have to make my mind up soon so that arrangements can be made, but it's not easy to decide what's best. I mean, there's no way I can leave Arnie, and yet I'm not sure if I can bear to send the kids away on their own . . . Our Dot's ever so good with them, but Freddie's only four, and they do say it might not be possible to board them all with the same family. Yet, I'd never forgive myself if I kept them here, and the bombers came . . .'

Finally, Kathleen said, 'Listen; if you like, I'll have a word with our Flora. I'm not sure how much freedom of choice she has, but it's worth a telephone call – she's pretty good at getting what she wants. At least if the children could go to her, you'd know they were well looked after – Mrs Meadows is a nice motherly woman. I don't know why I didn't think of it before.'

Flora's voice down the telephone was expressive. 'Five children under eleven, and no mother to look after them! Are you mad, Kathy? I'm already down for a couple of Civil Servants, and a mother and two children, including a baby.'

'Oh, come on, Flo – this is for Ellen. She's done so much for me, I'd like to do something to repay her. Her eldest daughter's ever so good with the younger ones – almost as capable as Ellen herself. Well, she's had to be. You've loads of room in your servants' quarters, and with the back staircase, they wouldn't get underfoot – in fact, you need hardly know they were there.'

'D'you want to bet?'

But there was humorous resignation in the question, and Kathleen knew she had won. Flora had even offered to come for the children, once they knew the date for certain. 'Peters is off to the army next week, but I wouldn't mind giving the Daimler one last fling before it's relegated to the garage for the duration.'

'That lovely car. It seems such a shame,' Kathleen said, finding it hard to imagine Flora without her beloved Daimler. 'Whatever will you do?'

Flora chuckled wryly. 'What everyone else will be doing, our kid. I'll be using public transport.'

But Ellen adamantly refused to accept any further favours from Flora. 'We'll manage fine on the train, honestly. Hester'd look out for Arnie while I'm gone. She's being a real trouper, in spite of her own trouble. Says having plenty to do takes her mind off things.'

In the middle of all the activity, Chris and Jimmy arrived home on a forty-eight-hour pass. No-one mentioned France, but Kathleen wondered how long it would be before they were sent to join the Expeditionary Force.

'Take care, now,' she said briskly, straightening Chris's tie as he stooped to kiss her goodbye. 'And think on – just don't go volunteering for anything heroic. We want you back in one piece.'

'Take care,' Liz whispered to Jimmy, and he grinned.

'You know me – always land on me feet. And listen, Dad told me to say you're not to worry – he'll see you all right for meat once rationing starts. Not that it'll take us long to see Gerry off.'

The war's first impact hit Liz within hours of its declaration when she had a visit from Fritz's daughter, who she had met when visiting Fritz, who had become very depressed. She remembered Mitzi as a plump cheerful woman. But now her eyes were bloodshot, and the signs of recent tears still stained her cheeks, as she told Liz that her father had suffered a stroke, and was in the Royal Infirmary.

'It had worn him right down – all the worry that he might be interned, and the cruel things that are sometimes said.'

Liz was devastated, and at once offered to go and see him, but Mitzi said that for the moment, it would be better not to. Such a visit might distress him.

'I still feel badly about what happened here. Your father is such a gentle man. No-one hated Hitler and all he stands for more than he did.'

'People do not always think rationally,' Mitzi said wearily. 'They simply wish for a scapegoat.'

When she had gone, Liz wandered down to the cellar, where everything lay spotless and waiting, and teasing aromas still lingered on the air – of vanilla and almond, chocolate and syrup and fruits. In her heart she knew it wasn't going to be practical to use this bakehouse much longer. She clutched the edge of the table as a great wave of disappointment, hopelessness and outrage swept over her. It wasn't fair! She had come *that* close – within fingertip distance of her dream, and it wouldn't have been possible without Fritz. Now he was ill, perhaps dying, and everything about this place seemed to mock her with memories of him. Liz bent her head and wept.

She stayed in the cellar for some time, and so missed the news bulletin announcing that the *Athenia*, bound for Canada with hundreds of women and children on board, had been sunk by a U boat, with a terrible loss of life. But her parents heard the news.

'Oh, Michael!' Kathleen's hands flew to her face. She felt her skin crawling with the horror of it, and the same horror was mirrored in his eyes as they met hers. 'That's the ship Laura should have been on. Oh, how dreadful. Suppose . . .' her voice broke on a sob, 'God help me, just suppose I'd driven her into going.'

Michael gathered her into his arms. 'Now, *acushla*, it's not a bit of use supposing anything of the sort. You'd do better to thank God that you talked her out of it, and that Laura and the twins are now safe in North Wales, at that place her mother found for her. At least Nick can visit her there.'

'Well, I tell you one thing – I'll never poke my nose in where it's not wanted again!'

Michael chuckled. 'I'll believe that when it happens.'

Some time later they heard Liz in the scullery. 'I'm just going out for a walk, Mam,' she called and her voice sounded strained and husky.

'Don't forget your gas mask,' Kathleen called, but the door had already slammed shut again. 'Oh, dear, I'm afraid she's taken it hard – about Fritz.'

But Liz was back in a very short time, out of breath. 'Mam, Dad, can you hear? There's a riot going on up Greaty!'

They all hurried through to the shop, and Michael opened the door. At once, they heard the sounds of crashing glass and timbers mingling with a frightening baying and shrieking, like wild animals on the loose.

'Mother of God!' Kathleen whispered. 'What is it?'

She saw Dandy across the street, flapping both arms urgently at them. He was shouting something, but there was a huge brewer's dray lumbering past, and his words were lost. Eventually, tin helmet askew and gas mask bouncing wildly from side to side, he dodged between the traffic to reach them, his usual jauntiness abandoned in his agitation.

‘Get inside, all of you, and lock that door!’ His breathing was laboured and he looked grey as he removed the helmet and wiped his forehead with a large red handkerchief. Kathleen made him come through and sit down while Michael pushed home the bolts.

‘Honest, Dad, you haven’t got the sense you were born with – all this ARP-ing and rushing about. It’s time you realized that you’re not a spring chicken any more.’ She was already busy with glass and whisky bottle, pouring him a generous measure. ‘Come on – get that down you, before you say another word.’

He savoured one long mouthful then, as a little colour came back to his cheeks, sighed and leaned back, content to sip the rest. ‘Never mind spring chicken – I’d have been dead meat if I’d got caught up in that lot!’

‘Has everyone gone mad?’

‘You could say that, our Kathy. It’s that ship, the one with the kiddies on – some of them from round here. The news’s made some of the Scottie Road lot fighting mad. They’re all bevvied up an’ bent on revenge, and they’re not too fussy who they pick on – Germans, Italians, anyone with a foreign name. They’d even do a Chinese laundry, the mood they’re in. Poor old Falavio – both his shops have been wrecked, an’ he’s got a lad in the RAF. I only hope they don’t take it out on you, because of old Fritz.’

Liz was appalled. ‘But can’t the police stop them? Surely Sergeant McNaughton wouldn’t stand for this.’

‘Have a heart, chuck. If they’ve any sense, the scuffers’ll be keeping their heads down. You’d need a regiment of soldiers to take on a mob like that.’

‘But that’s aw– ’ The crash of breaking glass almost drowned Liz’s scream. ‘Oh, God help us! That’s our window!’

‘Michael, don’t go!’ Kathleen cried, as he moved, pale but purposeful, towards the shop. ‘It’ll only get their blood up worse than ever, if they catch sight of you. Dad, come back! Have you gone crazy?’

But Dandy had already ducked past Michael and marched boldly ahead of him into the shop. He stood, arms akimbo, glaring at the jagged hole in the window, and then at the wild-eyed man who had thrown the brick which lay amongst the broken glass. The man, astonished to see anyone there at all, stared back. Behind him massed a sea of angry faces, waving hands clutching rough lengths of timber, bricks and other makeshift weapons. He could smell the danger.

Then the baying suddenly became muted as someone shouted 'Hey, gerrof – that's Dandy bleedin' Power, tharris!'

'That's right, me brave bucko. It's Dandy bleedin' Power. So, what are you goin' ter do about it?' He thrust his head forward pugnaciously, daring anyone to make a further move.

'Well, what we waitin' for? Eez only an old man,' came a cry of youthful scorn from the crowd.

'Shurrup! You don't know nuttin'. Yer only lukin' at the bonniest champion as ever lifted the roof off of the old stadium – and 'e in't so old 'e couldn't still do you with one 'and tied behind 'is back.'

'Ar, 'e could that. So, yoo watch yer gob, daft little nit! Why, if Dandy Power wus ter blow 'is nose, yoo'd fall over, I shouldn't wonder.'

There was some ribald laughter, and Dandy knew that most of the crowd were on his side.

'You're right, there, la. But we don't want trouble, do we? Look now, youse all know Michael Ryan – a good man, even if he is me son-in-law.' Another ripple of laughter greeted this. 'An' he doesn't deserve this kind of treatment.'

'Still an' all, 'e did 'ave that Gerry workin' for 'im.' There was a long growling murmur amongst the agitators, and for a moment it looked as though things were going to get out of hand again. But the voice of reason prevailed. 'Leave off, 'arry, Dandy's right. We're norr'after the likes of Michael Ryan!' And they went surging away down Greaty towards the market, the sound dying away.

'Dad, don't you ever do anything like that again!' Kathleen exploded, dragging Dandy back to the living room and pushing him into a chair. 'You could've been killed.'

The weathered skin on Dandy's head was beaded with perspiration as he picked up his glass and drained it. 'I reckon you're right there, girl.' He chuckled. 'It was a rare few minutes, an' if any one of 'em'd had the nous to have a go, they'd've murdered me for sure!'

'And if they hadn't, I would!'

Liz, her misery forgotten, was feeling pretty murderous herself as she surveyed the debris. 'You wouldn't believe one brick could do so much damage,' she wailed, climbing gingerly into the well of the window with dustpan and brush. 'Just look at these broken stands – and splinters of glass everywhere. It's going to take hours to clear. And after all those miles of sticky paper we licked trying to make it safe. Where's Shirley Anne? We could do with another pair of hands.'

'Gone to bed,' Kathleen said laconically, struggling to unfold a dust sheet. 'Anyhow, we'll get on quicker on our own. At least the sticky paper's glued some of the pieces together. Dump everything in this,' she said, spreading the sheet, 'and Dad can get rid of it. And for pity's sake, be careful. We don't want you cutting yourself on top of everything else.'

It took Liz ages to make certain there were no tiny slivers of glass left anywhere, but at last she and Kathleen were satisfied. 'Here now, let me be doing that,' said Michael, seeing them struggle to bring the corners of the dust sheet together so they could tie them. 'Joey's going to help me to board up the window, then I'll be away to see about getting a new one fitted. I can dump this on the way.'

'You gorrof lightly,' said the man Michael brought back with him to measure the window. 'Talk about bloody Hitler – I reckon that lot done as much damage as 'alf a dozen bombs. A right shambles.'

Late that night, as Liz was on her way upstairs, she heard a faint noise in the shop. 'Oh, no, not again!' Everyone had gone to bed except Dad, who was in the bakehouse. With heart hammering she crept along the passage. All seemed quiet. And then she saw an envelope lying just inside the door. It was addressed to Dad. She took it out to him.

Michael's hands were covered in flour. 'Open it for me, will you, Lizzie love?'

Inside were two ten shilling notes, folded in a grubby sheet of paper. Liz read aloud: 'Sorry, mate. We 'ad a whip round in the pub.'

Shirley Anne pressed the bell, and waited for Mrs Frith's maid to open the door. Her stomach felt all knotted. Coming back to Faulkner Square was rather like those last tense moments before going on stage. And maybe, she thought, remembering how ruthlessly she had made use of the old lady, facing Mrs Frith would be every bit as nerve-wracking.

There had been moments recently when she'd wondered if coming home had been such a good idea, but at the time, it had been an impulse born of desperation. She had no real friends in London, and the landlady, putting two and two together, had called her awful names and thrown her out. Shirley Anne, scared and reverting to childishness, had screamed back at her that nothing would persuade her to stay another five minutes in the dirty, smelly old rooming house that wasn't fit for pigs . . .

'Miss? Is it reely you, Miss?'

Shirley Anne pulled herself together to find Ethel, Mrs Frith's maid, staring at her, eyes as round as saucers. She said, brightly, 'Yes, of course it's me, Ethel. Is your mistress in?'

'Er . . . ' Ethel was clearly nonplussed, remembering the scenes there'd been when Shirley Anne had shinned off without so much as a word, leaving Madam up the chute, with concerts arranged and no-one to perform in them, let alone run round after her. And there'd been all that sobbing into sodden hankies, and cries of *ingratitude* – and *betrayal*. And now here she was back, pert as you please, as though nothing had happened.

'Well, is Mrs Frith at home, or isn't she?'

'I'd berra go an' see, Miss . . .'

But Shirley Anne knew what that meant. And she wasn't being fobbed off. All she needed was five minutes alone with the old lady, and she'd be eating out of her hand. She brushed Ethel aside. 'Never mind, I'll go myself. In the drawing room, is she?' Without waiting for a reply, she brushed past the maid, and stepped lightly across the hall.

The drawing room curtains were half drawn to keep out the sun, and Shirley Anne's feet made no sound on the thick carpet as she approached the sofa where Mrs Frith lay stretched out. Her dark skirt was rucked up at one side, exposing a good two inches of pink elasticated knickers, and her head nestled among the pillows, the blue-rinsed hair carefully contained by an invisible hair net. Her chin sagged and her mouth had dropped open, emitting little puffing sounds that weren't quite snores.

'Mrs Frith, dear – are you awake?' Shirley Anne said softly; waited, and then repeated the question.

The mouth shut abruptly on a kind of snort. Mrs Frith opened her eyes, and struggled upright, flustered at being caught at a disadvantage. 'It *is* you! I thought . . . why are you here? Ethel had no business . . .'

Shirley Anne crouched down to take her hands, feeling the resistance as she clutched them to her breast. 'Please, dear Mrs Frith, you mustn't blame Ethel. I simply had to get in to see you – to ask your forgiveness for the way I behaved' – the dramatic catch in her voice would have done credit to Bette Davis – 'deceiving you, letting you down, after all your kindness to me . . .'

'Dear me.' Mrs Frith looked into the angelic face, a little thinner than she remembered, but framed by that lovely shimmering hair, the huge blue eyes sheening with tears. 'Oh, dear me! You mustn't cry. To be sure, it was very wicked of you to behave as you did, but the young can be very thoughtless.'

'I was! Thoughtless and cruel! And if there is anything – anything at all that I can do to make amends. . . ?' Shirley Anne lowered her head meekly.

After a moment Mrs Frith tugged gently to release her hands. 'Oh, do get up, dear child, and we will say no more about it. My goodness, I have missed you. But you have been very successful, I believe. I read a small piece in *The Times* not very long ago – the critic thought you showed great promise! Are you home for long?'

'I – I have no definite plans at present. Everything is so uncertain . . .'

'Yes, of course. The war.' Mrs Frith sighed as she stood up and went across to the mirror above the mantelpiece to puff up her hair, which had got a bit flattened where she had been lying on it. 'It will affect us all. My committee's energies are now centred upon arranging concerts and comforts for our brave boys.' She turned, her manner almost beseeching as hope glinted in her eyes. 'I realize you can make no firm commitment, but if you would be willing to help for a little while you *are* here . . .'

'And where have you been all afternoon, madam?' Mam demanded when she finally arrived home. 'There's plenty to be done here, war or no war, and you're not home for a rest cure.'

Shirley Anne, well satisfied with her afternoon's work, accepted the reprimand in good part. 'Sorry, Mam. I've been making my peace with Mrs Frith.'

Liz came through from the shop as she was speaking, and Dandy, who was sitting by the fire, lowered his *Liverpool Echo* to cock a glance at her.

'I'm surprised Mrs Frith will even talk to you, after the way you treated her.'

'Well, that just goes to show how little you know, Liz Ryan. She was very understanding. As a matter of fact, she's asked me to help her with some concerts she's arranging for the troops.'

'That figures. You always were good at sweet-talking your way out of things, and they do say there's no fool like an old fool. You didn't think to tell her about the baby, I suppose?'

'No, I didn't – not that it's any of your business.'

'Come on, now, chucks – we don't want any skin an' hair flyin'.' Dandy stood up. 'I'm away for me tea.' He put the folded newspaper down on the table. 'I'll leave this here for Michael. I see Fred Munnings' son has done all right for himself – married into the gentry, or as good as. I suppose that's what going to a fancy public school does for you.'

The name, coming so unexpectedly, shocked Shirley Anne into immobility, and for a moment she felt faint. She forced herself to look at the photograph – Alec, smiling down at his bride in that lazy way she knew so well – and to read the caption underneath: *Mr Alec Munnings, son of Councillor Fred Munnings, and his bride Camilla, younger daughter of Brigadier Sir Algernon Boote, leaving St Margaret's, Westminster*. There was a brief account of the wedding, and an interview with Mr Munnings, who announced proudly that the wedding had been brought forward as his son had volunteered to serve his country and was awaiting his commission.

'Jumped up little twerp,' Liz said, coming to look over her shoulder. 'Volunteered, indeed. I bet his daddy-in-law's promised him a nice safe office job.' She suddenly noticed how still Shirley Anne was. Her face was chalk-white.

'Are you all right, our kid?'

'Of course I'm all right.' Shirley Anne jumped up, pushing the paper away. 'I'm just tired, that's all.'

'O.K. Don't bite my head off.' Liz had to keep reminding

herself to make allowances for her young sister. 'Look, you go and have a rest. We'll manage.'

When she had gone, Liz looked again at the picture. Alec looked positively smug – as well he might. But then, she was prejudiced. Odd, though, the way Shirley Anne had reacted, almost as if . . . But they'd never met. Or had they? Liz went cold. She had a quick look in the shop. Only one customer, and Mam was serving, but there was no-one waiting. 'I'm just popping upstairs,' she said.

Shirley Anne had moved into Rita's room when she came back from London, for both she and Liz had got out of the habit of sharing. She was sitting on the bed, still tense, plucking feverishly at the patchwork quilt and staring into space.

Liz pushed the paper under her nose. 'It was him, wasn't it? The loathsome toad who got you into trouble?'

'I never heard such a crazy idea! Why him, for heaven's sake?' But for once Shirley Anne's acting failed her.

'Because he wanted to get back at me. And because that's the way his pathetic twisted little mind works! Well, he won't get away with it! We'll see what Dad has to say.'

'No, Liz!' Shirley Anne wasn't acting now. She knew what Liz said was true. She remembered the look in Alec's eyes when he'd said *Why don't you go home and tell the bitch?* And her pride was shattered. Her throat worked convulsively. 'Don't! I don't want anyone to know – ever. I'll deny it if you so much as breathe a word to anyone.'

'But he ought to be made to pay. Oh, listen, love.' Liz sat beside her and attempted to put an arm around her shoulder, but Shirley Anne pushed it away.

'I mean it,' Shirley Anne sobbed. 'I don't want anything to d-do with him ever again. He's ruined my life. He . . .' her voice rose to an anguished wail. 'He *used* me!'

Chapter Ten

For a while everyone was on edge, waiting for the worst to happen. And when nothing did, life gradually reverted to normal – or as normal as was possible, with the occasional testing of the air raid sirens, the streets plunged into darkness each night, and the traffic lights and car headlights reduced to mere specks, with car bumpers and running boards painted white to aid visibility. Only in the cinema was it still possible to escape for a short while into the magical world of make-believe – the world of Fred Astaire, Anna Neagle, Errol Flynn, or Mam's favourite, Arthur Tracy, the street singer. Even there there was the Movietone News to keep everyone abreast of events.

'It's got nothing on our shop,' Liz said, as she and Clare emerged into the dank and dismal blackout of a November night during one of their rare get-togethers. Clare had done very well in her highers and had already begun her medical studies at Liverpool University. 'Most days, I guarantee you'll get to know more behind our counter about what's going on, than the Government ever does. Mam's threatened to put up one of those signs – *Careless talk costs lives*. Not that Nora Figg would take any notice. She's the first to hear and spread bad news. I'll swear she knew about the *Courageous* being sunk before the Admiralty did.'

Together, they pushed through the crowds and made for the nearest open café to snatch a quick cup of tea.

'I had a letter from your Chris yesterday – if you can call it a letter. More of a scribbled note, really. He's about as good a correspondent as our Francis.'

'Chris never was much cop with words.' Liz smiled and stirred her tea vigorously to cover the slight embarrassment she felt, for her own letters from Francis were frequently long and complex – not love letters, but strangely lyrical epistles, betraying a sensitivity she had become aware of only in brief glimpses. It was, Liz suspected, a Francis that his family never knew existed.

She heard nothing of Leigh. Many times she had resisted the

urge to ask Clare whether he had been back to visit the Whitneys. Monica Hazlett was now married, and the rest of the family had moved down to Wiltshire, so he would have little incentive to visit Liverpool. Anyway, Leigh was past history – a childish infatuation. It was Jimmy she loved, Jimmy she was going to marry.

'How's your Shirley Anne doing?' Clare asked, not noticing her friend's preoccupation.

'Surprisingly well in the circumstances. Once people started guessing at her condition, I expected her to – Oh, I don't know – want to hide away, I suppose. I mean, it's not very nice, having to put up with snide remarks. But not a bit of it.' Liz chuckled as she recalled the morning she and Mam and Shirley Anne had all been serving, and Mrs Killigan had said, with a full shop behind her, 'You're lukin' well, gairl. Putting on a bit of weight, though, aren't you?'

'It was quite obvious what she was getting at. You could have heard a pin drop. And then our Shirley Anne looked at her, cool as you please. "I suppose I am," she said. "It does tend to happen when you're expecting. But then, with all the practice you've had, you'd know all about that." I've never seen Mrs Killigan so silenced – gob-smacked, she was. There was a great sucking-in of breath behind her, and you could feel everyone's impatience to get served and get out, so they could be first to spread the word.' Liz giggled. 'That was one bit of news Nosey Nora didn't get hold of first.'

'It must have been a bit embarrassing for you and your mother.'

'It didn't bother me, and as for Mam – I thought she'd have a fit, but when the shop had cleared, she just gave Shirley Anne one of her looks, and said drily, "Well, that's one way of breaking the news".'

'I suppose she was always selfish – a bit of a law unto herself.' Shirley Anne had never been one of Clare's favourite people. 'And I daresay being on the stage has given her a tough shell.'

No, that's down to a toad called Alec Munnings. But Liz didn't say the words aloud.

'The news won't have pleased that old lady she's always been so thick with.'

'Oddly enough, Shirley Anne said that when she told Mrs Frith, she was very understanding – said that in such stressful times, accidents were bound to happen, and that as long as her young friend was happy to go on singing for "our boys", she didn't think *they'd* mind a bit.'

'Very broad-minded,' said Clare.

But some of the church's parishioners were less so. They seemed to find Shirley Anne's presence in their midst offensive. Three women, known mischief-makers, were at the root of the trouble. Liz had overheard their back-biting comments many times, but on one particular Sunday, as the two girls emerged from Mass, they didn't even trouble to lower their voices. 'Brazen, that's worrit is – her sort flauntin' her shame when decent folk're tryin' to worship.'

Shirley Anne gritted her teeth and made to walk on, but Liz had taken all she could stand. She swung round, incensed, bringing the three women up short. 'What do you mean exactly – her sort?' she demanded of the ringleader with ominous calm.

'Leave it, Liz,' Shirley Anne muttered. 'They're dead ignorant.'

'No, they aren't. They're nasty, malicious cowards, and I think it's time they said what they mean by *your sort* right out – to our faces.'

The sour-faced widow was by now puce. She clutched the bit of rabbit she called a fur collar tight up to her scrawny neck, bridling with righteous indignation. 'You know what – them as is no better than they should be. An' it's not right – your sister defilin' God's House with her wickedness!'

'I see. So you've set yourselves up as judge and jury, have you? And never mind love thy neighbour . . .'

A small crowd was beginning to collect, churchgoers as well as passers-by, their arms full of pickings from the market, who hung around in anticipation of a good barney to enliven the Sunday morning.

'Round one ter the young 'un.' Some wag from the crowd cheered Liz on.

'I'll be tellin' Father of you, Liz Ryan,' threatened Maggie Fitt, as fat as her crony was thin.

'You do that, Miss Fitt. But I'll not hold my breath. Come on, Shirley Anne, we're leaving.'

Shirley Anne was silent until they were almost home, then she said in a tight voice, 'You didn't have to stick up for me, you know, Liz. I – I don't care what a few old biddies think.'

Liz had squeezed her arm. 'Well, I do care. I'll not have my sister's name sullied by the likes of them.'

'Oh, Liz! I've been such a fool!' Shirley Anne was silent again for a few moments. Then: 'I suppose you wouldn't like to come to our Christmas concert for the troops? I'm sure old Ma Frith wouldn't mind me inviting you.'

'I'd love to,' Liz said.

'I hope you didn't mind my phoning you up out of the blue,' Leigh Farrell said, as Flora took his leather jacket and peaked cap and put them in the cloakroom.

'Of course I don't mind. I'm delighted to see you after all this time.'

'The thing is, I found myself with time to kill and nothing special to do. And I suddenly thought about you.'

'I'm flattered, young man,' she said drily. 'Go along into the drawing room and help yourself to a drink, while I see what Mrs Meadows can rustle up for supper.'

'Listen, I don't want to be any trouble . . . Things must be difficult enough for you.'

'It's no trouble. We aren't starving yet. Would ham and eggs be acceptable, if there isn't anything else?'

'Ham and eggs sounds wonderful.'

A few minutes later they were facing one another across the hearth where a fine log fire crackled and flamed. Leigh leaned forward, rolling his glass slowly between the palms of his hands and sniffing appreciatively. 'There's nothing quite like apple wood.'

'I agree. Caulderbank cut down a couple of very old trees last spring, so it's had all summer to dry out. There's no better fuel for a November night.' She saw that he was smiling at her – that long, slow smile that was part of his attraction. 'Have I said something funny?'

'Nope.' He sipped his scotch. 'I was just thinking how pleasant it is to be back here – to find that nothing has changed.'

Flora's immaculately plucked eyebrows arched in mock horror. 'Nothing changed? My dear Leigh, my maid and my chauffeur have joined the army, and the house is full of rampaging children and civil servants. This is practically the only room in the house that's still sacrosanct.'

He chuckled. 'Nevertheless, the warmth of the welcome is unchanged.' His eyes met hers, and grew serious. 'I wasn't at all sure that it would be.'

Flora didn't insult his intelligence by affecting not to know what he meant. 'Well, I did wonder at the time whether singling young Liz out the way you did wasn't courting folly.'

'And you were right. It was crass, self indulgent, and quite unforgivable. I have no excuse to offer.' Leigh pushed a hand impatiently through his hair, destroying the neatly brushed red thatch. 'Hell, I'm no novice – I knew the score. But I really wanted to see her again, and I was so damned sure I could handle the situation. Only I misjudged how deep her feelings went, and when I found out, I behaved like a raw kid on his first date, and blew it. After which I decided that a swift clean cut would heal the soonest.' He downed the rest of his drink in one swallow. 'I guess she took it hard?'

Flora wondered if he realized how vividly his own feelings were revealed in what he had, or rather had not, told her. Perhaps it would be wiser not to pursue that avenue of thought.

'Liz was very unhappy for a while, yes.'

'It wasn't that I didn't care. Quite the reverse, in fact.' He stared down into his empty glass as if seeking some kind of justification there. 'But it wouldn't have worked. My kind of life leaves no room for steady relationships. And she was so young – too young and too damned innocent to be fobbed off with anything less.'

'I agree. But you can throw away the hair shirt now.' She saw the quick colour come up under his skin – redheads were so very vulnerable that way – but she saw no point in being anything other than blunt. 'We can't, any of us, shield people from hurt. Nor should we try. Experience good or bad builds character, and Liz is none the worse for a little heartbreak. She's done a lot of growing up in the last year or so.' Flora told him all that her niece had achieved, and, lest he should be under any illusion: 'What's more, she is now engaged to be married, so you see, no lasting harm has been done.'

'I'm glad,' he said, not at all sure that he meant it. 'I suppose it's that guy she's been going round with for years?'

'Jimmy Marsden – yes, that's him. They finally decided to get engaged just before he joined the army.'

'And is he good enough for her?' The green eyes were suddenly very intent upon her face. 'It matters a lot to me to know.'

Oh, damn! Why, Flora wondered, did life have to be such a pig, sometimes? 'Liz obviously thinks so,' she said, replenishing his whisky glass, 'and she's a young woman with a mind of her own.'

'I guess so,' Leigh said slowly. 'I hope it works out for her.'

'So do I.' Flora, quite deliberately, changed the subject. 'And what about you? Are you over here on business?'

'Yes. I've been running a regular freight service for the last few months. Pan American have the biggest slice of the cake, of course, but we've built up quite a useful clientèle, and now – ' Leigh shrugged. 'Well, I guess it's no secret that we're supplying your Government with essential equipment, so one way and another we're going to be busier than ever.'

Just after Chris left, Michael had taken on Albert Keegan. He was a morose little man, not far short of his seventieth birthday, but a good workman, and as long as he wasn't expected to produce any fancy rubbish, he seemed content enough to work however many hours he was needed.

Liz still missed Fritz dreadfully – not only his creative skills, but his gentle presence about the place. Mitzi kept in touch with them, but she had no real news. Her father's condition had not changed, though there was some talk of allowing him home for a trial period.

'Of course, it is what we wish, more than anything, but how we shall manage . . .' She sighed.

Liz had worked like a beaver to get as many of the chocolates and petit fours as she could on sale back in September. Fritz had left her well supplied, and now, with Christmas getting closer, she spent every free moment supplementing them, for it soon became clear that, with shipping already being attacked and sunk almost daily, it would soon be difficult enough just to replenish essential supplies. There'd be no place for cocoa butter and other luxury ingredients, and without them, it was no longer practical to keep the cellar bakehouse going. Michael had already had it strengthened with steel girders, so that they could, if necessary, use it as an air raid shelter.

So at last Liz returned to the main bakehouse. In many ways it was like taking a giant step back, but she was resolved to go on producing the very best quality goods she could for as long as she could, in order to keep her little empire together. On the plus side, it was great to be working alongside her father again. She knew he was pleased to have her there. It showed in his eyes when she looked up and found him watching her.

Kathleen had installed her hens in the backyard and, once they had settled, was more than delighted with their yield. The hen run also provided an unexpected source of interest for Georgy. He would stand for hours, mimicking the clucking sounds, with his chubby fingers rapidly turning blue as he pushed them through the wire mesh, his discarded mittens hanging from the sleeves of his woollen siren suit.

'The little love,' Ellen said, watching him from the window. Kathleen heard the wistful note in her voice, and knew how much she was missing her own Freddie and the others, in spite of regular visits to them. It couldn't be easy for her, with only Arnie for company – and always at the back of her mind must be the worry of what might happen to him if they were bombed.

'Have you thought any more about having the children home for Christmas?' she said casually, as she came through from the stockroom with another side of bacon.

Ellen sighed and turned away. 'I think I'm goin' to have to risk it. Arnie says I should leave well alone – that it'll unsettle them more, coming back and then having to go away again. But I don't know that I can face Christmas without them, and surely even Hitler wouldn't bomb us at Christmas. Oh, I know I'm being selfish – there's lots worse off than me, who never get to see their kids, but . . .'

'But that doesn't really help the way you feel, does it? Why not wait and see how things go? Flora won't mind if you don't make up your mind till the last minute.'

'Perhaps that'd be best.' Ellen pulled her thoughts together. 'Have you noticed, we're getting low on sardines and condensed milk?'

'I know. The butter's going down, too, and one of the boats bringing dairy goods from Eire was hit two days ago, which will mean more shortages. Michael's been twice to the wholesaler. He says the warehouse is full one minute and half empty the next, and it's not just because of Christmas. People who can afford it are buying up everything in sight and hoarding it, which isn't fair on those who haven't the money to spare. I never thought I'd say it, but the sooner the Government brings in rationing, the better.'

Three nights before Christmas, Liz found herself in the lavishly decorated ballroom of a house in Sefton Park, loaned by one of Mrs Frith's friends. From her place near the dais, she looked back on a sea of uniforms, khaki and Air Force blue, a sprinkling of Navy blue, and the black and white evening dress of friends and helpers for the evening. Some of the men had brought wives and girl friends, so that brightly coloured gowns sparkled here and there like jewels. All were in party mood.

On the dais, a six-piece band, who would later play for dancing, provided backing for comics, conjurers and singers of varying degrees of competence.

Liz had taken particular care with her own appearance, as if it were in some way necessary to Shirley Anne that she should look presentable. Now that she had more money to spare, and under the combined influences of Aunt Flora and Alice, she had begun to develop a definite sense of style. Never had this been more apparent than in her present figure-skimming satin gown, cut on the cross, with narrow shoulder straps and a brief cape of matching cream lace. Her abundent chestnut hair, which most days she rolled up in a simple knot, was tonight drawn back into the sleek, sophisticated French pleat that Alice had taught her. It had taken weeks of practice before she managed to achieve the required degree of elegance. Already this evening she had been chatted up by several unattached officers, of whom one – a very young, shy subaltern – was presently sitting beside her.

'And now, ladies and gentlemen, lads and lassies' – the compère was in jovial mood – 'for our *pièce de resistance* – a little lady who is a big favourite with you all, star of the West End revue *Stepping on Air* – I give you your own, your very own, Shirley Anne Ryan!'

There were cheers and whistles, and shouts of 'Good on yer, gairl,' and 'Can I see you home, darlin''?'

'Your sister?' murmured her companion. 'She's very pretty.'

Shirley Anne stood quite still, smiling faintly, waiting for the noise to die down. A single light above her head turned her simply styled hair to pale gold, and her full-length gown of Alice blue chiffon was cleverly cut, scooped at the neck, back and front, and drawn in under the bust, falling in soft folds to conceal her thickening figure.

The moment she began to sing, Liz knew she needn't have worried. For more than half an hour, Shirley Anne held them all in the palm of her hand. She was, by turn, funny and sad, teasing and meltingly romantic, encouraging them to join in familiar lyrics from *We're gonna hang out the washing on the Siegfried Line* to *Alice Blue Gown*, and finishing with *I'll be seeing you*, the voices swelling, sweet and poignant –

> I'll be seeing you
> In every lovely summer's day,
> In everything that's bright and gay,
> I'll always think of you that way,

All around Liz, hands were being tightly held, and here and there an arm crept round bare shoulders, pulling a loved one close against rough khaki. The young subaltern moved closer and put out a tentative hand.

> I'll see you in the morning sun
> And when the night is new,
> I'll be looking at the moon,
> But I'll be seeing you.

With a lump as big as an egg in her own throat, her thoughts turned to Jimmy, but as her emotions soared, his face became blurred and took on another image. No, she pleaded. Please – go away. The applause was deafening, and as she joined in, the image receded.

That should have been the end of the concert, but because it was Christmas, Shirley Anne suggested a few carols, and ended by singing, very softly, *Silent Night*.

'And, oh, Mam,' Liz told Kathleen later, 'you could have heard a pin drop. I was crying like an eejut, and I wasn't the only one.'

Chapter Eleven

Rosemary Ryan bawled her way lustily into the world early on the first day of February, two full weeks ahead of time, when Shirley Anne, frustrated by inactivity and boredom, fell flat on her back after venturing out to the pictures against all advice, in icy conditions that would have taken the legs from under a much nimbler person. Liz and Kathleen took turns to sit with Shirley Anne through a long and trying night between Dr Graham's initial visit, when he assured them that the fall would not have harmed the baby, and his return many hours later to deliver her. By which time Liz, appalled by the drawn-out agony of it all, and unsure where pain ended and histrionics began, was convinced that her sister's screams must have kept the whole street awake.

Kathleen, her rosary beads never far from her hands, was surprisingly patient, gentle and bracing by turn, and her calmness reassured Liz. Never for a moment did she show the apprehension that might be expected after her own traumatic experience with Georgy.

Rosemary, immediately dubbed Rosie, was a beautiful baby, none the worse for being thrust before her due time into a cold white world, where the worst snowstorms for many years had disrupted traffic, and frozen pipes would keep plumbers in work for weeks. Michael had managed to get hold of enough paraffin to keep their own pipes from freezing, and a stove going full time in Shirley Anne's room.

There was certainly no shortage of warm shawls and bedding. Kathleen and Liz had been knitting and sewing in every spare moment. Shirley Anne had never been much use with a needle, but Aunt Flora and Mrs Frith had both provided layettes of wonderfully warm soft garments, lacy shawls of finest cashmere and Shetland wool, as well as luxurious bed jackets for Shirley Anne herself.

'She's a gorgeous baby,' said Ellen, who had crept up for a peep at the new arrival. 'A little blonde, just like her mother. You forget how tiny they are, don't you?'

'She's got a pair of lungs to rival her mother, too,' Kathleen said drily. 'I've a feeling we're going to have our hands full for the next few weeks. Shirley Anne's asleep at the moment, thank God, but I doubt she'll take kindly to having to feed the little one every few hours.'

'Ah, well, she's not much more than a child herself. But she'll learn. If you ask me, it's you that needs the rest. You look worn out.' Like a wrung out dish-rag, Ellen thought, though she didn't say so. 'Why don't you go and have a lie down? I can cope with the shop.'

'That's right, Ellen. You tell her. She won't listen to me.' Liz came through from the bakehouse with a tray full of sweet buns, and showing the same enduring stubbornness that had served Kathleen so well when her children were small.

'You've been up all night, too,' Kathleen said.

'Never mind about me, I'll catch up later.' Liz turned to Ellen. 'What d'you think about me being an auntie? Isn't it great? And Mam's a grandma.' Dark rings under her eyes proclaimed her lack of sleep, but she was ebullient as she put an affectionate arm round her mother's shoulders. 'Doesn't seem possible, does it? And, best of all, our Georgy only two, and he's Rosie's uncle!'

Aunt Flora arrived later in the day, driving an immaculate little second-hand car. Kathleen was at the door as her sister came lightly up the steps and through the shop with a smile for Liz, who was serving.

In the living room, Michael was sitting at the table, his pepper and salt hair ruffled into peaks by agitated fingers, sucking his pipe and poring over a pile of forms. But he stood up and crossed the room to greet her warmly.

'Flora has a car,' Kathleen said accusingly. 'What was it you said, our Flo, about using public transport like everyone else?'

Flora met Michael's amused gaze and gave an elegant little shrug. 'So I do, most of the time. But I saw this little gem of an Austin Seven in Goulder's yard – not a mark on it, and ridiculously cheap. So many people are selling their cars because they haven't anywhere to keep them. And as it happens, it will probably be very useful.' She shrugged off her mink, threw it over a chair and lit a cigarette. 'I've joined the Red Cross, and who knows where I may not be called upon to go at a moment's notice?'

'Oh, Flora, really! You – a nurse? Your bedside manner's about as restful as a gale coming straight off the Mersey!' Kathleen's mirth attracted Liz, who managed to snatch a breather from the shop for long enough to give her aunt a quick hug.

'What was that about nurses?'

'Your aunt has joined the Red Cross.'

'Well, good for you, Auntie. I think you'll be splendid at it – perk everybody up no end.'

'Thank you, Liz,' murmured Flora. 'Nice to know someone appreciates me. Mind you, my duties may not involve much actual nursing, though of course I'll have to go through all the basic training. It seems there's a lot of organizing to be done, such as liaising with the American Red Cross, who have promised to send supplies. They seem to think I might be quite good at that.'

'You'll be brilliant.'

'And how are you all managing? Still wrestling with the ration books?'

'We've more or less settled into a routine, now. Our regular customers have registered with us, so it's a case of working out each family's quota of tea, sugar, bacon and butter, and keeping accurate records. The next thing, we'll be needing to start on points for the groceries.'

Flora glanced at Michael. 'At least you've been spared bread rationing, for the moment. That must be a blessing.'

He smiled wryly, indicating the mass of correspondence scattered across the table. 'I'm not so sure about that. What with the Ministry of Food, and the Trade Board, wanting to know this and that about the business, I'm nearly dizzy with it all. If it wasn't for our own Master Bakers' Association doing all it can to help us clarify things, I'd be lost entirely.'

'Oh, come off it, Michael, you'll not let them beat you,' she said, and turned to Kathleen. 'And how is Shirley Anne?'

'She's fine. A bit fractious and tearful, but that's only to be expected. And little Rosie's a dream. Georgy is already besotted. The hens are going to have their beaks put right out of joint from now on. But we'll need to keep a bit of an eye on him – he doesn't really understand that she's not a toy – '

Flora didn't stay long; there were, it seemed, numerous tasks awaiting her attention. Kathleen thought she had never seen her sister look more alive. But before she left, Flora went dutifully to praise a sleepy Shirley Anne on her cleverness in producing such a lovely baby. And she remembered to ask Ellen how her children were doing.

Ellen had, after all, succumbed to having the children home for Christmas, and once they were home, she couldn't bear to let them go again. Like many parents, she was fast coming to the conclusion that the bombing was never going to happen.

'Well, I meant what I said – if it does, and you want them out of harm's way, just pack them off back to me.'

Their return did pose problems, however, as the schools were closed and many of the teachers were still away. A lot of children ran free, and shopkeepers began to complain about pilfering. The local Education Authority at last came up with a scheme using the few available teachers to teach small groups in private houses, volunteered by people who had a room to spare for a few hours each week. For the rest of the time, they were still free to run loose. But not Ellen's children – young Dot saw to that. Each day, she made them stay in and practise their sums and letters, and found various ways to keep them occupied. Much to everyone's surprise, Arnie did his bit, too, encouraged by Hester Whelan, who had offered her own house for use. 'I'm not good for much else,' Arnie had said grudgingly, 'but I can tell 'em what's what, an' our Dot can do the rest.'

'Our Rita's got nothing on your Dot,' Liz told Ellen with genuine admiration. 'She's obviously cut out to be a teacher.'

Nick came to wet the baby's head over at The Grapes with Michael, before going off to spend a couple of days with Laura and the children. He had been coming pretty regularly for Sunday dinner since his family had left for Wales.

'Are you sure, Kath?' he had asked when she first invited him. 'I mean, you and Laura didn't exactly part best of friends.'

'I don't see what that's got to do with anything. You're still my brother, and anyway, some would say I got what I deserved.'

'Not me. If you hadn't spoken your mind, Laura and the kids would've been on that ship, and I'd be – well, you know . . .'

Kathleen was brisk. 'Well, you're not. And the least I can do is see you get a good square meal occasionally.'

*

'Are you going to tell your Mam and Dad we're on embarkation leave?' Chris threw the question at Jimmy as they raced down the platform, past large notices demanding IS YOUR JOURNEY REALLY NECESSARY? 'Yes, it blooming well is,' he gasped, as they swung themselves on to the already crowded train just as it was leaving. 'Well, are you?'

'Dunno. Haven't made up my mind. Hey, shove, up, fella – do us a favour.' They pushed their way, encumbered by rifles and gas masks and heavy kit bags, along the freezing swaying corridor, packed with a writhing mass of humanity and lit only by a single blue light wreathed in cigarette smoke, which, together with the tightly drawn blinds, created an atmosphere fit to clog your lungs. 'If it gets any worse, I'll be getting me respirator out. Strewth, they're even six deep in the lavvies!' Finally, Jimmy commandeered a smelly corner in which to wedge themselves and their kit. 'Anyway, if they've been keeping up with the news, I should think they'll have guessed. Hitler's already on his way through the neutral countries like a dose of salts . . .'

'Ssh!' A frosty-faced ATS officer frowned at Jimmy. 'Careless talk,' she boomed.

'Silly old cow,' he muttered out of the corner of his mouth.

Joey saw them first. 'Hey, Mam – our Chris and Jimmy are here! They're coming in the back – and Jimmy's got a stripe up already.'

And then the living room was full of them, their kit scattered across the floor. Joey was marching round, wearing his brother's tin hat, and Chris was hugging Kathleen half to death, while Michael looked quietly on.

'You're looking great, old thing,' Jimmy teased, swinging a blushing Liz round in his arms. 'For someone who's an auntie!'

'Oh, you!' But he silenced her with a kiss that went on for ages. 'Give over,' she gasped. 'Just because you're a lance corporal! Everyone's watching.'

'So what? We're engaged, aren't we?' But he released her. 'I'd better get home. We'll continue this conversation later this evening.'

'Now then,' said Kathleen, when she and Chris were alone. 'Get that greatcoat off and let's be looking at you. Hm. Not bad. You've grown.'

Chris grinned. 'Not really. It's all that standing to attention.'

'And we're to have you for a whole ten days this time?'

'Yeh, I shan't know what to do with myself. How's Shirley Anne? Can I go up and see her?'

Kathleen knew he was changing the subject. But then, she didn't need to be told. 'Of course. She'll be glad to have you home. But change out of those boots, for pity's sake, or you'll frighten the baby.'

Shirley Anne had heard them arrive. A part of her longed to run downstairs to join the great family reunion. But she couldn't – not with Jimmy Marsden there, and her still looking like a sack of potatoes in her loose-fitting dress.

But when Chris knocked on the door and called softly, 'Can I come in?' she was out of her chair and across the room, flinging herself into his arms.

'Hey, steady on, our kid. Should you be. . . ?'

'Oh, I'm fine.' She stepped back, tossing her head with a flash of the old Shirley Anne. 'I'm just so glad to see a fresh face. Rosie's nearly three weeks old, but I feel like a prisoner, stuck up here most of the time. It's all feeding and changing nappies.' She wrinkled her nose with distaste. 'I'm bored. There's nothing to do but play Mam's old records. In fact, I'm so bored I was even pleased to see Lily Killigan. She came round one evening with a matinee coat she'd knitted, and some old *Picturegoers*. It was quite touching, really, 'cos I hadn't been very nice to her before I left Liverpool. Honestly, you'd hardly know her now – she's working on munitions at Speke and earning good money, and she's slimmed down and had her hair permed. She looked almost pretty.'

Chris smiled at the rather patronizing description. 'I can't wait to see the transformation.'

'She's not *that* pretty. Still, I said she could come again if she liked.' She sighed. 'Even Lily's better than no-one.'

'Well, I'll have to see what I can do to cheer you up while I'm home. Now, am I allowed to see my niece?'

Minute fingers wrapped themselves round his own large roughened one with surprising strength, and eyes as bright as periwinkles stared up at him. 'Well, what d'you know – she looks exactly the way I remember you looking, the first time I laid eyes on you.' He chuckled softly. 'I must have been four at the time, and I thought you were the most beautiful creature I'd ever seen. I still do.'

'Oh, Chris!' Suddenly she was in tears and clinging to him. 'I was so afraid you might feel awkward, ashamed of your little sister and her b. . . ' She couldn't say the word. 'You know . . .'

'Yer daft ha'porth,' he said, holding her close. 'Whatever gave you an idea like that? You've had a rotten deal, but us Ryans stick together through thick and thin. God willing, I'll always be there if you need me.'

Chris settled back to home life immediately, gravitating quite naturally to the bakehouse as if he'd never been away.

'It's grand, having you here, lad,' said Michael, watching the easy way he slipped back into the old routine, handing up the dough. They had great machines to do it in the army, he said. He had grown – not just physically, but as though, almost overnight, the youth had become a man. 'Like old times. Still, you don't want to be spending all your precious leave working.'

'Maybe not, Dad. But this beats dishing up bangers and mash for three hundred men. It's so peaceful in here. You've no idea how much I've been looking forward to that. It's one thing you never get in the army – peace, privacy. Time to yourself, to think your own thoughts, to be quiet. It's the thing I miss most.'

'But you don't dislike the life, otherwise?'

'Oh, no. They're a great bunch of lads.'

The silence of the bakehouse wrapped them round once more. A blessed companionable silence. A shame to break it, but for the question that hung, unasked, between them.

'Is it France, then, Chris?' Michael said at last.

Chris smiled faintly. 'Somehow I thought you'd guess. Does Mam know?'

'She hasn't said. But she knows.'

Jimmy had suggested the Grafton Rooms for old time's sake, remembering her birthday celebration. They had to queue, and only just got in before the 'House Full' sign went up.

Liz was spending every available minute with Jimmy, which meant either going dancing or to the pictures in the evening, and if the weather wasn't too awful, the odd day trip to Southport or New Brighton. And if all else failed, they could just stay in and talk, except that there was no privacy even at Jimmy's house, where his mother demanded all his attention.

It wasn't easy for Liz to take time off during the day, as a spate of rush weddings – the result of servicemen about to be posted overseas – meant there were constant orders for buffet wedding breakfasts. Sandwich fillings and savouries weren't yet too much of a problem, and it was still possible to manage a reasonable trifle and some pastries. The biggest problem was the wedding cake. Dried fruit was becoming scarcer with every day that passed, as the ships bringing supplies were bombed, and sugar for icing wasn't that easy to come by, either. But her fertile mind was already busy seeking ways round it.

'Great,' Jimmy said, when she tried to explain between dances. 'But do we have to waste precious time talking about it now?'

Liz was hurt. 'I thought you'd be interested.'

'I am. But not at this precise moment.' He slid an arm round her waist and led her on to a dance floor crowded with uniformed figures, women as well as men, so that she felt almost too frivolous in her bright red dress with the flaring skirt. The music was slow and smoochy, and many couples were dancing cheek to cheek. Jimmy did likewise, his voice seductive. 'Weddings I *am* interested in, though. To be precise, our wedding. It seems that, as the song says, *Everybody's Doing It* – why shouldn't we?'

'Oh, Jimmy! You know what we agreed.'

'What *you* agreed, darling. I just went along with it for peace and quiet.' He laid his mouth very close to her ear. 'But I wasn't on embarkation leave then.'

She had half expected him to use this argument. But even so – 'I can't spring it on Mam and Dad now, on top of everything else . . .'

'If you mean Shirley Anne's little problem, I don't see why not. If she was old enough to run away to London and survive, she's old enough to fend for herself, now, and look after the kid. She wouldn't put herself out for you.'

'That's a horrible thing to say!' But it was true, and in her heart she knew it. 'Anyway, it isn't just Shirley Anne, it's . . .

everything. Mam still isn't all that strong, I doubt she ever will be, and our Rita's miles away, and now there's Chris going off to fight – he's her favourite, you know, though she'd never admit to having one – and we've got all the worry about ration books and things . . .'

'All right. You've made your point.' Jimmy sounded cool. They finished the dance in silence, but Liz could feel his hurt. As they went back to their seats, she spoke his name tentatively.

'I've said, all right! I can't see how anything you've said makes any difference, but you obviously think it does. P'raps it's as well to know where I come in your scale of values. I sometimes wonder if you really love me at all.'

She stared at him, the blood draining from her face, then turned and ran from the room. Jimmy caught her up in the foyer, and swung her round to face him. The tears were streaming down her cheeks.

'I'm sorry. That was a terrible thing to say.'

'I didn't mean . . .'

'Nor did I.' He pulled her close, heedless of the interested stares of the cloakroom girl. 'Don't cry, please, Liz darling.' His voice was all husky and vulnerable, like that time in the bluebell woods. 'It's just that I want you so!'

His words raced round and round in her brain, and her chest ached with a welter of emotions. Perhaps it was this place – it brought back too many memories. And Jimmy's accusation had raised all kinds of confusion. If she felt as strongly as he did, surely nothing would keep her from him? And if not, how could she possibly tell him? If only everything didn't have to be rushed; if there wasn't so much to be done, so much to be organized, so many people depending on her. If, if, if . . .

'Liz – don't shut me out. Please!'

Jimmy's voice was urgent, and she drew a deep breath.

'I'm sorry. I didn't mean to. Maybe I'm just over-tired. It's been a tiring time, one way and another.'

'And you do too much.'

'Not as much as I did.' She smiled wanly. 'It's more of a mental tiredness, I think. Oh, Jimmy!'

'It's all right. You don't have to say it.'

She couldn't do it – couldn't send him away to fight without hope. 'I know. But I promise – when you come back – the very next time you ask me, we *will* get married.'

Chapter Twelve

Winter slipped almost unnoticed into spring, and life went on much as it ever had. Daffodils lifted cheerful heads in parks and gardens, bare branches sprouted tender leaves and riotous displays of pink and white blossom; the birds performed their courting rituals, and spirits everywhere lifted like the candles on the horse-chestnut trees. In Kathleen's window box, the fat buds of the hyacinths were already tipped with colour.

It had become known as the phoney war, and Liz, like everyone else, was becoming complacent. Rationing had become a way of life, tiresome but necessary. Even the shipping losses, tragic as they were, had taken on a kind of inevitability. She still took her part-time warden's duties seriously – there was little chance of doing otherwise with Grandpa Dandy, as divisional warden for the area, always around to keep her on her toes.

'There's no use thinkin' it won't happen, girl – it's what that devious beggar Hitler wants us to think. That's what Norway thought – and Holland and Belgium will break any day, which only leaves France, and I wouldn't lay odds on their will to fight on, even with our help. So we gotter be ready, because, mark my words, he's goin' to throw everything he's got at us. At least we've got Winston at the helm now to put some backbone into us, instead of that old woman Chamberlain.'

Liz remembered what Leigh had once said about the might of the Luftwaffe, and shivered involuntarily. But Shirley Anne, with the arrogance of youth, said it was just Dandy. 'He's loving every minute of it, strutting round in his warden's get-up with his gas rattle and his whistle, telling everyone what to do.'

'You can mock, young lady. But you might yet be glad that the likes of your grandad are prepared for the worst.' Kathleen sounded severe, though she knew much of her young daughter's edginess sprang from frustration. And small wonder, for never was any girl less suited to untimely motherhood.

Without condoning her behaviour, Kathleen realized that some of the blame must lie with herself. She had known Shirley Anne was up to something – nothing as drastic as running away to London, although the signs had been there: the restlessness, the hankering after fame and fortune.

From her earliest days Shirley Anne had been precocious, wilful and self-centred to a fault, almost always getting what she wanted with that cunning charm that made her seem older than her years. And the success she had achieved in a short time appeared to vindicate her belief in herself. Yet in many ways she was still an innocent, and her seducer, whoever he was, had taken full advantage of that. Small wonder that Shirley Anne was frustrated and bitter.

'I feel such a frump, Mam. I've only got two decent frocks that fasten at the front, and I'm not having them ruined with milk stains. I really don't see why Rosie can't have a bottle. It was good enough for Georgy . . .' Shirley Anne stopped, biting her lip. 'Oh, Mam, I'm sorry. I didn't mean to . . .'

'I know you didn't, love,' Kathleen said quietly. 'Just as I know it's tiresome for you, but it's not for much longer. Rosie's already sleeping right through the night. Bottles are an extravagance when you have plenty of milk, and your own is so much better for her.' She shook her head. 'You never did have much patience, did you? Heavens, girl, it's not three months yet. You need to get your strength back.'

'Oh, but I feel fine! And I know Mrs Frith is desperate for me to start doing the concerts again.' Shirley Anne fell to coaxing. 'Everyone seems to be working for the war effort, except me. I'd be hopeless doing what Liz does, but I could use the talent I have. Entertaining the troops *is* important, Mam! I mean, they do need cheering up. Suppose one of them was our Chris?'

And where is our Chris? Kathleen wondered bleakly. The news from France wasn't good. 'Well,' she said, weakening. 'Perhaps we could start Rosie off with a bottle for the evening feed. But I don't want you getting overtired.'

'Oh, I won't. I never get tired entertaining.'

As May drew to a close the news got worse, and they all began to dread turning on the wireless. And then the word Dunkirk was on everyone's lips, and they couldn't wait for the next bulletin. Kathleen was over at St Anthony's lighting candles by the dozen, and making special novenas for Chris and Jimmy, and everyone who came into the shop wanted to know if they had heard anything. Many of them had boys of their own with the Expeditionary Force.

Joey sometimes managed to tune in to a short-wave station where a man nicknamed Lord Haw-Haw, because of his posh English voice, had begun broadcasting the most dreadful lies about what was happening. 'It's only a bit of fun,' he protested, when Michael put his foot down and forbade him to listen. 'One of the lads at school has him off to a T.'

'War is not funny, my lad. Just you think on – this very minute, your own brother could be dying over there.'

This did sober Joey for a while, but although he was growing up fast, he was still young enough to find the whole idea of war exciting. Danny, his best friend at school, had an uncle who owned a two-berth cruiser, and often let Joey help him tune the engine. 'It's as well we've just given it a thorough overhaul, because Mr Freeman's off to help with the rescue. Just think of it, Liz. There's hundreds of boats gone already, including some of our ferry boats. I wish he'd take me with him!'

Liz rounded on him, eyes blazing. 'Don't even think about it! And don't you dare let Mam or Dad hear you. It's bad enough for them, worrying about Chris, without having you doing daft things.'

'All right, our Liz. Keep your hair on.'

Michael hadn't felt so helpless since the night Kathleen had told him she was pregnant with Georgy. He could think of little except that Chris was in danger and there was nothing he could do. Even prayer seemed inadequate. Soon, it became difficult to get two words out of him, and even Albert Keegan, a man of few words himself, began to find the silence in the bakehouse unnerving. Kathleen watched her husband anxiously, knowing there was no way to ease his mind.

Every news bulletin brought stories of unsurpassed courage on the part of ordinary men – and women, too – some making more than one journey to the beleaguered beaches, defying the Stukas which strafed them without mercy to help the Royal Navy bring home as many of the troops as humanly possible.

Two agonizingly long days passed, with everyone going through the motions of work, and Kathleen freezing each time the telephone shrilled. Little Georgy, not understanding, clung to her like a silent shadow, and when time allowed, she found some comfort in taking him on her knee and reading to him from a much-thumbed picture book.

In the end, it was Liz who took the call. The line was very bad, but she recognized him at once. 'Mam – ' she shouted. 'Mam, it's Chris! Chris, thank God! Are you O.K.? Is Jimmy with you?'

'Shut up and listen, I've not got any money . . .'

Kathleen snatched the phone from her. 'Chris? Where are you? Are you all right?'

'I'm fine, Mam. Just a graze. I'm in Folkestone, but I'll be home soon. Listen, Mam – tell Liz that Jimmy's . . .' The line went dead.

Kathleen ought to have worried about Jimmy, but all she could feel was relief that her son was safe. Liz had already run to the bakehouse to tell Michael, and as they returned together, she thought she had never seen him move so fast.

'He's safe, Michael. Our Blessed Lady be praised, Chris is safe!' And Mam was in his arms, laughing and crying, and his mouth quivering as he held her head against his chest, and there were tears in his eyes, too, as he looked across at Liz.

She wanted to cry, too, just looking at them. But she couldn't. There was still one question unanswered. 'Did he say anything – about Jimmy?'

Kathleen drew away, instantly contrite. 'Oh, Liz, love, I'm sorry. He was cut off just as he started to tell me. But Jimmy will probably ring himself any time now. I daresay the telephones are mad busy.'

But Jimmy didn't ring, and the Marsdens hadn't heard anything either. Everyone tried to be optimistic, but Liz knew in her heart that something dreadful had happened. It was only when Chris arrived home, almost a day later, that she was put out of her misery.

Chris looked dazed and bone-weary, and his uniform was stiff with dried mud and salt water, and other unmentionable things, and smelled atrocious.

'It's a disgrace,' Kathleen said. 'Wasn't there anyone to meet you, give you clean clothes?'

'Oh, Mam! I don't know. Maybe there was, but it was an

absolute shambles, with thousands of us wanderin' about. You've no idea. I managed to borrow some more money, but there wasn't a telephone free, and besides, I had to look after Jimmy. He's been taken to a hospital in Kent. They were all for leavin' him in France, cos his foot was in a bad way, but I wasn't letting Gerry have him. Me and some mates took turns carrying him. I have an address and telephone number for the hospital – ' He fumbled in various pockets and finally brought out a crumpled piece of paper. 'I promised I'd let his parents know – '

'Not another word, my lad. We'll see to all that.' Mam was suddenly brisk. 'You'll get out of those clothes and into a hot bath. There's plenty of water in the geyser. Your Dad will help you. And then it's a hot drink and bed for you.'

'Can you and Ellen cope for a bit, Mam?' Liz said, when he'd gone. 'I think I should go round to the Marsdens rather than phone them; they've been worried sick. And I could drop Chris's uniform into the cleaners. I'll take the van and go to the Candide on the way back.' Her lip trembled and she bit on it. 'Oh, Mam!' They hugged one another. 'They're alive.'

'And may the dear Lord have pity on the families who aren't so lucky,' Kathleen said huskily.

Liz waited while Mr Marsden got through to the hospital. He seemed to have aged in the past few days, and there was little evidence of the twinkling eyes and jolly manner that had long ago earned him the nickname Sunny.

'Well,' he said, hanging up the receiver and turning back to his wife and Liz, 'we're not much the wiser, except that his life isn't in danger. Like Chris said, there was great concern about his foot before he left France – ' Mrs Marsden uttered a piteous cry and Liz's heart sank. 'Now, don't go frettin' yourselves. Our Jimmy's a tough nut. But the time they'd got him to the hospital, it'd taken a turn for the better. An' if it goes on improving, there's talk of moving him nearer home in a day or two, so they've advised us to wait and see.'

'Well, they wouldn't say that if he was in danger.' Liz tried to sound encouraging, as Mrs Marsden's tears began to flow again. 'And we could still write to him. It wouldn't matter if he was moved before he got the letter. That's what I mean to do, anyway, as soon as I get home.'

Mrs Errol at the cleaners took one look at Chris's uniform and recoiled in horror. 'You can't expect us ter 'andle that. Gor, it don' arf pong! Our customers'd go mad if they was ter find out. It could be full of 'orrible foreign gairms or anythin', cos 'ose ter know wur it's been?'

'I can tell you exactly where it's been,' Liz said evenly. 'It's been in the sea off Dunkirk.'

The woman's face went very red, but if anything she recoiled even more. 'Well, I'm sorry, I'm sure, but such things is fer the army ter deal with. If yer ask me, it want's burnin'.'

Without a word, Liz turned on her heel, and went to Mitzi's, where she should have gone in the first place. By the time she arrived, the uniform was stinking the van out, and she began to realize that she was asking a lot of anyone. 'Look,' she said, 'if you feel you can't tackle it, I'll understand . . .'

'Why should we not tackle it? These poor boys do so much for us. I would be so ashamed to look any one of them in the eyes if we were not prepared to put ourselves out a little for them.' Mitzi took it without so much as wrinkling her nose. 'It will be ready for your brother tomorrow. I am pleased you have come. Papa is home only today from the hospital. You are welcome to see him for a few moments, if it will not upset you too much. He will know you, I think,' she said sadly, 'but you must not expect more.'

Fritz was in a small bedroom with a bright quilt on the bed and matching curtains at the windows, and family photographs everywhere one looked. He seemed to have shrunk, his mouth drooped at one side, and he dribbled constantly. Although she glimpsed momentary recognition in his eyes, there was no other response when she spoke to him. It made Liz more angry than sad to see this lovely man end his days in such a way. He, of all men, deserved to live and die with dignity.

At first Chris slept dreamlessly, but then the nightmare began. The bombardment as the sun rose, gilding the sand dunes, and picking out the khaki figures scurrying like ants towards the incoming boats and rafts – bombs blowing them to smithereens as the Stukas screamed in to splatter the sea and the boats and the men, turning sea and sand alike to red – wheeling away, and turning to come in again . . .

He was breast high in the water, pulling Jimmy along behind him, but the willing hands of a young naval rating outstretched to receive them suddenly weren't there any more. 'Hang on,' he yelled, clamping Jimmy's hands to the rubber fender. 'Don't you dare let go, d'you hear me? I'll get in and haul you up.' And then the Stukas were diving again, the bullets ripping into the rescue boat, into the rating lying helplessly spurting blood, missing his own leg by inches . . . then on to the next boat before swooping away, leaving only the screams of the injured and the more terrible screams of the silent dead, slipping beneath the waves, dragging him with them . . .

'Hush now, Christopher, my boy. You're safe home now.'

He came shudderingly to consciousness to find his father sitting close beside his bed. 'Sorry, Dad,' he mumbled. 'Was I making an eejut of myself?'

'Not at all, boy. I was on my way down to the bakehouse to make a start, and I heard you talking in your sleep. I thought there might be something you wanted.'

'Not now.' Chris sat up, elbows on bent knees, pushing his hands through hair darkened by perspiration. 'It was touch and go, Dad. I reckon it was only the Spitfires saved us . . . No more than a handful of them, but they were all over the Stukas, forcin' them to turn and fight, and I managed to cling on to Jimmy while someone came for us . . .'

Michael cursed himself for having no words to ease his son's distress. 'It was a brave thing to do, son.'

'No, it wasn't. It was pure bloody selfishness. I was scared of being left to die alone.' Swearing was as alien to Chris's nature as the harshness of his tone, but his father offered no reproach. Chris pushed back the bedclothes. 'Can I come down and help you, Dad?'

Behind the boy's eyes, Michael saw the lingering horror that could not be put into words – and they were sufficiently alike for him to know that Chris needed to work it out of his system in the way he knew best.

'Why not, if you feel up to it? Your Mam would skin the both of us alive if she knew you were out of your bed, but Albert doesn't come in until seven this morning, so I'd be glad of another pair of hands.'

*

Jimmy was transferred to the Promenade Hospital in Southport the following week, and everyone breathed a sigh of relief. Liz let Mr and Mrs Marsden go alone on the first evening, but she was there to see him the very next day. She didn't like hospitals, and in spite of Mr Marsden's encouraging report, she wasn't sure quite what to expect.

What she found was a Jimmy, paler than usual, but on the surface at least as irrepressible as ever – and from the number of nurses fluttering at his beck and call, being very well looked after. His bed was right at the end of a big ward with windows overlooking the Marine Lake and the sun shimmering on the sea beyond. She had to endure a chorus of wolf-whistles as she walked its length, her heels click-clicking on the polished floor, and her cheeks growing pinker by the minute. Jimmy's smile, however, had all the old charm.

'Hi, gorgeous.' As she bent to kiss him, he cupped her head with his hand, making the kiss last a great deal longer than was seemly, which raised a fresh chorus of whistles and shouts of encouragement. 'Let go, you fool!' she gasped, laughing. 'I've brought a big box of pastries for the whole ward. Sister has them, but if you don't behave, I'll tell her she's not to give you any.'

'Did you hear that, lads? My wife-to-be' – there were renewed whistles – 'makes the best pastries in the whole world, and she's brought some just for you!'

A cheer went up, and Liz blushed. 'Honest to God, if I didn't know better, I'd say you were here under false pretences.'

'Have a heart. I tell you, it's hell having all these pretty VADs around, and a dragon of a sister in charge who won't even allow them to comfort a fellow with a harmless kiss now and again.' He grinned shamelessly. 'Let me get a good look at you. My, but you're a sight for sore eyes.'

Liz had made a special effort with her appearance. The biscuit-coloured linen dress was new, softly and becomingly tailored; a natural straw hat sat perkily on her upswept hair, the narrow brim tilting forward; and her Henderson's handbag still looked as good as new. She saw his eyes stray to her legs – he had always admired their shapeliness, so she had worn a pair of her carefully hoarded silk stockings.

'Do try to be serious for a minute,' she said, sitting down beside him, and eyeing the big hump near the bottom of the bed where a cradle supported the bedclothes. 'Your foot really is going to be all right?'

'So they tell me. Funny, the way things turn out – they were all for chopping it off at the field hospital . . .'

'Jimmy, don't!' The thought of Jimmy, with all his small harmless vanities, maimed for life, was too awful to contemplate.

'It's all right, sweetheart. You know what I've always said – I'm lucky. Maybe the devil looks after his own.' His cheerfulness had a curiously hard edge that wasn't like him. 'Anyhow, the doc thinks being dangled in the sea for hours may have helped do the trick, though it's a remedy I'd as soon not repeat. So, you see, it's your Chris we should thank. I'd have gone under more than once, but for him. How is good old Chris?'

'Oh, you know – we hardly get a word out of him some days. But he'll soon work it out of his system. He's spending a lot of time in the bakehouse with Dad.'

'That's the trouble with your Chris, he's too soft-hearted – always was. An' it doesn't get you anywhere in this game.' Again, the unfamiliar hardness crept in. 'Look after number one – in't that right, lads?'

There was a chorus of approval.

'No use being squeamish.'

'Yeh. Fighting's a dirty business.'

'Get the b . . . . r before he get's you – savin' yer presence, Miss.'

Liz hated their offhand callousness. She knew it was probably bravado, but she had to bite her tongue to stop herself protesting that if Chris had thought that way, Jimmy wouldn't be here now.

'Anyhow, get the old so-and-so to come an' see us. I never did have a proper chance to thank him.'

It was still early when Liz left the hospital, and the golden June evening was far too beautiful to waste. There would be ample time to walk as far as Birkdale to see if Aunt Flora was home, and give her the good news about Jimmy. She wandered through the floral gardens along the promenade and down Rotten Row, and thought how sad it would be if the flowers had to be dug up to make way for vegetables.

At Rose Lodge, Mrs Meadows was delighted to see her. 'Seems an age since you were here.'

'I'm afraid life's a bit hectic these days, Mrs M.'

'You can say that again. All those poor boys!' She sighed. 'At least you got your Chris back in one piece. And your young man? How's he goin' on?' Liz's news was received with a lugubrious sniff. 'That Adolf Hitler's got a lot to answer for. But he'll get his come-uppance, you just wait and see. Your aunt's out in the garden, if you'd care to go through. Entertainin' a parcel of them American Red Cross folk to drinks on the lawn, she is, while we've still got drinks to give them – or a lawn, for that matter. They're already at us to dig it up and plant vegetables.'

'Oh, but that would be a terrible shame.'

'Mind you,' Mrs Meadows went on, opening the dining room door, 'Caulderbank's very near too feeble to use the mower, so there'd be small chance of *him* takin' on all that extra work.'

Liz walked across to the open french doors, pausing to glance in one of the two full length mirrors which graced the far end of the room. The long walk had brought a glow to her cheeks, warming her light dusting of tan. At least she wouldn't disgrace her aunt, she thought, twirling on the heel of one neat black court shoe to check that her skirt wasn't too creased.

A steady buzz of conversation, interspersed with laughter and the chink of glasses, came from the large oval lawn beyond the trees, and as she approached it by way of a path overhung with copper beeches, she saw upwards of a dozen people, men and women, gathered into small groups. Her glance moved from group to group, searching for her aunt's distinctive blonde Marcel-waved hair – Moved, and then stopped, a tingling sensation beginning to run through her veins, as the golden evening sun picked out one head from the rest, turning it to flame.

Chapter Thirteen

Leigh saw her coming across the lawn. He watched her with a feeling of inevitability, while his heart tipped and settled back into its natural rhythm.

He had fallen into the habit of coming here whenever his commitments allowed. Flora entertained him royally, and he found her company stimulating: he told himself that this was why he allowed himself to be drawn back, again and again. But, deep down, he knew differently – knew that if he came here often enough, one day Fate might allow him a second chance.

That he was behaving completely out of character made no difference. There had been many women in his life over the years, amusing diversions, but none had ever got beyond first base. But ridiculous as it sounded, young Elizabeth had touched the core of him at their first meeting, and imperceptibly, with each subsequent encounter she had grown into his heart, until that moment two years ago when he had seen her in the ballroom in her golden dress, and realized that he was in serious danger of falling in love. He should have quit then, of course, before it had all gotten out of hand.

Now, at last, Fate had been kind. She had come. No longer the enchanting half-child, half-woman he remembered, but a graceful young woman in a frivolous hat and a soft linen dress. A young woman, he sharply reminded himself, who was already committed – perhaps, by now, even married – to her childhood sweetheart.

Obviously Flora hadn't invited her; she knew the score, and there was no way she would have risked a meeting between them. So the choice was his. If he was not to risk hurting her a second time, the sensible thing, the honourable thing, would be to stay out of sight until she left. Yet, as he watched her cross the lawn, he knew that she was still his Elizabeth, and that he wanted her as much as ever.

And then it was too late. She had seen him. Her step faltered and, for an unguarded moment, one hand fluttered involuntarily to her throat. He watched her gather her courage and walk towards him.

'Hello, Leigh. What a surprise.'

'A pleasant one, I hope? I'm surely glad to see you.'

He didn't look it. He looked – almost angry. Liz had forgotten the impact of his eyes – their uncompromising directness that seemed to see right through her. Her legs trembled and the blood pounded through her veins. I ought not to be feeling this way, so soon after seeing Jimmy, she told herself. Yet her voice, when she found it, sounded quite normal, almost cool.

'I suppose you brought the American Red Cross?'

'Like bringing the good news from Aix to Ghent? It is a bit like that, I guess. Flora is keen to get every last cent of help out of them.'

'Then they don't stand a chance. Once my aunt sets her mind to something, she usually succeeds.' His slow smile at once exhilarated and disarmed her. She found herself responding, smiling back.

'You're doing your hair differently,' Leigh said abruptly. Again the hand fluttered to her throat, betraying her vulnerability, and he saw that she wore a small opal on her third finger, but no wedding ring. 'It looks good. But I still like *my* Elizabeth best with her hair blowing loose in the wind.'

'I – you shouldn't say things like that to me.'

'I guess I shouldn't. No, don't go,' he pleaded as she half turned away. 'We'll talk about something else. Anything. Flora was telling me about Chris – and your fiancé. I'm sorry. You must have been out of your mind with worry.'

'Yes, I was. We all were. But we are the lucky ones. At least we got our men back alive and more or less in one piece. Chris still won't say much about what happened, but he never was a great talker. He spends a lot of his time with Dad and Georgy. And maybe that's what he needs, just now. With Georgy he doesn't have to put on an act.'

'And – Jimmy?'

'He wasn't quite so lucky. But it could have been a lot worse. As a matter of fact, he's here in Southport, in hospital.' Liz spoke the words deliberately, her eyes meeting his. 'I've just come from visiting him. At first, the doctors thought he might lose his foot, but now the danger seems to be past.'

'You must be relieved – and very happy.'

'Yes, I am.' This was awful. They were like strangers awkwardly making conversation. She had seen a Noel Coward play once, where two people in love were . . . She said hurriedly, 'I'd better go and find Aunt Flora. She doesn't know I'm here.'

'I do now,' Flora said, coming up behind them. She looked from one to the other. My word! Were they aware, she wondered, that the air around them was crackling with suppressed emotions? Something would have to be done. 'Well,' she said brightly, 'I don't know what brings you, Liz, but you couldn't have chosen a better time.'

Liz explained about Jimmy.

'My dear, that is excellent news.' She glanced briefly at Leigh, but his face betrayed nothing. 'Now I wonder if you'll do me a big favour? Come and talk to my guests. They're nice people, eager to help in whatever way they can, and I'm sure that meeting someone who is actually involved at the sharp end, as it were, would give them even more incentive. You wouldn't mind?'

Liz assured her that she would not. Anything to get away from Leigh, who was promptly delegated to replenishing glasses. Aunt Flora's guests were charming, and their interest was so genuine that Liz found herself telling them about Chris and Jimmy's experiences at Dunkirk, in so far as she knew them, together with a great deal about the home front and people like Dandy, the backbone of the local defence. The Americans seemed impressed by her calm good sense.

'Do you suppose Germany will try to invade your country, Miss Ryan, now that France has surrendered?'

'They may try, but Grandpa Dandy says they'd be fools to imagine they could pull it off by sea. Our naval forces are too strong. He thinks Hitler will try to bomb us into submission first, but he says that won't work, either.'

'I'd surely like to meet your grandfather, Miss Ryan. He sounds quite a guy.'

'He is,' she said simply. 'But he's not the only one. There are plenty more like him.'

'The bulldog breed, eh?'

'If you like.'

'But aren't you afraid?' one of the older men asked.

'Of course. Oh, not so much of being killed. We all have to die some time. It's wondering how I'll cope with pain – my own, or other people's. We've had the odd air raid warning, and that alone is enough to set you shaking like a jelly, but nothing really awful has happened so far. I just hope I can stay calm when it isn't a false alarm, and I'm faced with dead people, or those who are badly injured, or made homeless.' She shrugged. 'Maybe I'm simply afraid of being afraid.'

'And yet you seem set on being, what was it – an air raid warden?'

Liz smiled. 'I know. Perverse, isn't it? Maybe I need to prove to myself that I can do it. Someone, I can't remember who, once said that the only thing we have to fear is fear itself.'

'Franklin D. Roosevelt, 1933.' Leigh's voice, close behind her, was cool. 'His first inaugural address – "Let me assert my firm belief that the only thing we have to fear is fear itself".'

'Well, fancy you knowing a thing like that, honey!' said one large homely lady, clearly delighted.

Liz sensed that for some reason Leigh was angry. It became increasingly hard for her to concentrate with his breath teasing the back of her neck. She said hurriedly, 'I suppose I learned it in school.' And as soon as she could decently do so, she moved away.

'Well, I think you can congratulate yourself on your contribution to international relations, young lady,' said Flora when she had waved off the last of the taxis taking the Americans back to the Prince of Wales Hotel, where they were staying. 'You certainly gave our friends plenty to think about. And as for coming out so pat with that quotation – pure inspiration. You could tell they were all tickled pink. Isn't that so, Leigh?'

He wanted to shout aloud that he thought Liz was crazy to put herself in so much danger. Instead he shrugged and murmured agreement; only his eyes said otherwise.

The setting sun clung to the top of the trees like a huge orange balloon; the air was still and heavy, drenched with the scent of stocks and roses and recently mown grass. But for Liz all the warmth had gone out of the evening, and suddenly she couldn't wait to get away.

'I must go, Aunt Flora. The family will think I've got lost.'

Flora kissed her cheek. 'Yes, of course. Thank you again for your help, my dear child, and for letting me know about Jimmy. Maybe I'll pop along to see him tomorrow.'

'I'll walk you to the station,' Leigh said abruptly.

'There's no need. It's only a few hundred yards.'

He picked up her bag and gloves and handed them to her. Liz accepted them in an awkward silence. Aunt Flora was watching them with troubled eyes, and not wanting to make a scene, Liz hugged her again then, with Leigh's hand firmly under her elbow, allowed herself to be led round the circular drive to the front of the house and out into the road. There, she stopped and shook herself free.

'This is ridiculous. I am not a child.'

'I know,' he said grimly.

'Well, then – '

She turned on her heel and began to walk quickly, turning the corner into Oxford Road and towards Birkdale Station, not daring to look back towards the shore, where the sunset was painting the sky with magical colours. Leigh fell into step beside her, and she was conscious of him with every nerve in her body. Except for a lone cyclist, the road was deserted. Finally, with the railway crossing no more than yards away, she could bear the silence no longer. She stopped again.

'I don't understand. Why are you so *angry*?'

He pulled her into the shadow of the station wall, and she looked up to find an expression of such glittering anguish in his eyes that she could hardly bear to meet it, and yet could not look away. 'Why? I'll tell you why, Elizabeth Ryan. Do you have the least idea how I felt back there, listening to you calmly telling those people about how you were going to be in the thick of the bombing, and how much the thought of it scared you?'

'But . . .'

'Be quiet.' His fingers were biting into her upper arms, but she was hardly aware of the pain. 'Dammit, don't pretend you don't know how I feel about you, because you do – because you feel the same way. And I'm angry because you're going to be in terrible danger and I won't be able to do a damn thing about it. Right this minute, I want to pick you up and fly you straight back to Connecticut where you'll be safe. But I don't have the right . . .'

'No, you don't.' Liz could hardly speak for the emotion

welling up in her throat. 'And if you had, I wouldn't go. My place is here.'

'Don't tell me.' He ground the words out. 'With Jimmy and your family and all your infernal responsibilities.'

And then she was in his arms. For a timeless moment his face swam heart-stoppingly close; a pulse over his temple seemed to beat in time with the blood thundering in her own veins, and in the instant before his mouth came down on hers, all she could see was the green of his eyes, blazing with a curious mix of love and exasperation. It found expression in a kiss of such bruising intensity as to rob her of all desire to resist.

One hand cupped her breast while his lips trailed delicious sensations across her eyelids, nibbled the ear-lobes against which he whispered sweet endearments, and moved down to the hollow of her neck before coming back to claim her mouth, gently, sweetly, parting it. And as before, everything was forgotten except this exquisite sensation surging through her body, inciting her to abandon herself entirely to him.

'Oh, my dearest girl,' he murmured, punctuating the words with kisses. 'I should have run off with you two years ago, when I had the chance. God help me, at the time I thought I was being noble. You were so young – too young, I told myself, to be dragged into my haphazard world. I didn't realize what I had lost until it was too late.' He drew back a little, lifting her left hand where the opal glinted. 'But maybe it isn't too late?'

His words stirred the deep recesses of her conscience, but at first she was too full of lightness and joy to heed it. He loved her. Really loved her. And then she heard the warning clang of a bell.

'Oh, no! I'll have to go. The crossing gates are closing. We'll have to use the underpass.' She took his hand and, like children, they sprinted down the steps and up the other side, to a deserted platform. 'I can hear the train coming, and it may be the last one. They're very unpredictable . . .'

'*Forget* the train. Sweet Elizabeth, we have to talk,' he said urgently. 'We can't possibly pretend nothing's happened.'

'Nothing has happened,' she said despairingly above the squeal of brakes. 'Please – let go of my hand.'

But still he held it, his thumb sensuously smoothing her wrist where a small pulse beat madly. 'Let the train go – telephone home to say you're staying over. We could go somewhere – that pub we just passed, or the beach – where better? It's a warm night . . .'

'No!' On the beach, her defences would melt away. 'Leigh, I can't! It wouldn't be any use.'

Several passengers descended and brushed past them unheeding, eager to be home.

'I'm off to London in the morning with my people,' he went on as though she hadn't spoken, 'and who knows when we'll get another chance . . .'

'Oh, stop it, stop it!' She was crying now. 'You're only making everything worse. It's too late – there are too many complications. Besides, I can't cheat on my promise to Jimmy – especially now, after all he's been through. I could never live with myself. And you'd hate yourself too.'

'Sanctimonious twaddle! Just try me. You'll be cheating on him anyway, if you marry him, feeling about me the way you do,' he insisted, his face a pale angry blur in the dark of the station as he grasped at her arm to keep her with him. 'What about me, Elizabeth? Don't you care at all how *I* feel? I don't want to lose you a second time!'

The despair in his voice so overwhelmed Liz that she almost weakened. To have come so close to being given a second chance – how could she bear to turn her back on him, and all that he meant to her? And then she heard again Jimmy's voice, proudly proclaiming 'My wife-to-be', and knew it wasn't possible.

'Are you two gettin' on or not?' The porter sounded weary. 'The train can't hang about all night.'

Tears streaming down her face, Liz shook herself free of Leigh and jumped aboard. The whistle blew and the train began to move. 'Dearest Leigh, forgive me! Of course I care. But please try to understand. You see, I love Jimmy, too – oh, not in the way I love you, but enough to make our marriage work. I promised him, you see . . .'

But Leigh had already turned away.

Shirley Anne grew more and more restless as the summer progressed. It wasn't that she didn't love Rosie: as babies went, she was quite an engaging little thing – except when she screamed, which was happening more and more often as she learned how to get her own way.

'That child's every bit as demanding as you were,' Liz said. 'Only you were more devious. I used to hate the way you could get anything you wanted with a whimper, a quiver of the lip and a well-timed tear rolling down from your big blue eyes. Rosie simply resorts to pure bad temper. In fact, she has a decided look of her father when she screams,' she added with a certain venom.

'Liz don't, for pity's sake! You promised you wouldn't breathe a word . . .'

'And I won't, don't worry. You haven't heard anything from him, I suppose?'

'There's no reason why I should. He'd already written me off. And it's hardly likely he'll lower himself to come back here, even to see his family, now he's gone up in the world.'

'True. Anyway, to get back to what I was saying, since you're out most evenings, now, it wouldn't hurt you to give us all a break by taking Rosie out a bit more during the day. Grandpa Dandy's got his hands full with his ARP section post. He can't even spend as much time as he'd like with Georgy at present, which is a pity – he can get more out of him than any of us. And we've certainly got enough to do without nurse-maiding Rosie.'

'But you're all so much better at it than I am,' Shirley Anne said ingenuously. 'She spits her food out when I try to give it to her, and I'm hopeless at changing nappies. They never seem to stay put.'

'Perhaps if you devoted as much time to changing nappies as you do to playing about, altering dresses and painting your legs, you might become more proficient,' Liz snapped.

'But it's important for me to look glamorous. It's part of my image. I can't keep buying new dresses, but it wouldn't do to keep appearing at concerts in the same ones. And since I've only got two pairs of decent silk stockings left, I have to paint my legs. I would take Rosie out more, but you know how I hate wheeling the pram. I can guess exactly what everyone's saying behind my back.'

'Oh, come off it! You must be used to that by now. You're just spoiled. Why don't you take her to Mrs Frith's when you go this afternoon? She'd love to fuss over Rosie.'

'And how do I get her there? Mrs F's hoarding her petrol, and you won't take me, and I can't possibly walk all the way to Faulkner Square with the pram.'

'There are such things as buses.'

'Carry her, you mean? Don't talk daft.'

'Other people manage.'

'Well, I'm not other people.' Shirley Anne flounced to the door. 'You know, you want to watch it, Liz. You're getting really scratchy these days.'

The criticism stung, but she was probably right, Liz thought wretchedly. With all the problems and shortages, life recently did seem to be one long dreary round of making do, and it was an added irritant to have Shirley Anne shirking her responsibilities, hankering after her old life. But that wasn't the real reason for her sharpness, and she knew it.

She had tried to put all thought of Leigh behind her, but it wasn't easy. He had written to her some time in the early hours of the morning following their traumatic parting, such a loving gentle letter:

> 'I can't bear to think of you miserable or guilty on my account. Your honesty was the quality that first drew me to you, and I wouldn't have you betray it now, for all that I want you so much. Perhaps there will be a time for us, in some distant bright tomorrow, for it seems to me inconceivable that Fate, having brought us a glimpse of what might be, will not one day be kinder to us both. But for now, be happy, my dearest Elizabeth. And may God keep you from all harm.'

For several nights she had tossed and turned, railing against that same Fate. She shed bitter tears over the letter until it grew sodden and crumpled. Then, as more immediate problems loomed, she dried her eyes and put it away with the rest of her memories.

Mam had looked at her oddly a few times, but it was Aunt Flora, waiting for her after her next visit to the hospital, who had taken her arm and walked her across the road to a seat among the flower gardens. It was another lovely evening, warm and mellow.

'So how are things with you, Liz?'

'Fine. Great. Jimmy hopes to be out before too long.'

Aunt Flora sniffed. 'I'm very happy for him, but don't flannel me, my girl. We both know what I mean. Leigh came back the other night as though all the devils in Hell were on his back. It took me a long time to get any sense out of him, but I did in the end.' She gave Liz a straight look. 'You are quite sure you've made the right decision?'

'Oh, Aunt Flora, I've gone round and round it all in my mind since that night, and, yes, I am sure.'

'Well, I'm glad,' she said. 'Shirley Anne might well throw her hat over the windmill without a qualm, but not you, my dear. And, in his heart, Leigh knows that.'

Chris had finally returned to his unit at the beginning of July in a relatively cheerful frame of mind, and was almost immediately posted to Scotland. But his departure had the effect of making Jimmy restless. His mind became obsessed with getting out of hospital.

'I can't think why they're keeping me here. The foot's fine. It's time we started making plans, Liz. Once I'm discharged, I could be off at a moment's notice.'

So Liz, after talking to the hospital doctor, went to see Fr Clarkson to arrange for the banns to be called, and the wedding date was fixed for the last Saturday in August. It would be a quiet affair, she insisted, not a bit like Rita's wedding.

'But you will be wearing white? I missed out on being a bridesmaid once.' Shirley Anne sounded aggrieved. 'I was sure you, of all people, would want a traditional wedding.'

Liz wondered what certain folk would have to say about an unmarried mother being a bridesmaid. Not that she cared a fig what anyone thought. 'I'm not sure it's right, all that extravagance.'

'Oh, don't be such a killjoy.'

Rita had stayed in Shropshire, though many of the children had come back home. She was now working part time in the office of a firm making munitions, and teaching English three afternoons at a private girls' school. But, as the school would be on holiday, she hoped to be able to take a few days leave to come home for the wedding. She sounded a bit diffident on the phone, and finally told Liz why.

'We're thinking of settling in Myndd Howe after the war.

Frank's spent his leave with me a couple of times, and he's really taken to the place. I'm managing to save a fair bit, and he reckons we could pick up a nice little house quite reasonably. His chance of getting a job there should be quite good, too.' She sounded half defiant. 'Would Mam and Dad mind very much, do you think?'

'I'm sure they'd understand. We've missed having you around, of course, but in a way, the break has already been made, hasn't it?'

Mam had said much the same thing.

'It's not for us to mind, Rita love. It's your life – yours and Frank's.'

The sinister wail of the sirens became more frequent, and Liz still hadn't entirely mastered the churning of her stomach each time the slow undulating whine began, and they waited for the slow throbbing drone of enemy planes. At first they did little damage, dropping their bombs for the most part in fields near searchlight batteries. People with nothing better to do even went out to peer at the craters.

But it was nothing compared to what was happening in the south of England. Dandy had been right about Hitler striking by air. For several weeks now, bombers had been coming daily in huge waves, wreaking havoc on shipping, and doing their best to destroy the new Radar advance warning installations and put the southern airfields permanently out of action. But again and again, by night, the airfields were repaired and the pilots, Francis among them, were able to take off again in their pitifully few Spitfires and Hurricanes the next morning, to harry and diminish the success of each new attack.

'We're all worried sick,' Clare confessed. 'Mother most of all. She's convinced the government are throwing away his life and the lives of all those young men for nothing.'

Liz could understand how Mrs Whitney felt. She wondered whether to mention the latest letter she had received from Francis, but the contents would hardly have reassured them; from its erratic swings of mood, she guessed it had been written over a lengthy period in those tense lulls between bursts of action. In early August he came home briefly on leave, and rang her to suggest they might go out for a meal.

'The old place, I thought, if it's still operating.'

'Fine. I'll meet you there – about eight?' Liz guessed he would be more than usually reluctant to meet her family and lay himself open to questions, and she could hear the relief in his voice as he agreed.

She swapped her warden duty with a friend, and took special pains with her appearance. She wore one of her prettiest dresses and her little straw hat and, not for the first time, blessed the person who invented the handbag that doubled as a gas mask holder.

'Liz, it's good to see you.' Francis took her hands and kissed her cheek lightly. 'You look wonderful.'

She wanted to say 'So do you,' but the lie wouldn't come. He had always been thin, but now his face looked drawn under its tan, and his quick, shy smile belied the haunted look behind his eyes.

The restaurant was fairly busy, but the proprietor, Mr Bernard, remembered them, nodded approvingly at the wings on his uniform coat, and showed them to a table in a secluded alcove. Although it wasn't quite dark, the windows were already heavily curtained, and the lighting subdued.

'I'm afraid I can't offer you much except sweet South African sherry as an aperitif,' he said, his disgust evident, and when they declined it, he lowered his voice to add, 'but I've still got a few bottles of decent wine tucked away.' The menu, too, was limited. 'Still, you've come on the right night, as it happens. I've a farmer friend who does a bit of pigeon-shooting – says they get among his cabbages – so there's a nice pigeon casserole, if you fancy it, with vegetable broth for starters.'

They said that would be fine. Liz didn't attempt to force the conversation. Instead, she talked quietly about all the ordinary goings-on of the family, and her forthcoming wedding, pretending not to notice that Francis ate little, smoked a great deal, and drank steadily. 'Only a week or so to go. Chris is hoping to get a forty-eight hour pass, so he can be best man.'

'And Clare's to be bridesmaid, I hear. Jimmy didn't mind me stealing you for this evening?'

She smiled. 'He doesn't know. He's to go before the medical board today. If they pass him fit, he'll be rejoining his unit soon after the wedding.'

Mr Bernard, coming to remove the plates, viewed Francis's scarcely touched meal with almost comical despair, but Liz gave a little shake of the head, and he seemed to understand.

'I may have to take over as temporary Flight Commander when I get back.'

'It sounds very important. They must think a lot of you.'

He laughed shortly. 'More like desperation. Our Flight's been nursing a grumbling appendix for weeks, and experienced pilots are getting a bit thin on the ground. D'you know how much training some of the new intake get? Six weeks. And six hours, if they're lucky, to convert to Spits and Hurricanes! God, Liz, they're only kids, most of them, thinking they know it all.'

'Would you mind having to take over?'

Francis shrugged. 'Not really. Put it this way, if it came to a choice, I'd a damn sight rather be out in front, leading the squadron, than get landed with the job of tail-end Charlie. He's the poor sod who flies above and behind the squadron, to signal any surprise attack from the rear, and he's usually the first to buy it.' Liz made a small distressed sound, but he went on talking as though he hadn't heard her. 'We can be scrambled five or six times a day between three in the morning and stand-down about ten o'clock, and each squadron has its regular patrol lines. There's quite an art, you know, to bringing down the Hun. You have to get up there ahead of them, well up, so that you can attack from above before they see you – thanks to Radar warning we can do that.'

He lit another cigarette, and Liz noticed that his hands were shaking. 'It's incredibly beautiful up there, you know, just after dawn. The sky is like a vast empty canopy, streaked with brilliant colour – so beautiful, so completely untouched, there's a kind of other-worldness about it. It's difficult to imagine anything evil in such a place.' For a moment she glimpsed the intense, lyrical Francis revealed in his letters. 'And then you see them way ahead, below you – hundreds of bright dots touched by sunlight, getting bigger as they come closer – bombers with fighter escort – '

'Francis . . .' But she never finished, for from the distance came the wail of a siren, taken up by others close at hand.

'Oh, shit!' he muttered, ashen-faced. 'I have to get out of here.'

'Yes, of course.' Liz saw the perspiration standing out on his forehead. He was shaking. She called Mr Bernard and quietly asked for the bill. She would have paid it, but Francis was already fishing his wallet out, fumbling with pound notes.

'If you wish, we have an excellent cellar . . .'

Francis pushed the notes into his hand. 'Thanks, but we'll be fine. Keep the change. Sorry about the pigeon – I just wasn't hungry.'

'Thank you, sir. Don't worry about it. Another time, perhaps.'

Outside, the darkness was made less dense by a brilliant half-moon hanging among the stars. The sirens had stopped, and from the nearby Grafton Rooms, where it was still business as usual, came the muted sound of the dance band playing *Somebody Stole my Gal*, almost drowned out by the buzz of laughter and conversation.

Francis staggered to the kerb and vomited. Liz allowed him to recover, and take out a handkerchief to wipe his mouth, before going to stand at his shoulder. He drew in several deep shuddering breaths. 'Good old Mersey air,' he said jokily. 'You can't beat it.' And then, without looking at Liz, 'I'm sorry . . .'

'Don't be,' she said, and tucked her arm through his. At first, she had thought it might be too much wine on an empty stomach, but he seemed as steady as a rock. 'Let's walk. You know, Grandpa Dandy says they've discovered lots of people who can't stand being in confined spaces.'

'Up there' – he jerked his head – 'I can cope, but down here, I feel so bloody useless. Sorry – my language has deteriorated, too.'

'Stop apologizing.' Liz, her ears attuned, heard the first distinctive throb of enemy planes. A shudder ran through Francis, but he made no comment.

'It's even worse, here at home,' he said. 'You know – Dad, as proud as Punch, keen to show me off to all his friends, and Mother being terribly brave and trying not to mind when I snap at her. I feel such a heel.'

'Oh, Francis, I'm sure she understands. Clare certainly will.'

'Sure. It's me that's out of step. At least I'm glad I never made friends easily. The way things are now, it's best not to get too fond of anyone. Do you ever see anything of Leigh Farrell?'

The question was shot at her so unexpectedly that her heart jerked painfully against her ribs. But she said calmly, 'Some-times,' and told him about Leigh's recent visit. A distant *crrump* came from the direction of the docks. 'He seems to be running a regular service these days – mail, much needed commodities, occasionally VIPs like this Red Cross group. Aunt Flora hinted that he's soon to be part of a scheme using all kinds of volunteer pilots to ferry bombers over. Bringing them by sea is proving too slow, and too many are being sunk. But I'm not supposed to know that.'

'It's the kind of challenge Leigh would relish. He's one hell of a fellow. It's thanks to him I got my wings, you know.'

'Yes, I did know. He once told me you had a real flair for flying.'

'Oh, I have. I'm pretty damned good at shooting down Huns, too. He'd never have guessed that. I certainly wouldn't.' An explosion much nearer made them both jump. 'I need a cigarette. Here – in this doorway.'

He fumbled for the packet. Liz took them from him, put one in his mouth and struck a match, careful to shield the flame. 'Thanks.' He drew deeply on it, coughed, and continued, his voice hurried, rasping, 'You know the best way to down a bomber? You head straight for his nose on full throttle, and at three hundred yards you have only seconds to fire and bank away. It's a bit like Russian Roulette, but it works as long as your reflexes are fast enough – if not, at least it's a quick clean death, and with any luck you'll take Gerry with you . . .'

'Francis, don't!'

The planes were much nearer now. Liz heard the whistle of a bomb – that fractional moment of silence, and then a crunching explosion that shook the ground and everything round them. 'Dear God,' she whispered, and Francis mouthed a stream of obscenities, and clutched her to him. Her hat went flying, as, clinging together, they sank to the ground in the rear corner of the doorway.

'I'll be glad to go back for a bit of peace and quiet,' he muttered against her hair, but Liz noticed that, although his voice shook, it had lost the frightening edge of hysteria. 'That was too bloody close for comfort.'

'About half a mile away, I'd say.' Liz swallowed her fear and forced herself to speak calmly. 'Over Walton way.'

Francis held her very tightly for a moment, and she could feel the unsteady beat of his heart, or was it her own? Then the sound faded and sanity returned. She sat back and wailed, 'Oh, my good hat!' and they both laughed hysterically because they were still alive, and hunted for it, finding it still in one piece a few yards away. And in the dark silence of the shop doorway he kissed her deeply, but without passion, and there was no need for explanations as he said shakily, 'Thank you, dearest Liz. Tell your Jimmy he's a lucky man.'

Chapter Fourteen

It was a quiet wedding but, perhaps because people needed reassuring that there was life beyond Hitler, it was a beautiful and touching occasion. Liz was very popular in the neighbourhood; she hadn't realized how popular, until presents and good wishes began pouring in as the day approached, including many small gifts from customers who had little to give. Even Nora Figg had pushed a crumpled parcel self-consciously across the counter. 'Knitted it meself, ev'ry perishin' stitch,' she muttered.

'If the smell of mothballs is anything to go by, she must have made it for her own wedding,' Kathleen said, as Liz unwrapped the paper to reveal a tea-cosy in violent mustard with a purple pom-pom. 'Lord save us, that's enough to put you off tea for life!'

Liz laughed. 'Never mind. Not many people can boast of getting a present from Nosey Nora.'

'Not many would want to.'

There had been a steady stream of weddings as men were called up, but seeing the beautiful fruit cake, one of several that Dad had made months before when ingredients were less of a problem, brought home once more to Liz the disappointment of many brides, for whom the traditional wedding cake had become a casualty of war. She decided to try out the idea she had worked out months ago. She had begged several hat boxes from Aunt Flora and from Mrs Frith, who, according to Shirley Anne, had mountains of them cluttering up her wardrobes. Clare managed to get her some plaster of Paris, and she had mixed it and piped each box with different designs. Then she had given them two coats of white gloss paint, and stuck a bride and groom figure in the centre of each, reserving a few coloured flower decorations which could be added to give a touch of individuality as required.

The result looked amazingly real – better than she could have hoped for; at a glance, no-one would guess that the facade concealed a much smaller, plainer cake. Liz persuaded her mother to let her put an advertisement in the *Echo*, and to her surprise and joy, a journalist came to interview her and took photographs. *Why let Hitler spoil your wedding celebrations*? the headline ran, and went on to describe how, by contacting Miss Elizabeth Ryan, at Ryan's of Great Homer Street, or enquiring at one of their branch shops, brides who wanted the illusion of a full celebration, could, so to speak, have their cake and eat it for a very modest charge. For the first few days the phone had hardly stopped ringing, and since then, the demand had remained steady.

Liz had finally succumbed to pressure from all sides, not least from Jimmy, to wear traditional white, and in Lewis's she found exactly the right gown in dull ivory satin, beautifully cut, with a high, Edwardian collar edged with lace, a fitted bodice and a gently flaring skirt without a train. She wore her hair up, and a short veil was held in place by a simple wreath of artificial orange blossom. Clare and Shirley Anne, her bridesmaids, both being fair and blue-eyed, had chosen pale blue taffeta. Jimmy and Chris wore their uniforms, and Joey was coaxed into a new suit, in spite of his – 'Aw, do I have to, Mam? I'll look a proper nancy boy, with a flower an' all!'

Rita, arriving the day before, made everything perfect by announcing that she was pregnant.

Kathleen had taken an unprecedented decision to close the shop for a couple of hours, so that Ellen shouldn't miss seeing Liz married as she had Rita. Michael quirked an eyebrow at her. 'I never thought I'd see the day.'

'Yes, well, this war's changed a lot of things.'

But it was Michael who insisted that Liz should take some time off before the day. 'I disremember when you last had any time to yourself, and all young ladies, so I'm thinkin', have things to do before such a great occasion.'

'Well, you're the boss,' she said with a grin. And hugged him, ruffling his hair.

'Am I, now? Well, there's a surprise. And me thinking all this time it was your Mam, with you pushing her from behind.' But the answering twinkle in his eyes faded as he kept hold of her. 'Listen now, Lizzie, my love – your happiness means everything to me, and – well, just recently I have noticed a look in your eyes when you think that no-one sees . . .'

She stirred uneasily, finding it hard to meet that steady blue gaze. 'It's been a worrying time.'

'True enough, an' all. But it wasn't that kind of a look. Ah, Lizzie, Lizzie, I may not say much, but I see a great deal, and I'm not easily bamboozled. All I'm saying is that I want you to be sure Jimmy is truly the one for you. Marriage is for life, girleen. There must be no looking back over your shoulder.'

He knew. She didn't know how or how much, but he knew. She kissed him and looked him straight in the eyes. 'I know that, Dad. But I do love Jimmy, and I intend to make him happy.'

Two nights in the Lake District.

It wasn't much of a honeymoon. And it didn't get off to the best of starts. The train was delayed for two hours by a de-railment, and they were stuck in the middle of nowhere, in a dismal carriage, too dimly lit to do anything but smile and holds hands, with nothing but growing blackness beyond the windows. They were both in unfamiliar territory, and when they stopped at yet another small station, they both peered anxiously at the painted-out name board.

'You wouldn't happen to know if this is Windermere?' Jimmy enquired of their sole fellow passenger.

The old woman smiled vaguely.

'Oh, hell! There should be a guard, or someone to ask.' Jimmy pulled the strap to let down the window. 'I can't see a thing. Hangon, while I do a quick *recce* . . .' He disappeared into the darkness, and suddenly the train belched steam and began to move. In a panic, Liz grabbed the cases and leapt out, just as Jimmy came running back.

'Not a soul,' he fumed. 'Hell, now what do we do?'

'There must be a stationmaster or porter,' Liz reasoned.

They made their way towards the dim outline of a building and knocked on the window. The door opened and a porter peered out, stifling a yawn. 'Well, bless me, where did you spring from?' He waved a dim torch over their tickets, and observed laconically, 'You'll have a tidy walk.'

Liz's heart sank. 'You mean this isn't Windermere?'

He shook his head. 'Oxenholme.'

'I don't believe it. Devil take this blackout!' Jimmy snatched the tickets back. 'So what time's the next train to Windermere?'

'Ten o'clock tomorrow mornin'.'

'Bloody Hell! Well, there must be a bus or something.'

'Buses don't run after dark.'

Jimmy swore again, but Liz laid a placating hand on his arm. 'I wonder – is there anywhere we can stay the night?'

The man pushed his cap back to scratch his head. 'There's a small commercial hotel up the road a piece – Mrs Wilson's place. That's if she 'ent closed her doors by now.'

Liz smiled wryly at Jimmy. 'It's that or the waiting room.'

Mrs Wilson, a raw-boned countrywoman, was abrupt to the point of rudeness, but their explanation brought about a partial thaw in the atmosphere. Her glance took in Liz's new red suit and the jaunty black hat with its bunch of shiny cherries, and moved on to Jimmy's best suit.

'On your honeymoon, you say, Mr – ?'

'Marsden. Corporal Marsden, actually.' He produced their identity cards, and her manner became, not friendly, but no longer frigid.

'Can't be too careful these days. As it happens, Corporal, I do have a double vacant on the second floor.' She led the way up the cheerless staircase, threw open a door and marched across to pull a pair of heavy curtains across the high narrow window before switching on the light. With the aid of the dim bulb they could just make out the ancient metal bedstead occupying the centre of a threadbare carpet that still bore traces of its original floral design. A solid oak chest flanked the bed on one side, with an equally solid wardrobe on the other. 'Seven and sixpence for the night. Chamber pot in the cupboard. Bathroom and WC down the passage. Bath, twopence extra.'

'We'll take it,' Jimmy said. 'I'll fetch the cases.' He gave her his most winning smile. 'I suppose you couldn't rustle up a cuppa – and maybe a sandwich?'

'Ah.' She sucked in her cheeks. 'I'll see what I can find.' Jimmy followed her out, and while he was away, Liz took off her hat and carefully placed it on the chest before sitting down to try the bed springs. This wasn't at all how she had imagined it would be. Maybe nothing ever was, but – Her mind shied away from forbidden territory and fixed on Jimmy. She was still sitting on the bed when he returned with their luggage.

Seeing the room anew in all its drabness, he stood at the end of the bed, thumping the iron rail with a clenched fist. 'Some bloody honeymoon this is turning out to be – a complete and utter shambles. The most important night in our lives, and we end up in . . .' He stopped, as his eyes met Liz's.

'Oxenholme,' she spluttered and went off into peals of laughter, 'with a chamber pot in the cupboard!'

After a moment he joined in, and they rolled across the bed, helpless with stifled mirth. He stopped, half on top of her, and with some difficulty removed her coat, flinging it aside before starting on the buttons of her blouse. She slapped his hand away.

'Jimmy, stop it. That gorgon could be back any minute.'

'So what? She's a married woman, she'll understand.'

'Not necessarily.' Liz struggled upright, just as Mrs Wilson knocked and entered carrying a tray bearing two mugs of tea and a plate of thick-cut ham sandwiches, her eyes studiously averted from the bed. 'That looks wonderful, Mrs Wilson. Thank you.'

'Breakfast at eight sharp,' she rapped out, and left.

'You're right,' Jimmy gasped, stifling his guffaws. 'If there ever was a Mr Wilson, I bet he never got inside *her* blouse.'

The ludicrous situation, coupled with a persistently creaking bed spring, eased away any slight tension and robbed Liz of much of her apprehension about the actual mechanics of making love. There was laughter as well as passion in their love-making, so that she found herself responding quite naturally to Jimmy's practised moves, and only momentarily did her heart betray her with a fleeting 'if only' . . .

'That was great, sweetheart, wasn't it?' Jimmy murmured. His fingers brushed her cheek in the darkness, and encountered a tear rolling down to soak the pillow. 'Hey! what's this? I didn't hurt you, did I?'

'Of course not, silly.' Liz reached up and drew his head down, her kiss reassuringly ardent. 'Girls cry for all kinds of reasons.'

Later in the night, their roles were reversed as she was roused from sleep to find Jimmy thrashing about and shouting obscenities. None of it made sense, but she knew Chris had suffered disturbed dreams, and guessed that both arose from the same cause. So she took him in her arms as if he were Georgy, and hushed him gently. 'You were dreaming,' she murmured as he half woke – and he turned his face into her breast and slept.

So each found consolation in the love of the other, and in the morning, Jimmy remembered nothing of what had happened.

Liz discovered a different kind of love in the two days that followed, as she beheld Lakeland in all its end-of-summer glory. Windermere was the first to weave its magic into her heart: the lake sparkling under a cloudless sky, surrounded by lush greenery, and wandering, hands swinging, through bracken beginning to turn gold and masses of purple heather. She loved the fells, smooth-bossed and dotted with sheep, and the rugged, mysterious peaks beyond, their mood constantly changing with the light. And then, on their second day, they took a bus to Keswick, and discovered Derwentwater and the remote and lovely Borrowdale, and Liz knew that she would never see anything more beautiful.

'You wait till we've got Hitler sorted,' Jimmy said, as they lazed together in the splendid isolation of a small inlet, skimming pebbles across the lapping water. 'I'll take you places that'll make this look like Blackpool on a wet Bank Holiday.'

But Liz smiled and shook her head, knowing that for her, nowhere in the whole world could be more beautiful. 'One day,' she whispered, 'I will come back.'

Back home, Liz quickly reverted to her old life, with only the wedding ring on her finger to remind her that she was married. She and Jimmy had both decided that while he was away in the army, it would be simpler for her to remain at home where she was most needed, and put their money into savings for the future. When Jimmy came on leave in early October, they moved into the flat over the Candide, which had remained unoccupied since Mr Morgan's death. 'Hey, it's great here, isn't it?' he said, lying back on his pillows in the pleasantly furnished bedroom on his first morning there. 'The old boy had some good stuff. Yes, this'll do us nicely for starters. Not big enough once the babies start arriving, of course,' he added teasingly. 'Liz Marsden, you're blushing.' His mind moved caressingly across her stomach. 'You're not. . . ?'

'No, I'm not,' she retorted, dismayed to find her body resisting the possessive intimacy of the gesture. She forced herself to say lightly, 'It's just – well, it sounded as though you were planning a baker's dozen.'

'Why not? A whole line of little Marsdens, as handsome as their father and as clever as their beautiful mother.' He grinned lasciviously and pulled her towards him. 'We could make a start right now.'

'Not now, Jimmy.' Liz gently released herself, and immediately felt guilty as a shadow crossed his face. 'I'm late already, and it'll take me a good ten minutes to walk home.'

He grimaced, but seemed cheerful enough as he rolled on to his back and reached for a cigarette. 'O.K. sweetheart, I can wait.' He lit up and lay back, watching her dress. 'I'll go and see the folks this morning, probably have my dinner there, so I'll get round to Fortune Street some time this afternoon.'

It was a while since Chris had written. He had apparently got over Dunkirk, but as he was quiet by nature, Kathleen was anxious to know what Jimmy thought.

'Oh, he's in fine fettle.' Jimmy grinned. 'Got himself a nice little ATS girl. Not exactly a stunner so far as looks go, but nice. Mary Clancy. You'd like her.'

'Chris never mentioned her when he was home,' Kathleen said. 'Or in his last letter.' Jimmy had many good qualities, but she didn't necessarily trust his judgement when it came to deciding who was the right girl for her son.

'Well, he only met her a couple of weeks back. Give him a chance.'

By the end of October Hitler decided to cut his losses. The bravery, skill and determination of 'the Few' had proved more than a match for the might of the Luftwaffe. The Battle of Britain was won. But many young lives were lost, on both sides. One of the last to die was Francis – in the manner he had described to Liz with such bleak but graphic eloquence. He was awarded the DFC posthumously, and Mr and Mrs Whitney went down to London to receive it.

Liz wept for the friend with whom she had exchanged confidences, sitting on the stairs one New Year's Eve a whole lifetime away – or so it now seemed – whose one and only dream had been to fly aeroplanes. And, on impulse, but with a total sense of rightness, she wrote to tell Leigh what had happened.

As Christmas approached, there was a mood of guarded optimism among the customers. November had been a bad month for air raids, ending with a night few would forget, when enemy planes had illuminated the whole city with flares before dropping landmines – killers that drifted silently down on green parachutes and exploded with terrifying consequences. A Junior Technical School received a direct hit, bringing three storeys down on top of the basement where over three hundred men, women and children were sheltering. Part of the basement roof caved in, fracturing boilers and furnaces, and killing well over half the people, and of the rest, only about thirty escaped unharmed.

'That 'itler'll burn in Hell hisself one day, for worr 'e done there,' Mrs Killigan prophesied, with some relish, as she waited for Kathleen to slice her bacon ration. 'An' if I could gerr'old of 'im this minute, I'd trim 'is bits off on that machine fer starters.' A crude threat, but the statement was echoed time and again as a great anger ran round the whole city.

Since then, however, things had been relatively quiet, and folk cautiously rallied, resolved to make the most of the festive season. Liz wrote to Jimmy every week, just as Mam wrote to Chris, and they wrote back. It seemed unlikely that they would get leave, but both were still in Scotland, in good heart, and safe, so Liz was able to set about creating some true Christmas spirit with all her usual enthusiasm.

It was almost like the old days, as the bakehouse became a hive of activity once more. The demand for Michael's bread was as great as ever, greater if anything. When rations failed to stretch, there was always bread and jam. The shortage of dried fruit meant that the Christmas cakes were lighter than usual, but each one bore a small ring of icing with a cheery robin on top.

'I think we should decide what we can most easily make, and concentrate on presenting those items as attractively as possible,' Liz said. 'I should still be able to make a limited number of petit fours, and there'll be no problem with the meringue Santas – I might manage some reindeer as well, this year. And choux buns and eclairs and most of the pastries. The Candide is doing excellent trade.'

'Well, I'm very happy for you, Lizzie, my love,' Michael said. 'As well to make the most of it while you can.'

'I will – and so should you. A lot of customers have been asking whether we'll be having your special pork pies this Christmas.'

'Ah, well, now, Lizzie – that could be a bit more difficult. I'd need to get quite a bit of pork over and above me allowance.'

'That's all right,' she said with a grin. 'Jimmy's Dad says he can let you have some as long as you make one for him. It seems Mrs Marsden's no good at making raised pies.'

'That's all very well, but . . .'

'I think we should just make them to order,' she suggested persuasively. 'That way, we wouldn't actually be selling them over the counter.'

'You've got a devious mind, young lady. Leading your old Dad into dishonest ways.' But she could see he was turning the idea over in his mind. 'We'll see what your mother has to say.'

Kathleen took the view that a small transaction between Sunny Marsden and himself hardly amounted to dishonesty. 'Any more than taking a few orders here or there. These days we have to make our living the best way we can, and our Nick was telling me of a thing or two you might pursue. All legal,' she added, as he began to protest.

So it was that, egged on by his wife and daughter, Michael began to keep an ear for any bargains going, such as the occasional auction of damaged goods, salvaged from bombed ships or warehouses. About two weeks before Christmas he came home in triumph, bearing a case of prunes.

The whole family was roped in to sit round the table and chop them up, including Shirley Anne, who protested that she would ruin her nails. When mixed with some of Kathleen's apples, stewed and bottled during the summer, some carefully hoarded allspice, and a little chopped suet from Jimmy's dad, they were able to make lots of excellent mince pies.

From time to time, Michael also brought home quantities of tins without labels, which might contain anything from stewed steak to baked beans to sliced peaches, and in order to generate a spirit of seasonal fun, Kathleen displayed these in a large basket, selling them for sixpence a time on a 'catch as catch can' basis – only one per person.

With less than a week to go, a peaceful Christmas had become a real possibility. Joey had festooned the shop with colourful streamers, to banish the gloom of the heavy window blinds and horrid dim blue lights near the shop door, and presents were wrapped and hidden away. Many shops closed early because of the blackout, but at half past six, Ryan's was more often than not still crowded. The talk was mostly seasonal, of turkeys and chickens, and whether the greengrocer might have any oranges for the kiddies' stockings. And out in the street, groups of children sang carols for pennies.

Kathleen was weighing Nora Figg's cheese ration, accompanied by Nora's usual moans about how 'a poor widder' could be expected to keep body and soul together on such meagre fare, when the sirens began to wail, the sound coming nearer and nearer.

'Oh, the Devil take Gerry!' muttered Kathleen, as some customers panicked and began struggling towards the door. 'Listen, now' – she had to shout to make her voice heard – 'there's plenty of room in our cellar, and you're all welcome to use it.' She lifted the counter flap. 'You can come through this way.'

Michael and Kathleen had long since let it be known that the protection of their cellar was available to anyone in Fortune Street who had no shelter, and found it difficult to get to a public one. Now a few took advantage, but those with families were anxious to get home. 'Ellen, you'd better get off, too. But do send the children along.'

'If I know our Dot, she'll already have them halfway here.'

Kathleen saw, with a sinking heart, that Liz was pulling on her warden's trousers and boots and reaching for her coat and tin hat.

'Do you have to go? It isn't your turn.'

'I know, Mam, but they don't usually come this early. I've a feeling they could mean business, in which case I'll be needed.'

'Your father's still out with the van.' Georgy was tugging at Kathleen's skirt, and absently she picked him up. He banged his head gently against hers – a sure sign that he was disturbed. 'Hopefully, Shirley Anne won't yet have left Mrs Frith's.' She put her head round the living room door. 'Where's our Joey?'

'He's already off on his bike.'

Joey had joined the Civil Defence Messenger Service, with some of the other senior scouts from his troop, as soon as it was formed. Their function was to deliver messages from one sector to another, especially when telephones were put out of action. Kathleen had protested strongly that he was too young, but to little avail.

'Oh, come on, Mam! What'll the others think if I chicken out?'

'If their mothers had any sense, they'd put their foot down, too.' She had looked into those melting blue eyes beneath the thick swathe of dark hair, knowing that, one way or another, he would get involved. The whole world had gone mad, she thought bitterly. 'But I can see I'm wasting my breath.'

Liz wasn't too happy about Joey being on the streets, either, but for different reasons. More than once, she had seen a familiar figure lurking in the shadows of houses left vacant when people took refuge in the shelters, and once she had caught him in her torch beam. Eddie Killigan on the prowl, his pockets suspiciously bulky.

'Just checkin',' he'd said cockily. 'There was an incendiary come round 'ere somewhere.'

But Liz knew he was up to no good, and she didn't want Joey to get involved.

But there was no time to worry about Joey, or anyone else. As Liz hurried to Dandy's Warden Post, her stomach churning, the sky was already alight with fire, and from the direction of the docks came a series of explosions that shook the ground beneath her feet.

Chapter Fifteen

Mrs Frith's informal gatherings were almost as popular as her concerts. They usually ran from about four o'clock in the afternoon until seven or seven-thirty, when people began drifting away to dinner. On this particular afternoon, with Christmas only days away, the drawing room was more crowded than usual, with friends and acquaintances, young and old. The atmosphere was festive; every nook and cranny festooned with greenery, a log fire crackling in the grate, and in one corner, a huge tree glittering with lights and silver baubles – a place where, but for the generous scattering of uniforms, it might have been possible to believe that the war was nothing but a bad dream.

The gentlemen allowed themselves to be generously plied with the contents of the cellars, judiciously stocked in happier days by the late Mr Frith; they flirted with the pretty young girls, and many a glance would stray to the exceedingly attractive long-legged blonde in a soft blue wool dress who moved as though she did not have a single bone in her curvaceous body, and who seemed always to be there to fill an empty glass with a smiling 'May I?'

Shirley Anne knew exactly how to attract attention to herself without ever seeming to do so, and she looked forward to these gatherings almost as much as she did to her concerts. It spoiled things very slightly when, as today, she was obliged to bring Rosie with her, but Liz had been quite adamant, and had for once brought them in the van. However, Ethel and Mrs Wright, the cook, doted on Rosie, and were more than content to have her down in the kitchen in a pram borrowed from a neighbour – an arrangement that also suited Rosie, who loved to be spoiled.

'Are you Mrs Frith's daughter?'

She turned to find a pair of audacious blue eyes watching her. He was slim, a little above medium height, wore Naval uniform, and was leaning with becoming nonchalance on a stick.

'Goodness, no. I just help out at these occasions.' She held out a hand. 'I'm Shirley Anne Ryan.'

'Ah.' He nodded, holding the hand a fraction longer than necessary. 'The beautiful and talented Miss Ryan. I might have guessed.' He inclined his head. 'Andy Rogers. Sub-Lieutenant.' She tugged, and he released her with a grin. 'Some of us hope to be at your concert on Christmas Eve, if Gerry doesn't put a stop to it.'

'Oh, we never allow Gerry to put a stop to our concerts.' Her glanced strayed towards his stick, and the grin became a wry grimace.

'I'd like to be able to boast of an injury acquired in the glorious defence of my country. In fact, I slipped on a patch of ice and sprained my ankle.'

She laughed. 'I'm sorry.'

'Don't be. It meant I got home leave for Christmas – and met you.'

Shirley Anne, well versed in the art of light-hearted flirtation, made some appropriate reply, which was cut short by the whine of the sirens.

Mrs Frith at once became agitated, her glance flying to the heavily curtained windows. 'Oh, what rotten luck,' she cried, the sleeves of her chiffon tea gown fluttering as she moved between her guests. 'So much earlier than usual, too. And after such a nice quiet spell. Should we go to the cellar, do you think?' She raised apprehensive eyes to a reassuringly calm and solid-looking colonel of artillery. 'It is quite cosy down there. Or should we perhaps wait? It could be a false alarm.'

But a young adjutant, who had been unobtrusively dispatched to investigate, came back to report that there was a heavy ack-ack barrage already under way, that bombs were exploding in the direction of the docks, and fires blazing all over the city. The colonel immediately made his apologies, advising that the cellar might be no bad idea. A number of people decided to leave with him, but the remainder carried on talking with studied non-chalance until several explosions set the glass chandelier tinkling.

At this, some of the guests began to show signs of distress, so Mrs Frith ushered everyone down to the large main cellar – which, being next to the boiler room, was surprisingly warm, and well furnished with a number of armchairs and little tables. Shirley Anne went to fetch Ethel and cook, and to help Ethel down with Rosie's pram.

'Perhaps you should ring your mother, dear,' Mrs Frith called after her. 'Tell her you will stay here until the raid is over.'

By the time Shirley Anne returned with Rosie, some of the younger people were dancing to music from a wind-up gramophone, which drowned all but the occasional bang. And then, in the middle of *The Continental*, a gigantic explosion shook the whole building, sending the needle skidding across the record.

'Oh, dear God!' one of the older men muttered. Some of the women were sobbing quietly, and one terrified girl began to scream. Rosie, who until then had been watching and rocking the pram, promptly took fright and joined in.

Shirley Anne felt like screaming too, but more from aggravation than fear. And when it became clear that no-one could control the girl, she walked across and slapped her face. 'Stop it at once!' she said, and went back to pick Rosie up. 'Can't you see how you're frightening her?'

'Well, really!' the girl's mother protested, rushing to comfort her daughter while the others watched, open-mouthed, and the men murmured, 'Oh, I say . . .' Mrs Frith, almost in tears herself, stammered, 'Shirley Anne, I really don't think . . .'

'I'm sorry,' Shirley Anne did her best to be graciously apologetic, whilst trying to quieten Rosie. 'But getting hysterical won't do any good. We're all still here, and in one piece, aren't we? If you really want to let rip, why not have a sing-song? Something rousing, and loud enough to drown the noise outside. Come on, let's beat them at their own game!'

Her eyes alight with enthusiasm, she began to sing *There'll always be an England*, and gradually most of the young ones joined in, followed rather self-consciously by the rest. 'That's great. Now, how about this?' Shirley Anne changed to *Run, Rabbit, Run*, substituting 'Adolf' for 'Rabbit', and urging them to sing louder every time a thud shook the building. Rosie bounced up and down in her mother's arms, her screams turning to crows of delight. From there they went on to *Little Sir Echo*, and Shirley Anne organized one half of the room to sing the song and the other half to be the echo, by which time the young ones were well into the swing of it, and able to carry on spontaneously. She stepped back, her face flushed and her eyes bright as sapphires.

Andy Rogers, having witnessed the slapping incident, watched her mesmeric performance – for that was what it was – with admiration. 'Your talents are wasted here. You ought to be in ENSA.'

She shrugged ruefully, the exhilaration gradually fading from her eyes. 'I shouldn't have gone for that girl, though. Poor kid.'

He quirked a laconic eyebrow. 'No younger than you, I'd say.'

'Not in years, maybe.' Shirley Anne looked across at the pretty, spoiled face. 'It's not her fault she hasn't got a mam like ours – she'd a short way with tantrums.' She turned to lay her now-exhausted daughter back in her pram, very much aware of the way his involuntary glance flicked to her left hand and then to her face as she straightened up. 'Yes, Rosie is mine, and I'm not married. Shocking, isn't it?'

'My dear girl, without knowing the circumstances, I wouldn't presume to judge.'

She laughed shortly. 'Thanks, but you don't have to be polite, or spare my feelings. The plain fact is, I behaved stupidly, and got exactly what I deserved.'

Kathleen was in the cellar, making hot Bovril and toast for everyone, when she heard sounds above.

'Watch that toast for me, will you, Dot?' she said, and hurried upstairs. 'Oh, Michael, thank God you're back safely,' she began, and then stopped, for he was covered from top to toe in what looked like brick dust and flour. 'Mercy on us – will you look at the state of you! You aren't hurt, are you?'

'Divil a bit, *acushla*. But there's a terrible thing happened in Bentinck Street. The railway bridge got a direct hit. All five arches destroyed. There's huge slabs of concrete everywhere, and God only knows how many poor souls buried beneath. It was a favourite place to shelter, d'ye see. Dandy's down there directing operations, and I'm away back to lend a hand, the minute I've changed into something more suitable.'

'You're going nowhere until you've had a hot drink and got something inside you! No, I mean it, Michael. If it's as bad as you say, it's not likely there'll be anyone alive, God rest them. Go on, now, and I'll have something ready when you come down. And a couple of flasks to take out.' She tried to sound casual. 'You haven't seen Liz or Joey, I suppose?'

'I haven't, Kathy, love. But they know fine how to take care of themselves.' Michael's eyes were compassionate as they caressed her troubled face. 'It's never easy, is it? Waiting.'

Liz never wanted to see another bag of sand or another stirrup pump. Her nostrils and eyes had accustomed themselves to the acrid smell of fire, and she'd long since lost count of the number of incendiaries she'd put out. As for fear – with a whole street to be evacuated after finding an unexploded landmine, she no longer had the energy to be afraid. Everyone was stretched to the limit, Grandpa Dandy had said the last time she'd called in at his heavily reinforced sector post, at the Scottie Road end of Fortune Street. He had just come back from doing his rounds and was covered in dust, and looking and sounding unbearably weary. He was only really supposed to do day duty, and she wanted to fling her arms round him, to love him better and urge him to go home and rest. But he'd only tell her, in his pugnacious way, to save her breath to cool her porridge.

'Your Dad was helping down at Bentinck Street when I left. A bad business. It'll be days before they clear the rubble and get the bodies out. I've just sent young Joey off to headquarters to see if they've anyone to spare, but there's small hope, I'm thinkin'. It's the same all over. St George's Hall's had a parcel of incendiaries, St John Market's on fire, and there's been a big explosion on Copperas Hill that's damaged part of the Adelphi. At least someone from the Navy's dealt with that landmine. If that had gone off, we really would be in trouble. You did well there, our Liz, helpin' to get all them people moved and settled somewhere for the time being.'

'It's amazing how many good folk there are, willing to help. We've been lucky so far down our street. Just a couple of incendiaries outside the Cassidys', and I soon made short work of those and no damage done – and Nora Figg's chimney's down, and her back window broken. She was crouched under her table, stubborn as ever, refusing point blank to come along to our cellar, for fear someone might steal her belongings. It's not as if she had anything worth stealing!'

'Ah, well, that's something you'll need to understand, chuck. What might seem like a pile of old junk to you, is probably some poor old biddy's treasure chest of memories.'

His reproach brought the sting of tears to her eyes. 'I do know, really, Grandpa Dandy. It's just, well, Nora's such an awkward old biddy, that if anything did happen to her, I'd feel twice as bad.'

'I know, chuck. Listen, now,' he said. 'It's gone eleven, time you got off home. No – I mean it. It wasn't even your night on duty, though we'd have been struggling worse than we are without you. The same goes for your Dad. Those poor buried souls, God rest them, aren't going anywhere except to their Maker. You both need to get some sleep, if you're to do your job properly. And it's important that you do. Folk still have to eat, and they'll need their bread and pies and cakes more than ever – something that's not much effort for them to prepare. So, just think on – that's your war work as much as any other.'

Back home Liz took off her tin hat, absently smoothing the tight ridge on her forehead where it had rested. Then she flopped down at the table, and sprawled forward with her head in her arms. Kathleen, heart aching, bustled into the scullery to heat some milk, watching the hunched motionless figure with a kind of angry pride.

'Here,' she said at last, pushing a mug of Ovaltine into her daughter's inert hands. 'Drink that, and then get down the cellar to sleep. The children are well away, and the few people who didn't leave during one of the lulls are dozing.'

Liz sat back, every bit of her throbbing with weariness. 'Oh, Mam, Grandpa Dandy is like a rock. I don't know how he does it – keeping everyone busy and cheerful, always checking.' Her eyes were dark hollows, gritty and bloodshot with the smoke. 'It's quite awful out there, you know. If Hitler means to keep this up, I don't know how we'll keep on coping.'

Kathleen stood behind Liz, where she would not see her anguish. Hands that had known many a hard day's work massaged her daughter's shoulders and then folded round her, holding her close. 'You'll cope, my valiant Liz. We'll all do it together.'

And cope they did. And through the next night and day, and the one that followed. Albert turned up without fail on his rickety bicycle, and somehow, with all the family pulling together, the baking got done and no-one went away empty-handed.

The second night was the worst. St Anthony's School was badly hit and the church and presbytery damaged. 'Sod the bastards!' cried a weary docker, fortifying his courage in a nearby pub. He staggered to the door. 'Come on, the lot of youse, we can't lerr'm burn the bleedin' church an' school!'

The school had received a direct hit, and fire engines and wardens, Dandy and Liz amongst them, were already busy helping to rescue Father Clarkson and two of his curates who were inside with the caretaker and his family.

Joey was among a team of volunteers eager to scramble up on the church roof to put out the flames. He found himself next to Eddie Killigan – the first time they had met in ages.

'Hey, it's great, this, isn't it?' Eddie panted, picking up one of the fifteen-inch smouldering incendiaries and throwing it down for someone to smother in sand. 'Like a proper adventure.'

It was like something out of a futuristic film, crouched figures scrambling across the roof amidst water and sand to douse the flames against a background eerily red with the light of many other fires.

'Don't mess about, Eddie,' Joey shouted. 'What've you got there? Another incendiary?'

'No, it's nothing.' Eddie stuffed whatever it was into his coat pocket and clambered across to join the others. Young Fr Glynn, his face streaked with dirt, was directing operations.

'This is a terrible night,' he said, close to tears. 'My two brother curates killed, and the caretaker and his family, too – may God have mercy on their souls. Father Clarkson has mercifully escaped with injuries and is on his way to hospital. I am sure he would want me to thank you for all you have done, and on Christmas Day, God willing, he will be able to express his thanks to you personally. God bless you all.'

'Come on, Joey, let's gerrout of 'ere,' Eddie muttered.

Fr Glynn's voice stopped him in his tracks. 'Eddie Killigan, isn't it? God bless you, Eddie – and you, Joey, for your help.'

Eddie fidgeted under the young priest's gaze. 'Yeh, sure. It was nothing, Father.'

When they were out of hearing, Joey grabbed Eddie's arm and swung him round. 'All right, what was it you nicked from the roof?'

'Nothin'. I don't know what yer on about.'

'Oh, yes, you do. I know you, Eddie Killigan. Always graftin'. But stealing from a church – and now, of all times. That's pathetic.'

Eddie shrugged him off. 'Leggo. It weren't nothin', I tell yer. Just a few bits of old lead. They come loose in me 'and. They'll never even be missed, an' it's worth a good few bob, is scrap lead.'

'That's all you ever think about, making a few bob! Well, this time you're going to give it back.'

'Oh, yeh? An' who's gonna make me – you?'

'If I have to.' Joey was scathing. 'You're no better'n Hitler, you – I bet you only went up on that roof in the first place on the scrounge.'

'That's a lie! I'll make you eat them words!'

'You can try!'

It was a scrappy fight, more guts than science, but a fight to the finish in red-tinged darkness, oblivious of the acrid smoke choking their lungs, and the occasional thud of bombs. Eddie was half a head shorter than Joey, but more thickset, and all the grievances, real and imagined, of the last few years, gave added zest to his wild swings, some of which found their mark. But Joey had the advantage of height and reach. He had also been well schooled by Dandy in how to keep a cool head, and make use of the long-armed jab. Soon Eddie's nose was bloody, and one eye was closing. His swings grew wilder with frustration.

'Have you had enough?' Joey panted. 'I don't really want to knock you down.'

'You couldn't knock a bleedin' coconut down . . .'

'Well, if that's how you want it.'

A moment later, Eddie was flat on his back without knowing quite how he'd got there. Joey crouched down. 'Are you all right?'

'Worra a bloody silly question. Course I'm norr' all right. I think yer just broke me perishin' jaw.'

'Rubbish. It was only a tap. I expect I caught you off balance,' Joey said generously, and held out a hand. 'Pax?'

'Yeh, all right.' Eddie scrambled to his feet and fished several lumps of lead out of his pockets. 'I suppose yer wouldn't tek this back for us?'

Fr Glynn was still busy clearing up when Joey got back. He explained somewhat sheepishly that his friend, Eddie, had found the lead in his pocket when he was almost home, and he'd volunteered to bring it back for him in case it was important. The young priest looked at him in silence for a moment, noting in the dull red glow the swelling coming up under Joey's left eye, and several other contusions that hadn't been there a short while ago. But he only said quietly, 'God is good. Thank you, Joey, and away home with you, now.'

Mam exclaimed over the state of his face, but he managed to imply, without telling an outright lie, that he'd done it up on the roof. And her distress over what had happened overcame any further inquisition.

On the last two nights before Christmas, the bombers left them alone, and gradually, everyone began to breathe again – and to hope. There was still a great deal of clearing up to be done, but the Liverpool spirit was more than equal to that. Dandy opened his house to families left homeless, and many others did the same.

As Kathleen sorted out the Christmas orders, helped by Ellen and Shirley Anne, the customers waited good-humouredly, and she listened to them swopping stories and marvelled at their resilience.

'. . . an' there she was, in all the glory of 'er bust bodice an' knickers, an' the firemen tryin' not ter luk. Bright pink, they wus, an' talk about our Nellie's outsize bloomers – if yer tied the legs t'gether, yer could of made a parychute of 'em, An' 'er so stuck up, too. Laugh . . . I nearly wet meself!'

This tale was received with gales of mirth and swiftly spawned others.

'. . . I told 'im, never mind the mess – broken winders'll mend. That little jumped-up Nazi perisher needn't think 'es gorrus finished that easy. We're 'aving a slap up dinner, turkey, puddin' – the lot . . .'

'Eh, don't mention turkey to our Fred! Ours wus ordered, only it got roasted down the market afor we even gorr'our teeth round it. Yer should've 'eard Fred . . . 'E were right by the market when it went on fire, an' the smell of them birds cookin' near drove 'im daft . . . Said 'ed a good mind ter go in an' gerr ours, there and then, fire or no bleedin' fire!'

'Honestly, Flo, you've got to hand it to them,' Kathleen said. 'If the rest of the country has as much courage as this lot, then Hitler will never win.'

Flora had come, as she always did, on Christmas Eve, to find Kathleen closing the shop earlier than usual.

'I think the customers are all like us – wanting to get in and finished. Ellen's taken Georgy home to have tea with her lot, so I'm on my own until the others come in. It was good of you to offer to have the children back, but I think Ellen was loath to be parted again, and they seem happy enough down our cellar. Michael and Liz shouldn't be long – they've gone round the other shops and the café to cash up.'

Flora was wearing a smart navy blue Red Cross uniform, and looked very brisk and business-like.

'I'd have come over to give a hand, but I've been a bit pushed, helping to find accommodation for the homeless.' She eyed her sister as she finished emptying the rack, hauled it back up, and brought the washing to the table to fold. 'For goodness sake, sit down before you fall down, our Kathy. I'll do that. You look all in.' And, seeing Kathleen's quickly veiled astonishment as she picked up one of Michael's shirts, 'You needn't look so surprised. I haven't forgotten how.'

Kathleen smiled, and sat down with a sigh of relief. 'We're all exhausted, even Joey and Shirley Anne.' She watched Flora's deft hands as they folded and smoothed. 'It's only the thought of having two whole days to ourselves that's keeping us going. Michael and Liz have borne the brunt, mind – out on the streets half the night, and coming back to start the baking, with only a few snatched hours of sleep during the day. They haven't been able to take things easy, either, with all the extra Christmas baking to catch up on.'

'And how's Dad bearing up?'

'Oh, you know Dad. You'd think he was fighting the Germans single-handed. But I do worry about him. He's not a young man any more.'

Flora grinned. 'Don't let him hear you say that.'

'More than my life's worth! At least he's coming here for his dinner tomorrow. Nick, too. Poor Nick, he sounded really down when he rang. He was to have gone to Wales, but with the docks taking such a pasting, they're all on standby for extra duties.'

Kathleen sighed. 'Christmas won't be quite the same, of course. We knew Chris and Jimmy wouldn't get leave, but neither could Rita's Frank, so she's gone to stay near him for a few days. But we got a lovely big parcel from our Mary, full of things we haven't seen in the shops for months.'

'Which reminds me.' Flora reached for her bag and pulled out two slim packages in fancy wrapping. 'Hide these, will you, before either of the girls come in? A little extra present. They're genuine American nylon stockings.'

'Goodness! However did you come by those?' Kathleen took them over to one of the sideboard drawers and slid them right to the back. 'Your American Red Cross friends, I suppose.'

'Never you mind. I'm afraid most of my presents are purely practical this year – money to spend, and lots of warm woolly jumpers and things, before they start rationing what we wear.'

'It hasn't been easy to know what to get. Except for Joey – he's always got a list as long as your arm, for his bike, mostly. And Shirley Anne is always happy with clothes or make-up. Incidentally, I think she's acquired an admirer.'

'Really?'

'There was a naval officer in the shop yesterday, asking for her, and when she saw him, I'll swear she blushed. Oh, is that the back door?'

Liz came in, followed by Michael, and as if not wanting to be caught in the act of helping, Flora folded the last towel very quickly, gave it a hasty pat, and stepped away from the table.

Liz was wearing a warm three-quarter-length red coat, a knitted bobble hat to match, and grey flannel slacks. Her face was pinched with cold, but there was nothing cold about her greeting as she hugged her aunt with more than usual affection.

'What a lovely surprise. And don't you look dashing in your uniform. Dad,' she swung round, 'doesn't Aunt Flora look dashing?'

'She does indeed.' Michael's approval was tinged with amusement as he noted her embarrassment. He came and kissed her cheek. 'How are you, Flora?'

'Oh, much as everyone else. Busy,' she said off-handedly. 'Not that I've had such a rough time as you've had here.'

'Flora is a great one for hiding her light under a bushel. Like not letting on that she's just folded that pile of washing for me,' Kathleen said, with unaccustomed mischief.

'Oh, for heaven's sake, Kathy . . .' Flora began to search in her bag for a cigarette. It had become much harder to get her favourite ones, and she was trying to ration herself. But now . . .

'That was a kindly thought, Flora,' Michael said quietly. 'Here, now.' He was beside her, sliding open a packet, holding it out to her. 'I saw these when I was down at the warehouse and, thinking you might be glad of a few extra, I managed to get hold of a hundred pack as a kind of extra Christmas present.'

She accepted the cigarette and stood there, holding it foolishly between her fingers while he took a spill from the jar on the mantelpiece and, smiling into her eyes, lit it for her before turning away to reach for his pipe. She inhaled and pulled herself together. 'That was a pretty kindly thought yourself, Michael Ryan.'

Liz had shed her coat, and was busy making a pot of tea. Flora wondered if it was the cut of the slacks that made her niece look as thin as a lath. She did not entirely approve of women in trousers, though in the present circumstances they did serve a practical function, and it had to be said that they looked particularly well on Liz's whippy figure.

'You're looking peaky, my girl. Lost weight, have you?'

'I shouldn't think so,' Liz sounded cheerful enough. 'We're all looking a bit peaky just now. It's been that kind of week.'

Flora declined to stay for tea. 'I've still got masses to do.' There was a general sorting out of presents, and then she kissed them all. 'Have a happy and, please God, a peaceful Christmas, all of you. I'll go out the back. Liz, you can walk to the car with me, if you like.'

Out in the road, she hesitated, then took a slim envelope from her handbag. 'I'm not at all sure I should be doing this.'

Liz's heart gave a sudden leap of joy, and her voice trembled with the force of it. 'From Leigh?' It wasn't really a question. She continued more steadily, 'I still had his address from years back, and felt I had to write and tell him about poor Francis. I daresay he felt he had to reply.'

'I daresay he did,' her aunt agreed drily, hiding her disquiet. 'He obviously didn't wish to cause trouble by writing to you here, so he posted it to me. Just so long as he doesn't make a habit of using me as a *poste restante.*'

'Oh, he won't, I'm sure.' Liz pushed the letter inside her coat and hugged it to her. And then, because she couldn't help herself: 'How is he, Aunt Flora? Have you seen him?'

'Not since he started ferrying those bombers over from Canada to Prestwich. It can mean a fast turn-round for the pilots, if there happens to be a ship going back. I've had the odd letter or call from him now and then.'

Liz wasn't sure which frightened her most – the North Atlantic flight, so dangerous in winter or the equally dangerous return by sea with the constant threat of U boats.

Flora, sensing her fear, was deliberately matter of fact. 'Leigh knows the score, my dear, and as far as it's in his power, he can take care of himself. That's as much as any of us can say at present. Besides, you have a husband to worry about now.' She touched Liz's cheek lightly and felt her tense at the implied reproof. 'And now I must go. Take care of yourself, too, dear girl.'

It was some time before Liz could take the letter up to her room. It had been posted in Prestwich two days ago, and was very brief, thanking her for telling him about Francis, and expressing his great sadness for the gentle boy who would have hated the killing, although – *I guess that flying was, for all too brief a time, everything that Francis had ever dreamed about. Few people get to achieve that much, so perhaps he is the lucky one.*

Liz crumpled the letter up, and then as swiftly smoothed it out again, knowing that it was her weariness, echoing his fatalism, that made her heart feel as though it would burst through her ribs, and her body ache with wanting him. She read the postscript again. *Have just learned about the dreadful bombing of Liverpool. Rang Flora, who says you are safe. Thank God!* She lay for a long time, dry-eyed, curled up on her side with the letter pressed against her face.

Midnight Mass was packed: St Anthony's reprieve from total destruction, and the tragic price that had been paid, seemed to have generated more fervour than usual. Liz noticed more than one non-Catholic in the congregation giving thanks. Perhaps, she thought, they were mourning their own lovely church of Our Lady and St Nicholas, which had been gutted. She had heard, with a faint prickling of the skin, that the first firefighters to go inside had found amidst the smouldering rubble, two blackened beams lying in the shape of a cross where the altar had been – almost like a sign. Though it was surely Hitler who needed the sign. But nothing could dim the spirit of Christmas, which came through strong and true that night in the joyous voices soaring up into St Anthony's charred rafters.

Soon after they returned home Chris and Jimmy rang, in ebullient mood. They had obviously been celebrating, and Mam warned everyone not to spoil their mood by mentioning the havoc of the past week. Jimmy told Liz he loved her at least six times, and perhaps because she was feeling a little guilty, she was extra loving in return.

Chapter Sixteen

Rosie celebrated her birthday in a style worthy of her mother, by taking her first steps. Dressed in the exquisitely smocked pink frock which had been a gift from Mrs Frith, she tottered across the hearthrug and collapsed against her Grandad's knee, gazing up at him with a beatific smile.

'She'll break hearts, this one,' said Michael, lifting her up and kissing her soundly. Rosie laughed as his moustache tickled her, and wriggled to be let down. Georgy watched gravely, then, 'Georgy kiss,' he said.

'Very well, dear, but don't hug her too tight,' Kathleen sighed. He was a big boy for his three and a half years, affectionate in his simple way, and he doted on Rosie. But he didn't always realize his strength.

All had been quiet since Christmas; bad weather had discouraged the raiders. But when the birthday excitement was over and the children tucked up in bed and asleep, Shirley Anne dropped a bombshell of her own.

The pile of plates Liz was carrying rattled and almost went flying. She set them down on the table with a clatter and turned furiously to face her sister. 'You want to do *what*?'

'Join ENSA. You know, the organization that . . .'

'I know what ENSA is. I just can't believe that even you have the gall to contemplate walking out of here without a thought for your responsibilities towards your daughter – or were you thinking of taking her with you?'

'Don't talk stupid. Of course I can't take her with me.' Shirley Anne flounced, a sure sign of guilt. 'I could be sent anywhere.'

'Well if you've thought it through that far, the rest is clear enough.'

'Mam?' There was a note of pleading in Shirley Anne's voice. But it was Michael who answered, quiet as always, but stern.

'Now don't be wheedling your way round your mother, girleen. She has more than enough to contend with, as have we all. I don't doubt the sincerity of your motives, but a child needs its mother. Your first duty is to Rosie.'

'But Dad, Mr Grace says they're desperate for experienced people . . .'

'Mr Grace?' Kathleen's voice was sharp. 'Do you mean to say you've been in touch with that man – after all that happened?'

Shirley Anne coloured up. 'What happened wasn't his fault. And anyway, he got in touch with me. He's organizing some of the ENSA tours, and I'm just the kind of artiste they're looking for, so he wrote to ask how I was placed.'

'Well, now can you tell him,' Liz said.

'Yes, but – ' She swung round. 'Oh, Mam, I'm a rotten mother, you know I am. Rosie minds you more than she ever will me. I'd be much more use doing what I do best. Even Andy says I'm wasted here.'

'Oh, well, if *Andy* says!' Liz knew she was being catty, but she couldn't help herself. 'It's the same old story, isn't it? You're selfish to the core – always have been, always will be! Everything's been fine while Andy Rogers has been around to dance attendance on you, but now he's gone back to his ship, you're bored.'

'That's not true! You've never understood!'

'Oh, yes I have. You don't really think we're stupid enough to believe it's pure coincidence that Mr Grace waggled his little finger just when you needed him?'

'I don't care what you think. It *is* coincidence. And if I am bored, p'raps it's because you're no fun to be with any more!'

'Shirley Anne, you will not speak to your sister like that.' Michael's voice held a warning, but she was too keyed up to hear it.

'But it's true, Dad. Liz wants to take a good look at herself. She's getting downright dull.'

That hurt. But Liz persisted. 'Maybe I am, but at least I wouldn't swan off and leave Mam to look after my daughter!'

'You haven't got a daughter!'

'Stop it, the both of you! You're no better than a pair of children yourselves!'

It was years since they'd heard that whip-crack sound in Kathleen's voice, and it pulled them both up short, to look shamefacedly at one another.

'Now sit down, for goodness' sake, and let's all look at the problem quietly and sensibly.'

'Kathleen – ' Michael began, knowing full well what she was about to say.

'I know, Michael, but we have to face facts. It would be foolish to deny that Shirley Anne has talent, and maybe she is right in thinking that it could be put to better use than it is at present. As for Rosie – ' She looked steadily at her youngest daughter, in whose eyes hope was already springing. 'I very much doubt that she will notice whether you stay – or go.'

If Kathleen had hoped to prick her conscience, she failed miserably, for Shirley Anne's only reaction was to rush joyfully across the room, fling her arms round her mother's shoulders and plant a smacking kiss on her cheek. 'Oh Mam, you're so good! I wish I could be more like you, but Liz is right, I *am* a selfish pig. I can't seem to help it, somehow.'

'Give over, now,' Kathleen said, pushing her away. 'We can do without the soft soap.'

'But it's true. I didn't mean all those awful things I said, Liz.'

Liz shrugged and half grinned. 'I guess we both went to town a bit. I should know better by now than to get mad at you.'

Michael stood up. 'Well, so. That's that, seemingly.'

'Dad?' Shirley Anne heard the flat finality in his voice and straightened up, her lower lip caught between her teeth.

He looked at her gravely. 'You know fine what I think, girleen. But I'll not go against your mother's decision.'

'Oh, thanks, Dad.' She hugged him, too, all enthusiasm now that she'd got her own way. 'Can I use the telephone? I might be able to get through to Mr Grace tonight.' At the door, she turned. 'One day I'll make you all proud of me, you'll see.'

She was like quicksilver, Liz thought with a touch of envy, all lightness and grace, eyes bright as gems.

In two days, Shirley Anne was on her way. Liz was surprised to discover how much she missed her; aggravating though she certainly was at times, life was seldom dull with her young sister around. But the ripples left by her going soon settled, and life went on very much as before. Though not quite as before.

If nothing else, Shirley Anne's words had made Liz take a good look at herself. The next morning had found her staring broodingly into the mirror above the piano, instead of getting on with her work. It was true. She hadn't taken much care with her appearance recently. In fact, she looked positively staid, with her pale morning face and her sensible overall.

On an impulse, she pulled the pins out of her rolled-up hair, and it slithered down in a shining aura about her face. At once, she heard Leigh's voice: *I like my Elizabeth best with her hair blowing free*. Oh, Leigh! She hastily gathered it up again, and was putting the last pin in as Mam came through from the shop.

'I thought I might get in touch with Clare, Mam,' she said casually. 'We haven't had a night out together for weeks.'

'A good idea, love,' Kathleen agreed, knowing exactly what had prompted the thought. 'It's time you had a little fun in your life. And as we none of us know how long this lull will last, you might as well make the most of it.'

Clare, in her second year at Medical School, was enthusiastic. 'If you like, I'll ask some of the crowd, and we could go dancing. If we get to the Grafton early enough, we should get in.'

Liz had been thinking in terms of the pictures, but it would be even more fun to get dressed up and go dancing. She hadn't been near West Derby Road since that last meal with Francis, but she'd heard that their restaurant had been gutted by the same explosion that had taken half the roof off the Grafton before Christmas and destroyed the Olympia Theatre, next door. Fortunately, Mr Bernard had been down in the cellar with his wife and some of the customers at the time, and they weren't hurt.

But Liz was determined to think only carefree thoughts that night. She made a real effort with her appearance, washing and brushing her hair until it shone, catching it high in front with two fancy clasps and letting it float loose. She applied her make-up with care instead of the customary quick dab, and wore her prettiest dress – a floral print with a halter neck and flared skirt. Even the discovery that Shirley Anne had filched one of her precious pairs of nylons couldn't damp her enthusiasm.

Clare's friends were great fun, the room was packed, and the atmosphere was wonderful. At least half the dancers, men and women, were in uniform, and everyone was out to have a good time. The mood was infectious and in no time Liz was joining in, all her dreary day-to-day problems forgotten.

'You know, I haven't seen you look so happy in ages,' Clare said as they paused, flushed, between dances. 'This'll do you the world of good.'

'Yes, doctor,' Liz grinned.

'I mean it. I suppose it can't be easy with Jimmy away.'

'No.' Liz instinctively shied away from intrusive questions. 'But there's lots worse off than me. I've been meaning to ask you, do you still write to Chris?'

Clare bit her lip. Liz remembered that half-guilty gesture from their schooldays, and thought how little Clare had changed – still the short, straight hair of the schoolgirl, still the single-minded dedication to becoming a doctor. 'Not as often as I ought. But I've got a very heavy workload this year, and to be honest, he isn't a very satisfactory correspondent. He hardly ever writes back.'

'Goodness, don't we know it. You don't have to feel badly about it. I only asked because Jimmy hinted, last time he was home, that Chris had a girlfriend, and I wondered if he might have mentioned her.'

It was well after midnight when Liz got home, but she still felt wide-awake and bubbling over, so instead of going to bed at once, she sat down and started a letter to Jimmy, the words spilling easily on to the page –

> 'Clare's friends were great fun. We laughed ourselves silly over the *Boomps-a-Daisy*. I even let a young airman called Clive flirt outrageously with me. He was very sweet, but he wasn't a very good dancer, and seeing all the couples cheek to cheek, I wished you had been there. *Goodnight Sweetheart* just wasn't the same without you . . .'

The shortages had been worse than usual in the weeks since Christmas, as Gerry compensated for a lack of bombing raids by sinking more ships than usual. And the weather didn't do much to lift people's spirits.

'Give us one o' them small tins of pilchards.'

'Fivepenny ha'penny, please, Mrs Figg,' said Ellen.

'Daylight robbery. Only a couple o' bites in 'em. Still, got ter 'ave summat. I dunno 'ow a poor widder woman's meant ter keep body an' soul tergether on two ounces of tea an' no more than a scrape of marge fer the bread. They didn't even 'ave no ciggies over the road this mornin'.'

'Oh, give over moanin', Nora.' Mrs Killigan pulled a face at Ellen. 'Things could be worse. An' I've never seen yer gerr'above two ounces of tea in all the years you've been comin' 'ere. Be a different matter if it was yer stout they rationed. Unbearable, you'd be, then.'

'It's easy fer some ter scoff – them as 'as families ter support 'em. There's that gairl of yours makin' a fortune on the munitions, an' your Eddie doin' alright fer hisself, one way an' another. I wonder the scuffers 'aven't gorr'im fer summat before now.'

Mrs Killigan's immense chest heaved. 'Don't you go slanderin' our Eddie, you foul-mouthed old bat. 'E's a good boy to 'is old Mam. As fer our Lily, she works bloody 'ard fer her money . . . an' so do I!'

'Honestly, it's like Fred Carno's Circus in there when the two of them get going,' Ellen said, coming through from the shop. 'Oh, sorry, were you adding up?'

Kathleen shut the ledger and stood up with a sigh. 'No. All done. That's the stocktaking out of the way for another year – not much adding up needed. It's a blessing bread's not rationed, or we'd be struggling to keep going. There's lots of small shops given up already.'

'Will you just look at the two of them?' Ellen nodded towards the corner beside the piano. Georgy was standing by Rosie's pram, as he would sometimes do for hours on end, patiently picking up the toys she threw out. 'You can see who's boss there, all right.'

'Little madam. Just like her mother. We won't be able to pin her down much longer, then she'll be ten times worse. I suppose I'll need to fetch down the playpen Dad made for Georgy, only it takes up so much room.'

'Have you heard from Shirley Anne recently?'

'Not since that scrawled note asking me to send on any letters from Andy. All we know is that Mr Grace welcomed her with open arms, and she's sharing a flat with four other girls, though I doubt she'll be there all that much if they mean to tour. She's about as good a letter writer as our Chris.'

The opening of the back door brought a draught of cold air. Dandy came in, his blocker at its usual jaunty angle, his face pink with cold in spite of his thick coat and heavy muffler.

'Dad, you look frozen. Come to the fire and get warm while I make you a mug of hot Bovril.'

'That'd go down a treat, girl. In the immortal words of Nora Figg, "it's brass monkeys out there".' He laid his hat on the table and unwound his scarf before going to take the poker to the fire. A tug on his coat made him turn to find Georgy looking up at him.

'Well, now,' he said, sitting in Michael's chair, 'and how's my young fellow-me-lad this morning?'

Georgy leaned against his knee and put the flat of his hand on the end of Dandy's bright red nose. 'Nose hurt.'

'Not hurt, me brave boy. Just cold. You'll need to give it a bit of rub – like this, see?' He covered the tiny hand with his own big paw, and gently rotated it. It made the little boy chuckle. 'That's the ticket.' He took Georgy's other hand and went through the same motions with his cheeks. 'Luvly.'

'Luvly,' Georgy repeated.

Rosie, having lost her audience, began to scream.

'That'll do, young lady.' Kathleen passed the Bovril to her father and went across to the pram. 'Here – have a rusk.' Eager hands snatched it from her. 'That won't keep her quiet for long. I think she's teething.'

Dandy watched her unconsciously stretch and rub her back. 'You've got your hands full, one way and another, our Kathy. Not too much for you, is it?'

'No, of course not.' But she spoke a shade too quickly. 'It's the time of year. I always did hate February.'

'I saw Liz pedalling away up Greaty just now.'

'She's taken to walking to the Candide recently, with Rosie in the pram, but this morning there was a bigger order than usual, and Michael had a full van.'

'Sounds as if trade can't be too bad. Any sign of those two lads getting leave?'

Kathleen shrugged. 'Chris had a forty-eight hour due, but he said it wasn't worth coming home. Most of it'd be taken up travelling.'

'You miss him, don't you, girl?' Dandy said softly.

She tried to smile. 'Oh well, at least I know where he is, and he's as safe in Scotland as anywhere. Jimmy's trying to wangle seventy-two hours. He'll probably get it too, being Jimmy. Not that I begrudge him. He and Liz have scarcely had any time together. If it was later in the year, I'd suggest they met somewhere halfway, but we'll have to wait and see.'

Jimmy did get home at the end of the month, but in the brief time they had together, it wasn't easy for either of them to adjust. He was full of energy, and talked endlessly about the great time they were having, and how hospitable the local people were. 'They've got some bonny wee lassies up there,' he enthused, and then, realizing what he had said; 'None as bonny as my lovely Liz, of course.'

Flirting was as natural to Jimmy as breathing. He wouldn't be unfaithful, Liz was sure – or almost sure. But the more she tried not to imagine him chatting up the 'bonny lassies', the more the thought persisted. It built a kind of barrier between them, so that she was almost relieved when the time came for him to return to Scotland.

'It'll be better next time, darling,' Jimmy murmured in her ear, holding her close and sensing her tension, as they waited for the train. 'We'll have longer together, and it'll be well into spring by then.'

A flurry of raids in March caused quite a bit of damage, though none in the immediate vicinity of Fortune Street, and with the days beginning to lengthen, the lighter evenings brought lighter spirits. The end of March also brought the signing of the Lend-Lease agreement with America. Before long, with any luck, some much needed foodstuffs should be on their way, if the Germans didn't sink them en route.

In March, too, Fritz Lendl died, as quietly as he had lived, causing as little trouble as possible. Mitzi came round to tell Liz and brought with her his recipe book, together with a complete translation, penned in Mitzi's large, childish hand, in two school exercise books.

'It was my father's dearest wish that I should do this for you,' she said, her voice cracking with emotion. 'I began it more than a year ago, in what time I could spare – and, to my joy, I was able to tell him, just days before he died, that it was finished.'

Liz clasped the treasure to her, moved beyond words. Then she put the books aside and hugged Mitzi, and they cried together for the loss of the man they had both loved.

'I'll never forget him,' Liz said, 'or his generosity to me. And I promise that as soon as possible, once this horrible war is over, I shall start up the Lendl Collection again – and your father's name will be known everywhere.'

Michael came back from his round one morning with the news that Fred Munnings had suffered a heart attack.

'How awful. When did it happen? Is it bad?'

'Pretty bad. He was taken into the Royal last night.'

Kathleen had never got on terribly well with the Munnings. They were older than them by about ten years, and Fred's wife Hilda was a terrible snob. She came from a good family and had never done a hand's turn in the business, that Kathleen could remember, even years back, before they expanded. On the few occasions she and Michael had attended a Master Bakers Association function, Hilda had been downright patronizing. Michael never saw it, of course, and for his sake, she'd kept quiet. But now her heart went out to Hilda.

'How will they manage?'

'As far as the bakery is concerned, things shouldn't be too bad. Fred liked to keep his hand in, I know, but they've got a pretty reliable team, and most of them beyond calling-up age. The same with the shops. He was at the Church Street shop most afternoons, behind the counter, chatting to the customers, but that was out of choice, too – good business practice, he said it was. And before the blackout, you'd see the light on in the office upstairs most evenings. Everything was run from there only with his say-so. But, for all that, he's got a perfectly good general manager and a couple of clerks.'

'Sounds as if he's been doing his best to work himself to death,' Kathleen said. 'A pity his son never shaped.'

'Ah, well, maybe he was never given the right encouragement. A fancy education isn't a ha'porth of use if it doesn't go along with a proper sense of enthusiasm and responsibility. And if Fred wouldn't delegate – '

Kathleen gave him a great hug.

'Now, what was that for, I wonder?' he enquired, imprisoning her with one great arm, and looking down at her in a way that made her blush.

'Michael, let me go, you great eejut,' she implored. 'Ellen might come in at any moment – or Liz.' And, when he still made no move to release her, 'Well, if you must know, I was thinking what a nice man you are, Michael Ryan. Soft as they come, but nice. Give over, now. It's hardly decent at our age.'

He kissed her a last time, and regretfully let her go. 'I wondered if I should call round – see if there was anything I could do,' he said.

And get your nose snapped off for your trouble, she thought. 'Well, if you think you should . . . Unless, would you like me to ring Hilda? I could pass on the message.'

Michael looked relieved. 'Would you, Kathy? That might be best.'

But the maid who answered the phone said that Madam was lying down, and not to be disturbed, which Kathleen did not for one moment believe. And two days later, Fred Munnings was dead. She wrote at once, offering their condolences and again expressing their willingness to help.

The funeral was very grand, and there was a two-column spread in the *Echo*, listing his achievements as one of the city's most prominent citizens.

'I mind,' Dandy mused, over dinner, 'when Fred's dad started that business, more than fifty years ago, off Wilbraham Street – a poky little place, it were, not as big as this was when you first took it. But Fred was ambitious. His bread was never a patch on yours, of course, but even as a lad, he was always grafting. And look where it got him – town centre, and half a dozen shops from here to Blundellsands and outlets way beyond. And a posh house in Woolton. But we all end up in the same place, sooner or later – six feet under.'

Georgy banged his spoon on the tray of his high chair, splattering gravy over himself and everyone else. The sound was like little hammers rattling inside her head. Kathleen shivered. 'Dad, please – not while we're eating.'

'Like it or not, it's the truth, girl.' Dandy used his knife to emphasize the point. 'Howsoever, now that you mention it, this is a bonny rabbit stew, our Kathy. I wouldn't say no to a smidgin more. If I'm to take this young lad out on the river this afternoon, I'll need a good lining to me stomach.'

'You're incorrigible, Dad. Oh, come on, give us your plate.' She went across to the big pot drawn to the side of the fire. 'Anyone else? There's more than enough left for Joey.' They declined and she tapped the ladle on the side of the pot and replaced the lid.

'I suppose Alec will be head of the firm now,' Liz said. 'That should suit him, as long as he doesn't have to do any work, and the money keeps rolling in while he's away doing his gallant bit for England.'

Michael quirked an eyebrow at her. 'It's not like you, Lizzie, to be sarcastic, especially at such a time.'

Liz cursed her impulsive tongue. 'Sorry. It was unkind.'

'I wasn't aware that you knew Alec Munnings.' Kathleen's eyes were as sharp as her voice.

'I didn't, not really. We met a couple of times at dances, you know how it is. I just couldn't stand that "I'm a cut above everyone else" manner of his.'

She thought Mam might pursue the matter once her father had left the room, and Dandy had taken Georgy to the bathroom to get him cleaned up ready to take out. But she was saved by a distraction in the form of Rosie, who woke early from her after dinner nap in a thoroughly grizzly mood.

'Enough of that, Rosie-Posie, you horrible infant,' she said, seeing Mam gather herself to deal with the imminent tantrum. 'I'm going to change that pongy nappy, then you're coming upstairs with me while I get ready. *Then*, your Gran's going to have a rest, and you and I will go to that nice café where all the old ladies spoil you rotten.'

The curiously pale blue eyes, spiked with tears, stared up at her out of a flushed face. Rosie's blonde curls were damp and flattened on one side where she had slept on them, and her lower lip still quivered ominously.

'Are you sure, Liz?'

'Of course I'm sure, Mam.' She unfastened Rosie's harness and hoisted her out. 'You look as if a couple of aspirins wouldn't come amiss. Ellen can manage the shop. It's never very busy round now.'

*

It was one of the those sunny, blustery March days. The little windmill on the side of the pram whizzed round, making Rosie laugh, and Liz was glad she had worn her flannel slacks and red woollen jacket, and tied her hair back with a red scarf. She went down Fortune Street into Scottie Road, then on to Byrom Street and along Great Charlotte to Ranelagh Street. As she was about to turn from there into Bold Street, she heard her name called. She knew who it was before she turned – as though talking about him had somehow conjured him up.

The uniform suited his rather effete slimness. No rough serge for him, she thought, eyeing the well-tailored jacket, shoulder pips shining in the sunlight, and the gleam of polished leather strapping. He was more sophisticated than she remembered, but the handsome face was beginning to show signs of over-indulgence.

'Well, well, if it isn't little Lizzie Ryan, all grown up,' he drawled offensively. 'Sorry, it's Marsden now, isn't it?'

She gritted her teeth, remembering his recent loss. 'I was sorry to hear about your father,' she said.

'Yes.' His eyes were speculative as he watched Rosie playing with the fringe of her blanket. 'Yes, it was unexpected.' He might have been remarking on the weather. Quite suddenly, he looked up. 'Yours or mine?' he asked softly.

The casual effrontery almost robbed Liz of words. 'I don't think that's any of your business.' She made to move on, but his hand gripped her arm.

'I might choose to make it my business. Shirley Anne at home, is she?'

'No, she isn't. And if she were . . .'

'Yes? Do go on, Lizzie.'

'Don't call me Lizzie,' she said through shut teeth.

'Very well – *Elizabeth*. You were saying, if she were. . . ?' So polite. So slimy – like a snake.

'If she were,' the words came out more smoothly than she would have believed possible, 'you are the last person on earth she would want to see – ever. Besides, your wife might not be too pleased.'

At that moment Rosie looked up, and pale blue eyes met even paler ones. Alec put a finger under her chin, subjecting her features to a long hard look. 'Camilla has been told she can't have children,' he said. 'She is so heartbroken, we have been considering adoption . . .' He looked again at Rosie. 'A pity she isn't a boy.'

Liz's heart was thudding. More than anything, she wanted to take the pram and run, which would be silly. She made herself meet his eyes.

'I don't agree. Boys grow into men, and men seem to be responsible for so many of the world's evils.' She saw anger leap into his eyes, swiftly veiled. 'I'm sorry for you wife – but doctors can be wrong.' She kept her voice steady. 'As for Rosie, she's a Ryan through and through, and will always remain a Ryan. And now, I really must go. I have an important appointment.'

Alec flushed and, with exaggerated politeness, stepped back and touched his cap. 'Then I mustn't keep you. Perhaps we shall meet again.'

'Oh, I doubt that very much.'

Liz forced herself to walk at a normal pace, straight-backed, in case he was watching. She told herself that his stupid hints were only meant to rattle her – he would never know how nearly they had succeeded. Rosie studied her face intently, then sighed and let out an enormous raspberry. And suddenly the whole absurd incident slid into perspective.

She laughed aloud. 'Oh, Rosie – how wonderfully appropriate! I couldn't have put it better myself.'

Chapter Seventeen

Chris had written to say that he was coming home on leave for ten days, and could he bring someone with him. Her name was Mary, and he wanted them to get to know her.

'Bringing her home for the seal of approval,' Liz said with a chuckle. 'Sounds as if he means business.'

'Oh, really, Liz. What a thing to say! I suppose she can have Shirley Anne's room, but it'll need a good clean out.'

Kathleen was talking to cover her sudden feeling of – of what? Apprehension? No, that was ridiculous. She wanted Chris to be settled, to be happy. At one time she had thought perhaps he and Clare – but that had come to nothing. But he was still young – not quite twenty-three. Plenty of time. She thought back to herself and Michael. He had been twenty-three. Oh, dear Blessed Mother, suppose I don't like her? Still, she has your name – and I only want him to be happy.

'I wonder if your father would have time to give that room a lick of paint?'

'Mam! She's just a girl, Chris's girl. I know that makes a difference, but she's not going to be looking at the paintwork.'

Kathleen needn't have worried. If she had chosen someone for Chris, she couldn't have chosen better. Mary Clancy was dark and rosy-cheeked, slight and trim in her ATS uniform, with an attractive smile and a straightforward manner.

'I hope we haven't put you to any trouble, Mrs Ryan. I told Chris, it's a bit of a liberty, imposing on you for the whole week.'

'Nothing of the kind,' Kathleen protested. 'As long as you don't mind taking us as you find us. There never seems to be enough hours in the day.'

Behind her back, Liz was making furious 'spit and polish' gestures to Chris, who nodded and grinned.

'Well, don't just stand there, Chris. Take Mary's case up to Shirley Anne's room while I put the kettle on. Your Dad'll be back soon.'

Mary soon endeared herself to everyone. She came from Gateshead, and was the eldest girl in a large Catholic family herself, so was used to coping with a certain amount of organized chaos. In no time she had slipped into the way of doing little unobtrusive things to help, and Georgy followed her round, apparently fascinated by her soft sing-song voice and the way she had of calling him 'Pet'.

'You should be out with Chris, enjoying yourselves,' Kathleen protested, when she found Mary one morning dealing with a pile of ironing.

'I am enjoying myself, Mrs Ryan, honest. It's nice to do homely things. Barracks is a bit like school. And I know Chris likes to help his Dad for the same reason.' She folded a sheet with brisk efficiency. 'Anyway, we've been out quite a lot. We've been to Southport to see Aunt Flora – she's nice, isn't she? An' your Liz's taken me round the shops. We're going dancing tonight, and tomorrow, if the weather holds, we're off to New Brighton. That's not bad going, I'd say.'

'Well, as long as you're not bored.' Kathleen hesitated. 'You're very fond of Chris, aren't you?'

Mary's eyes warmed. 'I think he's luvly. P'raps its something to do with being a baker, cos his Dad's luvly, too.'

'And, are you. . . ? No I shouldn't ask.'

'Are we thinkin' of getting married?' Her smile deepened. 'It's what my Mam wanted to know, right off. And the answer's yes. Chris hasn't actually got round to askin' me yet, mind, but he will.'

In the bakehouse, Chris was trying to broach the same subject, and his father, watching him work up to it, thought that army life hadn't changed him in that respect. 'If you mangle that dough much more, son,' he said drily, 'it'll be fit for nothing but the bin.'

'Oh, sorry, Dad.' He hastily handed it up and slid it on to the proving rack.

'It's a bonny lass you have there, Chris,' Michael said, helping him out.

'She's great, isn't she? I'm not usually all that good with girls, but we hit it off right away.' He looked hopefully at Michael. 'D'you think she'd have me – if I were to ask her?'

'Only one way to find out, son. I'd say you were in with a good chance. She puts me in mind of your mother when we first met –

not quite so bonny, maybe' – his voice softened – 'but then, there's no-one comes up to your Mam in my eyes, and isn't that how it should be?'

Chris thought of his Mam, her hair now more grey than black, the little worry lines between her eyes. Had she once been as bonny as Dad remembered? He tried to think back, but it really didn't matter. If he and Mary were half so happy – 'Dad, if she says yes, do you think it'd be fair to rush her? Only, I haven't said anything to Mam, but there's a chance we may get sent overseas before long.'

Oh, my gentle boy, thought Michael. And we'll have to go through the whole thing again. 'Well,' he said aloud. 'If you're both sure, and if your Mary is half the girl I think she is, she'll have her own ideas about that.'

So, with a lot of encouragement on all sides, the question was popped while they were out dancing that night, and a tentative date in July was set.

'But we'll need to ask Mary's parents,' Chris said. 'Would you mind very much, Mam, if we went back a day early, so we could call and see them?'

Kathleen was quiet after they had gone, wondering if it had occurred to anyone that her son's wedding would be in Gateshead – and there was small hope of her being able to get there.

Liz visited Jimmy's parents regularly. She often wondered whether Sunny Marsden's cheerfulness was a defence against his wife's continual gloom, for, like Nora Figg, she was only happy when she had something to complain about. This time it was Jimmy's leave – or lack of it.

'It's not that I begrudge your Mam, having Christopher home for a whole week,' she said, leaning forward to poke the fire, and pulling her cardigan closer about her thin frame, 'but it can't be right when our lad only got a measly three days . . .'

'I've told you, May, they have a system.'

'That's right, Mrs Marsden.' Somehow, Liz could never bring herself to call her mother. 'Jimmy'll get a longer leave soon.'

'Take no notice, chuck,' Sunny said as she left. 'It's just her way. It don't mean nothing.' A beaming smile lit his ruddy features. 'Now, what would yer Mam like fer the weekend? I've a nice shoulder – a drop of mint sauce, and it'd go down a treat.'

'That would be splendid.' Liz watched him crack the knuckle with his small cleaver.

'I'll not trim the fat – I've no doubt you'll find a use for it. Speakin' of which' – although they were alone in the shop, Sunny lowered his voice to a conspiratorial whisper – 'how are you fixed for cooking fat?'

'Well, we manage. Flour's not too much of a problem. Bill Sowerby's been as regular as clockwork up to now, but the fats do fluctuate a bit.'

'So d'you think your Dad might like a couple of gallon tubs of white fat? Good stuff, tell him.' He passed the wrapped meat over the counter. 'I've put a bit of skirt in there, besides – enough for a good nourishing stew, or a meat an' potato pie. What d'you think? Would Michael be interested? Say, a couple of bob a tub.' He winked and tapped the side of his nose. 'It's what you might call surplus to requirements.'

'Take it,' Mam said, when Michael demurred. 'If you don't, someone else will.'

'It's not much different from buying salvaged goods from time to time. And just think of all we could do with it, Dad.'

He looked from one to the other. 'Scheming Jezebels, the pair of you. It's to be hoped Sergeant Mac doesn't get a sniff of it when he drops in for his early morning cuppa.'

'Not him.' Liz grinned. 'Specially if there's a warm cornish pasty to go with his mug of tea.'

'Shameless hussy. You're worse than your mother – corrupting the police.'

'Rubbish,' Kathleen said. 'Sergeant Mac knows when to turn a blind eye.'

Shirley Anne had written with her usual haste, and in great excitement, to say that she was part of a small troupe that would be touring northern factories and army bases, and Liverpool would naturally be one of their venues.

'She doesn't say when, or for how long, or even where she'll be staying – just that she can't wait to see us all.'

'Give Rosie a kiss from me,' Liz read over her shoulder. 'That's Shirley Anne for you. Casual as they come. I expect their accommodation will be arranged.'

'She sounds happy enough, at all events,' Ellen said.

'Yes, she does. And it will be nice to see her.' Kathleen tucked the letter behind the spills jar on the mantelpiece for Michael to read later. 'I'm more concerned about Rita. It's a couple of weeks since she wrote.'

'When's the baby due?'

'Not for another three weeks, but the Ryan women seem to make a habit of springing surprises. I wish she wasn't so far away. I know she's made a lot of friends down there, but it's not the same as having family around.'

The shop bell rang, and Liz stopped what she was doing. 'It's all right. I'll go. You two finish your tea.'

'No signs there, yet, I take it?' Ellen said, low-voiced.

'No. And, God forgive me, but I hope there won't be while this war lasts. That really would be the last straw. Oh, Georgy, love, don't cling to my skirt. And don't whine. You're getting to be a big boy now.'

Ellen looked at Kathleen. She so seldom snapped at Georgy. Even when she was tired she seemed to have endless patience with him. Rosie was much harder work. 'I'm not sure I like the look of the little lad. It's not like him to grizzle, and he's been sniffly all morning, too.' She laid a hand on his forehead. 'I wouldn't be surprised if he was running a temperature.'

'Oh, no!' There was more than a touch of despair in Kathleen's exclamation, as she checked for herself. 'You're right, Ellen. It could just be his usual bronchitis, but if he *is* sickening for something, I hope he doesn't pass it on to Rosie.' She lifted him up. 'Come on, then, my treasure. Mammy'll get you a nice cool drink, and then you can lie down on the sofa while I send for Dr Graham.'

Rosie, hearing the magic word 'drink', set up a clamour of her own. She shook the bars of the playpen, chanting, 'Dink. Wosy, dink,' until Liz, coming back from the shop, told her severely to be quiet.

It was almost tea-time before Dr Graham arrived. Ellen had gone home, and Liz had taken Rosie to the bathroom to get her ready for bed. By now, Kathleen didn't need telling what was wrong. The fast-spreading rash on Georgy's chest was plain to see.

'Poor little chap. Not too comfortable, eh?' The doctor stood up after his examination. 'It's measles, right enough. I don't really need to tell you what to do, Kathleen. You've been through it all enough times, though Georgy's bronchial weakness may call for a little extra vigilance. Plenty of fluids, and bathe him down with a lukewarm solution of bicarb if he gets too uncomfortable. And keep him out of any strong light. We'll need to keep young madam under observation, too, in case she takes it.'

Kathleen's lack-lustre response made him look at her more closely. It was a while since he had visited her, but now he noticed that the fine-drawn look was back, as were the black circles under her eyes. 'And what of yourself? Doing too much, by the look of you.'

'Oh, I'm all right,' she said, but too quickly, and realizing it, attempted a smile. 'As all right as any of us can expect to be at present.'

'Hm.' He gently rolled down her lower eyelid, felt her pulse. 'How long is it since you stopped taking the iron tablets?'

'Ages. Well over a year.'

'Then I'd say another course wouldn't come amiss. Periods all right?'

'Reasonable.' She met his eyes – those all-seeing eyes – and looked away towards the bathroom, where she could hear Liz making fun of washtime. Finally, she lifted her shoulders in resignation. 'Well, a bit on the heavy side.'

'Which doesn't surprise me at all. You don't need me to tell you you're doing too much, taking on Shirley Anne's child as well as this young fellow.' The roughness of his words belied the gentleness in his eyes. 'The tablets should help, but if things don't improve, I'd like you to have a blood test – maybe even see Latimer.' He saw apprehension flicker in her eyes. 'Now, don't go leaping to conclusions, lass. Heavy mentrual bleeding can have any number of causes, especially in someone with your medical history. Latimer might be better able to help you.'

'I'll be fine with the iron,' she said stubbornly. 'And I don't want you saying anything to Michael. He's enough on his plate at present.'

Dr Graham was gruff. 'And you haven't, I suppose? Ah, Kathleen, what'll we do with you?' His bushy eyebrows came fiercely together. 'I suppose I'll be wasting my breath, telling you to rest more, but I'm telling you, just the same.'

As he spoke, Liz came out of the bathroom, carrying Rosie wrapped in nightgown and shawl, and looking as youthful and glowing as the child in her arms.

'That's right, Doctor, you read her the riot act. She won't listen to us.'

A bonny lass, Graham thought. As well that Kathleen had such a capable daughter to lean on.

Rita's son was born almost a week early, a healthy seven-and-a-half pounds. A friend rang the shop immediately to let them know, and Rita wrote the following day to tell her mother the things that all mothers want to know, and to tell Dad that she was calling her son Michael Francis. 'I don't know where Frank is right now, but I hope and pray he'll be back soon to see his son. Everyone's been great, but, oh, I wish you were here, Mam.'

It was so rare for practical, self-sufficient Rita to show any sign of homesickness that this lapse really upset Kathleen. She brooded on it for the rest of the day.

'Listen, our Kathy,' Flora said, on hearing the good news. 'If you're that bothered, why don't you go down there, just for a couple of days? Apart from anything else, the break would probably do you almost as much good as her. If you like, I'll come with you.'

'Yes, do go, Mam,' Liz urged. 'Georgy's over the worst now, and if Rosie had been going to take it she would have done so by now. We can manage, and it'd be such a lovely surprise for our Rita.'

It was the thought of the journey, as much as anything else, that made her hesitate. It was such a long way. But perhaps it wouldn't be so bad now she was back on the iron tablets.

'Listen,' Flora said. 'There's sure to be a nice little hotel somewhere not too far from Rita. Just think of it – being waited on, hand and foot.'

Kathleen could scarcely remember when she had had more than a day out with the children, let alone been waited on. It sounded awfully tempting, and in her heart she knew that Liz was quite capable of managing without her.

'All right,' she said. 'I'll go.'

Three days later she and Flora were on the train, bound for Shropshire, with a case full of baby clothes, Kathleen wearing a new navy costume and navy and white hat that Flora had talked her into buying. 'You want your grandson to see you looking smart, don't you?'

'Mam! Oh, Mam!' Rita cried, and promptly burst into tears, when she saw the small neat woman walk purposefully into the small ward of the Myndhurst Cottage Hospital. Kathleen gathered her into her arms and knew that she had been right to come.

'Oh, this is very silly – why am I crying when it's so lovely to see you? Except, I did so want you here, without ever dreaming . . .'

'It was your Aunt Flora's idea. She'll be in to see you later. We've found a grand little hotel near the river, and she's busy unpacking and generally making herself at home.' Kathleen sat back and smiled. 'Now, when am I going to see this fine son you've produced?'

It was an idyllic two days. The sun shone, and between visits to Rita, they took a bus trip round the beautiful outlying countryside. Kathleen could see why Rita and Frank wanted to settle in Myndd Howe. It was a small country town, almost village-like in its atmosphere. She liked Rita's friends, too, and when the time came to leave, she knew her daughter and grandson would be well looked after, though Rita was adamant that as soon as she felt strong enough, she wanted to bring Michael Francis to Liverpool to have him christened.

'It's a pity you couldn't have stayed longer,' Flora said, eyeing her sister keenly when they were back on the train. 'You look heaps better, after just two days.'

'I feel better.'

'I was beginning to get quite worried about you, taking on Rosie and all.'

'It wasn't just that.' Kathleen was evasive. 'It's been a trying time generally. Dr Graham thought I was getting a bit anaemic again, so he's put me back on iron tablets.'

'Good for him. There's not much gets past Graham.'

'No,' Kathleen said.

The resilience of ordinary people continued to surprise Liz. True, the raids had become spasmodic, but the threat was still very much there. Yet as customers waited to be served they would cheerfully air various theories about German strategy as though they were talking about a football match.

'They're only comin' now in dribs an' drabs. If you ask me, Adolf's shot 'is bolt.'

'Well, 'e's only a jumped up little decorator called Schicklgruber, when all's said an' done. Herr Hitler, indeed!'

'Stands to reason, 'e couldn't keep sendin' all them planes over – I mean, it's not just here. There's London 'an Birmingham an' Southampton, not ter mention poor old Coventry – must 'ave cost 'im a bleedin' fortune already.'

'Specially now our planes are bombin' his factories. Does me a power of good, knowin' they're gettin' a taste of what it's like.'

Liz couldn't share this sentiment, or their optimism. It was a bit like shouting into the wind, for terrible things were still happening. Only two nights ago, a stray raider had bombed the Sunshine Home for Blind Babies in Birkdale. Aunt Flora, with other local people, had been among the first on the scene, and the experience had affected her aunt deeply.

'It was quite dreadful,' she'd told them, her voice still shaking with anger and outrage. 'Three young nurses dead, and a miracle that none of the children were killed. Those of us who had cars wrapped them in blankets and took them to the cellars of the Palace Hotel, until provision could be made. I tell you, if I could have got hold of the man who dropped those bombs, I'd have killed him with my bare hands!'

Liz knew the feeling well. But it didn't do to dwell on such things. Good things were happening, too. Shirley Anne was at last coming to Liverpool, arriving in about ten days' time with four other ENSA members, to give concerts in a couple of factories and at one of the docks.

'D'you hear that, Rosie Posie? Your Mammy's coming home soon – well, not home exactly, but she'll be coming to see you.'

Rosie lifted a beaming, grubby face and reached with well-sucked fingers to smear Liz's cheek. 'Mammy.'

'No, not me, you little horror. I'm not your mother, thank goodness, though there are times when it seems like it.'

She made some salmon and shrimp paste sandwiches and lifted

Rosie into her high chair. Georgy now had an ordinary chair with a tray fixed across the front, and set well away from Rosie's disruptive influence.

It would soon be Georgy's birthday. Liz could hardly believe he'd be four. Rosie was catching him up so fast. She chattered away to him in a language that was for the most part incomprehensible to anyone else, and they were never sure how much Georgy actually understood, though he seemed happy enough to follow wherever she might lead, which was usually into trouble. Like last Sunday morning, when they'd let the hens out, and it had taken the combined efforts of the whole family over an hour to get them all back.

Ellen's eldest daughter, Dot, was minding the shop. She now came each afternoon after school, a wiry thin-featured child with straight mousy-fair hair. Dot was not yet fourteen, but she was quick and bright, and not afraid of work.

'She'll be leaving school this term, and it would be good experience for her,' Ellen had said diffidently when she had first suggested the idea to Kathleen. 'You wouldn't need to pay her much.'

'Don't be silly,' Kathleen said. 'Your Dot would be a godsend. In fact, if she likes the work I'd be happy to keep her on when she leaves school. Joey's hopeless behind the counter.'

'That would be great. In the meantime, I'd like to get her out of the house a bit more. Arnie's still terribly touchy.'

Liz knew this was an understatement. He had been brooding since his best friend had been killed in one of the pre-Christmas raids. She had been on the receiving end of one of his outbursts.

'If a bomb dropped on this house termorrer, I'd lay odds everyone'd be killed except me!'

'Mr Cassidy, you mustn't even think such things!' she had cried, shaken by his bitterness. 'It's like mocking God.'

'God? Don' ask me ter believe in a God as'd take a good man like Jack, an' leave me here ter rot!'

It was hard to refute such reasoning, and she hadn't tried. But it wasn't the best atmosphere for any of the children. Liz often wondered how Ellen managed to remain sane, let alone cheerful.

Chapter Eighteen

Leigh settled back in the sagging chair and stifled a yawn. It was almost like a second home, this shabby but comfortable rooming house presided over by a grizzled, long-jawed landlord, where he and his team of volunteers – barnstormers, sky-writers, civil engineers – whiled away the hours, sometimes days, between bringing the planes in and waiting for the big ugly brute of a Liberator that would take them back to Gander for the next run.

This had been a rough trip, unexpectedly so for the time of year. A freak storm halfway across had played havoc with the electrics, and two planes had gone down. Four good men lost – poor bastards. How eagerly they had sought this latest slice of adventure. Somewhere in the distance, an erratic series of explosions rent the night.

'Y're by yersel', then, laddie?'

The landlord's voice penetrated his thoughts. 'Yeh. I'm whacked. The others have braved the sirens and blackout, and gone looking for a bit of night life to round off that superb rabbit stew.'

Dougie Logan chuckled. 'On a Sunday night in Prestwick? Well, guid luck to them. There's little moves here after dark, as you well know. You'd maybe care for a wee dram?' He produced a bottle and a squat tumbler. 'Not a word to the others, mind. A malt sich as this would be wasted on the undiscriminating palate.'

Liquid gold glugged into the glass. As Leigh sighed with pleasurable anticipation, another crump of bombs came from the distance. 'Someone's getting it tonight.'

'Aye, poor devils. We're no too bothered here, most nights – an area of comparative calm, ye might say, between the devil and the deep, what with the Clyde the one side of us and Barrow, the other. Seems Gerry's going all out for the docks. There's a north west port taking a battering jist now. That'll be Liverpool, for my money.' The landlord turned towards the door. 'There'll be a news bulletin in five minutes, if you're interested, though they're no that forthcoming.'

Leigh's chest felt tight. He gulped the whisky in a way calculated to outrage Dougie Logan's sensibilities. It seared his throat, making him cough, but its spreading warmth had a salutary effect. When it caught the light, the amber liquid was the colour of Elizabeth's eyes. He sat forward convulsively and turned on the wireless. Music spilled into the room, and impatiently he fiddled with the knob, staying it as the dry, affected voice of Lord Haw-Haw came clearly into the room – 'There are riots on the streets of Liverpool. People are waving white flags, and troops have been brought in . . .'

He cut the voice off in mid-sentence, and was out of his chair, and into the darkened hallway. Not for one moment did he believe the slander, but nor could he contemplate flying back to Canada without knowing if Elizabeth was safe.

'Dougie? Can I use your telephone?'

But the operator told him there were no calls in or out of Liverpool. That did it. If the pick-up was early, they would have to manage without him for the next trip. He wrote a brief report, gave it to Logan with an explanatory letter to hand on to Sam Harding, his navigator, when he got back. Then he headed for the main road where the landlord, who clearly thought he'd taken leave of his senses, reckoned he might get a lift from a truck going south.

It was a Sunday morning like no other. The Ryan family dragged themselves to church red-eyed and silent, incapable of coherent thought or prayer, allowing the comforting familiarity of the Mass to enfold them. Even Rosie didn't wriggle, for once, but sat quiet and unmoving against Kathleen's breast, thumb in mouth, her eyes lacklustre.

At least they still *had* a church: many a weary worshipper, stumbling through the unfamiliar landscape choking on the acrid air, found only a smoking heap of rubble, or at best a roofless shell with gaping holes where stained glass windows had once cast their soft light.

After three nights of fire and mind-shattering noise, Liz found it hard to believe that so many buildings were still standing. Last night had been the worst by far. She tried to pray for the people she'd helped to dig out of the crumbling ruins of what had once been their homes, but her tired mind refused to focus.

The night had ended with a horrendous explosion that blasted Huskisson Dock to pieces. A damaged barrage balloon had fallen on the deck of the SS *Malakand*, laden with bombs and shells bound for the Middle East, setting it alight. Despite the fire-fighters' frantic and quite heroic efforts to prevent the fire spreading below, she had finally gone up after the 'all clear', with a series of terrifying reports that had scattered huge steel plates like confetti, for miles.

The cargo was still firing off as Liz set about preparing breakfast for the family – a thankless task, for no-one except Joey was hungry. Was it only three days since she had talked about celebrating the first of May?

'Oh, come on,' she said, her voice trembling with a mixture of anger and exhaustion. 'Mam – Dad – I've done boiled eggs for all of us. We need to keep our strength up, and we won't if we don't eat properly.'

'I'll have another one if they're going begging, Sis.' Joey looked up from dunking his bread soldiers, and stretched out a hand. Liz slapped it down.

'Don't be a greedy pig.' She carefully spooned egg into Rosie's mouth. 'You can have what's left of this in a minute. Rosie only eats the yolk. And there's plenty of bread while you're waiting.'

'Joey can have my egg,' Kathleen said as she helped Georgy.

'No, he can't.' Michael was firm. 'Liz is right. I'll not have you skimping on your food, Kathleen. It's little enough care you take of yourself, and there's plenty for all.'

She glanced across at him, half annoyed, but the look in his eyes silenced what she had been about to say.

'Can I go now?' Joey, already in his scout uniform, slid his chair back, helping himself to a last piece of bread. 'I'm sure to be needed after last night.'

'Grace, Joey,' Kathleen said without looking up. 'And look after yourself. Don't be taking any risks.'

Joey sketched a final sign of the cross, and grinned. 'I won't.'

'Boys,' sighed Kathleen, as the door banged behind him.

'I'll need to be away myself any minute.' Michael said, heaving himself out of the chair. 'To see if our shops have escaped damage.'

'As long as that's all you do. And you needn't look at me like that; I know you, Michael Ryan. Given half a chance, you'll be in the thick of it, digging away with the rest of them. You're not superhuman, for all that you might think it, and this is the only day you can snatch a bit of rest.'

Michael, hearing the sharpness of worry, came to stand behind her chair, his gentle hands kneading the tension in her shoulders. 'Listen who's talking – giving folk shelter, feeding them, keeping them cheerful.'

'That's different.'

He stooped to kiss the top of her head. 'Not really. We must all do the thing we do best. I can't stand aside, *acushla*, none of us can. Even your Flora's working all the hours there are, finding accommodation for the homeless. There'll be no rest for any of us until this lot's over.'

He was right, and she knew it. In a curious way, this terrible test of courage had brought everyone closer together. And throughout it all her faith had never faltered; she still insisted that they say the rosary each evening, her belief in Our Lady's power to intercede undiminished. Though after last night, she was finding it increasingly difficult to understand how God could allow so much suffering to continue, so much wickedness go unpunished.

As Michael prepared to go out, Dandy came in. His face was grey, matching his clothes, which were covered in a thick layer of dust, and for once all the bounce seemed to have gone out of him. Kathleen took one look at him and told Michael to help him out of his helmet and coat and sit him down, while she made a fresh pot of tea. She added a generous measure of whisky to his cup and put it in his hands.

'Drink,' she said, and didn't take her eyes off him for a second until he'd finished every last drop.

'Dan'y.' Georgy stretched out a hand.

'Not just now, pet.' Liz hushed him. 'Dandy's tired.'

The tea brought a little colour back to his face, but he still seemed too exhausted to talk. Sick with worry, Kathleen took him by the arm. 'Over to that couch, and I don't want any arguments.'

Before she had finished covering him with a blanket, he was asleep, and all the fury and frustration that was inside her finally boiled over. 'Honestly, Michael, wouldn't you think he'd have more sense at his age? He's not supposed to be on duty after midnight. If he carries on this road, it won't be a Gerry bomb that'll kill him – it'll be his own stubbornness.'

'Hush now, Kathleen – '

'I won't hush. You're all the same, you and Liz, even our Joey – trying your best to get yourselves killed. I think the whole world's gone mad!' She pushed past Michael into the scullery, where she began clattering dishes into the sink.

Liz stared after her, distressed by this outburst from Mam, who was the strong one. She would have followed her, but Michael laid a hand on her arm.

'Leave her, Lizzie, my love,' he said quietly. 'She needs to get it all out of her system. In a way, it's harder for her than any of us – waiting, worrying.'

Joey went first to the Fortune Street section post, passing Dandy on the way; he called to him, but for once his Grandad didn't seem to hear. The warden on duty said he'd nothing for him to do, so Joey decided to make himself useful elsewhere.

Cycling into town wasn't easy as so many roads were blocked by rubble, or closed by the police. His bicycle wobbled in and out of the debris, bumping over the dribbling hoses that snaked everywhere, and every few yards he stopped, awed by the destruction. Lewis's had gone, and Blacklers, and he had to mind his tyres as the roads were strewn with shards of broken glass shimmering like diamonds through the choking smoke, as firemen, black-faced and weary, still toiled to put out fires. If he hadn't been in his scout uniform, he'd probably have been stopped, but as it was he eventually got through to the divisional section where there was an air of tension. The telephones weren't working, all their messengers were out, and more water supplies were urgently needed.

'I can take a message.'

The policeman in charge looked at Joey and his bicycle. 'I've been trying to locate a motorcyclist. The lad who rode that' – he nodded towards the 250cc BSA leaning against the wall – 'fell off and cut his leg badly in the early hours, and was carted off to hospital.'

Joey's heart leapt. 'I could ride it.'

'You sure?' There was suspicion in the man's voice. 'We can't afford any cock-ups. How old are you?'

'Sixteen.' Well, almost, Joey added silently, fingers crossed, knowing that he looked it. 'I'm very good with machines.'

'Lerr'im go, Fred,' someone shouted. 'We've no time ter mess about.'

Minutes later, Joey was roaring off, weaving his way between obstructions, his spirits high in spite of the devastation all around him. A little beauty, the bike was. He'd ridden one before, of course, but only in the course of repairing or tuning them. The policeman called Fred had made a note of his troop, and he'd had to give his name, but they'd probably be much too busy to check him out.

'Great, Joey,' said Fred when he returned. 'We've more messages you can do, if no-one else is needing you just now.'

Joey finally cycled home in a state of weary elation, past the crowds who had congregated to watch a digger clearing rubble, ignoring constant appeals to them to leave. He'd been scared half to death more than once, and the motor bike had been harder on his muscles than he cared to admit, but it had been worth every fright, every ache and pain. Still, it might be wiser not to tell Mam.

It was around nine in the morning when Leigh reached Fortune Street. He would have been earlier, but the last of several drivers, who had picked him up in Preston, had stopped at his regular roadside eating house for breakfast, and it would have been churlish not to share his meal, although tension, combined with the long, bone-shaking journey, had left him with little appetite.

He had seen evidence enough of bombing on the way down, but it was nothing compared with the scenes of destruction they found on the outskirts of Liverpool. Again and again they were diverted, and finally the driver pulled up.

'I'd better drop you here, mate. I'll have to make me way to the docks best road I can – if they haven't all been blitzed to pieces. With luck, you might pick up a bus or a tram bound for Scotland Road.'

Many of the tramlines had become piles of twisted metal, or were overlaid with water hoses, but Leigh did manage to find a bus going in the right direction, past whole streets roped off and reduced to piles of spewed out masonry. The conductor clipped his ticket with a cheery, 'Yer in luck this mornin', Yank. We're takin' the scenic route. Hang on ter that ticket, cos there's a special prize fer guessing how many buildin's copped it last night. An' if yer go up top, you'll gerra better view.'

'It looks pretty bad, even from down here.'

'What d'yer expect? The number of flares Gerry's sent down, they know their way round better'n we do!'

His defiantly cheerful attitude was echoed by the passengers. Listening to the conversations around him, Leigh was astonished to learn that many were bound for work as usual, though they weren't even sure they still had a job to go to.

His relief at seeing Ryan's Bakery still in one piece was nothing to the joy his first sight of Elizabeth brought him. The shop was busy, but he was content now to wait, hands in pockets, his back against the wall, listening to the gossiping women. And again, marvelling at their spirit; weary and dishevelled they might be, but defeated they certainly weren't. More than once he heard a spontaneous burst of laughter.

But his eyes were all for Elizabeth. She was serving, with the help of an older woman, and hadn't yet seen him, so he was able to drink in the sight of her like a man slaking his thirst. Her hair was drawn back, rolled up in a kind of net, which made her seem paler, thinner, the planes of her face pared down to its fine bones. And then she smiled at some remark, and he thought she had never looked lovelier.

'I still wish you'd go to a shelter, Mrs Figg. One of the big ones, if you don't want to come here.'

'An' leave the likes of young Eddie free ter gerrin' an rob me of me bits and empty me meter? Norr'on your life!'

'That's slander, tharris. Anyhow, he'd be a long time gerrin' rich, robbin' the likes of you!'

Nora ignored the insult. 'I'm not shiftin', an' that's that. I've 'ad me incendry, an' it's a fact that lightnin' never strikes in the same place twice.'

'More like the devil lookin' after 'is own,' muttered the woman nearby, and again there was laughter.

'Well it teks one ter know one,' came the tart reply. 'Yer can give us a tin of conny, an' that's me lot. An' I'll thank you fer me tuppence change, Lizzie Ryan, or whatever yer callin' yerself these days.'

As the weird shawl-wrapped figure pushed past Leigh,

Elizabeth looked up and saw him. She couldn't have gone much paler, but she stood blank-faced, motionless, her eyes wide, her hands gripping the edge of the counter.

'You all right, Liz, love?' Ellen whispered.

'Yes, I'm – Yes, of course,' she said, joy flooding through her, galvanizing her into action. Her fingers flew, until all the customers had been served except one. He stepped forward.

'Hello,' she said inadequately, aware of Ellen's curiosity.

'Hi. I was – in the area and thought, why not call? See how you're all coping.' It was patently an untruth, but it would serve.

'Well, you'd better come through.' She lifted the counter flap and led the way into the living room, her voice falsely bright. 'Mam, you'll never believe who's here!'

Kathleen looked up from preparing the children's breakfast. She recognized him at once, the hair red as fire, the smile that must have charmed many a girl's heart – and one of them not more than a few feet away. Her daughter's casual manner might fool most people, but not her mother. Her anger against this man for coming back into Liz's life made her greeting sharp. His eyes told her that he understood.

'Have you had breakfast, Mr Farrell? We don't have anything very exciting to offer, I'm afraid . . .'

'No, really.' He put up a hand. 'I couldn't eat a thing. I can't stay more than a few minutes, but I heard things were pretty tough here, and decided to see for myself.' His glance moved to Georgy, and he went to crouch beside him. 'Hi, fella. My, how you've grown.'

Georgy considered him gravely. 'Hi,' he repeated.

'Me, me!' Rosie clamoured to be noticed.

Leigh looked up enquiringly.

'Rosie is Shirley Anne's child,' Kathleen said, without expression.

'Of course. I should have seen the likeness.' Leigh grinned. 'Hi, Rosie.' He stood up. 'I'll be off, then. I can see that I've chosen a bad moment . . .'

'There aren't many good moments just now. Two of our shops were hit last night. A real mess, Michael said, though no-one was killed, thank God. And we've just heard that my brother, Nick, is in hospital with concussion after a big explosion at the docks.

'I'm sorry.'

'Are you staying with Aunt Flora?' The words slipped out, and Liz was aware of her mother giving her a sharp look.

But Leigh answered easily. 'Lord, no. I guess she's got her hands pretty full right now, like the rest of you. This is just a spur of the moment visit. I'll book into a hotel overnight, then it's back to Canada by way of Scotland.'

'You're still flying planes over, then?'

'That's right.'

'Liz's *husband* is stationed in Scotland.' Kathleen, disturbed that Liz knew so much about his movements, deliberately emphasized 'husband'. 'And Chris.'

His slow quirky smile acknowledged her implied reprimand. 'I'd better go. I'm sorry you're having such a rough time, but from what I've seen and heard today, Hitler surely has to learn pretty soon that he's never going to win here.'

'I'll let you out the back,' Liz said, moving towards the scullery. 'You don't want to be going through the shop.'

Outside, Leigh said, 'Can I see you tonight? Just to talk.'

'I can't. I'm on duty every night at present – we all are.'

'Then let me come with you. In fact, that would suit me just fine. I want to – no, I *have* to – know and share what you're going through, if only for a short time.'

'Oh, Leigh! This is senseless.'

'No, it isn't, honey. Listen, I won't even touch you if you don't want me to, or get in the way of what you're doing. I might even be of some use.' He was very persuasive. 'And if anyone notices an extra body – what is it they say? In the dark, all cats are grey.'

The opportunity to be with him, no matter what the circumstances, for just a little time, was irresistible. After all, it wasn't as if she would be hurting or betraying Jimmy.

At midnight, Leigh was still sitting in his hotel room, wondering if there was going to be a raid that night. He surely couldn't wish one on these stoical people, even if it did cost him a few precious hours with Elizabeth.

An hour later, he was in the thick of it. He had seen newsreels, of course, but black-and-white film could never prepare one for the reality – the choking smoke and other indescribable smells, the eerie light of hundreds of fires, the whine and shuddering impact of high explosive that made the earth seem constantly to be moving beneath his feet.

'The blackest of smoke sometimes comes from "Mr Mitchell",' Liz said as he began to cough.

'Who in heck is he?'

'He's an *it* – a machine that belches black smoke, ten times worse than the smoke from fires. They trundle it through the streets on bright nights, or when the planes have dropped a lot of flares.'

She had borrowed a tin hat and a spare gas mask for him from her sector post – Alf Killigan, who was warden that night, was out on call, which spared her a lot of explanations. She took Leigh round on her nightly check of the street shelters, and his easy manner and willingness to join in the community singing brought a ready response.

'Want ter see me shrapnel, mister?' offered one young rip. And Leigh duly admired the jagged pieces of dull metal carefully stored in a tin.

He became an expert at dousing incendiaries, and helping to dig people out of their wrecked houses, and at the end of two hours, exhausted, he peered into Elizabeth's dirt-streaked face. His ears reverberated with the noise and over towards the town centre, the sky was blood red. It was like looking into the mouth of hell.

'How do you stand this, night after night?'

She shrugged. 'We just do. In an odd kind of way, you even get used to it. Some of the noise comes from the ack ack battery.'

'I'd never get used to it.'

'Liz!' Someone was calling her name. 'Liz, there's a couple of houses gone up in your street.'

'Oh, dear God, no! Come on!' She grabbed Leigh's arm and ran.

He had said houses, not the shop, but even so, Liz felt dizzy with relief to find it intact. Then she saw figures moving further down on the other side. *Not the Cassidys'. Oh, please, not the Cassidys'.*

But it was several doors on. Number nineteen had been reduced to smoking rubble, and taken half of Nora's house with it, slicing it through so that her bedroom hung pathetically exposed over the still settling masonry.

'It's a bad business, Liz,' said Hester Whelan who, with Ellen, had come to see if there was anything she could do. 'But at least the Parsons at number nineteen had gone to the shelter.'

'And Mrs Figg?'

'You know Nora,' said Alf Killigan. 'Stubborn old besom had no truck with shelters. Said under the stairs was good enough for her – guardin' that bloody meter.' He glanced curiously at her companion, and shifted uneasily. 'Listen, love, yer Dad's gone in with one of the firemen.'

'Oh, no!'

'He was in the bakehouse, see, when it happened, and came ter help. He and one of the firemen reckoned there wus just a chance of gettin' Nora out before the rest come down.'

'Dad wouldn't take risks – he's got too much sense . . .' But she knew he would. As she ran forward, Leigh caught her arm.

'Don't. There's nothing you can do.' He went over to the small group peering into the wreckage. 'Anything happening?'

A fireman shook his head and pointed. 'That's where they went in – see? Where that beam's holding up what's left of the staircase. They could just make it . . .'

Except that the space was limited, and Dad was a big man, Liz thought wretchedly, wondering how she was going to tell Mam, if . . .

'Hey, was that a light?' Leigh peered into the thick dust. 'There it is again – see?'

They all saw the faint flicker of a torch. 'Michael – that you?'

'No,' came the faintest of whispers. 'He's back there with the old girl. She's in a pretty bad way.'

'Can you get 'er out?'

'I think so, now. It's Mr Ryan – 'e managed to free 'er, an' ended up gerrin' 'is own arm trapped. Says he's O.K., burr' I'll swear I 'eard the bone crack. I'm gonna bring the old girl out now, if someone can lend us a bit of a hand. Then I'll go back to see what I can do.'

'I'm coming in,' Leigh said, not waiting for an answer.

'Leigh, no! Not you, too!'

'Now, hold on, Yank. This needs a bit of experience . . .'

Leigh's voice, like a sigh, floated back. 'I've been in tighter corners.'

Liz tried to pray, but no coherent words would come. Moments later – though it seemed like hours – a dust-caked figure emerged, half carrying, half dragging Nora's inert body. It wasn't Leigh.

'That Yank's crazy.' The young fireman fought for breath. 'He wriggled past me before I could stop him.'

Liz watched Ellen bend over Mrs Figg, and made herself walk across. A space on the flags had been cleared of glass, and a blanket laid down to receive her. The dim torch made her pinched face look like a *papier mâché* mask beneath its coating of dust, bits of mortar clinging like crumbs to the wispy beard. Just a wizened old rag doll, limp and lolling, her shabby shawl shredded, her skirt torn and bundled up round her chest, exposing voluminous black bloomers and torn stockings, all overlaid with the same grey dust. Ellen felt for a pulse, and shook her head.

This wasn't how death ought to be, Liz raged inwardly – without dignity or privacy. She tugged the skirt down as far as it would go, and out of instinct whispered, 'Eternal rest grant unto her, Oh, Lord . . .' while a baser part of her mind screamed, 'You stupid old woman . . . putting other people in danger! Selfish to the end! And if Dad and Leigh are killed, it will all have been for nothing.'

'There's an ambulance on the way, gairl,' the fireman said, misreading her concern. Inside the ruin, several loose bricks rattled down, and once again her prayers and her attention became entirely centred upon the two men she loved best in the world.

Then Alf Killigan said, 'I think there's somethin' movin'. God bless 'is socks, the Yank's done it!'

A moment later, Leigh was inching his way out, Michael's good arm firmly round his shoulder – and, as if it had been waiting for that precise moment, the holding beam shuddered and slowly crashed down behind them in a small avalanche of bricks and dust.

'It's a ruddy miracle, that's warrit is!' an awed bystander proclaimed.

The ambulance had arrived, and Nora Figg was being lifted on to a stretcher, while Michael, gingerly supporting his injured limb, protested with some vehemence that he wasn't going to hospital.

'Dad, you must. Even I can see your arm's broken.'

'She's right. It'll have to be set. But if it's a simple break, you'll be 'ome again in a few hours.'

'I must get back to Kathleen. And there's the bread . . . the dough'll need knocking back . . .'

'You can't make bread with a broken arm.' Liz was trying hard to keep calm. 'Oh, Dad, this isn't like you! Just go. I'll explain to Mam, and sort the bread out. Joey can go for Albert.'

'Look, I can't 'ang around argifying,' said the driver.

Leigh felt it was time to intervene. 'If this gentleman will just tell me where he's taking you, sir, I'll get myself some transport and bring you home.'

So at last Michael went, and so did the firemen, and as if putting period to the night's drama, the all clear sounded.

'Well, that's it fer another night,' Alf said, shining his torch down on his watch. 'Jus' gone four. You gerrof 'ome, Liz. I'll wait fer the Parsons, an' rope this lot off till the demolition lot get 'ere.'

Hester and Ellen lingered. 'Would you like one of us to come with you, Liz?' Ellen said. 'It's bound to be a bit of a shock for Kathleen.'

'Thanks, but you know Mam – as long as I convince her Dad's all right but for his arm, she'll be ready to give him the edge of her tongue when he gets home. You go back and try to get some sleep. I hope all this hasn't upset Arnie too much?'

'Well, you know how he is, times like this.' Ellen sighed. 'If you're sure, I'll go and get him a hot drink, but I'll be in extra early.'

'Her husband's paralysed,' Liz explained to Leigh, needing to say something as everyone melted away. 'He recently lost a friend, a docker, in the bombing.'

'That's tough.'

'Yes.' Abruptly, she turned for home, Leigh walking beside her in silence. Her emotions were in turmoil – anger, relief and a lingering terror all fighting for supremacy. She stumbled over a fallen slate, but when Leigh put a steadying arm around her shoulders, she tensed and tried to shrug it away.

'Don't. I can manage.'

'Of course you can. I think you're terrific.'

She shrugged him away. 'No, I'm not. Don't patronize me!'

Leigh stopped, pushed her back against a house wall, not roughly, but holding her firmly, her body rigid beneath his hands.

'Your father's going to be all right.'

'I know that.' Her voice was thick. 'But if you hadn't . . . Do you have any idea. . . ?' She beat at his chest with a clenched fist. 'Don't you *ever* do a crazy thing like that again!'

'Hush.' Leigh gathered her close, felt her trembling.

Liz fought against his hold. 'Oh, please, let me go. Don't make me cry. If I do, I may never stop!' But the tears were already slipping down her cheeks, choking her. 'You know the worst thing of all?' she gulped, her voice rising to an unsteady wail. 'Nobody even *liked* Nora Figg. There won't be a single person to m-mourn her p- passing!'

'Oh, my poor darling!'

'You mustn't call me that. I'm not . . . I never can be . . .'

His mouth came down on hers, silencing all her objections, and after a brief struggle she was kissing him back, straining urgently towards him as though she could never get close enough. It was Leigh who finally drew back.

Liz shuddered and laid her head against his chest. Her mouth felt bruised, her senses were on fire, and yet in a curious way, as she drew a long shuddering breath, she felt healed.

'Oh, Leigh, what are we going to do?'

They both knew what she meant, just as they both knew the answer.

He said softly, 'Right now, there isn't much we can do, honey sweet.'

'No.' Liz straightened up. 'Except carry on, and try to stay out of one another's lives. I must go and tell Mam what's happened.'

'I'll come with you. I know – ' He held up a hand. 'But I don't care to leave unfinished business – and anyway, after this, she's bound to get to know I was with you.'

As they walked back up Fortune Street towards the shop, they saw tired mothers straggling out through the back gate with their sleeping children, in the hope of being able to snatch two or three hours in their own beds before another day began.

Kathleen, standing at the gate, watched her daughter and the man who walked beside her. They weren't touching one another, weren't even close, yet she knew – perhaps because of the special love that existed between Michael and herself – that in every sense that mattered, these two were as one. Except that theirs was an impossible love.

'Let's go inside, Mam,' Liz said quietly.

Chapter Nineteen

Leigh took the family van and, having been re-routed numerous times on the way to the Royal Infirmary, finally arrived to find a state of chaos in the casualty department. The hospital had itself been damaged that night, but the staff were coping with admirable calm.

There was no sign of Michael Ryan, and the first two nurses he stopped, though promising to do all they could, were clearly run off their feet.

'Leigh? Is it really you?'

He turned to see Clare Whitney at his side, little changed from when he had last seen her. Only a new air of responsibility marked out the young woman from the child.

'Well, thank heaven for a friendly face! You don't happen to work here, do you?' She was wearing some kind of uniform, though not, he thought, that of a nurse.

She shook her head, and the curtain of short fair hair swayed and settled. 'Not really. I'm at Medical School, and drive an ambulance in my spare time. Listen, I'd love to talk, but I don't have a minute right now, so if you'd tell me how I can help – you aren't hurt or anything?'

'Not me. It's Elizabeth's father. I seem to have lost him.'

Leigh explained what had happened. Clare longed to ask what had brought him to Liverpool in the first place, but instead she went in search of Liz's father, and was back very quickly.

'I have to go, I'm needed. But I've found Mr Ryan. They're putting his arm in plaster right now, so he should be ready soon. I've told him you're here, waiting. Poor Mr Ryan. He won't be making bread for a while. I suppose that'll mean even more work for Liz. Give her my love. I haven't seen her for a week or two.' A wry smile lit Clare's eyes. 'We've all been a bit preoccupied lately.'

Michael eventually appeared, his forearm in plaster and supported by a sling. 'This is very kind of you, Mr Farrell,' he said. 'I seem to be doubly in your debt.'

Leigh stoutly refuted this. 'I'm glad I was in the right place at the right time, but others would have done the same.'

He half expected some kind of inquisition as to how he had come to be there in the first place, but Elizabeth's father seemed disinclined to talk on the way home, apart from giving directions when they were re-routed.

Kathleen stared at her husband's drawn face, and then at the plaster. 'Oh, Michael!' She moved to put her arms round him, her face half hidden against his chest while his good arm held her close, and he murmured: 'There, now, *acushla*. It's not half so bad as it might have been. And we've Mr Farrell to thank for that.'

She turned then, still in the circle of his arm, to find that Leigh, very much aware that he was intruding upon something special and private, was on the point of leaving.

'Mr Farrell, forgive me – '

He smiled. 'Leigh, please – and there's nothing to forgive,' he said gently. 'You are naturally concerned for your husband.'

'I am, but that doesn't excuse bad manners. Do, please, sit down. You must be exhausted.'

'Not really. I'm used to unpredictable hours.'

'Even so, a cup of tea is the very least I can offer you. Or coffee? My sister in Toronto keeps us well supplied.'

'Tea would be fine.'

'Michael, you sit in your chair, too, while I make it. We could all do with a cup, and then I'll get you to bed.'

'Where's Lizzie?' Michael said without moving.

Kathleen had hoped he wouldn't ask. She busied herself with the kettle. 'In the bakehouse – everything's under control. Albert will be here any minute – '

'I'd better just go and see.'

Kathleen swung round, eyes blazing. 'Michael Ryan, I forbid you to go near the bakehouse! You're not going anywhere but to your bed.' She turned distressed eyes to Leigh. 'Honest to God, what would you do with such a stubborn man?'

But Michael was already swaying. Leigh crossed the living room and got a shoulder under him. 'The couch, I think,' he said quietly. 'I'm not sure, but they probably gave him a shot of something at the hospital.'

Together they made Michael comfortable, and then Leigh said

not to bother with the tea. 'I really should go and see if my hotel's still standing – and set about getting back to Scotland.'

Kathleen went to the door with him. The haunted look had not quite left her eyes. 'I've never been very good at expressing my feelings.'

He frowned. 'There's no need.'

'Nevertheless, I'm sure you understand just how much Michael means to me – how much I owe you.' She watched his face, saw its sudden tautness. 'And I wish with all my heart that things might have been different for you and Liz. But . . . .'

'But they aren't,' he said harshly. 'Listen, I love Elizabeth with all my heart, and she loves me. Nothing can change that. Nothing ever will. We both know that, just as we accept that there's no use hoping for more. But since our paths will seldom cross . . . .'

'My dear Leigh, I'm so sorry.' Kathleen took his hand in both of hers. 'You'll want to say goodbye. She's in the bakehouse. And may God keep you from harm.'

Liz looked up from scaling off the dough, throwing each piece on to the table and tucking it quickly under a large cloth to keep it from chilling. She was flushed, her face streaked with flour.

'Oh – I thought you might be Albert.' Instinctively, her hands kept going. 'I'm sorry, I didn't mean – it's just a bit awkward to do this single-handed, when you're not used to it. I'm afraid I can't stop, or the whole batch will be ruined.'

'Right.' The bakehouse smelled warm and yeasty, bringing back memories of his grandmother's kitchen on baking days. A cat, black and wary, poked its head out from beneath the table, and as cautiously withdrew.

'I just came to tell you I'm leaving. With any luck I may get back before the Lib arrives to pick up the crew. We sometimes have a couple of days' wait. Your father is safely tucked up, and your mother's reading him the Riot Act.' It wasn't at all what he wanted to say. 'Oh, my dearest girl, do you have to work so hard? You must be almost out on your feet.'

'Breadmaking can be surprisingly soothing.' She scaled off the last piece and began handing up; smoothing, tucking the ends expertly underneath by rote, placing them one by one on a flour-dusted board, covering them with another cloth. 'They need time to prove, you see,' she explained. 'And if they aren't kept warm, the surface will crack and they'll spoil.'

'I don't give a damn about the bread! Elizabeth, I can't bear to leave you like this!'

'Perhaps it's for the best,' she said, keeping her eyes on what she was doing so he wouldn't see the tears. 'As long as you don't touch me, as long as I don't have to watch you go, I can just about bear it.' For a moment she thought he would ignore her plea. In the silence, she heard his ragged breathing. 'Please,' she whispered.

A moment later, the door opened and closed with a faint 'whoosh', and she knew she was alone.

Almost a week later, Shirley Anne arrived. She came breezing in, bursting with life and energy and managing to look fantastic even in uniform, bringing with her the aura of a different world. Her hair was shorter, and curled engagingly beneath the brim of her hat, which she promptly flung off before lifting Rosie high into the air.

'My precious! How you've grown!'

Rosie crowed with pleasure, and shouted, 'More!'

'Shirley Anne, do put her down. She's just had her tea; you'll make her sick.' Kathleen's voice was sharper than she'd intended. It was always the same with Shirley Anne – within minutes she had the place turned upside down. But to her credit, she didn't take offence, just grimaced, said 'Whoops!' and set her daughter down, and kissed Georgy, who stood patiently watching.

'So, how is everyone? The poor old home town's copped a packet, I see. I knew things hadn't been good, but it gave me quite a shock as we drove through – almost as bad as London.'

Her flippancy touched a still-raw nerve in Liz. Above Rosie's clamouring, she retorted in kind. 'We're fine, apart from Dad's broken arm, Uncle Nick's concussion, and Aunt Laura losing her parents.' She could hear her voice growing shrill, but couldn't stop herself. 'And, oh yes, we had a string of incendiaries on the bakehouse roof, and the Candide is closed, due to damage. But at least we've had three whole nights in a row without a raid.'

'Oh, Lor'.' Shirley Anne sat down abruptly, hardly seeming to notice when Rosie clambered on to her knee, though she put an arm round her. 'Nothing changes, does it? Five minutes home, and I'm behaving like an insensitive brat. But I didn't mean it. It's just that we're always being told to put up a cheerful front – that's what folk want to see from their entertainers, whether it's in air raid shelters or factories or hospitals. And it becomes a habit, even if you do sometimes end up feeling like a right Pollyanna. Sometimes it's the only way we manage to carry on, when there are bombs dropping all round, or you're performing for people who are terribly injured or disfigured . . .'

Her voice had gradually become more intense, and now a tear trembled. Rosie watched with interest, then reached up soft fingers to brush it away, kissing the place where it had been. 'Better,' she lisped, and Shirley Anne hugged her, burying her face for a moment in the curls so like her own, until Rosie wriggled free and climbed down.

For a moment Shirley Anne looked what she was, young and insecure – but Kathleen had also seen the pure steel beneath. She went to put her arms round her young daughter. 'I'd say you've finally grown up, love. And we're proud of you.'

'Of course we are. I didn't mean to sound off. My sense of humour's worn a bit thin lately.' Liz grinned. 'You be as cheerful as you like. It'll be good for us.'

'Oh, I have missed you all, and it is great to be home! Even if I can't stay long. We're in a grotty little boarding house off Paradise Street, and we have a rehearsal at five. So, tell me, quickly. What's this about Dad, and the incendiaries, and Uncle Mick, and – oh, everything!'

The shop bell rang. 'You tell her, Liz. Take her up to your room – you'll get no peace down here. Ellen and I will manage.'

So they curled up on Liz's cheery quilt, and Liz told Shirley Anne about Dad helping to get Nora out, though carefully omitting Leigh's name. 'She was a miserable old crow, but d'you know, I really miss her.'

'And how's Dad managing?'

'Well, he can't make bread one-handed, and he can't drive the van, either. At first it was sending him quietly crazy, but already he's becoming adept at a number of other jobs. And we've taken on another baker as well as Albert. Several big firms have been bombed, including that place where Sally used to work – you know, the one our Chris nearly went to. Badger's. That was awful.

Over a hundred of them working in the cellars, and a landmine fell on them. No-one got out alive.'

'Don't!' Shirley Anne shuddered. 'What about your incendiaries?'

'Oh, Joey climbed on to the roof and dealt with those before they could take hold. And an explosion close by shattered the side window. That's why it's boarded up. What a mess, even with all the brown sticky paper, nearly as bad as last time. It shook the fur from the oven roof down on to the bread, but we managed to brush it off, and the bread seemed none the worse.'

'You have had a time!'

'It had its moments,' Liz said drily. 'The new man, Steve Wilson, is from Munnings', would you believe? They've been laying off staff since Mr Munnings died, and the Church Street shop was damaged the same night as Cooper's, which won't help matters. Steve says there's no firm hand on the rein any more, and the staff all reckon that you-know-who is dipping his hand too freely into the till.' Liz saw Shirley Anne's face tighten at the reference to Alec, and wondered whether to mention her confrontation with him. She had a right to know.

'Little weed. I hope you told him where to go.'

'In no uncertain terms. Not so much of a weed these days, though. He looked every inch the officer.' Liz was curious. 'Would you really mind if he tried to claim Rosie as his daughter?'

'Well, of course I'd mind! Rosie's mine!' She stopped, aware that Liz was smiling. 'Well, she *is*. Just because I'm not very maternal doesn't mean I don't care!'

'O.K. Keep your hair on. I do like your hair, by the way. It suits you short and curly. I sometimes wonder if I should have mine cut.'

'Don't you dare. You've got lovely hair! I've always envied it.'

'Have you? You never said.' Liz peered at herself in the mirror. 'Ugh, it's not so lovely at present. I haven't had a moment to wash it.'

Shirley Anne moved uneasily. 'I don't know what Mam would do without you, Liz. It can't have been easy. And you had such wonderful plans.'

'I've still got them.' Liz slid off the bed, pulled out her pins, and began to brush her hair vigorously until the bright strands shone with life. On an impulse, she opened the drawer where she kept

Fritz's books. 'I get these out and study them sometimes, late at night.' Her chin came up. 'The war won't last forever.'

'Good for you. Oh, my heavens! Look at the time.' Shirley Anne jumped off the bed and smoothed down her uniform skirt, wrinkling her nose at its shortcomings. 'I must go, and we've hardly scratched the surface of the news. I wanted to hear about Chris and Jimmy, and – oh, lots of things. We're only here for a couple of days, but I will try to get along again before we leave.'

'And do try to see Mrs Frith. I take Rosie along whenever I can. It means a lot to her.'

'I'll try, but it won't be easy. And I must pop into the bakehouse to see Dad before I go, just in case I don't get back.'

'Shirley Anne, you are happy, aren't you?'

Her blue eyes widened. 'Yes, of course I am. Oh, the war's horrid, of course, and the digs can be appalling, but the actual performing – the audiences make everything seem worth while!'

'Have you heard from Andy Rogers recently?'

'Mm. He's with the Mediterranean Fleet. I try to write back, but you know what a rotten correspondent I am. And now, I really must go!'

She turned away so quickly that Liz couldn't be sure whether or not she blushed.

'That girl's like a whirlwind,' Kathleen said when she'd gone. 'And she still hasn't learned not to bang the door.'

Laura left the twins in Wales when she came home to arrange her parents' funeral. She had been devastated by the news that their Anderson shelter had been destroyed by a direct hit, the same night that Nick had been felled by a length of falling timber down at the docks. Kathleen knew she wouldn't want to be alone in their own house, and felt obliged to offer her sister-in-law the use of Shirley Anne's room, but was relieved when she decided to stay with a friend in Bootle.

'It will be so much more convenient,' she'd said tearfully.

'Especially as Michael isn't available to drive her hither and thither,' Flora observed with her usual perception, during one of her brief visits. 'Oh, I'm sorry for her, Kathy, but it seems to me she's obsessed with giving her parents a grand funeral. Concern for our Nick comes a pretty poor second.'

'I can only suppose she feels his condition isn't critical. Laura's closeness to her mother always was a bit unhealthy.'

'And she, God rest her, never loosed the apron strings. They stretched all the way to Wales. She was forever popping over to visit Laura and the children.' Flora caught Kathleen's eye. 'I'm getting to be a right sharp-tongued old cynic, aren't I? It's just when you see so many cases of genuine grief and hardship . . .'

'I know. Still, Laura can't help the way she is. And I'm a fine one to talk – I haven't been able to get to the hospital myself, yet, what with one thing and another. How *is* Nick?'

'Oh, a bit subdued, but that could be the concussion. He'll be as right as rain in a week or two. I usually try to pop in on him either coming or going from Liverpool. The staff are very good.'

Kathleen managed a wry smile. 'Michael's like a bear with a sore head. But I know how he feels, so I do try to be patient. Flora, I have to ask you – about Leigh Farrell . . .'

'Ah. I've had moments of guilt about that young man. I've grown very fond of him. In fact, I believe I knew how he felt about Liz before he did himself, which put me in a difficult position – or might have done, had he been less honourable. Tragic. Another time, another place, and no two people would have been more ideally suited – ' She shrugged. 'But don't go worrying yourself, Kathy – Leigh will never do anything to undermine Liz's marriage.'

'So I've come to believe. I'm glad, because I owe him so much, though he won't have it that he saved Michael's life. We talked a little – enough to convince me that he's very resilient. Like you, Flo.'

She grimaced. 'Oh, I'm a bit of a fraud. The truth is, heartbreak aside, I've enjoyed the challenge – being part of a team. And people have been so generous, both in this country and beyond – all our own Dominions, and America, too. I had a long talk the other day with Winthrop Aldridge, the President of their War Relief Fund, and he was most impressed by our various emergency relief stores, and the speed and efficiency with which we've been able to feed and clothe and even house people who have been left with nothing. I only hope the message gets back so that even more aid gets through – though I hope even more that it won't be necessary ever to work at that pace again.'

*

Flora's words were prophetic. From then on the raids all but ceased, as though Hitler realized he was never going to bludgeon the British people into submission. But even Dandy was taken by surprise when, in June, he invaded Russia without warning.

'I reckon that's his first real error.' Dandy rubbed his hands with satisfaction, and stuck the little swastika flag in place on the map he and Joey had hung on the scullery door. 'You'll see. Just like that other jumped up little dictator, Napoleon. He thought he could swallow Russia up easy, and have us for afters, and look where that got him.'

'Serves the Russians right for trusting Hitler. And it could keep the Germans off our backs.' Kathleen spoke absently, her mind more concerned with ration books. The Board of Trade had announced that clothing, cloth and footwear were to be rationed from the first of June, 1941, for everyone except children under four years old. There would be sixty-six coupons per head, and as a temporary measure, the unused page of margarine coupons in the current ration book would be used.

'I wonder if the bright spark who dreamed that up had the least idea how much chaos it would create? You wouldn't credit how many people have misunderstood,' she complained to Ellen.

'I know,' Ellen said. 'I've just have another one in, asking if she had to order her garments here. I'm glad they've excluded the little ones, and all the small haberdashery stuff, but it's a pity about wool. I knit an awful lot of our kiddies' clothes.'

Kathleen sighed. 'I suppose it'll all get sorted out next month, when they issue the new ration books.'

Ellen went into the store for some more bacon. 'That was a glowing write-up the *Echo* gave Shirley Anne. The *Post* had quite a good one, too. One of Arnie's pals came in last night, an' he was bowled over by the dock concert.'

'Ada Killigan's making the most of it, bragging about how Shirley Anne and her Lily were best friends before she went away. Lily's standing at the munitions factory went up no end after Shirley Anne spoke to her.' Kathleen sighed. 'Ah, well, it's the last we'll see of her for a while, I suppose. We'll have Rita next – she's decided to come up at the weekend. Michael Francis still hasn't been christened, and the priest down there has been on at her more than once. But she was determined to have the christening here, and we can't be sure when Frank will be home, so I've made arrangements with Father for Sunday. Chris can't get leave at such short notice to perform his duties as godfather, but Michael will stand proxy for him, and Liz is to be godmother.'

It was a lovely day, though Rosie, jealous of all the attention Michael Francis was attracting, had to be restrained time and again from poking him quite viciously in an attempt to make him cry. 'Just one more time, young lady,' Liz threatened, 'and it'll be home and straight to bed for you, and you'll miss the party.'

'I expect it's just over-excitement,' Ellen whispered.

'No, it isn't. She's like her mother. Never happy unless she's centre stage.'

The baby, on the other hand, was adorable. He had grown inches since Kathleen had seen him, and behaved impeccably throughout the ceremony. 'That's our Rita's teacher training,' Kathleen said proudly. 'She'll be a good mother.'

But the visit passed too quickly. Georgy haunted the baby's pram as he had done with Rosie when she was tiny, watching every move.

'How is he these days, Liz?' Rita asked when they were alone. 'I don't like to ask Mam.'

'Well, you can see for yourself – sweet-natured as ever, and in a curious way Rosie's quite good for him. She makes him talk, and badgers him into doing things he might not try otherwise. But he's never going to win any prizes. And Doc Graham thinks the measles may have left him with a bit of deafness in one ear.'

'Poor little chap, as if he hasn't enough. Mam'll have to tell his teacher when he starts school. All too often, children like Georgy get teased by the other children. Though they never tried it more than once when I was around.'

'Do you miss your teaching? It seems such a waste of all that training.'

Rita smiled wryly. 'Funny, the way things turn out, isn't it? The ambitions we both had. Still, the war can't last for ever. As it happens, Miss Hayes at the girls' school in Myndd Howe, would welcome me back with open arms, any time I like. She's desperate for an English teacher. But for now I've enough to do, looking after Michael.'

'I'm just sorry you can't stay longer,' Liz said, but it was obvious that Rita wanted to get back in case there had been word from Frank.

'I hope he comes soon. I've seen a little house that would be perfect for us, but I don't want to decide without him. Listen, though – I reckon he'll have been home and gone again by the time Chris gets married, so how would it be if I came up then to give you a hand? I take it Mam and Dad are going to Gateshead?'

'They are – if I have to put them on the train with my own hands. And I've told Mary to book them into the hotel for three nights. It'd be great if you could come. There'd be just the two of us and the children.' Liz crossed her fingers as she spoke, in case Hitler had another change of mind.

But life remained relatively peaceful, with only the occasional air raid, and the city, like a battered old war horse, struggled to its knees and then to its feet, scarred and not as spry as of old, but already getting its second wind.

The description might well have fitted Michael, too. At first he had prowled the bakehouse like a wounded animal – he could hardly bear to watch the others work, yet had to be sure everything was up to standard. He knew he'd been lucky to get Steve, and even luckier that he could drive, but Steve had been used to a dough mixer at Munnings' – something Kathleen had been on at Michael to instal for long enough.

'You're not getting any younger,' she'd told him more than once. 'And almost everyone uses them now.'

But to Michael the dough was a living thing, to be cherished and coaxed into exactly the right texture, and his reply was always the same. 'Well, I'll not be one of them, not while I've breath in me body. There's nothing in the world like the feel of that dough coming together under your hands. It's something no machine can equal.'

Now, as the days went by, and he mastered a number of smaller jobs one-handed, he was beginning to face the very real possibility that his arm would never again take the strain of hand-mixing, let alone lifting two-hundred-and-eighty-pound flour sacks.

Doctor Graham had already hinted as much, his eyes compassionate, his tone blunt. 'The arm's doing fine, Michael, but listen now – as we get a bit older, broken bones don't knit like they do in youngsters, so don't go expecting miracles.'

'You've been talking to Kathleen,' he said accusingly.

'She worries about you, sure enough – as you do about her. Which is as it should be in all good marriages. And, feeling as I know you do about her, that's all the more reason for not adding to her worries.'

Towards the end of June, the boys came home on their two weeks leave, and it quickly emerged that this was to be embarkation leave. The living room seemed very full, the evening they arrived, with everyone talking at once. They both looked very fit. Chris was more confident, and Jimmy was – Jimmy; jaunty, sure of himself, his black hair as sleek and Brylcreemed as ever, his moustache pencil-sharp.

'About time we got on with it,' he enthused. 'We've all had our fill of square bashing. Just let us at the Germans again, and this time we'll finish them for good.'

'Jimmy!' Liz pinched his arm. She had been watching Chris's face. And Mam's. 'Have a heart. You know how Mam feels about Chris, and the thought of him going into action. And it's bound to cast a bit of a gloom over the wedding.'

'Rubbish, sweetheart. You forget, Mary's an army girl herself. She understands how we feel about getting the job done.'

'How *you* feel, perhaps, but Chris is different. He's got a lot of Dad in him, and I know there's nothing he'd like better than to settle down here with Mary and raise a family.'

'And what makes you think I don't feel the same? Listen,' Jimmy said against her ear. 'Just let me get you alone for five minutes, and I'll show you where I'd rather be.'

'Hush.' Liz blushed. 'They'll hear.'

'Not them. They've only got eyes and ears for their number one son. Why don't we pop out for a drink – or something?'

Perhaps it wasn't such a bad idea. She hadn't yet broken it to Jimmy that the flat over the Candide wasn't safe to use. When Alice had come to tell her about the fire not long after Leigh had left on that awful morning, she hadn't really cared – not about that, nor anything else. The whole area was out of bounds until it could be made safe, and in a way, it was one commitment less, fewer fancy cakes to be contrived. When she did finally get to inspect it, she found the café itself wouldn't take much to put right – the smell was the worst, the mess mostly broken glass and water. The flat, however, was a different matter, and until the damage had been assessed for insurance, there was no point in even thinking about it.

Liz whispered in Mam's ear that they were off for a bit of a walk, and Kathleen nodded understandingly.

'We'll have to what?'

They had walked, skirting round roped off areas, towards the Pier Head. The setting sun softened the wounds of carnage all around them, but by the time they reached the still-busy river – bathed in a soft golden light, but with its own scars exposed as far as the eye could see – Jimmy was reduced first to an angry silence, and then to a stream of swearwords, most of which she didn't understand. Liz had never seen him in such a violent mood, and because it disturbed her, she sought to distract his thoughts. It was not, she reflected later, the ideal time to tell him.

'We'll have to use my room,' she said. 'It's got a double bed – Shirley Anne and I used to share it when we were little.'

But this in no way endeared it to Jimmy. He stopped dead in his tracks. 'I don't give a toss what you and Shirley Anne used to do. I mean, can you imagine us – well, you know! No way. Those walls are like paper – you'd be able to hear every sound!'

'You're exaggerating. I don't remember hearing anything when Mam and Dad – ' Liz stopped, blushing bright red.

'You didn't know what you were supposed to hear!' Jimmy pulled her close and kissed her almost brutally. 'And the things I want to do with you would be quite impossible with an audience listening in.'

Her reaction was instinctive, as she struggled like a wild thing to push him away. 'Jimmy, stop it! I don't want to know you like this!'

He drew a shuddering breath and let her go, turning to grip the rail so tight that the sinews in his arms stood out. After a few more deep breaths he turned, and though his eyes were still a bit over-bright, he was her own Jimmy again.

'Sorry, sweetheart. It's just – being away from you for so long. And then, seeing all this – it suddenly got to me! Oh, I knew you'd had it bad, but seeing it for real, knowing what you must all have been through. I love this old town, Liz – and I love you. And very soon, I'll be leaving you – really leaving you this time . . .'

'Oh, Jimmy!' She put her arms round him, and he held her very tight.

'Listen – I'm not short of a bob or two. Let's go somewhere for a day or two, you an' me. Blackpool, perhaps – anywhere, as long as we could be alone. Yer Mam and Dad won't wouldn't mind, would they? They've got Chris to fuss over, an' give them a hand if they need it. An' I'll have to leave you for a couple of days next week to go and be Chris's best man.'

'Of course you must go, love,' Mam said. 'It's only fair, when all's said and done. I'm just sorry you'll not be at the wedding. I still think . . .'

'No, Mam,' said Liz firmly. 'The plans are made, and I won't hear another word. You and Dad are going to Gateshead, and I'm staying here to look after the children and the business, and our Rita's coming to stay. No arguments. Chris knows we'll be with them both in spirit. But it would be nice if I could have a few days away with Jimmy before you go. I know he always seems very sure of himself, but inside, he's just like the rest of us.'

'I know, love. You don't have to explain.'

Liz hugged her, and resolved to make those few days memorable for Jimmy. And she did.

For two whole days while the sun shone, they went on the fairground and up the Tower, doing all the silly things that holidaymakers do in Blackpool. And at night they danced in the Tower ballroom. Even the squads of men in Air Force uniform drilling on the promenade couldn't spoil their pleasure. Liz felt closer to Jimmy in those two days than she had done for a long time, and he relaxed and was tender and loving in return.

The night before the party left for Gateshead, they had a slap-up family supper. Nick was still recuperating in Wales, but everyone who could be there, was. Mam killed a couple of her poor layers, and made a huge chicken casserole, with Chris's favourite jam roly-poly for afters.

When the last morsel had been consumed, Michael got to his feet and called for silence.

'It's usually Dandy who makes the speeches, so I daresay you're all as surprised as I am meself, seeing me in this unlikely role.' Dandy nodded sagely, and they all laughed. 'But this may be the closest we'll get to coming together as a whole family for quite a while, and there's a few things need saying. We've come through a lot over the years, and, mostly due to your mother's wisdom and love, we've done it together as a family. But these last few months have tested all of us more than usual, one way or another. And I would like you to know that I am proud of every one of you, not forgetting Rita – and Shirley Anne, who is doing us proud elsewhere, probably even as I speak.'

Liz shot a look at Mam's face, which mirrored her own choked state. 'Dad, you'll have the lot of us in tears at this rate!'

'There's no shame in tears, girleen, if they spring from honest emotions. In the same way, singling a couple of you out in no way detracts from my love and pride in you all.' His glance moved from his eldest son, to Dandy, resting a fraction longer on Aunt Flora, who lifted a quizzical eyebrow at him. 'I've already spoken of your mother, who is our strength.' His eyes warmed as they met hers, and then moved along the table. 'And now there's the little matter of Joey – '

'Hey, our kid,' Chris chuckled. 'What have you been up to?'

Joey sat forward, the long-lashed eyes wary. 'Me? I haven't done nothing.'

'Anything,' Liz murmured out of habit.

'Perhaps if you were to cast your mind back a bit, lad,' Michael continued blandly. 'And I'm not talking about the little matter of the incendiaries, though you showed great presence of mind – '

'Aw, Dad, you're havin' us on!'

'Not at all. I had a letter today, from your troop leader. He tells me that a Sergeant Fred Pringle has been in touch with him, concerning a member of his troop – a *sixteen-year-old* lad, name of Joey Ryan, who acted with conspicuous promptness and courage on the morning of Sunday, May 4th, by delivering a number of urgent messages in what he described as circumstances of considerable danger . . .'

'Joey!' Mam turned to stare at him. 'You never . . . Did you tell them you were sixteen?'

'Sort of. I had to, Mam, or they prob'ly wouldn't have let me . . .' He stopped, blushing.

'Ride the motorcycle?' Michael finished the sentence for him. 'Well, I daresay three Hail Marys took care of that little white lie, so we'll say no more, except that the sergeant felt your actions were deserving of some recognition.'

'Golly!'

'Oh, Joey!'

Chris nudged him. 'You crafty little beggar!'

'It was nothing. I enjoyed it.'

Michael eyed his errant son quizzically. 'So be it. Well that's about it really, except for a final word about one who, in her own special way, has helped your mother and myself through the last few trying years. I'll not embarrass you, my very dear Lizzie, by detailing how much we all owe to you' – his own voice was husky, now, as he turned to his most loved daughter – 'but, next month you will be twenty-one, and by then, who knows where we all might be? So this seemed an appropriate moment to wish you, as a family, all the happiness you deserve, and to give you this small token of our thanks and love.'

'Oh, Dad!' Liz could hardly see to open the little package. She drew out the little gold cross and chain, blinking at its splintering brightness. And as she recalled so many small and precious memories, the heartbreak and the happiness merged into one. Jimmy on one side, and Chris on the other, both hugged her. 'I didn't . . . I don't . . . Oh, Mam, Dad, everyone, it's a beautiful present, and I shall treasure it always. And now you really have made me cry.'

PART THREE

LEIGH
1942

Chapter One

Liz dusted the photograph and returned it to its position of prominence on the sideboard: two soldiers, one a corporal, wearing lightweight drill and smiling broadly into the camera, eyes creased against the sun. It had been taken on board ship, and had come with a heavily censored letter from Jimmy. Chris's letter had been similarly dealt with, as had the ones that arrived from Rangoon in time for Christmas.

The sideboard had become cluttered over the years, and now took ages to dust. To the original family photographs had been added the various wedding pictures – Rita's, her own, and now Chris and Mary's with Mary wearing a two-piece described by Mam as a pretty shade of pink, and a frothy hat. There was Joey in his scout uniform, several of Shirley Anne, including one with Andy Rogers and another in which she was reclining on top of a tank, her head thrown back in laughter. There was Jimmy and herself taken on that last holiday in Blackpool, and, of course, numerous photographs of babies at various stages of development.

And none of them mine, Liz thought, not sure whether to be glad or sorry. She had hoped, after that last leave, but it wasn't to be – not for the forseeable future, anyway. In purely practical terms, a baby would have created lots of problems, and they had more than enough to cope with as it was. Yet sometimes, when she wrapped Rosie into a towel, all pink and glowing from her bath, she longed for a child of her own.

There had been no word from Chris or Jimmy since the Japs had bombed the American Fleet in Pearl Harbour early in December – a flagrant act of war that had ended America's neutrality overnight. Now, Britain and America were united against both German and Japanese aggression.

Dandy and Joey immediately started a new map, covering South East Asia. In the weeks following Christmas, while the European map remained fairly static, with the swastikas still encircling Leningrad and Moscow, who stubbornly refused to yield to the Germans, little flags decorated with bright red suns began to oust the Union Jacks on the second map. First Kuala Lumpur had fallen – and later, unbelievably, Singapore. Liz hardly dared to look at her mother.

'The slit-eyed little devils crept down the Malay peninsula and sneaked up on us from behind,' Dandy said in disgust. 'Caught us on the hop with all our big guns pointing out to sea, waiting to blast them out of the water.'

She and Mam continued to send their airgraphs off each week, and as Mam grew tight-lipped, Liz suggested to Dandy that it might be more tactful if he put the maps somewhere less conspicuous than on the scullery door.

'But, Liz, Singapore's *miles* from Burma!' Joey exclaimed.

'Just do it, Joey.'

'Your sister's right, lad. It's not a game we're playin'. We've got our loved ones out there somewhere.'

It was perhaps fortunate that Kathleen had other things to occupy her mind. As well as ration books and the pink points books, she had been working her way through a sea of paperwork concerning subsidies. Now, they were being subjected to a whole new series of regulations. And something new was added to the baker's vocabulary: 'National bread'. The very words had a depressing ring to them.

'As far as I can see,' she told Michael and Liz, 'you can use up your white flour for now by mixing a quarter of it at a time with the new national wheatmeal flour. But after April, it's goodbye to white bread. And that goes for pastry and cakes, too.'

It was hard to say which of them was the more despondent. While Michael sat in his chair, sucking his pipe and brooding, Liz demanded angrily, 'Whoever heard of making cakes with wheatmeal flour? They'll be as heavy and flat as a fluke!'

Her father roused himself to say with surprising mildness, 'You never know what you can do till you try, Lizzie love. We all have to do our bit, and matters could be worse. At least bread isn't to be rationed, and we can still make the wheaten soda bread and farls.'

So he and Liz put their heads together with Albert and Steve, pooling their knowledge and experience. As soon as the flour became available, they began to experiment with it, trying the suggestions put out by the National Association to its members, as to ways in which the wheatmeal flour could be improved by the addition of a small amount of mashed potato, oats or barley. They found that potato worked particularly well in bread. Pastry and cakes proved more difficult. Fat and sugar were becoming scarcer, and there was still some confusion about what decoration, if any, could be added to cakes after baking. But Liz was ready to rise to the challenge, and the NA would be sending demonstrators round to advise.

Liz had finally managed to get the Candide open again, though the flat was still unusable. In spite of being freshly painted, Liz swore there were still traces of that awful smell that lingers after a fire. But no-one else seemed to notice, as the clients flocked back to their favourite meeting place, undeterred by the shortages and lack of choice on the menu. Reagan's café had been completely destroyed in the May Blitz, and many of his former customers swelled their number, until, with the approach of spring, the Candide was doing excellent trade.

When Michael picked up his morning paper, the headlines leapt out at him. RANGOON FALLS. At first, his eyes refused to function, to read on. He was alone in the living room, though for one instant it was as though he could feel Chris standing there beside him. He shook the notion free, lowered himself into his chair and took out his glasses. There wasn't a lot more – just the official press hand-out. He took off his glasses and stared unseeingly into the fire. How was he going to tell Kathleen?

She took the news rather better than he had expected, though he ought not to have been surprised: in time of trouble she was a rock, and now was no exception. Perhaps for Liz's sake, perhaps for all their sakes, she refused to think the worst.

'After all, like Dad's said more than once, Burma's a big country. And we don't even know for sure that our boys were still in Rangoon.'

Liz admired her mother's courageous approach, and backed it to the hilt. But inside she was less confident – and illogically wracked with guilt.

Shirley Anne arrived without warning, as she almost always did, on a February evening, when Liz and her mother were busy cutting down a couple of old dresses for the children, and Michael was sitting by the fire, glancing through the NA Review for any advice that might be of use.

'Well now,' he said, looking over the top of the glasses he now wore for reading, as the back door slammed and the whirlwind entered, bringing with her the usual aura of glamour, and an air of suppressed excitement. 'Here's a surprise!'

'The errant daughter returning to the bosom of her family – and very cosy it all looks.' Shirley Anne grinned as she bent to kiss his forehead, and hugged her mother. 'I was going to ring you, but I suddenly found myself with a couple of free days before we start our next round of one night stands, so I decided to bring my news in person.'

'I'll put the kettle on,' Kathleen said, half rising.

'Stay where you are; I'll do it,' Liz said, pleased to see her sister, but as always exasperated by the cavalier way she treated her home. 'Have you eaten? We haven't got a lot, but I can do you a poached egg on toast.'

'Lovely. I'm absolutely starving. The journey was depressing as always. A lady on the train had a thermos and insisted I share it with her. I'm not sure whether it was tea or coffee, but it tasted foul.' She prowled restlessly about the room, picked up a photo, put it down, and suddenly swung round. 'If I don't tell you right away, I shall burst! Mam, Dad, Liz – the most wonderful thing's happened – I still can't quite believe it . . .'

'Calm down, girleen, and let us all into the secret before we're killed with the suspense.'

She laughed. 'I'm going to make a film!'

Liz came to the scullery door. 'You mean one of those Government propaganda films?'

'Liz, really! As if I'd make a fuss about that. I mean a full length feature picture, with music, dancing, romance – everything!'

'And they've asked you to be in it?' Michael looked pleased. 'Well now, isn't that grand, Kathleen?'

'Not just *in* it.' Shirley Anne produced her trump card. 'I'm to play the lead.'

'You are?' Liz rushed to hug her. 'That's fantastic! Oh, damn, the toast's burning. Lay yourself a place on the end of the table, will you?' She ran to rescue the toast, calling from the scullery with sisterly candour, 'But why you?'

'It's all down to Mr Grace, really. I know you had your doubts about him, Mam, but he really has turned up trumps.'

'So it would seem,' Mam said drily, but they could tell she was pleased.

'The powers that be have decided that the longer the war drags on, the more people will need something to lift their spirits – something light, romantic, and purely English, with lots of singing and dancing . . . They're trying to get Ivor Novello to write the music.'

'Better and better.' Liz set down the plate on which reposed a rather singed piece of toast and two poached eggs, sunny side up. 'The hens are laying well at present.' She grinned. 'I suppose it should be caviar, but we're right out of it at the moment. So, who's going to play Fred Astaire to your Ginger Rogers?'

Her sister, knife poised, looked smug. 'Darren Wildman.'

'Oh, Shirley Anne! Is that definite? He's gorgeous! And famous. With him as the hero, the picture's bound to be a smash hit. You could become a star overnight!'

Shirley Anne's eyes were huge, and everything about her glowed. 'Oh, I do hope so!'

'Well, don't get too carried away,' Mam said, going back to her sewing machine. 'You haven't even made the picture yet, and there's many a slip . . .'

'I know, Mam.' Shirley Anne tucked into her eggs, accepting the rebuke with surprising meekness. 'And even if all goes well, it won't be for a while yet. There's rumours of us going to the Middle East soon. Oh, I'm not supposed to know that, so forget I spoke.'

Kathleen stared down at the garment she was making as though she had never seen it before. She put her foot down on the treadle and the machine began to whirr, and Michael absent-mindedly rubbed the slight ache in his arm. Liz noticed, and came to sit on the arm of his chair.

'Well, if you do become famous, *I*, for one, mean to bask in your reflected glory for all I'm worth,' she said lightly.

It was Shirley Anne's turn to grin. 'Fine.' She mopped the last bit of toast round her plate, popped it in her mouth, and laid down her knife and fork with a satisfied sigh. 'I thought I'd take Rosie round to Mrs Frith's in the morning, though I shan't tell *her* about the picture. She'd only blab it all round the place. And then, in the afternoon, I thought you and I could go out somewhere, Liz.'

'I do have to work, you know.'

'Oh, come on. One afternoon won't hurt. I'll have to go back on the evening train. We could do something really daft – do they still run those tea dances at Reeces?'

'Yes, but . . .'

'Right. We'll go there. You never know – we might get off with a pair of handsome GIs.'

'Shirley Anne, I'm married, or had you forgotten?'

The sharpness in her voice brought the nagging worry to the surface, and Shirley Anne was momentarily shamefaced. 'I should have asked. There's been no word, I suppose?'

'None,' her father said quietly. 'But then, the situation must make communication difficult.'

'I suppose so.' She glanced at her mother and away again to her sister. 'Oh, but I'm sure they'll be all right. And Jimmy wouldn't want you to mope. I didn't mean anything – about the GIs. But they're a long way from home, too; you could almost say it's our duty to dance with them. Oh, come on, Liz, it'll be fun.'

'Shirley Anne's right.' Mam's voice was muffled in pins. 'It'll do you the world of good.'

'But I haven't a thing to wear.'

'Rubbish. We'll go up to your room now, and look through your frocks.' Upstairs, she dug into her pocket and produced a lipstick, brand new. 'I've even brought you a present for the occasion.'

'Shirley Anne, you angel! I queued for over an hour the other day, and when my turn came, they'd sold out.'

'That's what I thought. We don't often go short. Make-up sort of comes with the job.' She began to search ruthlessly through Liz's wardrobe, her voice muffled. 'Talking of Yanks, what happened to that gorgeous man who took you to Southport years ago?' She half pulled out a cotton print, said, 'H'm, no, I don't think so,' and put it away again. 'He was friendly with Clare's family or something. I know I was madly jealous at the time. D'you ever hear anything of him, these days?'

Liz was profoundly glad Shirley Anne was so preoccupied. 'Not for a long while,' she said lightly.

Except once, she added silently. Last July, on her twenty-first birthday, a slim package had arrived – brought into the shop by a Scottish airman, who asked for her by name.

'It's mor'n my life's worth tay give it to the wrong lassie,' he'd said.

By sheer coincidence she had been alone in the shop at the time, Ellen having just gone to grab a cup of tea. She had recognized the writing at once, and had tucked it into her pocket, where it burned a guilty hole until she could find a moment to escape to her room.

Inside the package there was a faded blue velvet box, the kind Aunt Flora always kept her jewellery in. She opened it very carefully. On a soft bed of blue silk lay a lady's gold fob watch, beautifully engraved, on a long gold chain – the kind she had seen worn by elegant ladies in period pictures. On the back was an inscription. *To our dearest daughter Elizabeth, on the occasion of her 21st birthday, July 18th, 1861.*

It was, Leigh had written, his grandmother's watch.

> 'She died last year, a wonderful and formidable old lady. As you know, she raised me, and I loved her dearly. As you will see, you share her name as well as her birthday – and, I like to think, much of her character. Dearest Elizabeth, can it be mere coincidence, do you suppose, or was it some kind of affinity that drew me to you from the first? Whatever the truth, it seemed fitting that you should have the watch. Keep it always, and think of me sometimes with kindness.'

Kindness! Oh, Leigh! She had put it with her other treasures, and wound it nightly with loving care.

'Eureka!' cried Shirley Anne, emerging triumphant with a silky pale green dress with a flaring skirt. It was two years old, but Liz had lost a little weight, so it still fitted. 'Good. I always liked you in that.'

The following afternoon, they made their way to Clayton Square. Shirley Anne wore her uniform, as she would be leaving almost immediately afterwards. 'And anyway, it's a point of pride with us to wear it whenever possible, except when we're performing, of course.'

The tea dance was well attended, with uniforms of all kinds in evidence – men on leave with their wives or girl friends, and women on their own, perhaps hoping to pick up an American, as Shirley Anne had joked she and Liz might do.

The first American troops had arrived in Liverpool in January, billeted on the Grand National course at Aintree, and more recently, the USAAF had taken over RAF Burtonwood, near Warrington. Their arrival had delighted the younger female population, many of whom seemed to think they had come straight from Hollywood in their smart olive green uniforms, so superior to the British khaki issue.

'Thank God our Dot's still too young to go chasing after them,' Ellen had said, when a recent conversation in the shop had veered between approval and disapproval of the new bread, indignation at having to fork out eight points for a tin of conny, and fears that the arrival of the GIs would mean trouble for some.

'I 'aird that some of 'em came ashore with them *you know what's* stuck in their caps, brazen as yer please . . .'

'You don't want ter believe all you 'ear,' said Ada Killigan. 'Our Lily's goin' out with one, an' he's a perfect gent.'

There were a few sniggers from the back.

Ellen said, 'Well, I speak as I find, and I must say the ones we've had in the shop have been very polite.'

'It's times like this I really miss old Nora,' Liz said when the customers had gone. 'Can't you just hear her? She'd have had a field day, what with the bread *and* the Americans.'

Now, sitting at their little table sipping tea; watching Shirley Anne quick-stepping with a young naval officer, and carrying on an animated conversation at the same time; catching tail-ends of conversations in a wide variety of accents from scouse to French, Yankee to Southern drawl, Liz had to stop herself from listening for one particular voice. Where was Leigh now?

'Honey?' The voice was insistent, the accent familiar, and for a moment her limbs turned to jelly. But the young man bending hopefully towards her was a fresh-faced sergeant with a snub nose and an engaging grin. 'Would you care to dance?'

'Yes, of course. I'm sorry . . .'

He said his name was Aaron, and he was from Detroit. He danced with rather more energy than skill, but Liz found him excellent company. In the space of one quickstep, she learned that he had a mom and dad, four sisters and three brothers, of whom he was the eldest, and that he was obviously missing them like anything. So much so, that she found herself inviting him home to a meal on the following evening, if he could make it; gave him the telephone number in case he couldn't, and then spent the next half hour wondering if she would regret her spontaneous gesture, since he showed no disposition to leave her side.

In desperation she began to talk about her husband, but even this didn't put him off, and when Shirley Anne returned to the table, his eyes grew even bigger. 'Sweetie, you've got problems,' she murmured, and aloud; 'I say, Liz – that young man I was dancing with actually knew Andy slightly. Not that he could tell me much I didn't know. Things are pretty dicey in the Med just now.'

'Are you a real professional actress, ma'am?' Aaron asked, having watched her in awed silence for some minutes.

'Sort of.' Shirley Anne smiled benevolently at him, and stood up. 'I'll be back in a minute, Liz. Just going to powder my nose.'

Two dances later, Liz was at her wit's end when, with a sigh of relief, she heard Shirley Anne's voice, more animated than usual.

'Liz! Talk about coincidence – who do you think I've just found?'

And he was there.

'Major Leigh Farrell of the United States Army Air Force,' Shirley Anne announced proudly. 'I told him, we were talking about him only last night.'

'Hello, Elizabeth,' he said quietly.

'Hello. What a surprise.' Her voice sounded quite normal, which was odd, because inside she was a mass of seething emotions. Aaron, out-ranked, melted away, and Shirley Anne was re-claimed by her naval officer. So they were alone. Politely he asked after all the family, enquired about her father's arm, then:

'Elizabeth . . .'

'Oh, please, do stop towering over me; sit down.' This time she couldn't stop the tremor in her voice. And as he still hesitated: 'I'm sorry. It was just such a shock.'

'I know. For me, too. Look, if you'd sooner I went?'

But she couldn't be that strong. 'No.'

He sat facing her. 'I wasn't keen to come here today, but life's been pretty hectic since I arrived, and my fellow officers finally ganged up on me – as good as told me that all work and no play was making Leigh a very dull boy. So, since this is the last place I would have expected to find you, especially in the afternoon, I allowed myself to be persuaded.'

'I suppose I should have realized you'd want to be in the thick of things.' A grin as shameless as Joey's lit up his face. 'How long have you been here?'

'About six weeks. I don't suppose it's any big secret that we've taken over RAF Burtonwood. The base isn't operational yet, but soon it's going to be one *big* depot, and with time pressing, I guess they figured that my experience might as well be put to good use.'

So close for six weeks. And she had not known.

'Your sister's come on some,' he said, watching her doing a mean jitterbug. 'But then, I always thought she would.'

Liz told him about the ENSA work, and about the picture Shirley Anne was going to make, and he was impressed – so impressed that she felt a stab of jealousy, watching him watch her sister. Shirley Anne came back to the table, glowing with her exertions, her blue eyes brilliant, and as her sister chatted away, Liz had the oddest feeling that she had become invisible.

And then the band began to play *Just the way you look tonight*, and she looked up to meet Leigh's eyes. 'Shall we?' he asked. 'For old times' sake?' And, though she knew it was madness to give in to temptation, she was powerless to refuse.

He held her as he had done before, with her left hand folded close against his chest, his breath moving softly in her hair. 'You grow more beautiful every time I see you. *Oh, but you're lovely, never, never change . . .*'

'Please, don't!' she whispered. 'Shirley Anne will notice. She never misses anything. And she'll interrogate me quite mercilessly.'

'O.K.' He moved back a fraction. 'What shall we discuss – the weather? That *is* what the English discuss when all else fails, isn't it?'

'Idiot,' she said, laughing suddenly.

'I won't try to see you again. It wouldn't be safe.'

'No.'

Shirley Anne arrived back at the table just before them. Liz thought she was about to say something, but before she could, a voice lifted in a lazy Southern drawl. 'Hey, Red – isn't there a law here about keeping all the pretty girls to yourself?'

A couple of Leigh's friends had found him, and from then until the time for Shirley Anne to leave for her train, the conversation was general.

Liz seized the opportunity to leave at the same time, her eyes holding Leigh's for a fraction longer than the rest as they said their goodbyes. Outside, she kissed her sister lightly. 'I won't come to the station with you, if you don't mind. It's been a lovely afternoon, but I'd better get home. Goodness knows what that daughter of yours will have got up to by now.'

'To say nothing of her Aunt *Elizabeth*.' Shirley Anne looked at Liz with new eyes. 'Talk about dark horses!'

'It isn't . . . there isn't . . . Oh, I can't talk about it.' Liz bit her lip. 'Shirley Anne, you won't say anything to Mam and Dad? Not that I've anything to hide, but it's all a bit complicated . . .'

Her sister's eyes danced. 'And they might not understand?'

'Something like that.'

'Curiouser and curiouser. It's all right, Liz.' There was a sudden warmth in Shirley Anne's voice. 'You stuck by me when I needed you. A sister doesn't forget things like that.'

And suddenly they were hugging one another with genuine affection.

'I wish you weren't away so much,' Liz said, and meant it. 'We get on so much better now.'

'Don't be fooled, Sis – that's probably because I'm *not* around all the time to irritate you. I may have grown up, but I'm still a selfish brat underneath. Always will be, I guess.'

'At least you're honest about it. I've grown up, too – less of a prig, I hope. I'd like to tell you about Leigh sometime, though I'm not sure you'd understand . . .'

'Try me. I might understand more than you think.' Shirley Anne gave her another quick hug. 'Must fly. Bye, love.'

'Take care,' Liz called after her. Shirley Anne's hand lifted in reply, her laugh drifting back.

Chapter Two

'It is with the deepest regret . . .' Liz read the telegram for the umpteenth time, each time telling herself that she had missed some crumb of hope. Jimmy was such an *alive* person, too smart to get himself killed – by the Japs or anyone else. But each time the message had the same ring of finality. Corporal James Marsden had been killed outright by a sniper's bullet.

She hadn't cried at first. Not even when telling the Marsdens – an ordeal, but she insisted she must do it herself. Mrs Marsden had collapsed in hysterics and Sunny, shocked out of his normal cheeriness, cradled her like a child, in silence. But to Liz it seemed important that everything should go on as usual, and Kathleen, looking beyond her daughter to meet Michael's compassionate eyes, saw in them a silent plea to allow the girl to find her own road to acceptance.

There had been no word of Chris. Mary had promised to ring the moment she heard any news, good or bad, and Kathleen had no wish to add to her worries by pestering her. Instead she rang Rita, who now had her own little house at Myndd Howe. When Mary had been transferred to a camp near Shrewsbury, Rita had given her an open invitation to visit, and the two soon became good friends. Rita received the news about Jimmy quietly. Frank had been away longer than usual, and she knew he was on convoy escort duty.

'I'm only guessing, but he may be on a convoy to Russia, and knowing how dangerous that could be doesn't make the waiting any easier.'

'Rita love, I'm sorry to give you bad news when you're already so worried. It'll be just the weather holding them up. It can be unpredictable, this time of year.'

'Thanks, Mam.' Rita sounded a bit more cheerful. 'You're probably right. I'm just tired. Young Michael's teething, and I'm not getting as much sleep as usual. Leave Mary to me. She should be coming this weekend, so I'll use my discretion about telling her.'

'And if she should hear anything . . .'
'You'll know at once, I promise.'

It was, as often happens, something quite trivial that breached the barriers Liz had erected in her mind. For two days she had worked herself into a state of exhaustion, spending her evenings scrubbing bakehouse equipment that had been thoroughly cleaned by the men earlier, and then setting about the cellar, which she said hadn't been properly gone through since it had been used regularly as a shelter. At night she slept almost as soon as her head touched the pillow. By the third day, with nothing left to vent her energies on, she prowled restlessly, snapping at the least thing, while the rest of the family tiptoed round her.

That night sleep came less easily, and she tossed and turned until the bed springs protested noisily. In that moment she heard Jimmy's voice, as clearly as if he was in the room.

'I mean, can you imagine us – well, you know? No, way, sweetheart! Those walls are like paper!'

And the tears came at last – hard, painful tears, as she wrestled with her illogical conviction that if her love had been more whole-hearted, Jimmy might still be alive. She tried to imagine her endearingly cocksure husband as a corpse, and her sobs finally brought Kathleen hurrying in.

She held her daughter, rocking her in her arms, her head cradled against her breast, hushing her as if Liz were a child again, until there were no tears left, only emptiness. Then she made her a hot drink and tucked her up, watching until she slept.

'You never really know your own children,' Kathleen told Flora later on the phone. 'Liz loved Jimmy, I'm not saying she didn't, but it was never – ' She paused, hunting for the right words, and wishing she'd never started.

'The way you love Michael?' Flora suggested bluntly.

'Yes. Exactly that. And yet, to hear her crying – I don't know, it was heartbreaking.'

But Flora understood exactly. She was surprised that Kathleen couldn't see it for herself. But life was always very straightforward for Kathleen.

It was almost six weeks before Mary rang, her voice jubilant.

There had been a letter from Chris that very morning, from India. He had a badly broken ankle and had been ill with malaria, but he was well on the road to recovery, and should be coming home before too long. For Chris, the war was virtually over.

'Holy Mother be praised, he's safe, Michael!' Kathleen's voice trembled between thankfulness and joy. 'Not that I'll believe it until he's home!'

'Oh, ye of little faith,' he mocked, but his own mouth was not quite steady as he gathered her into his arms. 'God is good.'

'Indeed he is,' she said against his coat.

Tears prickled Liz's eyes as she watched them, but they were tears of happiness. Jimmy would not begrudge them this moment. And there was good news for Rita, too. In early July Frank's destroyer had come limping into port at last, with a great hole gouged in its side above the waterline, some of its equipment damaged beyond repair, and the loss of two lives. But Frank was safe and well.

A new surge of optimism ran through the house, and all the shortages and difficulties in the bakehouse couldn't diminish it. The regular customers, too, considering themselves to be an extension of the family, shared in their joys as they had in their sorrows.

Time was pressing, and Leigh had been working flat out with very little respite. But now the complex assortment of barracks, warehouses, repair workshops, control tower and runways was beginning to look like an operational Air Base, one of several dotted around the country, built to accommodate the B17s that would be crossing the North Atlantic on the route he had helped to pioneer. Goose Bay, Labrador, Reykjavik, Greenland, Prestwick – his flying muscles itched at the very thought of it. He'd been grounded for so long he was beginning to feel as though he'd lost a limb. His technical as well as practical know-how had been put to good and effective use, but now that usefulness was almost at an end, and he couldn't wait to get back where he belonged.

'I'm just a flier at heart,' he told Flora. 'Dad would tell you, I'm no damned good behind a desk, telling others what to do. I get fidgety and snap at everyone.'

As soon as Flora learned he was to be around for a while, she had told him that he was welcome to treat Rose Lodge as a home from home whenever he needed a break. Her evacuees had gone home, and the civil servants kept to themselves.

Flora's drawing room contained an excellent radiogram and a wide selection of records, her library was well stocked with books for all tastes, and there was a feeling of comfort and ease about the place, so that a fellow didn't need to worry about disarranging a few cushions. And if, as sometimes happened, she was out about her business when he arrived, Mrs Meadows would look after him in her own efficient, self-effacing way, and leave him to relax, put his feet up, and enjoy whatever took his fancy.

It was from Flora that he heard about Jimmy. He sent Elizabeth a brief note, expressing his sympathy, which in spite of everything was genuine. Too many young men, some of them little more than High School kids , were getting killed in this war, and there would be a whole lot more grieving wives and mothers before they were through.

'How has she taken it?'

'Much as you'd expect. When someone as young and lively as Jimmy dies, it can affect their loved ones in curious ways. The more imaginative they are, the harder it is not feel they must shoulder some of the blame. I've seen it happen a lot recently.' Flora gave him a straight look. 'It's going to take Liz a long time to get her life back into perspective.'

She watched his face. His jaw was taut, and his freckles stood out starkly against a skin grown pale. And then he sighed.

'I can wait,' he said at last. 'As it happens, I shall have to go back to the States just as soon as I've tied up all the loose ends here. And when I come back,' his voice softened to a kind of crooning, 'I'll be flying one of those beauties again. No-one, but no-one, is going to stop me getting into the action.'

He sat forward as he spoke, hands between his knees. His hair stood up in red spikes where he had leaned against the sofa back, and there was a gleam in his eyes that made Flora pity anyone who tried to get in his way. 'You really want it that much?'

'I surely do.' He grinned. 'Hell, they're not going to ground me. I may be going on thirty-three, but I'm one of the best damned fliers they've got.' Leigh sobered, staring down at his hands as though noticing them for the first time. 'So, you see, it's not likely

I'll be contacting Elizabeth for quite a while. In fact, I've decided it would be better all round to stay right out of her life until we've got the bastards licked. Flying bombers in wartime is no job for a man with commitments, and no way am I going to cause Liz fresh grief, or risk making her a widow twice over.'

'We are cheerful this evening. Has it occurred to you that she may not see things your way?'

His voice hardened. 'My dear Flora, she won't know if you don't tell her.'

'I never thought I'd hear such chauvinistic twaddle from you.' Flora was scornful. 'Liz has a mind and a will of her own – yes, and a right to be asked what *she* wants. If nothing else, this war is proving that young women like Liz are not delicate creatures who need protecting. You could end up losing her. Have you considered that?'

'I've thought about it,' he said doggedly. 'It's a chance I'll just have to take.'

Chris came home to late summer. His ship docked at Southampton and Mary, granted an extended leave, went down to bring him home. She was nervous, unsure what to expect. But all fear fled the moment she saw him. He looked bronzed and fit, and was walking reasonably well with the aid of two sticks, which he threw aside to hold her in a wordless embrace that went on and on, until she whispered gently, 'I'm not goin' to run away, pet.'

There was a snuffling against her neck, and she wasn't sure if it was laughter or tears, or a mixture of both, but eventually his hold slackened.

'I've dreamed about this so many times, I'm afraid you'll vanish if I let go,' he muttered, and then lifted his head and kissed her long and hard.

She said shakily, 'Then I reckon we've both been having the same dream. But it's over, Chris love. I'm not going anywhere without you.'

Once the first emotional reunion was over, however, Mary realized that it was going to take a while for him to adjust. They took the journey home in easy stages, reaching Myndd Howe on the second day, and staying in the little hotel where Kathleen and Flora had stayed. Rita gave him a joyous welcome, and when he rang home, he could hear the trembling in Mam's voice as she asked him in her prosaic way if he was all right.

'I'm fine, Mam. We'll be home in a couple of days.'

'Don't hurry, lad,' she said. 'We can wait, now we know you're safe, and your Mary'll want you to herself for a while.'

But he wasn't fine, not really. He had fantasized, in the stinking heat of the jungle, about making love to Mary, but the reality was a fiasco, and he turned away, shamed by his pathetic performance.

'It doesn't matter,' Mary insisted, cradling him like a baby. 'You don't have to prove anything to me. We've got the rest of our lives to *make* love. For now, loving itself is enough. I *love* you, and I've got you back, and that's all I care about.'

' 'E's comin' home, then, your Chris? I bet yer can't wait. Proper peaky, yer've been lukin'.'

'Aah, well, there's no-one but a mother knows warrit's like when 'er son's off, doin' God knows what. A son's special, when all's said an' done. Isn't that so, Mrs Ryan? Eh, yer wouldn't 'ave any of them sweet buns, would yer? Only our kids get that ravenous, an' the sweet ration goes nowhere with eight of them!'

Kathleen murmured to Ellen as they passed, 'I wish I knew how they get to know your news almost before you do yourself.'

'Must be something in the Mersey air.'

'We don't have no trouble gerrin' sweets an' that,' Ada Killigan was saying, her not inconsiderable chest puffed out in pride. 'Our Lily's American friend's ever so generous. Never comes ter the house but 'e brings us all kinds of things – ciggies, tinned salmon, chocs, and always sweeties an' chewing gum fer the kids.'

'Their Eddie's not doing so bad out of the Yanks, either, if what I hear is true,' Ellen said later. 'Lily's *friend* has introduced him to one of his mates, and between them, they're running a very nice little business on the side out of U.S. Army stores.'

'Until they get caught. But then, wheeling and dealing's been the breath of life to Eddie from the time he could toddle. I'm just thankful Joey doesn't have anything to do with him these days. It's a pity, though, because it could give the Americans a bad name, and most, like that Aaron our Liz invited home, are really nice – just a bit lonely and missing their folks. I always think, if it was our Chris, or one of the others . . .'

'I know what you mean. There's one called Rufus, a sergeant, came with one of Arnie's mates. He's been in to see Arnie once or twice.' Ellen was blushing slightly. 'Brought him some American cigarettes. Not that Arnie was at all grateful – said they tasted like something unmentionable. I wasn't altogether sorry, 'cos he smokes too much as it is, but he needn't have said it to the man's face. Rufus didn't take offence, though, and like Ada said, he's been ever so kind to the kiddies. He even brought me some make-up, though I don't know when I'll ever get to wear it. I wondered if your Liz might like some, knowing how hard it is to get decent stuff.'

'Thanks, but Shirley Anne sometimes has more than she needs, and she passes it on to Liz. You keep what Rufus gave you, and see you use it,' Kathleen said, thinking it was no bad thing for Ellen to have a nice man paying her a bit of attention. Arnie's friends only ever saw her as Arnie's wife – ageless, hard-working and kind, but hardly meriting a second look. Yet Ellen was only in her mid-thirties, and could be quite attractive if she made the effort. A little make-up and some kindly attention would do wonders for her.

Thanks to Mary's foresight, coming home wasn't quite such an ordeal as Chris had expected. Without telling him, she had rung Kathleen and asked her to play down the family welcome. 'I know it's asking a lot, but if you could try to make it normal, like he was just coming home on leave . . .'

'Chris is all right?' Kathleen's voice was sharp. 'Because if you're trying to prepare me for bad news, I'd sooner you just came right out with it.'

'No, no, really. He looks great. It's just that he's still a bit keyed up. He doesn't seem to want to talk about Burma. And, though he hasn't said, I think he's getting a bit worked up about facing Liz – having to tell her about Jimmy, so you'd better warn her. But there's nothing time won't cure, I promise. We should be home late afternoon or early evening.'

Kathleen swallowed the hurt of realizing that she was no longer the first woman in her son's life, and primed everyone to behave as naturally as possible. Michael had been out to an auction, and came home, triumphant, with a case of tinned salmon, a water-damaged tub of butter and a hundredweight of barley sugars.

'God in Heaven!' Kathleen cried. 'What are we going to do with that lot? We don't sell sweets.'

Michael smiled sheepishly. 'Well I was hoping to get some sugar, only there was none to be had. And it occurred to me that if we took off the wrappers, we could melt the sweets down. Use the syrup, like that maple stuff your May's always sending us.'

'But there must be thousands here!' she cried, horrified. 'Unwrapping them could take forever. Lord save us, Michael Ryan, have we not got enough to do? And our Chris due home this evening.' She told him about Mary's phone call. 'It all sounds a bit melodramatic, if you ask me. The young don't take things in their stride like we do.'

Michael shook his head. 'Mary's not like that. She's a sensible girl, so we'd best do as she asks.'

'I suppose so.' Kathleen sighed. 'Oh, for goodness sake, put those sweets away. We'll think about them tomorrow.'

She and Michael were alone in the living room when they arrived, which helped. Chris was a bit emotional at first – they were all a bit emotional, come to that; it was only to be expected. He limped about the room, unable to settle until the familiarity of it had wrapped itself round him. He ran his fingers over the piano keys, and paused for a long time by the sideboard, picking up one photograph after another, holding on to the picture of himself and Jimmy longer than the rest. There was a bleakness behind his eyes as he put it down and turned away, and Kathleen knew then that her daughter-in-law had been right to prepare them.

So they sat and talked about everyday things. Chris wanted to know how his father's arm was, and soon Michael was telling him about the problems of changing over to national flour, and they fell into a discussion about the various restrictions. And then the children came in with Liz, and what might have been a difficult meeting turned to laughter as Rosie studied her uncle for a moment with a predatory female eye, and then ran across to tug at his trouser leg.

'I'm Wosie,' she lisped.

'Mind your Uncle Chris's leg,' Liz said. 'It's poorly.'

'Wosie kiss it better,' she insisted.

Chris lifted Rosie on to his knee, glad of the distraction. 'The leg, or rather the ankle's, heaps better. And you're getting more like your mother every day, miss. A regular sauce pot.'

'Sauce pot,' she chuckled, while Georgy looked on wistfully.

Chris put Rosie down at once, and transferred his attention to his small brother. 'Not so small any longer, though, are you, my lad?'

'Georgy's going to school soon.'

'Five already? My goodness, how time flies. We'll have you working in the bakehouse before you know it.'

Taking advantage of the easy atmosphere created by the children, Liz came across and kissed him lightly. 'Welcome home, brother dear.'

He clasped her hand as it rested on his shoulder. 'Liz . . .'

'It's all right. We can talk later – much later, when you're ready.' And Mary smiled at her with gratitude.

It was a while before Joey came in, bringing Dandy with him.

Dandy now manned the sector post only two days a week, sharing the task with Alf Killigan and Alf's brother-in-law, and even that had become something of a formality. There had been no raids on Liverpool since January; and please God, would be no more. But the war went on for others, as the sight of his much loved grandson reminded him. Loquacious by nature, he now found himself lost for words, and could do no more than wring Chris's hand and tell him how good it was to have him home.

Joey, however, had come straight from cricket practice, and was so elated at having been promoted to the seniors' first team that he accepted Chris's presence almost as though he never been away.

'Old Misery Guts says I'm the best fast bowler they've had in a long time!'

'Joey!' Michael frowned. 'That is no way to speak of a coach.'

'It's what everyone calls him.' Joey, cheerfully unrepentant peeled off his pullover. 'No-one's ever seen him crack a smile – even when we wallop the opposition.'

'Well, you're the right build for a fast bowler,' Chris said with a grin. 'You must be almost as tall as me, now.'

'Don't encourage him, Chris, for heaven's sake. Joey, don't throw your pullover in a heap like that. It's got to last. At two coupons an ounce, I can't be forever buying wool to knit you another. I wish you put as much enthusiasm into studying as you do into sport, or scouts, or tinkering with those old engines.' Kathleen sighed. 'Goodness knows what your School Certificate results will be like.'

Her young rip of a son picked up the pullover with a good-natured shrug, folded it and put it on the stair. 'I told you, you worry too much. I'll get through.'

And Chris, already looking more relaxed, said with a grin, 'Good old Mam. Still hoping to produce a genius.'

'I gave that up a long time ago,' she said gruffly. 'As for you, my lad, home five minutes, and already full of cheek. A good job your Mary's well able to keep you in check.'

The one thing Kathleen refused to abandon that evening, even at the risk of upsetting her son's delicate balance of emotions, was the family's decade of the rosary, offered on this occasion as a thanksgiving for his safe return. But Chris showed no sign of breaking down, and she began to think Mary had exaggerated his mental state.

Over an early supper, Michael's latest purchases were discussed. Liz almost purred with pleasure at the mention of the butter and immediately fell to deciding how they could best use it, whilst the huge box of sweets had them all in fits of laughter. It was Chris who championed his father. 'I think it was a brilliant stroke, Dad. They'll make excellent syrup, melted down.'

'Hear, hear,' echoed Liz. 'Take no notice, Dad. Auntie May's maple syrup has been a life-saver more than once.'

'I agree. In fact, I don't see why we can't start unwrapping them tonight. There's sure to be something on the wireless we can listen to – '

'Henry Hall's Guest Night,' Liz said enthusiastically.

'Liz!' Kathleen was outraged. 'Putting Chris to work almost before he's through the door. I won't hear of it!'

'For God's sake, Mam, stop treating me like a visitor. I'm not ill, and I want to help.' His harsh voice and abruptness of manner shocked Kathleen out of her complacency. Chris had never spoken to her like that in his life. There was an awkward little silence, broken by Michael.

'I'm grateful for the offer, Chris. Seems to me I'm going to need all the help I can get, and many hands make light work, as they say. And the sooner I have the syrup, the better. I'm hoping you might have some ideas on how best to use it.'

Dandy backed him up. 'Well, I'm game, if the rest of yous are.'

The moment passed. And in the end, it couldn't have worked out better if they'd planned it. The mountain of sweets caused so much hilarity that they could hardly hear the wireless, and by the time Kathleen called a halt, all awkwardness had vanished, and they had accounted for about half the total, filled a big bowl with sweets, and an even bigger one with spent papers. And if the odd barley sugar found its way into a salivating mouth, no-one missed it.

Liz had moved her things into Shirley Anne's room, so that Mary and Chris could have her bed. No-one had mentioned how long they would be staying. She knew Mam hoped her son would be around for some time, but it wasn't that simple. Chris still had unfinished business.

His ankle, which had been broken in a fall during the long, dangerous trek from Burma to India, had been hastily strapped up by one of his companions en route, and had set badly, requiring painful re-setting later. As a result, it was doubtful whether he would ever recover full mobility. He was waiting to be called to one of the army hospitals – he hadn't yet been told where or when – for a comprehensive examination, which would almost certainly lead to the recommendation that he be granted an honourable discharge. In addition, he had been notified that his own regimental chiefs, together with certain War Office boffins, were anxious to question him. And when all that was over, he would surely want to be near Mary.

But the days passed, and he still avoided any mention of Jimmy. It was as though he had never existed. Liz became convinced that she would have to coax her brother to talk, for his own sake as much as hers. To her surprise, Mary agreed.

'The quiet ones are often the worst. I can see that what he went through is eating away at him,' she said with obvious worry. 'But he won't go to the doctor, and he refuses to talk about it to me, and I'm afraid that the longer it festers, the worse it'll get. It doesn't seem very fair to you, though.'

Liz assured her that she could cope, that she and Chris had

always been quite close. And so a plan was hatched. Mary persuaded Mam to go shopping with her in town, and Ellen said she and Dot could manage the shop.

'That just leaves us and the children, brother dear,' Liz said. 'Listen, I have to go over to Elizabeth's. It's too nice a day to keep the children indoors, but if you came too, we could take them with us – stop off in Sefton Park for an hour or so.'

He wasn't enthusiastic, but she insisted that the fresh air would do him good – a stricture that made him wrinkle his nose and call her 'bossy boots'.

It was an incongruous setting for grim recollections – an English park on a sunny day, alive with children's laughter. But in a way its very normality made things easier. At first they sat on a bench in the sunshine, watching Rosie picking daisies and imperiously ordering Georgy to do likewise, although Georgy was more interested in a roving dog of dubious parentage that came sniffing at his feet. Finally, Liz gathered her courage and began to speak.

'Chris, I know you don't want to be reminded, but I would like to know what happened, if you can bring yourself to tell me. You see, I find it very difficult to lay Jimmy completely to rest in my mind – '

She heard him make a choking sound, and without looking at him, put out a reassuring hand to cover his. It was knotted into a tight ball of muscle, but she persevered. 'You don't have to go into detail – in fact, I'd rather you didn't. But I have to know the truth. And I think Sunny would rather know, too.'

Chris's voice, when it came, was the voice of a stranger, brutally to the point, leaving no room for doubt. 'Jimmy never even knew what hit him. We were in thick jungle – and one minute he was alert, eager – checking every tree, every shadow that moved, inching us forward bit by bit . . . The next, there was a sharp rifle crack, and he was flat on his face with a bullet through his head.'

Liz swallowed and said, 'I see. Thank you for telling me. It sounds pretty awful.'

'It was. I mean, at least you knew where you were, fighting the Germans. But this – there'd be a skirmish, and then the little yellow buggers would just melt into the trees – silent and invisible. They didn't need to come into the open that often – it was easier to stay hidden and pick us off, one by one. But you could smell them, feel them all around you, and you'd wonder who'd be next. Christ! It's a bloody miracle any of us got away.'

The obscenities tripped so easily off his tongue; like Francis, like thousands of others to whom violence was anathema, her gentle brother had been irrevocably changed by war.

What Chris couldn't describe to her or anyone, not even Mary – especially not Mary – was the cringing mind-numbing fear. Not fear of death, but of what would happen if he wasn't killed outright. He had seen it mirrored many times in the faces of mates, too badly injured to keep up with the retreating army.

'Time and again, we had to leave the worst of the wounded behind.' Liz heard the break in his voice, the searing bitterness, and she knew that this was what was really eating at him. 'It made sense, of course – salvage what you can to fight another day – but I'm glad I didn't have to make the decision. Turning my back on those poor devils is the worst thing I've ever had to do. The look in their eyes still haunts me – I think it always will.'

Liz's heart ached for him. Had she been wrong, forcing him to bring this into the open? She kept her voice steady. 'You did everything you could. That's all any of us can do. Only God can work miracles.' He muttered something blasphemous, which she ignored. 'Listen to me, Chris. I know that my very worst experiences can never be compared with yours, but even I've seen, and heard, and forced myself to do things that will haunt me forever. The memory may never go away, but I promise you, love, it *will* fade to bearable proportions.'

He slumped a little on the seat, his head thrown back, and the hand she was holding convulsively gripped hers. They remained like that for some moments, until Rosie, curious, ran up to ask: 'Uncle Cwis sleeping?'

He choked on a half laugh, sat up, and said shakily, 'Not sleeping, little one. More like painfully waking up.' And as Rosie lifted her shoulders in a gesture of bafflement, and ran away again, he said quietly, 'Thanks, Liz.'

'What are sisters for?' she said lightly, but couldn't quite hide her emotion. 'Have you decided yet – what you'll do?'

Chris, still dragging his thoughts together, looked blank for a moment. 'Do?'

'When all the formalities are over. I suppose you'll want to be near Mary?'

'Well, I certainly can't face staying here without her.' He looked up suddenly, his eyes pleading with her to understand. And she did.

'I think you're right,' she said practically. 'Families can sometimes be stifling when they most want to be supportive.'

'Sounds as though you speak from experience,' he said wryly.

'Perhaps. I suppose, however old you are, your parents still tend to think of you as a child – though ours are more understanding than most. Dad, especially.'

'A wise old bird, Dad,' he agreed, visibly relaxing. 'It's not quite the same in the bakehouse now, though, with Steve and Albert there. I used to like it best when there was just me and Dad – and you, of course. But it's no use looking back.' He smiled suddenly. 'Speaking of which, however did you manage to talk Dad into installing a mixer?'

'That was Mam. She kept on until she wore him down. It makes sense, anyway. His arm will never be quite what it was, and Steve and I between us clinched matters by persuading him that it's perfectly possible to move with the times without dropping your standards.'

'The voice of experience,' he mocked gently. 'Poor Liz. This war's knocked your plans well and truly for six. Just when you were getting going so well, too.'

'My plans will keep. And, who knows, it may all be for the best. By the time I do get going properly again, I shall be that bit older and wiser.'

'I'd say you were pretty wise, right now.'

Liz felt herself turning pink. 'Thank you, brother dear. Rosie, do stop hitting that poor dog. He only wants to be friends with Georgy.' She stood up. 'Time to go home, I think.' A sudden thought struck her. 'Of course, there's always our Rita's. You'd be near enough to Mary there.' And I'll have a quiet word with her not to fuss you, she thought.

It was a good suggestion. Myndd Howe was the ideal place in which to recuperate, and well before Christmas, Chris had found a part-time job with a smaller baker in the high street there, and

Mary wrote that he was steadily healing in mind and body with every week that passed.

Dandy spent a lot of time listening to the wireless following the news avidly. He was jubilant when, in November, the Allies invaded North Africa, and Churchill said on the wireless that, 'This is not the end. It is not even the beginning of the end. But it is, perhaps, the end of the beginning.'

'And he's right, lad, you'll see,' he told his grandson as he helped him stick more Union Jacks in the appropriate places. 'Things'll start looking up now. Our Monty'll soon make short work of Rommel's army.' On the Far East map, too, one or two American flags had begun to brighten the scene around Midway and the Solomon Islands.

Chapter Three

The rumour had been around for a while, but soon after Easter, Steve came in full of it. Even then, it seemed too incredible to be true.

'Are you sure, Dad?' Kathleen demanded, when Dandy came in at dinner time with the same story. 'I mean, times are hard for all of us just now, but that business was always a little goldmine, and will be again one day. Alec Munnings must be mad!'

'Or desperate.'

'Not that desperate, surely? He couldn't have picked a worse time.'

'It could be he had no choice,' Michael suggested, as Liz settled the children and Kathleen dished up her version of Woolton pie. 'Steve's old workmates have been hinting for some time that young Alec's been bleeding the firm dry. And now that George Wilson's given notice . . .'

'But George has been doing their books for more than twenty years!'

'Maybe,' said Dandy, 'but a man can only take so much and George has had a bellyful. Creditors have been pressing since New Year, but he couldn't get Alec to take it seriously. Now they're threatening to sue, and George is a proud man – he's taking the shame of it personally. I've no wish to speak ill of the dead, but Fred gave that lad ideas above his station from the first, sendin' him to a fancy school to mix with the nobs. Small wonder he shot off to London when he came into that money.'

'That was Hilda's influence,' Kathleen said. 'Her only real pride in Fred was when she pushed him into becoming Councillor Munnings. Now he's gone. And he's probably left her that well off, she won't care if Alec sells the business, so long as it means she doesn't have to bail him out.'

Liz was very quiet. She wasn't all that surprised to hear about Alec. From the little Shirley Anne had told her, she suspected that even then his appalling vanity had led him to live above his means, and a lieutenant's pay wouldn't go far if he wanted to impress his fellow officers, or his posh relations. Perhaps he had hoped his wife's money would support his profligate ways, and had been disappointed. Whatever the reason, his present behaviour merely confirmed what she had always known – that he was a fool. And worse, a short-sighted fool, if he couldn't see that in selling the business he would lose the only asset he had, for whatever he got for it would soon go the way of the rest.

Out of curiosity, Liz asked, 'How much would a business like that fetch right now, Dad?'

Michael, surprised by the question, shrugged. 'Lord, Lizzie, I haven't the faintest idea. I wouldn't have thought anyone in their right mind would want to buy into the trade at all just now. But your Mam's the financial brain of this family.'

Kathleen said it was almost impossible to calculate without knowing all the details. 'They lost at least one shop in the blitz, and some of their retail rounds, too – a couple of the others have already come over to us. The main value lies in their bakehouse, which Fred took great pride in, and the Church Street shop. That's a prime site, and the damage it suffered was negligible. But against that, if the business is on the slide – and taking present conditions into account – ' She did a hasty mental calculation. 'I reckon Alec would be lucky to clear five thousand after settling debts – if he can find a buyer. His only hope might be a big company prepared to invest with an eye to the future.'

'I suppose so,' Liz said.

Dot was almost always cheerful. But one hot airless July morning she arrived later than usual, with apologies from her mother, and looking as though she had been crying. 'Mam's ever so sorry, Mrs Ryan. It's me Dad's lungs. Proper bad durin' the night, he was, an' she's waitin' on the doctor.'

Arnie's lungs had been causing concern for some time. 'It's the fluid – it collects, with him not being able to move,' Ellen had explained. 'You know how I've tried to make him give up his smokes, but he can be very stubborn, and he has so few pleasures. I thought the shortages might help, but his pals turn up, regular as clockwork of a weekend, with a couple of bottles of ale and his Players Weights. They seem determined to keep him supplied.'

But this wasn't just another attack. Ellen arrived an hour or so later, pale and in a hurry. 'Last winter took it out of him more than usual, and he's never really picked up. Doc Graham says there's no more he can do, Arnie'll have to go into hospital. It won't be the first time, of course, but I've never seen him this bad. The ambulance is on its way. I've left Hester with him while I ran to tell you, and she'll look out for the children. Only, I'll have to go with him. He's getting himself ever so worked up, and then he can't breathe hardly at all.'

'Of course you must go. And try not to worry.' Kathleen sounded more optimistic than she felt. 'Hospital's much the best place for him.'

Dot had come through in time to hear most of what her mother said. She stood biting her lip. Ellen ran to put her arms round her. 'Chin up, lovey. I'm counting on you.' And then she was gone.

Two days later, Arnie Cassidy died. 'Out of his misery at last, God rest him,' Kathleen said to Liz. 'Though he's been stuck there in that bed for so long, it's going to take Ellen a while to adjust.'

Aunt Flora, who hadn't visited Fortune Street for several weeks, finally arrived just as Liz was nerving herself to telephone her. Flora's car was laden down with good things from Caulderbank's kitchen garden, which had doubled in size with help from his grandson.

'Onions,' sighed Kathleen. 'Bless you, Flora, I haven't seen a decent one in ages. Cousin Tom has been keeping us fairly well supplied with vegetables, but his onions aren't doing well this year.' There were carrots, too, and runner beans, pounds of them, and early cooking apples, as well as tomatoes from the greenhouse. 'I know what Liz and I will be doing for the next few evenings. It's a good job we've plenty of bottling jars.'

Liz seized her opportunity as her mother took the last of the fruit through to the scullery. 'Aunt Flora, there's something I have to talk to you about. It's very important.'

The suppressed urgency in her voice was not lost on Flora. In all the months since Jimmy's death, she had not once asked about Leigh. Was this the first crack in the armour? And if so, how was she to deal with it? Leigh had remained emphatic about not resuming the relationship . . . However, she had never been one to duck out of a difficult situation.

'Kath? Can you spare your daughter for an hour or so when we've had a cup of tea? I'd like her to help me deliver some clothes to one of the relief centres. There's still a demand, even after all this time.' It wasn't entirely an untruth, for she did have to call in at one of the local centres.

'Could we go into town, if that's all right with you?' Liz said, once they were on their way. 'To Church Street?'

Completely mystified, Flora agreed. Perhaps Liz wanted to buy a special dress and needed advice, though the subterfuge seemed unnecessary. 'Anywhere special you'd like me to stop?' she asked drily as they turned Bunny's Corner.

Liz flushed and bit her lip. 'Just here would be fine. I haven't taken leave of my senses, though you may well think so when you hear what I'm about to say.'

Exasperation was fast setting in. Flora applied the handbrake, switched off the engine and turned to face her discomfited niece, in time to see her dark lashes flutter down in a kind of contained panic. 'Elizabeth Ryan, I'm a plain speaking woman, as you well know. Can't stand waffle, so for goodness sake, get on and say whatever it is.'

'Yes, of course. I'm sorry.' Liz had never felt so nervous, but she plunged in before her courage failed her. 'Aunt Flora, would you lend me some money – quite a lot of money, in fact?'

This was so far from what Flora had been expecting that she was reduced to silence. Liz glanced quickly at her face, and found it unreadable, which only increased her nerves.

'I don't – that is, it would be a proper loan, all legally drawn up, at a proper rate of interest – and I'd pay you back just as quickly as I could.'

'How much is a lot?'

Liz swallowed, and said in a rush, 'About six thousand guineas – maybe more.'

This time Flora made no attempt to conceal her surprise. 'That *is* a lot,' she conceded. 'And what exactly are you intending to do with this money, should I agree?'

'Buy Munnings'.' Voiced at last, the idea immediately seemed preposterous. Liz saw her aunt's eyes widen, and waited anxiously for some kind of reaction.

Flora slowly turned her head to look across the road at the shop in question, and Liz tried to see it through her eyes. Two of its leaded windows were now replaced by plain glass as a result of the bombing, and several of the windows above were boarded up, but it was still a handsome frontage.

I must be getting old, thought Flora. Even for Liz, this is a bit extreme. To give herself time to collect her thoughts, she said weakly, 'Whatever would you want with another shop?'

'Not just the shop. The whole business.' Before her aunt could condemn the idea out of hand, she hurried on to explain about Alec selling up, and why. 'It's been on the market for ages – He must be getting desperate.'

'Well I can see it's a tempting proposition, but I should have thought you'd all got enough on your hands right now without taking on an ailing bakery business.' Flora gave her niece an old-fashioned look. 'What do Michael and Kathleen think – or would I be right in thinking you haven't confided in them?'

Liz flushed. 'I wanted to sound you out first,' she admitted. 'You understand about buying and selling property, and besides, you know what Dad's like about borrowing money . . .'

'Especially from me,' Flora murmured.

'Years ago, it was one of Mam's ambitions to have a shop in the centre of town,' she continued, as if this counted as a point in its favour. 'Now even she would probably think I'd taken leave of my senses. But I haven't, Aunt Flora. I'm not exactly a novice, and I've given it a great deal of thought.'

'Hm. Well, come on, let's get out and take a closer look.'

'You go,' Liz said. 'Someone might recognize me.'

She watched her aunt cross the road and stroll past the shop, stopping to look in the window. She still had the kind of elegance that rose above clothes rationing, and had nothing to do with age. It was a look Liz had always envied, and tried to emulate, but it wasn't easy on sixty-six coupons a year. And anyway, clothes weren't everything. That kind of elegance came from inside.

Aunt Flora turned back, and Liz caught her breath as she went into Munnings', coming out a few moments later with a cake bag. She placed it on the back seat and slid back behind the wheel.

'Well, the staff seem to know their job – a bit slapdash, perhaps.'

'I'm not surprised. Slackness has been seeping through the whole business since Alec got his greedy little hands on it. There's no incentive to try, when they know the firm's debts are piling up. But there's nothing wrong with Munnings' that couldn't be put right with good management. The reputation for quality still clings, and there are still enough good men in the bakehouse to pull things round. They just need to feel that someone's in charge – and quickly.'

'And who would that someone be? You?' Flora was intrigued, in spite of her misgivings.

'In a way. Actually, I'd thought of asking Chris and Mary to run it.'

Flora chuckled. 'That would please Kath, once she got over the shock. Would Chris agree, do you think?'

'Once he was convinced he could handle it. And he could, with Mary behind him. She's got a lot about her, has Mary.'

'A bit like your Mam and Dad, in fact?'

'A bit, if you like. I'm sure Chris would love to come back to Liverpool. And you can see there's plenty of room above. I haven't been inside, of course, and it's partly used as offices at present, but it should make a splendid roomy flat.'

Flora was so pleased to see Liz enthusiastic again that she was loath to prick the bubble. 'You really have got this all worked out, haven't you?'

'Yes, I have. And you must admit it makes sense.' Liz leaned forward, her whole being intense. 'Aunt Flora, I know I'm asking a lot, but I really *do* want that business.'

Flora heard the quiver of intensity in her voice. It had been there earlier when she spoke of Alec Munnings. She had never thought of her niece as a vindictive creature, but it did arouse misgivings. 'Now hold on, young lady. I'm not lending you money so you can work off some kind of grudge . . .'

'You wouldn't be. I do have a powerful incentive, certainly, for reasons I can't explain. Not now. But that's only a part of why I want to do this. There are many other reasons. Good, practical ones.'

There was a long silence. Then her aunt nodded.

'I tell you what I'll do. I'll get Bill Yates, who handles my affairs, to make an approach. He can do that without naming his client, and he'll be given access to all the necessary books, records and so on. If he's satisfied, we'll authorize him to make an offer, and you'll get your loan.'

'Oh, Aunt Flora!' In the confines of the car, Liz couldn't hug her as she wanted to, but she squeezed her hand. 'You won't regret it.'

'Don't count your chickens, child. There's a long way to go. I just wish I knew why it matters so much to you.'

'It's not up to me, or I'd tell you.'

'Fair enough. And as for telling Kathleen and Michael, it might be as well to wait until we hear what Bill has to say.' Flora switched on the engine. 'Now I'd better take you home, and get off to the Centre with these clothes.'

As she was about to get out of the car in Fortune Street, Liz turned back suddenly. 'Aunt Flora, you've always been quite close to Leigh, haven't you? How is he these days?'

The question, coming without warning, caught her aunt unprepared. 'Lord, child, you've got a mind like a jack-rabbit!'

'Sorry. It's just – I know he was working at Burtonwood. I thought you might have seen him recently?' Liz persisted, trying to sound casual and not quite succeeding.

'Not recently. That job finished some weeks ago, and he went back to America.' Her niece, however, wasn't content to leave it there.

'But he will be back?' It wasn't really a question. Liz knew Leigh so well by now that she knew he would want to get in on the scrap. 'If – when he does come, would you ask him to – to look me up sometime?'

Flora sighed and eyed her keenly. 'Are you sure this is what you want, Liz?'

'Quite sure. When Jimmy died, I felt – a kind of guilt, I suppose. It was silly, really. He never knew I was in love with Leigh, and I never let it make any difference, if you know what I mean . . .'

'I believe I do.

'But now – well, war makes everything so uncertain, doesn't it?' Liz suddenly sounded very young. 'And if there is still a chance for us, it would be silly to let that chance slip away . . . Don't you think? So if you should see him, I thought perhaps you might tell him I'd be happy to hear from him.'

Flora cleared her throat. 'I'll certainly tell him, if I see him.' But I know what his answer will be, damn him. And damn the war.

'You're very quiet,' Kathleen said later that evening as they sat together, slicing runner beans and pressing them into jars between layers of salt. 'Nothing wrong, is there?'

Liz came to with a start. It had been a long while since she had allowed thoughts of Leigh into her conscious mind, and now he wouldn't go away. She had been trying to block him out by concentrating on her future plans, but without much success.

'Nothing at all, Mam. I'm just a bit tired.' But a faint flush stole up under her skin as she spoke.

It was very strange, sitting in the darkened cinema, watching a beautiful young girl laughing, loving, dancing, singing, and trying to convince yourself that the lovely creature on the screen was your sister.

Shirley Anne's picture had been premiered in London several weeks earlier, and received wonderful reviews. '*Mayfair Melodies*,' wrote one correspondent, 'is a tonic for these uncertain times, conjuring up the heady froth of champagne; a delightful extravagant feast, guaranteed to revive weary minds and hearts. And much of its success may be attributed to the little lady who lights up the screen with an appealing combination of talent, magical singing and dancing, and a youthful zest for life. Truly, a new star is born.'

The first showing in Liverpool was on a raw November night at the Paramount in London Road, and what the occasion lacked in London polish was more than compensated for by the warmth and fervour of the welcoming crowds, for Shirley Anne was one of their own, coming home in triumph. For hadn't she been 'doing her bit', entertaining the troops in the Middle East, after the Allied assault on El Alamein and more recently in Tunisia. That she had arrived home just in time to make a personal appearance in this dreary winter of 1943 endeared her even more to those who, unable to get seats, waited in the pitch darkness to catch a glimpse of the golden-haired figure who stepped out of the chauffeur-driven car, her pale skirts floating on the night air.

The family were present *en masse*. Rita, Chris and Mary had come up for the occasion. Chris had rung up two nights earlier, bursting with news.

'It's Mary, Mam – she's going to have a baby!'

'Chris! That's wonderful news. When's it due?'

'Oh, I'm not sure. She's only just had it confirmed – sometime next spring, I suppose.'

Men, thought Kathleen. 'So she'll be leaving the ATS?'

'Very soon. We'll tell you all about it when we come.'

There had been lots of juggling with clothing coupons, to ensure that no-one let Shirley Anne down. Everyone insisted that Mam, at least, was to buy something special for the occasion, and Flora went with her to make sure she didn't take the first thing that came to hand. They came back with a simple lace frock in a pretty shade of grey-blue, with which she could wear all the accessories she had worn for Liz's wedding, and a hairdresser friend of Ellen's had offered to do her hair.

Liz had already decided to alter her favourite two-year-old cream satin, and Flora volunteered a couple of her evening gowns, to be altered for Rita and Mary if necessary.

'There are some great ideas for creating new dresses out of old in Mam's *Home Chat* this week,' Liz told the girls when they arrived. 'And the material in these frocks of Aunt Flora's is really beautiful. I thought perhaps the blue silk for Mary, and this lovely purple colour for you, Rita. We could soon run them up between us.'

Mrs Frith had been invited to sit with the family during the showing of the film, and had the pleasure of seeing Shirley Anne step up to the stage to make a short, witty speech which was greeted with cheers and thunderous applause. She also went with the family to the official reception at the Adelphi afterwards, decked out – as old Nora might have said – like a May horse, in clouds of grey chiffon.

'Wonderful!' she murmured over and over, dabbing at misty eyes with a lace handkerchief. 'Like a fairy story! If only Miss Eglantine could have been here tonight.' The dance teacher had been a victim of the bombing.

Joey, having been dragooned into attending, overheard her tremulous paeans, and couldn't have agreed more about the fairy story bit, though he had to admit their Shirley Anne was good. Even so, it had been a bit embarrassing, having his sister in a soppy film. He had resigned himself to the fact that his form-mates in the lower sixth would rib him rotten, but to his surprise some of them had actually tried to bribe him to get them a signed photograph.

'Looks like you finally made it, kid.' Chris grinned. 'You always were a right little show-off. Are you proud of her, Dad?'

Michael, slightly ill-at-ease in his best suit amongst all the City big wigs, watched his young daughter flitting gaily from one to another of the dignitaries, saying all the right things. Then he turned back to regard each of his children in turn.

'I'm proud of every one of you,' he said quietly, and with a special smile for Chris and Mary, 'Your mother and I are indeed blessed.'

'I'll second that,' said Dandy, who was at his most dapper, and having the time of his life. And as Shirley Anne came back to them: 'But tell us, now, chuck, doesn't it give you a funny feeling, seeing yourself up there on the screen like that?'

'Mm, a bit. Darren Wildman said I was one of those rare creatures that the camera loves. Wasn't that sweet of him? And Mr Grace agreed. Oh, Mam, Dad, everyone' – she hugged them all – 'It *is* a bit like a dream. I have to keep pinching myself. I'm contracted for another picture, though I'm not quite sure when. I've been halfway round the world since I made this one. In fact, I don't seem to have stopped for months.'

Michael and Kathleen exchanged looks. 'Seems to me you're due for a good long rest, young lady,' Kathleen said.

'Oh, but I enjoy the tours!'

She tried to explain, but it was impossible to convey adequately the exhilaration of not knowing quite what one would be doing next. She had been everywhere from Coventry to Cape Town, appearing at the Cairo Opera House one week, and the next performing high kicks in spangled tights on the back of a truck, or on some rickety platform out in the desert under a frizzling sun, with a sea of eager sunburnt faces watching and cheering every move. Even the discomforts of the journey out and back in convoy were a part of the novely, with the ever present threat of U boat attacks, and being obliged to rehearse in odd corners of the comandeered liner, wearing life-jackets.

'I met Andy Rogers in Alexandria,' she told Liz later, feeling quite at ease on the shaky camp bed in one corner of her old bedroom, while Liz occupied the other, and Rita and the baby had Chris's old room. 'He was spending part of his leave there.'

'I bet he was delighted to see you.'

'I believe he was. Poor lamb, he looked whacked. It's been pretty hair-raising, trying to keep the links with Malta going. In fact, I'd say he's lucky to be alive. They lost four ships in one convoy last August. He said the Maltese are wonderful – and never was a George Cross more deserved. We wanted to give a concert there, but it was considered much too risky.'

'I should think so!' Her sister's seeming imperviousness to danger never ceased to amaze Liz.

'Anyway, Andy took me to most of the places he said one should see while in Eygpt. We watched the sun setting over the Nile – oh, Liz, it was fabulous!' And so was making love under a blue-black sky shimmering with stars, she added silently. Strange – after Alec, she had vowed that no man would get that close to her again. But with Andy, making love was fun. And safe. No strings, she had said, and he felt the same way.

'You look very pleased with yourself, little sister. And I do believe you're blushing.'

Shirley Anne pulled a face. 'Well, I've plenty to be pleased about, big sister. How about you? Have you seen that dishy American lately?' She remembered Jimmy and bit her lip. 'Sorry – "foot in mouth" time!'

'Don't be silly. Anyway, the last I heard, Leigh was in the States.'

And so offhand did she sound that Shirley Anne wondered if she had been wrong about them.

In fact, Liz had more immediate things on her mind. She intended to broach the subject of Munnings' this weekend, while everyone was at home. The transaction had been approved by Bill Yates, the offer provisionally agreed, and it only remained for the papers to be drawn up.

Now came the difficult bit.

Chapter Four

'You want to do *what*?'

Aunt Flora had offered to be there to back her up, but Liz knew this was something she had to do on her own. Now, as she repeated her news, she was already half wishing she had decided otherwise. Her father seldom raised his voice, and she had never seen him this angry.

It reminded Kathleen of his outburst the night she had told him she was pregnant with Georgy. And she suspected that Michael's anger was in part due to what he regarded as an act of betrayal on the part of his favourite child.

Only Liz wasn't a child any longer, and once over the first shock, Kathleen surprised in herself a secret admiration, even perhaps a twinge of envy. It was a bold move on the part of her daughter. If she had been twenty years younger and fitter, it was the kind of vision she might have shown herself. But it was no use telling Michael that.

'So you went behind my back to Flora.'

'Not behind your back.' Liz was determined to stay calm and stand her ground. 'You have so much to cope with, both of you, and until I knew whether it was a viable proposition, there seemed no point in troubling you. As Aunt Flora's done a lot of dealing in property, she seemed the logical person to consult.'

'That seems reasonable enough to me, Michael,' said Kathleen, above the noise of everyone talking at once. 'Do be quiet, all of you!'

'And now Flora's given it her blessing, and her money, you've condescended to tell us?'

'To ask for your approval and support, yes,' she said quietly.

'Well, that's grand! I just hope you're not expecting Ryan's to be a part of this great venture.'

'Well, as a matter of fact, Dad, that's exactly what I am hoping – that it will all become a part of Ryan's. Aunt Flora's come up with an excellent idea, but we can discuss that later; we need to get the important part sorted first.' She turned to her brother. 'Chris, how would you feel about coming back to Liverpool? Because I was rather hoping that you would take over at Munnings'. I didn't know Mary was expecting when I thought of it, but that makes things even better.'

Kathleen's admiration for her daughter increased; she had been watching Michael's face. It wasn't always as easy to read as now, with anger giving way to blank astonishment, until, with the realization of the splendid opportunity being offered to Chris, she could see that he was beginning to accept the situation.

'Oh, Chris,' Mary said.

'It's not as daunting as it sounds,' Liz went on. 'The shops and the bakehouse are staffed, and there's lot of room above Church Street. It would make a lovely flat . . .'

Chris had taken Mary's hand and turned to his father – dazed, but with hope leaping in his eyes. 'Dad, do you think that I – *we* could do it?'

It was not what Michael had hoped for. It had always been his dream that he and Chris would eventually work together as a team, but with his son's marriage and a baby on the way, the situation had become less clear-cut. He looked at Chris, the light of ambition in his eyes, and at Mary, not showing yet, but with the bloom of approaching motherhood already giving her a special beauty. And he remembered how it had been for Kathleen and himself, starting out. Things were very different, then, and he wouldn't wish those hard times on anyone, especially Chris. This latest scheme of Liz's, like most of her notions, was a little grandiose for his taste, but it would be a splendid opportunity for his son to become his own man and yet remain a part of the family team. And with a home for the two of them thrown in.

'You will do very well, my boy,' he said deeply. 'You've a fine wife at your side, as I have always had, and if she is in favour . . .'

'I think it's a grand idea.' Mary stood on tiptoe to kiss his cheek. 'And I think it was lovely of Liz to think of us . . .'

Liz grinned. 'You might not say that when you discover all the hard work involved.'

'I've never been afraid of hard work.'

'And I'll be around to give a hand with the paperwork – I might even persuade George Wilson to think again about leaving.' She went across to her father, unsure if he was still angry with her. 'Dad?'

There was a fractional pause while they looked into one another's eyes. Then he gathered her close. 'Ah, Lizzie, my love, there's one thing for sure, life is never dull for long with you around.' And she felt an immense relief, as though a load had been lifted from her chest.

Kathleen blinked several times and viewed them with satisfaction. 'Well, that's settled. I think we could all do with a nice cup of tea.'

'Tea? Have we nothing stronger to toast the great adventure?' Shirley Anne protested.

'Tea will be fine,' said Liz, misty-eyed. 'We don't want to tempt fate by celebrating before the deal is signed and sealed, however certain it all seems. So, please, don't tell a soul about it until then.'

'Well that's something you're good at, anyway,' said Rita. 'Talk about tight as a clam!'

'I hated all the secrecy, but we didn't want the whole thing to go off at half-cock, and the less anyone knew, the better.'

Shirley Anne had been surprisingly quiet throughout. Now, she asked abruptly, 'Will Alec Munnings have to know who the buyer is?'

Liz looked steadily back at her. 'Not, I hope, until it's too late to back out.'

The beginnings of a smile lurked in her sister's eyes. 'He'll be livid.'

There was an additional idea which Flora had suggested early on, though Liz had thought it better to let Dad adjust by degrees, so she hadn't yet mentioned it. It was that they should use her solicitor, Hayfield and Wynn.

'Rupert Wynn is a good man, and the fact that he isn't local will attract less interest. And since you are so keen to preserve your anonymity until the deal is completed, he has come up with an excellent suggestion, which is that you should form a limited company, with yourself as the principal shareholder, and Chris, your father, and myself each holding a five per cent interest. It would also give you a measure of security if, God forbid, anything should go wrong, and negotiations can be conducted in the name of the company, which may be called anything you like.'

It was an idea that appealed to Liz – partly because it might, in the fullness of time, enable her to add another name to the list of shareholders. And to her surprise, and with very little prompting from Mam, when she did tell her father, he quite took to the notion of a limited company. A lot of discussion followed before they finally came up with *CHOICE FAYRE, Ltd* as the company name, but once that was approved and registered, everything happened quite quickly.

Meanwhile, there was plenty to keep Liz's mind occupied. Christmas was looming on the horizon, the fifth Christmas of the war, and each year it became more difficult to overcome the shortages and create something festive. After a lot of experimenting with wheatmeal flour and dried eggs, she had become quite adept at producing an acceptable swiss roll, so, as they weren't too badly off for cocoa powder, Liz decided to make chocolate logs and decorate them with a dusting of sugar and trickles of white icing. She made little paper robins on skewers, and painted them: holly leaves and berries were made from scraps of material or wool, and stuck on to a small circle of white paper, frilled round the edges, which was then anchored to the log with the robin's skewer. She also made tiny round Christmas puddings from cake crumbs and a few chopped prunes soaked in enough syrup to bind them without becoming too sticky. These too had a trickle of icing and a little white hat decorated with red woollen berries, and were very popular with the children.

Georgy had started school a year late in September. Liz could only guess what it cost her mother to send him out on his own amongst a crowd of strangers, even though his teacher had promised to keep a special eye on him.

Kathleen had snapped at everyone that first morning, and they had all conspired to keep her out of the shop, in case any of the customers took umbrage. And Rosie didn't help by making a scene because she couldn't go, too.

'I don't know what you're worryin' yourself about, our Kath,' Dandy told her. 'The lad's that good-natured, he probably won't notice if the kids do rib him a bit.'

But she wouldn't be mollified. 'Don't try your soft soap on me,

Dad. I *know* how cruel children can be. Young Freddy said he'd look out for him, but he's in the juniors, and Georgy's so defenceless.'

'Well he can't go through life with you fighting his battles for him,' Dandy insisted. 'Tell you what, let me go for him, dinner-time. Him and me, we understand one another. I'll suss out how he's gone on.'

Georgy was quieter than usual, though otherwise he seemed to have survived relatively unscathed. But after a couple of days he succumbed to one of his bronchial attacks, and this seemed to set the pattern for his early schooldays, as he picked up every cough and cold and germ that abounded in the classroom, and spent more time at home than at school. And it was Dandy, with more time on his hands now that air raids, please God, seemed to be a thing of the past, who took the little lad under his wing once more. Together they developed a daily routine of gentle exercise, after which Georgy was allowed to stick the little flags in Dandy's maps, removing the swastikas and red Japanese suns almost daily now, and replacing them with Allied ones. His Grandad also encouraged him to draw pictures and make small models out of plasticine, for which he showed a surprising aptitude.

Liz, having several times watched the way her slow, ungainly brother painstakingly shaped the plasticine, called her father to come and take a look.

'Dad, have you ever thought of taking him into the bakehouse to try his hand – like you did with Chris when he was small? I don't suppose he'd be able to do anything complicated, but he does seem to enjoy making shapes, and it might please him to think he was helping you.'

Michael's smile was warm as it rested on her. 'It might indeed. I sometimes wonder what we'd do without you, Lizzie, my love. You always seem to spot the obvious before any of us.'

Georgy loved the bakehouse, and because he was a docile child, Charlie and Steve had no difficulty accepting his presence about the place. The only problem was the flour, which sometimes aggravated his asthma. But the benefits on the whole outweighed the problems, and his strangely shaped bread rolls were greeted and consumed by the family with genuine pleasure.

*

Ellen found it hard to adjust to life without Arnie. 'Every time I turn my head, I expect to see his bed in the corner,' she had said at first. 'Getting rid of it was almost like losing him all over again.'

But work kept her going, and by Christmas she had begun to lose that furrow of worry that had been a fixture for so long. Her hairdresser friend persuaded her to have her hair permed, which made her look years younger, and Hester helped her sort the living room out. The older children contributed by giving the walls a lick of paint, and Aunt Flora found her a second-hand carpet from a pile of goods salvaged from bombed houses.

'It's a bit stained, but it's made all the difference. The room looks really nice, now. A room I can ask people into – ' Her mouth trembled very slightly. 'Does that sound awful? Only I can't wish Arnie back, can I? Not the way he was.'

'Of course it's not awful. It's very natural,' Kathleen said robustly, and hoped that Ellen wouldn't hear any of the unkind comments, admittedly few and made by their more catty customers, about Sergeant Rufus Grant, who had been seen in the vicinity of No 23, Fortune Street, laden down with Christmas presents. 'No-one could have done more than you did for Arnie.'

'I find I can think of him occasionally, now, as he used to be – a fine, vigorous man. That's how I want to remember him.'

The firm of solicitors acting for Alec Munnings had offices in Castle Street. Gloomy, old-fashioned rooms, they were not made any brighter by dark oak panelling within, and a January sky heavy with the promise of snow beyond the tall narrow windows.

Alec was late. He arrived in a hurry, rapping out a terse greeting with no hint of an apology. 'Damned trains,' he snapped. 'Well, let's get the formalities over. I don't have much time.'

George Wilson had tried many times to find some trace of Fred Munnings in this hard, toffee-nosed young man in his fancy uniform, but, by now, any lingering trace of allegiance had vanished.

'Mr Garth has everything ready,' he said.

The solicitor, whose manicured hands constantly fidgeted with papers, sat forward, eyeing his elusive client. 'Do please sit down, Lieutenant Munnings.' He indicated a vacant chair. 'Mr Yates,' he nodded towards a heavily-built man sitting near George

Wilson, 'has been empowered to sign on behalf of the purchasers, Choice Fayre, Ltd. Does this meet with your approval, sir?'

Alec, slouching in the chair, shrugged. 'If you're satisfied, it's fine by me. I don't give a damn who signs, as long as the business gets done.'

And he can get his hands on the money, George thought. Old Fred could be an awkward, tight-fisted old cuss, but he was honest in all his dealings. Thank God, he wasn't alive to see the child upon whom he had lavished so much, behaving like a cheap money-grubbing street trader.

'You will already have studied the copy of the agreement I forwarded to you? May I take it that you have no objection to the terms stated therein? Five thousand guineas, with all debts cleared?'

'If I objected, I wouldn't be here.'

'Then it only remains for both parties to sign and exchange the contracts. If you would care to examine them – no?' He sighed. 'Very well. If you will sign there, I will witness on your behalf, and Mr Wilson will witness for the other party.' Mr Garth indicated the place, and Alec scrawled his name, prowled the room impatiently and finally flung himself into his chair, fumbling in his top pocket for his cigarette case, which he offered round. When they were politely declined, he took one, snapped the case shut and flicked his lighter.

'Thank you. And Mr Yates, if you will. Now, it is a simple matter of exchanging the contracts.'

A door behind Mr Garth opened. Through a plume of smoke, Alec saw the figure of a slim young woman, dressed with simple elegance in a dark coat and skirt, a narrow-brimmed hat with a pale grey bow perched above neatly coiled hair. Behind her, a tall man whose sandy hair was liberally sprinkled with white.

He let out an oath, his chair scraping across the polished floor as he came to his feet. 'Lizzie Ryan! What the devil are you doing here?'

'I wanted to witness the completion of our transaction,' she said calmly.

'Your. . . ? But you can't be . . .' His face suddenly twisted. 'This whole thing's a bloody conspiracy! I'll sue the lot of you. Give me those papers!'

But Mr Garth had judiciously placed the contracts beyond his reach. 'Everything has been conducted according to the letter and spirit of the law, Lieutenant Munnings. Mrs Marsden is the majority shareholder and managing director of Choice Fayre, Ltd.'

'As I daresay you might have discovered if you hadn't been so eager to get your hand on this.' Liz opened her handbag and drew out the cheque, not flinching at the venom in his eyes as she held it out.

'You scheming little bitch!' he snarled.

Michael stepped forward, hackles rising, but Liz stayed him with a hand. 'No, Dad. Leave it. I don't mind Alec calling me names. He is understandably upset.' She laid the cheque down on the desk. 'I'm sure you would love to tear that up,' she said, still watching him, 'but you won't. And I reckon it about squares our account. Don't you?'

Chapter Five

Leigh watched the green signal flare shoot up from the control tower into an early April sky still tinged with pink. 'That's it,' he said to his co-pilot, Lieutenant Beeman, on his left. The plane began to roll down the runway, and the flutterings in the pit of his stomach immediately settled. 'More juice, Lieutenant,' he murmured, and into the radio: 'Red Leader commencing take off.'

Behind him, the words were picked up by rest of the squadron, and as he accelerated for lift off, the next B17 was already revving its engines. The move was repeated at thirty second intervals, and soon the sky was buzzing with Flying Fortresses and Liberators. Once out of the turbulence, Leigh took up position at the head of the formation. It was going to be a long, tough, and decidedly uncomfortable haul – eight hours of claustrophobic conditions and considerable danger for the crew. Their target, Hanover – a giant munitions factory.

But before that, they would have to fight off everything the Luftwaffe could throw at them. Leigh had been flying these combat missions out of East Anglia since January, and with many miles of coastline to choose from, had become adept at plotting a different course each time, in the hope of postponing the moment when the Messerschmidts and Focke-Wolfs found them. An escort of P47s gave cover as far as the German border, but then they had to turn back for want of fuel, and they were on their own. From then on, it could get pretty hairy, with only a few brief respites when the German fighters returned periodically to base for refuelling.

Leigh had always considered the Fortress a masterpiece of engineering, easy to handle even at high altitudes. 'Keep it tight,' he told the formation as they crossed the Channel at 10,000 feet. 'New crews especially. And tail gunners, watch out for anything sneaking up your tail. Short bursts – don't waste ammo, it's got to last a long time.'

By the time his navigator had pinpointed the target, they had lost one B17, accounted for three FWs and a couple of ME210s, and flak was now their biggest problem. But they delivered their bombs smack on the button, tightened formation in order to protect the unfortunate craft who were flying on fewer than four engines, and altered course for home.

They were almost over the Dutch coast when a Focke-Wolf squadron came at them out of nowhere. Leigh's intercom crackled. 'Tail gunner to pilot – Jeez, Major, five FWs at nine o'clock!'

'Mark them. And stay cool.'

'Focke-Wolf squadron at six o'clock,' came another voice, 'levelling out nine . . .'

'Fighter high, coming in fast . . .'

The plexiglass crazed under a hail of bullets, and Leigh felt something scorching-hot pierce his flack-jacket. He wasn't conscious of pain, just a numbing ache, and a warm trickle running down inside his combat dress.

'You all right, Major?'

Hank Beeman's voice penetrated his consciousness, dragging him back. He wiped the mist from his eyes, relieved to find that it was mostly sweat.

'I've been better, Lieutenant. But we've got the sea below us now, so the worst should soon be over.' As he spoke, a Lib went spinning past them, trailing smoke. He counted one, two – four parachutes. 'Take over the controls, will you, Hank, while I concentrate on getting as many of us as I can back in one piece. Red Leader to all crew – keep it tight. Make it hard for them to get at you. And if anyone does drop out, close up fast. Hang in there, guys, we're almost home.'

Flora was on her way out when the phone rang. She hesitated and a strong gust of wind tried to tug the door out of her hand. Mrs Meadows came labouring up from the kitchen.

'I'll take it, madam. You'll be wanting to get on.'

But something made Flora linger. The swirling wind was doing its best to ruin the early almond blossom. April was a capricious month – forever changing, as though it could never decide which season it belonged to. She hated indecision. Mrs Meadows was saying, 'Oh, yes, I see – Well, madam was just on her way out, but I'll fetch her.'

'It's one of them Yanks from up the Palace Hotel – you know . . .'

Flora took the telephone from her. 'Mrs Hetherington speaking.'

'Ma'am. This is the American Red Cross Club. We have a Major Farrell on the line for you.'

Oh, dear God, what now? 'Put him through,' she said.

'Hi, Flora? Is that you?'

Liz was delighted with the way everything was working out. Chris and Mary had settled in well in Church Street. Dandy, who always seemed to *know* someone, had found a semi-retired builder and joiner who, with a little cunning and a lot of know-how, had transformed the upper two floors into a pleasant and spacious flat.

Chris had been accepted in the bakehouse almost without question, once the staff found he knew his job and was prepared to work as hard as they did. And Mary, with some initial help from Liz, soon learned the ropes, and had made herself popular with the shop girls. Also, George Wilson had agreed to stay on until everything was running smoothly, and Liz had mastered the books. And the customers, it seemed, had accepted the change with no more than the occasional comment, mostly favourable.

The sign above the door now read: RYAN's BAKERY, (formerly MUNNINGS). And a discreet notice on the window, and inside on the counter announced: *The name has changed, but the quality will remain the same*.

In practice, it would now have been simpler to supply the Candide from Church Street, but Liz resolved to go on providing her own personal touch in this one small area. The Candide was her very own, left to her by Mr Morgan, and remained linked in her mind with Fortune Street in a very special way.

A letter from Aunt Flora was a rarity: she invariably picked up the phone or called in to the shop. But as Liz read the contents of the letter, her eyes blurred and her heart began to thump. She went hurrying in search of her mother.

'Mam, could you manage without me for a few hours?'

Kathleen thought fleetingly of the sheets they had been going to turn sides-to-middle. Then she looked at her daughter's face.

Liz misread the hesitation. 'I'm sorry. But I really do need to go to Southport.'

'Problems? I thought the business was all settled and done with . . .'

'It isn't that, Mam. It's Leigh.'

Oh, no! Kathleen's heart went out to her. It couldn't be happening twice. 'He isn't. . . ?'

'No.' Liz spoke quickly, as much to reassure herself as her mother. 'It isn't that bad. He's been hurt, but . . . Mam, he said he didn't want to see me! I can't believe that, and neither does Aunt Flora. She thinks I should go over.' She was gabbling; stopped and drew breath. 'Everything should be all right here. I've made up the order for the Candide – if Steve could deliver it . . .'

'Oh, for heaven's sake, of course you must go.' Kathleen cut through her rambling. She looked at Liz and cupped her face with unusual gentleness. 'It'll be all right, love.'

It was afternoon when Liz arrived at Rose Lodge, by which time her palms were sweating and she had convinced herself that Aunt Flora had been trying to prepare her for the worst. And when she saw Flora looking out for her, opening the door before she could ring the bell, then taking her into the morning room and closing the door – then, Liz was certain.

'Where is he?' she demanded.

'In a moment, Liz. I just wanted to explain. Leigh doesn't know I sent for you.'

'He's in the drawing room, isn't he?'

'I'm still not entirely sure if I've done the right thing . . .' But her aunt, for once curiously indecisive, didn't deny it, and Liz left her in mid-sentence.

The drawing-room door opened without a sound, and she closed it behind her just as quietly. The large mirror above the mantelpiece reflected a good part of the room, including the sofa set at an angle in front of the fire. There, Leigh lounged against a pile of cushions, reading. He was casually dressed, his shirt open at the neck, an unknotted scarf draped over it, the very picture of comfortable indolence. Her feverish gaze sought arms and legs, and confirmed that he still had two of each. She released a little of the breath she had been holding.

Leigh looked up at that moment and saw her. He laid the book aside and came slowly, and somewhat cautiously, to his feet. This should have further reassured Liz, but instead she was filled with a wild unreasoning anger. It carried her across the room to within a few feet of him, where she stopped, eyes blazing.

His face told her little, except that he was very pale beneath the mass of freckles, but his voice was firm enough, with even a hint of wry humour.

'So Flora ratted on me. I might have guessed as much.'

That did it. All her pent-up emotion spilled over. 'How dare you, Leigh Farrell! How dare you look so – so *normal*, when I've just spent the last few hours worrying myself silly!'

He frowned. 'Now, hold on, Elizabeth. It wasn't my idea to worry you. I wanted to spare you, which is precisely why I asked Flora not to get in touch.'

'To spare me?' Liz flung the words at him. 'That makes you feel better, does it? Well, bully for you!'

'Elizabeth . . .'

But she swept on. 'And what makes you think you have the right to protect me from my own feelings – to assume that if I don't know anything, that somehow makes everything all right? I'm not a child, I'm nearly twenty-three years old. Do you really think it makes things any easier for me, not knowing what crazy risks you're taking?'

'Honeysweet, if you'll just – ' he tried again, though this time his voice was less certain.

But she didn't hear the hesitation. She was fast running out of steam, and tears were beginning to threaten. Leigh seemed to be half swaying before her blurring eyes, but she hadn't quite finished all she wanted to say.

'Well, if that's what you think, you couldn't be more wrong. And if you didn't look as though a feather would knock you over, I would *hit* you!'

'Elizabeth – ' This time there was no mistaking the shake in his voice, or his unsteadiness. 'Darling girl, I *do* love you quite desperately, and I've missed you like hell, but right now, I simply have to sit down.'

In an instant she was at his side, steadying him as he lowered himself back on to the sofa. For the first time she realized that the scarf was in fact a sling.

'Oh, what a fool you are, Leigh Farrell!' she exclaimed, dripping tears all over him as she straightened the cushions, making him slide his arm into the sling, watching him lean back with a sigh. 'Whyever did you let me go on shouting at you?'

He grabbed her hand with his good one as she was about to step back, drawing her down beside him with surprising strength, and circling her waist. Not that she had the least desire to escape.

'I guess, because even if they were a mite loud, they were the sweetest words I'd ever heard.' He chuckled softly. 'No-one down there at the Palace Club has anything like such a beguiling bedside manner.'

'Fool,' she said again, but very softly. Now she was close to him, she had only to turn her head to look into his eyes, to lay her mouth against his. There was no fierce passion – time enough later for all that. Now, there was just a deep thankfulness and the sweetness of loving – of knowing that mind and heart and soul were at one.

Flora had not, of course, been listening. But she had heard the raised voices; it would have been difficult not to, even through the stout oak door. However, all had been quiet for some time now, so she ventured in and found them pressed as snugly close as a couple of love-birds.

'She's finished giving you the round of the houses, then?'

Leigh grinned weakly. 'Like ten rounds with Joe Louis. How come she can look so demure, and fight so dirty?'

'She gets it from her mother. A right little firebrand, our Kathy.'

'It's not nice, making personal remarks about people as if they weren't here,' Liz complained.

'A drink – that's what we all need,' Flora said. 'I've asked Mrs Meadows to oblige.'

'Aunt Flora, Leigh has asked me to marry him.'

'I thought he might, once he could get a word in edgeways,' she said drily.

'And I've said yes.'

'Of course you have.' Flora looked into her niece's shining face.

Mrs Meadows knocked and came in, with a bottle and three glasses on a tray. She declined to join them, but wished the couple very happy.

'Champagne, Flora?' Leigh's smile was quizzical. 'Wasn't that taking a bit of a gamble?'

'Not really.' Flora eased the cork up until it popped and the wine spilled over. 'Once I got the two of you together, I knew what the outcome would be.'

'Clever Auntie.' Liz kissed her cheek, and took a glass over to Leigh. 'And lovely bubbly.'

'I'm down to my last half-dozen,' Flora sighed. 'Still, I can't think of a better reason for cracking one.' She raised her glass, beaming at them. 'I do wish you very happy. Not that you need my wishes, looking at the pair of you. So – I suppose the next step is to put in for a dispensation?'

Liz bit her lip, and glanced anxiously at Leigh. 'We haven't even begun discussing details, Aunt Flora.'

'And I can mind my own business. You're quite right, my dear. Tact never was my strong point. But do bear in mind that the wheels of the Church grind exceeding slow.'

'So, what *is* this dispensation?' Leigh wanted to know.

'It's . . . well . . .' Liz glanced appealingly at her aunt.

Flora was by now wishing she had kept her mouth shut. 'It's exactly what it says, Leigh – a dispensation from the Church, granting Liz permission to marry a non-Catholic.'

'Hell!' He sat forward, wincing slightly. 'Does that mean what I think it means? That we'll have to wait?'

'I'm afraid it does. I had to get a dispensation to marry John, but mine was a little easier, because there was no question of children coming along to complicate things – ' She saw Liz blush. 'Amongst other things, you will have to undergo a certain amount of instruction, and agree to let Liz practise her religion, as well as bringing up any children as Catholics. Perhaps there's a padre you could talk to about it?'

'Never mind talking,' Leigh snapped, his head thudding as tiredness began to take its toll. 'I haven't got time for all that rigmarole! I just want to marry Elizabeth. A simple civil ceremony would suffice . . .'

'Leigh, I couldn't!' Liz was shocked. 'It would break Mam and Dad's hearts! And, anyway, I just couldn't! I wouldn't feel married.'

Liz felt panic rising in her.

'Great! Maybe it would be simpler to forget the whole thing.'

This was supposed to be a celebration!. How could everything have changed in so short a time? She threw her aunt a look of sheer desperation.

'Nonsense,' Flora said, as if Leigh were about ten. 'You've just had too much excitement for one day, my boy, and you're worn out. Time I took you back to the club.'

Her briskness reduced his grievance to the level of a tantrum. He half smiled, and then saw the misery on Elizabeth's face. 'Honey sweet, I'm sorry.' He held out a hand and she flew across the room, remembering in time not to fling herself on him. 'Flora's right. I'm not fit company for anyone – especially you. And don't worry – I can see this dispensation thing means a great deal to you. We'll sort it out.'

Liz was anxious not to neglect her work, but she spent every free moment with Leigh, sometimes at Aunt Flora's and sometimes, in the evening, at the Palace Hotel. It was strange seeing the beautiful hotel turned into a rest and convalescent club for American fliers. Leigh was getting stronger with every day that passed, and whilst Liz welcomed his return to full health, a tiny part of her was dreading the moment when he would be pronounced fit to fly again. Already, he was beginning to show signs of restiveness.

'Do you remember the last time we were here?'

They had left the grounds and turned towards the beach. It was an evening not unlike the last time – the end of a beautiful day, with the sun just beginning to set in a blaze of colour.

There were a few couples strolling along the wide stretch of sand. Leigh's arm circled her shoulders, drawing her close so that she could feel the warmth of his body through her thin cotton dress.

'I was very young, then,' she said, in mitigation.

'And I well and truly loused things up.' His hand tightened momentarily. 'It could be I'm about to do the same again.'

She glanced up swiftly and saw that he was staring out to sea, his face taut. There was a squeezing pain inside her chest. 'You're going back to active duty.'

'Not immediately, but it won't be long now.' Still without

looking at her, he said, 'Elizabeth, will you come away with me? Soon. Somewhere quiet and peaceful, just for a few days?'

'How soon is soon?' she answered without hesitation.

Leigh seemed to sigh. And then he turned to her. 'Just like that? No reservations?'

'No reservations.'

He pulled her close and kissed her, deeply, passionately. 'I was half afraid you'd say no, and I do want you so much.'

'And I, you. We can neither of us be sure what tomorrow will bring, and I'm not going to risk losing you again.'

She was looking up at him, and in the rays of the setting sun, her eyes were pure molten gold, and unflinching. 'I don't deserve you.'

'Silly,' she said. 'Have you any idea where you'd like to go?'

It wasn't easy, telling Mam. Good Catholic girls don't even contemplate such behaviour. But Kathleen, not for the first time, surprised her. Liz said so.

'Did you think I wouldn't understand?'

It was an incongruous place for such a momentous discussion, but the scullery happened to be where they were when Liz plucked up the courage. She put her fingers over her mouth to stop it trembling. 'I was so sure you would disapprove.'

'Ah, well, disapproving's a different thing altogether.' Kathleen turned briskly from the sink with the kettle, setting it on the stove before wiping her hands on her pinny. She reached up to brush back a strand of her daughter's hair – such lovely hair, too nice to be pinned up all the time.

'Listen to me, love. I've watched you over the years, always trying to do what was right, even when it wasn't easy – keeping this family together when I wasn't able. And you've always done it cheerfully, and with love, lifting us when we've been down.'

'Mam!'

'I know. But it's true, for all that. I know, too, what you gave up for me. You may well blush. All these years, I've never let on, but your Dad left Sister Imelda's letter in a pocket and I found it . . .'

'I told him to burn it,' Liz said shakily.

'Yes, well, knowing your Dad, I suppose he couldn't quite bring himself to do that. I was upset at the time, and yet I was proud of you, too.' Kathleen busied herself with cups and saucers. 'Anyway, that's all water under the bridge now. I never was one for wearing my heart on my sleeve – even with your Dad, though the love we have for one another is very special. And without taking anything away from Jimmy,' she said, looking steadily at her daughter, who flushed, then went deathly pale, 'you never looked at him the way I've seen you look at Leigh. And it's quite obvious that he feels the same.'

'Oh, yes, Mam, he does! And he's being so good about waiting . . . But now he's almost fit to go back on active duty, and anything could happen . . . A few days, that's all we ask . . .'

'Well, it's your decision, love. You're old enough to know your own mind. I probably shouldn't say so, but this war's made nonsense of a lot of old values, and I reckon it'd be a mean God who wouldn't forgive the odd lapse from grace.' The kettle began to whistle. 'I'll say no more. As it is, that's about the longest speech I've ever made in my life.'

Liz hugged her. 'Mam, I love you!'

'Give over, child, do.' Kathleen blew her nose. 'That kettle's going to drive us both daft.'

Liz rushed to move it off the gas. 'What about Dad?'

'You leave your Dad to me.'

Chapter Six

They set out very early on a perfect day in May, leaving from Southport to avoid fuelling speculation among the likes of Ada Killigan. Leigh had borrowed a friend's car, a shabby green Bentley with a full tank, and enough spare petrol coupons to last them a month. Liz didn't ask where he'd got them, and in any case five days was as long as she could manage. For the journey she wore her grey flannel slacks and red jacket, and tied her hair back with a scarf. They didn't have a lot of luggage, although Aunt Flora had taken her shopping beforehand.

'I've enough clothes to last me a lifetime,' Flora insisted. 'And a good dressmaker who can take them apart and re-model them.' Ignoring all protests, she parted with half her ration of clothing coupons (now cut to sixty to last for fifteen months), and more money than Liz would have contemplated, buying her two Dereta dresses for best and several sets of exquisite underwear, so soft and clinging against her skin that it seemed almost sinful to wear it. And for fun, a Jacqmar scarf with lip and finger motifs, based on the 'Careless talk costs lives' posters. Her half-hearted protests were dismissed with 'Nonsense, there's utility and utility, and if you want to look your very best, it's no use buying cheap rubbish.'

Leigh didn't seem to mind where they went as long as they were together, but Liz knew exactly where she wanted to take him. They drove north, sharing the driving so that Leigh shouldn't tire himself. They stopped within sight of the Westmorland fells to stretch their legs and drink some of the coffee Liz had brought along in two large thermos flasks. She had also brought enough sandwiches to fortify an army.

'They're mostly Spam, I'm afraid,' she said. 'And a few egg ones.'

'Honeysweet, I don't care what they are. This air surely makes you hungry,' Leigh said, as they sat on a dry-stone wall eating the contents of one small pack, and watching the puffy clouds race across the face of the sun, their shadows undulating over the green, smooth-bossed fells dotted with sheep that stood out like white stones. 'It's so peaceful – a different world. I love it already.'

'The best is yet to come,' Liz promised him.

The road rose steeply over Shap, and at the top they ate the remaining sandwiches sitting in the car, looking out on a different terrain; bleak, austere, windswept. And then they drove by country lanes to Keswick, and the scene changed yet again to the rugged beauty of Cumbrian peaks and crags.

Leigh was enchanted by the little market town of Keswick, with its ancient Moot Hall, and Liz promised they would come back to explore it later. But they were almost there, now, and she couldn't bear any delay.

Derwent Water and the valley beyond were every bit as lovely as she had remembered – a small world set apart, with high screes and little knots of woodland towering over them to their left, and the lake in places almost lapping their wheels on the right. The road wound constantly and each time the scene subtly shifted, the sun spearing the treetops with brilliant shafts of light.

About two miles out of Keswick they found a simple country hotel, perched on a promontory overhanging the lake, and surrounded by fir trees that reached out like genteel ladies to dip their toes in the water: a square house built of the lovely grey lakeland stone, that had weathered long years of exposure to the elements with grace and fortitude.

The owners, Mr and Mrs Woodman, made them welcome.

'It's a pleasure to have some young company, my dears,' said the buxom Mrs Woodman, as Leigh signed the register and Mr Woodman went to collect their luggage. American, she thought, her eyes flicking to Liz's third finger. The wedding ring wasn't all bright and shiny new, yet they weren't no old married couple – she'd stake her reputation on that. She'd seen enough newly-weds, or them passing themselves off as newly-weds, to recognize the signs. Not that she was one to pass judgement, not with the war and all – and anyway, she'd taken to this pair on sight. 'We're quiet just now. Just the one gentleman, and he keeps himself to himself – spends most of the day walking.'

She offered them a choice of rooms, and Leigh had no hesitation in taking the largest one, overlooking the lake. It had its own bathroom, but exuded a kind of shabby comfort that saved it from opulence. A faded blue carpet found sympathetic echoes in the chintz curtains and furnishings. The huge, comfortable-looking bed was covered with a hand-worked cream lace counterpane and when Liz exclaimed at the beautiful workmanship, Mrs Woodman blushed with pleasure and admitted that it was her own. There were squashy chairs either side of a fireplace, the fire ready laid, and a gleaming copper bucket filled with logs.

'There's matches on the shelf,' she said as she left them. 'Just you put a light to it, if you feel the need. We serve our evening meal at seven, but it's a fair old while until then, so if you should feel peckish betweentimes, and folk hereabout often do, just pop down and I'll do you afternoon tea.'

Liz felt like pinching herself, as she stood at the dressing table removing her scarf and shaking her hair free. Such luxury. It couldn't be more different from the awful room where she and Jimmy had spent their wedding night. But no shadows of the past came to cloud her present; no guilt, just a warm feeling of benevolence, and instinctively she knew that Jimmy understood, even approved. A faint smile curved her mouth.

'A penny for them?' Leigh's voice broke into her thoughts.

'Not for sale.' She turned, her hair swinging.

'Well, then? *Are* we feeling peckish?' He was looking at her in a way that filled her with a sudden leaping panic of shyness, and brought the colour flooding from the tips of her toes to the crown of her head. And then he drew her towards him, and the feel of his long, sensitive hands holding her made everything all right. Liz wound her arms about his neck, drawing his head down until his lips met hers. 'It's a fair old while until dinner time,' he murmured against her mouth.

A bubble of joyous laughter welled up in her. 'I daresay we can find some way to fill the time.'

'Oh, my lovely Elizabeth, what have I done to deserve you?'

There was a dreamlike quality about those first moments together. They shed their clothes unhurriedly, taking a mutual pleasure in each other, in each new revelation, and through the long windows, the sun, bouncing off the ripples in the lake, dappled their bare skin with watery light. His shoulders were broader than she had expected, and, oh – her heart contracted – there was the scar, almost level with his armpit, healing well, but still livid against the pale, almost transparent skin that went with his colouring. His stomach was taut, his legs long, his hips narrow – and his need of her was very evident. She caught her lip between her teeth, and blushing suddenly, looked up to meet his eyes which were full of tender laughter, and adoration – and something less definable that made her pulses race.

'You are even more beautiful than I had imagined,' he said simply, and came to gather her up.

'Leigh – your shoulder – you mustn't – ' But he refused to be denied. 'Well, at least let us move that lovely counterpane! I couldn't bear to spoil it.'

'Dammit, woman!' he cried, exasperated. 'I am trying to bed you! How can you contemplate practicalities at such a time?'

Liz giggled. 'But, Leigh, the poor woman probably spent years toiling over that lacework.'

Very carefully he set her on her feet, went across to fling back the bedclothes and, lifting her up again, dropped her on the bed so suddenly that her giggle became a tiny shriek. 'How ungallant!'

'Ungallant be damned. By now, my manhood is suffering severe crisis of confidence!

Liz, half shocked by her own boldness, and almost dizzy with joy and love, allowed herself a quick peep. 'Liar,' she declared triumphantly.

'Baggage,' he retorted, and came to lie beside her.

She had never known it could be like this. Jimmy's lovemaking had been accomplished with a kind of exuberant expertise that was not unpleasing, though she had always sensed that he was more concerned with his own satisfaction than hers. And in her naivety, she had supposed that this was how it was meant to be.

But with Leigh she was introduced to a whole new experience – a mutual voyage of discovery and delight and tenderness, each seeking to please the other: he, the teacher, and she a most willing pupil, as he showed her how to give and take pleasure, to emulate the way his hands and mouth invited, encouraged, explored, the touch of his long sensual fingers returning unerringly to those places that roused her senses to peaks of desire, so that when at last he entered her, she cried out with a fierce joy.

They came back to reality in time to present themselves for dinner in a cosy, heavily-curtained room furnished in dark red plush. Liz looked radiantly bridal in a soft cream dress, demurely fastened high at the neck, and, for the first time, she wore the beautifully engraved watch on its heavy gold chain that had belonged to Leigh's grandmother. His eyes warmed as she lifted it from its velvet bed, and he came to take it from her and slip it over her head. 'I've waited a long time to see you wearing this,' he said softly.

Liz was surprised to discover that she was ravenously hungry. 'I always thought that being in love was supposed to take away one's appetite,' she whispered across the candlelit table.

'Old wives' tale.' Leigh's slow smile set her pulses racing. 'Stands to reason, you gotta keep your strength up.'

'Leigh!' She glanced across the room, but their elderly fellow guest was either deaf or very discreet.

She had come armed with seven days' ration cards, which Mrs Woodman had accepted gratefully, but the meal she served that night went far beyond the realms of rationing. An exquisite soup was followed by a superb casserole of chicken, with lots of fresh vegetables, finishing with apple pie and cream. There was even goat's cheese to finish, but this they politely declined. And to drink, they were offered Mr Woodman's homemade parsnip wine, which Leigh declared to be as fine as any French vintage.

'He's won prizes for his wine,' Mrs Woodman explained proudly. 'Always keeps it five year before he uses it, he does. As for the cream and that, we've kept a couple of Jersey cows and a goat or two. And hens, of course.'

The standard never faltered during their stay: fresh eggs and thick, crisply browned rashers of bacon for breakfast, with homemade bread that Michael Ryan couldn't have bettered; picnic lunches that would have served four with ease; and dinners fit for a king, contrived out of very little, that intrigued the professional in Liz.

That first evening they walked for a full hour after dinner, pausing for a while to lean on the stone sill of Grange bridge, looking towards the heart of Borrowdale. With double summer time, the light was mellow, the air soft, and they seemed to have the whole world to themselves. 'A tiny bit of heaven on earth,' Leigh said, taking her hand as they followed the path along the River Derwent, meeting no-one, stopping here and there to kiss as lovers do, until the light began to fade. And then they returned to their room to resume where they had left off earlier.

Later, when he slept, she lay quiescent in the curve of his arm, marvelling that such perfect happiness could be. A shaft of moonlight fell across Leigh's body, and she lifted her head to look at him. His face in sleep was free of any lingering pain or worry lines. She leaned across with care to lay her lips against the scar, and at once he turned to her, and her senses, so finely tuned, began to melt into need. 'Yes, please,' she whispered, as he slipped easily, half-sleepily inside her, and her back arched to meet his growing arousal.

For three days the weather remained perfect. They visited Keswick, exploring its quaint little streets, and took a boat out on the lake, Leigh insisting that a bit of rowing would do his shoulder a world of good. But most of the time they were content to explore the valley on foot. A passing walker, hung about with backpack and various cooking implements, was persuaded by Leigh to take their photograph at the foot of the giant Bowder Stone, a curious thirty-five-foot high boulder standing on end near the head of the valley.

On the second afternoon, they lazed on the pebbled shore of one of the lake's inlets, skimming flat stones across the water and watching a moorhen among the reeds, tugging her young family back and forth on an invisible piece of elastic. Their sorties made little wavelets to disturb the glass-like surface, which reflected the blue of the sky and the hump-backed serenity of Catbells facing them on the other side. Liz told Leigh about Mrs Tiggy-Winkle, who washed and ironed her clothes and laid them out to dry somewhere beyond a little door hidden in the hillside. 'A hedgehog!' he exclaimed, his mouth quirking derisively. And she rose in defence of Beatrix Potter, and the tales of Peter Rabbit, Squirrel Nutkin, and Jemima Puddle-Duck and many others that had peopled her formative years.

Occasionally, disembodied voices carried across the water, and they would turn, eyes shielded, to see tiny dots climbing halfway up a distant craggy rockface, one above the other.

'Rather them than me,' Leigh drawled, and she teased him for his cowardice, which led to a brief skirmish, ending in the inevitable way. With every word spoken, every touch of hands, every meeting of eyes, they discovered some new delight.

On the fourth day it rained, soft Lakeland mist swiftly turning to a sheeting downpour that moved across the lake in a visible mass.

'Such a shame,' said Mrs Woodman, when they came in soaked to the skin. 'Your last day, too. Bring your clothes down and I'll dry them for you.'

But even this didn't matter. Amid great hilarity, they shared the permitted five inches of water in the great bulbous bathtub, and while the rain lashed the windows, towelled each other dry in front of the fire. Liz attempted to brush her tangled mane, until Leigh took the brush from her, teasing and caressing her hair with long smoothing strokes until it shone, and individual strands crackled and lifted like spun silk.

'I feel like a pampered courtesan,' she sighed, stretching with cat-like abandon. 'I wonder what the customers would say if they could see me now.'

'You'd be run out of Liverpool on a rail as a Jezebel,' he teased.

Liz had spoken without thought, but the mention of Liverpool brought the first intrusion of real life. Her mood changed abruptly. She sat up, turning her head away.

'Hey!' Leigh's sensitive fingers were on her neck, pushing up into her hair, drawing her round to face him. 'What's this? Tears?'

'Pathetic, isn't it? I was going to be so sensible.' She blinked, tried to smile, but her mouth wobbled, and she wailed like a child, 'I don't want it to end!'

He gathered her close. 'Oh, honey sweet, how can anything this wonderful end? Few people are granted even one day of perfect happiness, and we've been allowed five. Whatever the future brings, nothing can take that away from us. I am forever a part of you, as you are a part of me.'

The fear that had receded for this brief time, threatened again, but she thrust it away, murmuring into his shoulder, 'I'm as bad as Rosie. I want my goodies, and everyone else's share as well.'

Leigh chuckled, though his arms tightened about her. 'When we've got this war licked, I promise you all the goodies you could ever wish for.'

That night brought a new intensity to their lovemaking, a fulfilment that Liz had never dreamed could exist within the bounds of reality, as though every facet of touch and taste, of ecstasy and cherishing, must be explored, lingered over, and committed to memory.

Leigh had to report back soon after their return. And the good Lakeland air, and the exercise, had done him so much good that he was immediately passed fit for duty.

Kathleen didn't know quite what to make of her daughter, who had thrown herself back into her work with renewed zeal.

'I expected her to be utterly wretched, once he'd gone,' she confided to Flora. 'But there's a kind of serenity about her that nothing seems to shift. She handed out presents for the children – for all of us, in fact – and talked a lot about the excellence of the hotel and the food and the countryside. But she's hardly mentioned Leigh – as though she's deliberately avoiding anything personal.'

'It was the same with Leigh. But you've no call to worry. I had the advantage of seeing them together, remember.' Flora lit a cigarette, and inhaled reflectively. 'I'm not a fanciful woman, as you know, our Kathy, but there was a kind of absolute fulfilment about them, as though they had been granted a glimpse of Shangri-La, and nothing else mattered.'

'I'm not sure if that's good or bad. I mean, with Leigh going back to active duty, anything could happen. You'd expect her to be really down. But if she is, she's hiding it well.'

Rita's Frank had been lucky so far: now, just when the war seemed to be on the turn, it seemed his luck had run out. She rang, tearfully, to say that his ship had been sunk by a U boat. There had been survivors, but it would be some weeks before she heard whether he was a prisoner of war. To make matters worse, she was three months pregnant. Liz tried to find the right words, but it wasn't the same as being there. However, Rita seemed to be bearing up very well.

'Never mind, chuck,' Dandy said, seeing Liz's expression as she put down the phone and told him the news. 'At least there's hope. And it's only a matter of time, now. Things are all going our way. See them Allied flags young Georgy's been stickin' all over southern Italy? I said they'd throw in the towel once Mussolini was given the order of the boot – not that he was ever more than a big bag of wind. It won't be long now till we take Rome, then we'll have the Germans on the run. You'll see.'

Liz smiled and agreed, but she knew that this was only part of the story. The daily and nightly bombing raids over Germany were, if anything, being intensified, and she hadn't had a letter or a telephone call for over a week.

Chapter Seven

'It's happened at last!' Dandy was jubilant. 'We've landed in France!' He tossed his hat on to the breakfast table and swaggered through to put the first flag on the coast of France. 'Normandy, June 6th, 1944. That's a day that'll go down in history, that is.'

It had been rumoured for weeks. The south coast harbours had been filled with landing craft, and no amount of camouflage could disguise the fleets of tanks and lorries clogging up quiet lanes in the surrounding countryside. Now 'Operation Overlord' had begun, and optimism ran high.

'Now don't be getting carried away,' Michael warned, once the first excitement was over. 'There's a long road ahead before we can claim victory.'

Kathleen thought about Rita, who had just heard that Frank was a prisoner of war, with Michael Francis two years old, and another baby on the way. How old would they be before their father was released and brought safely home? But at least Frank was alive, and Rita would be able to write and send him parcels through the Red Cross. It was selfish of her to be glad that none of her own children would be involved in the fighting this time – except Shirley Anne, of course. You never knew what that one would get up to next. And then she caught sight of Liz's face. There would be no rest for the bombers, and Leigh would be in the thick of it.

The news of the invasion filled Liz with a mixture of hope and apprehension. She saw less and less of Leigh, though they kept in close touch by letter and telephone. As if by unspoken consent, they both avoided mention of the dispensation. Liz had heard nothing, and didn't like to keep bothering Fr Glynn – and Leigh's mind was filled with more immediate priorities.

Shirley Anne's first picture had broken all records, and in the early summer, after yet another tour, she had been released to make a second one, again with Darren Wildman. She also promised to get home for a week's holiday, and arrived just in time to wet the head of her brother's first-born. Peter Michael Ryan was a bouncing ten-pounder. He had given his mother a hard time, but she came through the difficult labour splendidly. Chris was dazed and exhausted after a sleepless night, but he was over the moon with joy when he arrived with the good news.

'Chris, love.' Kathleen reached up to cup his face, drawing it down to kiss him – and he hugged her fiercely in return. There were hugs all round, even from Michael who was clearly moved.

'I couldn't be more delighted,' Liz told him warmly, suppressing the tiny worm of envy that moved inside her. And Shirley Anne teased Chris about being a daddy.

'The bakehouse staff have kicked me out for the day,' Chris said with an embarrassed grin. 'They're all pleased as Punch – the shop staff, too. Been rooting for a boy, they have.'

Word had reached Fortune Street before the shop opened for business. Dot and Ellen were run off their feet. 'Another little Ryan ter keep the firm goin',' said Ada Killigan. 'I berr 'is Gran's made up. Soon be as many Ryans as Killigans.' She shook with laughter.

'Ar, 'e's a good lad, is Chris, God love 'im,' said another. 'Tell 'im we'll be wettin' the babby's head in The Grapes ternight, if 'e 'appens ter be passin'.'

'Give us one of me usual, will yer, Ellen? And I'd better 'ave a dozen of them tarts. What's in 'em, or shouldn't I ask?' Ada shook again. 'Only Hymie, that's our Lily's fella's comin' fer tea. The Ryans aren't the only ones with good news.' She looked round to make sure that the shop was good and full. 'You can tell Shirley Anne when you see 'er, that Lily and Hymie are gettin' married next month, an' she'd be very welcome ter come.'

'That's a bit sudden. Got ter gerra move on, 'as she?'

Ada swung round, almost knocking those nearest to her off their feet. 'I 'aird that, Nellie Biggin! You want ter wash your mouth out, spreadin' filthy rotten lies . . .'

Liz decided that while Shirley Anne was home, she would bring up the question of Rosie's future. 'Help me take the order to the Candide, and I'll treat you to coffee.'

Her sister raised a quizzical eyebrow, but offered no objection.

'You've got it looking pretty swish again,' she said, looking round at the painted walls tastefully flushed with pink. It was early, and they had the place to themselves. 'Done anything with the upstairs yet?'

'Not yet. I may eventually turn it into a function suite.'

'You are getting big ideas,' Shirley Anne drawled.

'Not really. I doubt I'd ever use it as a flat. With Mam's health a bit up and down, I can keep a better eye on things living at home, and we've room enough for when Leigh comes up.'

'Mam *is* all right, isn't she?'

'It's mostly the anaemia, I think. I know Doc Graham wants her to see the specialist, but you know Mam – '

'*The iron pills'll do me fine*,' they chanted together, and smiled.

'He's given her a tonic as well, and I'm working on her,' Liz said.

Alice brought the coffee, and stayed chatting for a few minutes, wanting to know all about the picture. When she had gone, Liz explained to her sister what she had in mind for Rosie.

'What do you think?'

Shirley Anne's head came up slowly. She had grown her hair again, and now wore it in a 'Veronica Lake' bob which she brushed back with a sophisticated flick of the hand to give Liz a sharp look.

'You'd really give up ten per cent of your shares to provide for Rosie?'

'Yes, of course. It's the least I can do – a large part of the company was once her father's business. I intended to do it from the first, but I couldn't without telling the family the whole truth. That's why the decision must be yours.'

'You're full of surprises, our kid,' her sister said with affectionate mockery. 'Every time I think I've got you sussed, you come up with some new ploy. First you and Leigh Farrell going off together, bold as brass – I bet that took a bit of swallowing on the parents' part, especially after my little débâcle – and now this.'

But Liz wasn't about to allow any probing about Leigh. She just said, 'You might be surprised about Mam and Dad. But it's Rosie we're talking about. What do you say?'

Shirley Anne lit a cigarette and sat back, watching the smoke curl up. 'Oh, what the hell! I don't suppose it matters a toss, now, if they all know. But you don't have to do it, you know.' She tossed her hair back again, her blue eyes twinkling wickedly. 'I have a feeling I'm going to be very rich one day.'

'You could well be right. Even so, I think Rosie is entitled to something. Of course, it'll take a while before the profits amount to much, but if her ten per cent were to be wisely invested until she's twenty-one, it could give her a nice little nest egg of her own.'

Shirley Anne stubbed out her cigarette. 'Well, you're the business brain of the family these days, sweetie. If that's the way you want it, I'll break the news about Alec to the parents, and the rest is up to you.' She dropped the flippancy suddenly. 'And thanks.'

The identity of Rosie's father came as a shock to both their parents, especially to Michael, who found himself remembering the flare of hatred on Alec Munnings' part when Lizzie revealed that she had bought the business.

'You've known all along, haven't you, Lizzie?' he said quietly. 'That Alec was Rosie's father?'

'I have. But I promised I wouldn't tell. I think she was afraid you might want to see right done, and she hated him so much by then, she wanted nothing to do with him.' Liz knew the way her father's mind was working. 'That wasn't the only reason I wanted that business so badly. I had a few grudges of my own to settle, too. But even that wouldn't have made me take such a big step. I really was looking to the future. The war can't last that much longer, and I did, and still do, believe it was a chance not to be missed.'

Michael shook his head. He still found it difficult, coming to terms with the fact that his little Lizzie was not only a grown woman, but a woman with a very strong will of her own, and more business sense than many a man. Yet, much as he loved her, he was still troubled by the thought of her marrying Leigh Farrell. Not that he had anything against him – quite the reverse, in fact. Didn't he owe the man his life? But Farrell was an American – and after the war, wouldn't he want to return to his own country, taking Lizzie with him? It was a prospect hardly to be borne.

Dandy's initial euphoria over D Day was soon marred by a new German obscenity – an unmanned flying bomb, the V1, soon nicknamed the Buzz-bomb because of its engine which cut out moments before it fell – launched against the south of England. It had no purpose but to terrify and kill indiscriminately. Many were brought down by anti-aircraft guns, but many more got through. In September, they were followed by the more sophisticated V2, a rocket that came in silence.

It was now Liverpool's turn to play host to some of the many thousands of evacuees from southern England. Dandy opened up his home again and so did Hester, and anyone else with room to spare. Flora was once more in demand to find billets, and Kathleen worried about Shirley Anne, who could be anywhere, and was a hopeless correspondent.

Leigh came up to Liverpool for two whole days, around the time of her birthday, and stayed in Chris's old room.

'I thought you deserved a treat,' he said. 'And I happened to hear that Glenn Miller was playing at Burtonwood, so I got me two tickets.'

Liz had seen *Orchestra Wives* and *Sun Valley Serenade*, and she and Joey often listened to the American Forces Network programme, and knew all the big American bands. But Glenn Miller was her favourite.

Liverpool girls had been going to the Burtonwood dances in droves, since the Americans first arrived: that was how Lily had first met Hymie. Special trains ran from Central Station, packed with excited young girls, often lying about their ages, their painted legs with black seams drawn up the back with eyebrow pencil, unless they were lucky enough to find themselves a GI who could provide them with nylons. Make-up was hard to come by, but they sooned learned that a slick of Vaseline on their eyelids was almost as effective as eyeshadow – if you could find the Vaseline.

But for a Glenn Miller concert you needed an invitation. Leigh had, as usual, managed to borrow himself a car. It was a magical night, one she would always remember; laughing and jiving their way through a lively version of *In The Mood*; their dreamlike closeness during the beautiful *Moonlight Serenade* and *At Last*. But the best was saved until last, when, with everyone clustered round the platform, Glenn Miller announced a special item.

'Ladies and Gentleman, we have a request. This tune doesn't normally figure in our repertoire. But this is a rather special occasion, so we practised a little, and here' – he smiled straight at her and Leigh, the light glinting on his glasses – 'from one Major to another, is a birthday surprise for a very special young lady . . . *Just The Way You Look Tonight.*'

Liz had known, even before he said it. And she didn't even notice when everyone stood aside to let them dance alone. All that mattered was that it was their song, and they were dancing it somewhere far away in their own world.

Clare passed her finals that summer and became a fully fledged doctor. Mrs Whitney gave a garden party to celebrate and Liz was invited. She had been to the house many times over the years, but for some reason, that particular occasion was haunted for Liz by the ghost of Francis – that shy young man with his head in the clouds. And of another red-haired flier, who had captured a young girl's heart, and who at this moment might be over Germany, in terrible danger . . . She slipped away from the crowd, into the house, and it was in the dining room that Clare found her, staring out of the window.

'Memories?' she asked with unerring accuracy.

'Silly, isn't it? After all this time. I just suddenly felt like being alone.'

'I'll go away again, if you like,' Clare said.

Liz shook herself. 'No, of course not. Anyway, the mood's passed.' She sighed and turned to look at her friend. 'So what happens now, Doctor Whitney? Have you made up your mind what kind of doctor you want to be?'

Clare shrugged. 'Not definitely. I'd quite like to specialize in obstetrics or women's diseases, eventually, but I've a long way to go before that.'

'You'll have to come and give Mam a good talking to. She's still having terribly heavy periods, and they're making her so anaemic, which in turn makes her tired, which in turn . . . but I don't have to tell you, do I?'

Clare was sympathetic. 'I'll talk to her, if you like, but if she won't listen to Doc Graham, it's hardly likely she'll take any notice of me.' She looked closely at Liz. 'And what about you – really? It can't be easy, listening to the talk of new air offensives, reading the papers – and knowing that Leigh's in the thick of it.'

Liz shrugged. 'No, but I'm not alone in that, and I've plenty to keep me busy.'

'We haven't had a word from Shirley Anne in weeks. The last we heard she was off on a tour of factories in the south of England. That's how vague she is . . .'

Flora had called and was staying for tea. And as Kathleen spoke, Joey arrived too, the back door opening and banging shut as he strolled in, filling the room with his great height, and his case and sports bag, which he dropped on the floor. 'Joey, how many times have I told you – ? It's no wonder Rosie's so untidy, with you for an example.'

Flora grinned sympathetically at her nephew, and said, 'Shirley Anne'll be all right. She always lands on her feet. That Rosie's going to be just like her.'

Kathleen busied herself setting the table. 'Well, it wouldn't hurt her to phone. She must know we'd worry, what with the Buzz-bombs.'

'Michael,' Flora said, 'will you shake her, or shall I?'

He looked up from the book he was reading and eyed his elegant sister-in-law, who never seemed to grow any older. 'It never occurred to me before, Flora, but if Rosie's like her mother, I reckon they both take after you. Seems to me you all thrive on excitement, even danger.'

'Well, I suppose being misjudged by one's nearest and dearest is a cross one has to bear,' she said, adopting an aggrieved expression.

'Ah, now, Flora, girl, I didn't mean . . .'

Kathleen gave him an exasperated look. 'Michael Ryan, after all these years, can you still not see when my sister's winding you up? And leave that bread and marge alone, Joey. There'll be none left for anyone else, the way you're going.'

He grinned and pulled a face behind her back. 'The flying bomb's a tremendous revolution in technology, though, isn't it?' he mused, his mouth full of bread. Joey had passed his highers with excellent marks, and had just started a full-time engineering course. 'I mean, just think of it, being able to guide unmanned rockets over that kind of distance? And someone was saying today there's a V3 being perfected that's even more powerful.'

'Is that all you can think about? How clever it is?' Kathleen, white-faced, could hardly get the words out, she was so angry. 'There are people being killed, maimed, scared out of their wits . . .'

'Easy on, Kathleen,' Michael hushed her. 'The lad just didn't think. You can't expect him to see things the way we do – '

'Then he ought to see. He's not a child.' But she knew Michael was right.

Joey came and put his arms round her. 'Sorry, Mam.'

'Oh, get on with you.'

To lighten the atmosphere, Flora said, 'Listen. D'you want to hear something really funny? And I'm not winding you up this time, Michael, gospel truth. Someone's come up with a story that Hitler had Southport earmarked as one of his invasion towns, if he'd ever got this far. How's that for a laugh?'

Liz worried about the Buzz-bombs, too, and not only because of Shirley Anne – Leigh could also be in their line of fire. But she tried to keep busy, to keep her spirits high. And every time Leigh rang and she heard his laconic, 'Hi, honey sweet,' she sent up a quick, 'Thank you, God, for another day.'

And then, in November, Leigh's father had a severe heart attack. Leigh managed to get compassionate leave, and flew to the States in time to see him before he died. Afterwards, he stayed on to arrange with lawyers for the settlement of his affairs. In 1942 Farrell-Drew-Farrell had merged with one of the major aircraft corporations, where Charlie Drew's skill as a designer was easily absorbed. Mr Farrell senior had been allocated a seat on the Board of Directors, with special responsibility for marketing – which sounded very grand, but meant little more than being paid a handsome retainer for turning up when he felt like it to sign a few papers.

'That wasn't Dad's style,' Leigh said, having come back via Burtonwood and sneaked an extra day. They were stretched out on the fireside rug in Mam's parlour, their backs resting against the sofa. 'He was at his happiest when it was just the three of us, and he was wheeling and dealing, thinking up new ideas. The merger made him a rich man, but I reckon he died of boredom and frustration.'

'Oh, my dear love!' Liz knew exactly how she would feel in his place; Leigh's father had been his only kin, and they had been very close. She put her arms round him and rested her head against his shoulder. At least she had some good news for him.

'I'm not sure if this is the ideal moment, but in a curious way, it might be exactly right. Leigh, how would you feel about a Christmas wedding?'

He propped himself up on one elbow to look down at her, his expression almost comical with disbelief. 'It's come? The dispensation?'

'Two days ago. I've been terribly frustrated, not being able to tell you.'

'And we can go ahead any time we want?' He still sounded dazed.

'Uh-huh. I thought Christmas would be a good time, if you could get leave.'

He laughed exultantly. 'Tomorrow would be better.'

'Honestly! There are certain formalities and preparations to be . . .'

Liz tried to sit up, but he gently pushed her down onto the rug, sliding a hand beneath her breast where her heart was now thudding furiously. His kiss was long and lingering, and with his mouth still against hers, he murmured, 'Hang the preparations. I think we should celebrate right now.'

'Leigh! We can't! Not here. Mam might walk in any minute.' But her body was already responding in the most dangerous way.

She slipped from his grasp and came to her feet, side-stepping out of reach of his long arms. He leaned back, content to watch her, and as she met the look in his eyes, her colour mounted and she rushed into speech.

'Christmas is a very busy time for us, of course, but it's a lovely time for a wedding. I . . . I've already had a word with Father Glynn, and he's sure it can be arranged.'

'I might have known. You've got a lot of Flora in you, young lady. I do hope you won't turn into a managing wife.'

'How unkind.' Liz pretended outrage, but laughter got the better of her. 'And after she's been so good to you, too. Anyway I shall be much too busy with my own career to manage you or anyone else. It hardly got off the ground before Gerry put a stop to it, but I'm determined that one day the Lendl Collection will be famous. And I want babies, too.'

Leigh laughed aloud.

'Honey sweet, you can conquer the whole darned world and have as many babies as you want, as long as it makes you happy. Hell, maybe we'll found our own dynasty.' He stretched out a hand. 'Come back. I promise to be good.'

'Have you thought what you'll do after the war?' Liz asked, when she was safe back in his arms again. 'I can't see you twiddling your thumbs on some Board.'

'No way.' His green eyes were quizzical. 'I daresay I'll be offered some kind of position, but I'd rather do my own thing. I rather thought I might stay in England – start up my own freight business. How does that idea grab you?'

Her heart leapt. 'Could you do that? Wouldn't it cost an awful lot of money to start a business like that from scratch?'

Leigh laughed softly. 'That's my girl – always practical! But the money's no problem. And air freight's really going to take off after the war. Dad would've liked me to be involved.'

A coal settled in the hearth, and Liz said, her voice choked, 'I wish I could have met your father. From all you say, and the photographs you've shown me, I think he must have been quite a man.'

'He was that, all right. I told him about you, and he said "Your Elizabeth sounds as if she's got guts – just like your Mom". He always reckoned women were the strong ones.' Leigh could still hear the frail thread of that once vigorous voice. He reached for his jacket and took out a small box. 'He wanted you to have this.'

Inside was a sepia photograph of a young woman with a sweet yet strong face, framed by dark wavy hair drawn back into a knot, almost too heavy for the delicate neck to support. Liz picked it up and studied the face. 'How sad that you never knew her.'

'Yeah. I sometimes think she might have been a little like your mother.'

She leaned across and kissed him. 'Oh, darling, I do love you.'

He reached into the box. She hadn't noticed the wedding ring. It was almost new, and the realization of how short a time his mother had worn it brought a lump to her throat.

'Do you mind, sweet Elizabeth?' Leigh asked, sliding Jimmy's ring off her third finger. She put it in her pocket, and he slid his mother's on. It fitted almost perfectly. Their eyes met. 'As if it were meant,' he said softly, removing it again. 'So we'd better have a word with this priest of yours before I leave.'

That night she put Jimmy's ring back on, but on her right hand.

Her parents were happy about the wedding. Even the fact that it was their busiest time could not detract from their pleasure. They had never been comfortable with the way things were, though the circumstances had been unusual from the start, and Liz was no longer a child, to be told what to do. It would be a family affair, but the radiance in their daughter's face broadcast her joy to all.

Almost as important – in fact, more so to Rosie's way of thinking – was the Nativity play. Rosie had started school the previous January. Now, three-quarters of the way through her first year, she was very much the class leader, bright, intelligent, and full of her mother's guile at getting her own way. Which was how she came to be playing Mary – not an ideal choice in terms of humility, but this was compensated for by her ability to remember her lines – and everybody else's. There had been one awkward moment when Rosie had demanded that Georgy should play Joseph, until it was explained very forcibly to her by Kathleen that, in the interests of fair play, only one person from each family could take a main part, and in any case Georgy would be much happier as a shepherd.

To give Rosie her due, when Georgy's health permitted him to attend school she was very protective of him: half his size, she would guard him like a hawk. No-one but herself was allowed to boss him about, and woe betide any child who tried to make fun of him.

'Georgy belongs to me, an' you let him alone,' she would insist, steely-eyed, daring anyone in the class to defy her, or chant 'Uncle Georgy-Porgy' at him in her hearing.

'She's going to be a handful, that one,' Ellen said, when Kathleen had gone out the back to take the two of them to school.

Liz thought she sounded a bit down. 'Is anything wrong?'

Ellen cocked an ear towards the shop, where Dot seemed to be coping. 'It's Rufus,' she said quietly. 'Liz, I think I've been a fool. And your weddin's brought it home to me. Before he left, Rufus asked me to marry him – and I couldn't make up my mind, so I refused him.'

Liz wasn't sure what Ellen wanted her to say. 'I thought you were fond of him?'

'I was – I am. And he's been ever so good to us, me and the kiddies. He really made me feel I was someone – you know what I mean?'

'So?'

'I don't know what came over me. When he proposed' – she blushed – 'I suddenly thought of how it was with Arnie and me when we first met and fell in love. You won't remember how he was, before . . .'

'Oh, but I do, very clearly. He was so handsome, very sure of himself.'

'Right.' Ellen's voice thickened a little. 'I adored him. And I knew I didn't feel that way about Rufus. Now, I realize that there's different kinds of love, and I miss him – more than I would have thought. Only he's somewhere in France, and I can't tell him that I've changed my mind. Do you think, if I was to write, he might get it eventually?'

'Yes, of course. You could maybe send it care of Burtonwood. I'll ask Leigh, next time he calls.'

'Bless you, Liz.' Ellen hugged her.

Shirley Anne's new picture, *A Nightingale Sang*, had its premier two weeks before Christmas and was an even bigger success than the first. There was a poignant theme to the story this time, which gave her a chance to prove her ability to act, as well as sing and dance.

'Mr Grace is dead chuffed. He reckons that, come the end of the war, I could have Hollywood knocking at my door. It was his idea that I should record the song that runs through it,' she said casually. 'I thought I might take Mrs Frith a signed copy for Christmas.'

'Oh, she'd be thrilled!' Liz said. 'Poor thing hasn't been too well lately.'

It was the first time in years that Shirley Anne had been home for Christmas, and it couldn't have happened more opportunely. With Rita visiting too, the whole family would be together for the wedding.

They were sorting through the decorations, the best of which had already been used in the shop. 'My sister, the Hollywood film star,' Liz said in a posh voice, swaying round the room, draped in faded crêpe paper streamers, 'is to honour me by attending our simple ceremony. She's got no side on her, you know – thinks nothing of washing up when she's at home. But then, she never thought much of it when she was a nobody!'

They both collapsed in laughter, and Rita, heavily pregnant, came in to find them helpless on the floor, almost drowning out Bing Crosby singing *I'm Dreaming of a White Christmas* on the wireless.

'Honestly,' she said in her best schoolteacher voice. 'You two don't get any better.' She picked up a squashed lantern. 'Ugh. Is this the best we can do?'

' 'Fraid so.' Liz got to her feet. 'Still, we'll manage. The kiddies won't notice how tatty they are, and Aunt Flora's brought us that little tree from her garden. We've still got a few silvery baubles, and I bought a whole lot of red and green ribbon ages ago when T. J. Hughes got a new lot in. I've used most of it for cake decoration, but there's still a few yards left.'

'Mam's really made up, having us all home together, and lots of kids around again,' Rita said. 'I just wish . . .'

'I know,' Shirley Anne put in quickly. 'But we're having no long faces. Just think – by next year, the war'll be over, your Frank'll be home, and there'll be lights everywhere.'

'Listen to her. Shirley Anne Ryan, star of stage and screen – and eternal optimist.' Rita still hardly dared to look that far ahead, although everything did seem to be going the right way. 'At least the black-out's more of a dim-out now, down our way. Even here, it's become less rigorous, and they're talking about doing away with the hoods on car headlights, and allowing public transport to be properly lit again.'

Perhaps it was the expectation of all this that made Christmas seem a bit easier and a bit jollier this year, despite the shortages. For the first time in ages, there had been a delivery of oranges – just in time for the children's stockings – and Aunt May and Uncle Liam had been more than usually generous with the parcels they sent to all the members of the family. The resources, when pooled, proved invaluable, and with the wedding imminent, couldn't have come at a better time.

Sunny Marsden, too, continued to be generous. He was genuinely pleased that Liz was to find happiness with someone else.

'But we'll always think of you as one of the family, lass.' He sighed. 'Christmas is a sad time for us, now. Mother's never really come to terms with our loss. She keeps saying, if only she had a grave to put flowers on – '

'That's the worst part,' Liz admitted. She tried to visit Mrs Marsden regularly, but the poor woman's continuous grieving made her feel guilty that she had accepted Jimmy's death so comparatively quickly. And now, having to tell her about Leigh . . .

'Listen, young Liz,' Sunny said, after a particularly gruelling session, 'don't let Mother get to you. You were a good wife to our lad, but life has to go on, and our Jimmy'd not want you to waste yours, mourning him. You need a man and babbies like any other young lass.'

'Thank you.' She reached up to kiss him, and he chuckled with pleasure.

'Now, how about a bit of pork for yer Dad? Enough to make a few of those special pies. And I've some of that fat, if he needs it.'

Liz kept busy to keep herself from getting nervous – and there was plenty to do, trying to provide at least some attractive Christmas fare. The practice of adding mashed potato to the bread dough had proved so satisfactory that she had eventually tried it out in pastry, and found that ten ounces of mashed potato added to the same of fat and two pounds of National flour, made an excellent short paste. This was particularly useful at Christmas for making very good mincemeat fingers, which were much more economical than mince pies. She would pin out the pastry and line large baking sheets, and mix three ounces of cake and bread crumbs, adding lots of extra apple to every pound of mincemeat, to spread thinly and cover with another layer of pastry. It was quick to make, and cut into slices, brought an excellent return. She also used the potato pastry to make savoury puffs, by cutting it into rounds, placing a little grated cheese and some flaked haddock or minced chicken or Spam in the centre, and pinching the edges together before baking them in a hot oven. These were extremely popular during the cold weather, particularly with the ladies at the Candide, as were Dad's boxty.

Liz was increasingly optimistic that Ryan's, trading as *Choice Fayre, Ltd*, would thrive. Even now they were holding their own, in spite of wartime restrictions. It never ceased to amaze her how quickly the queues formed whenever the rumour went out that anything extra was available in the way of confectionery. The first year's takings in the new company had been better than expected, largely because of the work Chris and Mary had put into pulling their side of it together. Young Peter thrived, and Mary seemed to have no trouble managing him as well as the shop. It was something to build on for the future.

Food had started coming in more regularly, as fewer ships were sunk: the Germans now had more urgent priorities. In fact, the speed with which the docks had recovered was little short of miraculous. In no time, it seemed, they were shipping out armaments and troops, and handling essential foodstuffs, with all their old efficiency. Ellen heard from one of Arnie's old mates that part of the Mulberry Harbour, which had been assembled so successfully off the coast of Normandy, had been dispatched from Liverpool. So well were things going that the docks were actually starting to recruit more men. Ellen's second-eldest child, Ned, had been taken on as an apprentice fitter.

'It was his Dad's trade, and he was determined to take after him,' Ellen said. She was quietly cheerful these days, having had a letter from Rufus.

Nick had tried several times to get his old job back, but each time he failed the medical. He still had headaches and dizzy spells, though they were becoming less frequent. He clearly hated the North Wales job, and was desperate to get back to Liverpool and his mates.

'I doubt they'll come to the wedding – not that that's much loss, though I'd have liked Nick to be here,' Kathleen said, when she and Michael were alone. 'Laura's going to lose him altogether, the way she's going on. The trouble is, with the money and property her parents left her, she holds the purse strings now – and she wants to sell the Bootle house and stay in Wales.'

Michael puffed on his pipe. 'It's a sorry affair altogether.

Especially for the kiddies – I suppose they'll be well settled at school there.'

'Children soon adapt,' Kathleen said, unwilling to see any side but her brother's. 'Perhaps, now the docks are reviving, Nick'll be able to get a less physically demanding job.'

'Well, it's not our affair, *acushla*, so don't you go interfering. They'll just have to work it out for themselves.'

Chapter Eight

Liz and Leigh were married in the early afternoon two days before Christmas: the night before, Liz had removed Jimmy's wedding ring, putting it carefully away with her other treasures.

The actual wedding service had to be held in the vestry because it was a mixed marriage, but Fr Glynn made everything as warm and welcoming as possible, and when Leigh slid his mother's wedding ring on to her finger, she felt that nothing else mattered. The blessing that followed in the church itself, with all its festive decorations, simply added the perfect finishing touch. And if it seemed strange to Michael to be giving his Lizzie for a second time, the shining radiance that hung about the pair of them was a sure indication that this was no ordinary love.

Everyone had been up earlier than usual, so as to get all the Christmas orders for that day ready and out. Steve and Albert were coping in the bakehouse, and Ellen and Dot swore they could manage the shop. It was a little easier for Chris and Mary, as they had more staff.

Liz had been in an agony of indecision over what to wear. There was little hope of buying anything new; Christmas had left everyone low on coupons. She had almost fixed on the nicer of the two dresses she had bought to go to Borrowdale, when Shirley Anne settled the matter by vanishing upstairs, to reappear a few minutes later with a beautiful flowing silk dress in a soft bronze shade billowing on her arm. It fitted Liz perfectly, and brought out the colour of her eyes.

'Oh, but are you sure?' Liz sounded dazed as she twirled to let the soft folds settle about the legs. 'It looks terribly expensive.'

'Fruits of success, sweetie,' Shirley Anne said carelessly. 'Something borrowed. You can't possibly refuse. And that frothy little cream hat you had last year will go with it beautifully, though I doubt Leigh will be looking at what you're wearing.'

He had arrived the night before, accompanied by his co-pilot, Hank Beeman, who was to be his best man.

'Very dishy,' Shirley Anne murmured, looking the lieutenant over with a predatory eye.

'Hush, he'll hear you.'

For the ceremony, both wore full dress uniform, and in spite of wishing to keep the affair quiet, the noisy, good-natured crowds outside the church threatened to block the street.

Leigh had wanted to save Liz and her family work by booking a wedding breakfast at the Adelphi, where he had taken a suite for what would be a very brief honeymoon, but Kathleen was adamant that the wedding breakfast must be at home. It was a bit of a squeeze, even though the piano had been moved into the parlour, but there was just enough room to fit in an extra table. 'And many hands make light work,' she said.

There was quite a spread. Sunny Marsden had contributed an ox tongue and some rib of beef, and Cousin Tom had produced a large ham shank, together with lovely fresh leeks and Brussels sprouts.

Dandy, under the influence of the wine provided by Leigh, became loquacious and made one of his speeches, combining his pride in the further extension of the Ryan family across two continents, with the confident expectation that the war would soon be over. Laura and Nick did come, after all, though they left the children with friends in Wales.

'I bet when all came to all, Laura couldn't resist the chance of meeting Leigh, and bragging to her friends about her niece marrying an American major,' Flora said.

'I've been offered a job at last,' Nick confided to Kathleen, catching her on her own in the scullery. 'In me old yard. Warehouse foreman. I won't get the overtime I got with the old job, of course, but just the same, it's what I wanted.'

'I'm glad. What does Laura think?'

'We've compromised.' Nick didn't quite meet his sister's eyes. 'She wants to sell our house and move out Waterloo way. We could afford it, if we use some of the money Laura's parents left.'

'I see. Well, I hope it all works out, Nick. You've had a rotten time.'

With the meal at an end, Dandy master-minded the washing up, helped by Flora and a reluctant Laura, while Kathleen was made to sit down, and Rita and Mary attended to their little ones before taking over in the shop, so that Ellen and Dot could have a well-earned break. The customers were in high good humour.

'God love yer, Liz, gairl, be 'appy!' and other similar expressions of affection, and demands to see the bride, were continuously being shouted through from the shop. And occasionally, Liz persuaded Leigh to make a brief appearance.

Soon, the piano was going full belt. Hank played *In The Mood*, and Liz remembered how Glenn Miller, eyes smiling behind his glasses, had played Leigh's request only a few months ago. Now he was missing – lost just over a week ago, flying to France to entertain the troops. But her sadness was fleeting – nothing could spoil today. Shirley Anne was flirting outrageously with Hank, who had already promised to take her out for the evening, and Rosie was getting over-excited. Georgy, to everyone's surprise, had attached himself to Leigh.

'I help my Dad make bread,' he told him gravely.

'I'm sure that *is* a great help to him,' Leigh said with equal gravity.

'He's got Steve and Albert, of course, but anover pairs of hands is always useful.'

'I bet it is. Especially when they're very busy.'

'Christmas is busy,' Georgy said. 'And weddings is extra busy.' After a moment, he asked anxiously, 'Are you taking Liz away?'

'Not far, and only for a day or two.'

This seemed to satisfy the child, who smiled and trotted away.

'Honey sweet,' Leigh murmured, capturing his bride as she flitted from one to another. 'Your parents had given us a wonderful time, and your family are great, but this is all getting to be a bit like Grand Central Station! How long before I get to have you to myself?'

He was joking, but she could hear the weariness in his voice.

'I'll have a quiet word with Mam and Dad.'

She found her father in the bakehouse. Steve and Albert had gone, and he was alone, looking a little lost.

'Dad?'

He held out his arms to her, and she went into them. 'My Lizzie. This time, God grant you all the happiness you deserve.'

She laughed shakily. 'If I was any happier, I don't think I could bear it. You won't mind if we slip away? Leigh is very tired.'

Kathleen, back in the parlour, had seen the tiredness for herself and pre-empted the question. 'Off you go, the two of you. That man of yours looks as if he could do with a bit of peace and quiet.' She hugged her daughter. 'I don't have to say "be happy", do I? It's shining out of you. Go on, now. We'll see you sometime Christmas Day.'

Flora was able to snatch a moment with Leigh. 'I'm not much given to making speeches, but you know how fond of you I am, and Liz has always had a special place in my heart. So if you ever want a couple of quiet days together, just let me know, and Rose Lodge will be at your disposal. I'm very good at becoming invisible at a moment's notice.'

Leigh, seeing the caring woman beyond the elegant perfumed facade, enveloped her in a great bear hug. 'Flora, you're an angel,' he said, and bent and kissed her.

'Well, if I am,' she said huskily, 'you'd better give over before you crush my wings.'

For almost two days they didn't leave the suite at the Adelphi. Room service arrived discreetly with a meal when summoned, but between times they were hungry only for the sight and touch and taste of each other.

Liz had sometimes wondered if the magic of their previous interlude together had been accentuated by time and place, never to be repeated. But with Leigh's very first caress, she knew that all that had gone before had been but a prelude. There was an instant fusion, a perfection in their lovemaking that seemed to reach new heights with each coming together, as night ran into day, and into night again.

'It's Christmas,' she murmured, her lips trailing softly against his skin. 'Would you mind – could we go to Midnight Mass?' And as he groaned softly: 'It wouldn't take too long, and I have so much to say "thank you" for.'

So they slipped in at the back of the crowded church, and as the voices soared, the joy of the occasion moved Leigh as it moved everyone there. And afterwards they slipped away again, to celebrate in their own special way.

In February there was a massive raid on Dresden. The Russians were advancing fast, and a huge Allied air offensive was launched to pave the way for them. Many people cheered, remembering how they themselves had suffered, but many more were disturbed by such wholesale destruction.

Liz knew that Leigh would be involved; knew, too, how much he would hate it. He had been very edgy on the telephone, not at all himself, and she hadn't pressed him to talk. It was at times like this that she wished East Anglia wasn't so far away, that he hadn't been so adamant that she should remain in Liverpool, where she was needed.

'Look, you wouldn't know what to do with yourself down there, honey sweet, all on your own. And as things are at present, you wouldn't see much more of me than you do now. I'll hitch a lift up here any chance I get, and we can talk on the phone.'

It all made perfect sense, but it didn't help.

When he did manage a brief visit, towards the end of March, Liz was shocked to see how drained he looked, his eyes wary behind a blank facade. 'How long have you got?' she asked and, finding it was a mere forty-eight hours, she had a quick consultation with Mam, and got on to Aunt Flora. Within a couple of hours they were at Rose Lodge.

'I've laid you a supper out in the drawing room, by the fire,' Mrs Meadows said, taking their coats and generally fussing round them. 'A good hot casserole. You might have to search for the meat, but there's some of me special dumplings, and lots of good fresh vegetables from the garden. And Madam said you'd to have a bottle of the Margaux.'

'Lovely, Mrs M.,' said Liz.

'I wish I'd known you were coming,' she said reproachfully. 'What with Madam being called away so sudden and all. I could've put off going to my sister. It's not as if she knows what day it is, anyway.'

'We wouldn't hear of it. I'm not exactly a stranger to my aunt's kitchen. Besides, Major Farrell and I will probably eat out quite a bit.'

'Well, if you're sure . . .'

'Darling, I thought she'd never go,' Liz giggled when the door finally closed. And then Leigh pulled her close, and all desire to giggle left her. At last, he released her, except for her hands, which he held on to very tightly. His green eyes picked up little darts of light from the fire, which gave them an added intensity.

'Food first,' she said firmly.

But he only picked at the casserole, and later, despite his desperate need of her, he finally flung away in disgust, his arm shielding his eyes. 'What a bloody fiasco that was! I should never have come.'

'Don't say that! Don't ever say that, Leigh Farrell!' Liz loomed over him, tears of anger coursing down on to his chest. 'As if that's all I want of you!' And he swore softly and pulled her close, cradling her until she grew quiet. And early the following morning, they made love with a particular sweetness.

Much later, he confessed that it was more than tiredness – he was becoming sick to his stomach of the constant bombing. 'For long enough it didn't bother me. In fact, I took a pride in planning a strategic exercise, pin-pointing specific targets – aircraft factories, munitions, railway yards. Now, our brief is becoming less and less discriminating, and a lot of ordinary folk are being killed.'

Her heart ached for him – and for those poor innocent people caught up in the kind of terror she and others had endured. In an attempt to salve his conscience, she said quickly, 'It's what they did to us.'

'Honey, that just makes it worse. I've been there, remember? I saw and heard and felt what it was like. And I'm not sure how much longer I can keep on sending those bombs down, knowing what I know – '

'Oh, Leigh, darling, you're just tired out.' She could feel his heart beating erratically fast. 'It's ridiculous! They ought to stand you down for longer. Two days isn't anything like enough time to relax.'

He laughed, a harsh sound. 'Would you care to tell Colonel Radner that? His language can be a mite colourful, when he's roused. Anyway, it's better to keep going. A longer lay-off just makes starting up again that much worse.' He lifted her away, holding her where he could see her in the fading light. 'Take no notice, honey sweet. I'm just in a foul mood. Once I climb back into the good old *Lullabelle*, I'll be fine.'

Chapter Nine

But it wasn't that simple. After he went back, his calls became more erratic. Liz told herself that he would be bone weary after a raid, not wanting to talk. She told herself not to worry. If anything had happened, she would have heard. For days, she went through the motions of work, of serving in the shop, of talking brightly to customers – she even made extra jobs for herself so that she wouldn't have to think, except that nothing could blot out the unthinkable. Not even the birth of Rita's baby early in March – another boy.

Every time the phone jangled, she froze, waiting for someone else to answer it. At last, Kathleen said, 'For heaven's sake, Liz, why don't you telephone the base? You have the number.'

'I can't.'

Kathleen's heart went out to her. But she kept her voice brisk. 'Of course you can. I've never known you to run away from anything in your life, however unpleasant.' And when Liz still hesitated, 'Ah, come on, love. Anything's better than not knowing.'

And so she rang the air base, and after a lot of crackling noises, and being passed from one clerk to another, Leigh's voice came down the line, faint but clear. Relief robbed her of the power to speak. She felt dizzy.

'Elizabeth? Is that you?'

'Yes,' she managed at last. 'Oh, Leigh, it's so wonderful to hear your voice!'

'Likewise.' He sounded puzzled. 'Are you all right? Has something happened?'

She laughed weakly. 'No, everything's fine. I feel wonderful. Leigh, you'll think me a perfect fool . . . I just wanted to hear your voice.'

'I don't think it foolish at all, honey sweet. I was going to ring you this evening, anyway. I've just been a bit tied up – long debriefing sessions, you know the kind of thing?'

She said 'Of course,' and didn't voice her fears. It was enough to know that he was safe. And the shining glance she threw her mother told Kathleen all was well – this time.

A week or so later, when the children were in bed, and Mam had gone to the weekly vigil to Our Lady of Perpetual Succour, the phone rang around Leigh's usual time and Liz ran to pick it up.

'Is this Mrs Elizabeth Farrell?'

The voice was American, but not Leigh's. She turned hot and then cold, and found that she was trembling all over. 'Speaking,' she managed.

'Mrs Farrell, I'm Colonel Vincent Radner . . .'

She knew at once. 'It's about Leigh, isn't it?'

'He particularly asked me to call you if he ever went missing . . .'

'You don't have to wrap it up in fancy language, Colonel,' she said, suddenly quite calm. 'Leigh's dead, isn't he?'

'I wish I could be that specific, ma'am. The truth is, we don't know, not for certain – that's why I've delayed this long. The *Lullabelle* went down over enemy territory, along with several other F17s, about thirty-six hours ago, during a very heavy concentration of ground fire. The returning crews reported seeing several parachutes open . . . We have no way of knowing from which plane, of course . . .'

'Except that Leigh wouldn't jump unless everyone was safely out of the plane. We both know that.'

'No, ma'am, he wouldn't.' She thought she detected a note of something like admiration in his voice. 'But Red's a pretty resourceful guy, so I'm not prepared to write him off yet. Radio contact wasn't good, but another pilot thought he heard him say that he had two badly wounded crew members, and that he was going to try to land the plane, even though it was in pretty bad shape.'

'I see. Then we must wait. You will let me know, if you hear anything definite?'

'I surely will, ma'am.' The colonel cleared his throat. 'Red told me you were a very gutsy lady. May I say that I wholeheartedly agree with him?'

Liz put the phone down and walked slowly back into the living room. Michael had just put on the wireless to listen to *Scrapbook*. He was about to fill his pipe when he caught sight of his daughter's face. He laid it aside and went to her.

'Lizzie?'

She didn't seem to hear him at first. *Oh, dear God*! He took her by the shoulders, shook her gently. 'Lizzie, my love, something's happened. Is it Leigh?'

She leaned her head against him for a moment, and then straightened. 'They don't know for sure.' She looked up at him, dry-eyed and astonishingly calm. 'I think I'll make a pot of tea. Mam'll be in soon, and she'll be cold.'

Michael let her go, feeling helpless, as he always did at such times. He listened to her moving about, heard the water gushing into the kettle, the scrape of the match, the spoon rattling in the tea caddy. Then she came through with the milk jug and began to lay the cups and saucers on the end of the table.

A cold rush of air brought Kathleen hurrying in just as the kettle began to whistle. 'Oh, bless you Liz, you're making the tea. There weren't many of us tonight, which is no surprise. It's more like January than April out there.' She took off her hat and stabbed the hatpin back into it before unwinding the thick woollen scarf from around her neck. Only then did she notice the atmosphere. She looked to Michael, then Liz, then back again to Michael. 'Jesus, Mary and Joseph! Not. . . ?' He nodded.

'Oh, my poor Liz!' She reached out her arms.

Liz allowed herself to be held briefly, then drew away. 'I think if you don't mind, I'll take my tea upstairs.'

She sounded so calm; too calm. Kathleen watched her go, then turned to Michael with so much grief in her eyes that he gathered her to himself. 'Should I go to her? I'm sure it isn't good for her to be alone.'

'Let her be, *acushla*. It's not above fifteen minutes since Leigh's colonel rang. She needs time to take it in. There's still some slim chance, but slim is the word, I'd say, or he wouldn't have called.'

'Dear God, Michael, will it never end? This war – this wicked, wicked war that has ruined so many lives?'

'Soon. But not soon enough, maybe, for our dearest Lizzie.' Michael shook his head. 'This will break her for sure. They were so much in love – had so many plans.'

*

But Liz didn't break, not even when Colonel Radner came in person to tell her that the *Lullabelle* had been found by advancing Russian troops, burned out in a field with no survivors. She took him through into Mam's parlour. Mam had offered to support her, but this was something she had to do alone. He seemed to fill the room – bluff, red-faced and clearly ill at ease as he perched on the edge of a chair built for a much smaller man.

'Red spoke about you a lot, ma'am. I'm only sorry we have to meet in such tragic circumstances. But I felt I had to come myself – to tell you and to bring your husband's personal effects.'

'I appreciate the thought, Colonel,' she said politely. 'It's kind of you, when you must be so busy. Can I offer you tea – coffee? Or something stronger, perhaps? I believe we have a little whisky . . .'

'Thank you, no,' he said, getting to his feet a little too quickly. 'Time is pressing.'

'If you're sure. You would be very welcome to stay and have a meal with us.'

'You're very kind, ma'am, but I have a plane waiting to take me back.' The colonel cleared his throat, and wrung her hand with obvious emotion. 'I don't have to tell you how much I'm going to miss Red. He was one of a kind – and not just because he was the best damned flier we had, begging your pardon. I valued him as a friend. It can get awful lonely at the top, and to have someone you can talk things over with – ' He shook his head. 'The men liked and respected him, too – trusted his judgement. That means one hell of a lot in a tight spot, I can tell you. My report will include the highest possible commendation for gallantry.'

Liz murmured all the right things, and couldn't wait for him to go. Then, without a word to anyone, she took the familiar shabby leather bag upstairs to her room and put it down on the bed. And because, if she didn't do it at once, she feared she never would, her hand reached out for the clasp and opened the bag wide.

Like a genie released from a bottle, the essence of him enveloped her, seeming to fill the room with the smell and the feel of him, like a physical presence. Her breath caught, held, filling her chest almost to bursting . . . *If I can hold it long enough, he'll take me with him*. But even as the thought took shape, she glanced down at the bag and saw a pair of photographs that had spilled from Leigh's wallet – two of the many he had taken at Borrowdale. The first of herself leaning on Grange bridge, laughing into the camera, her love so transparent it was almost unbearable. She pushed it aside, and saw the two of them, snapped by the young hiker beneath the Bowder Stone. Leigh seemed so heartbreakingly real, looking down at her with that quizzical smile – so real that if she turned her head just a fraction, she was sure he would be there, telling her that this wasn't really the end. What was it he had said, that last evening? 'Honey sweet, how can anything this wonderful end?'

With a shuddering sob, she let her breath go, and with the void it left behind came the first unbearable sense of loss. She wrapped her arms tight around herself, rocking back and forth in a dry-eyed, almost silent keening release of her grief.

When it was over, she was able to take up the letter that lay beneath the wallet, with her name scrawled across it in his own distinctive scrawl. This she picked up with a steady hand, slitting it open.

> 'My lovely Elizabeth, you will know by now that things haven't gone quite the way we'd hoped. But remember that you will never be alone – a part of me will always be a part of you, urging you on to fulfil your dreams. So live your life to the full, honey sweet, for my sake as well as your own. And if, in time, another man should come along, don't shut him out because of me – you are too precious to squander your warmth and generosity on memories . . .'

There was much more, but her eyes were misting and she couldn't see the words clearly. It would wait until later, as would the large official-looking envelope that had lain beneath it.

She propped the two photographs up on the little chest beside the bed, the last images she would see before she slept, and the first to greet her when she awoke. And then she went downstairs again to get on with her work.

Word of Leigh's death got round, as such things always did, and the customers were warm in their sympathy. Kathleen arranged with Ellen and Dot to keep Liz away from the shop as much as possible for the first few days. Fortunately, Lily Killigan, now Lily Mullins, had recently given birth prematurely, and endless calculations about the time difference between the dates of the wedding and the birth of her daughter provided an endless source of entertainment, and took some of the pressure off Liz. The Killigans were also in the limelight for another reason.

Eighteen-year-old Eddie, who had been lving the life of Riley as a result of the deals that had for so long supplemented his messenger's job, was about to have his comfortable existence rudely shattered. Like many other men between eighteen and twenty-six he was to be drafted down the mines. Kathleen was relieved that Joey would be spared because of his engineering course. But Eddie had no cause for exemption.

'Your Eddie down the mines – that's rich, tharris,' chuckled Ada Killigan's latest tormentor. 'Talk about black market! 'E won't find it so easy ter gerr'away with a sack of coal.'

'You want ter wash your mouth out, Nellie. An' anyway, 'e won't pass the medical. Delicate chest, has our Eddie – a martyr ter the bronicals, just like Kath's little Georgy. Coal dust could be lethal to a chest like that.'

'Gerr'away. 'E never found brick dust any problem, when we wus bein' bombed.' Nellie chuckled. 'Ar, an' with 'is luck, I shouldn't wonder if your Eddie strikes gold.'

'I haven't told Michael, but it can't be healthy, the way Liz is behaving,' Kathleen told Flora.

'You mean she's created a shrine?'

'Well, not exactly. The photos aren't surrounded by flowers and candles, or anything like that, but even so – I just feel there's something very odd about it. I mean, when I think how she almost broke her heart when Jimmy died. This time, I don't even know if she's shed any tears at all. If she has, I've seen no evidence of it. Apart from being a bit subdued, she seems to be carrying on almost as though nothing's happened. Michael hasn't really noticed, but then he wouldn't, being a quiet man himself. I wonder if I ought to get Fr Glynn to have a word with her. She seems to get on quite well with him.'

Flora stubbed out her cigarette. 'If I were you, our Kathy, I'd let her be for now. You remember what I said when they came back from the Lakes – about the kind of fulfilment that seemed to surround them? That may have something to do with the way Liz is reacting. We all have to handle our grief in our own way.' Her face crumpled momentarily. 'Leigh was like the son I never had.' And then, pulling herself together; 'She's coming to Southport next week to see Bill Yates. He's handling the complexities of Leigh's will for her. Ironic, isn't it? From what he's told her, it seems as if Liz is going to be a rather wealthy young woman.'

Chapter Ten

There was no longer any doubt about an Allied victory. By April, it was simply a matter of how soon it would come. Dandy avidly scoured the papers and listened to BBC news bulletins. Not all of them gave cause for celebration. Even as the troops converged on Berlin, there was widespread sadness, early on the morning of the 13th, when it was announced that President Roosevelt had died.

'He wasn't a well man, but it's a pity he couldn't have seen it through to the end.' Dandy shook his head. 'Winston'll miss him – a tower of strength he's been. I only hope this Truman feller knows what's what.'

As the prison camps were liberated, Rita waited daily for news of Frank's Stalag number. When it came at last, she joyously rang home in case they had missed it.

'That's really great news, Rita,' Liz said warmly. 'You'll have him home before you know it. And little James to welcome him.'

'Yes.' Rita's voice went suddenly flat. 'I'm sorry, love. I forgot, just for the moment.'

'Good. I'll be glad when everyone else stops walking on eggshells. Honest, the last thing I want is for folk to feel guilty every time they rejoice over the return of their loved ones.'

But there were terrible discoveries, too: concentration camps where unspeakable atrocities had been committed against Jews. Liz thought how, but for the grace of God, Fritz might have been one of them.

'It does not bear thinking of.' Mitzi was close to tears when Liz visited her. 'Did you hear that nice American journalist, Edward Murrow, yesterday? The horror of what he had seen at Buchenwald was in his voice. So many of our friends, treated like animals – worse than animals. As well Papa did not live to know of such things.'

As Liz was leaving, Mitzi called her back. 'I almost forgot. I have received a letter from a young friend of Papa's, Josef Werner. He went to Switzerland before the war, but they kept in touch. It was a long time before I could bring myself to go through Papa's papers, and so found his letters. Naturally, I wrote to tell him what had happened. Papa must have mentioned you to Josef, because he now writes to say that should you wish to further your knowledge of confectionery, he would be more than happy to assist you. Here – ' Mitzi pressed the letter into Liz's hands. 'It may be that you will want to go away for a while at the end of the war. If so, he says you would be most welcome to stay with his family for as long as you wish.'

Liz took the letter, to put it with the books Fritz had left her. She had made no definite plans. Originally it had been so simple; she would open up the cellar bakery and carry on where she had left off. Since then, many things had changed. With Leigh's death, it seemed that her ambitions had died, too.

But now Mitzi had put this idea into her head, and it wouldn't go away. Idly she began to turn the pages. It was a long time since she had really looked at the books. The names sprang out at her – pretzels, noix de Zurich, petit fours, glacés, praline, torte . . . luscious, luxurious names. For the first time since Leigh had gone, she felt a stirring of excitement. Josef Werner's offer was very tempting. She would have to wait a while, of course, until everything had settled back to normal, and she was sure that Mam and Dad could cope without her.

Money would be no bar. She still hadn't come to terms with the idea that she was a wealthy woman – quite how wealthy, she wasn't sure, as negotiations between the English and American lawyers were, to say the least, protracted.

'I can't seem to feel anything,' she told Aunt Flora, after yet another visit to sign more forms. 'The money means very little without Leigh. We had such plans . . .'

'I know, Liz. But that will pass.' Flora's heart ached for her. Why, oh, why, did life have to play such dirty tricks? There was Shirley Anne, talented, single-minded Shirley Anne, who was already halfway to stardom, and destined for Hollywood and her heart's desire, all with seemingly little effort. And here was Liz, who had never put herself first, and had fought her way through every obstacle until now, when her heart's desire had been denied her. Perhaps this re-awakening of her early ambitions, if she could be persuaded to take advantage of it, might be her salvation.

'I think the whole idea of going to Switzerland is an excellent one. It's time you put yourself first. Get away. Start a whole new life. Kathleen and Michael will have Chris and his Mary to keep an eye on them.'

'I'll think about it,' Liz said. 'The war isn't over yet.'

By the end of the month, however, people were getting out their flags and bunting in readiness for the great day. Every new rumour was discussed with relish among the customers.

'Italian partisans got that pompous little perisher, Mussolini – strung 'im up, an' good riddance.'

'I 'eard Hitler hisself 'ad committed suicide, killed his mistress, an' all. Serve 'er right, silly cow. Good riddance ter the lot of 'em!'

So many wild stories abounded that Dandy refused to believe anything, unless he had actually heard it given out by Alvar Lidell or Stuart Hibberd on the BBC news. It wasn't until the 7th of May that the pronouncement was finally made – the surrender terms had been signed, and the following day would be celebrated as VE Day.

'Well, that's it then,' he said, with a little nod of satisfaction. 'It's official. Mind, we still have to finish off the Japs, but that won't take long.'

That same evening Rita rang to say that Frank had arrived home, just in time for the celebrations. 'He looks fine, Mam,' she said, half in tears. 'Quite brown, in fact, from being out of doors so much. We'll be up as soon as . . . Well, you know.'

Kathleen said not to worry, and had a quick word with Frank before ringing off. 'I've never heard our Rita sound so happy. Thank God. And Our Blessed Lady. It's taken longer than we thought, but I said she wouldn't let us down. And she hasn't.'

As they knelt to say a decade of the rosary in thanksgiving, the room was alive with ghosts: Jimmy, and Leigh, even poor Nosey Nora – and many more, for few families had come through entirely unscathed. Liz had a lump as big as an egg in her throat, for only she remembered that it was exactly a year ago to the day that she and Leigh had set off for the Lakes.

'Well now,' Michael said. 'If we're to get enough bread made for tomorrow, we'd all better get busy. Folk'll be on the doorstep at the crack of dawn, I shouldn't wonder.'

*

Incredibly, some people hadn't heard it was VE Day, and turned up for work. But not for long. Every church bell that hadn't been destroyed was pealing for joy, and on the Mersey itself the ships' sirens deafened everyone. Even the early morning rain failed to dampen spirits.

'Are you going to let your hair down and come into town this afternoon, Liz?' Joey said, when the bread was all gone, and the shop closed. 'There's a whole crowd of us going – all ages.'

'I don't think so. There's lots to do here, and I've promised to go to the Candide later this morning to put up some decorations. The ladies are going to listen to Mr Churchill and then have a party. I've even arranged for a pianist, so they can have a sing-song.'

'We're having a party in the street,' Rosie announced. 'An' Georgy and me are helping, and I'm going to wear my new pink dress that mummy sent.'

Joey wrinkled his nose. 'I grew out of street parties years ago.'

So did I, thought Liz.

Clare rang in the afternoon to ask her much the same thing. Mr Churchill's speech, which had been blasting out of every wireless in the street, had just come to an end, and everyone was singing so loudly that Liz could hardly hear what she was saying. 'I would have been in touch earlier, but the hospital switchboard's been jammed! Listen, I'm off at six, and we're making up a party to go down to Hamilton Square. You'll know some of them. Do say you'll come.'

'I'll think about it,' she prevaricated.

'Liz! I refuse to take no for an answer. Leigh wouldn't want you to mope.'

'It isn't that.'

Clare was right in a way. She wasn't moping, but her emotions had been all at odds for days now. And only today had she realized why. Her period was almost two weeks overdue. In all the fuss and excitement, she hadn't given it a thought. Even now, it was too soon to be sure, to admit the possibility that she might be carrying Leigh's child. If she was wrong, the disappointment would be unbearable.

'All right,' she said in a rush. 'You've talked me into it.'

'Good. We'll pick you up.'

*

It was a night like no other. You couldn't move in Lime Street, and Hamilton Square was a sea of ever-moving colour, as more and more people pressed in, waving flags, eager to see the victory illuminations – shop girls and city gents, housewives and sailors, GIs and dustmen. The sky was red with the light of numerous bonfires, and everyone was singing and dancing, strangers were kissing one another, and a huge impromptu conga wove its way down Basnett Street, led, someone told Liz, by the Portuguese Consul and his wife.

It was easy to get carried away amid so much uninhibited joy, and she laughed and sang and kissed with the rest until very late. Clare wanted her to go back to the Whitney house to carry on celebrating, but it was after midnight and there was baking to be done for morning.

The house was in darkness when she got back. Mam would have gone to bed long since, but the light was on in the bakehouse. She wandered through and found her father already at work. He looked up and smiled at her, his heart full as he saw the light back in her eyes, her cheeks rosy with her exertions.

'Lizzie, my love, you're a sight to behold. Sure, there's no need to ask if you've enjoyed yourself.'

'Yes, I have,' she said, surprised to realize that it was no less than the truth. For the first time in weeks, she had really let herself go. 'It's impossible not to be happy tonight.' She reached up to kiss him, and, just for a moment, was tempted to confide her hopes.

'Well go on now, and get your head down for a few hours.'

She was on her ways upstairs when the phone rang. At this hour it could only be Shirley Anne. She'd never had any sense of time. Andy Rogers was home from the Med, and she was celebrating with him in London. Liz ran to answer it before it woke Mam. It was a terrible line.

'Shirley Anne? Is that you?'

The crackling grew worse, cleared momentarily, and a distant voice said, 'Elizabeth?'

The blood raced through her veins, swelling up until she could hardly breathe and everything swirled around her. I'm going mad, she thought. It was thinking too much about the baby that did it –

some trick of the sound waves – a wrong number – someone playing a cruel trick.

'Elizabeth, darling? Can you hear me?'

'Who *are* you?' she whispered piteously.

'Could you speak up, please. Is this Ryan's Bakery?'

'*Leigh*?' But that was impossible. Ghosts didn't make phone calls. The voice came again, repeating her name. She cleared her throat. 'Leigh? But you're . . .'

'Honey sweet, it *is* you. Thank God. Listen, I'm calling from Germany . . . haven't got long . . .' The crackling came and went, but he had called her 'Honey sweet'. No-one else would know that. '. . . been with Russians. Couldn't speak English . . . no way . . . pass message.'

'You're alive?' It was an inane question – a bizarre situation.

'Fine. Poor love . . . worried sick . . . Must go . . . coming home. Love you.'

Liz slid to the floor, hunched up in the corner, still clutching the receiver. Which was how Kathleen, coming down in her dressing gown, found her.

'Liz, whatever are you doing there? Been celebrating too well, by the look of it.' She prised the receiver from her daughter's hand, and hung it up. 'Come into the living room and I'll make us a hot drink. I heard the phone. Was it Shirley Anne?' Only then did she see the tears streaming down her daughter's face. 'Liz? For pity's sake, what is it? My dear, you'll make yourself ill if you cry like that!'

But Liz couldn't move, let alone speak. She stared up at her mother, eyes red and blurred. 'It was such a bad line . . . Germany. All the bombing, I suppose. But he *did* call me honey sweet. No-one else ever did that . . .'

Kathleen, now thoroughly frightened, ran to the bakehouse. 'Michael! Please come – it's Liz. I think she's – Oh, dear God, I don't know what to think!'

No-one got much sleep that night.

Michael eventually went back to his baking, and Kathleen sat with Liz, who didn't dare to sleep in case she woke up to find she had imagined the whole thing. She tried to call Colonel Radner, but the lines were jammed.

It was about eight o'clock the following morning when Colonel Radner called her. Liz was first to the phone.

'Mrs Farrell? I guess you've already heard the good news?'

'Then it really was Leigh? I could hardly hear . . . couldn't believe . . .'

She heard him swear. 'I guess it must have given you quite a turn. Gave me one hell of a shock, I can tell you. The most incredible set of circumstances.'

He told her briefly, then, how Leigh had crash-landed the *Lullabelle*, and been pulled, unconscious, from his seat by a couple of farm hands seconds before the whole crate went up in flames. 'These guys carried him back to their farm on a cart. He'd taken a nasty crack on the head, and had a sprained wrist, but the family looked after him until he was in some kind of shape, which was pretty damned decent of them in the circumstances. He had enough German to make himself understood, but they were out in the middle of nowhere, and there was no way he could get to a phone. Then a small contingent of Russkies came to the farm in search of food. They didn't speak anything but Russian, but he managed to convince them he wasn't German, and they let him tag along with them, hoping to contact an English or American unit. By the time that happened, the whole shooting match was over.'

Liz could hardly take it in.

'One of the reasons I rang, ma'am, was to say that your husband is due in here sometime this afternoon, and I've arranged for you to be picked up about an hour from now, and flown down. Can you be ready in time?'

Could she? She laughed aloud. 'Ready and waiting, Colonel,' she assured him huskily.

It was a beautiful day. Warm, serene – a perfect Lakes day.

At the air base, there was a great bustle of expectancy, and everyone was exceedingly kind to Liz.

There hadn't been time even to wash her hair, but she had brushed it until it shoned, clipped it back off her face, and seized the first dress that came to hand, which happened to be the cream one she had worn at Borrowdale. Finally, she slipped the fob watch over her head. As usual, a crowd had collected to see her off and shout encouraging messages, which she scarcely noticed. Miracles didn't happen very often.

Colonel Radner made her as comfortable as possible in his office and left her there, so that she could meet Leigh alone. 'I've given orders so you won't be disturbed, ma'am.' He smiled wryly. 'I'm sorry it's not a mite tidier.'

But Liz couldn't have cared less.

From the window she watched the plane land and taxi round. It was very like the one she had come down from Liverpool in – not at all like Monsieur Giroux's little Avro. Her chest felt so tight, she couldn't breathe.

The plane stopped, the door opened – and there was Leigh, all in one piece, and taking the steps almost at a run. He was wearing a leather flying jacket, his cap pushed to the back of his head so that the sun turned his hair to flame. Until this moment, she hadn't really dared to believe. She watched the colonel return Leigh's salute before gripping his hands in an emotional gesture of welcome. He said something, and pointed in the direction of his office. Leigh nodded, and strode across the tarmac.

He opened the door and closed it quietly behind him, his eyes devouring her as she stood there, unable to move.

'Elizabeth.'

His voice broke the spell, galvanizing her into action. He opened his arms, and she flew into them like a homing bird, clinging to him with every ounce of her strength, and he was solid and real.

'I've dreamed this dream so many times, but always, when I woke, you were gone, and I told myself I'd never see you again.'

Leigh's arms tightened until she could scarcely breathe. 'Who? Me? I'm not got rid of that easily.' He bent his head until his mouth mets hers, and the kiss went on and on, as if neither of them could bear to end it. Finally, he drew apart long enough to murmur, 'Is that real enough for you, honey sweet?'

'Just about.' Liz took a long tremulous breath. 'But I hope you aren't going away again for a long time, my very dear and wonderful Leigh, because I am going to need constant reassurance.'

'I guess that can be arranged.' His long, slow smile was less steady than usual. 'In fact, I think we should seriously consider making a start on founding that dynasty. What do you say to that?'

'I think it's a wonderful idea.'

Liz's smile had a particular radiance about it. But this was their special moment, to be savoured, treasured for all the years to come. Her news would keep until tomorrow.

A.O.C.